THE GREEN KINGDOM

THE GREEN KINGDOM

Edited, with an introduction, by Nancy A. Walker

THE RACHEL MADDUX SERIES
VOLUME 4

The University of Tennessee Press / Knoxville

TO **KING BAKER**

Efe yw'r to sy'n cysgodi'r aelwyd siriol.

LIBRARY OF CONGRESS CATALOGING IN PUBLICATION DATA

Maddux, Rachel, 1913-1983
    The green kingdom / edited with an introduction by Nancy A. Walker.
—1st ed.
        p.   cm. — (The Rachel Maddux series : v. 4)
    ISBN 0-87049-780-4 (alk. paper)
    I. Walker, Nancy A., 1942-   . II. Title.
    III. Series: Maddux, Rachel, 1913-1983. Rachel Maddux series; v. 4.
PS3563.A3395G73   1993
813' .54—dc20   92-26664
                                      CIP

CONTENTS

AND WHEN I TOLD THEM OF THE GREEN KINGDOM,
THEY ASKED ME WHERE IT WAS—IN WHAT STATE
OR BY WHAT RIVER. AND I ANSWERED THEM:

THE GREEN KINGDOM LIVES IN ALL MEN'S
HEARTS, FOR IT IS LESS A PLACE THAN A
CONDITION. IT IS GOOD HEALTH INSTEAD OF POOR;
IT IS FREEDOM FROM DEBT, OR A RAISE IN PAY.
IT IS A SYMPATHETIC RATHER THAN A NAGGING
MATE. IT IS AN IMAGINATIVE SUPERIOR. IT IS
THE FAITH OF ONE'S FELLOW MEN. IT IS
THESE THINGS WHEN THEY ARE LONGED FOR.

IT IS THE HARMAS FOR FABRE. IT IS A LITTLE
RESPITE FROM THE ANXIETY OVER NECESSITIES
FOR VAN GOGH. IT IS AN INTELLIGENT LISTENER
FOR MENDEL. IT IS JUSTICE WITHOUT CAPRICE
FOR JOB. IT IS THE CITY FOR THE PEOPLE IN
SMALL TOWNS, AND THE COUNTRY FOR THE PEOPLE
IN THE CITY.

IT IS THE LONGING FOR WHATEVER CONDITIONS
UNDER WHICH A MAN BELIEVES HE COULD DO
MORE OR BETTER WORK THAN HE IS DOING
WHERE HE IS.

OR, AS JUSTIN MAGNUS SAID IN THE ONLY
SPONTANEOUS SPEECH HE EVER MADE IN PUBLIC,
IT IS THE PROMISE BORN OF MAN'S LONGING
THAT HIS FATE SHOULD BEAR RELATION TO HIS
OWN ACTIONS AND HIS BELIEF THAT, GIVEN A NEW
CHANCE, HE WOULD CHOOSE TO THINK OF
HIMSELF AS GRAPPLING, RATHER THAN BUFFETED.

IT IS THE CLIMATE OF POTENTIALITY.

INTRODUCTION

On December 14, 1953, Rachel Maddux wrote to a friend, "If I should die tomorrow, I feel that life and I are even. We do not owe one another anything more. I have had my heart's desire." The occasion of such fulfillment was her completion of the manuscript for *The Green Kingdom*, her first novel and by far her longest work of fiction, which she had begun to write in 1941. Altogether, she estimated, the novel had consumed 18 years of her life—"7 years of thinking and 11 years of writing"—so that her relief at its completion is understandable. Understandable also was her subsequent frustration with the length of time it took to find a publisher for the novel. Finally, in the spring of 1956, Simon and Schuster accepted *The Green Kingdom* for publication, on condition that Maddux make drastic cuts in the manuscript and change the ending. Her anger at this and other publishers' unwillingness to take a chance on a largely unproven writer's long and, in many ways, experimental novel seemed to Maddux to validate "what the book is about, that the forces of sterility are ruling the world."

The concept of "sterility" would seem at odds with the lush promise of a "green kingdom," and indeed the tension between aridity and generative creativity drives the novel. But Maddux's comment springs as well from her experiences during the years she spent conceptualizing and then writing *The Green Kingdom*—years that began in the Depression and extended through World War II and into the McCarthy era. Against these public events were set Maddux's private struggles, which at times intersected with the the public ones. Forced by health problems to withdraw from medical school in the late 1930s, Maddux was determined to become a writer, supporting herself with a series of jobs in Kansas City. Following her marriage to King Baker in 1942, she adopted the nomadic life of a military wife, and when King was sent over-

seas she settled in California, where she worried about his safety
and attempted to resolve what she regarded as conflicting desires
to have children and to finish the novel.

These experiences inform a number of elements of *The Green
Kingdom*. To someone living through the Kansas dust bowl of the
1930s, as Maddux did, utopia might well take the form of a completely green world, and even though the novel apparently begins
during the Depression, the deaths of the sons of Justin Magnus—
one of the central characters—in "the wars" seems to refer to the
Second as well as the First World War. The fierce desire of the
central female character, Erma, to have a child reflects Maddux's
own yearning for motherhood during these years, and Erma is
named for Maddux's older sister, whose importance in Rachel's
life is described in Maddux's autobiography, *Communication*
(published by the University of Tennessee Press in 1991). Further,
the characters' ambitious project of capturing the details of everyday individual experience in the "Human Record" originated in
Maddux's own practice of maintaining a detailed personal journal.

In addition to being situated in such personal and historical realities, however, *The Green Kingdom* also draws upon several long-
standing literary traditions. One of these is the utopian tradition,
which began with Sir Thomas More's *Utopia* (1516). "Utopia" literally means "no place," and utopian fiction typically describes a
society that the author imagines as ideal, such as the all-female
culture of Charlotte Perkins Gilman's *Herland* (1915) or the har-
monious society based on the principles of behavioral psychology
in B. F. Skinner's *Walden Two* (1948). The Green Kingdom of
Maddux's novel is utopian in its offering of an unspoiled countryside with the resources to provide for the physical needs of people
who manage to find their way into it. But what seems utopian to
some may seem quite the opposite to others, and the isolation of
the Green Kingdom from what the characters come to refer to as
"the World" causes some of them to regard it as the antithesis of
utopia—as the worst rather than the best place that can be imagined. The tradition of the dystopian novel, as exemplified in George
Orwell's *Nineteen Eighty-Four* (1949) and Margaret Atwood's *The
Handmaid's Tale* (1986), is more dynamic than the utopian, which
tends to consist of static description, and much of the conflict in *The*

Green Kingdom arises from the characters' different responses to their environment—their own perceptions of utopia or dystopia.

By isolating her main characters from the rest of the world and forcing them to interact without the mediation of external events or other people, Maddux also participates in what might be called the "ship of fools" tradition, in which an author places a group of characters in an environment they cannot escape—often a ship or an island—so that they necessarily become involved in each others' destinies. The device is frequently used to construct a moral allegory, with forces representing good and evil confronting each other in close quarters. Such is the case in Herman Melville's *Moby-Dick* (1851), William Golding's *Lord of the Flies* (1954), Katherine Anne Porter's *Ship of Fools* (1962), and Marianne Wiggins's *John Dollar* (1989). But Maddux is less interested in moral absolutes than in the potential for human creativity and the forces that either nurture or stifle that potential.

Yet another literary tradition that informs *The Green Kingdom* is the *Kunstlerroman*—the novel that describes the development of the artist. In quite different ways, the two central characters are artists who discover the wellsprings of their creative energy. Justin Magnus is already, at sixty, a well-known composer when the novel begins, but the experience of the Green Kingdom allows him to emerge from creative paralysis and complete his finest symphony. Music and stories are continually transmuted into one another. Justin's grandfather's stories of the Green Kingdom had inspired Justin to begin a symphony with that name, as they later inspire a search for the actual place, and ultimately the novel itself comes to represent the symphony—its four sections bearing the titles of the four movements of Justin's symphony: "Discovery," "Time of Innocence," "Time of History," and "The Fulcrum." In a sense, then, Maddux invites the reader to "hear" her novel, just as she heard the music of her fiction before writing the words. In one of her notes on the manuscript for *The Green Kingdom*, Maddux comments on her process of composition:

> The Time of Innocence was, to me, the most satisfying of the volumes, that is, it most perfectly suited the music which preceded it. It was given to me to hear the four movements of Justin's symphony.

Unfortunately, I am unable to control or capture such experiences and, as the music fades from my memory, there is a feeling of terrible loss. The music for The Time of Innocence was very different from that of the other movements and, so far as I know, unlike any I had ever heard at that time.

Justin Magnus thus becomes a kind of coauthor of the novel.

Whereas Justin is a public artist—he meets the other principal characters while on a concert tour—Erma Herrick is a private, instinctual artist, unaware on any conscious level of her artistry until late in the novel. Others, however—primarily Justin—note her natural talents: the artful arrangement of a plant in the bathroom of her apartment, the designs on the tops of the loaves of bread she bakes in the Green Kingdom. But Erma's major work of art is accomplished in secret, in a cave that becomes a temple to a goddess of fertility.

Seeking at first simply a hiding place for a wounded animal, Erma begins to enlarge the cave and to sculpt on its walls images of the animals and plants in the Kingdom, all about to give some kind of birth. The centerpiece of the sculptured wall is the figure of a pregnant woman, "rounded, full, and voluptuous," representing the fertility that Erma does not believe she has. Toward the end of the novel, shortly before she learns that she, too, will give birth, Erma carves the figure of a woman out of driftwood—no longer in secret, but for Justin Magnus, who muses on the change he perceives in her:

> How wonderful to see how the too lush literateness of the dark
> cave had become, above ground, this restrained, powerful beauty,
> how the hidden, wound-licking process of secret consolation had
> metamorphosed into a joyous process of work.

The carving looks like Erma; her ultimate artistic creation is symbolically and actually herself.

Rachel Maddux's focus on the self-creation of the woman artist is one of several elements that make *The Green Kingdom* seem to belong to decades more recent than the 1950s. Indeed, a contemporary reader might well take issue with Justin Magnus's characterization of Erma's cave sculpture as a "too lush . . . wound-licking process of secret consolation," and view it instead as a celebration of female sexuality and an evocation of the female-centered goddess religions of earlier centuries. For Justin, the drift-wood sculpture is completely different from those in the cave; it has an "extreme delicacy" and "the physical weight of a bird's skeleton." But Erma connects the two art forms. Referring to a curve in the driftwood body, she remarks, "I remember learning that line . . . on the big torso, on Her thigh. I remember exactly how it felt."

Despite Justin's seeming frequently to be the authoritative voice in *The Green Kingdom*, often apparently speaking for the author, a reader today is likely to find Erma and Gwen—and the conflict between them—coming to the forefront and providing commentary on the role of women in both traditional and experimental cultures. Erma is creative and nurturing, but at the same time strong; Gwen is wholly self-absorbed and calculatedly helpless: "Between Gwendolyn and the things she needed or wanted, there had, all her life, been a person: the person who got them for her. . . . The conception of one's facing the world directly, without this intervening figure, had actually never occurred to her." Thus unfitted for the challenges of settling a new world, Gwen exerts the strongest force away from the potential harmony of the Green Kingdom. Although she is capable of populating the kingdom, she is never a part of it; Erma, in contrast, is as one with the green world, replicating its forms and processes in her art.

Also striking to readers today is Maddux's sensitivity to environmental protection and ecological balance. One of the fascinations of the novel—as of any novel that features the inhabiting of a new landscape—is curiosity about the practical realities of everyday existence. What is edible? Of what can shelter be constructed? How does one cook, keep clean, care for the sick or wounded? Maddux provides rich detail regarding these activities and many more. The "soaproot" has cleaning properties; the cattlelike "mossbacks" provide milk, and their hides are made into sandals; melons and "clusternuts" abound; and various substances provide paper, ink, and even a form of beer. But the five adults who live in the Green Kingdom are not careless of these resources. They save and plant the seeds of fruit and are careful not to deplete useful plants by overharvesting. They are aware, too, that the Green Kingdom is a closed ecosystem, removed from the "World." When, toward the end of the novel, Justin and Erma consider digging a tunnel to the outside, they quickly reject the idea, fearing damage to the environment. "If you tamper with nature," Justin says, "you never know what forces you're letting loose." Their realization that the shells of the clusternuts contain a chemical capable of killing vegetation is a sobering one, and Maddux remarks that "it is a significant time in the history of a settlement when man has it within his power to dominate the landscape."

But, as much as Maddux is concerned with the physical landscape of the Green Kingdom, the interior landscapes of her characters provide the central focus of the novel. As she makes clear in the prologue, the Green Kingdom is more a state of mind than a geographical location; it is a metaphor for whatever circumstances can make a person feel that he or she has some control over his or her fate. To live in the Green Kingdom is to inhabit "the climate of potentiality"—and to read *The Green Kingdom* is an intense experience, not least because we imagine our own responses to living in the land that Rachel Maddux so carefully delineates.

Nancy A. Walker
Vanderbilt University

1. Discovery

SITTING at his desk in the university where he had been vaguely uncomfortable for ten years, Justin Magnus reread the letter he had been carrying about with him for two weeks. The letter contained an offer of a concert tour in the interior of the country and so made it possible for him to prolong unchanged his present illogical existence by adopting a future which would be, to him, still more illogical.

The making of a decision requires at least two alternatives. This was Justin's trouble. He could imagine the future if he accepted the terms in the letter. But if he did not? He had been trying for weeks to face the alternative and he could not. In the great shift of emphasis to the physical sciences after the war the guiding heads of the university had decided that it was a luxury for the pupils to study the musical compositions of others but an absurdity for them to study their own, and Justin had been notified that the spring quarter, just beginning, would be his last.

To a man of such fame, how could this matter? He had never had the true passion for teaching. Nor can one imagine that the composer of the three greatest symphonies of his time could be so much baffled at the loss of a salary, however seriously his fortunes might have suffered during the long wars. A concert tour was distasteful to Justin Magnus; more, it was frightening. He believed himself a mediocre performer, and knew the offer came because of his fame and not his skill. Why, then, did he not refuse the offer and have done with it? He was sixty years old. He had done a great work and he was tired.

Yet Justin Magnus did not exist alone in the world, and to know him, as few people did, was to know his history. He had lost four sons in the wars and these were all the children he had. Other men have also lost all their children. In truth, the blows had fallen on Justin Magnus more with the force of dullness than of sharpness. They did not explain the man's bafflement, his appearance of receiving life through a translucent curtain. Not only the death of his sons but their lives as well had come to him through this same curtain. There were, in fact, only two things which had not. One of them was his music, while he was composing it. The other was his wife.

A small, extraordinarily delicate woman, not half Justin's size, Edith Magnus gave the appearance of being composed completely of conductivity and elasticity, while at the same time having been carved out of white chalk. She walked without sound, yet there was nothing soft or silken about her, and the bony structure of her face and hands had a cruel nakedness. Her black eyes burned through the chalk of her face, and the little head, as though to compensate for the bitter economy of flesh, was wrapped round with luxurious coils of thick black hair. Her hair was a magnificent incongruity, a cruel joke on the face of propriety, as though the top of a telephone pole had suddenly burst forth with blossoms.

Edith Magnus was insane. She constantly believed herself to be either pregnant or in the pains of childbirth. There were a few days when she knew that her sons were all dead and, strangely enough, these were the days when she appeared the least sane. Such was the force of the woman's personality that Justin often found her juggling with time to be more reasonable than his own. She rarely seemed insane to him, so logical was she in her madness. His life for many years had been an effort to produce for her the outward manifestations of her illusion. He had, in fact, exhausted his savings on it. It had been only in the last two years that he had given up hopes of a cure. When he was finally convinced that a cure was impossible he spent what money he had left from medical treatment in soundproofing the house and substituting trained nurses for the servants. His whole effort now was concentrated on maintaining the illusion without change. In a world where many sane people had little to eat, Justin fought bitterly to provide his wife with white lilacs and no longer questioned the rightness of it.

Edith did not remember the war, nor was she aware of the great spiritual fatigue called peace. She never saw a newspaper. She thought of herself as a young mother, the wife of the brilliant Justin Magnus, secure and often happy. She wished the house to be filled with flowers constantly and thought they were well able to afford it. She thought herself most fortunate in her servants and most of the time she thought it was spring.

Had Justin been a young man he might not have considered his wife's illusions necessary for her life. Even if he had, he might have considered their perpetuation less valuable than his freedom to compose. At fifty he had not thought so. At sixty he thought still less so. Viewed from this light, the letter with its offer of the concert tour made possible the perpetuation of the illusion a few months longer, perhaps even a year. To refuse the offer meant the loss of the house, the loss of luxury, the loss of nurses. It meant committing Edith to the barrenness of an institution. This was the alternative that he could not bring himself to face.

Well, he would go down to the sea. He knew he would never be able to make the decision sitting at his desk. The knee space of this desk, which he had used for ten years, was an inch and a half too short for Justin's legs. He had never found this out. He believed he could think better if he walked by the sea. The sea offers a target for the eyes, always directly ahead. Justin thought of himself as a *direction* projected on a level with his eyes. He was not concerned with his feet or the way they were able to carry him places, and the things that happened to them he never took personally.

See him now—a huge, gray lumbering force propelled slant-wise downward to the sea, unmindful of the hazards in the sand. The March wind blew violently against him, tearing at the open letter he carried in his hand. This also, being below eye level, hardly concerned him. Even at the piano he always thought of the music as coming straight out of his eyes. The sea was gray also, today, like Justin, yet the March wind bore a spring promise. There was an odor, almost an odor of warmth, that Justin was immediately sensitive to. Standing on the shore, he gradually grew calmer. The need for a decision became less urgent. The wet salt wind blew over him and made his problem small, and then it came to him, like the news of peace, that he would go and talk it over with Max Staats. This was, with Justin, an old formula, yet he never recognized it. He always took his problems from his uncomfortable desk down to the sea, but he never settled any of them there. It always came to him with a certain joy, this second step, this going to talk it over with Max Staats.

As soon as he had thought of this, he felt as though he had already settled the problem and he put the letter into his pocket.

He found a large rock and sat down. A fiddler crab came out of its hole and rattled over the sand toward him. Justin looked at the crab, and the crab's two eyes on their long stalks stood up like periscopes and looked, apparently, at Justin. The crab moved a few steps nearer. Justin sat perfectly still. The crab reached up its two small front feet, took hold of its long eye stalks, laid them down in their external horizontal sockets, brushed the sand particles from them and hurried, sideways, down its hole.

It was as though the crab had pulled the letter, the university and the uncomfortable desk with him. Justin stood and began slowly to walk down to the shore. He was aware now of the sea and nothing else. The tide was coming in, and with the swelling movement Justin was filled with an inexplicable joy and, somehow, hope. These things were strangers to him, so long forgotten as to be new. Immediately he was filled with shame at his own unconquerable vitality. From what audacious depths had he summoned the courage to feel, of all things, joy? How many sons would he have to have killed, how many cherished wives would he have to watch crumble into insanity, how poor would he have to be, how *old* would he have to be, before he could put a seemly face on life? There are some people to whom resurrection is the inevitable sequence to crucifixion. Such people cannot be killed in sections. They live when no one else can. They are ashamed of it and powerless to stop it. In a world where no hope is, they hope. Justin Magnus had nothing to hope for, yet he stood there with the sea spray bursting about him and he was filled with hope. Finally he recognized it. His was the simplest, most elemental hope: the hope that spring would come. He shook his head and started up the sandy slope toward Max's house.

A small, dark, sallow man, fifteen years younger than Justin, Max Staats was as definite as Justin was amorphous, as directed as Justin was aimless, as concentrated as Justin was nebulous. Their friendship was of long standing and had grown out of a mutual love of music. Strictly speaking, Max's great passion was mathematics, the difference between the two fields being, to him, almost nonexistent.

Max sat now at home, at a desk big enough for Justin. Through the thick lenses of his glasses his myopic eyes made out Justin's approaching shape and gait. Without moving his eyes from the figure, he reached for the telephone and called Justin's house.

"Mrs. Norris?" he said. "Max Staats. How's Mrs. Magnus? Good. Justin is at my house."

He replaced the receiver, got out brandy and a glass, placed them by the chair Justin would occupy, and was again seated at his desk when Justin walked in without knocking. Justin went directly to the chair without taking off his coat, and sat down.

"Been down to the sea," he said. "Wonderful weather."

"I saw you coming," Max said. "Have a drink."

Justin poured himself a drink and stretched out his feet. "Had the damnedest feeling down there," he said. "Felt as though I could go on forever. Felt glad it's almost spring. Glad, can you imagine?"

He took a drink of the brandy and sat knocking the glass against his knee. "Just stood there feeling ashamed of it," he said.

Max took a cigarette neatly from his case. With one sustained, circular movement he fitted it into his cigarette holder. "Easter is less a matter of history than of chemistry," he said. "Why should you be different from the wheat?"

"Easter," Justin said. "Well, then, if I was only responding to the vernal equinox, I needn't have felt improper."

"Will you excuse me if I take off my glasses?" Max said.

Justin laughed. "You should know by now. I always have to laugh to think the first time I heard you say that."

"Well, since I cannot see a thing without them," Max said, "I feel just as impolite as if I had turned my back when you were speaking."

"But surely you no longer need to see my face in order to understand me," Justin said. "You must have all my different expressions memorized by now."

"That's true," Max said. "There aren't so many. Besides, it is so restful this way."

Max smoothed his closed eyelids with his fingers and sat back in his chair. He looked in Justin's direction and smiled. It was a smile of incongruous sweetness which transfused his face completely for an instant. Justin thought of the fiddler crab and the thought filled him with tenderness for Max. He sipped his brandy and looked into the fire. Both men were at rest. There was quiet in the room and perfect relaxation and the accumulated mutual friendliness of ten years. Justin looked into the fire and the flames leapt in him and diminished and leapt again the way the tide had been in him, surging with hope and with joy. He remembered an Easter when his boys were little and Edith . . .

And then the thing came again, the awareness that was always at the back of his brain, that went with him everywhere, and he jumped from his chair.

"My God!" he said. "I forgot to call the house."

"I called for you," Max said, "just before you got here. I saw you coming."

Justin sat down again and lighted his pipe. "Thanks," he said. "What would I do without your efficiency?"

"You would do all right," Max said. "People like you always give their friends the illusion of being essential. It is, however, only an illusion. I am convinced that if you were completely alone in the world you would somehow bungle your way to safety."

"That reminds me," Justin said. He began to search through his pockets for the letter. When he had found it and tossed it on the desk Max put on his glasses and reached for it.

"This letter is two weeks old," Max said.

"I've been worrying about it for some time," Justin said, "but I didn't realize it had been so long."

Max read the letter through carefully, which was enough for him to memorize it, folded it, and handed it back to Justin. "You'll go, of course," he said.

"You make it sound very simple."

"Well, what can you do?" Max said. "You are the way you are."

"Yes," Justin said, "I suppose in the end I'll go. I remember so well when I was a young man and sat up all night with a friend of mine whose wife was insane. I remember explaining to him how the private institutions were no better than the state ones, how really the only sensible thing for him to do was to put his wife in a state asylum before he was absolutely penniless. It is easy to tell another what is reasonable, what is sensible. Yet, when it is your own . . ."

"No," Max said, "it is not merely being unable to take your own advice. It is something else, I think. The thing you don't know about another man's wife when you're young is that the bones do not go insane."

"Ah, that's it, Max. That's it."

Max was glad that he had his glasses off and that he was unable to see Justin's face. He swung the glasses by the ear pieces once to the right, once to the left, and they remained there, balanced a moment, before they swung down against his hand.

"I think you're very lucky to have this offer just now, Justin," he said, "even though it means hard preparation for you and is not exactly to your liking. There is nothing for you here and it might be six months or a year before you would find another permanent place. This concert tour will tide you over and Edith can stay where she is. That's the thing you want and that's why it is so useless to argue, because in the end that is what you will choose."

"I know it," Justin said. "I suppose I really knew it all the time."

"The reason it is so useless to discuss it is that you want it for yourself, Justin, as much as for Edith. No matter how ill she is, she is still the—"

"She's still the only one left," Justin said. "I know. You're right. Much of my desire to care for her is selfish, I know. I would be very lonely without her, without that house. And you know, Max, when I am with her, except for the bad times, she . . . she doesn't seem insane to me. It is difficult to explain."

"Why should you explain, Justin? She has the record. She is the proof of your past. Even if she keeps the record inaccurately, it is still a record that no one else in the world has. It cannot be replaced, it cannot be substituted. You will cling to it as long as it is there, naturally. A man needs proof that he has lived."

Max put on his glasses and abruptly lighted another cigarette. "Here," he said, "give me back that letter and I'll answer it for you. When you get your itinerary, let me have it. I'll watch after Edith while you're gone and keep you posted. It will be only a few months. Then you can return with a little money and, in the meantime, perhaps a permanent place will turn up. At any rate, there's nothing to do right now but answer that letter before they change their minds."

Justin tossed the letter onto the desk. "Thanks very much, Max. I always had an awful time writing letters. Edith always used to write all my letters, except the ones to musicians, and now . . . I never write any."

Justin stretched and sighed. He dreaded the long hours of practice and preparation and travel ahead of him. "Oh," he said, "that my grandfather's Green Kingdom were real and that I could take Edith and go there and never come out."

Max spread the letter out carefully and placed it at the left corner of his desk blotter. He would answer it as soon as Justin had gone. Perhaps if he worded his reply carefully, he might be able to get the offer raised a little; the terms were low, even for the times. He laughed sharply, a little bitterly.

"Oh, yes," he said, "you mentioned the Green Kingdom to me before. Some kind of utopia, wasn't it?"

"I hardly know," Justin said. "I was only about ten years old when my grandfather died, and now I can't remember how much he told me and how much I made up. I used to dream of the place a lot when I was a boy, and then, later, I always thought I would get it all down in music sometime and now there is no one left to ask about it."

"Oh, you could ask almost anyone about it, I imagine," Max said. "I don't suppose there is any person alive who doesn't have some such conception he carries around with him—some place free from the cares of the world—"

"No, there was something different about my grandfather's place. He was so . . . so tenacious about it. He had such a detailed picture of it, even to the animals and the trees."

"Literature is full of descriptions of paradise," Max said, "complete to the design of the plates one eats off."

"I know, but you have to die to get there. Now, that was the wonderful thing about my grandfather's Green Kingdom—that a live man could go there. Of course my grandfather insisted that he had been there."

"And what did your grandmother say?"

"My grandmother said that he was an irresponsible, no-good, drunken lout and that he had simply run off to get out of working, and that after he had roamed around the country for ten years in God knows what kind of company he had got tired and come back home, trying to excuse himself with this fantastic tale that nobody believed. She wouldn't allow him to mention it in her presence. Neither would my mother, so he used to take me off secretly and tell me about it. I suppose that's what made it stick so, all that secrecy."

"How did your grandfather explain his ever having left such a desirable place, do you remember?"

"Oh, yes. At least I think I remember that part. He was supposed to have been searching for gold when he came on the place. As nearly as I can remember it, he heard from some natives about a mountain which split open every ten years. They were afraid of it. My grandfather's story is that he went to the place out of curiosity and, sure enough, it happened. Something like a split caused by an earthquake—that's as near as I could get to it, but perhaps I made that part up. It's been such a long time. Well, he went through the split and it closed up after him."

Max began to chuckle. "Some kind of door on supernatural hinges, no doubt," he said. "Oh, I'm sorry I didn't know your grandfather. Go on. What happened then?"

"Well, then he was shut in there and he would tell me what it was like, but of course it is possible that my picture of it is my own invention. Anyhow, no matter whose it was, I remember it was all green inside; the animals were green, the flowers were green. The thing I dreamed of most often was a great, green tree —green leaves on green twigs on green branches on a green trunk."

"And the people," Max asked—"were the people green, too?"

"There were no people. That I remember very clearly. Always, my grandfather insisted, there were no people. He was alone. I think that must have been the part my grandmother couldn't swallow, the idea that my grandfather could have taken care of himself for ten years."

"I am beginning to have a great sympathy for your grandmother," Max said.

"So had everybody else, except me. I believed my grandfather. He seemed a tragic, misunderstood figure to me. You see, his story was that he lived those ten years for the day he could go back and get my grandmother and all their friends, wait ten years, and then return to live in the Green Kingdom. Only, after ten years of loneliness and planning, he came back and no one believed him, not even my grandmother. For a long time he tried to convince people until finally he came to be the laughingstock of the town, a kind of buffoon. Long before my time, of course, he had quit trying. I must have been a satisfaction to him, even if I came along after he was completely embittered."

"I wonder he could believe in it himself by that time," Max said.

"Oh, I think he did," Justin said. "Of course a child's mind is hardly accurate, but there is one thing I remember that I know really happened. When he was dying he made a great fuss and

swore at my grandmother and my mother until he got them out
of the room, and then he gave the map to me and made me promise never to show it to either of them."

"A map?" Max said. "You mean he had even made up a
map to go with his story?"

"Well, it was a map of something. Of course as soon as he
died my grandmother and my mother started in on me and began
to tell me how he was crazy and had been for a long time and how
I mustn't believe anything he told me, but I never showed the map
to anybody. It wasn't much, as I remember—pretty sketchy and
smeared and dog-eared."

"What happened to it?" Max said.

"Oh, it's around somewhere. Probably in the attic."

"You never mentioned the map before," Max said.

"Well, it's been so long since I looked at it myself. Perhaps
it isn't anything but some lines on paper. I'll look it up again
some day."

The phone rang only once before Max picked up the receiver. He said, "Yes, right away," and replaced the receiver.
"It was Mrs. Norris, Justin," he said. "They want you at home."

Justin stood immediately. "Thanks for taking care of the
letter, Max," he said. "I'll let you know how things are."

He walked rapidly to his own house. Apprehension made his
gait more hurried than usual; yet he did not run, as once he had,
for the apprehension had long ago become familiar. As soon as
he was inside the door he could hear Edith screaming. He took
off his coat and went into the kitchen for a glass of water. He
drank it very slowly, aware of the beating of his heart, and, as
always, he had that strained expectancy, that terrible need not to
make any mistakes. He went slowly up the stairs, listening carefully, and forcing himself to be calm. Just outside the door he
waited for Mrs. Norris to come out to him.

"How long?" he asked her.

"About half an hour," she said.

"Has she said any *words*—any words at all?"

"Something that sounded like *greer*."

"Thank you," Justin said. "I'll be in in a moment."

He went into his own room and sat down on a chair. If Edith
had said *Greer*, then it was David's birth she was in now, because
Greer was the housekeeper they had had then. It was strange how
completely, how accurately Edith made these journeys back in

time. Everything that he insisted upon in her treatment depended now on the accuracy of his memory. But it was usually David's birth, the first one, the one he was most practiced in, so he rose almost immediately and went into the room. He had it all clear before his mind, like a painting.

Edith was kneeling on the floor in the far corner of the room, both arms crossed over her belly. Her long hair fell in tangled strands over her shoulders. There was a bleeding scratch on one cheek. She looked up at Justin without recognition and, as he walked slowly toward her, she shrank back and moaned.

"Animal Eyes," he said now, walking slowly toward the woman, "I've called the doctor." *What was the doctor's name? Dr. Carlsmer.* "He's coming right away."

He held out his hands to her, but he did not touch her. The wild look of her eyes was fading and in its place came one of puzzlement, of lostness. She breathed heavily and looked about her.

"Greer," she said. "I can't find Greer. I've been calling and calling."

He moved his hands slightly in front of her. "Greer's getting everything ready for the doctor," he said. "The doctor said you must lie down now. Come, let me help you."

Edith looked at Justin questioningly and then slowly she put her hands in his and he lifted her up from the floor. As soon as she was standing he picked her up in his arms and began slowly to walk across the room to the bed. Now he must get everything right.

"I can hear the doctor's carriage," he said. "It is snowing out, Animal Eyes. It is a beautiful white snow and in a minute Dr. Carlsmer will be here and Greer will be here and they will help you."

Edith was crying soundlessly. Her eyes were closed. Justin put her down on the bed very carefully and made a sign to the nurse who stood ready at the door. Within a few seconds Mrs. Norris had given Edith a hypodermic injection and disappeared from the room. Justin sat by her bed suspended in an old past time on the day that David was born. When he looked out the window he could not reconcile the obvious early spring with the snowfall that had for a few moments been so real to him.

Well, he had done it. He had proved once again that there was no need of force as long as he was there. He was suddenly very tired from the effort to remember everything exactly. If this happens while I am on tour, he thought, they will use force on her. They will have to. What did it matter that they said she wouldn't remember the force, that she wouldn't *know* it? How did they know? Even if they were right, did that change the *force* any? Hadn't he proved with fantastic success that his way was superior?

He sat now in a chair by the bed, looking at the calm, quiet face of his wife. Max had said she was his record, the record of his past. Was he not also hers? And was he not her only one? No one else knew their times. In all the world, he alone knew that important thing, that it was snowing on the day that David was born. Who else knew the doctor's name was Carlsmer? Who but they knew that Greer was in the kitchen boiling water? These things they had had together, though the proof of them was dead, but such things had made their time together, made it theirs and no one else's. He knew really that it was spring of the present year and that the quiet of his wife was not a good quiet, had been induced by a drug. Yet, as he put a light coverlet over Edith carefully, he felt the snow falling outside.

"How can I leave you?" he said. "How can I go away and leave you to these people who do not know the moments and the happenings, the persons, the names, the *weathers* of our time?"

Mrs. Norris came in and attended skillfully, quickly to the long fingernail scratch on Edith's cheek. Justin got up very slowly from the chair and walked into his own room. He trusted Mrs. Norris beyond any other nurse they had had. He had himself chosen her. Yet as he walked into his own room, he was quite aware that she thought him ridiculous and he knew that he would never be able to make her see the value or the importance of the thing he had just accomplished. He was very tired now and he undressed slowly and went into the bathroom and took a hot shower. He did not bother either with the soap or sponge, but stood there, tired and still, under the hot water. When it became intolerable, he turned his body around. It was a great and powerful body, heavily covered on the chest, legs and forearms with thick gray wools of hair. Steam rose in the room, covered the mirrors, coiled in drops upon the tile, and Justin continued to stand under the hot water. One hand came up aimlessly and scratched his chest. He yawned and turned around. Presently he would dress and go down to dinner. He and Mrs. Norris would eat together and he would tell her about the tour. Would she stay on? He must get her to stay on.

And all the time there would be that slight patronage in her. Why was it she did not know, could not see? Max knew. Max would never have thought he overestimated the importance of those few moments. If only there were such a nurse as Max. What was it that Max understood, that Mrs. Norris could not appreciate? Mrs. Norris saw Edith in her own terms. The thing was she did not see *him*. That was the thing that Max had that Mrs. Norris did not. Max saw it his way. What was the clear, wonderful thing Max had said? *The bones do not go insane.* If only Mrs. Norris knew that. If only Mrs. Norris could see *him* instead of Edith, then she would know how much it meant to him, those few moments in there when, by his special knowledge and his sudden backward walking through Time, he had been with Edith in her insanity so that, sharing it, she had not seemed insane.

Mrs. Norris would never see that, but, so long as he was successful, she would not try to change the method. That was why he was so tired now, of course—that terrible compulsion to make no mistakes, that desperate need to prove that it could be done his way. But if, as they said, Edith would not know about the force, why was he so afraid of failing? It was for himself, that he should not have to witness force upon her body, because then . . . then he too would see her differently. He too would believe her insane and outside himself. And the illusion that he had worked so hard to preserve, that he was going on a concert tour in order to preserve still longer, had he done this for himself? He had. Max knew it. Now he knew it himself. That's why it had been so easy for Max to say, "You'll go, of course."

Justin ducked his head under the stream of hot water. He rubbed his face and scalp and turned the faucet. In the sudden silence he shook his head violently and then stepped out upon the bath mat. Naked, in the steamy room, he walked over to the window and rubbed a clear space on the glass and stood looking out on the early spring evening. In the brilliant light of the room, separate spherical drops of water shone where they hung caught upon the hair of his chest, the tip of one ear, on his elbow and knees. His hands felt aimlessly over his naked body for his pipe. Finding no clothing and no pockets, they gave up the search.

Then it was borne in upon Justin's consciousness that he wanted to smoke. He reached for a towel and began to rub it over his body.

Where would Edith come out? Yet this was not what he meant. It was not where but *when*, what place in Time, for it was not a continuous time she followed, nor a predictable one. Because she had a while before been in that day of David's birth, the day of Greer and Dr. Carlsmer and the white snowfall, did not mean that she would resume a waking state on the day after David's birth. Once before, another time when it had been David's birth, she had come out into Tommy's diphtheria, which had happened ten years later. There was no way of predicting.

But it would not be for hours yet. Justin dropped the towel on the floor and, naked, went into his room and lighted his pipe while he began dressing. Standing before his mirror, tying his tie, he stopped suddenly, took the pipe out of his mouth, and stared at his own face. *How does she reconcile my face? I wonder,* he thought. *What do I look like to her? Do I look as I did then? Does she see me at all, really? Surely it must be confusing to her, frightening, to see me the way I look now when she is in the old Denley Street house in Greer's time. Especially,* he thought, resuming the tying of his tie, *especially since her own face has changed hardly at all.*

He had kept Mrs. Norris waiting but he was not aware of it. During dinner he told her of the concert tour and she said that she would stay on. Justin felt much better after he had eaten and did not go to bed immediately but went instead into his studio. What, then, would he choose for the tour? He must begin soon to prepare himself. The choice was limited in many ways. There would be no orchestra; he must carry the whole thing alone. He knew almost nothing of the interior of the country, but the letter had said that they were mostly small towns. What did they want to hear, these people?

The hot shower, the dinner, and the certainty that Mrs. Norris would stay on had combined to give him a feeling of well-being. He reached into his pockets, one after the other, in search of a match, and, finding none, he walked across the room to the table where his smoking things were kept. He lighted his pipe and puffed on it slowly, and slowly he waved the match back and forth in the air to extinguish it. With his hands in his pockets he walked the length of the room very slowly, turned, and retraced his steps. "I wish," he said, "I wish that I had *The Green King-dom* ready."

It had been many years since he had even thought of working on *The Green Kingdom*. It had been almost ten years since he had worked on anything of his own. He doubted that he were capable now of doing it. He had been quite certain for a long time that his creative streak had run dry. Yet, today by the sea and again in front of the fire at Max's, had there not been the old stirrings?

He walked out of the room and up the stairs quietly and past Edith's door. Edith was as he had left her. Mrs. Norris sat in a chair at the far end of the room, reading a book.

"Is midnight all right?" he said to her. "Or would you like me to relieve you earlier?"

"Well, really," she said, "it's not necessary at all. You want your sleep."

"I'll come in at midnight," he said.

In his own room he set the alarm, undressed, and fell asleep immediately. At 11:30 he awoke suddenly, turned off the alarm before it could ring, arose, washed his face, shaved, dressed, and went into Edith's room. He sat in the chair by Edith's bed and settled himself while he waited for Mrs. Norris to assure him that it was unnecessary for him to be there. He did not protest. He settled himself and looked politely upon her and waited for her to go.

Now the room was quiet and it would perhaps be several hours before Edith would awaken. He had forgotten to call Max to let him know how Edith was, as he had promised. Well, it was too late now. He would call him in the morning. He did not feel like reading. He waited. *Where would she come out?*

In a little while, perhaps an hour or so, Edith would begin to stir and to climb slowly up through the cloudy layers of the drug, and then, then she would perhaps say a word, a sentence, a name, and everything in him must be waiting and attentive and yet relaxed. For if his mind were absolutely open and clear, then the slender ribbon of their time would slide through his mind and catch upon the right notch. Justin was almost grateful to the woman for her timing of this last attack so that her coming out should be in the quiet, undisturbed hours of the night, for it was at such a time as this that he was best able to taste and feel and meet the challenge.

The form on the bed made no signs of movement or unrest yet, and Justin moved his chair over to an open window so that he could look out upon the night. Because of the light in the room he was unable to see out, and so he went over to the wall switch and clicked the room into darkness. He did not need the light to know when Edith would stir, for in their long years together he had become attuned to many ways of knowing. He had, through long practice, developed an awareness of her movements composed of so many small, unrecognized components that it was like a special sense of its own. He knew it so, as an awareness, a special thing, and had never split it into its components: the rate of her breathing and the slight variations therein, the sound of the mattress if she moved, the slight shifting of the head's weight on a pillow, the dragging of the sheet over a moving foot, the sudden plumlike odor of her hair freed into the air by a movement of her head. How many countless other minute details, unrecognized and never separated, go to compose and resolve into the very vibrations in the air which beat upon another so that he says, "My wife stirs, my wife dreams, my wife is awake"?

Where would she come out this time? Would she come out again into Tommy's diphtheria? He hoped most fervently that she would not. Perhaps it would be later than that. Perhaps it would be the winter they had all been in Greece. Since it was useless to predict, he might as well predict pleasure instead of disaster. He wished it might be that Christmas in Athens. He wished that by some studied, careful concentration he could have the power to make it so.

It had seemed incredible to them to have Christmas out of doors, they who had always been accustomed to snow. All of them together had had a picnic, a picnic right out of doors under the trees on Christmas Day. Edith had sat on the grass, leaning her back against a tree, and she had been wearing white. She was holding Tommy on her lap and he was struggling and straining in her arms to get his hands into the food. And such food! Edith was laughing and struggling with Tommy, whose hands were perilously near the wine bottle.

"Ouch!" she said. "You devil. You kicked me in the stomach."

"Here," Justin said, "give him to me." He put his pipe in his mouth and stretched out his arms for the struggling child.

"Justin," Edith said, handing the heavy child over to him, "make them quit fighting."

David and John were rolling over and over each other, punching poorly directed, good-natured blows into heads and bellies and any chance unprotected spot.

"They're not fighting," he said. "They're wrestling."

"I don't care what they're doing," she said. "They're going to land right in the . . ."

And then they had; so that Edith had finished the sentence with a squeak, and while she and David had become very businesslike trying to disentangle John from the delicacies of the feast, George had suddenly broken the silence with his laughter. George had always been so. Rarely had he ever joined in the noise or activity, being content to sit perfectly still in one place, until suddenly there would be a disaster or a silence or a breathing spell and right in the middle of it would be George's laughter, loud and long and not easily controlled. It seemed to Justin that George had always laughed alone in other people's quiet places. The boy, like his laughter, had always been a puzzle to Justin.

Some one, or several, of the thousand components that went to make up that special awareness of Justin's was now brought into focus and set vibrating, and Justin moved silently over the carpeted floor and stood by Edith's bed. The pattern of her body under the light coverlet had shifted. The sharp line of one knee was there, where it had not been before. It was beginning then, the long ascent upward from sleep. He went back to his chair by the window. It would be some time yet.

It was strange, now that he had been thinking about George, to realize how seldom the violent attacks of Edith's were associated with George's birth. Perhaps it was because George's birth had been the easiest for Edith. Yet it was not their births but their deaths which mattered, he knew that. Their deaths had come in rapid succession just as Edith had approached her forty-fifth year, and somewhere in the time of disorder and uncertainty and shock she had transferred the violence of their deaths to that of their births. It was an imagined violence, of course, for even now he knew very little of the actual conditions under which, individually, they had died.

Where would she come out? Perhaps it might be back, 'way back, before David's birth even, back to the time when he was working on *The Knife and the Grapes,* before he had even started his first symphony. Perhaps that night he had brought home the barbaric earrings. A slight, silent, spring breeze tossed itself into the room against Justin's face and then became still and died. A smile crossed Justin's face in the same manner. They were terrible, those earrings. Much too heavy, too bold, for the delicacy of her face. Only a very young man would have bought his wife such earrings. She wore them, though. In great pride and with quick movements of the head, she had worn them out onto the street with him, out . . . where had they gone? Was it to a restaurant?

Some old disquiet and discomfort hung about Justin's memory. He could not place it. He sat very still waiting for it to come clear. And the slender ribbon of their time coiled and slid through the old pathways of Justin's memory and caught itself upon the right notch and in his mind's ear he heard an ancient lullaby.

> *Rock-a-bye, Baby, in the tree top,*
> *When the wind blows, the cradle will rock.*

That was it. Walking by his side, the new, incongruous earrings swaying heavily, Edith had started to sing the old nursery tune.

> *When the bough breaks, the cradle will fall.*

"How brutal!" she said. "Isn't that a brutal song to sing to children, Justin? When the bough breaks. Listen to how those words sound together, even if you didn't know what they meant: bough breaks, bough breaks."

It was no wonder that the memory had made Justin feel apprehension, for after Edith had become insane he had come upon her one day sitting very contentedly with her arms cradling empty space, singing to the same tune, as she had done many times since:

> *One for the Loyalists, one for the Poles,*
> *Two for the Russians, Pegasus' foals.*
> *I've dropped a child on every war,*
> *But no more now, no more, no more.*

The myriad components of that special sense of awareness became forceful and Justin moved again to his wife's side. The pattern under the coverlet had changed again. She had moved one arm. She had shifted her head a little. It would not be very long now, perhaps half an hour, before she would begin climbing up, layer by layer, through the strata of sleep. Justin got his chair from the window and placed it by the bed.

But perhaps it would be none of these times he had thought of. Perhaps she would come out to a much later, more recent, time, even to this very day where he was now. And before he had censored the thought, it was there and it was over with and past retracting. Conscious of a great guilt, he realized that he had hoped that this would not be so. He could not now retract it. In the honesty that is bred only in the dark and silent lonely places of the night, he had to admit that he did not want her to be sane.

He did not want her to be living in the dull and disorganized wreckage of the present, or to read each day in the newspapers the short-sighted measures of hatred, vengeance, bickering, and compromise that had been substituted for the International Plan. He did not want her to haggle and search and wait in the markets for their daily food. He did not want her to be without flowers all through the fall and winter and secretly add up columns of figures on the backs of old envelopes. He did not want her to be fifty-five years old.

In guilt and shame he had to admit he did not want to spend his days in bungling puzzlement at the university only to come home to sit with her through the long evenings in constant deadening grief for their sons. He did not want to sit with her in sorrow and endless grief while they waited for each other to die. And in the silence of the dark and lonely places of the night, he faced his guilt and knew it for what it was. It would be, henceforth, a thing he lived with, as for many years now he had lived with the knowledge that he had never known his son George.

And then Edith stirred and she put one of her skeleton chalk hands up to the scratch on her cheek. Instantly Justin's self-accusation and all the accompanying thoughts vanished. For there must be nothing in his mind now but reception. His whole body and his mind were tensed into active, waiting, suspended reception. There was nothing in the man now of being old or disillusioned or tired or defeated.

He was listening. Like the very thread of life and youth and tension, he was suspended in a waiting listening. He was waiting for the first words, the first clue, so that he could tell her where she was and, telling, be there with her.

JOE ROBERTS walked down the shady side of Maple Avenue, on which there was not a maple tree in sight, in the town of Drury. The town looked like an aerial photograph of itself, which is to say that it was squat, spread out, and contained a preponderance of right angles. Its buildings were for the most part limited to three stories and its entertainment to one movie. It is located about an inch and a quarter west of the exact heart of the continent on the customary atlas-size map. However, the customary map does not show Drury at all.

Before the entrance of the Herrick-Roberts Printing Company he stopped, carefully pinched the fire off his cigarette, scrutinized the butt, and dropped it into his pocket. Then he went in. Behind the soil-dimmed window of the Herrick-Roberts Printing Company were displayed a few dusty boxes of stationery and several forlorn and fly-specked Easter greeting cards. Inside the door one entered a small, dark room which bore some resemblance to an office. There was a desk here with a worn typewriter on it and a large ledger. There was also a counter with an assortment of unrelated and dusty objects sitting on it. Prominently displayed at eye level was a huge cardboard sign:

THIS IS

A PRINTING OFFICE

CROSSROADS OF CIVILIZATION

REFUGE OF STUBBORN TRUTH:

TO THIS PLACE

ANY FREE MAN MAY COME

WITH WORDS TO BE PERPETUATED

AND MULTIPLIED IN COLD PRINT

THIS FACT ALL TYRANTS KNOW

AND HAVE KNOWN FOR FIVE CENTURIES

HENCE THEY HATE AND PERSECUTE PRINTERS

O LOVERS OF LIBERTY

YOU STAND ON SACRED GROUND

THIS IS A PRINTING OFFICE

No one was in the room, and Joe Roberts had apparently not expected anybody to be, because he went directly through the door at the rear. Here everything changed. Joe entered a large room, well lighted and in the most immaculate order. Two presses stood in the room, one quite old, one relatively new, both singularly free from dust. Along one whole wall was a system of shelves, pigeonholes and type cases. The wooden floor was swept clean and a large wastebasket sat in the middle of it. In one corner there was a washbasin, and beside it, on nails, hung a large towel and two printer's aprons. Between the washbasin and the window there was a solitary shelf upon which, in a neat row, stood some twenty large loose-leaf notebooks waiting for the daily entries of their owners. Each notebook bore a number. Before the window sat a large battered desk, its top clean and bare. At the desk sat a young, dark-haired man chewing on a yellow pencil in a dogged, discouraged, and somewhat hungry manner. This was Arthur Herrick, co-owner and founder of the Herrick-Roberts Printing Company.

Joe pulled a high stool over by the desk. He slid onto the seat, hooking his heels over the top rung of its supports, put his elbows on his knees, and fitted his jaw into the cup of his hand.

"No luck," he said.

"You mean you couldn't collect the bill or he wasn't there?"

"He was there."

"Well, didn't he even offer to pay part of it?"

"The son of a bitch is bankrupt," Joe said. "He bummed a cigarette off me to prove it."

Arthur took the yellow pencil out of his mouth and threw it across the room. Then he stood up. "That's the last one," he said. "We're done. We're beat."

He put his hands into his pockets and began to walk up and down the room. He walked over to the shelf containing the identical loose-leaf notebooks. "Only twenty of them," he said, "and I'm through already. I'm broke. And even these aren't half full. They're only started. Nobody came in today; nobody yesterday."

Joe stayed perched on his stool. Finally he reached into his pocket and extracted a cigarette butt. He examined it critically and finally lighted it. "We've got to find some other way to do it," he said. "There must be some way we haven't thought of yet."

Arthur strode back and forth in the room following the yellow pencil. He would walk over to where he had thrown it and pick it up and throw it again. Then he would follow it. Once it fell close to the shelf of notebooks and he stood staring at these for a long time.

"The People's Library," he said. "The Human Records." He hit the shelf a blow with his fist. "Jesus, how could I miss so far? From a million down to twenty volumes in six quick months. And even these," he said, picking up one of the notebooks and shaking it at Joe, "even these aren't full. They're only started."

"They're full of crap, I'll bet," Joe said.

"That doesn't matter, Joe. I keep telling you. It doesn't matter if it's crap or not. If you got enough of them, it'll be valuable. Lies are valuable. Deception is valuable. Anything human is valuable if you've got enough of it."

"Yeah, I know," Joe said. "You keep telling me. I keep believing you right down to my last nickel. Just for Christ's sake quit chasing that little yellow pencil around your cage and let's talk sense for a change."

There was a sudden jubilant sound of hurried steps coming down the rear stairway, the door burst open, and Erma Herrick dipped into the room. She brought with her obvious news, good news, secret and personal and joyful news. It was in her triangular eyes and her full mouth and in the raised heel of one foot arrested in the middle of a step. As soon as she saw the two young men and the bitten pencil, the news slid off her exactly as though she had stepped out of a wet bathing suit. She completed the arrested step and, with its completion, the news was hidden, put away. It was not the right time to tell the news that Justin Magnus was actually coming to Drury and that she might really meet him.

The most significant thing about Erma Herrick was that people remembered her as slightly larger than life size and were always surprised when they saw her after an absence to feel their mental readjustments jogging into smaller-scale corrections. This illusion was aided by the fact that her head was a shade large for her body and the effect was heightened by her long, curly, undisciplined, almost red hair. She was not really exceptionally tall and she was actually rather thin, yet no one ever remembered her so. Even Arthur, who knew perfectly well in his muscles her exact size and her surprising frailties, had first described her to Joe as: a rather big girl—sturdy, I mean, not fat.

Her secret safely put away, Erma walked over to Joe, put her hand into his coat pocket, and took out a fine, long, straight cigarette butt.

"Hey," he said, "that's my prize. I was saving it for after dinner. You do it every time without even looking."

She reached into the pocket of her apron for a match, scratched it on the underside of the desk, and laughed. "You see what valuable things you can learn by practicing the piano?" she said. "I've got touch, Boy."

"You got nerve, too."

Something very pleasant and confiding flashed back and forth between these two, something that no one, probably, would ever dare flash at Arthur Herrick and certainly not expect to have returned. There was ease in it, a kind of ease that the woman's husband would never possess or experience. Yet it was only an obbligato to the real thing. The real thing was just as quick and just as sure. It was the knowledge that Joe had been unable to raise any collection money to carry on the work.

"Supper's pretty soon," Erma said to them both. "You're going to stay, aren't you, Joe?"

"You know I haven't got a cent," Joe said.

"You want me to call Gwendolyn for you?" Erma asked. "You want me to ask her over to eat with us or you want to get her later?"

Joe's eyes slid over to Arthur. "Call her for me, will you?" he said. "Tell her I'll come over and get her about eight."

Erma started out of the room. Just at the place where she had slid out of the wet bathing suit of her secret, she hesitated, as though to let it crawl up her body once more, and then she began to climb the stairs.

When they heard the street door open Joe said, "I'll get it," and went out of the room.

He returned in a few minutes followed by a little old man who stood tentatively in the doorway. This little man's motif was a certain pattern of creases which was repeated all through him. This crease pattern was a line which forked into three divisions. It was across the tops of his heavy work shoes. It was repeated at the knees of his trousers, the elbows of his coat, twice on his neck, once for each corner of his mouth, once at the outside of each eye, and once on his forehead.

"You are Mr. Herrick?" he said to Arthur.

Arthur was so surprised that the man had called him mister that he got up and put his chair to one side for him. "Yes, sir," he said. "Come in."

The little man began to move toward the chair slowly and all his creases breathed together. "My boy, Pete," he said. "He work for you."

"Pete Dobenski?" Arthur asked.

"You keep a record on him," the little man said, standing beside the chair. "I come to get it back."

Joe moved over to the little man. "Sit down, Mr. Dobenski," he said. "Did Pete ask you to get it for him?"

Mr. Dobenski sank into the chair and Arthur leaned against the desk. "I'm sorry, Mr. Dobenski, but I can't give it to you. You see, I promised everybody to begin with that their records would never be given to anyone else and I can't break that promise. Pete'll have to come himself and get it."

"He can't come," Mr. Dobenski said. "That's why he sent me to get it."

"Well, what does he want it for?" Joe asked.

"He want to destroy it, to burn it up. So I have come to get it."

"Destroy it?" Joe said.

"That's his privilege, of course," Arthur said. "They were all told that any time they wanted their records back they could have them. All he has to do is to come and get it himself."

"So then give it to me, please," the little man said, "and I will take it to him."

"But I can't do that, Mr. Dobenski," Arthur said, raising his voice. "In the first place, I wouldn't give Pete's record to anybody but Pete, and in the second place I couldn't give it to you if I wanted to. I don't even know which one is his. They just have numbers on them. They don't have names."

"It's number 17," Mr. Dobenski said. "He told me to tell you."

"Look, Mr. Dobenski," Joe said, "you tell Pete all he has to do is come in and get it. He can have it any time he wants."

"He can't come in," Mr. Dobenski said. "He's in jail for stealing a typewriter."

"Jail?" Arthur said. "Oh, I'm sorry, Mr. Dobenski. Why didn't you say so at first?"

"Well, if he's in jail," Joe said, "what the hell does he care where his record is?"

"Mr. Herrick," the little man said, "maybe there are some things in there that Pete wrote. Maybe there is something which would make it harder for him by the police."

"But the police won't ever see it," Arthur said. "How would the police get it?"

"I don't know, Mr. Herrick. I don't know what you use them for."

"But I don't use them for anything, Mr. Dobenski."

"Mr. Herrick, we all got our work, I know. We all got to eat. Please don't tell me that you pay my boy five dollars a week to write you a record and then you don't do nothing with it after you paid for it. Just because I'm an old man in work clothes and worried about my boy, please don't try to make a fool out of me."

"I'm *not*, Mr. Dobenski. I've got on work clothes, too. Now you just bring me a note from Pete asking me to give you his record and I'll give it to you."

But the little man did not intend to be taken in so easily. He sat very solidly in his chair. He smiled and wagged his head back and forth to show that he knew the joke.

"But I already told you the number now, Mr. Herrick," he said. "Who knows what will happen to the record while I am gone over to the jail?"

He reached into his pocket and brought out a fat, round purse. It had two compartments and a double nickel clasp on the top. From one side he took out a dirty twenty-dollar bill and carefully put it on the desk.

"Now, Mr. Herrick," he said, leaning back in the chair confidently, "perhaps you feel different about it."

Arthur had the bill crumpled and stuffed back into the little man's pocket in one quick movement. "Take your money and get the hell out of here," he said.

"Hey, use your head," Joe said, pulling Arthur away from the little man. "We've got to find out what's going on here. Go cool off, for God's sake."

Arthur walked over to the window and stood there with his back to the little man. He had been accused of being a dreamer, an idealist, a fanatic. But he had never been called a stool pigeon. Never had anybody questioned his integrity, let alone offered to buy it for twenty dollars. It was too much. Especially on this day it was too much.

That it should have come to this. Six months ago in this very room he had gathered the faithful ones, fifteen in all. "We are the first," he said to them then. "We will begin the Keeping of Human Records." One by one they had drifted away from him, all but Erma and Joe. They said they were too tired after working all day. They said it was hard for them to write down their thoughts. Some of them had really been in earnest. A few had lasted as long as four months. But it had been an avocation, something they did last after everything else was done. When they had all quit except Joe and Erma, he had been discouraged, but not as he was now. Because he thought he knew what was wrong. He hired five unemployed people. Now it will *be* their work, he said to Joe. Now it will be the most important thing to do because it's all they have to do. He paid them five dollars a week, all he could afford, to write in their secret, unexamined books a daily record of their thoughts. For several weeks he paid them out of the printing business and then, when the profits were insufficient to do it longer, he and Erma moved over the print shop so he could use the rent money to pay them. Now there was no money coming from the business. There was nothing else he and Erma could give up.

And it was this day, when he had come to the place where he knew he had to tell them, that a little man had the gall to hold a twenty-dollar bill under his nose, a bill that would pay four men to keep the Records for one more week.

Joe sat down on the stool opposite Mr. Dobenski. "Your boy must have written something pretty bad in that record to make you so scared," he said.

Mr. Dobenski began to have hope again. "You work with Mr. Herrick?" he asked, and his hand began to search once more for the twenty dollars.

"Just leave your money be, Pop," Joe said. "I don't want it either. What I want to know is, what are you scared of or what's Pete scared of? You tell me that, maybe we can get somewhere."

"Well, you see my boy's in jail. He gets to thinking; he gets scared. He thinks how he wrote in that record for Mr. Herrick—

only what's in there, it ain't true. It ain't Pete, what he done. It's all copied out of a detectiff magazine, you know. Pete, he said he didn't know what to write, so he just copied some of this magazine down about a man that was poisoned."

Joe looked over at Arthur's back. It was no longer the back of an angry or defiant or insulted man. It sagged. "Well, that's a hot one," Joe said. "Twenty-five bucks we paid for a detective story we never read."

"You see," Mr. Dobenski went on, "Pete, he gets to thinking in jail maybe the police might come here or Mr. Herrick, he might give Pete's book to the police and they wouldn't know it was only a magazine story. Maybe they'd think Pete poisoned that man."

Joe went over to the row of notebooks, chose number 17, opened it, and held it before the little man. "Is that Pete's writing?" he asked.

"That's it, all right," Mr. Dobenski said, and moved his hand toward the book.

"You got nothing to worry about, Mr. Dobenski," Joe said. He knew Arthur had turned around and was watching them, but he paid no attention. He ripped the sheets from the book and tore them in two. Then he put them into the ash tray and set them afire. All three men watched the pages burn and no one spoke.

When all the sheets were blackened Joe said, "Well, you satisfied now, Mr. Dobenski?"

"I thank you," the little man said. "I'll tell Pete." But he sat on in the chair. Perhaps they had made another one on their typewriter just like this. Such things could be done. Perhaps they were tricking him some way he didn't know, since they would not take his twenty dollars.

No one moved or said anything. Only Mr. Dobenski sat there with his many creases, hating to leave the room until he was sure. Meanwhile the blackened paper burned gray at the edges. Finally the little man stood up.

"But, Mr. Herrick," he said, "I don't see . . . I don't know what you get out of it."

"Why don't you tell him, Arthur?" Joe said. "Go ahead. Here you got a perfect laboratory. Why don't you use it? Tell him just like you told me. Go ahead."

Arthur came over toward them. "All right," he said, "I'll try." He climbed wearily onto the stool and sat facing the little man. "Sit down, Mr. Dobenski, and I'll tell you what I get out of it."

"I'll go tell Erma to hold the food," Joe said. "Give him all you got. We've got to find out where we missed on Pete."

Arthur had used a lot of ways trying to explain the Human Records to people, but he had never tried before to tell it to a man who thought he was selling information to the police. Mr. Dobenski sat watching Arthur trying to form and aim exactly the right words and he was puzzled. He had never seen anything like it.

"Well, now, I'll tell you this way," Arthur said. "One night my father woke up and he couldn't sleep. He lay there a long time in bed by my mother and finally he got up very quietly so as not to wake my mother and he lit his pipe and walked across the room in his bare feet. It was summer and the window was open and my father stood there by the window in his bare feet and he was thinking about something."

"Yes?" Mr. Dobenski said.

"But I don't know what he was thinking about, Mr. Dobenski. And now my father is dead and he never told me and it is gone. He didn't leave any record of it anywhere and now I will never know what he was thinking about."

"Don't feel too bad, Mr. Herrick," the little man said. "Sometimes, you know, fathers when they do that, they don't think about anything. Sometimes they just stand there."

"We'll try your father," Arthur said, a little encouraged by the fact that the man had at least replied, had perhaps even recognized something familiar in the story. "Do you know what your father thought about the night you were born? Do you know what your father thought about when he was sick? Do you really know how it was with him to eat peaches or to hear the violin or to think of dying?"

"It's so, I don't know those things," said Mr. Dobenski. "I never thought about it before."

"Well, do you wish you knew those things about your father, if you could? Or do you wish you knew how Pete feels about being in jail?"

"Well, Pete, he feels pretty bad."

"You see, Mr. Dobenski, it isn't just that I wish I knew about my father. I wish I knew about your father, too, and hundreds of other men."

Mr. Dobenski shifted one foot forward. He looked toward the door.

"Look, Mr. Dobenski," Arthur said, "some day there will be a great big building, bigger than the cathedral, and it will be full of Human Records. It will be a People's Library. People like you and me, they can go there on Sunday with their children and look up on the shelves and point to their own records, records like this. . . ."

Arthur went over to the shelf and selected notebook number 1. "Here," he said. "Here's my own. I've kept it for three years now. It's got all the things I think about in it, and some of the things I do. Imagine the People's Library, bigger than the cathedral, full of thousands of these. Doctors could go there and students and teachers and businessmen and writers and farmers and painters and they could read whole lives. Kids could study them in school just the way they study geography. Suppose it's a hundred years from now and your record was there and a young man read in it how you felt the day your barn burned down and your cow burned to death?"

"That was a terrible day," Mr. Dobenski said.

"People do keep records all the time," Arthur said. "They do feel the need to. Only they keep all the wrong things. They keep rent receipts and pedigrees on their cows and dogs. They keep their bridal dresses and their baby's shoes. They keep snapshots and posed photographs. They keep recipes and tinfoil and stamps and string and old sheet music and deeds of sale, but nothing of themselves that is uniquely theirs. Sometimes when a man dies you can go through his things and find out every penny that he spent and what he bought with it and the names of his relatives and his friends on their letters, but the man himself is gone and you can never find out what he really wanted or how close he came to getting it."

Mr. Dobenski had never seen anything like it. It made him shy to see the young man trying so hard. He looked out the window.

"Well, Mr. Dobenski," Arthur said, "you asked me what I get out of it. That's what I get out of it. I want to make a start, that's all. Really, I don't get anything out of it, because I suppose it will be a hundred years or so before there's enough of them to mean anything. Only somebody has to start it, that's all. Somebody has to begin the keeping of Human Records, not the way that history is written or the way that novels are written, but the way that lives are written: a little at a time."

Mr. Dobenski stood up, assembling his thirteen repeated crease patterns. "It's getting dark," he said. "I should go home now."

"You aren't afraid any more, are you, Mr. Dobenski? You don't think I'd do anything to hurt Pete?" Arthur asked.

"No, Mr. Herrick, I believe you . . . only . . ."

"Only what?"

"Only I think you should maybe build the building first."

"The building?"

"That building bigger than the cathedral. Then maybe people would be afraid to trick you."

Something had hit home, then. Arthur was filled with affection for the little man. "You're right," he said. "Only I have no money. I have no money to build a building and no land to put it on. All I've got is an idea and a handful of people, Mr. Dobenski, and an ebbing faith."

The little man began to move toward the door slowly. Finally he stopped and turned around. "Mr. Herrick," he said, "please don't get mad with me. I don't want to get you mad again. But I think you should take the money now for a different reason."

"Why?" Arthur said.

"Well, my boy, he cheated you, Mr. Herrick. You paid him and he didn't do what you paid him for. He copied out a story from a detectiff magazine, so I figure he owes you some money."

"Well, thanks, Mr. Dobenski, but you don't owe me anything. Look, I'll tell you why. If we had that big building I told you about, if we had thousands of boys keeping records, I'll bet you that same detective story would show up someplace else. Maybe if you took all those records that had that same detective story in it, maybe all those boys had something else alike, too. It might be a good thing to know. You can't tell. You see, you just can't tell what's going to be valuable ahead of time."

"Well, good night, Mr. Herrick. I think you should take the twenty dollars, but then . . ." The little man moved his creases slowly through the darkness of the front office and out the door.

Arthur locked it after him, turned out the lights in the rear room, and, with notebooks 1 and 2 under his arm, started up the rear stairs. He was very hungry.

"Where's Joe?" he said to Erma.

"He went out," she said. "He said he'd be right back."

When Joe came back to the shop, he let himself in with his key, went quietly into the darkened back room. Here he stood a minute, listening, and then suddenly he turned on the lights and walked over to the shelf of Records.

The Herricks were already eating when Joe climbed the rear stairs. "How'd you come out with old man Dobenski?" he said as he sat down.

"Pretty good, I think," Arthur said. "You'll never guess what finally caught his interest."

"What?"

"The building. The People's Library Building. He thinks we should build it first and then collect the Records."

"Well, I'll be damned," Joe said. "Jesus, Erma, you should have seen them. The old man offered twenty dollars for Pete's record and I thought Arthur was going to kill him."

"Where you been?" Arthur said.

"Down to the jail to see Pete. He tells the same story as the old man, except for the twenty dollars. He didn't know his old man had twenty dollars and it really made him sore. I talked to that guy for an hour and I can't find out where we went wrong. I can't see what we did ever made him think we'd peddle his record to the police."

Erma poured herself a cup of coffee and made a little whirl-pool in it with her spoon. Was there never going to be a good time for her news? How long would she have to hold in this secret, waiting for it to be assured a receptive audience?

"Arthur," Erma asked, "why is it that you and Joe and I can keep the Records and nobody else can stick to it, or haven't we tried enough people yet?"

"I know why it is," Arthur said, "but I don't know how to change it. It's because, with us, it's the most important or one of the most important things we do. It's one of the first things. With other people, it's a last thing. That I don't know how to change. If only there were a place, a new place, where we could go and start out with the idea that the keeping of the Records was a first thing. With me, now, it took about six months to learn how to do it. First you keep lying and putting the emphasis on events and then finally you have occasion to refer to your own record and you make the discovery that you cannot trust it, because you have omitted or distorted the truth. After that you begin in earnest to tell the truth and then finally you come to the place where you either have to change your life so you can bear to record it, or else you come to feel that you can bear to record the truth as it is. After that, you get a kind of second wind and then the writing gets easy. With me, it took about six months before I got that second wind and I suppose it is near that with most people. Now we simply can't get them to stick it out long enough for it to come easily because it is not a first thing with them.

"It makes you so furious," Arthur went on. "At least twice there's been a chance in the history of the world when it could have been a first thing and no one even tried it. Once was when learning was confined to the monasteries. If only those monks had written down themselves instead of illuminating with that painstaking gold lettering the same book over and over. Again, when large sums of government money had to be put out to unemployed people right here in this country, they could at least have tried to get the people to give something important of themselves for it."

"Lots of those people couldn't write," Joe said.

"All right. You're the practical one. If you want to be practical, look what a stimulation would have been given to literacy. A lot of people could learn to write in about three weeks if their food depended on it."

"That's pretty tough on the people, though, Arthur. That's pretty high-handed, I mean," Joe said, "to hold out requirements on top of misfortune."

"Living is tough on the people," Arthur said. "They might just as well be trying. Oh, well, what are we arguing about? They didn't do it. I just wanted to point out that at least twice when there's been enough power to do it, they didn't even think of it. Now we've thought of it and we don't have the power to do it."

"Power?" Joe said. "What fools we are. We're sitting on top of a printing press and you say we have no power. I'm not so surprised I didn't think of it, but I don't see how in hell you could have missed it so long. Give me a piece of paper, man. I want to do some figuring."

Erma got up from the table and got Joe a scratch pad and pencil. Then she began to carry the dishes out into the kitchen so that the two men could have table space.

"You mean a book? A book explaining the whole thing?" Arthur asked. "Why didn't we think of that before?"

"Suppose you started out as though you were trying to explain it to Dobenski," Joe said, "and then kept adding new stuff."

"Yes," Arthur said. "Sure. And there's no need to confine ourselves to this town at all. We could mail it all over the whole country. We could mail it to foreign countries if we wanted to. Erma!" he called toward the kitchen. "Come listen."

How curious, Erma thought, that Arthur had never thought of writing it in a book. How strange that the type of prophet should vary so little through the ages, that always a solitary man should return from his revelation in the wilderness alone with a desire to *tell*, to look in the eyes of his friends and *tell* them, to go from group to group, speaking, speaking, so that always it had been left to a follower, a disciple, a student to write down the revelation.

"We could mail them to all different kinds of people," Joe said. "It wouldn't be any trouble to get lists. We could get classified directories of other cities. Hell, there's no limit to what we could do with it."

"That's right," Arthur said. "You can't tell what will happen. We may run into some other people already trying the same thing."

Joe pushed the chair back from the table and balanced it on its two back legs. Erma watched him as always in fascination. In the hundreds of times she had seen him do this, he had never once fallen.

"Listen," Joe said, "we could do all the labor ourselves, see. Keep the cost down, but make a beautiful job out of it."

"I'd set it by hand," Arthur said. "Cloister, I think. And for the front I'd use that thing of Virginia Woolf's: 'The strange thing about life is that though the nature of it must have been apparent to every one for hundreds of years, no one has left any adequate account of it. The streets of London have their map but our passions are uncharted. What are you going to meet if you turn this corner?' "

Arthur sat quiet for a long time. He reached over and picked up Joe's sheet of figures. "Well," he said, "it looks beautiful on paper. I wish we had the money we've soaked into those Records downstairs. We can't even buy the paper to print a book on. And very likely all those downstairs are just like Pete's. Copied out of magazines or maybe the encyclopedia."

"No, they're O.K.," Joe said.

"How do you know?" Arthur said. "I don't have any faith they're on the level."

"I looked at them," Joe said. He straightened his chair and sat looking at the table top. Erma looked away from him. Oh, now there would never be a good time for her wonderful news.

"When?" Arthur asked.

"After I came back from jail," Joe said. "Just before I came up here."

There was a terrible silence in the room and Erma finally got up and went into the bedroom. Joe slowly raised his eyes to Arthur's. "Well," he said, "it's done. I've already done it. It's over with. There's a limit to how long we could have gone on beating our brains out when they might all have been detective stories."

He did not move his eyes from the other man's and gradually the color came back into Arthur's face. There was a look of defeat there, for a moment, a look of sorrow, and then suddenly he smiled.

"I don't know why I'm sitting here in righteous indignation, Joe," he said. "You did it and now I never have to. I can always tell myself that I wouldn't have. They were really all right? All of them?"

"I just read a page at random in each one," Joe said. "Mostly they're too much like an ordinary diary—'got to work late, came home, went to movies' sort of stuff—but they were all real as far as they went. They weren't copied out of detective magazines, I can tell you that."

"It beats me," Arthur said, "how we never thought of a book before. It's got such possibilities. Suppose we send a book to a guy that's not capable of keeping a record or that's not interested. That doesn't mean it ends there, the way it would if you tried to tell him about it. Maybe he'll give the book to somebody. Maybe he'll throw it in the trash and the trashman'll read it."

"Sure," Joe said. "That's the beauty of having a press of our own."

"Only," Arthur said, "where'll we get the money to print the book?"

"We'll raise it," Joe said. "This isn't something we've got to do tomorrow. You've got to write the book first. Listen, I got to

go over and get Gwen. Tomorrow we'll figure the whole thing out
—the cost, I mean."

Erma came back into the room and she looked from one face
to the other, but there was no way of telling what had happened
or how they had got over the terrible time.

"Erma," Joe said, "what time did you tell Gwen I'd be over
there?"

"Eight, and it's eight-thirty now."

"Oh, Lord. I haven't even shaved. Better to have the bristles
on my face than Gwen's back, I guess."

But he did not seem to be very much troubled and he left the
room at his usual good-natured, leisurely pace.

Whatever it was that had happened between them, it was all
right now to tell Arthur her secret, for she had rarely seen him
look so happy. She went up to him where he was standing by the
bookcase hunting for his volume of Virginia Woolf with which to
verify his memory for the front of the book. Erma kissed him on
the back of his neck and he turned around suddenly to her.

"I've been saving a secret to tell you all day," she said, "only
every time I started, you were in some more trouble. First, Joe
couldn't collect any money and you thought you'd have to give up
the Records, and then that Pete Dobenski trouble and then, after
that, that time with Joe."

"I'll tell you about that later," he said, "but it's all right now.
Everything's better now. What's your secret?"

"Justin Magnus is coming here."

"*Your* Justin Magnus? Your composer?"

"Yes. Oh, Arthur, I don't know why or how it ever happened
here, but he's coming in two months and he's going to give a concert. Think of it. Justin Magnus. I'll really hear Justin Magnus
and surely he'll do some of his own work."

"I'll get you a seat in the first row, Erma, I promise. If I've
got to print a tissue job, I'll get you a front seat."

"We'll both have front seats," she said. She reached into her
pocket then and brought out a little roll of bills, very neatly
creased. "Arthur," she said, "would this pay for your book?"

He unfolded the money as though there were constant danger that it would fall in a fire or be swept away by a tornado.

"A hundred dollars! My God," he said, "where did you get
a hundred dollars? What is it?"

"Will it do it?" she said.

"Well, it'll come close. I mean, if we do all our own labor, we could make it do it. Why, you can perform a miracle with a hundred dollars. Where did it come from? What is it?"

"It's . . . it's savings," she said. "I've been saving it a long time, but only for something very important."

"But, Erma, you need it for yourself. You need so many things."

"You get me a seat on the front row to hear Justin Magnus," she said, "that's all I need. How do you suppose they ever got him to come *here?*"

Arthur was hardly listening. He stood looking at the money in his hand. "Erma," he said, "is it really all right—the money, I mean? You must have meant it for—"

"I meant it for something important," she said. "And this book, it is important, isn't it?"

"If I didn't believe that," Arthur said, "my God, where would I be?"

It was one of the things she prided herself on—that she had finally learned to distinguish between the questions that Arthur asked of God and the ones he asked of her. She reached out and touched his shoulder with an awkward little gesture. "Do you want any coffee or anything," she asked, "before I go to bed? This has been a day."

"No, thanks," he said. "I can get it if I do. I put your Record on your dressing table when I came up."

Erma sat at her dressing table combing her hair. The top of the table had, not so long ago, been the underside of a bread-board, but it was anchored firmly to the wall and served equally well for a desk. Its skirt had been a tablecloth belonging to Erma's mother and it was fastened in neat pleats around the breadboard by thumbtacks. She opened her Record and began to write of Justin Magnus and, after this, of the lesser events of the day.

And when I gave Arthur the hundred dollars, he asked me, "What is it?" And I did not know how to answer you, Arthur. Should I have said, "A hundred dollars is a baby"? I don't know just where I got the idea that I had to have a hundred dollars to have a baby, but it's a fixed sum in my mind. The two are so synonomous with me that once I wrote baby instead of hundred dollars when I was typing a letter for you. But I can't tell you this, Arthur, because then you could not take the money and also you would think that I must have the baby right away or that I am thinking about it all the time. And suppose you failed with the Human Records? Suppose you had to give it up because the baby had mastoid or pneumonia or whatever else babies have that is expensive? Then would not the baby mean to you something that you did not get to do? A baby must be something that you did get to do. And I can wait until you either win or fail of yourself with the records and have it settled, just as I had to wait until I had admitted that I was not a great pianist. I could not dare to run the risk of believing that I could have been if it had not been for the baby. No baby should be asked to equal all its life some negative thing in its parents. I will wait. Perhaps by that time I will have another hundred dollars, or perhaps I will not believe any more that I need it.

Or should I have said what the hundred dollars was? It was rayon instead of silk. It was margarine instead of butter. It was not going to the movies. It's taking off your stockings as soon as you come in the house so that they will last longer. It's being without cold cream and putting off going to the dentist. It's standing out in the alley trying to do dry cleaning with an inflammable fluid and remembering all the people that have been killed that way. It's regular instead of air mail. It's passing beggars on the street without looking into their eyes. It's reading the price column of a menu first and pouring the cream off the top of milk bottles and hoping that people will come to see you after dinner. It is not having insurance and wearing shoes that are too wide for you and never buying a magazine with its slick new smell. It is a limp toothbrush and no perfume and only vegetables in the garden. It is an untuned piano.

But why should I tell you these things, Arthur? You have a list of your own. So I said it's savings.

Across the town Mr. Dobenski was also awake, not, however, because he was writing his record of the day, as Erma Herrick was. Mr. Dobenski was awake simply because he could not sleep. Like Mr. Herrick's father, he thought, I'm awake in the night, only I got no wife in the bed to be quiet for. Also, like Mr. Herrick's father, he climbed out of bed, lighted his pipe, and walked in his bare feet over to the window. As he had told Mr. Herrick, fathers sometimes just stand there. Only Mr. Herrick's father did not have a boy in jail.

What had he, Dobenski, done wrong that his boy should be in jail? Had he beat him too much, or not enough? And what in the name of a holy thing had Pete wanted with a typewriter? That was the thing he could not find the answer to.

His son, Pete, was awake too, lying on his bunk in the city jail, saying over and over to himself: The bastard, the dirty little bastard, the son of a bitch. He had a twenty-dollar bill on him all the time. He could have *bought* me a typewriter—at least a secondhand one.

But this is not recorded anywhere, nor is there in Pete Dobenski's record any explanation of why he had placed such great importance on the possession of a typewriter. The only record Pete Dobenski left was an account of the murder, by poisoning, of a man in a detective magazine. And this man, the magazine led Pete to believe, did not die from the poison of hatred or the poison of envy or the poison of defeat or humiliation or frustration or from any poison of his own. He died, so the magazine says, from a strange poison in no way concerned with him, not of his own making or of his own knowledge or of his own body. He died, so the magazine says, from a poison out of a glass bottle, bought in a drugstore for seventy-five cents.

And Arthur Herrick sat late at the dining-room table writing, writing, long after Erma had finished and gone to bed, for he had decided how he would begin the book:

The rocks keep an accurate record. Fossils hold facts. Calcareous strata and the rings of trees and the great loop-folded streams of lava know the value of the moment. Mankind, alone in nature, relies on retrospect.

Man will speak with tenderness of his childhood, with amusement of his adolescence, and with appreciation or regret of his youth, but the ring in a cross section of a tree trunk that was laid down there in the spring of 1912 is the spring of 1912 and not a memory of it.

Mankind alone blunders on its way to death content with memory in huge lumps, while the unique essence of its individual times goes unmarked and dissipated like a sigh upon the wind and a breath upon the night.

CHAPTER THREE

JUSTIN MAGNUS lay on a hard and strange bed in a strange and uncomfortable hotel room, waiting for midnight. His long legs extended over the foot of the too-short bed and an electric light shone directly in his eyes, yet he was hardly aware of these things. He had just finished the third of his concerts on tour, but even though he had felt himself playing well tonight, he was not able to relax now that the ordeal was over once again.

Every night at midnight he called Max by long distance, this being the only time he was ever sure of being undisturbed. Leaving Edith had proved to be almost impossible at the last moment and it was only this nightly talk with Max that made the tour endurable. Max alone he trusted to tell him the truth. He felt that Mrs. Norris would be unable to resist protecting him. Mornings were possible, somehow. He was concerned with the coming evening's concert or with rehearsals or, often, with traveling accommodations, but in the afternoon, just before dusk, apprehension would begin to rise in him both for his performance and for Edith and it would be a slow and continuous crescendo of tension until he was actually on the stage. Often, during the concert, he would be aware of Edith to the point of forgetting his audience and forgetting his fear of it. After the concert, he would have a time of fondness for the people in the audience, as though he and they had been through a great ordeal together, and sometimes he had an hour's relaxation at this time. It was then, just after the concert, that he would realize his hunger and he would go out alone, if he could manage it, and eat. But after dinner he would begin to wait for midnight. Often he had only a few moments to wait; but tonight he had half an hour.

There was mail which Max had forwarded but he was unable to be attentive to it. He had plans for the next day to think on, too, and a little packing to do, but he lay there stiffly on the small, uncomfortable bed, his arms behind his huge gray head, the electric light shining in his eyes, unable to concentrate on anything but the telephone call he would soon make. Finally it was time and the reassuring voice of Max was inquiring about the concert.

"A little better than the last one," Justin said. "And Edith?"

"A little better, also, I'm glad to say," Max said. "Mrs. Norris called at eleven. Edith was asleep. She has been making a blanket today, Mrs. Norris said. She is sewing words into the blanket with colored thread."

"Oh, yes," Justin said. "She made them for Tommy, I remember. That's good, then. That was a good time. She worked all winter on the blankets, it seems to me. That's fine, Max. Thanks so much for that. And did she eat her dinner?"

"Yes, Mrs. Norris said she ate lunch and dinner both today, though a light dinner. She went to bed immediately after."

"Do you think it worries her, Max? I mean does she ask where I am?"

"Not today, Justin. She asked yesterday, I told you. Mrs. Norris told her you were on tour and it seemed to satisfy her. When do you get your train out of there?"

"In the morning. Well, thanks, Max. I'll call you tomorrow night."

"Good luck," Max said. "Get some rest."

Now he *could* rest. He lay down on the bed for a moment, but it was all changed now. He was aware that it was hard and strange and small. He was painfully aware that the overhead light was shining in his eyes. He thought of the mail, still unopened, and the packing, still not done. He swung himself to his feet, turned out the light, undressed, and lay down naked on the bed. It was very hot in the room and finally he shifted his huge body so that he was lying diagonally across the bed, and then, at last, he could rest. Lying there in the dark in the quiet of a small-town night, he felt himself sinking down heavily into tiredness. He crossed his arms behind his head and closed his eyes and began to think of Tommy's old blankets.

Edith had said she felt dauncy and she was impatient because she could not go out of doors. It seemed to him that she had been confined to the house almost the whole of that winter after Tommy's birth. She had had a bad cold and later influenza and she had taken the continuous dreary weather as a personal insult.

"There are those damned thank-you letters for Tommy's baby presents that I still haven't written," she said. "I really can't keep putting them off this way."

"Well, I'll help you," Justin said. "Let's do them and get them off your mind."

She had got them out then, all Tommy's presents, and ticked them off against a list, and then she had said that she simply couldn't tackle the notes without a cup of tea. She had sat there by the fire, holding her cup of tea, looking very thin and petulant and dauncy, eying the presents.

"Seven baby blankets, actually, Justin. Seven! My God, there is nothing in the world so dull as seven baby blankets. And always, always, the same procession. There is the white one with the wool fringe and the blue one bound in blue satin and the pink bound in pink satin. Why doesn't someone make a rainbow baby blanket or a scarlet one or a paisley one?"

"Well, at least," Justin said, "you can have a different one for each day in the week."

"We *will* have one for each day in the week," she said. "After all, they don't have to be so dull." She had run upstairs then and returned a little later, out of breath, carrying a basket of bright-colored threads.

"What are you going to do?" he said.

"You'll see."

"What about your letters?"

"Oh, the hell with the letters. I'll do them tomorrow; tomorrow I'll feel better about the blankets."

So she had begun the slow work of stitching into the blankets the story of the creation. Almost the whole winter she spent on it, sitting with him in the evenings, her lap covered with the brilliant threads, while he worked on his symphony.

"How do you know where to change colors?" he had asked her once.

"Oh, there's no plan," she said. "Every time my needle runs out of thread I change color. That way I don't lose interest, you see, because I never know how it's going to come out."

And Tommy had loved his blankets. They were his comfort and his bedtime stories and later his first reader. "Read me my blanket," he'd say at night. So many nights had Justin sat by the child's bed "reading his blankets" that even now he could say them all from memory, like old prayers.

A cool wind came into the room and Justin reached out and pulled part of the bedcover over his naked body. He was too tired to get under the covers properly or to get up and find his pajamas. He closed his eyes and worked his head into a hollow of the unfamiliar pillow while the old, old words slipped through his mind. He could see clearly before his eyes the brilliant letters stitched into the blankets, though in the center of each blanket was superimposed the red after-image of a light bulb.

In the beginning God made the heavens and the earth. The earth was without form and darkness was upon the face of the deep. God said, *Let there be light,* and there was light. And God divided the shadows from the light and He called the light Day and the shadows Night. This was the first day.

This had been the Monday blanket, the blue wool one. Strange how furious David had got over these blankets later on. Full of facts from his new Christmas encyclopedia and hero worship for a brilliant teacher, he had insisted that Edith make them all over, make them, as he said, "true." He had even written them out for her "the way that they ought to be."

"No, Davie," Edith had said. "You're my intellectual. You were a long child; Tommy is wide. Tommy is a snuggler." Tommy and I don't want to lie under a blanket of scientific facts. We want a nice, warm, soft God just now, a nice old man sitting on a rock, with his hands on his knees, his white hair cut in a long bob and his belly full of mashed potatoes.

Long before he could read them, Tommy could tell the blankets apart and he resented any discrepancies in their order. Once they had heard him screaming in terrible temper at a new nurse, "But Tuesday is pink! Tuesday is pink, I tell you!"

Then God said, *Let the waters gather unto themselves and let the dry land appear.* And he called the dry land Earth and he called the waters Sea. This was the second day.

Oh, it would be good to be home now, to be with Edith again in the time of the creation blankets. He used to carry her upstairs that winter. While she was brushing the bright threads off her skirt, he would swoop on her and lift her up and always she protested. She had to turn out the lights or put out the milk bottles or squeeze the orange juice for morning, or something. But he would carry her up anyway and then later, if he remembered, he would come back to do whatever it was.

And on the third day God said, *Let the earth be covered with*

green, and it was so. And He made the trees of the forests, the
grasses of the fields, and the flowers of the meadow.

It seemed such an extra waste, for Justin, that the boys had
been so distinctly individual. He swung his feet over the side of
the bed and sat up. He must do something to change his thoughts
or he would never get to sleep. He reached for his pipe and sat
on the edge of the bed smoking in the dark, trying to weigh and
choose among the various mental tricks he was accustomed to use
to get his mind free of his sons' deaths. He decided that he would
say the creation blankets straight through, like prayers.

The next morning on the train he still held over a little of
that secure feeling of the dauncy winter and the creation blankets,
and he was glad that he had not tried to go through his mail the
night before because now it would be a diversion for the journey.
He came to a letter addressed in an unfamiliar and curious handwriting. Max's small, neat forwarding instructions on the envelope
were in great contrast to the spacious, almost vertical, hand of the
original address. The letter was postmarked *Drury,* which he
recognized as being one of the towns on his tour. He read:

MY DEAR JUSTIN MAGNUS:
At night when I am lying awake in the dark it
seems quite reasonable for me to write to you. It seems
then that I will write a letter of such sincerity that it would
be unmistakable to you. It also seems that you will like
the letter and read it with sympathy. Yet each morning I
become self-conscious about it and I feel that I will write
a silly letter and that you won't like it.
To be truthful, this is about the twentieth attempt
and this one I am writing at dusk, so as to strike midway
between overconfidence and fear. The request is very
simple, really. It is only to ask you to stay with my
husband and me while you are in Drury.
I suppose you get a great many such requests and I
suppose it will be difficult to convince you that this one is
motivated neither by romanticism nor social ambition.
But I'm going to try all the same. In fairness, of course, I'll
have to list your alternatives.
There's the hotel. It's terrible. It's run down, old, dirty
and next to the railroad track over which a freight train
rattles at three in the morning. Our place is also old and run

down. In fact we live upstairs over my husband's print shop.
But it's clean and we're several blocks from the railroad
track. True, the vibration of the presses shakes the floor,
but while you're here we won't run the presses.

Next, I suppose, would be Mrs. Clyde Robinson's
house. Rachmaninoff stayed there one night before the war
when the trains were stopped because of a flood. Mrs.
Robinson got up at dawn so that she could be sure to have
everything perfect for his breakfast, but he said he only
wanted shredded wheat. It's a nice room, though, very
large and quiet, with a fireplace in it. We don't have a
fireplace, but on the other hand, we have never had
Rachmaninoff for a guest either, so you wouldn't have
any competition.

The next largest house belongs to the Gerards. They
also have a large guest room. It doesn't have a fireplace but
it has a Beautyrest mattress. However, Mrs. Gerard leads
the choir at the First Methodist Church and it is just
possible that she might sing for you.

But it is much more difficult for me to compete against
Mrs. Perry's house. It's an old farm house on the edge
of town and Mrs. Perry has an apple orchard. I suppose you
could have a whole wing of it to yourself because all of her
children are gone away now. She can't sing either. She's
just a wonderfully sweet and gentle old lady and I wouldn't
be surprised if she had two fireplaces in each room and
mattresses of white swan's down.

Only she couldn't have been fifteen years old the way
that I was fifteen years old. Because just before I was fifteen,
my mother died. My father was a piano tuner but when
the war broke out nobody cared any more whether their
pianos were in tune or not and my father was busy all the
time trying to find some other kind of work. It was the first
birthday that I hadn't had a cake. I was too big to play with
dolls and all the other little girls were too embarrassed to
talk to me because my mother had just died.

I was alone all that day, but at dusk my father came
home and he brought me a recording of *The Knife and the
Grapes*. We played it and then he and I left the house and
walked out past Mrs. Perry's apple orchard and on to the
country. And on the way home I thought I would grow up

to be very great and write a concerto for train whistle and flute.

You have saved many many days for me. Since I have known you were in the world I have always felt able to make my own birthday cakes.

That is why I would like to have you be at our house. Perhaps it is not really so different from the way Mrs. Robinson felt about Rachmaninoff; I also would like to make your breakfast.

Sincerely,
ERMA HERRICK

The letter still in his hand, Justin Magnus turned and looked out the train window. Such land as this that child had walked over, at dusk, with the notes of *The Knife and the Grapes* fresh in her mind, the notes lying there lightly on top of grief and death and loneliness and no birthday cake. If only he had had this letter before the first concert. If only he could hold fast to the belief that one's music truly . . . truly touched. This was what they never told you, the only kind of comment which is of any possible good to an artist.

A piano tuner had got it for her. That, to Justin, was more remarkable than all the rest. How often had he sat watching a piano tuner work, wondering how he could bear to listen to the sounds he made. He had, in his lifetime, been exposed to hundreds of piano tuners and never had he heard one of them express the faintest interest in music. They were, as he remembered them, curiously lacking in conversation.

Just where you weren't looking for it, there it was, in the hidden and forgotten places, the hearing ear, the weapon against one's ever-wakeful doubt. Perhaps in the town last night there had been such a person as this girl, perhaps more than one. It was good to know. He read the letter over again. For no matter his age or his fame, one thing stays constant with an artist all his life: that if there be an ear to hear what he meant to speak, he is grateful for it. It had been more than thirty years since he had written *The Knife and the Grapes,* and yet it had meaning to this girl today. He looked out at the country with a sense of calmness and of weight. What had this one thought of his fourth symphony? he wondered. Had she heard it? Yes, surely, he would stay with these people his one night in Drury, though such a thing was not his custom.

Later than usual today the thought of Edith came upon him. She would be awake now. He hoped that she would go on with Tommy's creation blanket because it was good to think of her so. Perhaps had Edith not been ill, he would have *The Green Kingdom* finished by now. Yet it was unfair to blame this on Edith. One got old. One ran dry. One lived on beyond one's time.

He folded Erma Herrick's letter and put it in his pocket, and over the crackling of the envelope came very clearly the first few notes of a theme. He left his hand suspended over his pocket, so as not to interrupt the stream of notes, and gradually he closed his eyes to blot out the countryside and the noise of the train. He could hear it quite clearly, the theme, as belonging to *The Green Kingdom,* yet it seemed familiar. Many miles the train carried Justin over the country while he sat motionless, listening. Finally he opened his eyes and turned to the window. Then once more, quite clearly, the whole theme repeated itself, and suddenly, as the train came even with an isolated farm house, he saw the shadow of a maple tree thrown in darkness on its slanting roof and he recognized the theme. It belonged to *Lazarus.*

Many years ago, after Justin had written *The Knife and the Grapes* and before he had begun his first symphony, he had begun an opera called *Lazarus.* He had, however, felt himself disoriented in the opera form and, once he had begun work on his first symphony, had discarded *Lazarus* unfinished. The symphony was right for him, belonged to him.

Once he had recognized the theme as part of *Lazarus,* he began to have a feeling of excitement, for the parallel between the figure of Lazarus as he had conceived him and that of his grandfather in *The Green Kingdom* was very striking. His preoccupation with the figure of Lazarus dated far back into his childhood with a child's curiosity as to a story's continuation and a child's disregard of a story's climax. His grandmother had told him the story of Lazarus, the brother of Martha and Mary in Bethany, who had been miraculously raised from the dead by Jesus.

"And then what?" he had asked. "Then what did Lazarus do?"

"He went on working, I suppose," his grandmother said, "the same as he had before."

But it had not satisfied the child. He could not think that anything, to Lazarus, would be the same as before. The question had nagged at him for many years, and then one day, after the first flush of his success with *The Knife and the Grapes,* he had found his answer. He saw the figure of Lazarus quite clearly and he began work on the opera of which, until now, he had hardly thought in thirty years. He had conceived of Lazarus as a quiet and rather timid man, content to live with his two sisters in Bethany, not overanxious to start a household of his own, beset with little troubles and the tasks of daily living, dying without much struggle, his body wrapped in linen bandages moistened with the tears of his sisters, and resigned to the tomb with unostentatious grief, the heavy stone rolled quietly and with finality against the tomb.

To this quiet, simple, uncomplaining man came suddenly the notes of the resurrection music (it was this theme that Justin had heard so clearly on the train) and the blinding light of the miracle, and he stumbled out into the dazzling light to stand before the people he had known all his life. While they disentangled the loosened linen bands which held him, he heard still in his ears the trumpets, the angelic voices of the resurrection miracle, and his eyes still held the white, strong light of rebirth.

Cast suddenly into a fame he had never anticipated, the character of Lazarus gradually began to change. His sisters and their old friends made much of him, hardly dared believe this wonder. From miles around the people came to see this marvel, to bring little gifts of food for the pleasure of hearing his own account of the resurrection. A hundred times he had to tell it over. In the streets of Bethany they followed him and for the simplest task he had a wondering, silent audience. Because of him many people were converted to the Christian faith, and to these new ones he was constantly being asked to give advice. Through all this early time he conducted himself with a simple, quiet dignity.

But cattle must be tended, children watched, houses cleaned and food prepared. One sees a miracle and wonders and, for a time, forgets oneself. Yet, in a while, it is one's own life that becomes important again. There were not so many people in Bethany but that in the space of a week they had all heard the story, most of them from Lazarus' own lips. Gradually the crowd thinned, the people returned to their own work, and Lazarus was sometimes left without an audience. The people of Bethany began to be accustomed to living with a miracle in their midst. Even Mary and Martha could not remain forever in a constant state

of awed suspension. Did he not get hungry like any man, this
Lazarus? Did he not leave his clothing fallen on the floor to be
picked up? Did the dust not cover his sandals so that his feet
cried out for washing, as any man's? Moreover, they were concerned now with the fate of Christ, whose persecutors were using
this Lazarus incident against Him.

With the crucifixion of Christ and His resurrection, the miracle of Lazarus was eclipsed. More, such was the fear caused by
the trial of Christ that people for their own safety began to avoid
Lazarus, began publicly to deny acquaintance with him. Even in
his own house there was little attention for Lazarus, his sisters being bowed in grief for the loss of their Lord. And they wept in
fear that they had hastened His end. Had they not said to Him,
"Lord, if Thou hadst been here, our brother would not have
died"? Had they not practically asked Him to raise Lazarus from
the dead and had not this very thing been used against Him?

It was at this time that Lazarus began to lose the simple dignity which had carried him so far through his sudden fame. It is
difficult for a man who has heard the angelic trumpets and seen
the miraculous white light to convince himself that it is necessary
and important for him to milk a goat or to weed a garden. His
standard of what is urgent is changed. Domesticity exists only because of the capacity of a great many people to believe in the
urgency of its small necessities. As the weeks went by, his few
friends who had the courage to speak to him began to bring him
disturbing tales from the town. There were some, they said, who
doubted the authenticity of his resurrection. The eyewitnesses,
they said, were a small number, and of this number two (the sisters) were so overcome by grief as to be incapable of an accurate
account. One witness was said to be half-witted. Later it came to
Lazarus' ears that there were some who said that he had never
been dead and some who hinted that he had never been sick.

It was this that brought about the final change in Lazarus. He
found himself unable to resist speaking of the miracle. At the
slightest pretext he would bring the conversation to illness, death,
resurrection, miracles. He began to insist on it. He questioned
people if they did not believe him. His sisters pleaded with him
to think more upon Christ and less upon his own small part in
Christ's life, and, as the great burden of the work fell heavier upon
them, they began to show their impatience. Lazarus could
scarcely eat a crust of bread without feeling the need to justify his

right to it. He became morbidly sensitive and believed that his sisters regretted his resurrection. Slowly, for the people of Bethany, the miracle turned into the nebulous and doubtful mists of past events. More emphatically than ever, but to fewer and fewer people, Lazarus repeated and insisted on his miracle. Within a year after his resurrection, he was reduced to the half-witted witness and an old whore for audience. These two he had constantly to be buying with wine.

In contrast to the gross and sordid voice of Lazarus' boasting before his sodden, disreputable audience would sound again the clear triumphant notes of the resurrection theme. It was this theme which had now transferred itself to *The Green Kingdom*, and Justin, thinking on the obscure processes of the mind, saw how clearly also the whole foundation of the opera had come through this curious alchemy. Lazarus was discarded and taunted; his grandfather they called a drunkard and a crazy man. Lazarus sat at last with only a half-wit and a whore for audience, and these bought; his grandfather had a small boy and the wine of secrecy.

Perhaps, Justin thought, he was not finished as a composer, then, not drained. He had always regretted the unfinished opera. They should hear again, perhaps, from Justin Magnus. There would be other children to walk through the countryside as Erma Herrick had walked, and in their ears the memory not of *The Knife and the Grapes* but of *The Green Kingdom*.

When the train stopped at the next of Justin's concert towns he was the first to alight, and in one glimpse he took the little town in gladness to himself, for it was here that he would begin, after a silence of ten years, to work again. His concert was not until the following night, which meant that he could begin work immediately. He began to work that evening and it was the first night since he had begun the tour that he was not held and dominated by the tension over Edith. He called Max at midnight with a feeling that, surely, everything must be well.

"How are you?" Max asked.

"Fine," Justin said. "I've begun *The Green Kingdom*."

"That's good," Max said. "Good. How did it happen?"

"It's built on the framework of an old opera, Max, that I started a long time ago. I told you of it once, I think—the Lazarus opera. How's Edith today?"

"I went over to see her this afternoon, Justin. She was resting. She seems all right, only a little tired. She did not know me."

"Oh," Justin said.

"She thought I had come to see you. And it's very curious. You know she told me that you couldn't be disturbed because you were working on an opera and could not get it to come right. I wondered at her saying *opera* because I'd forgotten you ever worked on one."

"How strange, Max. How very strange. I wonder if you'd mind having the doctor drop by tomorrow and see her. I'd feel better about it."

"I will," Max said. "I'll tell you what he says when you call tomorrow night. And good luck with *The Green Kingdom*. I think the tour's doing you good."

Justin came away from the telephone very much shaken. Even now she was with him, almost as though she had *caused* him to think of the Lazarus opera and, through it, to be able to work on *The Green Kingdom*. It was strange and horrible, this feeling he had, as though two people could be so inseparable that their thoughts could compel each other. For what if he were to lose his perspective, his common sense? What if it worked backward, and his working with what had once been the Lazarus opera could keep Edith in the time where she was?

For it was not a good time. It was just before David's birth and she must not come to David's birth alone, without him there to help her. But she did not follow a continuous time, he knew that. Tomorrow she might be in another time altogether. Besides, tomorrow Max would have the doctor in. Yet the fear came back to him. He became obsessed with the idea that if he would quit work on *The Green Kingdom*, if he would stop any connection with *Lazarus*, he could release Edith into a different, safer time.

The floor was littered with sheets of manuscript and he stepped through them to the window and looked out over the town where he had felt such joy awaited him. He could not see a light any place. Tired, Max had said. His Animal Eyes, *tired*. He would quit, though it might be superstition. He would destroy the music he had written. He would deny it. He would *will* Edith to be in another time. He saw her chalk face against the yellow-white of the pillow. He saw the dark hair swept to one side. He saw her eyelids fall slowly, *tiredly*, over the animal eyes.

And even as he saw it he heard in his mind the continuation of the music where he had left off working to call Max. Denying it, he heard it, heard it clearly. He moved across the room and sat down on the floor and began furiously to cover the paper with notes so that his pen made a scratching in the silent room of the silent, darkened, sleeping town.

By the time he got to Drury, where the Herricks lived, he had finished the first movement of *The Green Kingdom*.

CHAPTER FOUR

ARTHUR met Justin Magnus at the train and waited with him through the interview with the local concert manager and the inquiry about departing trains. He went with him to try out the piano in the auditorium and to test the acoustics, and through the hot summer afternoon they started together to the print shop. The heels of Justin's shoes sank into the soft asphalt of the street as they crossed it and waves of heat came up to him from the pavement. He did not feel like a young girl's hero and he very much regretted having accepted the invitation. He had worked constantly on *The Green Kingdom*, and now that the first movement was finished he was suffering a letdown. Also, he had stepped into the intense heat from an air-conditioned train. He dreaded the night's concert. It did not seem possible that he would be able to get through it.

He wished he had the energy to be pleasant to the young man who was walking so quietly beside him carrying his bag. They entered the print shop and, by contrast with the street, it seemed cool. Arthur led the way through the office into the shop and the sharp odor of fresh ink came to Justin, but he was too tired to identify it so that it became only part of the town's heat and his own fatigue. He had forgotten that there were to be stairs and he began to climb them slowly, making a conscious effort not to bend over.

As he made the turn he saw Erma standing at the top of the stairs. In his tiredness she was only a white blur to him, except for the reddish hair, though he was aware of some incongruity, something almost like shock. He saw that she had one hand out toward him. It was not that he took it in greeting so much; it was that he used it to help him make the last step.

He was older, of course, than the way Erma had him in her mind unchanged from a photograph she had seen when she was fifteen, but he was obviously, shockingly tired, even to a stranger's eyes. She did not let go of his hand or offer any word of greeting the way that she had lived it so many times in advance. She kept his hand and led him into the bedroom.

"You must rest," she said. "We will be sure to call you an hour and a half before your concert, so you can go to sleep in confidence if you're able to. I saw you coming from the window and so I ran the water for your bath."

And then she was gone and the door closed behind her and Justin sank down on the side of the bed. For a long time he sat with his head bent over and his eyes closed. Finally he opened his eyes and looked at his shoes. He reached one hand down and began to untie the laces. After that he did not need to think any more. His undressing was accomplished according to an old pattern, and when he found himself in the bathtub with the air coming in from the open window upon his wet body he knew that he would be able to make it all right. It was only a temporary thing. When he opened his eyes the room was no longer blurred and he noticed a low table by the side of the tub. There was a fat, brown earthenware coffeepot on the table and, beside it, a cup and saucer. He poured a cup of the steaming coffee, glad to find that his hand was quite steady. He sat in the tub taking small swallows of the strong, rich coffee, and gradually the tight band he had felt all day above his eyebrows began to loosen and he remembered that he had several hours yet, that there was no longer any demand between him and the night's concert.

The room began to come into focus for him. Finally he realized that the green spots he saw against the sides of the bathtub were actually leaves and he followed them up to the window sill above. They were tendrils of a green vine which spilled luxuriously over the sides of a white bowl set in the window sill. He had never known anyone to put flowers or plants in a bathroom before and the idea of it pleased him. He set his empty coffee cup back on the table beside the tub and began to splash the bath water up on the leaves. The water slid off the leaves into the tub and a few drops remained and hung on their tips for a while.

But of course she would not be a child any more. That had been years ago she had walked in the country with her father. And even then, *The Knife and the Grapes* was already old to him. Naturally she would not still be fifteen, gangling and walking across the countryside, feeling together the greatness of life and the grief of death. He splashed the water upon the green vines once again and reached for the soap. He spread the lather thickly over his face and suddenly, lavishly, nostalgia swept over him and a great sense of longing, but he could not place it.

Shaved, and in his robe, he returned to the bedroom. He searched through the pockets of his coat until he found his pipe and his tobacco. He walked about the room looking for a match, and saw some on a table by the window. By the table was a chair and he sat down, fearful that if he were to smoke his pipe lying down he would fall asleep. The window was open and the smoke from his pipe climbed in a slanting spiral to it. It was good of them to leave him alone like this. He hardly knew what he had expected, but it was not this.

The room was small and the low ceiling sloped. Yet he did not feel cramped in it as he usually did in small rooms. There was nothing in the room except the table and the chair where he now sat and, across the bare, scrubbed floor from it, the low, wide bed. He looked with pleasant anticipation toward the bed with its clean, white, coarse covering. On the scrubbed floorboards beside the bed was a large circular rug of a rich brown color and it looked soft to the feet. Yet he could not remember having stood on it when he was undressing.

He was thirsty and he put out his hand before him on the table where he wished the water to be and it was there, a large pitcher of it, frosted and damp, the cold sweat running down the sides in channels. He poured out a glass of it and the sound of the ice was pleasant. When he put the glass back on the table he saw the huge wooden bowl, full of ice. On the ice were the most magnificent fruits he had ever seen. In the center there were great ripe peaches, red on one cheek, and around them were small blue tight-skinned plums. At the outer edge of the bowl were clusters of grapes, almost black. He spread both hands over the bowl to touch them all, to feel the coldness coming up from the ice. He took a large peach, the center, highest one, and bit into it. It did not seem possible that there could be such flavor left in the world. He tasted each bite slowly, thoroughly. Soon he would begin the second movement of *The Green Kingdom*.

When he had finished the peach, he dipped his hands into the ice to rid them of the juice and he rubbed them roughly over his mouth. He plunged his hands in the ice again and held them over his eyes for a moment and then he walked across the room to the bed. He sat down on it and took off his slippers and then suddenly he stood up again and walked barefoot across the cool bare floor to the table. He took a cluster of the heavy black grapes back to bed with him and lay on his back looking up at the sloping ceiling while he ate the iced grapes one by one, biting them off the tough, heavy stem with his teeth. There was no sound in the house. The cold black liquor of the grapes lay in his throat like the gratitude he bore these people for this quiet time alone.

He dreamed that he was in his grandmother's house and that outside his door he could hear his grandmother's serene and steady tread while she walked about at her household tasks. When Arthur knocked on the door Justin awoke with a feeling of security, a feeling of time, and while he dressed, although the heat was still oppressive as it had been before, he knew that he would play well.

He did not go to the auditorium with the Herricks but left earlier with the local concert manager, and he had only a moment with them to receive their good wishes. When he first came out on the stage and seated himself, waiting for the audience to settle into silence, he saw Erma immediately. She was sitting in the second row looking excited and expectant and, he thought, proud. It was a good audience, he could feel that almost immediately, a shy but hungry audience, not used to concerts and with few musicians in it. He was sorry for them a little, sitting so politely in their good manners and their too warm clothing, for the first half of the concert was heavy, he felt. But it was also familiar and perhaps the familiarity and the conservative nature of it would balance its heaviness. If their good manners would hold through the heat until the second half, then he would make it up to them.

As the concert progressed, two things began to battle for his attention. One was the girl Erma; the other was the steadily progressing heat. They were both strange. He was well into the concert before he began to feel the girl's attention, like an intent, unmoving light upon him. He had never known such attention. It was like singing into a shell. Slowly, it began to blot out the rest of the audience, the slightly defective acoustics, the small physical interruptions. About even with his right shoulder he could feel it, like a poultice which draws the skin. Each time he left the stage the spell was broken and he became aware of a counterforce, the heat. It was increasing constantly with a foreboding pressure, and off stage he wiped his face and hands and

drank water and still there was no help for it. The house was un-
usually still. Erma's attention and the heat alternately battled
against each other for domination of the man, equally strange,
equally intense, equally powerful. Gradually the two seemed less
at war with each other than degrees of the same thing. He stood
off stage before his last number and he felt drained with the heat,
with the heaviness of it, the silence of it. He became engulfed in a
sense of unreality, as though he were standing under water.

"The windows must be opened," he said to the manager who
stood with him. "The doors must be opened. The heat is impossible in there."

"I don't know what to do," the man said. "I know you must
be playing under great difficulty, but if we open more windows
the noise will come in."

"I can play over the noise," Justin said, "but I don't think
I can play again in this heat. I don't see how those people are
standing it."

He had taken off his coat, which was wet clear through, and
now he threw water on his face in an effort to stop the terrible
sense of unreality that hung over him. At his orders the man was
now having all the doors and windows opened, and suddenly,
standing there in his wet shirt, Justin was wrapped in a little
whirlwind of cool air. Nothing had ever felt so good. He could
hear the audience begin to stir and a wave of movement and low
laughter went over them like wind in a field of wheat. Justin remembered them with great affection and he wished in some way
to be generous, to be close to them. The moving air came sweetly
on his forehead, under his armpits. With exultation it surrounded
him. A door banged. He took off his tie and unbuttoned his collar. He threw more cold water in his face and pushed up his shirt
sleeves to have the water on his wrists. The pulsation at the back
of his head ceased and the feeling of heaviness and unreality left
him and then he knew what he would do.

While he waited for the attention of the audience, now distracted by the opening of the doors and windows, he saw many of
the faces look at him in puzzlement and some of them were smiling. Only then did he realize that he had come onto the stage without his coat or tie, his shirt open, his sleeves pushed up to his elbows. He had a moment's panic and a desire to run backstage into
the security of his coat, but he did not leave the stage. A great gust
of wind blew in at the open door and swept over the audience. Be-

neath the sound of it there was a sighing, moving wave of relief. Almost at once Justin felt the audience to be a unit, bound by a thread of excitement at the storm's coming. There was a continuous murmur through the house and, unable to speak over it, Justin made a pantomime of pointing to his own clothing and inviting the audience to follow his example. Immediately there was established between Justin and his audience the element which had been missing all his concert days. For the first time in his life he stood perfectly at ease before an audience, without feeling inadequate or apologetic.

He rolled up his shirt sleeves securely so that they should not fall and hinder his playing and he looked down into Erma Herrick's face. It was perfectly still, waiting. Quite clearly, like the silver beads that are put on children's birthday cakes, he saw the drops of sweat clustered where the hair sprang out above her forehead. Later it seemed to him that the audience had caught its quiet from her, for while he stood watching her he realized that they had, all at once, become still. Then, easily, he began to talk to the audience.

"The war has left most of us with few possessions," he said. "Some of these are shabby and many do not fit us any longer. Yet some are more valuable to us by being old. That is why in the earlier part of the concert I tried to bring you the familiar and well-loved music of a different day. But in a way I have been dissatisfied ever since I began this tour, for I wanted also to bring you something new and untried, something you had never heard before. There is youth here tonight, the way that there is always youth. We are constantly forgetting this, that there is always some youth left, because we have seen so much of it lost. And this youth, if it is scarred, is scarred by something not of its own making and therefore it is never scarred as deeply as we think. Tonight with your leave I should like to discard the rest of the concert as it was planned and play for you a kind of synthesis of a symphonic work not yet completed called *The Green Kingdom*. You are the first to hear it and, in fact, this is my first time to play it."

There was applause now and with the rapidly changing temperature in the room there was strong attention in the audience and a feeling of anticipation. The applause jolted Justin from his assurance and he had a moment of doubt. Far off in the distance the first thunder sounded and the recognition of it flashed between Justin and his audience.

"I would like to tell you a little about the Green Kingdom," he said. "It is a land of which my grandfather told me when I was a boy, a land that he said he had seen. I came to imagine it as a kind of geological fault, a bubble formed in the earth's surface when it was molten and hot, a hollow place that cooled into a perfect sphere, like the bubbles that are sometimes found in home-made bread. Inside this land no other man had ever seen and, to my grandfather, it was revealed spectacularly by a sudden split in the wall. In this kingdom everything was green—the trees, the flowers, the grass, and the huge green birds. All the shades of green there are—pale and deep, yellow and blue, soft and hard— were blended. The animals and the insects and all the living crea-tures were green, too. It was a fertile, thick and luxurious land with strange voices and a strange quiet. It was like the morning of the world and there was nothing barren in it. It is the promise born of man's longing that his fate should bear relation to his own actions and his belief that, given a new chance, he would choose to think of himself as grappling, rather than buffeted."

Justin turned and walked to the piano. He took out his handkerchief and dried his hands. Then he looked out on the audience again, so still, so wonderfully quiet, that outside he could hear the trees bending suddenly before the wind. He looked at Erma Herrick and suddenly he faltered and the strange and unaccustomed freedom and exhilaration left him, for, after all, could he do it? Could he remember it all? He thought that she smiled at him, but it was such a fleeting thing between two wait-ing seconds that he was not sure.

"The first movement is called 'Discovery,' " he said, "and I should like to dedicate it to my hosts, Mr. and Mrs. Arthur Her-rick."

Then he seated himself and put his hands out before him and it seemed to him that he was his grandfather. There were many that night who were never able afterward to remember which was the storm and which the music, so well did the elements serve Justin Magnus, for the thunder restrained itself and approached with threatening measure until its time, and the fierce crescendos and silences of the wind alternated with the score as though they followed its tempo and not their own. The clouds split in a yellow crackling streak to herald in the trumpets of the discovery theme, which once had been the trumpets of the angelic choir summoning

Lazarus back to life. Of all these things Justin was unaware, except for this last: as the Kingdom in all its fantastic greenness lay discovered to his grandfather, the odor of the storm came into the room and it was the odor he had always believed to be that of the Green Kingdom.

There was sudden silence when he had finished and then, as suddenly, the whole house was on its feet and Justin sat on at the piano stunned to think of what he had done, of how free and confident, even coherent, he had been. Outside the storm burst and the first rain spewed in at the windows in pulsating sheets. Only then did he succumb to the most intense stage fright of his concert days, so paralyzing that when Arthur Herrick came backstage for him he begged him to find an exit by which they could avoid the crowd. Nor could he bear to wait the storm out. Beaten by the wind, the two men clung to the railing of the narrow fire escape and descended to an alley.

"If you want to wait here," Arthur said, "I'll go around front and find a car for you."

"Isn't your place close?" Justin asked. "I mean, since we're already soaked, couldn't we make a dash for it?"

"That suits me," Arthur said. "We can go down this alley to the back of the shop and you won't have to meet anyone at all. Erma's likely to give me hell, though, bringing you home dripping like this."

"Where is she? Where is your wife?" Justin asked.

"She went on ahead when the concert was over so that you could eat as soon as you got home."

"But you must eat with me," Justin said. "We must go and get your wife and find a place."

"There's no place that Erma feels has food good enough for you," Arthur said.

The first fury of the storm had died and the footsteps of the two men rang out upon the silence.

"We are a soggy pair," Justin said, stopping under the shelter of a doorway. "I must thank you for finding that fire escape. To tell you the truth, I had a bit of stage fright back there. I never made such a speech before."

"It was a fine speech," Arthur said. "It was a fine thing for you to do."

"We are all more sensitive to the weather than we make allowance for, I suppose," Justin said. "Some people are frightened by storms and others gain a false courage from them, a kind of elation."

"Joe says it's the only way he can enjoy a good fight without having to pay for it."

"Who is Joe?" Justin asked.

"Oh, he works with me in the print shop," Arthur said. "We've been together a long time."

While he was changing into dry clothes, Justin discovered that he was very hungry and that his feeling of unreality was quite gone. Though he was still amazed at what he had done, he had so far adjusted himself to the idea that, as he entered the room where Erma Herrick was waiting for him, he felt glad that he had done what he had. Erma's hair was still wet from the rain so that it seemed much redder and of a deeper color than he had remembered it. Water droplets clung to the loose ends, and, to catch these, she had fastened a huge white towel about her shoulders. The folds of the towel and the wetness of the heavy hair molded to the lines of her head gave her a sculptured, timeless quality.

Justin had meant to protest at being guest instead of host, as he had meant to apologize for having dripped water all over the floor, but as he stood there looking at her it seemed to him that she already knew these things, that they were not worth saying.

"Sit down," she said.

"Where's your husband?"

"He's putting on dry clothes," she said. "He'll be here in a minute. Isn't it wonderful, this coolness?"

"I thought I should never live to see it," Justin said.

When Arthur came in they all began to eat and he, who had been a little hungry for a long time and knew so well that Erma had too, wondered that she ate so little. Erma was trying to give Justin a chance to eat, seeing his great and obvious hunger. She repressed her question as long as possible, but finally she could wait no longer.

"Where is it?" she said.

"Where is what?" Justin said.

"The Green Kingdom," she said. "Where is it? Where is the land your grandfather found?"

"Oh," he said, "did you think it was real?"

"Yes," she said. "I did. Isn't it?"

"I used to think so when I was a boy," Justin said. "I've got out of the habit of thinking of it as a place since I began thinking of it as music. I didn't realize you would take it literally."

He was abashed at the look of obvious disappointment on the girl's face, as though he had been guilty of misrepresentation, and he was a little resentful, too, for surely it was the music that mattered.

"But you said your grandfather saw it," she said.

"*He* said he saw it. But he was not a very reliable man. He was inclined to . . . to boast a bit."

"At any rate," Arthur said, "it's real now."

"Oh, of course it doesn't have anything to do with the music," Erma said, laughing, "only it was such a shock, you know, your saying it wasn't real because I was so sure while you were playing that I knew just what it looked like. Why, I even smelled it."

"My grandfather would be glad of your faith if he were alive," Justin said. "He was always trying to convince people that it was real and he never succeeded with anyone except me."

Erma put her hand under her hair and shook it back from her neck. "What made you change your mind?" she asked.

Justin had just lighted his pipe and he blew out the match before answering. "I guess it was my grandmother," he said, dropping the match into an ash tray. "My grandmother, and getting older. But I don't remember when I changed, it was so gradual. There never was one certain day when I didn't believe in it any longer."

So he began to tell them the story of his grandfather and his grandfather's Green Kingdom, much as he had told it to Max Staats, months before. But with the thought of Max, his new freedom and courage and confidence and the glory of the night's accomplishment were instantly gone and he was filled with shame.

"What time is it?" he said. "I have to make a telephone call."

He was only a half hour over his customary time in calling Max, and Max did not even mention it, yet the guilt that Justin felt for it never quite left him. For Max said that Edith was very restless and that he had had the doctor come in, and he felt that it was necessary to take the Herricks' telephone number and to call Justin back next morning before he left town. Justin relayed this to Erma and Arthur and then he left them abruptly and went into the room they had given him. But sleep would not come, and he went over and sat by the window at the table where only that afternoon he had found the bowl of iced fruit and taken new life from it.

He had forgotten Edith. For the first time he could remember, he had forgotten her. While she was restless and in danger, he had not thought of her. He sat in the dark by the open window with his incredible guilt for company and sought in some way to excuse himself. "It was so hot," he said, as though he could tell her. "It was so terribly hot, Edith, and it was like walking downhill, under water. And then there was that girl's attention and I wanted to be powerful and to count for something again, as an artist. It was only a few hours, only a little time, that I let loose of you, my darling. I would never have done it except for the storm and the terrible heat and wanting to feel a composer again."

No forgiveness came to him from the silent town, and his position before the window suddenly reminded him of the night that he had begun writing *The Green Kingdom* and of how he had felt then that if only he were to destroy the music and stop any connection with the Lazarus opera he could free Edith from a bad time. But he had not done it. And now he had added to his crime. For the flattery of a stranger's child and the illusion of creation he had taken away his hand from his wife and left her to tread alone the dark and perilous road of her secret, lonely time.

"What am I doing here?" he said. "What good are all the things *to her* I hoped to perpetuate by making this tour? If I had stayed with her, even in change, it would have been better." He put his big tired hands over his face in the darkness. And immediately he was swept again by that nostalgia which he had felt earlier in the afternoon. Now, without the pressure of time upon him or the battle to survive against the heat, he was free to question the curious nostalgia and finally he was able to identify it. It came from his hands, from the odor of Erma Herrick's soap. It was the soap that his grandmother had had in her house. His grandmother was solid. To lie in bed in his grandmother's house, waking from sleep to hear the sturdy, solid tread of his grandmother going through the halls, going about her work, was the greatest security he had ever known. He found that it was to memories of his grandmother, rather than his grandfather, that he now clung in the hour of his self-disgust. Aligned as he had always been on

the side of his grandfather, Justin had never felt close to his grandmother. Now it seemed curious to him that in all the years he had
never had a revaluation of his grandmother. With the smell that
had always been that of his grandmother's skin so close to him that
by moving his hand he could recapture it at will, he wondered
that, in relation to his grandmother, he had not thought to change
in fifty years. The one thing his grandmother had above all others
was, simply, health. The robustness of which he had been so much
ashamed that day by the sea was probably not, as Max had said
then, any primitive urge to celebrate Easter, but only his grandmother's health speaking again in him. She had lived to be old,
very old, but never feeble. The last time he had gone to see her,
he had come into the house unexpectedly and his grandmother's
voice, talking to another old lady, had come to him quite firm,
quite clear. "Sliced cold," he heard he say, "I love it. There's
nothing in the world more edible than cold roast beef."

In the darkness Justin smiled at that memory, suddenly filled
with tenderness for his old grandmother, and he wondered at the
years in which he had never prized her. And then he remembered.
His grandmother had not liked Edith. "She's too quick on her
feet," she said. "She'll never steady. The cream will never come
to the top."

And this was enough for Justin to be with Edith now, the way
that he always was, as though he had never left her in the madness
of the heat, in the confidence of the storm, had never begun a work
in which she had no part. As though Edith herself were sending
him a token of forgiveness, he saw her in an old picture. Out for a
walk once, they had turned a corner on a crowd around a huge
trained bear. Leading the bear by a chain was the frailest of street
urchins, his dark eyes quick to measure the audience, his free
hand catching the coins in the air, never missing. "Look," she
had said, pointing, laughing, "that's us."

You laughed, my darling. You liked that. You laughed. But
not now. She was not laughing now. He must help her. He must
share this with her, the way that he always had. It was ridiculous
to have thought of sleeping, as ridiculous as . . . as his being in
this town. For now he wondered that he had ever considered this
trip; he could not think how the lack of money had so muddled
his head. How could he have thought it would be so terrible to up-
root Edith from her surroundings that he had done a much worse

thing and uprooted her from himself? He leaned back against the chair and ease washed over him, over his bowed head and his giant's shoulders. "Edith," he said, "I'm coming home."

Once he had made up his mind he tasted the sweet pleasure of knowing he would never again give another concert. Quietly he moved into the room where the telephone was, but there was no train until ten o'clock the next morning. The decision was the thing that mattered, though, and now he could rest. It was easy, once the decision was made, for him to fish back into Max's conversation for the reassurance that the doctor had been there. And in the morning there would be the reassurance of another call from Max. It was really better to wait than to start the journey in uncertainty, for by now they must have quieted her.

He awoke in the morning as he always did, immediately, with an instinctive consciousness of the weather and a pleasant hunger, the way that his grandmother had always awakened. "By the time I get my shoes buttoned, I know how the day will go," she said once to Edith, said it sharply, for Edith had always fought her way up to the top each morning, stratum by stratum. And the top was always a blank new sheet to Edith, as though she died each night and was born again each day, without memory, innocently, into an alien world.

The first thing Justin remembered on awakening was his decision and the freedom it had brought him. Like a bridegroom who goes forth to meet his bride and on the way invests all the things in his path with his own joy, Justin now cherished the room, the clean, bare quality of it. While he was shaving he could see the green plant reflected in the mirror, and this, too, he remembered with affection. It was all suffused with a kind of golden charm, the patient audience last night, the Herricks, this place.

Like the golden light of his own cherishing, the sun fell in a broad yellow shaft upon the breakfast table, the white cloth, the yellow plates, and the two mounds of ripe strawberries, upon the fat sides of the earthbrown coffeepot and the steam rising up from the spout of it.

"Good morning," Justin said.

"Oh," Erma said, turning to him. "I'll just give them the signal downstairs and then we can eat."

She went over to the wall and flicked an electric switch on and off a couple of times and he was surprised to see how different she was than he had remembered her. She kept changing all the time. It had seemed to him last night that she was taller, more subdued. Sitting across the table from him, her reddish hair interrupting the shaft of sunlight, she seemed altogether lighter, gayer and much younger. There were only two places at the table.

"But wasn't that the breakfast signal?" Justin asked, nodding toward the electric switch. "Isn't your husband coming up?"

"Oh, no. He and Joe have already had breakfast. That was just to tell them you're awake and up so they can start the presses. I like the sound of them, but of course I'm used to it. Hear them?"

"I didn't know what it was," Justin said, listening consciously to the slow boo-den-ty-*bump*, boo-den-ty-*bump* that gradually speeded up and became a steady booden*bump*, booden*bump*. "You can feel it in the floor," he said. "You're right, though: it's a good sound. They needn't have held off their work on my account."

"I don't really think they had an urgent job," she said. "To tell you the truth, I think they made it up so that I could have you to myself for breakfast. Arthur can talk to any number of people, but Joe's like me. He can't say anything real unless he's alone with a person."

"Oh, yes, Joe," Justin said. "Your husband mentioned him last night. They work together, don't they?"

"Yes," Erma said. "I'll give them the signal again when your call comes through, don't worry. I hope your wife is better this morning. I hope your news is good."

"Thank you," Justin said. "I hope so, too. But don't bother to give them the signal, please. I shall be able to hear all right. It sounds like the sea, you know. It makes me homesick. From my house you can hear the sea all the time. At night you can always hear it."

"Is there water in the Green Kingdom?" Erma asked. "I don't suppose there is a sea, but are there lakes or rivers? Surely there must be."

She poured coffee into a cup and handed it to him and from a blue bowl she took the cover exposing, under a cloud of steam, a yellow mound of eggs, as though the brilliant shaft of sunlight had turned fluid and coiled upon itself in folds.

"Ah, poor Rachmaninoff," Justin said, "with his shredded wheat."

She was pleased that he had remembered her letter and a look of sudden shyness crossed her face.

"Well, tell me about the rivers," she said, "or the lakes, or whatever there is."

"Perhaps you know better than I," he said. "After all, you said you knew what the place smelled like. Maybe you know what the rivers look like better than I do."

"Oh, no," she said. "I mean, what did your grandfather say about them?"

"Well, let me think now. It's all so long ago. You know, I think you're more interested in my grandfather's Green Kingdom than you are in mine."

He handed her his empty cup to be filled and he was teasing her. He was laughing at her because she was so much a part of the sunlight and it was all yellow and fresh and free, the whole room; it was all delicious and light, now that he was going home. That was what he wanted to tell to the girl, to Max Staats, to anyone who would listen—that he was going home.

But she was not part of his mood, and it was with a kind of gravity that she handed him his coffee cup and looked at him so seriously, saying over the throbbing of the presses, saying into the innocent yellow sunlight, "I believe in yours and I believe in your grandfather's. I think they are the same place and I think if I ever saw it I'd recognize it."

It was always more than you bargained for, he thought, that intensity of youth, more startling, more demanding, and he was thinking whether to temper it or to feed it, when the telephone's ringing cut short his uncertainty.

"You take it," she said, "and I'll flick the switch." She heard him say hello and then she listened for Joe to cut the power. Still standing by the switch, she heard the booden*bump*, booden*bump* slow to boo-den-ty-*bump*, boo-den-ty-*bump*, boo . . . den . . . ty . . . *bump*. Then she went back to Justin.

He sat bent over, his mouth open, his face gray. Both hands were clutched around the telephone receiver from which came a buzzing sound. Erma uncurled the man's big fingers and replaced the receiver on its hook. It made a small clicking sound. The presses had stopped. The floor was still. The shaft of yellow sunlight pinned fast everything it pierced.

The three of them, Arthur, Erma, and Joe, packed Justin's bags and took him to his train and put him on it. Joe took his wallet out of his pocket and bought his ticket for him. When they asked him a question he answered, and when they told him to do something he did it, but it was obvious that he did not comprehend any of it and that he had no idea where he was. Now the three of them stood outside on the platform even with his window, but he did not see them. His eyes were closed.

"God, I wish we'd had time to buy him a bottle of whisky," Joe said.

"Maybe there's still time," Arthur said. "Got any money?" He reached down into his own pocket and fished out a dollar bill. "I've got a buck," he said.

"So've I," Joe said.

But just then the train started and Erma suddenly turned from the window. "Let me have it," she said. She grabbed for the two dollars and swung herself up on the moving car.

Inside the train she walked to Justin's seat and sat down beside him, but he made no sign. When the conductor came through she asked Justin for his ticket and he gave it to her, but then he turned and stared out the window. Erma gave the conductor her two dollars.

"How far will that go and return?" she said.

"Tilbury, Ma'am. Ticket to Tilbury and return. Comes out even and no change back."

There was nothing to say. Nothing, nothing to say. Maybe whisky would have been better. Two dollars only goes to Tilbury, Ma'am, but whisky goes on to the sea. To sea, to say, nothing to say. Once Justin roused himself.

"It was only a few hours," he said, turning suddenly to Erma, "not more than two or three hours that I let loose of her."

"Yes," Erma said. She took one of his big hands in both hers and held on tight.

And another time he said, "They must have forced her. They must have come at her the way that they said she wouldn't remember, she wouldn't know. They never believed what I did was necessary."

"Yes," she said.

More horrible every minute came the approach of Tilbury. But at Tilbury Justin's eyes were closed and his hand in hers was quite limp. She did not dare to rouse him in case he had found some moment's oblivion. It was Tilbury and she had no paper or pencil with which to write him a note and nothing to say if she had. It was time to leave him alone with his bewildered, uncomprehending grief. The train had stopped and no one else was getting off. And suddenly Erma reached to her neck and jerked loose a locket on a chain, breaking the chain, scratching her neck, and this she put in his hand and closed his fingers around it and then she left him, not looking back.

And what good would a locket do him with her father's picture in it—a man he had never seen? Still it was all she had to leave with him, some proof that he had not been the whole time alone. It was all of her that they would let ride free to the sea. Tenderness must wait at Tilbury, Ma'am, but grief rides free.

There was no place for her to hide her sorrow going back, not even a coat that she could have thrown over her head nor a hat to pull over her face. How could she have left him alone? Wouldn't it have been better to take the train fare out of his wallet the way they had for his own ticket than to leave him alone on the train in the state he was in? If only someone else had got off at Tilbury so that she would have had time to think.

When she was home again Arthur said, "You've got a cut on your neck."

"I wish it went clear through," she said.

M A X met Justin at the station. "I'm going to take you straight to my house first," he said.

Justin sat in his old chair and poured himself a drink and when Max asked him if he wanted to eat he said no. Max asked him if he wanted to lie down and he said no. Max knew what he wanted. He took off his glasses and laid them on the desk.

"It was the way you said it would be, Justin," he said. "She had another bad attack and they tried to give her a hypodermic without you there to quiet her first, the way you always said it had to be done. And she jumped out of the window. She was not left alone and no one was careless. She was dead before they got there. No one had dreamed it was possible, Justin. She went right through the screen. No one had any idea she could be so quick, as ill as she was."

"Where is she now?" Justin said.

"She is at home in her own bed."

"Is anyone in the house?"

"No, they are all gone. I have paid them all and they are all gone."

"Thank you, Max. And will you cancel my concerts?"

"I have already done it."

"Well, then, Max, I think that I'll go home."

Quietly and with great calm Justin climbed the hill to his own house and let himself in as though it were any other time, as though they had sent for him and she in great need of him. Steadily, now, as though it were any other time, he climbed the stairs, not needing the handrail, no more than at any other time. And evenly he walked to the door of her room. But he had never gone into her room with dirt on his hands, with travel dust upon him, and he would not do it now. He went into his own room, as though it were any other time. He bathed and shaved and put on clean clothes. And then, softly, as though she had great need of him, as though it were any other time, he walked down the hall and opened her door and walked in.

As though it were any other time she lay in bed, the lines of her thin body making geometrical patterns under the coverlet. Only they had not parted her hair right. Strangers cannot part a dead person's hair right; he'd noticed that when his father died. Strangers should not try.

He walked about her room, not approaching the bed yet. And finally he got his chair and her hairbrush and went over and sat down in his old place by her side, as though it were any other time. He began to brush her hair, long, even strokes. Always before the children were born he used to brush her hair, hours on end. It swirled about the pillow, the way that she liked it to, *the way that was right*. But there was always a place at the nape of her neck that he could not reach and he would always lift up her head and do that last. It made him uncomfortable to think of that one spot left unbrushed, and he put his hand under her head to lift it, as though it were any other time.

But it was not any other time. The brush clattered to the floor and the sound of it echoed through the silent house and, after it, the agony of a man's heart splitting, the same as that of an ox or a bull or any other giant creature who finds himself caught in the one, unique moment that is *not* like any other time. Long, long the man knelt on the floor, his arms thrown across the body of his wife, his head upon her breast in which no heart beat now nor trembling quickened to his touch, from whence no comfort came. Slowly the violence of his weeping spent itself and he began to stroke her arms, monotonously, as though to comfort himself.

He opened his eyes and saw the long scratches on her arm and these he kissed with great tenderness. Tenderly he touched her body under the coverlet, tenderly he cupped his hand over the sharp line of her knee. "The bones do not go insane," Max had said to him once. Nor, for the beloved, do they ever die, he thought. He began to stroke her shoulders gently, evenly, with his hands, to touch the line of her cheek. He kissed her eyelids, closed now and dark, covering the animal eyes. And slowly and tenderly, in the way that he had always done, he undressed her. She had a pear-shaped belly and, long ago, before he had called her Animal Eyes, he had called her his golden pear.

The golden pear was cool against the skin of his face and he closed his eyes. "Edith," he said, "let me lie here where all my sons have lain, each in his turn, for I am tired."

When he awoke there was black darkness in the room but his head was instantly clear. He was not afraid. His wife was dead and he knew it. Life had taken from him now everything but itself and that was without value to him. He began to dress his wife in feverish haste, in a white robe. Then he lifted her in his arms and wrapped her carefully, securely, in the wool coverlet, like a sleeping child.

"Oh, they will never put you in the ground," he said. "You never belonged to the earth. You didn't even like to garden. They will never cover up your face with earth and leave you there alone, stifling. Oh, no, my darling."

Carefully he carried her in his arms down the dark stairway and out of the house and down to the sea where he had kept his old boat. He put her down gently on the sand until he found the boat and loosed it, and then he picked her up in his arms, and, standing in the boat, let it drift out to sea.

"It's an old boat, my princess," he said. "Not a good boat. It will never bring us home again. But a leaky boat is good enough for us, eh?"

He nestled her close to him, almost gayly. He turned his back upon his home and slowly, slowly the boat drifted out to sea. The night was solidly black and a cold wind blew over the sea. Justin pulled the coverlet up to shelter her head.

"You never liked the wind to blow on your cheekbones, my lovely," he said. "Did you? You used to cover your hands over your cheekbones. And you never liked the gull's cry. You used to stop your ears from the gull's cry. There's a storm coming, a fitting storm. Once the storm is here you won't be lonely any more and I won't be lonely either."

Once he turned around and looked back. "See, my darling?" he said. "It's too far back now. I shall be heavy with all my clothes on and you shall be safe and dry in your white blanket, in your boat."

The boat was taking the big swells now and each time that he kept his footing Justin's exultancy rose. And suddenly they were engulfed in the storm and it was all around them so that he must yell if she were to hear him.

"We've had enough, haven't we, darling? We had enough a long time ago. Hold tight, my lovely, hold tight, hold tight."

Then he could see it, a great black wall of a wave coming on them and they were part of it. Justin's arms were empty in the icy water; his voice was gone. Once in a flash of lightning he saw the little boat high above him, but if she were in it or not he did not know.

I shall be heavy with all my clothes, he thought, and then he did not think for a long time, but later he found himself naked in the water so that his own body must have struggled in spite of his will. He did not want to fight and he could not stop fighting. He did not know how to make himself heavy and his arms began to pull with fierceness and direction. They would not stop. He could not make them stop, though there was only fire in his chest and nothing, nothing in his mind. Finally a wave caught him and threw him hard upon the shore and then his arms stopped. Oh, strange are the ways of the sea and inscrutable are the tastes of the sea that will gobble up puny boys and spit out the free gift of a giant.

Justin awoke in bed in Max's house, and of how he came to be there or how long he had been there he had no memory. He saw Max's face and he tried to put up one hand in greeting but it fell back on the bed.

"Hello, Justin," Max said.

He tried his voice but it was only a hoarse whisper and pain shot through his chest. "There's more of it yet?" he asked.

"There's more of it yet," Max said.

The sea had refused him and now, above everything, above his loss, his grief or any curiosity as to his own rescue, he felt foolish. He had never before asked of his arm that it should move, of his voice that it should speak, and had them fail him.

The truth is, he thought, I don't know how to die. Death, also, must be a thing that has to be learned.

He, who had never been apologetic, who had never been ashamed, he was now foolish—foolish and feeble. In the first moment, only the knowledge that he was alive had flooded his mind and the recognition of Max had been a complete thing in itself, but once this sense of shame had entered his mind it flooded out everything else. He could not bear to face it. He could not bear to have Max look at him. He closed his eyes and retreated into sleep. The gray folds of sleep wrapped him, covered him, shrouded him in anonymity, made him blind and deaf, made a blank sheet of him without history. Twice more that day he opened his eyes, twice more he slid out onto blankness, recognized the room, recognized Max, felt the pain in his chest, remembered his shame, and crawled back willfully into the gray escape of sleep. In his dazed, ill state he had not begun to taste the bitterness of his present being. Each day would bring a greater wakefulness, each day the speed of orientation would be accelerated so that his shame would flood over him sometimes even before his eyes were open. And each day the path backward into the escape of sleep became more difficult, so that his very effort to be on the path made it longer.

Once, when he awoke, he felt immediately the hard metal surface of the urinal between his thighs and his face was hot with the knowledge of it. Was there a nurse, then, here, a strange woman, who had placed it there, who had moved his thighs apart to make room for it without his even knowing it? Or had Max had to do this for him? Had Max, then, with his small, quick, efficient hands, had to carry this thing out of the room, walking carefully so that the contents should not slosh and spill on the carpet, the odor of it in his winged, sharp nostrils? And how long? How long had they had to do these things? How long had Max or unknown strangers looked upon his body and prodded it and cared for it while he slept? He felt of his face and it was covered with a thick beard. It had been days, then, that he had been like this, weeks, perhaps, that he had been a helpless, foolish blob of weight, a catalogue of endless bodily functions without secrecy, without dignity, without shelter of any kind.

There are people in hospitals like this, he thought, all over the world. There are whole rooms full of them, floors of them. There are *acres* of people like this in the world. How do they stand it? How do they stand the suppliant humiliation of it?

I have to get out of here, he thought. I have to find my clothes. His anger and his great will made the first lunge possible. He was at last sitting upright. His breathing made a terrible sound and each sound was a path of fire through him. The room swam about him and he began to shake all over but he would not stop. He held on to the head of the bed and slid his legs over to the edge, knocking over the urinal, flooding the bed with its contents. In his fury he was more determined than ever and reached out to the bedside table for support, but his arm missed by inches since he could not make it obey him and, while the bottles of medicine and a heavy water pitcher crashed onto the floor, his fury dissolved into weak tears flowing, without control, over and into the wild mass of his beard. And he had to know that Max saw him so. He had to try to apologize while the confusion of his brain would let no words come and the no words coming increased his furious frustration, increased the flood of weak tears. He had to be told to lie down and, falling, had to obey while his legs traversed again the guilty secret of the empty urinal and slowly, with what strength he had left, he turned his body to the wall and prayed in awful concentration that he would escape in sleep. But he could not and then it was that in all these days he came to have his first thought, not a chance wave of memory, or a flood of emotion or a blundering, groping question, but a thought arrived at and conceived by a mental process. *If he could not sleep, he could at least pretend to sleep and therefore escape was not denied him.*

He had a weapon. A man with a weapon is not helpless. A man can hide behind a weapon, hold his council, observe and learn. He need not ask questions, need not be at another man's mercy. A man who can think once can think again. A man who can think can plan. While the doctor took his pulse, while the bed was changed, while the urinal was carried out, he pretended to sleep and in this way he learned that Max alone took care of him. He, who had always depended so much on women and to whom women had always been essential, he now found himself grateful for the male household. One morning he awoke and he was hungry, and so at last he opened his eyes to Max. Max looks so old, he thought. He looks so tired.

"Hello, Justin," Max said. "How are you?"

Justin opened his lips and realized that his chest was lighter, that the pain had let up. "I'm hungry," he said.

"That's good," Max said. He left the room and returned, not with the steak of which Justin had dreamed, but with broth and gruel. These he left within reach of Justin and then he went away. Justin was again grateful to him that no eye should see the invalid's trembling, clumsy hand lift the invalid's food to trembling lips, that no waiting eye should witness in pretended ignorance the trail of spilled invalid's food through the tangled mass of beard onto the bedclothes. He had never realized before how complex a thing is eating, of how many distinct and finely calculated motions it is composed.

He slept, but in a few hours he was hungry again, and so the days slipped away from him and he took no note of them, though his shame eased. Max was in and out of the room all the time, but their conversation was of the barest quality. "Are you better?" "It is a fine day." "The doctor says." "Are you hungry?" And in all this time their eyes hardly met. Their eyes slipped off each other in a kind of dance. Though Justin often tried to speak of the knowledge which lay between them, Max never did.

One day Justin was allowed a newspaper. It was a far better escape than pretended sleep. The mind could hang onto one word at a time, then another, then another, memory and shame lost in *robbery, man, dog, taxes, drought, new, fire,* while the minutes slipped easily, silently away. He had never had much time for newspapers, never had the patience to sit over them except long ago when he was a young man and had feared the critics and, later, for a time, when his sons were at war. Now he read every word. He read of a flood in a town which he had never visited, read with great concentration how a Mrs. Mabel M. Werrenright, aged 87, had been marooned in the second story of her home, how she had been rescued by a young man in a boat. He saw her crawling stiff and old, her bottom uptilted, through the window, saw in another picture how she sat stiffly in the boat clutching the side, saw her old tomcat sitting in the boat, too, saved in a second trip by the same young man. Justin read of a man who had invented a new kind of lawnmower. He read how to get a complete dinner in thirty-seven minutes, and an exact description of a wedding gown worn by a scrawny, thin-lipped girl, and he read how children should be brought up. He read of a plan to educate more people in less time and he read all the legal notices of properties to be auctioned and he read the number of miles of railroad in India. He read every word of the advertisements and wondered how it was possible to say in so many different ways that a coat is warm, realized for the first time that this wording made up the whole lifework of numbers of people. In this way he negated the mornings and the evenings.

One day he read about Dr. Ivan D. Yorshly and after that he stopped reading the papers and began to think. Dr. Yorshly was in prison. A cleaning woman had discovered in his room the mummified body of a woman covered in many layers of wax. It was said that Dr. Yorshly had been engaged to a young woman some ten years earlier and that she had died the day before their wedding. Upon opening her grave, they found it to be empty. The people of the town said that Dr. Yorshly never went anywhere except to call on his patients. He spent every evening at home. He had no hobbies, no recreation, no friends. He was known as a formal person, a good doctor. He had many patients, most of them poor. Except about medicine and the weather he was never known to enter into conversation with anyone. Now he was in prison. A young woman had spat in his face while they were taking him into court. The courtroom was packed. Dr. Yorshly had nothing to say.

But why have they got him in prison? Justin thought. Why do they spit on him? Don't they know that that face does not look horrible *to him? I can understand it perfectly well. Is there something the matter with me that I cannot tell what is criminal any more, what is sane?* He felt as though he were being watched. He felt vulnerable and exposed. They must know that I took Edith out in the boat, he thought. Is that also illegal? I didn't notify the authorities. You have to notify the authorities when someone dies. Then he remembered he had heard that in some states attempted suicide was illegal, that a man could be imprisoned for failing if he tried to kill himself. He did not know the law. He would be utterly helpless against the law. *Dr. Yorshly had nothing to say.*

Then why did the police not come? He had to talk to Max. He had to find out from Max as soon as possible. But when Max came into the room he had the doctor with him and they said that he might try to sit up in a chair. He made it from the bed over to the chair, sank down in the chair breathing heavily, and looked out the window to the sea. It gave him a wonderful feeling of accomplishment. Later, alone with Max in the room, he thought: It is lying on your back that makes all those fears. He and Max sat in the room, the two of them looking out at the familiar sea. Still, though, there was a lot he would like to know.

"I have been reading about that Dr. Yorshly in the newspapers," he said.

"Yes," Max said, "I saw it. A terrible thing. Terrible."

Justin started to speak and then stopped. Did Max mean it was a terrible thing that the people had done to Dr. Yorshly or a terrible thing that Dr. Yorshly had done? He did not know and he was suddenly afraid to ask.

"I wonder, Justin," Max said, "if you are able to see Tim Corkin. He's been here every day to ask after you."

"Tim Corkin?" Justin asked. Tim Corkin had been his favorite student when he was at the university, and the thought of appearing in his feeble condition before the boy made Justin very uncomfortable.

"He rescued you," Max said. "I forgot you didn't know that. Naturally he, as everyone else, thinks that he rescued you from an accident at sea. Since he doesn't know how little you valued your life, I suppose he rather expects you to be grateful. Can you manage that?"

"They think it was an accident?" Justin said. "Everybody does?"

"Everybody but the doctor. Having known you and Edith for so long . . ."

"Oh," Justin said, "Edith. How is Edith?"

Max looked at him and waited for the mind to right itself. He saw Justin look down in embarrassment, saw him frown and shake his head and put his hand up to his mouth.

"I'll go and tell Tim another day," Max said, "when you're feeling stronger."

I must quit talking, Justin thought, until I have control. How did I happen to say that? Why, Edith is dead. Edith has been dead for days, for weeks now.

The next day Max had a barber come and shave Justin and it was then, as the barber held the mirror for him, that Justin had the corroboration of a thing he had suspected and evaded for several days. He had a slight head tremor. It served to make the hugeness of his head a little more conspicuous, as though the weight of it were too much for the neck to balance with security.

Justin sat in the chair again, looking out to the sea, and Max sat with him. Between them lay the questions Justin wished to ask and his unexplained slip of yesterday about Edith, but neither man spoke of these things yet and finally Max said, "Would you like to see your mail? There's quite a lot of it."

"Yes," Justin said, "I would."

When he saw Erma's handwriting again he had the day back on the train, that wonderful day when he had started to work again. He had looked out the window that day, too, but the sea had not been there. There had been a house with a red roof on it and on the roof the deep shadow of a maple branch. He had started to work again that day. He had been a composer, a creator, a strong and a well man.

Dear Justin Magnus:

Joe and Arthur wanted to get you a bottle of whisky

that day but I took their two dollars away from them
and jumped on the train as it was pulling out and I sat by
you as far as Tilbury but I don't suppose you remember
that. At Tilbury my two dollars was up and I could not bring
myself to steal from you for the rest of the fare and I could
not bring myself to leave you alone either, but nobody
else got off at Tilbury and they were waiting on me so I
tore the locket off my neck and put it in your hand and I
suppose you wonder how you came to be sitting with a
picture of a strange man in your hand. It is a picture of
my father and I knew that it would be of no help to you and
yet . . . I wanted to leave you something and it was
all I had. I know how it was when my mother died and I
know what it was like when my father died and yet I know
this is not the same thing as if Arthur died. For one thing
I heard all the things that people said, all the stupid things
that they never mean you to listen to, only to hear the
tone of voice and take comfort. It comes to us all,
they said, over and over again, it comes to us all, as
though that were comfort, as though that made it all right.
And I was angry and young and without tact and I
yelled at them: That doesn't make it any better. If five
hundred people die, it makes it five hundred times as bad.
Then they were hurt and they told me that a young girl
in *my* position was in *no* position to scorn sympathy and
I said the hell with their sympathy. I wasn't sorry; I was
mad. Mrs. Perry came and took me away from them, took me
to her house and she gave me an ax, a new ax with a
keen blade and a solid handle. Go out and cut down a tree,
she said, a young tree, a live tree, a little tree. Go on.

But if it had been Arthur, I would never have heard
what they said and if I had, *it comes to us all* might
sound comforting, as they meant it. I cannot say.

I try so hard to know what it is like with you, but I
can't make it. I don't know. I cannot be your sorrow
and your death as you were once my consolation and my
life. I do not know enough.

There is only one thing that I know, one tiny little
piece, but it will show you that I'm trying. When I was a
very little girl, about five, I went to the railroad station

with my mother to meet a train. The train was late
and we had to wait a long time. There was a woman
there I had never seen before. She was a young woman
dressed in black and she wore a long veil. There were
four or five people standing behind the young
woman, moving when she moved, turning when she
turned. They were constantly putting their arms out in
front of them as though to be ready to catch her if she
fell. I asked my mother why she had that thing on her head
and my mother said that she was in mourning, that
probably her husband had died and they were sending his
body home. My mother said she thought they were waiting
for the train to come in and it would have the
man's body on it.

The train was very late and I was tired waiting so I
watched the woman with that blend of innocence and
cruelty that you are when you are five years old. I had
heard about death and about mourning, but I had never
seen it yet so I tried to imagine what the woman
would do when the train came in. I thought when the
train comes in some man will carry her husband's body
off but he won't be able to step down the steps because
he'll be dead. The woman will put her hands together and she
will cry and then she will take off her veil and tear it up
and then she will fall down and those people
will pick her up and carry her away, but what will they
do with her husband?

The train came in and all the passenger cars went way
ahead of where they usually stopped and finally there was
a flat car with nothing on it but a huge box. When
the flat car got even with the woman the train stopped.
She walked forward slowly and with no need of assistance.
She reached up her hands and held to the top of the
big box and then she put her breasts against the box and
pressed them hard against the box and she closed her eyes.

My aunt got off the train and my mother said,
"Say hello to your Aunt Martha," and then she took my
hand and started to walk away. "Don't stare," she said and
she shook my arm a little and then we went home. When we
got home I went out to the pear tree and reached up

my arms and rubbed my chest against the pear tree.
The bark scratched my ribs. I could not
understand it.

When you are five years old, it is what you do *not*
understand that you remember. And what you don't
understand comes to stick in your mind like a foreign body,
like those people who live for years with bullets in their
hearts or pieces of glass stuck in them somewhere.
It gets walled off from the rest of your mind,
encapsulated.

I sat by you on the train, on the way to Tilbury,
and I had your hand in mine but you did not know it and
once you moved your hand. That was when the capsule
was dissolved. That was when the foreign body was no
longer foreign, but dissolved and freely mingling with the
things that were my own. I saw the woman again at the
railroad station and what she did seemed right and
logical and easily understood and I was, though twenty-five
years too late, ashamed that I had stared.

I have read in the papers that you have canceled your
concert tour and that I can understand. But I have also
read that you are ill. Is this true? I try to believe this, but I
cannot imagine it. To me, you have always been . . .
indestructible.

> Sincerely,
> ERMA HERRICK

Max came into the room and saw Justin sitting with the letter
in his lap, saw him staring out to the sea, saw that the head tremor
was very pronounced. He sat down by him in the other chair and
waited. Finally Justin raised one arm in a jerky, awkward way
and pointed out to the sea.

"Is there anything to keep me from walking out there?" he
asked, still looking at the sea.

"Not if you dress warmly," Max said. "I'll get your things
for you."

I even have to ask someone else where my clothes are, Justin
thought. I have to stand like a child and wait to be dressed. He
was impatient to be out of the room and the house, to be alone
and free from any human eyes, however helpful. He shuffled
through the rest of his mail, not caring about it now. When Max
came back with his clothes Justin put Erma's letter into his coat

pocket. His knees trembled on the stairs and for the first time that he could remember he held on to the banister. He could not wait to get out and yet when he had his hand on the doorknob he hesitated. The wind blows cruelly on a man outdoors; the light is harsh and without subtlety or tact; strangers' eyes are free to look upon him. There is no wall to lean against, no shade that can be lowered; there is no softening, no conditioning of the blow, no muting of the elements. Justin turned the doorknob and went outside. Exposed, without protection of any kind, he put his eyes upon the sea and began to move after them.

But he had forgotten the smell of the sea and the high salt taste of it and he had forgotten the sound of it, the rushing, surging, swishing, urgent, washing sound of the sea. The sea gave him personal, intimate greeting. He was the prodigal son whose sins have all been forgiven him, the sin of living in closed rooms, the sins of dependence, feebleness, of having desired shelter. He climbed up on a rock, leaned back against another, and closed his eyes. The rocks were warm from the sun. The weight of the sun pushed him back against the rock and the rock pressed forward gently to support him. Before his closed eyes everything was red and shimmering and his ears held only the sound of the sea. When these two became interchangeable, red sound and roaring light, all, all was forgiven him.

To me, you have always been . . . indestructible.

She does not know, Justin thought. The world took on a different aspect because Erma Herrick did not know of his humiliation, had not seen him lying sick and feeble with the furious tears of impotence matted in his beard. He took out her letter and read it over. The sun beat down on him and eased him and he remembered vividly the day he had lain back against the cool porcelain of the bathtub in Erma Herrick's house and felt the tight band leave his head while he put out his hand to trickle water over the green leaves spilling down from the window sill. Beside the tub that day there had been a low table with a brown coffee jug upon it.

I will go back and ask Max for some coffee, he thought. He could taste it now in anticipation—strong and black and full flavored with the steam rising from it. No, he could not ask Max. For weeks he had been able to ask Max, although usually Max had anticipated his wishes so that the words were unnecessary. How is it that a man can, for weeks on end, ask of his friend:

Where is my coat? Where are my clothes? Help me to sit up. Help me to eat. Keep my secrets for me. And then one day he puts on his clothes and goes out of doors. He looks at the sea and sits in the sun and chokes over asking for a cup of coffee.

He did not want to go back into the house. For if he did go back he would ask for something, if not for the coffee. When you are in a house, he thought, you are constantly needing things, and when you are in a stranger's house you are never able to find them. But he did want the coffee. He wanted it badly and he stepped down from the rock and stretched himself and turned his back on the sea. Then he saw his own house. Why, he had a house, a house of his own where, if he needed something, he would know where to look for it. He began to walk up the slope away from the sea, toward home.

But long before he reached the top he changed his course. He had not reckoned on the uphill climb, and he found himself suddenly very tired. Besides, he had no key. He thought with pleasure of getting back to his room in Max's house and lying down. And, after all, if he wanted a cup of coffee, all he had to do was ask Max for it. When he opened the door to his room he caught Max in the act of making his bed. Max, who had always seemed to Justin so deft, so graceful, so quick of movement, was very awkwardly trying to stuff a pillow into a fresh pillowcase. Both men were embarrassed.

"I'm not very good at this sort of thing," Max said, "and I find that I do not improve much with practice. There is simply something lacking in my make-up."

"Hold on a minute," Justin said, "till I get my coat off and I'll help."

"You'd better sit down," Max said. "You're winded. I'll have the struggle over with in a minute and then we can have some coffee to restore us both. I made a pot against your return, though I can't vouch for it, either."

He had not to ask for the coffee, then, after all. Justin was ashamed at the thoughts he had had by the sea. He said, "Whatever happened to that woman who used to come in to cook for you?"

"Mrs. Johns? Well, I told her not to come for a while," Max said. "She's quite a talker, you know, and I wanted to keep you from publicity if I could."

Justin came over to the bed. He on one side, Max on the

other, they made an attempt to draw the bedcovers up smoothly.

"You've had to do everything alone, then, all this time?" Justin said.

"Well, as it turned out," Max said, "I overestimated the danger. I thought you might be in for more serious trouble than you were and I simply didn't want the reporters here or a lot of talk going around until I found out. How about it? Can you make it downstairs or shall I bring the coffee up here?"

"I can make it," Justin said. Both men turned away from the bed in obvious relief. On the stairs Justin asked, "And what did you find out? How much trouble am I in?"

"None at all," Max said. "I think you'd even be free of reporters now. I should imagine you could go anywhere, be free to do what you pleased. There was a little irregularity with the health department, that's all, not having a burial permit. I put an attorney on it right away."

"An attorney?" Justin asked.

"Well, yes, there was the business of your concert contract, you know, and you were fined by the health department. It's all cleared up now. Everything is paid out of the money you left with me to take care of Edith and . . . and of your house. I've a statement of everything when you want to see it."

Justin sat at the table and Max poured the hot coffee for them and then sat down too.

"That's all right," Justin said. "I don't need to see it. Just tell me—the house. Do I still have the house?"

"Oh, certainly," Max said. "Certainly."

"Well, I was thinking, I believe I'll go up there for a while, Max. I've upset your house long enough."

"You mean to stay? You want to go up to your house to stay?"

"I don't know," Justin said. "I thought I'd just go up and look around for a while."

"Oh," Max said, reaching into his pocket. "Well, here's your key. You ought to take plenty of time to get well, you know. You're welcome to stay here, more than welcome. There's something ridiculous about two men living in two big empty houses. Might be you could rent yours later on for an income and live here with me. I'd get Mrs. Johns back to cook for us, now that you're getting well, and—"

"And to make the beds," Justin said.

Max fitted a cigarette into the end of his holder. "By all means to make the beds," he said.

"Well, I don't know, Max. Thanks, of course. I have to go up there and look around a while and . . . and see how it is."

"Certainly," Max said. "You see how it is. See how you feel tomorrow."

Next day Justin sat on the rocks again in the sun by the sea tasting with a delicious joy this strangeness, this thing so foreign to him, this tolerant, prideful acceptance of convalescence. When he began to walk up the slope toward his house it might have been any day. He might have been out for a walk and just returning home again as in the old days, except for the feeling of excitement he had, except for the feel of the key under his fingers.

By the time a man is Justin's age his fingers are full of odds and ends of old knowledge that he is never aware of until the need arises. The fingers are no heavier for it. A man puts his hands into his pockets, hands laden with many years' knowledge of the feel of things, and yet there is as much space left in the pocket as though he had just begun to live. Always with the front door it had been necessary to put the key into the lock, turn it a quarter of the way around, and then lift up on the doorknob at the right moment with one hand while the other hand turned the key past a difficult place. Justin did not have to experiment; he got it right the first time. He felt the catch give and the knowledge of it flooded into his hands and up his arms. He pushed the door open and walked inside.

It was not dark or silent or horrible as he had feared. He was simply a man who comes home, a man who walks about the rooms of his own house looking at things, touching a chair, a clock, an old table, picking up an old pipe and some tobacco and stuffing them into his pocket, a man breathing easily, glad to be home. He was a man walking easily, naturally, out of the living room across a hall into his own studio, as though this were what he had come for. He was a man sitting down at his own piano, settling himself, opening his coat, stretching his hands over the keyboard and striking a solitary note to taste the flavor of it, to prolong the sound of it, different from a sound made in any other room in the world.

As though it were born from this note, the mother note, without conscious effort on Justin's part, he found himself playing

The Lullaby of Edie-Davie, the first of what Edith had called
the "Strictly Family Music." This he used to play for her before
David was born. Edie-Davie it had had to be then, for Edith was
just as certain on some days that the child would be a girl as she
was on others that it would be a boy. If she were lying down upstairs resting and he had had to leave her alone overlong while
he was working, he would break off and play *Edie-Davie* for her
so that she would know he was thinking of her.

And suddenly she *was* lying down upstairs, listening. Justin's
fingers grew careful and precise so that each tone would be clean,
so that she would miss nothing. And then *The Lullaby of Edie-
Davie* coiled upon itself, turned and rolled and became a fugue
and the fugue lost its simplicity and grew solid, grew big and split
asunder, urging from itself by accelerating contractions an un-
militant march, the march which had been the introduction to
John's song:

> *On my birthday can I have ten pounds of butter?*
> *All the yellow butter that I want to eat?*

But this one also refused to stay simple and, like the lullaby,
began to grow and fuse and change, so that Edith would be surprised, lying up there listening—*and she was lying up there listening*—following to see what he was doing with the family music,
hearing how it was full of surprises for her and strange journeys
and old jokes, like the suddenly interpolated

> *Don't cry, Tommy, it's only a movie*
> *Don't cry, Tommy, it isn't real.*

And she *was* up there listening, recognition in her, special
knowledge in her, peace in the house. And she would be pleased,
he knew, to hear what he and Bach together were making out of
George's

> *I'd rather play checkers than listen to music.*

Whether because he had let Bach into the Strictly Family
Music or why, he did not know, there was a resentful note, a note
of rebellion. Or was it contempt? How had George said it, originally? Justin could not remember, for this was one of those events
that the whole family had adopted so that the original was over-
laid with strata of special applications. It had become part of
the family vocabulary used for inferior concerts, used for going

to the dentist, for any unpleasant job: *I'd rather play checkers.*

Well, had it or had it not been said in rebellion? It was originally either one way or another and he had to know. Justin left the piano and began to walk upstairs. He would ask Edith. Edith would know. Perhaps it was only to him that George had seemed a mystery, laughing in other people's quiet places, sitting still while other people fought, being tranquil when they yelled, laughing when they were quiet. Had Edith understood George all the time, intimately and well?

But Edith was not upstairs. It was a woman's bedroom Justin entered, empty and foreign. No one was there. He turned around and went back downstairs. Instantly he touched the keyboard, Edith was real again, lying upstairs, resting, listening. Like a man who constantly tries a sore tooth, Justin would put his hands on the keyboard and each time the presence of Edith was constant and real. He would give a concert for her every day. He would come in from the sea and sit at the piano and immediately she would be listening to hear all the things he had planned for her. But he would not seek her in the room upstairs again nor question her any more.

On the way back to Max's he could not get it out of his mind: Had George said it in rebellion, in hatred, in contempt, *or hadn't he?* Justin stopped and turned his face out to sea and his past fell away from him. So long he had held onto it, cherished it. Now he did not trust his knowledge of it. Had any of the others, besides George, hated his music? Had George hated *him?* He tried to remember the last time he had seen George. He remembered standing by the railroad train. Edith was with him and Tommy was saying good-by to a girl. He could remember the angle at which George stood, he could remember the size of him, the uniform he wore, the way he put one hand up to wave. But where the face should have been, there was nothing. He could not remember his face.

"I am alone," Justin said. "I am really alone." While he stood there looking out to sea he seemed to feel the faceless figure of George retreat slowly up the hill, leaving him in the late-afternoon light, alone. He straightened himself and turned back to Max's house. The world had never seemed so quiet. The distance before him stretched out like a great chore and he took a deep breath and tried to steel himself for this last push. He dreaded the time ahead after dinner when Max would go straight to his desk with his usual display of energy while he would sit aware of his own idleness and indecision and convalescence while he courted sleep. Now that he had discovered himself to be alone, he wished that he had something he must do, every minute, right up to the time he died. And it would not be music, he felt sure of that. It would never be music again.

So it was with eagerness that he welcomed Arthur's book when it arrived a few days later. He allowed himself to read the note from Erma on the fly leaf, and then he put the book aside to save for the evening time so that he too could have something ahead that he must do. That evening he sat in his old chair by the fire, opened the book, read the title: *The Keeping of Human Records*, read the front, turned the page and began:

The rocks keep an accurate record. Fossils hold facts. Calcareous strata and the rings of trees and the great loop-folded streams of lava know the value of the moment. . . .

The fire crackled. Max lighted a cigarette without taking his eyes off his papers. Justin turned a page and another. Suddenly he told Max good night and took the book upstairs with him. In his room he moved the big chair under the lamp and sat down again with the book. He was excited and he wanted to be alone:

For if a man's son dies, where is the truth about him, and if the man wishes to know the truth, where will he seek, now that it is too late to ask his son? Shall he start, then, at the beginning? Shall he go to the courthouse and walk up the gray stone steps which, even in his time, have been worn into a deep wave by the passing of many questioning feet? Shall he ask for the record of his son's birth, hoping to discover in what way it was significant? No man is so foolish as to seek out the truth of his son's birth in a courthouse. In the hazy shades of years he questions his memory and the nearest that he can come to it is that the rain shone black on the pavement under the streetlight all through the long November night.

If not the courthouse, then, the toy chest. Seek in the toy chest, Old Man, for a clue. But this also bears false witness, for only the things he did *not* use are left. What he used, what he loved, he wore out.

So look in the clothes closet, Old Man. See if the truth about your son is there. Here it is as it was with the toy chest. The clothes he loved best, he wore out. Even his smell is gone from these, care-fully removed by a conscientious dry cleaner. It is true that from what is left it can be learned that your son leaned on his elbows, that he ran over his left shoe heel on the outside, but you know this. This is not what you seek.

Oh, pick in the seams, Old Man. Feel among the crevasses of the pockets. Here are tobacco crumbs (Is it Burleigh? Is it latakia?). Here is dust (Is it limestone? Is it sand?). But where is his mar-riage, Old Man, his violent and short-lived marriage to the open-faced and vulgar woman with the cherries on her hat?

You, Old Man, sitting there gathering in and storing up the warmth of the late-afternoon sun against the coldness of the night, admit it now. He could have been another man's son for the things you knew about him. He could have been any other man's son, ex-cept that you fed him, except that you clothed him, except that you mourned his death.

But, Old Man, he knew as little about you. He knew even less about you.

Justin put his finger against the page to keep his place, and closed the book on his hand. I want to smoke, he thought. All this time since his illness he had been forbidden to smoke, but now he had such a hunger for tobacco that he was reckless of his health. Then he remembered having seen his old pipe at the house this afternoon, remembered having stuffed it into his pocket auto-matically as though he had known in advance how much he would need it now. He got out the pipe and lighted it hungrily, not mind-ing that the tobacco was stale nor fearing the rawness of the smoke as it hit his throat. Though he was shaken clear through by what he had just read, he sat there enjoying his first taste of tobacco and the sense of excitement and discovery which made him feel more alive than he had in weeks. Of a sudden he remem-bered coming down the fire escape in Drury, beaten by the fierce rain and his stage fright.

On into the night Justin sat reading *The Keeping of Human Records*, reading of the original idea, reading of the first ones who gathered together and failed so soon, reading of Mr. Doben-ski's visit to the print shop, reading of the plans to write the book, to mail it out, reading of the dream, the People's Library and of the schools where, along with spelling and geography, one might study human beings the way that they really are. He finished the book and switched out the light and sat in the darkness by the window smoking his forbidden tobacco. He was thinking of George and of Arthur Herrick and also, most clearly, of Mr. Dobenski. How well he knew that fathers, as Mr. Dobenski had said, when they go to the window at night, often are not thinking of anything but are just standing there.

Justin did not know about getting people to keep records, whether it was possible or not or whether a young man such as Arthur Herrick even did well to spend so much of his time trying to get them to. The People's Library was far less real to Justin than it was to Mr. Dobenski. But Justin knew that what he suffered now in impotence and questioning futility about his son George was suffered also by other men. And he knew that Arthur Herrick knew about that suffering. Whether it was possible to do anything about it, as the young man believed—well, Justin Magnus doubted that. But at least to have one's need recognized— that was something. It was a great deal coming from a man who was so young, who was perhaps not so much older than George had been, not so very different perhaps from the way George had been.

At last Justin got up from the chair, knocked out his pipe, and went to bed. Just as he was falling asleep the faceless figure of George came in to haunt him and, gradually, as it stood there, the blankness began to give way to cloudy features. But that is not George's face, Justin thought. That's Arthur Herrick's face. And then, just as the figure faded away and left him, it occurred to Justin that he need not suffer this tormenting uncertainty, for surely in his own house there were photographs. Tomorrow he would go to the house and hunt until he found a photograph of George. Then he would remember. Then he could put his mind to rest.

But as he walked into the house next day, he saw the open door to his study and it came back to him how, just by putting his hands on the keyboard, he had made the presence of Edith real. Without taking his coat off he went directly to the piano and placed his hands on the keys. Instantly Edith was upstairs in her room, listening. He sat down and played her *The Lullaby of Edie-Davie* again. His loneliness left him. A feeling of well-being came over him.

Why, he thought, I have never played *The Green Kingdom*

for Edith. She has never heard it. He took out his forbidden pipe and lighted it and walked about the room. He was not sure he could do it after all this time. Now and then as he walked about the room smoking he would go back and touch the keyboard just to be sure she was still there. Finally he thought that he could do it, at least the first part of it, and he put down his pipe and sat again at the piano. How surprised Edith would be, hearing this new work for the first time.

He began to play. At first he was concentrating so intently on remembering, on directing the notes all new and clear straight up to where his wife lay resting, that he didn't notice. After a while he gained confidence, for it was coming easily the way that it had in Drury and he was able to relax a little. Then he noticed it. It was too loud, like music played in an empty house. For no one was listening. Edith was not there. *The Green Kingdom* had not been composed in her time, was none of hers, and so she could not stay to listen but must leave the bed where she had been resting, leave the room, leave the house and return once more to the boat that rode forever and forever outward on the pathways of the sea.

Justin felt betrayed and deserted. It was as though they were conspiring together, his dead, against him: Edith refusing to listen to his *Green Kingdom* and George withholding his face. It was this that he had come for, he remembered now—to find a photograph of George. He turned his back on the piano and began to climb the stairs to the attic.

He had no idea where to begin to look, for all the photographs had been stored away soon after Edith became insane. Justin stood in the dark and dusty attic as though he held its low ceiling on his shoulders and therefore dared not move. He was smothered and confused and he did not know where to begin. When you are reduced to seeking for them in an attic, he thought, then they are really dead.

He longed for the sight of something familiar in this gloomy, silent place, and so he began to walk around cautiously, as though the boxes and the crates were people sleeping. Suddenly he came upon an old trunk from his student days and it seemed to welcome him, to give him companionship in the empty, silent room. He tried the lid and should not have been surprised to see that it came up easily because even in those days he always lost his keys and never remembered to lock anything. He pushed the lid back and a shower of dust fell off it into the air. Old manuscripts and notations were there, and he leafed through them thinking it would be good to play some of them again but he hated to think of playing ever again on that piano. There were old photographs, letters, and some newspaper clippings, some old gloves and a pair of ice skates. All these things which had once been so dear to him that he could not bear to throw them away were now hardly recognizable. Yet when his hand came upon the corner of something much older than these, he knew it instantly and pulled it forth free from the other things. For no matter how vaguely he had spoken of his grandfather's map of the Green Kingdom, still when he saw only a corner of it he knew it.

Haloed in a sphere of suspended dust, he sat down on a packing box in the dark attic and he was ten years old. That day had never faded from him, the day his grandfather had given him the much-folded map of the Green Kingdom. How true and real it had been for Justin then. Now he carefully unfolded the old piece of paper, fearful lest there should be only a line or two scrawled out of the head of an old drunk man to hold the audience of a child. The marks were so faded and the light in the attic so poor that Justin got up and made his way among the boxes to the door. The yawning top of the trunk received the gently falling dust into its mouth. The attic door, also forgotten as Justin went down the stairs, yawned on its hinges.

Downstairs, Justin started into his study, but changed his mind and went out of doors instead. Here the clear afternoon light and the sea air battled with the dust upon the man, and this time he stopped and closed the door of his house and carefully locked it. He tried to hold the map but the wind beat at it, and in fear of its tearing he put it in his pocket and hurried toward Max's house.

"A letter came for you," Max said. "It's up in your room."

"Thanks," Justin said. "I'm going up anyway." He wanted to be alone with the map. He wanted to be inside his room with the door shut and to sit down and take his time over it.

As soon as he recognized Erma Herrick's generous handwriting on the envelope he became conscious of the dust on his hands and washed them. Even before he saw the head tremor in the bathroom mirror, he saw the dust on his face. The record was there on his face: the streak across the forehead, the mark of his fingers where his hand had cradled one jaw. He did not remember having touched his face, was completely unaware of all the little mannerisms which he had built up recently in an unconscious effort to quiet the shaking of his head.

Now that his hands were clean he could not decide whether to read Erma's letter first or to look at the map. He took the map out of his pocket, still folded and creased, and put it on the table beside the letter. Then he picked up the letter and carried it over to the chair by the window.

DEAR JUSTIN MAGNUS:

Last night I dreamed of your Green Kingdom or rather, this morning, for I awoke with the dream still upon me.
I cannot remember ever having dreamed in color before.
I was walking on a vast plain and I came on a huge bird, standing on the ground. He was all green, only instead of the usual feathers, his were quilted. His wings were scythes.
He turned his head and looked at me. It's not surprising that I should have dreamed of your Kingdom because the night before we were all talking about it.

Arthur and Joe have their mailing list finished and Gwendolyn (Joe's girl) and I were helping address labels. First Arthur was so afraid he wouldn't get the book written right and then he was afraid the printing wouldn't be perfect and now he's suffering an agony of doubt that none of the people he sends it to will answer him.

Joe was trying to reassure him and he painted a beautiful picture in fun of how we would collect all the people who answered and all of us would go off to your Green Kingdom to keep the Records. After a while it wasn't a joke any more and we began to talk of how wonderful it really would be, until Arthur and I were all for packing up and starting out right then.

Gwendolyn brought us back to earth. She thinks we are all cracked but then she's so beautiful that we don't mind. Besides, she can outwork all three of us. Well, anyway, the books are in the mail now and it is just a matter of trying to anesthetize Arthur until the first replies come back.

Oh, I hope you are well, now. I try to imagine how it is with you but I cannot.

Sincerely,
ERMA HERRICK

If there was anything that Justin Magnus understood perfectly about people, it was Arthur Herrick's agony. Had he not lived through it at the publishing of each new work, at every concert?

I must write to him, he thought, and tell him how much his book meant to me. But how could he tell anyone about George? Then he remembered that he had not found a photograph of George, that he had forgotten it in his excitement over finding the map.

At any rate, I can write them about the map, he thought, and it is too dark now to see anything in the attic. I shall have to go back tomorrow. He got up from the chair and went to the desk. Carefully, he began to unfold the map. He was relieved to see that it looked like a real map; at least it was not a careless, drunken, unintelligible scrawl as he had feared.

Mrs. Johns had been restored to the household and, since that time, the meals had improved a great deal. When she went to Justin's room to call him for dinner, she found him hunched over the map in such deep concentration that she startled him.

"Oh, yes," he said. "Yes, Mrs. Johns. I'm coming right now." He picked the map up, folded it, and stuck it into his pocket. Surely Max would not be able to disparage *this*.

After dinner the two men sat together by the fireplace smoking and drinking their coffee. Justin had completely forgotten about his pipe's having been forbidden him, and Max never mentioned it. Once he started to and then he thought, If it were me, I would not go out of my way to prolong my own life. Why should I try to prolong his?

"You're looking very well tonight," Max said. "Better than I've seen you in a long time."

"I feel well," Justin said. "I feel first-rate." He had his hand in his pocket, fingering the folded edge of the map, savoring the secret knowledge that he had in store for Max.

"Well, possibly," Max said, "it's that Mrs. Johns has taken over the cooking again, though I hate to admit it."

"Oh, no," Justin said, "it's . . ." He was afraid to tell Max. He was afraid that Max's cleverness, on which he had counted so many times, would penetrate right through the map, would easily expose it for a fraud. He did not want it to be a fraud. At any rate, right now he did not want it to be a fraud. He did not mind there not being any Green Kingdom there but he wanted to hunt for it. He didn't mind not getting *in* it, for he himself did not really believe it was there, but he wanted to go *to* it.

Max took off his glasses and pressed his thumb and index finger against his eyelids. "Yes?" he said.

"I was just thinking," Justin said, "I'd like to take a little trip."

"That's a good idea," Max said—"a change of scene, a little vacation. Where are you going?"

"Well, I'd like to get the car and just start out. Some of that country where I was on tour, I liked it out there."

I do not even need my glasses on, Max thought, to know what a bad liar he is. "Surely," he said. "It sounds good. I think I'll take a vacation myself, once the summer term's over. A couple of weeks somewhere up the coast."

What would Max do on a vacation? Justin wondered. What would he be like, not working? He had a sudden picture of Max alone in a boat, fishing, sitting up straight in the boat, impatiently trying to get the fish to pay attention and concentrate and do what they were supposed to do so he could get on to something else. Justin smiled.

"You'll have to have your car checked over," Max said. "It hasn't been used for so long that I doubt if it's safe." Perhaps, he thought, it is only that he wants to be away from the sight of his house, away from the sea.

What do I care if it's safe or not? Justin thought. If it breaks down I'll walk. His grandfather had found the Green Kingdom on foot. Why shouldn't he? But the young people. *If they would go with him, if they were there,* well, then, of course, the car would have to be safe.

"I'll do that," Justin said. "Better do it tomorrow."

"You're going soon, then?" Max said.

"Well, yes. Pretty soon," Justin said. Tomorrow, he thought, if the car were ready, if the car were safe. Justin stood up. "Well," he said, "I'd better go up. I've got a letter to write."

Why don't you write it down here? Max wanted to say but he could not bring himself to do it. He put on his glasses and went to his desk and straightened himself as though he and the desk were in some kind of combat.

It took a week for the car to be made ready and in this time, though Justin often went down to the town to make purchases and was constantly preoccupied with packing and with getting ready to go, he never went to his own house.

Perhaps I should offer to go for him, Max thought, to go over to his house and bring back his things, for apparently something unfortunate has happened to him there. But this also he could not bring himself to suggest. Nor could he imagine what Justin had been doing in the house to have come back with dirt all over his face.

When Justin sat in the car ready to leave, saying good-by to Max, he wanted more than anything to tell him where he was going, to speak of the map which even now lay safe and folded in his pocket, but he could not do it. They said the things that men say: "Well, let me hear from you and thanks for everything and have a good trip." At last, to put an end to them, Max stood back.

In the rear-view mirror Justin caught a glimpse of him standing looking at the ground for a moment and then abruptly going toward the house. In his mind's eye he saw him going inside, going to the desk, taking his glasses off, sitting there at his desk alone in that big house.

I should have told him about the map, Justin thought, as he began to drive faster away from the sight of his own house. I don't know why I couldn't do it. As he drove on alone he began to think of Max and to wonder about him. Max had always been, in the ten years he had known him, exactly as he was now. It had never occurred to Justin before to wonder if he had always been the same. But now it seemed strange to him that Max lived alone in that big house and even stranger that he had never asked Max if he had ever had a wife or a family.

Max had not gone to his desk. He stood by the window watching the place where the car had been, thinking: I should have got him to tell me where he is going. I should have made him see the doctor first. But Max could never bear to do what had to be done in order to make people tell him what they meant. He cursed the sense of delicacy that had made him all his life unable to say, "Don't lie to me, my friend. I am concerned for you and I have a right to be."

Mrs. Johns came into the room and stood there with her hands crossed over her stomach. "Am I to put the things back now?" she asked. "Your sister's things, the way they were, or is Mr. Magnus coming back?"

"No," Max said, "I don't think he's coming back. I don't think so."

He was still looking out the window and finally Mrs. Johns turned away and went out of the room. Silently she climbed the stairs and began methodically to restore the room to the way it had been. From closets and drawers she took the things that had been put away and replaced them: the sister's portrait on the wall, the little footstool, the sewing cabinet, the ivory desk with the quill on it bearing the long gray feather.

CHAPTER SIX

JOE came into the room where Erma sat sewing, alone in a circle of lamplight. He had one hand in the pocket of his jacket. He wore no necktie, his shirt was open two buttons down, and his yellow hair, as usual, stood straight up in a pattern of its own.

"Hey, look," he said. "Look what I found." He pulled his hand out of his pocket and in it was a small, bedraggled kitten.

"Oh, Joe, you shouldn't have taken it," Erma said. "It's too little."

Joe sat on the floor rubbing the kitten's fur the wrong way. "Hell, I didn't take it from anywhere," he said. "It was lost." He held the kitten up, his big hand encircling its whole body. "Look at her squirm. You got some milk?"

"There's some in the icebox," Erma said, "only it's too cold. You have to heat it for them when they're little like that."

Erma could hear Joe in the kitchen going from the icebox to the stove, trying to do all the operations one-handed since he still held the cat. Presently he came back, balancing a skillet before him, the cat still dangling at his side. He put them both down on the floor. It was funny about Joe, Erma thought, the way you could never say, Not in here, Joe. Don't make a mess, Joe. Even though she was trying so hard to keep everything clean for Justin Magnus' arrival, the best she could do was to hope the kitten would be quick about it so she could get it all cleaned up again.

The kitten walked up to the skillet, backed off tentatively, sniffed the air, and finally put both front feet in the milk and began to lap it up.

"Look at her eat," Joe said. He reached behind the kitten and lifted her hind legs in the air. The kitten's whole face went into the milk and, upon having her legs restored to the floor, she looked up at Joe with all her whiskers frosted. Joe began to laugh.

"You've got enough milk there to feed a grown dog," Erma said. "Don't let her eat any more, Joe; she'll get sick."

Joe picked the kitten up in his hand and Erma took the skillet into the kitchen. When she came back she had a towel with her. "Here," she said, "let her have this for a bed."

Joe put the kitten down on the towel and it sat washing its paws and its face for a while and then it went to sleep. Erma went over to the window and pushed the curtain aside.

"I thought he'd be here by now," she said. She came back to her chair and picked up her sewing again.

"You really think he'll let me go?" Joe said.

"Sure he will, Joe. I wrote to him about you. He'll want you to go, all right."

"What did you say?"

"I said you could fix cars."

"I never wanted to go any place so bad in my life," Joe said. "You get to thinking about it, it gets hold of you, a place like that. I just want to see what's there."

"So do I," Erma said, "especially now that he's found the map."

"I've just got to go this one last place," Joe said.

"What do you mean?" Erma said.

Joe began to scratch his head violently. He turned and walked over to where the kitten was and with his toe just gently disturbed it so that it changed its position.

"Listen, Erma," he said. "I got to talk to you about Arthur."

"What about Arthur?" she said. She put the needle securely into the sewing and folded the cloth. Men always thought if you were doing anything with your hands you couldn't listen. Joe stood looking at the kitten, his hands stuffed into his pockets.

"Well, hell," he said. "Gwen wants to get married."

Erma reached into her pocket and got out two cigarettes. She handed one to Joe and lighted her own. "Well, that shouldn't surprise you," she said. "What's the matter? Don't you want to get married?"

The cigarette seemed to have freed him of his restlessness and he sat down astraddle a straight chair, leaning his arms on the back of it. He put his chin down on his arms and then he raised his head and took a drag off his cigarette. "Well, yes," he said, "I guess I want to get married, but, Christ, Erma, I don't know if I do or not."

"You love Gwen, don't you?"

"Sure I love Gwen. I loved Gwen the first time I saw her.

But marriage is different. I mean you get to thinking how nice it would be to have someone pull the shade down if the sun was in your eyes and you think about those awful hot mornings when you're too tired to kick the sheet off and there'd be somebody else there to kick it off for you, but then you get to thinking how final it is, how you couldn't go running off with the circus any more. Hell, there was a carnival one time after the war and I just went off with it for a couple of weeks. You get married and you couldn't do that any more. That's why I want to go on this crazy trip so bad, hunting for something that only exists in the brain of a dead man, sort of a farewell performance."

"Joe, anybody that loved you would never try to keep you from going off with a carnival if you wanted to. You'd always come back."

"That's not what I mean, Erma. It isn't that anybody keeps you from going. You get married and after a while you don't want to go. Carnivals just don't appeal to you. You get a little routine and you get so you like it, so you don't want to leave."

"Well, if you know in advance that you'll like it, what do you care?"

"Well, I don't know if I want to like it," he said.

"Besides, Joe, maybe you're wrong. Maybe it isn't marriage that does it; maybe it's just getting older."

"Nope," Joe said, "you're wrong. There's a hell of a lot of old guys with carnivals. Real old guys. I don't want to talk about carnivals; I want to talk about Gwen. Look at it from her side. She's got all those sisters. She's different from you; you just had yourself. It must be terrible having all those sisters knowing about you, asking you when you're going to get married. I mean it would be almost better for a girl like Gwen to get married and make a mess of it than to have her sisters keep asking her year after year."

"Oh, Joe, that's no reason to get married."

"I know it," Joe said. He went over and picked up the kitten and stood scratching its neck. "What I started to say is, Gwen wants to get married and I guess I do too, and what the hell am I going to do about Arthur?"

"Why? What's it got to do with Arthur?"

"Well, I've got to get a job," Joe said. "I've got to quit fumbling around and get a real job where you get up every morning and put on your pants and run down to work on time and do what they tell you so that you can wake up next morning and put on your pants and run down to work . . . Erma, I can't support Gwen out of this business. I can't support myself."

"I live off it," Erma said.

"I know," Joe said, "but three of us is all it will stand if it will stand that. Besides, that's not the point. You aren't Gwen. Gwen is scared. She doesn't think tomorrow will be different. She has to have it different today. She can't help the way she is. She wants a house, a house of her own, a house that her sisters would think was a house."

"Well, Joe, there's nothing wrong about a woman's wanting a house."

"I know it's not wrong. I just say she isn't like you. Nobody's trying to make her be like you. But Gwendolyn thinks if you start out using boxes for furniture, you'll still be using boxes in ten years."

Erma got up and went over to the window. She was looking for Justin but at the same time she was looking, in her mind, at her own house. And suddenly it didn't look, as it always had to her, a triumph of ingenuity. She saw it in Gwendolyn's eyes and it looked like bare and eternal makeshift.

"Well, maybe she's right," Erma said. She turned away from the window and sat down again in the chair.

"Will you talk to Arthur for me? You've got to help me, Erma. Hell, I don't know how to say it so he'll understand. There aren't any jobs here. I'm going to have to go into the city. Arthur and I, we've been together ever since the war. We were always going to work together. We weren't ever going to work for anyone else, just ourselves. We've got to make something with our own hands, Arthur said. That's the only way to live. Then when you work all day, at night you can take something in your hands and hold it up to the light and say you made it. We bummed over the whole country together after the war. We've been every place together. We saved our pay to start the business with and we bummed. And then that night we hit here and they picked us up off the freight train and put us in jail and Arthur couldn't sleep. That was the night he thought out the Human Records. Then in the morning when they let us out we went by here and saw this shop for sale and we decided that was it, so we learned the printing business."

"Maybe the business will get better, Joe."

"It won't, Erma," he said. "It isn't that we don't work hard. There simply isn't any place in the world for a two-man print shop. On a big job you're up against a big shop, on a little job you're up against amateurs. When we bought the old man's shop here, we should have asked him why he wanted to sell it. We just asked him to teach us how to print. When you're first out of the army you think you can do *anything* if you can just do it by yourself, and it takes a long time before you'll admit that some things are no longer possible. You stand down there in the shop when the presses are still and you think there ought to be some way you could grit your teeth and double up your fists and make it be better, but it isn't in your hands. It just isn't a two-man problem and that's all there is to it."

Why did it have to be today? Erma thought. *Today,* with Justin Magnus coming and Arthur not home yet. She had never known Joe to be depressed before, and now with this talk of boxes and crates it was coming off on her so that she couldn't even think straight.

"But, Joe," she said, "we're forgetting the work. It isn't just a printing business. The thing that makes it all right to have boxes for furniture and all the rest of it is the work, the Keeping of Human Records. The work makes it all different."

"It's *Arthur's* work, Erma. You forget. It's not mine, and it sure as hell isn't Gwen's."

"But, Joe, I thought . . . I thought it was your work, the same as it's Arthur's."

"I guess it was, Erma," he said, "in the beginning."

"*Was?*" she said, and now she knew that it could not be put off to another day, could not be ignored. "Joe, it's serious, isn't it? I mean it's more than the money and the business and getting married?"

"Yeah, I guess so, Erma. But I didn't mean to let that slip. You don't need to pick away at it. The job and the money, that's plenty; that's all I have to talk to Arthur about."

"You mean you don't believe in the Records any more, Joe?"

"Oh, hell, Erma, I don't know. Believing or not believing. It's just that something's gone. Something's wrong about it."

He was moving his hands in a helpless way, so unlike him that Erma felt unreasonable fear rise in her. "Was it the Dobenski boy, Joe?"

"No, no," he said impatiently. "It's all of them. It's me. There's something unnatural about it. I can't explain it. Maybe Arthur's right. Plenty of times there's been one man right and the whole world wrong, but it's just the way people are, Erma. The Records, they're against *action*, that's it. The work doesn't make any . . . any energy. It takes away energy; it runs down. Erma, tell me the truth. Don't you ever wonder? Don't you ever——"

"No, Joe," she said. "No, I've never doubted it. And I think the book will help. I think it will locate others."

"It's a funny thing," Joe said. "I thought it would, too, and then . . . Well, the thing is, Erma, I hope it does. I hope he finds the people it is meant for, because, no matter how right it is . . . It's right to Arthur and it's right to you, and it may be right to somebody else, but it just isn't for me any more. I got to quit kidding myself."

"Joe," Erma said, "Joe, what is it you want?"

"That's it. That's the trouble. I don't know. Arthur knows what he wants and he's such a hell of a spellbinder I thought I wanted it too. And now I'm going to do it again, Erma. I'm going to think I want what Gwen wants. It's my own fault. I ought to know what it is I want and maybe I'll never find out, but I know one thing and that is it wouldn't ever again be anything you had to talk people into. I don't want to convince people to do what they don't want to. I want to help them do what they *do* want to do. All I know is, for me, it ought to be fun; it ought to make you feel good. And if I can't find that, at least I ought to make some money with what I do know how to do."

There was silence in the room between them and at last Erma said, "All right, Joe, I'll help you. I'll talk to Arthur for you, but I dread it. Does it have to be right now? Couldn't you wait until he gets a few answers from the book? He'll feel so different then."

"I know, Erma. I wanted to wait, too, but he's forcing my hand."

"How?"

"Don't you know where Arthur is right now?"

"No," she said, "I don't. He went out this afternoon, early."

"He's gone to the bank and God knows where else. He's trying to mortgage the big press."

"Oh, Joe, really? But he shouldn't do it now. It'll be only a few days until he begins to hear from the book."

"But he *has*, Erma, and he's thinking that I'll be with him to help pay it off. He's got to know."

"I have to think about it, Joe. I'll help you, but I won't promise right now when it will be. Besides . . ."

She began to smooth out the folded cloth on her lap, her eyes watching her hand.

"Besides what?" Joe said.

"Maybe the Green Kingdom is really there," she said. "Maybe you'll never have to tell him."

Joe stood again at the window with his back to her. "Sure," he said. "Sure, with a great big Easter Bunny sitting right in the middle of it."

"I'd like to see your face if it were," she said.

"Well, anyhow, Magnus won't come now," Joe said. "It's going to rain to beat hell."

Erma put her sewing on the arm of the chair and went over by Joe. "I don't suppose he will come now," she said. "He's been sick, you know. He may have to take it slower than we counted on. He might not even be near."

"Jesus, it would have to rain. Every night I have to wait, it gets that much harder to face Gwen. She doesn't want me to go. She wants me to get started on this job business right now. You can't blame her. It's almost time for her vacation. She wanted to take it and not go back to work. I know how she feels, but God, how I wanted to go on this one last chase! What'll I tell her? What'll I say to her now?"

Erma turned away from him. "Tell her to come to dinner," she said. "I got a lot of food in, thinking Justin Magnus would be here tonight. Anyhow, if Arthur went to mortgage the press without telling me, it'll be easier for me to act as though I don't know it if there's someone else here."

"O.K.," Joe said. "I'll go get her. Can I leave the cat here?"

"Oh, sure," she said, looking over at the kitten. "I forgot about her."

Joe looked down at Erma and opened his mouth to say something, but instead he put his big hand on top of her head and, with neither gentleness nor grace, he moved her head back and forth a couple of times and then he gave a little snort through his nose and turned away and left her.

Erma stood looking out on the purple clouds. The whole town had turned a sickish lavender in anticipation of the storm, and the wind was inhaling now, steadily and quietly, getting ready for the moment of violent exhalation. She thought of Justin Magnus trying to drive against the storm. She thought of Arthur trying to mortgage the big press. She thought of Gwendolyn and the windows of furniture stores. But of how Arthur would take Joe's leaving, she could not bear to think. The kitten maiowed.

"I'm tired," Erma said. "I'm tired."

One thing they had in common, these four people sitting around Arthur Herrick's table, and that was a deep, a genuine, admiration for food either good or abundant. For food good *and* abundant, they had reverence. In its presence they laid aside their cares and their preoccupations automatically; such things can always wait. Spread before them was the food which had been bought and borrowed and saved for Justin Magnus; it was no time to be disconsolate. Let the feasting be over and the time for tobacco; then would be ample time to resume their thoughts.

"But aren't you afraid to go, Erma?" Gwendolyn said. "I mean, you said yourself that day he left here, he didn't know what he was doing. And on top of that, he's been sick a long time."

"You haven't seen him," Erma said, "or you'd know he isn't the kind of man who goes crazy."

"Who cares?" Joe said. "Let him be crazy, just so he'll take me along. You really think he will, Erma? You really think he'll let me go to the Green Kingdom?"

"If you're Joe and you can fix cars, you've got an invitation right now," Justin Magnus said from the doorway.

They had not heard him come in over the noise of the storm and they were all unable to speak, their eyes focused on the wet, shaggy figure standing in the doorway. Water ran down his face, water squeezed out the seams of his shoes.

It was just as he had remembered it—the place, the light, even the rain. Only Erma was different, smaller somehow than he had remembered her.

"Well," Justin said, "I'm here. I made it." He laughed a little and shook his head so that the water flew in a spray about him. And this released the others from their spell so that Arthur was able to jump up and take his coat.

"But you're soaked through," Erma said. "You must put on dry things. Where are your clothes? Where are your bags?"

Well, he had made it. He found that he was very tired. He was also cold, he realized, and hungry. He sat down. Immediately he saw Gwendolyn sitting directly across from him looking like an advertisement for a perfume called Dark Symmetry, and he realized that his clothes were wet, that he was getting the chair wet, that he had left a puddle of water in the doorway where he had been standing.

Then Erma saw for the first time the slight head tremor. This is new, she thought. This is different.

"Forgive me," she said. "Gwendolyn, this is Mr. Magnus."

"How do you do?" Justin said, and he stood up and went back to stand in his original puddle, though he could not have explained why.

Gwendolyn always had a disturbing effect on strangers. There is a certain type of beauty so startling in its utter perfection that it causes an immediate self-questioning in those who see it and results usually in unjustified isolation for those who possess it. Strange women on buses seeing Gwendolyn often resolved to begin anew to diet or to change their face creams. Though she was aware of the effect that she had on most people, particularly men, she honestly did not realize what caused it and was quite powerless to help it. All she said to Justin Magnus was hello in her own exquisite and fastidious way, and he felt like an old water rat. Even Arthur still sometimes suffered from a kind of timidity in her presence.

Joe had missed it all. The one man Gwendolyn had ever been able to love was, of necessity, the only one who was blind to the essence of her beauty. He recognized the beauty but he simply had no awe in him. No one could ever have explained to Joe that it is all right to eat popcorn in a second-run movie house while watching a Western but that it is not all right to eat popcorn at the opera. To Joe it was a matter of whether or not you liked popcorn. He did.

"I'll get your bags," Joe said.

"But you can't," Justin said, still standing in the door. "They're miles from here. The car stalled."

"And you *walked?*" Erma asked. "You've been *walking* in this storm?"

"Well, it was more like fighting," he said. "The storm came on me all at once and flooded the engine. It was farther back to the last town than it was on to this one and . . . well, frankly, I just didn't have enough sense to quit. I kept thinking the next turn would be it."

"Never mind that now," Erma said. "You must have a hot

bath and something hot to drink." She went into the bathroom
to start the water running.

For the last three miles he had been thinking of that bathtub
with the green vine trailing into it, of the hot coffee sitting in the
brown pot beside the tub. He had been fighting his way to them.
But now he stood rooted to his puddle as though the angle of
Gwendolyn's vision were a wall he could not pass.

"I hope the map is safe," Arthur said. "Is it in the car?"

"Oh, my God," Justin said. "I had it in my pocket."

He could move now from his puddle and he took the map
from his pocket and spread it out on the table. It was damp but
apparently still legible.

"I'll get a big blotter," Arthur said, "and we'll dry it out
while you're changing."

Erma came back into the room and took Justin's arm and
led him away. "Just leave your clothes in the bathroom," she
said. "I'll dry them out later."

When she came back the others were clustered around the
map. It was apparently a real map but she did not have time to
be puzzled over it now. What concerned her at the moment was
what Justin Magnus would wear. There was not even a place they
could borrow clothes for him, for in all the town there was not a
man his size. Though Joe was about as tall as he, he was only
about a third as broad.

"Gwen, help me," Erma said. "I've got to heat this food
and set the table in that room. He's had nothing to eat."

"Is he going to eat in there alone?" Gwen said.

"Well, he's dead tired and I think it would be better," Erma
said. "Besides, there's nothing dry for him to wear. He'll have to
wrap up in some blankets."

As Erma set the hot soup down on the small table, Justin
came out of the bathroom wrapped in his blanket. He was barefoot.

"Won't you stay," he said, "and keep me company?"

"Well, all right," she said. "Did you get warm?"

"I am on the outside," Justin said, sitting down at the table,
"and as soon as I have had some of this soup I will be on the inside and by then—"

"By then you will be sleepy," she said.

"I don't know," Justin said. "While I was trying to get here
I thought if I ever reached this room I should fall on the bed in

exhaustion, but now I'm beginning to feel more awake every minute."

"If only you don't have pneumonia in the morning after that terrible walk in the storm."

"Well, if I do," Justin said, "I want to be buried just like this. I'm extremely comfortable. I have always maintained that a man should be buried naked, wrapped in a blanket. You wonder how people can say they have 'laid a man to rest' in a full suit of clothes. Just imagine—*to rest*. It's not possible. Think of the shirt collar, the necktie, the belt around the waist."

He looked down at his feet and spread his toes. "And think of the shoes," he said. "That's the worst of all."

In the other room they were still bent over the map. "By God, Arthur," Joe said, "there *must* be something there."

"I'd give my right arm," Arthur said, "to know what *is* there. Just imagine what it would mean right now if two hundred people out of that thousand should answer about the Records. Imagine being able to write back to them with something concrete, with a *place* to go."

"Well, in a week or two we'll know," Joe said. "By the time we get back there'll be some replies waiting for you."

"I've got to go home," Gwen said. "*I've* got to go to work in the morning. Come on, Joe."

When they passed Justin's room, Joe stopped. "If you'll give me the keys to your car, Mr. Magnus, I'll go out first thing in the morning and see if I can bring it in."

"Thank you," Justin said. "The keys must be in the car. I can't remember taking them out."

"Have you any idea how far out on the highway it is?"

"No," Justin said, "I haven't. There wasn't any place open or I would have called a garage. All I can remember was that I had just passed a schoolhouse."

"My God," Joe said, "that's five miles from here."

"Well, good night, Mr. Magnus," Gwendolyn said, going into the room. "Oh, please don't get up."

Justin drew his bare feet under the table. "I hope you have an umbrella," he said.

"It's not raining," Gwendolyn said. "It's stopped."

"Oh," he said, "so it has. I . . . I didn't notice." He picked up his coffee cup and, seeing that it was empty, set it back in the saucer.

"When are you leaving?" Gwendolyn asked.

"Well, it depends on the car, I suppose," Justin said.

"Oh, Joe will fix that," Gwendolyn said. "He's quite wonderful with cars. Well, I hope you all have a pleasant trip."

"Why don't you come along?" Justin said. His toes had begun to ache from being held rigidly in a cramped position.

"Why don't you, Gwen?" Erma said, looking at the girl and then at Joe. "You could get your vacation a little early, couldn't you?"

As he and Gwendolyn walked toward her house, Joe said, "What made you change your mind? Was it the map?"

"I didn't say I'd changed my mind about the Green Kingdom," Gwendolyn said.

"Or was it Mr. Magnus? He's a great guy, don't you think?"

"Listen, Joe, I think you ought to stick close to him. He's the kind of man who can get you a good job, get you out of this hole."

"Aw, Gwen, you got him wrong. He's a great man, all right, but not like you think. Why, I doubt if he could get himself a job."

"That doesn't make any difference," Gwen said. "He knows important people. That's the way you get jobs, Joe, because you know people. You don't get a job because you're good at something; you get it because you know somebody."

"Tell me more, Mamma," Joe said. "Tell me more about the bad, cruel world."

"Joe, be serious. I'm desperate. If I have to go back to that same office again after another vacation, I'll . . . Oh, Joe, I hate it so. I can't stand it any longer."

Joe turned to the girl and he put his arms around her. "I'll get you out, Gwen," he said. "Honest I will. I'll make it somehow. Why don't you go with us, huh? Why don't you get your vacation early and come with us? Think what a wonderful time we'd have. Then when we come back, I'll go to the city and get a job and we can get married."

"Somebody'll see us, Joe," she said. "Don't."

Justin Magnus had gone to sleep and Erma had hung his clothes to dry and washed the dishes. Now she and Arthur lay in bed, both of them too excited to sleep.

"When do you think we'll go?" Erma said. "I ought to be

planning but I don't know what to take, whether we'll need warm clothes, or what."

"Depends on the car," Arthur said, "and on how Magnus feels. You don't think he's going to be sick, do you?"

"Oh, I hope not," Erma said. "He should never have made that long walk in the rain."

"Still, he seemed all right, didn't you think? My God, the man is like an ox. Do you realize he walked five miles in that storm?"

"I know," she said. "I know. If only he's all right in the morning. He's changed a lot since he was here last. It breaks your heart."

"Did you notice his head?" Arthur said. "Maybe it was only tonight, because he was so tired, but it—"

"Yes," she said. "I saw it. As soon as he came in, I saw it."

Arthur stretched his arms above his head and turned a little in bed. "I keep telling myself," he said, "that this is a vacation, this is just a jaunt. But I can't help wishing that it—"

"Would you be very surprised if it were real?" Erma said.

"It's funny," Arthur said. "If there isn't anyone around to accuse you of being a dreamer, you accuse yourself."

"Even if you have a map?"

"What do you believe?" Arthur said. "Do you really believe it's there? Do you think we'll find anything more than a fertile valley when we get there?"

She lay in the darkness, in the quiet house, staring up at the ceiling, trying to think what exactly she really expected to find. "Well," she said, "I know this. If we came to it and it turned out to be just as I have imagined it, I don't think I would be surprised. I would be glad."

"If only we could know right now what *is* there," Arthur said.

"I like it better this way," Erma said. "I'd rather have the discovery, the hunting."

"But, Erma, if I knew! If even I knew there were a valley where men could survive, think what a difference. One wouldn't need to be a dreamer failing in a print shop, struggling with a handful of people. Imagine how it would be to take a hundred, two hundred people there to keep the Records. To promise them a living, to promise them a work, to go there for the purpose of keeping the Records, to do it right, on a scale that matters."

"Maybe there are people already there, Arthur. After all, it's more than seventy years since Justin's grandfather was there."

"I forgot about that," Arthur said. "Of course it can't be the same."

"Reach me a cigarette," Erma said. "I'm not sleepy, are you?"

"Here," he said, lighting the cigarette and handing it to her.

"Thanks. Well, anyhow," she said, "even if there aren't any people there, you and I will keep the Records. That's what we'll go there to do and that will be our work."

"You and me and Joe," he said.

Erma thought of the big press (and was it mortgaged now?) and she thought of the mailbox, empty again today of answers from the book. And she thought of Joe. She leaned over her husband and kissed his eyelids.

"I wonder if Gwen will go," she said. "Weren't you surprised when Justin asked her?"

"I was more surprised when you urged her to come," Arthur said. "Joe wants to get away from her; I thought you knew that."

"What makes you think so?" Erma asked.

"I know Joe."

"Arthur, maybe we don't really know Joe. It's so easy for me to say: Joe, will you go to the grocery for me? Will you get me a cigarette? I forget that isn't enough for Joe. Why wouldn't he want a wife of his own? Why wouldn't he want . . . well, things we don't even know about?"

"It wasn't Joe we were talking about," Arthur said. "It was Gwen. What made you urge her?"

"I don't know, Arthur. Maybe it was to get Justin Magnus out of an embarrassing situation and get Gwen moving. There he sat wrapped up in his blankets, and you know how Gwen never feels any obligation to make things easy for people."

"She won't go," Arthur said. "Don't worry about it. She'd hate it."

"I wish I could be sure you're right," Erma said, "but I'm not. I don't know anything about her, really. I don't understand her."

"What's that noise?" Arthur said.

"It's that cat Joe left here," Erma said. "I forgot all about it."

Erma knew the house by heart and, her eyes accustomed to

the darkness, she began the search for the kitten. Oh, don't let it be in *his* room, she thought. All over the living room she went, and the kitten's voice, like that of a cricket, seemed now in one place, now in another. Finally she traced it to the door of Justin's room. She stood by the door, hesitating whether or not to open it. The cat would surely awaken him, for now its voice grew petulant, demanding. Erma turned the doorknob by degrees while she held her breath and pressed her lips together. She felt the latch loosen under her hands and she pushed against the door slowly.

Not familiar with the sounds of the house, Justin had been lying awake for some time before he located the sound. He felt, rather than saw, Erma come into the room. She stood in the doorway for a moment trying to locate the sound, and Justin lay there thinking *By the window; the cat is by the window*, but he said nothing. Erma moved into the beam of light cast by the street lamp. She wore a long robe which showed a light blur in the darkness and it made her seem much taller, more as he had first remembered her. He saw her go directly across to the kitten and pick it up in her arms and he was afraid to breathe. The kitten ceased crying.

Justin saw her silhouetted against the window, stroking the kitten in the rhythm that his own heart was beating, and he grew anxious for her to leave the room, for he had held his breath until now it was a revolving wheel inside him, but she did not leave. He could see her moving slowly toward the bed and, full of guilt, he closed his eyes. He could feel her standing by the bed and he was aware that his legs and arms were threatening to fly loose from the leash of his control and betray him. Erma put one hand out toward the bedcovers and then she withdrew it. She turned and went silently to the door, and Justin heard the knob turn in her hands.

By the time Joe and Arthur got the car back to the house next morning the map was dry enough that it could with safety be lifted up from the blotter. It was then that they saw, for the first time, a kind of calendar marked on the reverse side.

Arthur saw it first. "What's this?" he said to Justin. "This list of dates."

"Let me see," Justin said. "I never noticed it."

Arthur handed him the map. Justin had put on clean clothes, brought from the car, and, having arisen very late, was just finishing his breakfast. He wiped his hands on his napkin, spread the map out face down on the table, and bent over it.

"Why, those must be the times of the split," he said.

"Oh," Erma said, "the door that opens every ten years."

"Yes," Justin said. "That's it. I remember now he wrote them down for me, oh, very seriously. See, here are the two he actually saw, with stars beside them, and here are the ones he forecast."

"I don't remember about any door," Joe said.

"Neither do I," Arthur said.

Erma looked at them in disbelief. She looked to Justin Magnus and back again to Arthur. "Why, that's the most important thing of all," she said, "the door or the split, or whatever it is. That's the whole point!"

Who can say how a man listens or for what he listens when you speak to him? Where is the listening mind that speakers imagine: the mind that lies clear, untroubled, and receptive like a newborn pool of water? It is nowhere. It does not exist. The pool is muddy; it is full of fish. The spoken pebbles that are cast into it it receives with dissolving acids, it obscures in clouds of mud, it engulfs in the bellies of quick-moving fish, it encrusts with mineral deposits of its own, it overgrows with algae. The roughness of the pebbles is worn smooth, the sharpness is dulled, and on the smooth places arise new prominences. The pebble is changed or it is obscured or it is lost. It is neither embraced nor returned the same as it was cast in, for the listening pool is never really still nor can it be newborn unless a man can be born without parents, without generations before him, without regard to Time. Each man fills the listening pool with the waters of his own dream, according to his needs.

Erma came around to Justin's side of the table and bent over the dim list of dates. "Well, when did he forecast the next one?" she said. "Are we going to be in time?"

Justin ran his big finger down the list slowly. "Here it is," he said. "According to his calculation, August twenty-sixth of this year."

"Then we haven't much time," Erma said. "Only ten days. Are you rested enough to start right away?"

"What is this split, this door, or whatever?" Joe said. "What happens?"

"Oh," Justin said, "God knows what really happened. But

my impression of it is a kind of vertical split caused by an earthquake. It is, by my memory, mountainous country. A split was
supposed to open up in the wall of a mountain and stay open at
least long enough for a man to get inside, and then, according to
my grandfather, it closed up again."

"How?" Joe said.

"That I don't know," Justin said. "My own idea was that falling rocks blocked the way. Of course we mustn't expect anything
too spectacular. After all, frankly speaking, my grandfather was
a sot. He also had the reputation of being cracked. Or, it may only
have been that he had to make up a good story to explain a temporary desertion of my grandmother. I personally do not much
care. I'd like to be there on the appointed day, out of sentimental-
ity, just as I'd like to follow this map whether it's the shortest
route or not."

And, too, he thought, maybe on the journey it will come
back to me, as I had it before, and I can begin the second movement of the symphony. What comes after discovery? he thought.

"You mean," Joe said, "that there's a chance we might get
in some place we couldn't get out of?"

"Of course," Erma said. "That's what I keep telling you."

"You mean it would be all right with you," Arthur said, "if
we got shut in some place, if we couldn't get out?"

She saw Justin lift his coffee cup and she knew if there was
any coffee in it that it was cold. She saw him watching her over the
top of the cup. "Why, yes," she said. "It would be all right with
me."

"I don't know," Joe said. "I think I'll take along some dynamite, just in case."

Justin was still watching Erma. He had not moved. He did
not know if there were coffee in the cup or not.

"Joe," Erma said, "you've got to do something with that
kitten."

"Jesus, I forgot all about her. Where is she?"

"She's in my clothes basket in the kitchen. Maybe Mrs.
Perry would take her."

"I'll find a place for her," he said.

Erma followed him out to the kitchen. He reached into the
basket and picked up the kitten. "Listen, Erma," he said, "don't
say anything to Gwen about this door business, this split, or whatever it is. I just got her talked into going along last night, and

now if she heard us talking about getting shut in that place she'd back out again.''

''But, Joe, you can't do that. You can't take somebody into a place they can't get out of without even warning them.''

''Why, you believe it,'' he said. ''Don't you?''

''Oh, it's not so much that I believe it, Joe; it's that I hope for it, I guess.''

Erma had a long and confusing day trying to pack for the Green Kingdom. She put in a copy of Arthur's book and a Limoges teacup given her by Mrs. Perry because they might never come back. She packed little to read because they might be back in two weeks. She packed a wool sweater for Arthur because it might be cold there and also her bathing suit because it might be hot.

She wanted to clean the house before dinnertime and she could not very well do it with Justin Magnus there. It was ridiculous to insist on cleaning the house now and she knew it, but still they might be leaving it forever; one couldn't be sure. She felt that Arthur would understand, so she went downstairs to the print shop to ask him if he would take Justin Magnus out of the house for a while. But Arthur was concerned with his own leave-taking. He had put the shop in order, cleared his desk, and now he was cleaning the big press. The sight of him there with his pile of ink-stained rags and his squirt can of gasoline endeared him to her as nothing ever had.

''Where's Joe?'' she said.

''He was here a while ago, but he's gone out again,'' Arthur said. ''He says he knows a place where he can get some dynamite.''

''Dynamite?''

''Yes. I wanted him to help me clean the press, but he said it would be dirty again in two weeks when we got back and in the next breath he says he's going after dynamite to blast us out of the Green Kingdom. I said if he was so sure we'd be back in two weeks why was he so hot to get hold of the dynamite, and he said he wouldn't even go to a hypothetical place without a means of escape. That's Joe. One minute he'll tell you that door is a lot of crap and the next minute he's trying to find a key to fit it.''

Well, she would certainly not ask Arthur to leave his press, and if Joe did come back, Arthur would need him. Of course, she could simply explain it to Justin Magnus, this need of hers to leave her house as though she were leaving it forever, ask him to go out somewhere and walk around a while until she got it cleaned. But, dear God, he might offer to help her. She gave the whole thing up and sat down on the stool near Arthur. It was a thing she often had to tell herself: some things are more important than others.

"Listen, Arthur. We've got to do something about Joe. This morning he said he's going to take Gwen into the Green Kingdom without telling her about the door. And we simply must not let him do that. If there's even the slightest chance of our being shut in, we can't allow anyone to walk in unwarned. He told me this morning that he'd just got Gwen talked into going and that if she heard about the door she'd back out."

Arthur began to laugh. "He got *her* talked into it?"

Erma reached into her pocket and took out a cigarette. "I learned something about Joe this morning," she said. "I never realized it before. Everybody thinks Joe's irresponsible. He keeps telling you how irresponsible he is. It's part of his charm. And then Gwen comes along and depends on him. He likes it. He feels responsible for someone and he likes it."

"Well, you don't need to worry about Gwen," Arthur said. "Joe changed his mind after he talked to you. He met Gwen when she got off work at noon and he told her about the door."

"What did she say?"

"She just laughed and said she'd like to see any place that could hold Joe if he wanted to get out."

"You see what I mean?" Erma said.

"I see all right," Arthur said. "Now the guy's got to spend the whole night hunting up dynamite just so Gwen won't be wrong. Otherwise he could have helped me clean the press."

But Joe's labor was all in vain. Next morning the men were arranging the luggage in the trunk of the car and Joe said, "Be careful of those caps, Arthur. Don't put them so close to the other box. We've got to keep them away from the dynamite."

"Dynamite?" Gwendolyn said. "Are we going to ride in a car full of dynamite?" Whereupon she refused to go. She would not ride in the same car with a box of dynamite and that was all there was to it. Explanations were to no avail. Justin, too, finally expressed himself as being a little uneasy, and so finally they left the dynamite behind.

Who can tell the effects of daylight on a man's night thoughts? What man has not lain long awake staring into the darkness of the night building himself a plan, a dream, a house, only to see it melted, wilted, made ridiculous by the morning light? A case of dynamite—well, that is a wonderful thing at night. It proves that a woman can put her faith in you with safety. How different it looks in the early-morning sunlight, like a box of firecrackers, like a child's weapon against an enemy that is not there. They left it behind. They buried it in the yard.

They got into the car and started off, gaily, joyfully, in a holiday mood, under the bright summer sun. They were going to the Green Kingdom, these five, whatever the Green Kingdom might be; they were going to retrace the grandfather's journey as long as the map bore any resemblance to reality.

They had nine days.

O R T H E Y had a lifetime. For who can measure, really, nine days unmarked, unticketed, in the future? *Tomorrow* a man can hold in his head as a definite measure. But nine days, blank and free and unpredictable—the mind cannot hold such a measure. Gwendolyn was better able than the others to measure the quantity of nine days, for to her it was nine-fourteenths of her vacation. To the others it was a total—that is, it was if they cared to be there by August 26, if they cared to be faithful to the grandfather's prediction.

The first day, of course, they did not care much. Whoever stops to order his coffin on the way to kindergarten? When they started from Drury, Justin was driving, but, on stepping out of the car when they stopped for lunch, he turned his ankle. Although at the time it seemed to be a slight thing, by the middle of the afternoon he was glad to relinquish the wheel to Joe. They had planned to make, that night, one of the grandfather's stops, a town called Westgate. In the grandfather's time this name had been chosen with romanticism and prophecy and faith in the future, and, in the grandfather's time, it had really been a gate to the West, but now, as they compared the recent state map with the grandfather's, they could not even find the town.

Oh, the bitter irony, the alchemy of Time upon a name. All men have seen it in the past and yet they never believe it for the future. If they did, they would call all their new things small, knowing they will become so. They would label their fashions ridiculous, knowing they will soon be so. They would never give their children childish names, knowing they will not stay so. But they do not believe it. It is a thing they all know, but they know it in only one direction, so they build a new theater and call it *Palace*, and in twenty years the very name *Palace* means old, dirty, and rat-ridden. Time brings only roughnecks to lodge at the

Elite Hotel as the paint gets old, while, next door, hash and cabbage are the mainstay at the tables of the De Luxe. Men found a
town and make it out of their own spirit, and for this spirit they
call the town Independence. And in fifty years it is a suburb,
suckling its very life in utter dependence from another city. They
name their children Hope and Faith and watch patiently while the
seeds of war are planted for them. What short-visioned man has
designed a piece of furniture and called it Modern, not being able
to see that, while he is still sitting on it, perhaps, the very word
will come to mean outdated? With what wonderful audacity have
men called things *new, late, futuristic, fast and speedy,* as though
the world would end tomorrow.

Numbers are safer. It would have been better to call a town
Thirty-Seven than to call it New Hope and see it deserted, leveled
to the ground, grown poverty-stricken and diseased. Better Fifty-
One than Bella Vista looking out upon the soot of slag heaps.
Better Three than Whitewater with the creek bed dry. Better One
than Westgate, for Westgate, when they finally found it in the
smallest print on the map, was not even on a highway, and led
nowhere.

"Well, what do you think?" Joe said. "Do you want to risk
it?"

"How far out of the way is it?" Arthur asked.

"Oh, it's only fifteen miles off the highway," Joe said. "It's
not the time. It all depends," he said to Justin, "whether you want
to risk the tires or not. The road's not even paved."

"The food's probably awful," Justin said, "if there's anybody alive there to cook it."

"Oh, let's go," Erma said. "Let's not desert the grandfather
so soon."

Justin's ankle had become quite painful now and, hating to
complain, he had been consoling himself with a vision of a good
bed and a hot bath. Before Erma spoke he had been about to suggest stopping at the nearest large hotel.

"Oh, well," he said, "let's go to Westgate. What's thirty miles
to us? Of course—" he turned around to look at Erma—"you'll
patch the tires for us."

"I'll lend you my nail polish," Gwen said. "I brought a new
bottle."

It was all like a dream to Mr. Fenway. Just like a dream.
Very often in the years after they moved the highway, Mr. Fenway

had had this same dream. A car stopped in front of his hotel. A man got out, a big man, well dressed and prosperous-looking, with new luggage. He had a party with him. They all wanted rooms for the night, the best rooms. Only, of course, in the dream he had been ready for them. The rooms were clean and aired, the kitchen was full of food. The lights were all on, the elevator worked, and when he gave the bell a smart tap, a uniformed boy appeared. Also, in the dream there was a new point in the pen.

Now it was really happening to him. There was the big, prosperous-looking man, though he was bareheaded and seemed to limp, and he had a party with him. They were not trying to find the highway or a garage or a place to buy liquor or cigarettes; they actually wanted rooms. Only he wasn't ready. No smartly uniformed boy would jump to his tap on the bell, and, for a fact, the clapper of the bell had come loose and been lost long ago. The elevator had not functioned in three years. The rooms were all shut tight upon their hoard of dust, and most of the light bulbs were symbols only. He was beside himself with anxiety, as are all men who foolishly discount their dreams. He began to cry frantically for Mrs. Fenway, who had, long ago, come to think of the hotel as her home, the only home that she would ever have, since no one else would buy it.

Justin and his party were surrounded in a continuous flutter of apologies. On the stairs it was no longer possible for him to hide his ankle. He hated it now, the pain and the disability, and it seemed to him that, ever since he had been ill, his life had been filled with these petty accidents and inconveniences. He was glad that Arthur carried his luggage, that Erma held his arm going upstairs. He was glad they had noticed his ankle so that it was not necessary to explain about it. He was very tired and hungry and he wished that the Fenways would stop their endless, fluttering apologies and leave him alone behind a shut door so that he could get his shoe off and groan in peace.

Bad as the stairs had been, still he was glad they had come to Westgate, for the young people, and particularly Erma, were thrilled with the rooms. Dusty and old and dimly lighted, they were immense by modern standards. An old and faded elegance pervaded everything in a gentle, quiet manner: the high ceilings, the furniture designed exclusively for giants, the ornate fireplaces, the once luxurious hangings.

"I seem to have drawn the bridal suite," Justin said, looking about him. "I wonder if we could all eat up here?"

"I'll go down and find out," Erma said. "Surely you can, anyway. You're not to climb those stairs again. Why didn't you say something about your ankle? We should have stopped long ago."

"Oh, it'll be all right, once I get my weight off it."

When he was alone, Justin sat in the biggest chair and pulled off his shoe. He was disgusted with the swelling; it seemed to him out of all proportion to the accident. To get the sock off, now, that would take some doing. First, he would take off his coat. If only he could go to sleep in this chair, take a short nap, before he had to get up again. Once a man is really ill, he thought, he begins to break up all over. He felt as though he were falling apart and it would not have surprised him if his teeth had all begun to ache, too, or if he should have a cold in the morning. He wished that he had a footstool or, lacking that, he wished that he had energy enough to pull a chair close enough to rest his ankle on it. He leaned his head back against the chair, and just before he fell asleep Erma knocked at the door and then came into the room. She had a teakettle in one hand and a foot tub in the other. She went into the bathroom and put a little cold water in the foot tub, and then she came back and knelt down before Justin and began to roll up his trouser leg.

"Here," he said, "what are you doing? You needn't have done that. I'll just get into the bathtub."

"The water's cold," she said. "They've lighted the tank, but it will be an hour or two before it's hot. I've got more water on the stove downstairs. Arthur'll bring it up." She touched the swollen ankle gently and looked up at Justin's face. "Have you got a knife?" she asked.

"No," Justin said.

She jumped up from the floor and went out of the room. When she came back she slit Justin's sock neatly down one side. "That's the nice thing about Joe," she said. "He's always got a knife." She poured some water from the teakettle into the tub. "Put your foot in," she said, "and then when you get used to it I can make it a little hotter."

"You shouldn't have gone to all this trouble," Justin said. "Aren't you tired? Ouch! Women never have any idea how hot anything is."

"Leave it in," Erma said. "It's not too hot. It won't do you any good if it isn't hot." She put her hand into the water and began to splash it up higher on his leg so that he would become accustomed to it sooner.

"After you've gone to all this trouble, I suppose the least I can do is allow myself to be scalded," he said. He could see the straight line of the part in her hair when she bent her head over his foot, and, under the water, her hand had become narrow and elongated, the fingers like toothpicks. It felt good, the hot water, wonderfully good. But he was no sooner accustomed to it than she poured in more from the teakettle, and he was no sooner used to that than Arthur appeared with another steaming bucketful.

"That's fine," Erma said. "Bring it over here, Arthur. Now I'm going down to see about food for us and you keep pouring a little hot in all the time, will you, Arthur? Don't let him talk you out of it."

"I'm long past that," Justin said. "I can see now, even if the flesh all falls off my bones, that there's nothing to do but submit."

"That's right," Arthur said. "If she's decided something is good for you, there's nothing you can do about it."

When Erma had gone, Arthur put his hand into the water to try it. "Jesus," he said. "How do you stand it?"

"If you won't give me away," Justin said, "I don't mind telling you that it feels pretty good now. As a matter of fact I was thinking of putting the other foot in, too, just for pleasure. Won't you join me? I hear there's going to be no bath water for some time."

"I can't yet," Arthur said. "There's still another bucket getting hot."

It really was good, Justin had to admit that, and with both feet in the hot water it was even better. It was amazing how just to have your feet in hot water could make you feel rested all over. He reached for his coat and got his pipe and tobacco out of his pocket. When he hit the exact center of the fireplace with the dead match, he knew that those fears about a cold and a toothache were nonsense.

"Can you stand a little more, now?" Arthur asked, and, at Justin's nod, he poured in more water from the new bucket.

It was taking less time to get accustomed to the increased heat. "I'm glad you're here, Arthur," Justin said. "This is the first chance I've had to talk to you about your book. I started to write to you just after I finished it, but I'm not much for letters. It meant a lot to me, that book—meant a great deal."

"I . . . I guess I will join you," Arthur said. He unlaced his shoes, pulled off his socks and rolled up his trousers. While he was letting his feet down gingerly into the hot water, he said, "There ought to be some preventive quality to this. I ought to get credit for two sore ankles."

"That's a different kind of record, I'm afraid," Justin said.

"I'm awfully glad to hear you talk about the book," Arthur said. "You're the first person I've heard from that's read it."

"It's a great idea," Justin said, "and an ambitious one. It's so ambitious it makes my head swim. I don't know if you could get hundreds of people to keeping Records or not. I rather doubt it. But then as you grow old you lose faith in people."

"But you," Arthur said, "did you feel a desire to begin the keeping of a Record yourself?"

"Well, what I felt was a regret that I had not kept one. It hardly seems worth while to begin now, for me. The thing I was thinking about most was not so much how your book applied to me as how it applied to one of my sons. I kept thinking of how my sons had left no record, almost none. You see, there was one of them—George—that I hardly knew. I never felt close to him and when I was ill I got to thinking about him and I couldn't remember his face. I couldn't really remember what he looked like. It was just then that I began to read your book, and right there at the beginning, you know, is that part about the old man and his son. Well, I was amazed that a man so young could write like that."

Arthur reached for the bucket and poured in a little more hot water. Both men shifted their feet away from it. "Well, it works both ways," he said. "You can learn it being a son just as well, I suppose, as you can learn it being a father."

"Oh," Justin said. "Well, perhaps that's true. I wish it were all possible, your idea. I'd like to see you have a real chance at putting it into effect."

"But still, you yourself don't think that your own Record is worth keeping now. You felt no desire to begin."

It was Justin's turn to hide behind the hot water. "What will we do when we get to the top of the tub?" he said.

"Pour it out and start over, I guess."

"Well, you see," Justin said, "I've always thought that in someone like me, my music *is* my Record. In a way, it seems to me that the people who create things do keep the record for other people and have always kept it, that this is their real function."

"That's an argument I've never thought about before," Arthur said. "Still, though, the kind of Record I mean, I don't really believe one person can do it for another. Surely the fact that most people are shocked by their own behavior, so shocked they constantly try to avoid responsibility for it, is almost proof that they have failed to recognize it in an artist's Record."

"Well, of course," Justin said, "an artist has to keep reminding himself constantly what a small per cent of people are concerned with his work."

"But there you are," Arthur said. "All the people are concerned with living."

"Well, I don't know," Justin said. "You see some of them and you begin to wonder if they're concerned about anything at all. But I'd like to know more about your work. Tell me, how did you happen to begin it?"

Arthur lighted a cigarette and leaned back in his chair. He scratched his head. "It's hard to say, exactly, just the moment an idea comes to you," he said. "Little things add up together and then finally you get the sum. In the army, when you're first in, you see all those millions of guys. It seems to you that the army is making them all alike, making them lose their individuality, but after a time you see it's just the opposite. Because of the pressure, they have to resist, have to assert themselves. They become more unique and separate and individual than they would be outside the army. And then they begin getting killed and dying of accidents and illnesses and for a while you get them all mixed up. You can't remember who's alive and who's dead.

"And," Arthur went on, "your own memory does not seem a safe enough place to hold this. Things slip away from you. You want to rebel, to resist against the speed with which these men are lost. Most of all you begin to fight the ease with which they are replaced because you know that no man can be replaced. You want to make a little plaque for each man that dies: 'Toby kept a turtle in his bed.' 'Larson cried for Helen in his sleep.' And then it begins to dawn on you what a fraction your Record would be compared to their own, if they had written it down. The waste of it, the mass-scale waste of it, creates a fury in you."

"Yes," Justin said, "the waste, the awful waste. That's what appalls one. I lost four sons, you know, almost as though they'd never lived at all. Tell me, did you speak to any of the soldiers about your idea?"

"Well, no," Arthur said. "It really wasn't clear to me until afterward. At that time, when I was in the army, it was just beginning to come to me. I hadn't got very far with it then. I saw it only as a protest, a means of slowing things down, just as though a man on a station platform had taken a pencil and drawn a pair of eyes on the side of the train, to prove he'd seen it, that he'd been there when it slipped past."

"I thought perhaps you might have talked to other soldiers about it," Justin said. "I'd like to know if they felt the waste, if they expressed this urge to leave a mark."

"I think everybody has the urge," Arthur said. "That's how I really came to the idea in the end. That was in jail. Joe and I bummed the country after the war and once we got thrown in jail overnight. I got to looking at the walls there in the jail, reading all the things written on them. 'Frisco Kid, 1906, just passing through.' Things like that. I got to thinking of all the men who had been in that room and of how some hundred or so of them had been compelled, for some reason, to record upon these walls the fact that they had been there. I twisted my neck and damned near stood on my head and I read it all, the anger and the filth, the protests and the jokes, the names of girls, greetings and dates, the heavy-handed humor. It didn't seem to be accidental. It added up. It began to spell out a universal urge, a man's desire to leave a mark, of *any* kind, but a mark upon the wall of Time. I thought what if each man had left something of his own there, what if the Frisco Kid had left his thoughts there when he was just passing through? Just passing through to where? I wondered. To what? How much I could have learned that night if I had had those men's thoughts to read on the wall.

"And why don't we have it? I thought. Why haven't we had it all this time? Why are the maps only in geography books? Why does a child have to try to learn what a man is like from reading *The Little Red Hen?* Why can't he have the man to read instead?"

"It's always wonderful," Justin said, "to see how a man's mind works, to find out, for example, that the People's Library was born of a jail-cell wall."

Gwendolyn's laughter froze them, turned their eyes to the door. She stood there, trying to keep from dropping the tray of food she carried, while she laughed at the sight of the two men sitting knee to knee, their legs bare, their feet soaking.

"Well," Justin said, beginning to laugh, too, "I suppose we aren't a very impressive sight."

"Oh, God," Arthur said, "I've let the water get cold. Here, quick, put your foot in this bucket before Erma gets here. It's a little warmer. Gwen," he said, "for the love of God, put that tray down and throw me a towel."

Mrs. Fenway, all of a flutter still, had managed to produce from cupboards and cellar an assortment of food, mostly jellies and preserves. There were eggs and ham and fried potatoes and bread, but mostly there were jellies and preserves. Mrs. Fenway had been a great hand at preserves, once, everybody said so. Mr. Fenway said they ought to make it a specialty of the house. But no more had she got the cellar crammed with them than the highway had been moved. She'd been most apologetic about the food tonight, and then she had remembered the cellar and, in a happy effort to redeem the meal, she'd run down to the cellar and got out the preserves from under their layers of dust and cobwebs and, if the truth be told, a further layer of thin mold, scraped off and cast hurriedly into the garbage. She did so hope none of them would be poisoned, but then everybody said sugar mold was harmless, and they did say old Mrs. Adams up the road was so miserly that she ate it. But, there, you couldn't just give people eggs and ham and potatoes. You had to have *something.* She did hope that Mr. Fenway wouldn't take a fancy for any of it, because she would never in the world have the courage to tell him why he shouldn't. She'd just have to watch him and wait it out.

After supper, when the water in the pipes finally got hot, it got very hot, and though it burst out in a strange, brown color from the rust in the old pipes, still, Erma and Arthur didn't mind, for they had never had such a big tub to play in, such marbled, ornate elegance.

Erma got in first. "Oh, it's wonderful," she said. "The water's soft, even if it is a strange color. I wish we had a boat."

"Put some cold in," Arthur said. "I can't get into that."

"Oh, all right. You men, you all want everything lukewarm. You're just like Justin Magnus."

Arthur began to laugh. "He was complaining about the heat of the water and I almost said to him, 'That's nothing. You ought to take a bath with her.' "

Erma turned the cold faucet and then slid up to the front of the tub to mix the water. "What do you think about his ankle?" she said. "Do you think it'll be all right?"

"Sure," Arthur said, climbing into the tub and letting himself down into the water cautiously. "Only he ought not to drive."

"That'll suit Joe fine," she said.

The tub was so big that they could both be submerged side by side. Nobody had to take the faucets in his shoulder blades.

"God, this is wonderful," Arthur said. "I never want to get out."

"I love this hotel," Erma said. "I'd like to stay here."

"Say, I forgot. There's some money on the dresser. You must be clear out."

Erma slid the bar of soap over her belly. "I saw it," she said.

"I gave half of it to Joe," Arthur said. "It's from the big press. I mortgaged it."

"Why did you, Arthur? It's such a little while until you'll have some answers from your book and maybe then you wouldn't have had to."

"Well, it was partly this trip. I couldn't start this trip without any money, and Joe needs money, you know. He can't very well be dependent on Justin Magnus in front of Gwendolyn."

"Oh," she said.

"Well, there's no need to blame it on Joe," Arthur said. "I know Justin Magnus invited us all. I know he knows we're poor. It would have been all right if he'd been my hero, I guess, but . . ."

"But he's my hero," she said. "Is that it?"

"That's it," Arthur said. "You can't be dependent on your wife's hero, somehow. It just puts everything in the wrong place. It—"

"Do you remember, Arthur, that first place we had, how we used to bathe by candlelight? That was the best, wasn't it? We ought to have it like that again."

He leaned over her and kissed her closed eyelids to taste the salt of the tears that he knew she held there.

"Sure," he said. "That was fine. We ought to have it like that again."

The morning of the third day, in a hotel more modern than the Fenways', and in a room much smaller than she had had there, Gwendolyn lay alone in her bed sleeping. Free from apprehension, she lay on her back with one arm thrown above her head, her face turned to one side, and her fine, black hair strewn over the pillow. The long black eyelashes lay at rest now over the dark shadows under her eyes, and the black mole showed prominently at the corner of her mouth. It was still a girl's mouth, especially so it seemed in her sleep, a young girl's mouth, not yet set, not yet finished, still several years behind the eyes, belonging more to the smoothness of the throat, to the young girl's breasts set high and wide apart like two little apples under the nightgown.

She stirred a little in her sleep and suddenly frowned, and then, with one movement, she threw the bedcovers back and leapt from the bed. She bent over and pulled the nightgown over her head, all in the most frantic, hurried way.

"Oh, God, how do I do it every single morning?" she said, almost crying in anger and regret at having overslept. She tossed the nightgown onto the bed and turned to the place where her clothes should be, but they were not there, and suddenly she realized where she was. At once a softness came over her whole body, erasing the angles of hurry, erasing the frown of regret. The sweetness and youth and unfinished quality that it had had in sleep came back to her mouth, and Gwendolyn laughed and lay down on the bed. It was only the third day of her vacation. She locked her arms around her knees and stretched her head toward them, rubbing her nose against one knee. Then she stretched out on her back and effortlessly raised both legs to a vertical position, holding them straight from hip to ankle. Pointing first the toes, then the heels, toward the ceiling, she felt a delicious pull in the calves of her legs. Slowly she brought her legs down to the bed. She put her arms back of her head and stretched, luxuriously and fully. She closed her eyes, relaxed, and smiled.

She could see them all in the office, working right on through her vacation. She hated them all and today she would not be with them, nor tomorrow, nor the next day. She would not be with them for eleven more days and maybe something wonderful would happen to Joe and she would never see them again. But what if nothing wonderful happened to Joe? What if everything just went on and on the same? Gwendolyn shivered and pulled the covers over her. She turned on one side and pulled her knees up. How was it it all went wrong, one's life? Where did it start? Whose fault was it? It was not the way they had planned it when they saved her hands from the dishwater, or when she studied her lessons, even the dull ones. It was not the way they had planned it that she was still working, suffering the terrible patronage of the already married ones. And now, if she married Joe, she would not even have a house to live in.

Surely it was not wrong to want a house. She was asking for a house that grew smaller as she grew older, a house and a little security. It was the next year that she dreaded; it was the twenty-sixth year that the house and the "security" dwindled and became unreasonable. She had seen it happen to others; she knew what it would be like. She put her hopes in Joe and Justin Magnus, having no place else to put them, and went back to sleep.

All that day they rode through the flat lands, the static, silent prairies. It was all of a sameness for Justin. The heat was very oppressive to him and the miles of yellow wheat constantly tracing the design of the hot wind blinded him. Yet he saw Erma exhilarated by it.

"What do you see?" he asked. "What is it? It all looks the same to me. How do people live here with never a woods, never a mountain?"

"My mother came from this country," Erma said. "She said it was the only place she dared to take a deep breath and that she felt if she tried it in a woods or near mountains she might draw them right up her nostrils."

"I think," Arthur said, "people like it because the landscape is so negative, so monotonous, you *have* to think. It's all right for you to think big because there's nothing to remind you of your smallness. It's natural to be timid before a mountain, but on a prairie a man looms large against the sky and so his thoughts can dare to be heroic. When you have nostalgia for this land, it's not nostalgia for the land itself; instead, you have nostalgia for the things you thought upon it."

"Well, yes," Justin said, "I suppose so." He was not attending, for the word *nostalgia* had suddenly given him a shock. He did not feel it. He had no longing to see his home, he suddenly realized, or the sea. There was no place in all the land that he cared to champion or to claim. For if I have nostalgia, he thought, it is not for any place. It is for a time, a different time from this.

Erma turned from the car window and gave a little laugh. "My mother would never say 'prairie,'" she said, "because she thought it must be farmer talk. She did so wish to be distinguished from the farmers, and because they said Sarie for Sarah and Mandie for Amanda, she was always very careful to say 'prarah. I saw a prarah fire when I was little,' she'd say, or 'all night long we could hear the coyotes on the prarah.' "

Because they traveled at a different rate of speed than the grandfather had, their night stops no longer coincided, and it was still in the heat of the afternoon that they came upon the Big Blue River where the grandfather had camped. But it was not as it had been in the grandfather's time. The river bed was almost dry and only a little muddy stream ran down the middle. They got out of the car and stood on the sand where, in the grandfather's time, the mighty blue waters had roared past. Now there were only the serrations of a sandbar like the bare back bones of a huge dead animal. The hot wind blew against them, never ceasing, and Justin found it very depressing, as though the Green Kingdom would be also shrunken now, changed and dry.

"I keep thinking," Erma said, looking at the ground, "that maybe he dropped something out of his pocket and we'll find it."

"Well, I wouldn't waste any time looking for it if I were you," Justin said, "after all these years."

"It's fun to have time to waste, though," Gwendolyn said. "When I woke up this morning I thought I was late for work again, and then all of a sudden I realized I didn't have to go to work at all. Not for days yet."

"Oh, we've got plenty of time," Joe said, "only let's go waste it somewhere where there's a cold drink."

Later that day they began to climb into the mountains, a slow transition, and about dusk they hit a pocket of coolness and the prairie was gone, no longer visible when Erma looked back. Just before they stopped at a lodge in the mountains a deer ran across the road, its eyes green and startled in the headlights, and Joe swerved the car sharply to avoid it. They were all of them shivering from the cold and glad of the fire burning in the huge fireplace of the dining room.

While they were having dinner Justin realized that his ankle was practically back to normal. "Maybe we ought to take a day off," he said. "After all, there's no need to drive ourselves. We're on vacation."

"Yeah," Joe said, "we've got to have the car checked over pretty soon and this looks like a good place. Anyway, it's cool."

For Gwendolyn liked this place, Joe saw. She was gayer than he had ever seen her, excited and responsive. It had been a wonderful day for Joe, hot winds or not, for the three others had sat in the back seat and he and Gwendolyn had been alone. It seemed to Joe that as they got farther away from Drury, Gwendolyn gradually softened, as though each mile she was releasing a little of the long rope that held her tight and stiff. He had felt fine, Joe had, behind the steering wheel of the car, money in his pocket, and Gwendolyn's hand lying palm up waiting in the seat beside him. When they saw the deer, she put her hand on his knee in fear that they would hit it, and afterward, when it was safe, she had left her hand there. In the darkness, he had pressed his own over it and known that Gwendolyn was thinking just as he was that this was their car and their vacation and their room waiting in the mountain lodge.

He thought this was the night, though it surprised him it had come so soon after Drury. Alone in his own room he bathed and put on clean clothes and then he went downstairs. When he came up he had an armload of wood and he built a fire in his room. He sat down and waited a long time when the fire was laid, and then he stood at the window listening to the night sounds. He waited until he thought they were all asleep because there must be no sisters coming home this time, no fears and no hurry. Then he lighted a match to his fire and turned out all the lights and quietly went out of the room. In a minute he came back and picked up all the clothes he had left lying on the bathroom floor when he changed. He stood a moment with the clothes in his hand, but the fire had caught fast and was roaring, so he threw the clothes inside the closet and shut the door on them.

Outside Gwendolyn's door he was suddenly afraid that it would be locked. He had been so sure all through dinner that it wouldn't be locked and now he held his breath and slowly turned the knob. The door slid open and there was no light in the room. Gwendolyn sat naked in the darkness weeping, weeping that she had found herself envying Erma Herrick who slept not alone in the darkness, who lay not alone in the mountain darkness, hearing the wind through the pine trees, breathing the clear, cold smell of the pines. She wept to find herself envying a woman who had nothing and would never have anything.

She was shivering with the cold, and Joe picked her up and carried her over to her own bed and put the covers over her. Then he lay down beside her in his clothes and, while she clung to him, he waited for the crying and the frantic trembling to subside while he stared through the darkness at the ceiling. In his mind he could see the fire, so carefully laid in his room, going out now, going into embers and to ashes with no one there to see it. He thought of the wild deer, frightened and running into the woods.

"Go to sleep," he said. "Go to sleep."

By the time the rest of them were ready for breakfast Joe had already taken the car to the garage and had it checked and ready to go. He wanted to be moving, driving ahead. All he hoped was that Justin Magnus wouldn't want to drive. Erma, too, wanted to get started.

"We've only got five more days," she said. "Something might happen to the car. You can't tell. We ought to allow for delays."

"You mustn't build your hopes too high," Justin said. "The Green Kingdom may turn out to be another Big Blue River."

All the fourth day they were still in the mountains, and with every hour Justin felt more withdrawn from everything that he had ever known. He did not feel tired, only quiet. He did not know if the others were affected in the same manner or not; he was hardly aware of them. He kept his eyes focused out the window most of the time, and perhaps, he thought, that is all it is, a kind of hypnosis brought on by eyestrain. He felt exhilarated and at the same time withdrawn and still. At last he recognized his detachment for what it was. It was not hypnosis brought on by eyestrain. It was the hushed and waiting time before the work begins. Well he knew it, this waiting time, the formless matrix of potentiality. Its special identifications are as yet unannounced, its qualities are just barely inaudible, its visions one inch beyond the threshold. Many things may, in the potential time, come from such a matrix, yet they will all bear in common some general character, for one thing is known of the matrix, even in the waiting time, and that is its tempo. Though it cannot be known yet what will arise out of the matrix, still it is clear what cannot possibly arise from it. The hushed and waiting time before the work begins is like the shape in space that a ball will take, a ball that has not yet been thrown.

Only the tempo is known now, but even so it is already established that from this matrix will not, cannot, come either the Discovery music of *The Green Kingdom* or the resurrection trumpets of *Lazarus*. The tempo is known. From such a matrix might come the blessed, languid time of the arisen Lazarus when children touched his robes and followed him on the road, or the golden and enchanted years in which the grandfather was received and graced by the Green Kingdom, when all the wonders were like strange, ripe fruit to be tasted and savored and embraced. It was a matrix of ripeness. Who could say at this time what would arise from it: a quiet sea with the waves steady, a full and warm and spherical breast with the heartbeat beneath it, the night walk of a lioness down to the water hole, or melons lying ripe and heavy beneath their hairy leaves? All these could have been in it. The tempo was known. The curve of the ball is established before it is thrown.

The car stopped suddenly. "How's this?" Joe asked.

"It'll do," Erma said, and then, turning to Justin Magnus, she said, "We thought we'd stop early tonight. You'd like to, wouldn't you?"

"Yes," he said, "I guess I would. Why?"

The others were all climbing out of the car and getting the luggage out of the trunk.

"I thought maybe you wanted to work," she said.

"I believe I might," he said. "What made you think so?"

"You've been whistling all afternoon and I never heard it before."

"Oh," he said, "have I?"

Standing at the desk in the strange hotel, Justin was only vaguely aware of the discussion about rooms. There were only three vacant rooms, and quite suddenly Erma had arranged that she and Gwen should share one, Arthur and Joe the second, and that Justin should go straight up now to the third. She would have some food sent up to him later. She also would select it. There was nothing officious in her manner, just a sense of urgency, as though to make the transition from the car to the room as easy for him as possible. He was pleased by it and he hoped the others didn't mind.

He took a hot shower and it was pleasant standing there, turning his body slowly, knowing the work was coming, anticipating the pleasure of it. He put on a pair of trousers and, naked from the waist up, sat down at the rickety, too small desk before the window. There were some small objects on the desk and these he put down on the floor beside him. Then he put his elbows on the desk and sat looking out at the mountain opposite his window.

The mountain was just now beginning to grow hazy in the coming dusk. While he was looking at the mountain, the matrix went away. It went quietly away and left him empty and alone, looking at the mountain. The hushed and quiet time was gone; the work was gone. At first he could not believe it. It was like having a loose tooth pulled when one is little. At first it does not hurt and you do not feel any different. It is only later, as the tongue begins to explore, that you realize there is a big hole there.

He could not believe it; he had been so sure. The whole afternoon had been stamped with authenticity. Now it was gone. He was a man, an empty man, who eats and sleeps and washes himself. He heard the elevator labor up its shaft. He heard someone cough in the next room. Now he believed it. Now it was the matrix that seemed incredible, and the work itself. He did not think he would do any work now. He did not think he would ever do any work again, and it seemed hard to believe that he ever had done any. He was a dull, old man, an empty, dull, old man who ate and slept and washed himself, and who would as long as he lived. Why had he ever thought different?

There was a knock on the door and Justin started guiltily, but it was only the waiter with a tray of food. "Maybe I am hungry," Justin said. "Maybe after I eat I can work." But he did not believe it. He ate mechanically and then he lighted his pipe and went over to the desk again. The mountain was gone now, lost in darkness. Justin was overcome with weariness. Maybe if I had a nap, he thought, then I could work. But he did not believe it. He went over and lay down on the bed and closed his eyes.

What would he say to her in the morning? He could hear her now asking eagerly, "Well? Did you work? How did it go?"

He got up from the bed and took the manuscript of the first movement of *The Green Kingdom* out of his bag and put it on the desk in case he wanted to refer to it. Shame covered him at the piece of obvious posing done in case Erma Herrick should come to the room. If he needed to refer to the first movement, he wouldn't have used a manuscript. He would have used what was in his head. He began to resent the woman as he had never resented anyone in his life. He did not owe a symphony to Erma Herrick. Let her spill her encouragement over a younger head. He was an old man, an empty, old man who ate and slept and washed himself. He'd done enough work already for a lifetime. He did not need to do any more, and no one could force him to. After all, what did she know about writing a symphony, she or her piano-tuning father, either? Did they think it could be turned on just by a little interest? What was he doing here anyway? What was he doing in a strange hotel forcing himself into a ridiculous and shameful pose by placing a manuscript so obviously on a desk?

He picked up the manuscript and threw it into his traveling bag. He took off his clothes and turned out the light and threw the covers back on the bed. He lay in the darkness empty and weary and full of resentment. It was quite late. Where had the time gone? There was still a kind of haste in him rolling around on top of the weariness, as though he must get something done before morning. He dug his fist into his belly and stretched his legs. It was hopeless. He would never in this world work again. If only he would never see the morning; if only he would die in the night and never face another empty day.

To me, you have always been indestructible. Just behind his eyelids he could hear her saying it. Perhaps if he went to sleep now he would wake up in the night and be able to work. That had happened before. It had often happened that when he was stuck like this he would go to sleep and dream the work and the dream would wake him up. That was it. He was stuck, that's all, the way he had been stuck a thousand times before. It wasn't ready yet. He'd thought so this afternoon, but then he'd been mistaken. He'd simply been mistaken. No good to force these things.

And that was what Joe was thinking, too—that it was no good to force things. While he and Arthur sat over the detail map, reviewing the landmarks, planning out the mileage, he was thinking that he didn't know whether to be relieved or resentful at the room arrangement. It was a strange situation for Joe because the one thing Joe had always known for sure was just exactly what he thought he ought to do. It was always the thing he wanted to do and this he knew, too. Now he didn't know any more. The whole thing with Gwendolyn had slipped away from him and he didn't know how it had happened.

Right from the time he'd asked her to come on the trip he'd known what it was he wanted. He wanted to touch reality with Gwendolyn and he knew only one way for it to happen, for it to have a chance to happen. They had to be together, the whole way, not furtively or hurriedly, but slowly and gently and all the way together. And afterward, then he was sure they wouldn't talk about her sisters or the office or the people in the office or Drury. He thought they would just be quiet, and then when they began to talk they would talk about themselves and then he thought she could hear him. He could never get her to hear him in Drury, not clearly, because he was always talking through the office and the town and other people rattling coffee cups and music coming out of jukeboxes and she was always worried about what time it was. Well, then that day, was it the third day out? Anyhow, sooner than he had expected, she had forgotten to care what time it was. But how should he know he would find her crying in the darkness, 'way beyond hearing him, far off in some strange and lonely place of her own, some woman's place where he could not go?

"Tomorrow ought to put us more than halfway there," he said to Arthur. "Do you think it will?"

"I don't know," Arthur said. "Stopping early tonight set us behind a little. As far as the mileage goes, we're O.K. The last two days won't be on highways, though. I figure we ought to be through the Salt Desert tomorrow, and the next day we start north and we ought to hit Name Rock."

"What the hell do you think that is, Name Rock?" Joe said.

"I don't know," Arthur said. "Can't be the name of a town, or at least not one of any size, because it's not on our map. Then, on the seventh day, if we don't make any more early stops like tonight, we ought to hit that Indian village. That'd give us two days to hunt out the rest of Grandpa's landmarks to the Entrance."

"Grandpa's landmarks get less convincing the closer we get to them, I've noticed."

"Well, anyhow, we know the Salt Desert's there because it's on our map, too, and that's all we have to worry about tomorrow."

In the morning the car slipped right out of Joe's hands, for Justin decided to drive, at least for a while. He wanted something to do. He wanted to have the road ahead to be busy with, so that he could hide his shame from Erma Herrick. There had been no need to feel resentment against her, to fear her questions. She had seen his face at breakfast, and then she had lowered her eyelids and looked at her hands. She had not said anything. She had not asked anything. She had not looked at him at all.

They had seen it on the map and they had talked about it, but none of them, on this the fifth day of their journey, had really been prepared for the Salt Desert. They were driving in the lush, green coolness of the mountains, driving downhill, and suddenly it was on them, sharp and hard and white, and the mountains were gone like a crowd held back by a rope from a street parade. It was so startling that Justin slammed on the brakes. Joe let out a low whistle.

"What is it?" Gwendolyn said. "Is it really salt? It looks like snow."

But snow is soft. Snow is a blanket of warmth and protection for the tender new wheat lying in the earth. Snow is for children to play in, a shield against bruises. This was salt, dazzling, crystalline, bitter testimony that the earth, like man, also knows desolation. As far as they could see, it stretched ahead of them in the glaring sun, absolutely flat, absolutely white. Nothing grew on it. No thing moved upon it. There were black lines across the whiteness: one for the railroad, one for the highway, one for the telephone poles. The lines were parallel. Justin started the car up slowly, as though it were hardly safe to bear down the car's weight on such a surface in this silent place. He had the feeling that they might fall through and disappear.

"Well," he said, "don't forget Lot's wife. Anything could happen here."

As they penetrated the Salt Desert, they began to be more aware of the heat. It increased insidiously, steadily. The sky was cloudless, too blue, too close.

"It's strange you don't see any other cars," Joe said.

"I've noticed it, too," Justin said. "I suppose they take it at night. Maybe we'd better go back and wait till evening."

"There's a town shown on the map," Joe said. "It's thirty miles. It isn't as though we had to cross the whole desert without stopping."

"This is where I'd like to live," Arthur said. "I wish I'd known about it a long time ago."

"Here?" Gwendolyn said. "Are you crazy?"

"Right in the middle of it," Arthur said. "Right out there in the bare middle of it. I mean it. I'd like to live here."

"You couldn't," Gwen said. "How would you live? What would you do?"

"Work in the salt mines, I guess," Arthur said. "They must be somewhere near. I'd carve a house out of the salt. How about it, Erma?" He turned to her. "Let's come back here some day. What do you say?"

"I don't know," Erma said. "You'd have to be tough to live here. You'd have to be—"

"That's just it," Arthur said. "You'd *have* to be."

To Arthur it was as though he had at last found the landscape for which, without knowing it, he had always hungered. It would be the ultimate place, the last of the shifting layers after the fine-mesh sieve. Here there would be no comfort, no refuge from the final question. One could not hide behind any petty accomplishment and so evade the question. Without solace, diversion, subterfuge, bare and naked, a man would be down to the core, at last. A man would know if the core were solid.

"Could you really make a house out of salt?" Erma said. She could see it, built of white blocks. It would have a white tower under the blue sky, and, inside the thick walls, there would be the sudden, blessed coolness.

"I don't see why not," Arthur said. "I doubt if it ever rains here."

"You can have it," Gwen said. "Especially the heat. I'm sick of it already."

"I've heard about this place," Justin said. "A man I knew married a woman he met out here. I saw her only once. He took her to live at his parents' house because they were too old to live alone. It was a huge old house, one of those solid brick houses full of mahogany and walnut, surrounded by trees so old that no one knew who'd planted them. They hadn't been married very long, he told me, when the woman got sick. She said she was homesick, but her husband insisted that she be treated by a doctor. She got worse and worse, but she kept insisting that there was nothing the matter with her except that she was homesick. Finally the doctor told her husband he'd better let her go, that maybe she *was* homesick. By this time she could hardly walk, he said, though the time I met her she was all right, just awfully quiet. I don't know why he was so stubborn about letting her go. Perhaps he knew what would happen. He could not leave his business at the time and finally he sent her off alone. He told me he got a postcard from her saying as soon as she smelled the salt she was all right. And that's all he ever heard. She never wrote again and she never came back."

"That *is* a story," Arthur said. "It must have been terrible for her to be hemmed in by the old trees, to be always cold in the dark shade of those old trees."

"Well, didn't he try to find her?" Gwen asked. "Didn't he come out after her?"

"I don't know," Justin said. "I didn't ask him. He was drunk at the time."

"Maybe he couldn't leave the elm trees." Joe said. "Maybe it worked both ways."

Erma laughed. "How did they get to be elm trees all of a sudden, Joe?"

"I don't know," Joe said. "Didn't you say they were elm trees, Mr. Magnus?"

"I don't know," Justin said. "Did I?"

"There are elm trees at home," Gwen said, "at our house." Oh, when would it end, this glaring furnace? She felt hot and ugly and rumpled. Something had gone wrong with her vacation. She said, "Five days. It doesn't seem like it's been five days, does it?"

Joe looked at her. He had to get her out of this desert. He had to get her to a cool place where there was something alive to look at, something green, or he never would reach her. Here he was, with a decent suit of clothes and money in his pocket for once. He had managed to get Gwen away from Drury and somehow the whole thing had got out of hand. He knew how the man felt, all right, the man under the elm trees, up against something too strange for him, losing out a little every day. And he knew how drunk he would have to be, too, to keep from getting on a train and doing the same thing all over again. How many times could you lose the same woman? he thought.

Suddenly on the white flatness a huge billboard loomed up:

COOL DRINKS
5 MILES AHEAD

"That's a welcome note," Joe said.

"What I like is how cautious they are," Justin said. "Cool, you notice. Not cold."

"That must be the town on the map," Erma said. "Do you suppose?"

"It's high time," Justin said. "The engine's getting hot. I hope we can get water here."

"Whether we need it or not," Arthur said, "we've got to stop long enough so I can talk to somebody. After all, this is where I'm going to live some day. I've got to see what the people are like."

"I can hardly wait," Joe said. "According to your theory, they all ought to be giants—tough, enduring giants with great big souls."

"They can all be feeble-minded," Gwen said, "just so they give me something cold to drink."

"Cool, Gwen," Arthur said. "Don't get your hopes up too high."

The "town," when they came to it, was a combination filling station and lunchroom. If there was more of it somewhere else, it wasn't visible. They left the car in the shadow of the filling-station roof to cool off and went to look at the thermometer hanging by the lunchroom door. It said 115°. The lunchroom was small, and, after the white glare outside, it was very dark. There were stools before a long counter and they all sat down. Behind the counter, in old wicker rocking chairs, sat two boys and a girl. The boys wore jeans, no shirts and straw hats. The girl wore a faded cotton dress. She was vaguely blond and her face also looked faded and too old for her body. One boy was reading *Life;* the other was reading *True, The Crime of a Hidden Sin*. The girl was reading *Wuthering Heights*. The three continued to read. They were all about seventeen years old.

Gwen looked at Arthur and raised her eyebrows. Arthur cleared his throat. The three readers sat quietly reading.

"What do you have cool to drink?" Arthur asked of the room.

True turned his head to Life. "They want something cool to drink," he said.

Life nodded toward Wuthering Heights. "They want something cool to drink," he said. "What do you think of that?"

Wuthering Heights turned a page daintily. "So get it," she said.

True had now reached the bottom of his page so it was possible for him to look at the customers. He looked at them with hatred, but whether it was really for them or for the criminal of the hidden sin, they did not know.

"We got pop," he said, "and it's twenty cents a bottle. You want it or not?"

"O.K.," Arthur said. "Sure. What kind?"

True lifted a tired arm in the air, and with a tired finger pointed to a sign on the wall, which listed the kinds of pop.

They all chose the first one on the list in the hopes that by paying twenty cents a bottle for something they couldn't drink they would then have the right to ask for water. After the choice was made, Life, True, and Wuthering Heights kicked around the question of who was to lift the bottles onto the counter. Finally Life stood up and shuffled out to the back room, reappearing with five bottles of very warm pop. He handed Arthur the bottle opener and returned to his chair. They all tasted the hot liquid and set the bottles back on the counter. It was too sickening to down. There was complete silence in the room.

"Could I have a glass of water?" Gwen said.

"She wants a glass of water," True said to Wuthering Heights.

Wuthering Heights got up languidly. She put her book face down open on the chair, pulled her dress loose from her bottom and minced out to the back room. She came back with one glass of water and put it in front of Gwendolyn. Then she watched her.

Gwendolyn took one swallow and, keeping a straight face, handed the glass to Joe. "Have a taste, Joe," she said.

Joe took one swallow, unsuspectingly, and immediately spat it out through the screen door. "Jesus Christ," he said. "It's boiling. Haven't you got any cold water?"

"I don't know what we'd use to cool it with," said Wuthering Heights.

Gwendolyn had started to laugh at Joe and now she couldn't stop.

"Why, you're leaning on an ice chest right now," Joe said. He had just noticed it. Bubbles of cold sweat covered the outside surface.

"Giants," Gwendolyn said, throwing her head back and laughing hard. "What do you say now, Arthur?"

Wuthering Heights didn't change her expression. "We have to haul our water and our ice twelve miles from the railroad," she said. "And it has to last us four days. We keep it for ourselves."

They were all a little sobered by this, a little ashamed. After all, they should have had a thermos jug. Even Gwen stopped laughing. Arthur looked at Erma. The girl behind the counter stood staring at them, her heavy face still expressionless. Life and True had not looked up from the printed word during the whole time.

"I noticed you're reading *Wuthering Heights*," Erma said into the silence, hoping to make up a little for Gwendolyn's laughter, hoping still to salvage something for Arthur.

"Yeah," the girl said.

"That's a wonderful part," Erma said, "where Heathcliffe says, 'How can I live without my life?' "

"That's over in the back," the girl said.

Suddenly Arthur sat up straight and leaned forward a little, putting his elbows on the counter. "Oh," he said, "then you're on your second time through? You've read it before?"

"No," the girl said. "I seen it in the movies."

Gwen started laughing again. "You and your theories," she said to Arthur.

Joe threw enough money on the counter to cover the drinks. "Come on," he said. "Let's get out of here."

Outside they stood around trying to decide whether to wait until the next town to put water into the car. There was no attendant in the filling station, though there was some water. They decided to risk waiting.

Arthur walked away from the car and stood looking out on the white desert, looking at the three still parallel lines under the flat, blue sky. Erma walked over and stood by him, feeling his disappointment like the sickish, sweet taste in her mouth.

"I forgot," he said. "There always is a refuge. One can become stupefied, one can become brutal and full of hatred."

Joe picked up the water can and filled the radiator. "What the hell," he said.

He had to redeem Gwen some way. The rest of them—they were older. They'd been married a long time. They hadn't spent night before last sitting alone in a dark room naked, crying, trying to make up their minds.

Just as Arthur got into the car he saw the sign in the window. It said:

MAN IS MADE OF DUST

DUST WILL SETTLE

BE A MAN

All the fifth day they drove through the desert. After a while they stopped talking to one another. Each time they came to a "town" they filled the car with water and rinsed their mouths with lukewarm soda pop. The men took turns driving by unspoken

agreement, keeping a grim and deadly order in their turns. To
Joe it was a great deal like the way Life, True, and Wuthering
Heights had shifted the questions around. It was getting crazy in
his mind now, the little refrain bouncing around like the glaring
red spots in front of his eyes: I'll be Life and Justin be True and
Art can be Wuthering Heights.

In the afternoon Gwendolyn went to sleep, and when she
woke up she was sick. They had to stop the car so she could get
out. Joe stood there holding her around the waist while she vomited onto the hard, metallic whiteness of the desert.

"It's only a little while more," he said. "I'm driving as fast
as I can. The very first place, we'll stop." He wiped her face off
with his handkerchief and then he put her in the back seat of the
car.

"Here," Erma said, "put your head in my lap and lie down,
Gwen."

Joe was driving. He kept a careful eye on the temperature
gauge and drove as fast as he dared.

As abruptly as the desert had begun, it now ended. They
were in green coolness and they were climbing up. Joe turned
around and looked in the back seat. Gwen was asleep. He was almost past the little hotel before he saw it, and he slammed on the
brakes.

"Sorry," he said. He wasn't asking any questions. He was
getting Gwen into the first place he saw, and if the others didn't
like it they could go some place else.

After her bath, Gwendolyn felt much better, and she put on
her new blue negligee and brushed her hair and made up her face
carefully. Then she put out all the lights but the bed lamp and
lay down on the bed looking up at the ceiling. Stealthily eying
the door, she pushed the negligee off one shoulder. She put her
cheek against her bare shoulder and closed her eyes. She was beginning to get cold, after the warm bath, but she did not like to
cover up the beautiful negligee with the incongruous and practical
blanket. Also, she had been too sick to eat before and now she
was hungry.

Joe came into the room trying to walk quietly on the balls of
his feet. He sat down on the bed beside her. He leaned over and
kissed the bare shoulder, and Gwendolyn put her hand on the back
of his head and opened her eyes.

The first thing Joe did was to cover her up with the ugly and practical blanket. "Are you going to be all right?" he said.

"Oh, I'm better," Gwen said. "Lots better. I'll be all right."

"I brought you some food," Joe said. "Could you eat it?"

"That was sweet of you, Joe."

He lifted her up in the bed and propped the pillows behind her. Then he put the tray on her lap and lighted a cigarette while she ate. "How's your head?" he asked.

"It's better, Joe. I just got too hot, that's all, on that damned desert."

"We won't do it again," Joe said. "We'll take it by night going back and take our own water along. Everybody's pretty well beat down. Even Arthur's already turned in and he can't wait to get back to the place."

"I always did think he was crazy and now I know it," Gwen said.

"He's not crazy," Joe said. "He's just got an admiration for the hard way. Hardway Herrick, we used to call him. You don't understand about Arthur," he said. "The thing about Arthur is he can't ever take it for granted that he's going to be as brave or as cowardly or as strong or as weak as most other guys. He can't let it rest. He's got to tear at himself over each thing, and the result of it is he always makes himself come out 'way ahead. Only it never convinces him. Say, are you going to be able to make it tomorrow, do you think?"

"I'll be all right, Joe. It was just too hot and . . ."

Joe took the tray away and arranged the pillows so that Gwen could lie down, and then he sat by her again and began to stroke her forehead.

"And it didn't seem much like a vacation, did it?"

"No," she said. She put one hand up to his face and Joe held it there, against his mouth, kissing it.

"Poor baby," he said. "You go to sleep now. Tomorrow's going to be different. You're all right, aren't you? You're going to be all right?"

She had never felt so secure in her life. Wrapped in her illness and her blue negligee, she had never been so sure that she was completely, utterly safe.

That night Joe dreamed of Gwendolyn. She was sitting under the elm trees in a blue dress. Her face was as white as the salt desert, and her long black hair was divided in three strands down her back: one for the railroad, one for the highway, and one for the telephone wires. "I don't like the Hardway," she said. "I like the white meat. I like the breast."

On the sixth day they came to Name Rock, and if they had not been actively hunting for it they would never have noticed it at all. They did not know what they were looking for, and, unused to the simplicity of the grandfather's day, none of them had expected the fulfillment to be so literal. It was a huge rock, sitting back some little distance from the present road, and on its surface were the faded markings of many penknives. In the grandfather's day, of course, it had not been so unpretentious. Sitting as it did at the crossroads of the only two trails, it was a calendar and a timetable, a history, a guide, and, above all, a concrete reassurance. Then the markings had been clear, deep-cut and easy to read. Now they were faded, eaten away by the wind and the years, blurred by the dust.

JONATHAN ANDERSON, 1840, was the first one they could make out clearly, and under it, in huge, deep-gouged letters: 2 GUN SAWYER GOIN SOWTH 1842.

Beneath this, in smaller, neater letters, was JORETH AMES, Sept., 1850 WELL.

And then they all saw it together, not so deeply cut as 2 Gun Sawyer's nor yet so elegant as Joreth Ames's fine carving:

WILLIAM MAGNUS 1870　　←———

And farther down again:

WM. MAGNUS 1880　　———→

One arrow pointed in the direction of the Green Kingdom and one arrow pointed back, toward home.

They were all of them strangely affected. A hundred maps could not have touched the power of this twice-repeated name upon the rock, telling so much in its economy, telling in the deep, careful letters of the first line how he had been proud to have come so far, how he had cared to the extent of all that labor to join the company of Jonathan Anderson and 2 Gun Sawyer (who was goin sowth) and of Joreth Ames (who was, praise God, well). Ten years later the knife had been dulled and the quality of the labor so well remembered as to condense William to Wm.

Gwendolyn was the first to say out loud what they were all thinking: "Why, he was really here."

"Oh," Erma said, "to think of his even abbreviating it the last time in a hurry to get home with his news, his wonderful news, and then not to be believed." She went up to the rock and put her hands on the letters. She brushed the sand out of the homeward arrow.

"The one I like," Joe said, "is Mr. Ames. I'm glad he was feeling well. I certainly am. Imagine sitting here with your name all carved, waiting to add something to it, wanting to say something. Think of the things that must have run through the guy's head, things too long or too hard to carve, things he didn't know how to spell. Well. Hello, World, how are you? I am well. *Well*. Every day, forever, I am well. Imagine feeling so good you want to carve it on a rock."

"Oh, I wish we had a camera," Erma said. "Didn't anybody bring a camera? Think how wonderful it would be for your book, Arthur."

Arthur looked at her and smiled, but he was too full of the moment to speak.

Name Rock marked the beginning of a real difference in their journey, for now they began seriously to hunt. They ceased looking at the landscape and began to watch the road. Vacation turned to search, hunger and fatigue were translated into delay, and they became concerned with time. It was now possible for them to believe that something, whatever it was that the grandfather had called the opening, was going to happen on August 26 and not on any other day. Each of them felt a secret guilt for whatever individual part he had played in the fact that it was now the twenty-third of August. Justin, who had had a lifetime to get here, now tried to remember whether his grandfather had mentioned whether the opening had taken place in the morning or in the evening, but he could not.

The men decided to take turns at the wheel and to keep driving until they hit the next landmark, the Indian village. They kept going all that night, driving and sleeping in turns, and at noon the next day they found the first trace of it. Stiff, hungry, weary, dirty and discouraged, they stumbled into the only café of a small, bedraggled country town. They wanted news and something to keep them awake, and they wanted to stop driving for a while. They had the café to themselves except for the proprietor.

"You folks come up for the fishing?" he said, and it hit them all at the same time that the man himself looked exactly like a fish. His watery eyes were flat in his face and his ears were so close to his head that he seemed not to have any. His skin also was scaly and mottled purple and gray, and, as though trying his best to act the part, he was chewing on a piece of string with his round, lipless mouth.

"Well," Justin said, "we—"

"Because if you did, I've got just the place for you. Course you're a little late for the season, but then what I always say is, there's always some fish don't know what day it is, ha ha. Now I got the best cabins anywhere around here down on the river."

"You see," Joe said, "we—"

"Course they're a little dusty. Not many comes this far any more—road's pretty bad—but it'll only take an hour or so to brush out the cabins. What I always say is nobody's looking for a de luxe hotel on a fishing trip, ha ha."

"Have you got anything to eat?" Joe said. "And some coffee?"

"Sure thing. Fix you right up. You ladies want to wash up or anything, it's right around in back. Now," he said, "what'll it be?"

The man had to go into an adjoining room to get the food, so they had a respite from the fishing talk for a few minutes, but as soon as he came back he started in again. He was a man who loved fish, who knew all about fish.

Finally Arthur broke through the constant talk. "We didn't come to fish," he said.

"You didn't?" the man said. He couldn't believe it. He stood there with his mouth open, and his flat, colorless lips kept making little fish-mouth circles of astonishment.

"We're hunting for an Indian village somewhere around here," Joe said. "Ever hear of it?" He had to strike fast while the man was stopped in midstream.

"Oh," he said. "You're from the Department of Health, I guess. Hasn't been any of them up here for a long time. Right after the big epidemic there was a lot of them here—doctors and nurses and all—but it's been a long time since . . . Say! You mean it's started again?"

Even as tired as they were they could see his fear. The man's knees were trembling and he slid into a chair and stared at Justin exactly as a fish slides under the shadow of an old log when the darting kingfisher swoops. "Not again!" he said.

"What?" Arthur said. "What's started again? What do you mean?"

The man looked all around him furtively, even out at the

white, dusty road through the dirty glass window. "The fever,"
he said. "You guys don't talk much, I know. But you can tell me.
I won't start no panic. Has the mountain fever started again? Is
it here?"

"Fever?" Gwendolyn asked. "What do you mean, fever?"

"Ain't you from the Public Health?" the man said. "Honest,
ain't you?"

"Listen," Joe said, "you got us all wrong. We . . .
we're . . ."

"We're just on vacation," Erma said. "We heard about this
Indian village from the gold-mining days. We just wanted to see
it, that's all, out of curiosity."

The fish ceased trembling his fins. He looked in all their
faces for reassurance. When he came to Gwendolyn, saw her
black hair, he hesitated. "You ain't Indians, any of you?" he
said. "Or part Indians?"

"No," Justin said, "not that we know of."

"How about this place?" Arthur said. "Is it near here? Can
we get to it in a car?"

"It ain't there any more," the Fish said. "Nobody's ever been
up there to prove it ain't there, but I don't see how it could be
after what we done to it."

"You mean there aren't Indians there any more?" Arthur
said.

"Not unless they're made out of asbestos, ha ha."

"What's this about a fever?" Gwendolyn said. "That's what
I want to know. If there's any fever around here, I want to get
out. Of all the places I would hate to get sick, this is the place."

"Oh, there's no fever here," he said. "We saw to that. That
was years ago. Why, that was before the war. Them damn savages, they lived up there in the mountain. They kept to themselves. Nobody minded. Once in a while people like yourselves
would go up there out of curiosity, but they never stayed only a
few hours. So long as the Indians stayed in their own place we
left them alone. And then one day two of 'em come down into
town, said they wanted medicine and food, said they was all sick
up there. The preacher he heard about it. He said he'd go back
with them. He stayed several days and when he came down he
started right away for the city to get the Public Health. But he
never came back. He died there. Well, when he didn't come back
the Indians started down the mountain, them that could still walk

or crawl. We figured they would and we was waiting for 'em. We had a fire started around the base of the mountain and we kept driving them back. We burnt out the whole mountain, burnt it clean—Indians, animals, trees, ticks and all. So you don't need to worry," he said to Gwendolyn (can a fish smile?). "There ain't no fever here."

"Oh, it was tick fever?" Joe said.

"Spotted fever, some calls it," the Fish said. "Mountain fever, tick fever, whatever you call it, it kills you."

"You *burned* them?" Erma said. "The ones that were crawling, the ones that were lying down, you burned them alive?"

"Sure," he said. "We would all of died of it, just like the preacher. Why, they was savages," he said. "Why, you'd have done the same."

But Erma did not hear him. She was gone. She was standing outside, leaning against the building, shaken to find herself capable of such violence. If I kill him, she thought, we'll never find the Green Kingdom in time. She became aware of her cramped hand and, looking down, saw the fork clenched in her fist. She opened her hand and let it fall in the dust, where it shone like a gray fish in a dirty pond.

When she walked back into the restaurant Justin Magnus was saying, "Well, since he thinks we might possibly be able to follow the road still, I think I'll have a look at the place."

"I'll go with you," Joe said.

"But the fever!" Gwendolyn said. "You're surely not going up there where the fever was?"

"Oh, that was years ago, Gwen," Joe said. "Before the war, even. My God, I'm not going to get this close and miss seeing what I came for."

"I don't like to urge any of you," Justin said. "I think I'll go on while there's still light and come back here this evening. At my age it doesn't make much difference. I'd just as soon die of a tick bite as arteriosclerosis."

"Why don't we leave the girls here to get some sleep and the three of us go have a look and come back?" Arthur said.

And so it was agreed. The Fish took Erma and Gwendolyn down to the cabins. They chose the least dirty one and fell immediately onto the two cots just as they were. While they slept the Fish's wife cleaned the adjoining cabin. Several hours later Gwendolyn awoke out of a deep sleep. She did not know where she was and she was frightened and depressed. She saw that Erma was still asleep and got up quietly and took her bag outside the cabin. There were no signs that the men had come back yet, and Gwendolyn was glad because she wanted to be bathed and dressed before Joe got back.

The cabin next door was an improvement over the other one. It had been hastily cleaned, the windows were open, and someone had drawn a bucket of fresh water and set it on the rickety little stove. Gwen lighted the stove and began to undress. She opened her bag and laid out clean clothes, and then she sat down to smoke a cigarette while she waited for the water to get hot. Now she was awake enough to notice the quiet. In all her life she had never been alone in such silence. It was a rotten way to spend a vacation. And it was half gone! Seven days almost gone now, time to turn around and repeat the miserable journey in reverse.

It was not right. It was not the way people did things. When you took a vacation you planned it, you picked out the place. I'm going to the Lakes, you said. I'm going to the Springs. And then you went there as quick as you could and you spent your vacation in that place and then you came home. How was your vacation? they asked you, and you said, Fine. Where did you go? they said, and you said the name of a place, not just a long road going and coming. And what did you do? they said. And then you told them. On the first night, you said, and on the second night, you said. You met new people, you ate different food. You danced, you had a good time, you wore your new clothes and you hated to leave. That was the way to spend a vacation. Not like this. Even if they found the most wonderful place in the world now she couldn't stay in it. She wouldn't have time.

She could hear the water spitting out onto the hot stove, and she threw her cigarette out the door and went over and began scrubbing herself, standing by the stove, dribbling the water over the floor, wishing for a bathtub, wishing for a good hotel, wishing to be almost any place where there were other people around and a little noise. When she had bathed and dressed she began to wish that Joe would come back or at least that Erma would wake up so that she would have somebody to talk to. At home she hardly ever dressed alone. One of her sisters was always sure to be there and they would talk to each other's reflections in the mirror while they dressed.

Gwendolyn went outside the cabin thinking to walk down to

the river, but the silence defeated her. She went into Erma's cabin, but Erma was still asleep and the cabin was so dirty that Gwendolyn feared soiling her clean clothes. She returned to her own cabin and tried to write a letter to her sisters, but she could not bear to admit this dreary excuse for a vacation to anyone. It was really too dark in the cabin to write anyhow. There was only a coal-oil lamp, and, not knowing how to light it, Gwendolyn was afraid to experiment. Finally she went outside and sat on the step of her own cabin to wait for Joe, and, as the darkness increased, her fear increased. The sound of the cicadas began and mounted in a crescendo. She kept straining to see the path on which Joe would come, and when the darkness cut even this occupation away from her she had nothing but her fear left. She began to shiver from the cold, but she could not bring herself to go into the dark cabin for her coat.

Where *was* he? Where was Joe? Was he starting down the path now? Was he almost here? Was he back at the restaurant?

Or was he still on the mountain, the mountain where the fever was?

For the first time it occurred to her that something might have happened to Joe. She stood up and tried a few steps along the path. Nothing must happen to Joe. It could not be. Not now. Denying a lifetime of caution and all the mannerisms that made her own personality, Gwendolyn was actually reaching out. Even physically her arms were stretched forth in the darkness. She began to run along the path, carelessly, wildly, bent forward and tripping over vines and tree roots. As she ran she cried as she had never allowed herself to cry, so that she ran blindly into Joe without having heard him on the path, felt herself held by him, pressed hard against him.

All the different times he had wanted it and hoped for it and sought it and despaired of it had made Joe long ready to know the turbulent surrender, and he was glad that he had left Arthur and Justin Magnus talking with Fish-face and had come up the path alone.

"Oh, Joe," Gwen said. "I thought something had happened to you."

*

Arthur tried to feel his way around the dark cabin. "Hey, Erma. Wake up," he said. "We found it."

"What?" she said. "Arthur? Oh, you're back." She sat up on the cot. "It's so dark," she said. "I can't see anything."

"Listen," he said. "We found it. We found the village—what's left of it—and we think we've found the path up the mountain."

"You did!"

"Now you're awake. Here's a cigarette."

"Where's Justin?" she said.

"He went down to the river to wash. Let's us go down too. I'm filthy."

"So'm I," Erma said. "I just fell on the bed and I haven't been conscious since. Light the lamp, will you? It's over on the table. Did you bring anything to eat? I'm starved."

"Yes, that's what took so long. We stopped off at Fish-face's and got some food. He's going to round up some camping stuff for us to take tomorrow."

"You really found it?" she said. "It's really there? Oh, Arthur, were any of them—are any of them up there?"

"No. It's an awful sight, Erma. All burned out and black, but there's a kind of altar. You can tell where the village was, all right. Come on," he said. "Let's go down to the river and have a swim and then we can all eat."

Alone, Justin Magnus swam out into the cold waters of the river, washing away the dirt and the sweat of the long, eventful day. It was the first time he had been in the water since he had tried to drown himself, and it was the first time that he had been really glad that he had failed. Seeing the burned-out village this afternoon and finding a path that might be the right path up the mountain, he had begun to believe that really there would be something at the end of it. He wanted to live to see it. It was a strange feeling. Even the water, cold as it was, was pleasant, and so was his pride in finding himself not so tired as he had believed. He was anticipating the morrow, a thing he had not done for a long time. He was even anticipating the evening when they would all be sitting around the lamp eating and planning how to get up the mountain past where the car could go.

And this moment, right now, he was looking forward to the next moment when Erma Herrick would be coming down the path, her red hair dim in the darkness, her voice calling out to him, asking if the water was cold. Justin turned on his back in the water and floated quietly, looking up at the sky. The first stars were showing.

Now that his taste for life had returned, now that he was himself again, it was unthinkable that he should let another night go by without writing to Max. As soon as they had all eaten he would write to Max and he would mail the letter tonight, too, even if it necessitated getting out the car and driving some distance—for Old Fish-face could certainly not be trusted. Through the soft night sounds of the country Justin remembered his leave-taking, remembered the restraint in Max, the delicacy that would not permit the questions, and himself acting like a stubborn child, taking advantage of the delicacy, withholding information, content to leave Max with his burden of concern. But now that he was himself again, now that he was *all right*, he knew that this very night he must get the letter off. A man who is *all right* does not treat an old friend this way, does not ignore his right to feel concern.

CHAPTER EIGHT

I N A vast sea of blackness, their fire was the only light. Wrapped in the Fish's blankets, the five sat or lay huddled about the fire in various degrees of fatigue, cold, and excitement after the long day's climb. Halfway up the mountain they had been surprised by the abruptness of the mountain night, which none of them had anticipated, and now they were trapped on a jutting shelf of rock from which they dared not move.

"Well, what are we going to do?" Gwen asked.

"There's nothing to do," Joe said, "but stay put. We'll be all right."

"We wouldn't dare to go back now, Gwen," Erma said. "We'd break our necks."

"I suppose we should have started back about noon," Justin said. "I should have realized. But after we found the shell bridge and sighted the mound of red rocks, I kept thinking the next turn would bring us to something decisive."

"So did I," Erma said. "I've felt that each step would be it. I forgot all about the night. Besides, I had no idea it was so late."

"I knew what time it was," Arthur said, "but I didn't know it got dark all at once like this. Besides, what does it matter? We're safe here as long as we can keep a fire going and we've got blankets, and we won't starve to death for missing one meal."

"I don't know," Joe said. "I'm practically starved now."

"Oh, but somebody will see our fire," Gwen said. "Fish-face knows we're up here. He'll send somebody after us."

"That coward?" Arthur said. "With what he's got on his conscience he wouldn't come near the place. Anyhow, they're used to overnight campers around here. They probably don't think it's unusual at all. Even if they did, I doubt very much if this shelf is visible from the village."

"So do I," Justin said. "Oh, well, it's only a matter of a few hours until it's light. It isn't as though we were lost. As soon as it's light we can go back down."

"But we can't!" Erma said. "We don't have time. We have to be here tomorrow. We can't spend tomorrow going back and the next day coming up again. We'll miss it."

"Maybe this is it," Joe said. "Maybe we passed it this afternoon. After all, the last landmark on the map was the mound of red rocks and we passed that hours ago."

"Whatever we decide to do tomorrow," Justin said, "we ought to get some sleep now."

"We'd better sleep in shifts," Joe said. "Somebody might roll off, and, besides, we ought to keep the fire going."

"I'll stay awake," Erma said. "I'm not sleepy."

"Neither am I," Justin said.

"Who the hell is?" Joe said.

It was true. They were not sleepy. They were tired. They had climbed all day, sometimes in spurts of excitement, sometimes in grim, steady progression, yet they were not sleepy. There was an excitement which held them all awake.

"Must be something about the air up here," Arthur said.

"Yeah," Joe said, "I guess so. I've felt about half tight all afternoon."

Maybe it was the air, Gwendolyn thought. Yet, did the rest of them really feel as she did? She didn't think so. Even this morning she had felt this way, as though she had just discovered the road—that all she had to do was keep her feet on it, keep moving ahead, and everything would be all right. She pulled the blanket closer around her and lay down with her head in Joe's lap. She hoped no one saw their fire. She hoped no one came for them. She wanted to stay just as she was, danger of fever or not, staring up at the stars. The stars were new. She was new. The world was new. Every step she'd climbed all day had been in a new world. She didn't care if she were late getting back to the office. She didn't care if she never got back at all. Joe was responsible for her now. She was not alone and she would never be alone again.

It was a son-of-a-bitching life, Joe thought, when you could put your hand out and touch a woman, touch her throat, touch her breast, and know the fight was over, know from the very feel of her skin that she was yours now any time, any time, and all you could think of was how you wanted a plate of ham and eggs. He had never been so hungry in his life. Suddenly he remembered the underwear that he had stuffed into the closet of his room back in the mountain lodge. For all he knew it was there yet.

They watched the fire and gradually they stopped talking. Now they were waiting. As they grew colder, they grew quieter. Automatically they fed the fire with whatever was in reach. They were waiting and therefore they were wakeful. One cannot really wait and do anything else at the same time. Each man learns this in his own way and then forgets it as soon as he can. He calls it the strangeness of the mountain air. He calls it not being able to get anything done. He calls it insomnia. But the inner chambers of the mind, the waiting inner chambers of the mind, do not forget. They wait in a positive manner, according to a pattern. They wait with the memory of other waiting times.

Like the arcs of perfectly aimed tracer bullets, their waiting times came back to them, the arcs meeting on the rock shelf, projected there from various places and from various times. When they reached the mountainside, the arcs became five circles, entire and separate from one another.

Joe's arc came from the war, from a lost battle when he and Arthur and many others had trudged wearily back and back in defeat through the miles of hot fine dust, no words for one another, all of them focused upon the command, which never came, to stop and rest. He had been hungry then, too, really hungry. And thirsty, his mouth and nose and eyes filled with the dust, the sound of it loud on his teeth. Well, he was thirsty now, especially so since in the night quiet he had become increasingly aware of the sound of water somewhere near. Yet he did not dare to seek it in the darkness on the unfamiliar mountain paths.

Gwendolyn felt him go away from her, felt the shape go out of his hand upon her breast as though, to him, it lay on a table or on a stone. She felt him become detached from her along his own particular waiting arc. It frightened her. It made her remember the mountain fever, made her imagine the bites of deadly mountain ticks, made her remember her headlong flight in panic down the path from the cabin the night that Joe had been so late.

Waiting is a thing that people do alone, and, in turn, the very act of waiting makes one isolated and alone. They did not share their arcs of memory, these five. As though they sat surrounded by individual hoops, they sat in their individual worlds like five closed circles on the mountainside.

To Erma, this night was like the night her father's house burned down. She had wanted to save things, to clutch at a few things, but her father had taken her hand and led her out. "It is hopeless," he said. "At such a time everything is equally valuable." She followed him then away from the house. They walked until they came to a rise in the ground. They turned and watched the fire. There was no anger in her father, not even sorrow, just a kind of grim attention not to miss any of it. He could not leave the spot until the house was all gone.

This is the way I used to sit for Edith, Justin thought. This is the way I used to wait for Edith to come out after she had had an attack. Looking at the darkness and waiting. It seemed a long time ago to him that he had sat at attention in the darkness ready and waiting for Edith to come out on the fragile silver ribbon of her special times. The strangest thing about it was the certainty, new to him, that he would never sit by Edith's bed again, never be essential to Edith again. He was also certain that he would never see that room again or go inside their house.

Had he got any mail at the shop? Arthur wondered. In the constant movement and strangeness of the last eight days he had forgotten the deadly time of waiting in Drury, waiting for the answers to his book. Surely when they got back there would be some. It was not possible that you could cast a question in a thousand directions and have not one answer. It was not true that men talked and wrote always to the wind. Or was it? He saw himself going back to Drury, going up to the shop, taking the key out of his pocket, opening the door. There on the floor opposite the mail slot . . . there was nothing. No, it was too maddening even to imagine. He imagined that there were ten letters sprawled on the floor at angles. Finally, there in the darkness, sitting on the jutting rock shelf, inviolate in his hoop circle, obedient to his individual memory arc, he cast caution to the stars. He let himself imagine a stack of letters, a hundred at least, piled up one on another, tumbling over one another.

And what would he say to them, all those people? Well, he could not know until tomorrow. Perhaps after tomorrow . . . He let himself dream. He let himself hope. What was the harm, since he couldn't sleep? After tomorrow, after they had seen the place, then he would say to the people: Come with me. I will lead you to a place that I have found. Come with me, climbing up, away from what binds you, away from what defeats and exhausts you, what makes you die too young. Come with me past the Indian village. Cross with me the bridge of colored shells built by the Indians. Climb with me to the red rock mound on Grandfather Magnus' map. Sit with me through the night on this very ledge where once I planned our journey, where once I dreamed through the night of our accomplishment. In the morning I will take you to the Green Kingdom. No heaven, this. No fantastic paradise, but a place where men can work for what is essential, for their shelter and their clothing and their food *directly*, so that they need not lose sight of them in the translating. Here we will live. Here we will begin the Work. Here we will start to keep the Records.

If he could say this to them, then nothing had been lost. Nothing he had ever done had been wasted.

"It's getting light," Justin said. "Have you noticed?"

"Yes," Erma said. "You can begin to see shapes. I'm glad. I'll be glad for the sun. I'm cold."

"That water," Joe said. "My God, the sound of it has been driving me mad. I'm so thirsty I could die and for all I know it's only a few feet away."

"Better wait, Joe," Arthur said. "It's still too dark to move away from the fire."

"Oh, I'm cold," Gwen said. "And stiff. How long will it be until we can move?"

"Not very long now," Justin said. He stood up and stretched and turned, facing the mountain. "Well, Grandfather," he said, "were you a liar or not?"

Erma, too, stood up. "To think," she said, "today. That it's today we're going to know."

They found the water by following the tantalizing, elusive sound of it, and while they knelt there splashing their faces and tasting from their cupped hands the sweet, cold flavor of it, they did not think that they would remember it all their lives, that they would come to remember it, some of them with a terrible bitterness, as the last thing they did in a world where it was still theirs to choose whether to go ahead or back, whether to climb farther or go down.

They heard the rumbling and they felt the ground tremble

beneath them and they were paralyzed, all of them looking up in the direction of the roaring, their hands halfway to their mouths, the water running out between their fingers. Then without any words they began to run up the tangled, dim path toward the noise. They could hear rocks falling and crashing near them, and they stumbled, as they ran, over many rounded stones. It was hard to run in the thin air to which they were not accustomed, and the effort of breathing made conversation impossible. Even when they were on it, they were all too startled, too puzzled, to talk to one another.

For it was, more literally than any of them had dared imagine, a split in the mountain, a vertical tear. They were surrounded in dust and none of them could see through it yet. Cascades of dust fell from the ragged edges of the rent, and the sound of crashing stones below profaned the mountain silence.

Justin was the first. They saw him put up his hand to the side of the great, gaping hole, saw him walk straight ahead until he was lost to them in the falling, blinding dust. Afterward he swore to them that he could not remember going in. He could remember being outside, he could remember being inside, but he could never remember entering. He could never remember saying, "Now I will go. Now I will go in."

Erma could remember. She could remember going after Justin impulsively, going headlong, just as she had jerked the two dollars out of Joe's hand that day in Drury and jumped on the train after him, the day that Edith died. It was the same movement. It was the same need. She remembered it always as a moving forward of the body.

And Arthur remembered a moment of conscious decision. He remembered the realization that *there must be something there*. He had doubted it really, all the time, the more so as he hoped for it, as he needed it. There is something there, he thought. I can tell the people now. I can promise them a place. It had seemed to him, as he groped his way through the dust toward the greenish light ahead of him, that he was not alone. He had them with him, all his people. He led them to the place where they would do the Work. He led them in triumph. He saw Erma turn toward him. He saw her haloed and bathed in the strange, green light, her hands stretched out to him, and then he stumbled and fell. He began to roll down, down, before they could stop him.

Joe, following Arthur, suddenly remembered Gwendolyn. He turned back and helped her up the path. She stumbled and clung to him and then he heard Erma scream. He left Gwendolyn standing at the entrance and ran ahead through the dust, feeling his way along the mountain wall. He saw Erma and Justin hurrying toward Arthur, and he ran past them and ahead of them, part of his mind curiously aware that *his feet made no sound.* It was as though he floated down to Arthur, who lay dazed and motionless on the soft, green feather grass.

Gwendolyn stood alone outside. She was afraid to go in, though the dust was clearing now and she could see that it was not dark ahead, that it was strangely light, with a light that she had never seen before. She turned away from it and leaned against the wall, looking back the way they had come. But it did not look the same. Joe had been with her then. Now she was alone and the mountain was alien. The rocks were no longer crashing down the mountainside and the new stillness was menacing, terrifying. She was afraid to move. She was paralyzed with panic. Under the alien sky she was lost, microscopically lost. She tried to call for Joe and her mouth would not open. Her throat was stiff. In her mind she was surrounded by rattlesnakes and death-bearing ticks. A sudden cold wind blew against her and it was the breath of sheer terror. Suddenly the scales shifted; the balance became reversed. There *was* no unknown danger with company as horrible as being alone. She had never in her life been absolutely alone before, the only creature on the landscape. The knowledge that she need not be, that *this* terror could be ended, dissolved her paralysis, and with a violent jerk she wrenched herself free from the alien hold of the mountain and went running into the green light where the others would be waiting, where Joe would be waiting, where she would not be alone.

Arthur sat up.

"My God," Joe said. "I thought you were dead."

"No," Arthur said, "I'm all right. Something's wrong with my leg, but I'm all right. Jesus! Look!"

As soon as she saw the rest of them, Gwen was ashamed of her panic. She was able to go down to the others almost calmly. She watched her feet and walked carefully, and the wild beating of her heart gradually quieted.

How can it be said *in words* what they saw spread out before them? How is it possible? Imagine that you have been starved—not just hungry but *starved*—for many weeks. You are a bundle of bones, your skin is a terrible color, and you can no longer stand. Even your voice is almost gone. You are kneeling before a bakery window. With your bony fingers you are clawing at the glass which stands between you and a windowful of bread. The bread is in large loaves with a thick, brown crust. The sun is shining on the crusts, lighting it up in shiny spots. I say to you: There is no glass in the window. Reach in.

That is what the Green Kingdom looks like.

Imagine that you are lost on the desert. Your water is all gone. Your horse is dead. The heat on the white sand is merciless. Before you, you see a mirage. You have seen it before; you have learned before that it is a mirage. It is a roaring waterfall, foaming and white. I say to you: It is no mirage. Truly. It is real. Reach out your hand. Feel the wetness.

That is what the Green Kingdom looks like.

You are a seamstress. All your life has been lived in poverty. Your hands are rough in a thousand places where the needle has pricked your skin. Your eyes are dim from the long hours spent in a bad light. All your life you have made beautiful clothing for other people and yet you yourself have never worn anything but the cheapest, the roughest cotton. Before you I begin to unfold a piece of finest velvet. Not a yard or two, but a whole bolt of it. It falls in folds, soft, soundless folds at your feet, over your hands, all around you. You are surrounded in it. You rub your cheeks in it. I say to you: It is yours.

That is what the Green Kingdom looks like.

You are a soldier. You are tired. Not, as a civilian, tired as you used the word then, but tired as you are now, as you never knew you could be and live. You were exhausted day before yesterday. Yet you are still walking. You have walked through snow, through dirt, through rain, through mud. You have been beaten from below by hard pavement. You no longer know what you are walking in or on. You were exhausted day before yesterday. Or was it week before last? Yet you are still walking. And not in quiet, either, nor in safety, but in a constant hell of unrhythmic and unpredictable noise. So long you have been doing this that in the rare times that it really stops, the noise, you continue to hear it in your head.

I say to you: Turn right here. Walk twenty steps. You are in a quiet place. There is a bed there. On the bed are springs. On the springs is a mattress. On the mattress are clean sheets. Over the sheets is a down quilt.

That is what the Green Kingdom looks like.

You are deaf. You have always been deaf. You have never heard anything. I take away your deafness. I point to a harp. I place your hands upon the strings. You move your hands across the harp.

That is how the Green Kingdom looks. And this:

As though a giant, moving hand had held aloft a honey jar and let the honey fall and coil upon itself. The honey is green. The coils, wound and roped upon themselves, are each of a different shade, a different tint. All the greens there are are there. The yellow greens, the blue greens, the gray greens, the green of the first spring pussy-willow buds, the green of new lettuce just showing in the weeded garden rows, the green of thick grass where it is standing in the evening and also where it bears the imprint of a body lying down, the green of the laurel in the sun and the waxy dark green of rhododendron in the dark and shady and secluded woods, the black green of wet evergreen, wet from the forest snow, and the white green of a new peeled, fragrant twig. And they are not arranged in order. They are mixed and coiled upon one another, wound around and woven into one another.

Look closer. Come down from the giant hand holding the green honey jar. The coils are textured, from the fine feather grass underfoot to the bayonet leaves of the greatest trees, from the smoothness of moss to the viciousness of spikes, all the textures are there: horny, hairy, rough and smooth, the textures of silk, crepe, cotton, linen, wood, glass, wax, fur, paper and oil and stone, pebble and spike. They are all there.

Coil upon coil the lush vegetation lies there before the five people. It is heaped upon them to excess; it is piled upon them in a giant crescendo, wave on wave, coil on coil, in jagged peaks and in low mounds, under foot, at eye level, over their heads. It is largess, it is excess, it is beyond appetite and freely given. And it is all strange.

Well hidden in it to their unlearned eyes, secret and hidden because of the early morning chill and because of the intrusion, are the animals: the winged and the hoofed, the flying and the running, the slithering and the crawling. They also, hidden now in their warm and secret places, they also are green.

The five people had come in on a steep slope, and Justin now began to go down, down to the level ground below, down to the many-greened plain below, walking with his headlong, lumbering gait, walking without sound over the green feather grass. Tears streamed down his face and he made no effort to stop them. He who had shed no tears for the death of his four sons, he cried now out of shame for his small faith. He cried out of a bitter and terrible love for his grandfather. If only he could take the little old dried-up, disillusioned man in his great arms, carry him like a baby in his great arms, hold him close to his bursting chest. If only he could say to him: Yes, yes, it is so. Just as you said. It is so.

As she had followed him on the train for the journey to Tilbury, as she had followed him into the Green Kingdom, instinctively, now, Erma took two steps after Justin. Then she blushed, turned and knelt by Arthur.

"Oh, Arthur," she said. "Your leg." She burst into tears, violent and sudden tears.

"But, Erma," Arthur said, "it's only my leg. It's just a sprain. Why, Erma, you never cry. You never cry like that."

As the sound of the opening had held them all paralyzed when they were drinking at the stream, so now they stopped and turned their heads toward the source of a hissing noise. In curious, frozen postures, they watched the stream of hot lava shoot into the opening, fill and cover it, seal it and drip down over the edges of the rent like the dripping wax from a candle flame.

Justin saw it too, just as the others did, though he was much farther down the slope. He was the first to recover, being now beyond shock, beyond surprise. Why should he be concerned with getting out when he could not even remember coming in? He turned back to the view below him and began again his fast and lumbering descent.

Ahead of him he could see a river or a lake, green water moving slowly, changing constantly under the changing light. It was this he sought. It was this he wanted. When he came to the bank, he stood still, his feet wide apart. He looked into the green water. His hurry was over. His bitter anguished tears had ceased. Gradually his breathing quieted, slowed down, became finally a great sigh. He reached up to his throat, pulled his necktie loose, and dropped it into the water. He could see it being borne away from him out of his sight, floating and bobbing and partly swallowed. It was none of his.

He reached into his pocket and pulled out his keys and these he let fall into the water. They went straight down.

Then he took out his money and let it fall slowly, idly, through his fingers, seeing the bills dancing and sliding along after the necktie, seeing the coins make separate, ineffectual splashes one by one.

Max Staats had, with difficulty, controlled his anxiety through the days of silence. When the letter came at last he tore it out of its envelope and scanned it hurriedly until he was satisfied that all was well with Justin. He sighed with relief and allowed himself to light a cigarette and turn on his desk lamp before he settled down to a careful reading.

Dear Max:

I hasten to plead that you think me less a clod and a boor by sending you this overdue bulletin. I suppose it's natural that one who waits until he's sixty to have an acquaintance with illness would not handle it with any grace, but, Max, I am genuinely sorry for any unnecessary anxiety you may have had since I started on this trip. I am fine.

It was childish of me not to have told you about the map. The last time I was in my house I found my grandfather's old map of the route to the Green Kingdom and I couldn't face the possibility that your sharp mind might expose it for a fraud. I knew that I had to have something to go toward, to get moving, or I would rot, and I seized on this because I didn't have anything else. About the map, so far it's been accurate. We've found all the landmarks and are getting pretty close to the end now. No matter what the Green Kingdom turns out to be, the trip has already served its purpose as far as I'm concerned.

You may remember on the old concert itinerary the

town of Drury where I stayed with the Herricks. Well, I stopped in Drury and Mr. and Mrs. Herrick and two friends of theirs agreed to join me for the rest of the trip. So we are five.

Right now my feeling is that I probably will not return to live in the old house, at least not permanently. When I know what may plans are, I'll let you know, and of course in the meantime I'll keep you posted.

Max, my gratitude for your long friendship and all the ways you showed it during the past months is very great. I'm sure that it will be no surprise to you when I say that these seemingly erratic roamings are vaguely directed toward the hope of finishing the symphony I started before Edith died.

Keep yourself well.

JUSTIN

Max leaned back in his chair and laughed, letting his anxiety explode from him to think how the old giant had walked about in this very room with his secret map tucked safely in his pocket, afraid to show it to him. I must have been close enough to touch it, he thought, many times. And here while I've been worried about him, possibly sick and alone somewhere, he's had not one but FOUR companions.

He folded the letter and put it back into its envelope, and, holding the envelope under the lamp, he tried to decipher the postmark. He could make out the state, but the name of the town had been imprinted over the stamp and was illegible. He pushed the envelope neatly into the right-hand corner of the desk blotter. It was his custom to destroy letters as soon as they were answered, for he disliked clutter, but this one, of course, could not be answered until he should again hear from Justin.

With the greatest possible economy of movement he reached out and turned off the desk lamp. Then he took off his glasses and pressed the knuckles of one hand against his closed eyelids. He moved his chair so that he would be facing the sea.

He could not see it, but he knew it was there. He was not laughing now, for the words I PROBABLY WILL NOT RETURN TO LIVE IN THE OLD HOUSE had come out of the letter to sit with him, and the thought that the shaggy bulk of Justin Magnus might not again loom up between himself and the sea, as it had so many hundreds of times in the past, gave him a deep sense of regret.

The quiet room grew gradually darker about him as he sat, quite motionless, in a mood of gentle sadness, remembering the long years. He remembered the times he had taken Justin's mail up to his sickroom and of how Justin had pawed at the letters, slipping them aside without interest, coming to rest on the envelope with the big square handwriting in what had looked then only a random choice. That curiously incongruous smile of great sweetness suffused Max's face for a moment, transforming it completely. It hardly seemed possible that he had found himself envying a man whose measure of suffering had been so great. But it is true, Max thought. I do envy him.

Day after day Mrs. Johns carefully dusted over the letter and reset its top surface parallel with the blotter's edge. On the desk behind the letter, like sentinels, stood Max's especially favored books: Whitehead and Russell, Gauss, Riemann, Poincairé, LaPlace and Von Neumann. Leaning against these giants, somewhat timidly because of its worn condition, was a slender little copy of Schroedinger's WHAT IS LIFE?

2. Time of Innocence

CHAPTER ONE

L IKE the beads of blood that rim the lip of a freshly made
wound, the tears of lava dotted, in frozen suspension, the
edges of the seal upon the Green Kingdom. So far below it that
it was no longer even visible to them now, the little group sat
huddled together by the shore of the green river. Here they had
quenched their thirst and here, on the soft feather grass, they had
tried to make Arthur comfortable. Now, in the green lighted
silence, they had nothing to say and they avoided one another's
eyes.

So it was true then, Justin thought, staring into the green
swirling water beneath him. It has been here all this time, waiting. In all the years of sorrow, in all the terrible time, it was here
and I did not believe it. I could have brought Edith here. I could
have brought the children. And they would be here now.

Joe was the first one to break the silence. "How's your leg,
Arthur?" he said.

"It's all right," Arthur said, sitting up. "I just twisted it.
The trouble was I must have hit my head on something. Feel sort
of dazed."

Their voices brought them back to Justin with a shock. He
had forgotten them, the young people. And now it was not the
reality of the Green Kingdom that he must consider; it was the
reality of the seal upon it. How would they take it? Would they
hold him responsible? Would they blame him? He looked first
at Gwendolyn, for hers was the accusation he most feared, and
she was looking straight at him, her eyes wide, her lips afraid to
speak it lest they make it certain. Justin looked at her and he did
not know what to say to her, and finally she looked away from
him.

"Give me a cigarette, Joe," she said.

"While they last," Joe said, offering the package around.

"That's right," Arthur said, taking a cigarette, "we'll be out of them soon. I don't suppose anyone stocked up on cigarettes or anything else."

"Cigarette, Mr. Magnus?" Joe said.

"No, thanks," Justin said. "I have my pipe. I hope I have my pipe." He searched in his pockets until he had found it. "And, Joe," he said, "I think you might call me Justin now since it looks as though we are going to know one another so well."

"Looks like we're trapped, all right," Joe said.

"No!" Gwendolyn said. "How can you just sit here and say you're trapped? You haven't even tried. It isn't true. It isn't true." She stood up in hatred and defiance of the others. "I've got to get out!" she screamed. "I've *got* to!"

She turned and darted away from them, running back and up, the way they had come. Joe looked at Justin and then he started after her.

Well, he knew about two of them, Justin thought. Gwendolyn was hysterical with fear and Joe felt trapped. He had to know about Erma now; he couldn't wait any longer. He turned to her, but she was sitting with her back to him, very alert and quiet.

"Well, Arthur," Justin said, "I . . . I don't know what to say. I feel responsible for . . . Believe me, I didn't believe it. I never really believed it."

"Shhh!" Erma turned toward them and then turned away again. "Look," she whispered.

Coming carefully, slowly toward them, all their heads held high and questioningly in the air, was a small herd of animals such as they had never seen before. They were about a hundred yards away, grouped behind a leader. Smaller than horses, yet looking something like horses except for their curled, spiral horns, they were all green and each had a long green feathery mane. Their leader halted and all the others waited. Erma got up very slowly and began to move toward the animals so gradually, so soundlessly, that it was almost as though she were floating. Arthur made a sudden motion to follow her, but Justin restrained him.

"Better not to startle them," he said.

"But do you think it's safe?" Arthur said. "They might hurt her."

"I don't think they will," Justin said. "Not the way she's going at it." For it was exactly the way in which he had been

accustomed to approach Edith, and he felt within him how it was
with Erma Herrick. The two men sat as though their stillness
could protect her.

Erma was up to the animals now, within a foot of their
leader. She watched him as he was watching her, seeing with
great clarity the green, silky hide, the long bushy tail, the slender
delicate legs, the lovely spiral horns, the pale-green eyes. Finally
the leader took one step nearer her. Very slowly she lifted her
hand so that it was just beyond his head. Very slowly he stretched
his neck and placed his head under her hand. She let her fingers
fall lightly upon his head and then remain there for a moment,
and, because she could resist it no longer, at last she touched the
feathery green mane. Now they were all around her, leaning
against her, circling around to be nearer. She stood in the midst
of them, her hand, trembling with excitement, still on the leader's
mane. Behind her she heard Joe's voice, and at the sound the
leader instantly turned and fled, the whole herd at his heels.
Within a few seconds they had vanished from sight. Erma stood
alone for a moment, and suddenly she realized that she had been
holding her breath for a long time. She heard Joe call her name
and turned back toward the others.

"Hey, Erma," Joe said. "Come help me. Gwen's gone sort of
crazy. I . . . I had to treat her kind of rough, she scared me so.
Will you watch her while I get some wood? I've got to get a fire
started. She's shaking all over."

"Of course, Joe," she said, walking with him back to where
the others were. "We've got to think about tonight. There's not a
blanket, not anything. And she's hungry, Joe. We're all hungry.
We've had nothing to eat since yesterday. Joe, look!" Erma
pointed to the ground. There, nesting under huge furry leaves and
lying on the ground, were many small, pale-green melons.

"Do you suppose they're good to eat?" Joe asked.

"Let's take them back anyway," Erma said.

"Come on," Joe said, "we've got to hurry. I've got to get
back to Gwen."

The stems of the melons were tough, and Joe reached for his
knife.

"Thank God you've got your knife," Erma said. "I'll bet
it's the one useful thing we have."

They took five of the melons and started back to the others.

"I'm sorry about Gwen," Erma said. "I should have stayed

with her, paid more attention. It was just . . . Oh, it's so beautiful. I forgot everything."

Joe needn't have worried that Gwendolyn would again try to run from them and become lost. She was now quite incapable of movement. She lay on the ground with Justin's coat thrown over her. She was rigid and shaking with cold. Her eyes were wild and there was no recognition in them. Her long hair was disheveled and there were scratches on her face.

Justin leaned over her, rubbing her arms. "Arthur's gone for firewood," he said. "You'd better go too, Joe. We've got to get this girl warm."

Erma knelt on the other side of Gwendolyn and began to rub her other arm. "The grass is all wet here," she said to Justin.

"It's the dew," Justin said. "Must be going to get dark very soon. Probably the dampness explains the thick growth everywhere. We'll have to keep a fire going all night, since we've no shelter."

"Look," Erma said, "across the river."

Clouds of mist were rising in all directions, as though a million kettles had been set boiling at all levels.

"Do you think you could manage alone?" Justin said. "I ought to help with the wood. We won't be able to see in a short while."

"Yes, go on," Erma said. "Hurry. Maybe you and I can get a small fire started to guide the others. If they've gone far I'm afraid they'll be lost. And Arthur. Arthur shouldn't have gone at all. Did he seem all right to you when he left?"

"Stay with Gwendolyn," Justin said. "I'll be back as soon as I can."

All this time Erma had been rubbing Gwendolyn's arms and legs, trying to get some warmth into them. Now the two women were alone, and at last Gwendolyn's teeth stopped chattering.

"I think I've found us something to eat, Gwen," Erma said. "Gwen, you'll be better in a little while. We'll have a fire and get you warm."

She could feel the rigidity gradually leaving the girl's arms, and she kept talking, kept saying her name over, aware now and very conscious of the danger of the men's getting lost. How could she have been immersed in the Green Kingdom like that, unaware of the others, as though she were alone? She was surprised to see that the wild look was completely gone from Gwendolyn's eyes and that in its place was focused one of pure hatred.

"Are you all right, Gwen? Are you better now?"

"You knew," Gwendolyn said. "Didn't you? You knew all along."

"Knew what, Gwen?"

Gwendolyn raised herself now and pulled Justin's coat around her shoulders. Her face was very close to Erma's.

"All of you," she said. "You all knew we couldn't get out before we started, didn't you? Everyone knew it but me."

"I see you're better," Justin said, behind them. "We'll have you warm in a little while. I found Joe and Arthur," he said to Erma. "They'll be along soon."

"Thank God!" Erma said.

Justin started to build the fire. He gave Erma a quick, direct look. "I think," he said, "you could help them, Erma, if you'd go right up that way."

Now he was alone with the wild one. He who was old enough to know the principle of peace at any price, he who knew the therapy of lies and compromise—this was his job. Let the young ones gather in the wood.

"Are you getting warm now?" he said to Gwen.

"Yes," she said. "Thank you for your coat. I . . ."

"Now, see here," Justin said to her. "You're only to think of tonight, you know, to get yourself rested for tomorrow. We dare not leave the fire, any of us, for fear of getting lost. We must all stay close together tonight."

He walked around the fire and sat down close to the girl. She turned to him, looked up at him, and, even in her present state of exhaustion and hunger, there was a physical desirability about her that was so incongruous, so out of place in the circumstances, that Justin was repelled by it. He had an impulse to hit at the girl, to hurt her. And that made it easier to do what he had to do, to start her down the long, slow, cynical path of gradual acceptance. He was the only one who knew that there is nothing as efficacious as prolonged hope to break the spirit.

"You know," he said, "before the mists came up it was light, and so the light has to have some way to get in here. So there must be an opening above us. And that river there beneath us, it goes somewhere. You'll have to be strong and rested before we can explore, but it's something for you to think about."

He was not prepared for her violent reaction. She threw her arms around his neck.

"You'll help me," she said. "Won't you?"

He could feel her breasts against him. Christ, he thought, I could have her. I could have her right now if I promised to get her out. He had to grit his teeth in order to be gentle with her as he unclasped her hands and kept them imprisoned in his own. I could break them, he thought, easily.

"You'll help me," Gwen said. "The others, they don't understand. They don't have families. They're all alone. It doesn't make any difference to them where they live. But think of my mother, think of my sisters. Think how terrible it will be for them."

She bent her head and began weeping in a strange, lost, pathetic way. The confusion of physical desire and hatred left Justin instantly, and there was nothing in him but sadness at her childish crying. He put his hand on her head and patted it. Trust me, he thought. Trust me. I can't get you out, either.

"Now," he said, "you go down to the river and bathe your face. The others will be back soon."

He helped her to her feet and saw her going unsteadily down to the river. She was safe to leave alone now. By virtue of her own weeping and her dependence on him, she was as safe as if he'd had her on a leash. In his mind he had a sudden picture of her, a lost, disconsolate, bedraggled little figure squatting on the ground, urinating and staring sadly out at the lonely, hostile river. He spat into the fire and shook his head. God damn Joe, he thought. Why would he pick out one like that? Wrong for the place from the very beginning. Wrong straight through. But he knew. He knew very well why Joe or any man would pick her, and he hated having the knowledge now on the first day, in the time that should have been a holy time.

When they were all huddled together around the fire, their only weapon against the cold, against the unknown dangers, the only break in the blindness of the mists, Justin took one of the melons and broke it open. He meant to do it quietly without attracting any attention, but as he took the first bite he heard Gwendolyn gasp, heard her say, as he had known she would, "It might be poison."

"It's a marvelous taste," he said, "even—" he turned to Gwendolyn—"even if it should be poisonous. Anyhow, I much prefer poison to starvation."

He held the other half out to Erma. "First fruit," she said, taking it from him. She took a bite and then she turned to Arthur.

"Oh, it's wonderful. A little bit like mangoes. No, that's only the texture."

"Wait a second," Arthur said, "till I catch up with you."

"Why did we only bring five back?" Joe said. "Now I've had a taste of food, I'm ravenous. I wish I'd brought a gun. There must be all kinds of game we could eat."

"But not my feathermanes," Erma said. "Don't kill my feathermanes."

"Where is the place the melons are?" Arthur said. "Could you find it again, Erma?"

"I'm sure I could," she said. "Get Joe's knife and let's try."

As soon as they were out of range of the firelight they turned instantly to each other in close and meaningful embrace.

"Oh, I've wanted this so long," Erma whispered to him, "wanted us to be quiet and alone."

"I know," he said, "I know. You've taken it in already. I watched you walk up to those animals—"

"You know," she said, "they smell like horses, a little."

Arthur started to laugh, and then he kissed her and he could feel the longing in her, the hunger, in answer to his own. "Oh God," he said, "they'll be hunting for us if we don't get back."

"Never mind," she said. "We'll have a house of our own soon. We'll . . ."

He felt her slipping away from him. They stepped carefully, feeling their way.

"I think it's about here," Erma said. "Let's get down on our hands and knees. They're right on the ground. Have you got a handkerchief?"

"Yes. Why?"

"Well, give it to me. I've no pockets and I need both hands. I want to tie something up in it." She handed him back the knotted handkerchief. "You won't lose it?" she said. "You'll be careful of it?"

"What is it?" he said.

"Oh, it's the seeds out of the first fruit. I thought we ought to keep them, you know."

Gwendolyn was asleep when they got back, but the rest of them sat around the fire eating of the first fruit, eating until in thanksgiving they were actually hungry no longer. Arthur said he would take the first guard duty, and they agreed each man should take two hours in rotation to keep the fire going. Then it was they discovered that none of them knew the time, nor did they know how to mark the passing of it in this place. Arthur had no watch. Joe's was in hock in Drury. Justin's had stopped.

"I didn't think of it," Justin said apologetically. "I never thought to wind it."

And suddenly, because of a watch that did not tick, because of a small inanimate thing he held in his hand, he was in a new place. No longer was he alone in the Green Kingdom, in communication with his grandfather, making his holy gestures of silence and acceptance. He was the criminal. His was the blame. Young people, *young* people he had led into this place carelessly without forethought, without making any preparation for their needs or their comfort or their escape. And when they said to him, "How will we get out?" he would only be able to say, "I didn't believe it would happen."

It was a monstrous thing. How had he been capable of it? He who had been so careful of other people all his life? And what was this terrible rule that no one learned and everyone knew, the rule that held even here in the Green Kingdom, the rule that monstrous things must not be spoken of? Why was it he couldn't say out loud that he stood accused before them, that he recognized his guilt? It had been the same with his four dead sons. You must not speak of your four dead sons killed in the war because it was embarrassing to other people. It had always puzzled him about grief; now it puzzled him about guilt. You must not speak of grief or guilt before others, for it is embarrassing to them. Why is it so? he thought. It is all right to kill people; it is all right to imprison them, even; but the thing you must not do— you must not embarrass them. And now he did not know what time it was. He was ashamed and he had lost his communion and his joy because he did not know what time it was.

"What the hell," Joe said. "What do we care what time it is? Set it for twelve. Just so we each take two hours."

"Sure," Arthur said, for he too had sensed the apologetic tone in Justin's voice and had the desire to reassure him, the desire which comes as an automatic response to apology, the quickest weapon to ward off embarrassment.

Justin had done the same thing too, many times. Sometimes you forget, when you have had four sons killed, sometimes you let something slip, and if you do people are quick to try to make some gesture, some embarrassing gesture, and to ward them off you always said, "It's all right." Every time Justin had said it he wondered how he could possibly have said it. Surely he had not meant to say that it is all right to have four sons killed.

"Don't set it," Erma said. "What does it matter whether we take equal turns? The point is to keep the fire going."

As though a projectionist had changed the focus of a movie they were watching, the three men looked at one another and smiled, for at that very moment the fire was in need of more wood. Joe threw on another stick.

"You're right," Arthur said. "This is a silly place for a watch. I've already wound it now. I'm sorry I did."

"Don't be sorry after two o'clock," Joe said. "Wake me up then. I'm going to sleep."

It was not the time for a man who had been careless of their very lives to make a gesture of taking infinitesimal and unnecessary responsibility, Justin decided. The best thing he could do was to lie down and at least pretend to sleep until it was his turn to tend the fire. He had to take turns now. He was not the father, not the husband, not even the host. He was a member of a group. He must remember that. The way to begin was to go to sleep until he was called. But with his eyes closed, silently, in his heart, he thanked Erma for taking the load off him about the stopped watch. "The point is to keep the fire going," she had said.

Arthur felt Erma's head go heavy against him as she sank into sleep. It was curious to feel them all slipping away from him into sleep, leaving him alone and awake to keep the fire, to guard against what they did not know. In all the Green Kingdom he was the only man awake, and, from the silence that crowded against his back, perhaps the only creature. He had the fire for company and he had Justin's watch, the watch that was so out of place here, methodically ticking out the wrong time. "Please don't start it," Erma had said. He could hear her saying it now as he looked down at her and longed to touch her. He could feel the lump of the knotted handkerchief in his pocket, the handkerchief that held the seeds of the first fruits. She already lives here, he thought with wonder at her adaptability.

Tomorrow, the first thing, before any exploration took place, a shelter of some kind must be made against the heavy dew. A communal shelter at first, Arthur thought. One was all they should attempt on the first day. Another day should not be allowed to slip away to find them tomorrow night unprotected. Better to build it on this very spot rather than waste any time in choosing another. He remembered the huge, heart-shaped leaves on a plant he had noticed when they went for wood. They looked tough enough. If they could utilize a kind of natural bower and rein-force it with those leaves (they must have been a foot and a half across), he and Joe and Justin together could surely get a tempo-rary structure fashioned in one day while the girls hunted food.

How would Gwendolyn take tomorrow? he wondered. Would they be able to manage her so that they could concentrate on the shelter, or would Joe be chasing her all the time to keep her from getting lost? Christ, why had they brought her? And if Joe couldn't manage her, who could? Well, they had to have a base—that much he knew. And he had to make the others see it in the morning if they had to tie Gwen to a tree. No one knew how long they'd be here, trying to find a way out. They had to have a place to work from. It made him feel better to have something decided in his own mind. It was a great relief to have his head cleared at last after the dazedness that he had suffered as a result of his fall. He was not at all sleepy and was surprised to see by the watch that half his time was gone. He felt good now, excited and wakeful, alone and waiting in a kind of suspension. How familiar it was, this awareness, this suspension.

The ledge. Of course it was familiar. They had had a fire, too, on the ledge. But it had been on the other side of the seal, on the outside. They had still been in the world that night; they had still had the power of decision in their own hands. That night they had been within only a day's journey of Fish-face and the cabins. *That night. That was last night.* It did not seem possible. Was it true? Was it only twenty-four hours ago that they had sat on the ledge waiting for morning, waiting to find the opening?

Confusion crowded on Arthur. He longed to awaken Erma, to ask someone else if it had been only last night that they had been on the outside. Yes, surely. This was their first night in the Green Kingdom. This was the first day. But he could not remem-ber what day of the week it was. The harder he tried to pin it down, the more elusive it was. He stared at Justin's watch, asking it the day, and it went on methodically giving him the artificial, arbitrary minutes. He had to make a mark on something for this one thing he knew for sure: that they had spent one day inside the Green Kingdom—while he still knew that for sure. They were already hopelessly lost in the hours; he had to keep straight on the days. And he dare not let it wait until there was further chance of doubt. He felt through all his pockets, trying to be methodical about it (was it Friday or Saturday?), but there was no pen, no pencil there. Even if there had been, there was no paper to mark it down on. *A stone. He would put a stone in his shirt pocket for every day.* As far as he could reach without disturbing the others, he felt about him on the ground, but his hand met nothing except the deep grass now soaked in dew. *A stick, then. He would put a twig in his pocket for every day. But a twig will break. A twig will snap in two, making two days for one. A twig is not an accurate record.*

There it was. The word. Record. It walked across the fire to him and settled down upon him, the weight of doom, destroying his clarity, his confidence, killing the wakeful, suspended joy of the first vigil. His book. He saw the letters coming into the print shop, saw them dropping through the slot, piling up on the floor of an empty room. No answer to the letters, no carrythrough. The faith of all the writers broken, the shop empty, the emptiness noticed, commented on, kept track of. The rent unpaid. The press . . .

The press! They would think he deliberately mortgaged the press, deliberately left town with the money. What if they were trapped now with no way out? Not in ten years a way out. What if it were true?

He looked at the sleeping figures, trying to read from their postures how they stood on the question, as though a vote would make it so, one way or the other. Were they trapped? Did Justin think so? Did Erma? Did Joe? Not Gwendolyn. He knew Gwendolyn did not believe it, and because he knew that she did not, because he took her for a fool and feared her for the disruptive powers she had already manifested, he suddenly did believe it. He accepted it and, with it, the stillborn death of his book and his work and the guilty weight of the money he had borrowed on the press. His elation all gone, he traveled down a swift spiral of despair.

The minute Justin's watch said two o'clock Joe sat up, shook his head and signaled for Arthur to hand him the watch. Arthur stretched himself out beside Erma, trying not to disturb her. If only they were alone so that he could wake her and tell her his load of despair. *The Work, Erma. The book.* In her sleep she stirred and turned her face toward him so that the firelight fell on it. For the first time that he could remember he felt truly estranged from her. She was smiling in her sleep. *What if it were true?* he had said to her in Drury before they started out, and now he could hear her saying it again: *I would be glad.* He closed his eyes. He was alone as he had never been. And suddenly he remembered that he still had Joe's knife which he'd taken to cut the melons. He turned his back on Joe and slipped the knife out of his pocket. In the darkness he opened the blade and felt for the point, and before he went to sleep he made one sharp scratch on his arm where it would be covered by his sleeve. Once, for one day, for the first day of exile.

During Justin's guard duty Gwendolyn woke up. She sat upright and stretched her cold, cramped body. Justin made a sign to her of the others sleeping so that she would not begin to talk. He dreaded the time when Gwendolyn would talk. By the very fact of their being here, there was the making of a struggle. Gwendolyn against the rest of them, or would it be Gwendolyn and Joe against the rest of them? The trouble was that there would come, he knew, because of the struggle, a need for authority, and who was to assume it? How, among friends, can one take authority without seizing it? he thought. For here the ordinary grounds were missing. There was no inequality among them either of their possessions or of their knowledge of the land. In time, he knew, there would come to be inequalities among them. In time they would come to have relative positions to one another. And the amazing thing was (and this was the only thing he knew for certain after sixty years of living) that no one could say in advance, despite the obvious indications of their individualities, no one could really say.

He broke open one of the melons and smiled at Gwendolyn as though to say, You see, I am still alive, and held the melon out to her. She took it from him with a little reluctance and lifted it to her mouth doubtfully, and then ravenously she devoured it. He handed her the other half and she reached for it quickly. Justin put more wood on the fire. He was sorry that Gwendolyn was cold and uncomfortable, sorry she had forced herself to such painful hunger. What a curious thing it was about the girl, he thought, the way her thoughts and her actions were opposed to one another. He wondered if Joe, too, were torn between antagonism toward her and a desire to comfort her, the way that he was.

In the way she had suddenly abandoned herself to crying last night, in the way that she had eaten so greedily just now and then fallen instantly asleep, there was a quality of such childlike defenselessness, so directly appealing, that it was hard to believe she had only to utter the simplest sentence to fill him with anger. He wished that the others could find it in their youth to soften the morrow for her, but he doubted it. They were too direct, themselves, and too young. He was afraid they were going to force an admission of their fate from her, an acceptance of their condition, in the way that he had watched each of the others accept it for himself. They were direct people and they were young and he was afraid that that would be their way.

He was the one who ought to do it. He was the one who knew the great efficacy of the long, winding road of gradually diminishing hope. For had he not in his time been led down it by experts, by the finest doctors in the land? *I cannot say your wife's case is hopeless, Mr. Magnus. We must always allow ourselves to believe, in cases of this kind, that the unexpected can happen. No one can say, my dear Magnus, how long. The best I can give you is an opinion. Certainly, we must go on hoping. Certainly.*

Reason would not bring acceptance to Gwendolyn, he knew, the way that it would, he thought, to Joe. Nor a *fait accompli*, as it would to Erma. Nothing would bring acceptance to Gwendolyn but the weight of the days, another and another and another. He was sorrier than ever, now, that she was cold. Tomorrow, she must have a shelter, a warm place, and, as an antidote for the forthrightness and bluntness of the others, gentleness, gentleness.

During Joe's second duty it began to get light. All around him things began to take shape and project out of the darkness. Slowly the greenness flooded into them. A dawn such as he had never seen, strange and eerie, with no visible sun on the horizon, insinuated itself. It was as though the vegetation gave off its own light. And yet it was dawn, real enough and familiar enough in its feeling so that Joe found himself waiting for the sound of a solitary truck. Instead, he heard a bird call and, a second later, heard another answer it, but though they sounded very close he could not see anything. He turned his back on the fire and saw below him and far to his left the solemn, silent procession of the feathermanes going down to drink at the river.

Everything will have a name in time, Joe thought. It's only a little while that I can sit like this in the Green Kingdom. After a while it won't be a whole; it will be this particular place and other particular places. He turned toward the fire and the circle of sleeping bodies. Gwen's face was dirty and her clothes were rumpled. He had never seen her face dirty. Even on the desert when she was sick she was still somehow flawless. Now she was real, at last. Now she was his. I have a wife, he thought. It's different now.

He was to have Gwen now, the way he had always wanted her, without the competition of her sisters and her job at the office, but not because he had left Arthur Herrick to sink alone with the print shop, not because he had gone away and got a job in the city. It was not because of anything that he had done, but because of the place where they were.

He knew how Arthur and Erma felt about Gwen, and now he was ashamed that he had never protested it. In their minds, he knew, there were the three of them, and then, outside, there was Gwen. Even Magnus had somehow fitted right into it, too. There were the four of them, and then, yes, outside, there was Gwen. He and Arthur and Erma had so long been close to one another that it was almost as though he and Arthur had both married Erma. If Erma and Arthur thought of Gwen as something isolated, some attribute of his like an odd hat that he put on and took off, he could see that it was his own fault. Because they were wrong. If they turned him loose right now with the whole world to choose from, he'd come up with another one just like Gwen. Gwen was no fluke, no mistake. It wasn't Gwen they didn't have in focus; it was him.

He couldn't imagine making love to Erma Herrick even though he knew there was no one like her in the world. He couldn't even imagine Arthur's making love to her. It would be like taking a special ladder and wearing special equipment to pick apples and then having them all fall square into the basket of their own will. There wouldn't be any fucking in it—that was the thing. There wouldn't be any triumph. It took a big guy to take a gift, and maybe Arthur was that big a guy—he didn't know. *He* wasn't though. He was a limited guy. Funny it didn't make him sad, taking his own measure like that, but it didn't. He even felt good about it, relieved. Now he knew. He knew quite a lot of things, all of a sudden. All he had needed to get his head cleared was to have Gwen be mussed up and helpless.

He knew what to do, too, but he couldn't do it with an

audience, not even now. He'd taken his own measure and he knew his place and there was no sense in turning right around and substituting Arthur and Erma and Justin for Gwen's sisters and Gwen's office and his poverty. He couldn't fight them all. He could fight Gwen, all right, if they were alone, or at least he thought he could. And the way to do it was to let her try to get out, let her keep right on trying to get out and stick with her till she gave up.

And how was he going to get this through Arthur's head? How was he going to say to Arthur: Listen, for the first time since we've been together I can't help you. I can't help you build a shelter, I can't help you gather wood, I can't help you figure things out. I have to take care of my wife. Listen, Arthur, it's all different now.

In the end he did what he always did. He tapped Erma on the shoulder and when she opened her eyes he motioned for her to follow him down to the river.

"Listen, Erma," he said, "you've got to help me make Arthur understand."

CHAPTER TWO

THE days were really short, they had agreed on that. It was not just that they seemed short because there was so much to be done. They were so startlingly short that they knew now the Kingdom must be shaped like a bowl or a vase, wide at the bottom and narrowing at the top, for the morning light would appear suddenly only on one side of the Kingdom. Since this was above the base camp, they knew themselves to be on the west side of the Kingdom. Their desperate dependence on the light made the terms *morning, noon, afternoon* meaningless, and very shortly they came to refer only to *west-sun, deep-sun, east-sun* in their talk with one another. For the light meant everything at this early time, and their lives were a constant race with it.

There was a certain place on the bank of the river, below the base house, a level place, all grass-covered, about as big as a table top; and it was here that Erma came to bathe. There was a time during west-sun each morning when this roomlike place was in its brightest light for a short while, and Erma had learned to time it exactly so that she could have her bath in the warmth. Always as she crawled out of the water and lay in the grass getting dry she could feel the sun going away, and she longed for the time when she and Arthur might follow the light in a straight path, down, down, down and, she supposed, up again. The river would have to be bridged and, as with most things she waited for, Joe and Gwen would have to come back. She envied them, when the sun path or any far thing beckoned, that they did not have to keep the base camp going, that they did not have to wait at the lookout stations for the signal fires, that they could sleep in a different place every night and in the same bed together, without Justin Magnus in the room.

She washed out her underwear and hung it on a tree from which she took the slip that she had washed yesterday. As she pulled it over her head she found herself wondering what Joe looked like with a beard. When she laughed out loud there was a frightened rustling in the bush near her and she saw a small green bird fly crazily away. She stopped laughing and lay back on the grass to close her eyes and steal a moment's rest. The time was always stolen, it seemed to her, even if one stopped for a second. There was so much to be done—the smallest thing took ages to ac- complish and nothing was the way she had thought it would be. Nothing. Yet it was not the Green Kingdom that was different; it was herself in it and the others, too. It seemed to Erma that there was something incongruous and ineffectual about everything that she did and thought, like the way that in this magnificent place she dreamed every night of saucepans, rows and rows of them. Sometimes they were on a shelf and sometimes they were hanging against the wall by their handles. They were all sizes and shapes. God, how she needed a pan, a bucket, a skillet, a jug, a bowl— anything that would hold something. Near the base camp there was the huge plant with the thick heart-shaped leaves full of dew every morning, so that all you had to do was tip the point of a leaf for a spout. Yet for want of a bucket to store the water in they saw it evaporate and by night had to go to the river to drink.

When they had lamps, then it would be better. It was hard to work with only the firelight at night. When they had light. When they had warm clothing. When they had enough covers. When they had a portable firebox perfected so that they need not remember every moment that they had given Joe all the matches and that the fire must never be allowed to go out. When they could get Justin's house finished so that she and Arthur could be alone. When Joe and Gwen came back so there would be more hands to work. It was an endless list. There was nothing that they could do that did not necessitate doing something else first, and this gave them a sense of hurried frustration all the time.

She could not lie here any longer with all the things that had to be done, so she got up quietly in case the bird had returned. She put her hand up to her head, as though to ease the feeling of tightness, because it was always now as though she wanted to cry and couldn't. For it was not really the lack of a saucepan, the lack of enough covers, the lack of enough light.

It was Arthur. And the terrible depression that hung over him because of the work lost and the money borrowed on the big press, and his anger at Joe's desertion. There was no way for

him to ease himself of it because the whole day must be spent
in work that they might live through the night with a little more
comfort: the wood to be gathered tediously, laboriously, with
only the aid of one knife, the walls of the shelter to be strengthened, the animals to be hunted and trapped and stolen upon,
without weapons, without a gun, while the precious hours slipped
away. And he could not bring himself to talk before Justin, to
complain of what was hopeless.

Justin knew, though. Erma knew that he did. But another
house meant twice as much firewood to be gathered, and the
building of it meant time stolen from the trapping for food. And,
though they had not discussed it among themselves, another
house meant too much permanency, for they all felt (or did Justin? she wondered) a sense of temporary waiting until Joe and
Gwen returned, as though having stayed away this long (it was
two weeks now) they would surely come back with some news
that would change things. And yet how could they? At least when
they did come back she was sure that they would all move. They
would be free to leave the base camp then and explore the land,
and surely if they were nomads it would be more the way she had
thought it would be.

But it wouldn't. Arthur would be the same. His work was
lost in Drury the same, if they lived at the base camp or if they
roamed the land and found a new place. It would be the same
even if they could be alone and not have Justin in the room with
them. But no, it would not. It would *not* be the same if only she
could hold him close in her arms. If only she had all of his body,
freely, without self-consciousness. Then she could help him.
Surely she could help him, or what was it for, this longing? What
was it for to be married, to love a man, if it didn't help any?
What was the good of it?

Now she lay on her belly and leaned over the river to drink,
and as she put her hands down to cup up the water she could see
the reflection of her own face broken up so that for a second it
was as though there were many faces there, all like hers. She let
the water fall through her fingers and she did not drink but rolled
over slowly on her back and shifted her position slowly so that
her head would have support. She closed her eyes and let the
deep, sweet languor flow through her. Now it could be. Yes.

She smiled and opened her eyes and looked up at the lush

greenness all about her. The knowledge had been here all the time and only now had she found it. Wasn't it strange that she hadn't known immediately about the children? For the old reasons, the old barriers, the old frustrations were all gone because their poverty was gone. They could be rich with a child. And richer and richer. She stood up slowly and began to climb toward the base camp. Nothing hurried her, nothing drove her. She needed the time to look well at the land where her children would play and laugh and run over the feather grass.

Whatever it was that had to be done, why, they would get it done. Whatever was needed, of course they would find it, have it, make it, take it. She felt this slow sweetness, this competence, this great size and weight of herself so upon her that it seemed to her that Arthur must know the minute he saw her. But if he did not, she would keep it. She would wait until they lived alone. Or perhaps he too had thought of it. It would keep, though. There was plenty of time now. They lived here in this land. This was their home.

It was all so different, so easy and so right, that she did not even hurry or question when she saw the big green turtle coming toward her. She kicked once with her foot and turned him over on his back, and then she pulled her dress off over her head and wrapped him up tight in it. Keeping him upside down, she tied a knot in the dress and slung it over her shoulder, for his shell would make her a pan, and she knew when she got back to the camp there would be a way to cut it free and punch a hole in one side to anchor a handle by *because it was needful* that it should be done.

It was as though all her life before this moment she had been walking six inches above the ground. She shifted the burden on her shoulder and paused to taste her place in space and time. The first thing she noticed was that nothing seemed wasted now. The bungling and the fumbling, the waiting and the failures and the small experiments that had been her childhood and her youth, they led somewhere. They led right up to here, or down to here, whichever it was (does one ascend or spiral down to reality? she thought).

"The road is straighter than you think when you are traveling it," she said aloud to the rich and wonderful greenness around her, "and nothing is really wasted." And though she had never admitted before that she thought he had been wasted, she said now in a jubilant and triumphant discovery, "Nor was my father wasted."

Not her father or his inarticulateness, even. Not the pianos he tuned or the night that he stood by her on the little hillock watching their house burn down. Not the house, either. It was as though Life sent you a notice to be awake on a certain day and you went to a place like a railway express office. There was a man there who lifted up the grilled window and slid toward you a big box, a box of the days and the nights you had lived, with all their secrets and their actions and their failures to act. And you said, "Yes, it belongs to me. I'll sign for it. All right." And behind that box was another, smaller and farther away. It was your father's. And you said, "I'll sign for that one, too."

Climbing up to the base camp, she felt taller than she had ever felt, and heavier. Yet it was no sudden mood, she knew; it was here to stay. She had a hold on things. It was amazing what a difference it made in every way, how it brought the base camp into focus, for example. She replenished the small fire automatically and inspected the clay fireboxes which were drying. She saw immediately what the trouble was with the coverlets she had tried to weave to supplement the few hides they had. The fibers were too thick. No real warmth would ever come from fibers like that. *It was needful* that there should be smaller, more resilient fibers, and so she would find them. Even the heavy ones she had used because they were close and plentiful, even these would be improved by soaking, perhaps by beating. They should be separated. The need was not for twigs, nor vines, but for cloth. She untied the turtle, keeping him on his back until the men should return with the knife (what was Joe doing without a knife?), and, as she put on her dress, she knew it was high time that she had begun to think and think in focus about cloth, for the dress had many torn places in it and the men's clothes, too, were torn now and dirty.

And the child . . . Blankets would be needed, and diapers. Erma sat down on one of the pallets and put her hand on her breast. She bent her head over and her fingers pressed hard on her breast. Arthur did not know yet. How strange that seemed. Arthur was still floating around six inches off the ground and she had it in her power to shove the ground up under his feet—or was it to push his feet down to the ground? She wanted it to be soon now because, not knowing, he seemed far away from her. He seemed . . . not her size.

Later, standing at her lookout station, watching for the signal fire from Joe and Gwen, she had a great feeling of tenderness for Gwen, such as she had never known before, simply because Gwen, too, was a woman. Gwen, too, might know the things she felt. Would they have children together? Would their children play together in this rich and wonderful land? Then she saw the smoke and she called to the others and climbed down from the tree where she had been watching.

There was always, each night, a crescendo of anxiety built up in them as they climbed their trees and took up the watch for the signal fire that meant Joe and Gwen were still alive, still within some range. Privately, Justin called it the shrew fire, and each night he wondered if Gwen were tamed yet and if it had occurred to Joe to plant in the girl's mind the hope of rescue from the outside, the way that he himself would have done. It seemed to Justin that the fire was closer tonight, but he must compare notes with the others on this. They always had a little time of gaiety after they'd seen the fire, a shared feeling of release.

Now Arthur and Erma went down to the tree to mark this day on the calendar carved there. Arthur had used the skin of his arm only once; the second day he had peeled the bark from a square space on a tree and had started a calendar. He was glad of Erma's presence there every night, not only because it might be their only time alone together but because, since his first panic over the confusion of the days, he felt the need of a witness. If the panic should come again he could ask of Erma, "Did I mark today?" and she could answer, "Yes." It was only in the evening now that they went. They did not count the day until it was over.

Arthur took out the knife and made the mark for the fifteenth day that they had spent there. Each night they walked back together to the camp and Erma would begin the preparation of whatever animals they had killed and what fruits or vegetables she had found. Then she would build up a big fire while the men went down to the river to bathe, for as they came back the white mists of the night would already have begun to spout up in the distance and the coldness would have crept upon the camp. But this night she lingered by the calendar tree. It was only six inches now, whether she pressed his feet down or pressed the earth up.

She smiled up at Arthur. "Can't you put a star there?" she said. "Can't you make this day special?"

Well, there it was for him again, the need of the Record, the lost work in Drury, but he knew she had no cruelty in her, and if she reminded him of the lost work it was for some reason of her own.

"A star?" he said. "Sure. Was it—is it—a special day?"

"Oh, yes," she said. (And, after all, it was quite easy.) "To-day I thought of the children, of how there is no reason any longer why we cannot have children. I was leaning over the river to get a drink and . . ." She leaned against him, relaxed and pleasantly tired. "Oh, Arthur," she said, "it is all so easy now. As though I had been hurrying always and now I have plenty of time."

If she kept her eyes closed, he thought, it would give him time to catch up, or if he kept his mouth shut, maybe he could travel in silence over the first blunders. For he had not known that she still wanted children. Christ, had he failed her too, along with the bank and all the people he'd sent the book to? He had not thought of children (why children? he wondered. One thinks of a child. One child at a time) since the early years of their marriage and then it was with dread that they might have a child and not be able to feed it, with dread that he would have to give up his work for the child's sake. But Erma? Had she wanted a child all this time? Had she accused him that she did not have one? Why had she kept it secret?

"Wouldn't you be afraid?" he said. "If we can't get out of here? There's no hospital. There's no doctor."

Still leaning against him, Erma opened her eyes and looked out over the Green Kingdom. She could see the first white mists already beginning in the last of the east-sun light. There is no poverty here, either, she started to say. But that was not what he had asked.

"Oh, yes," she said, "I expect I will be afraid. But it doesn't keep you from having them, you know, being afraid doesn't. It doesn't concern the baby. The baby comes just the same if you are afraid or not."

He held her very close to him, so close he could feel her heart beating. "I don't understand it," he said.

It always stopped him, the way she spoke of fear as though it were similar to measles. He wouldn't be surprised to find that she thought of fear as a warm thing, even. He had to keep telling himself. She did not know the cold-sweat fact of fear. And maybe that was what kept her always young and malleable and potential.

"You know," she said, "I must find something to make good cloth out of right away. Something with a smaller fiber. And soap—what do they make soap out of? Grease and what?"

"Lye, I think," he said. "I mean they used to."

"And paper," she said, "for your work, and ink."

"Paper?" he said.

"Naturally," she said. "Do you think I want to lose a single day of this child or get it mixed up or let time make it different than it was?"

*

Now, Justin thought, now that at last he had a place of his own, surely his insomnia would be better. When or if Joe and Gwendolyn returned was no longer of any importance to him. Nothing mattered to him but sleep. Every day he worked harder than he had worked in many years. Exhausted, he and Arthur would return to the base camp. Somehow he would manage to pull himself up to his lookout station. After they had seen the signal fire they would bathe and eat, and then, once on his bed, his mind would come maddeningly awake. If only he could smoke! If only he dared swear or roll or toss or walk the floor! And finally, if it were for one night or twenty, if Arthur had to hunt without his help, he did not care. He had to be alone, and he built himself a small shelter in a desperate frenzy and gathered a little firewood, though he would not need much. Either they had grown accustomed to the climate or else the weather was actually milder, but really he no longer cared if he froze to death, just so he could sleep.

It was not having any tobacco. He had had insomnia before, but always he had reached for his pipe or got up to sit in a chair by a window and smoke. And he had slept alone too long. He simply couldn't sleep with other people in the room—that was all there was to it. That, and having no tobacco.

"I'm set in my ways, I guess," he said to them. "I've been alone so long. I can't seem to sleep when there are other people in the room."

He had thought somehow that it was going to be awkward,

pulling out, going off by himself, but they had been almost too eager to help him, pressing the warmest animal skins on him, making him a softer, thicker grass bed.

Well, naturally, they wanted to be by themselves, he thought. If only his brain were not so drugged from the prolonged insomnia, he would have realized that long ago. Curious how out of place that made him feel. It was nice of them, though, to have concealed it so well.

He placed his bed where he could see the fire, lay down on his back, felt his tired muscles snap and jerk into settling down, and closed his eyes. Well, of course they wanted to be alone. Naturally. All this time they had not slept together that he knew of. Well, let them. Let them. Sleep, sleep, there was no luxury like the consciousness of oncoming sleep, to feel oneself sinking down.

His eyelids began to twitch as though tiny fingers were beating a tattoo on them, and in his ears he could hear a constant high note—G sharp, it was. When he paid attention to it, it was no longer constant, but came and receded in rhythm: yes sir, yes sir, yes sir. It was like the locusts in the summertime at his grandmother's. People called them locusts then but they were really cicadas. Cicada, cicada, cicada. That was much closer to it than yes sir, yes sir. Cicada, cicada, cicada. It was the fire, probably, that kept him awake. He wished he had not built one at all.

If only he had some tobacco, he could smoke until the fire died down. To smoke. The hunger for tobacco went all through him, the terrible longing and need for it. If only he could smoke and then go to sleep in absolute blackness without the firelight. Once he had met a man on a train who told him that he could sleep only in an absolutely black room. The tiniest pinpoint of light kept him awake, he said. When he traveled the man used to carry black cloth with him to put over the edges of window shades. Justin had laughed at him.

Someone (Who was it? He could not recall the face. Some man sitting in the big chair to the right of the fireplace), someone once said to Edith when she spoke of insomnia, "Oh, sure, I have it, too. But it doesn't bother me. I just turn on the light and read awhile."

And Edith had laughed, a quick, contemptuous laugh. "If it doesn't bother you," she had said, "it isn't insomnia."

Well, he understood what she meant now. If there'd been a

whole library here and a good electric light, he couldn't have read a book.

If you count, they say. One, two, three, four, one, two, three, four. One, two, three, four. But no, it's better to count toward some number continuously, perhaps. In the cartoons the sheep were always labeled in the thousands. One, two, three, four. Cicada, cicada, cicada, cicada. Maybe there was something wrong with his heart. He had never thought of it before. Never thought of dying gradually, ailing. Strange, the effect of the firelight. As it changed, it made the ceiling look as though it were falling. It might fall. If there were a wind it might blow the whole thing over into the fire.

He'd lost count already. No wonder it didn't work for him. He couldn't keep at it. One, two, three, four, five, six, seven, eight, cicada, cicada, cicada. Sometimes Edith used to sleep with her legs thrown over him.

There was not a chance. Not a *chance* of their being any tobacco in his pockets. He'd been through all that. The skin on the back of his left leg itched. He was sleeping in his clothes for warmth, and he could not get to the spot to scratch it. That was probably half the trouble, sleeping in their clothes the way they did. (But were *they*, tonight?) Well, he had lost track again. Eight, nine, ten, eleven, twelve, thirteen, fourteen.

Let them. So let them. Naturally a third person (not third; fifth, it was). Joe had been right. Take her away. One and one. One and one. Fifth was fifth. Now the skin on his abdomen was burning. Well, there was nothing else for it. He'd have to get up and take off his clothes, even if he froze to death. And certainly, who cared? Surely the dead did not suffer insomnia. But he would have to get up to take off his clothes. How could he fail to go to sleep when he was this tired? How long can a man stay awake? Surely there is a limit.

It took him a long time to get his clothes off and when he did he was cold. He went over and squatted down by the fire. It was a devil's game to make you so drowsy the minute you were upright and so wide awake as soon as you lay down. He turned his head quickly. Nothing. There was nothing. It was terrible, this feeling of portending disaster he had, as though the roof would fall in, as though his heart would stop beating, as though a woman were going to scream. If he didn't sleep soon he would lose his mind.

The feeling of danger hung over him so that he wanted to be outside his shelter. He wanted to look around. He could not see out because of the firelight. He came back and threw dust on the fire to smother it. He did not want the fire, anyway; maybe it was the fire that kept him awake.

He stood in the doorway trying to accustom his eyes to the dark. Then he saw it. He had been right: there was something happening. Off to the right there was a light, a glowing. Not right for fire. Surely it couldn't be fire. He began to run toward the light, fear in him, panic in him. Was there some kind of fire here they didn't know about? A volcano that glowed palely before it began to erupt? He ran on and on and the glow seemed to recede from him, dance and elude him. At last, he reached it and fell on his knees with exhaustion and relief and wonder.

Before him stretched a field of phosphorescent flowers. Each blossom stood about two feet high, was solitary on its stalk. The huge petals, flat and pale green, were together about the size of a large plate. In the center of each flower stood a solitary, glowing pistil. The whole field seemed to be shimmering, full of movement. Justin closed his eyes and sank back on his heels to get his breath. The relief of knowing that it was neither fire nor volcano was in itself exhausting. When he opened his eyes he could see that there was really movement of some kind among the flowers and he fastened his eyes on a single one, trying to catch it. Lying horizontally around the vertical pistil were the shimmery, phosphorescent stamens, and, one at a time, rotating in order about the circle like ballet dancers, they rose up and touched the pistil and let fall a constant shower of bright-green pollen. It was like watching luminescent spirals, for the motion was flawless, without hesitation.

Suddenly Justin sprang back and stood behind a tree, for he had heard footsteps and remembered his nakedness. His fingernails bit into the bark of the shielding tree, and he held his breath and leaned against the tree while he watched Erma Herrick come alone and out of breath, naked and running as he had run, kneeling in wonder as he had knelt, and catching her breath sharply at the glowing wonder of the fertilizing spirals ascending and descending in the green, showering pollen.

She stood and waded straight into the flowers, into the heart of them. She had her back to him and now he could go. He took his hands down from the tree but he did not move. He saw Erma break off three of the huge flowers (the snapping of the stems made a crackling noise in the silence) and knot the stems together around her waist, and then she held her hands in the showering pollen and he heard her laugh, a way he had never heard her laugh. Low, sweet, and secret. Naked, she seemed much taller. He had not known she was so tall. She rubbed the pollen on her breasts in circular movements and then she began to dance around and around in a circle, heedless of the flowers, brushing them, shaking the pollen into the air (the pollen on her breasts was still phosphorescent), and then suddenly she stopped and ran back through the flowers, right past him. He could see the glow of the flower girdle she wore dancing ahead of him, like a firefly.

The weakness all through him was shameful. His body was bathed in sweat. He had to start walking back, back to his shelter. He must not lie down here. He must not be found here. He was shivering with the cold and he had to make it to his shelter somehow.

So this was the end? So this was the triumph of a long life? A man worked hard and long and honestly for sixty years. He saw his wife go insane, he lost his four sons—for what? So that at the end of it all he might be a peeping Tom, spying on a young girl dancing naked in a field of flowers. This was Justin Magnus. Would he never make it back to the shelter? Never? And there was no fire. He had put out the fire.

He stumbled into his own shack and knelt down by the fire pit, trying to feel a little warmth from the embers. As tired as he was he tugged and pushed at the bed to move it from its place. He had never liked the way that their beds were always out in the center of the room, like the blades of a fan, around the fire. He liked a bed to be by a wall. He put on his clothes for warmth and fell on his bed. In his terrible tiredness he tried ineffectually to cover himself with the mat and the animal skins, and then he turned his face to the wall and closed his eyes, pushing into his eyeballs the most terrible loneliness he had ever known. So this was Justin Magnus, the great Justin Magnus, alone and cold and without tobacco. *So let them, let them, let them, then.*

Oh, certainly, certainly and by all means, oh, certainly let them enjoy each other, let them cling close to each other and thrust themselves toward each other. Let them lie naked and together in the secret nearness of their youth. Let them rest, then,

too. And yes, yes, let them sleep easily and innocently and without history and not wake alone in the night. His clenched fists began to uncurl and the warmth of his body was spreading to the
bed, and out of the man there came a tremendous sigh.

What was *he* doing here? That was the question. He had
come—oh, yes, now it could be remembered from long ago—he
had come to explore the Green Kingdom. And, in the name of
Christ, *why?* For what does the vegetation matter to the lonely?

He rolled over on his back and lay there with his eyes open.
Max Staats would never have made a mistake like this. Max
Staats was a smart man. A lonely man, but a man who knew what
to do with loneliness. Loneliness belongs in a lonely place. Let it
be contrasted with an empty house. Let it be contrasted with an
ocean.

"Why don't you stay with me, Justin?" he had said. Max
had his loneliness in a lonely house, properly. And Max had his
work. Well, had not he his? What of his own work? Had he no
work any more? What *was* it that came after discovery?

Suddenly he slept, deeply, heavily, as he had longed to sleep
for so many terrible nights, and very early, during the first of
west-sun, he awoke rested, with calmness on him. He walked out
of his shelter and washed his face under the spout of a dewplant
leaf, and he climbed up where the path of west-sun was and stood
in the warmth. He stood there, smiling and getting warm, and it
was already there with him before he knew it was coming, the beginning of the second movement of the symphony. It was there
with him in the early-morning west-sun quiet, the same as if he
had always been confident it would come, the same as if he had
never feared its death.

Now he knew what came after "Discovery." It was this, that
he was hearing now. This. A quiet and a restful thing, and not his
own. Loneliness and insomnia and discomfort may have been *his*
sequel to discovery. Not this. This was Erma Herrick's sequel to
discovery. The young may discover a place, but they find there a
time. A new time, new and innocent, without history, like the
length of a child's summer day, his own to mark.

Justin tasted the sound of Erma Herrick's new time that he
had with him now, and in his eyes he felt the smarting of the tears
of thanksgiving to be at work again. The years and the knowing
fell away from him, and it was no longer shameful that he had
watched her dancing in the phosphorescent flowers. The theme

he had with him and already a promise of what came after it. Rest it was. That which comes after discovery: to rest without possessing the knowledge of tiredness, to rest without knowing it, to taste a different time, a time that has no history yet.

In their own new time Erma and Arthur awoke to each other and, seeing the deep green stains around her body, Arthur said in fear, "What is the matter? What happened?"

"Where?" she said. "Oh, the conception flowers. Oh, Arthur, you were asleep. There was a whole field of them and . . ."

She told him of the phosphorescent flowers and of how she had named them, but he kept his eyes on the stains where the stems of the flower girdle had pressed against her skin, and he frowned and reached out his hand to touch them cautiously.

"What is it, Arthur?" she said, for he was not listening to her. "I'm not hurt."

He looked from the stains to her face and he smiled at her. "I was thinking," he said.

And from having lived with him so long, she knew that he was thinking of something he knew to be irrelevant to the conception flowers and of her naming them. But in the joyousness of this morning she put her disappointment carefully aside, reminding herself that Arthur had not, after all, been with her, had not seen the wonder of the flowers, had not danced among them.

"I know what you're thinking," she said, and she was glad now, for it meant that he had made a gesture of belonging here, of living for even the time of a thought some place besides the print shop in Drury. "You're thinking it will make ink," she said.

CHAPTER THREE

FROM THE RECORD OF ARTHUR HERRICK, THE THIRD DAY OF THE SECOND MONTH OF THE FIRST YEAR:

This is the first paper, made from the inner bark of the paper tree, written on with a quill and the first ink from the stems of the conception flowers. The paper is too heavy as yet to be practical and we do not even know if the ink is permanent, but still it is to be at work again. Not in the way nor on the scale that I had hoped for, but still, work, and our own.

Erma is already miles and years ahead of me on the work. She has peopled the Green Kingdom with our children already, trained for the work of the Records from the very beginning. She has Joe and Gwendolyn having children too, and, in ten years, when the opening is made again, she says that one adult couple could go into the world and bring back new people for the work. The failure in Drury is still too new for me so that I cannot allow myself to jump into the great dream so soon. In moments of depression I think Erma could live just as well without it and has only taken it up to give me heart. Yet it is fine to hear her speak of it so confidently and so often now that we are alone, Justin having made his own house.

It seemed to us all last night that the signal fire was much closer. Surely Joe and Gwen must be coming back soon. It will be good to have Joe back, now that the work is started. I've got to talk to him about the work. He has always been with me since the work began. He has always believed in it. I suppose I took it for granted that he always would. Now, in this different place, I don't know for sure. He might say no. What would I do if he did? Would Erma and Justin be enough? I'm not even sure of Justin.

ERMA HERRICK'S RECORD, THE TENTH DAY OF THE SECOND MONTH OF THE FIRST YEAR:

Joe and Gwen got home last night with a thousand new wonderful things. There never was anyone like Joe. He's got something to use for tobacco and he says he's found something we can make beer of. You'd think he had lived here all his life to see him sitting by the fire smoking his little mud pipe. In comparison, we are certainly slow and unadjusted. I think how Arthur and I worried because we had Joe's knife, and here he comes back with a whole set of tools made of animal bones and parts of fish skeletons. Why, even their clothes are marvelous. They both have beautiful soft *tailored* suits of animal skins and the seams have been *sewn.* Gwen looked so beautiful and so smart in hers. I am ashamed of our old rags. Joe has made bone needles for her and, by soaking the edges of the leather and sewing them together with a fine strip of the same material, she's made perfect, tight seams.

The wonders they tell of: hot springs to bathe in (this is what makes the white mists at night. Funny we didn't figure it out), and eggs of a large green bird, good to eat. Joe even shaves. He has the sharpest knives I ever saw. They carry a portable tent with them, made from the skins of an animal they call the mossback, with the fleece side outside, and they've got a better soap than ours that I made so laboriously by treating animal fat with wood ashes. Theirs comes from the root of a plant. Joe found it by accident when he was trying out everything systematically to smoke. During this process, besides finding the soap, he said he got himself sick, drugged, and poisoned.

The only things we had to show with much pride were the portable fireboxes which are really quite efficient. The clay hasn't cracked yet on the new ones and we seem at last to have figured out the right size for the vent holes. But when you come to think of it, these we made out of fear because the thought of being without fire in this damp place is so awful. Joe's things are different. He goes at it from—from pleasure.

We talked until all hours last night, but for me the most wonderful part was just as we were saying good night. "Well, Erma," Joe said, smiling that way he has, "when did it happen for you? What day?"

"When did what happen?" I said.

"Why, when did you first realize that we aren't poor any more?"

"Oh, on the fifteenth day," I said. "We made a mark on the calendar, a star for it. I can show you."

"That's about right," he said. "It was the greatest thing ever happened to me. I was trying to outrun a mossback. Didn't have any good tools then, no weapons. I got so I could outrun the bastards and wrestle them until I got them down, and then I'd hit 'em on the head with a rock. Well, this was the first one I ever killed, and I was sitting down on him, breathing hard, and all of a sudden it came to me: Christ, I'm not poor any more."

It was strange I couldn't tell Joe how it came to me, not that we weren't poor but that we were rich because we could have children. I don't know just why I couldn't tell him. I didn't tell Gwen, either, but then we weren't really alone long enough.

Gwen and Arthur had a row about the calendar. Gwen kept one, too, and she says that ours is a day ahead. At the end of the argument, Gwen suddenly said, "Oh, what difference does it make? They'll surely be here soon and then we'll *know*."

It was a shock to find that she is still hoping someone will rescue us from the outside. The clothes and all their discoveries had me fooled. I thought she was so much better reconciled to living here than we were, but I guess these are all Joe's things. Still, though, she made the clothes, but maybe it was only to look attractive for her rescuers. I started to say something to her, but I caught Joe's eye just in time and he gave me, I think, a signal. Apparently he's encouraged her to hope for deliverance. Maybe he knows best. It seems wrong to me.

Justin was so pleased to have a smoke. I looked over at him when we were all sitting around the fire and suddenly I noticed that his head does not shake any more. The tremor is gone. Now that I think of it, it seems to me it has been gone for some time, maybe ever since he started to work again on the symphony.

JUSTIN MAGNUS' RECORD, THE FIRST DAY OF THE THIRD MONTH OF THE FIRST YEAR:

This is my first try at Record keeping. Joe and Arthur have so far improved the paper that there is a sufficient supply to allow meandering. When it was scarce I found the idea quite impossible. Besides, by common consent, I was allowed a special dispensation while I was working on the symphony. But now I have come to a temporary stopping place in my own work and so I, too, will try my hand at the Records. For one thing, I believe it is necessary for Arthur Herrick that we all do it. He was accustomed, apparently, in their old life, to being the leader. Yet he has never had this position by assertion but by virtue of the love that Erma and Joe have for him. I don't think he realizes the difference. He should not, this early, be forced into asserting authority, I think, for if he made the gesture and failed in it something disastrous would happen to him. The time is soon coming when Gwendolyn will rebel against Arthur and against Arthur's work and I do not care to be the one to give weight to her argument. Therefore, I conform. Why Gwendolyn does, I have no idea. I was much surprised to see her joining in. What trump Joe is holding, to take the place of her hope of rescue when it is finally worn out, I can only guess. I dare say he will be able to handle it, as so far he has managed everything else.

Joe is, to me, a source of wonder and great personal satisfaction, for to me it seems as though he knew the score of the second movement and followed it exactly. I feel almost as though I had written all his thoughts for him because he, even better than Erma, for whom I had originally intended it, exemplifies the "Time of Innocence." There is no way, in imagination, that I could possibly improve on Joe. He has even a new stride and a new stance here, not at all that of a conquerer, but that of a true discoverer who has come, by some self-drowning or submitting process, truly to belong. To see him take hold of any physical problem that befronts us is a moving experience. His own quiet joy is the most noticeable thing about him. Everything that he does and says is like his tools, the function dictated to the need exactly. Of course to me he would be wonderful in any case, for he brought back what passes with us for tobacco.

The more that I watch Joe, the more (though this is heresy to the work that should unite us) I cannot help but wish that Arthur Herrick could be more like him, could be content just to live, to be submerged and molded by the land. Yet, how can *I* wish that Arthur Herrick could change his work? How can *I* believe he would be better off? I would not change my own work according to geography. Nor would I give it up, had I a choice. Why do ease and the lack of struggle seem desirable for someone else?

GWENDOLYN ROBERTS' RECORD, THE FIFTEENTH DAY OF THE THIRD MONTH OF THE FIRST YEAR:

Yaw yaw yaw yaw yaw. It's easier to pretend to do it than to make a fuss. They don't know what you write and if they do I don't care. The quick brown fox jumped over the lazy dog. The quick brown fox jumped over the lazy dog. Now is the time for every man to come to the aid of his party. Now is the time. Now is the time. Now *is* the time. Oh, why don't they come? Why don't they come for me? Gwendolyn. Gwendolyn Roberts. Gwen Roberts. Main Street, Market Street, Poplar, Topeka, Baltimore, Laurel and Reece. Main

Street, Market Street, Poplar, Topeka. Oh, nuts. a b c d e f g h i j
k l m n o p q r s t u v w x y z.

ERMA'S RECORD, TWENTY-THIRD DAY, THIRD MONTH, FIRST
YEAR:

I was so sure I was pregnant. How could I have been fooled like
that? Why, I even imagined that I had morning sickness and I was
delighted. I suppose that should have told me, that if I could be
delighted it wasn't real. I *felt* pregnant. How can one's instincts be so
far off the mark? I told Arthur that I knew I was pregnant, that I
was sure, and, though he is still apprehensive about the lack of
medical care, still we were very close to each other, very happy. Now
I feel as though I had done something fraudulent. I told Gwen, too,
like a fool. She was so terrible about it. Oh, it is all ghastly and a
bitter disappointment. Everything has somehow combined to make
the loveliest days of my life ridiculous, and that is hard to accept.
I wish I had not told Gwen before I was absolutely sure. "You mean
to tell me," she said, "that you've got the curse and you're not *glad?*"

It has always set my teeth on edge the way Gwen calls it the
curse. Maybe it is only a word that she uses unthinkingly, and it
could as well have been another, but how can it be an unthinking
matter?

I want a child so much. I cannot think of anything else. Surely
by next time. Surely. Maybe it is, as Arthur said to console me, just
as well that it doesn't happen until we have moved and are settled
in the new place, for at first there will be a lot of hard work to do
and then things will be so much easier. Joe says we are to have a hot
spring right inside the house. Such luxury. I made the mistake of
speaking of this to Gwen, and she said she thought it was ridiculous
to go to all that trouble for such a short while. She has not budged
a bit from her hope of rescue. She is really not living here at all,
merely waiting. I wish I could ask Joe what his plan is, but somehow
it seems wrong in this place to talk about Gwen behind her back. Oh,
I wish, for all the years ahead, that it could have been a woman I
could love with all my heart, without reservations or criticism.

Something is worrying Arthur. He has not been sleeping. Maybe
it was only for thinking about the child, maybe it was only excitement and planning. I wish I knew.

ARTHUR'S RECORD, FIRST DAY, FOURTH MONTH, FIRST YEAR:

I can't get it out of my mind. Gwen says my calendar is a day
off. She kept one when she and Joe went off by themselves, and hers

is one day behind mine. I've never taken Gwen's word for anything else. Why should it make such a difference to me about her calendar? But Records are my business. They're my work. After all the time I've spent working and writing and thinking about Records, if I can't even keep track of the time I might as well quit. There must be some basis for my self-doubt or I wouldn't get into such a state about it. Every time I try to discuss it with Gwen, to go back where we can find some landmark in common, we get into such a fight that it takes me hours to get over it.

Gwen always knew what time it was in the world—that's what keeps taunting me. I remember particularly noticing it and even being annoyed by it because it seemed to me to be proof that she was wrong for Joe. There is something terribly wrong with a woman who *always* knows what time it is. I even said that to Joe once. I can remember it. He said, "It's handy, though; my watch is in hock."

I can remember the corner where we were walking and the bugs around the streetlight. In the one quality in the world for which I would have given Gwen authority, she disagrees with me. And she is very positive, not to say insulting. Of course she resents our twenty-eight-day month, thirteen-month calendar. But it is so much more sensible here and leaves less chance for error. We don't have to remember if it's a month with thirty or thirty-one days. All we have to do is remember to add one day at the end of each year. It ought to be a feast day. A holiday of some sort. Also, the moonlight is not just a romantic curiosity here. The little we get is of vital importance for hunting and looking after the pit traps.

But mainly the new calendar is a sign of adjustment, and admission of where we are. We are not in the world any more, and the more things that make us realize that, the faster will our ability grow to live better here. You can't live two places at once.

JOE'S RECORD, TENTH DAY, FOURTH MONTH, FIRST YEAR:

Well, what am I doing playing the bitch's role like any dame holding out in bed for the price of a new hat? How the hell did I get here? It must be the bitches all say too that it's the only weapon they've got. And this isn't the first time either. My wild stubborn girl, she cannot stand to be alone. She cannot bear to be ignored. How can a man bear to do a thing like that deliberately, for I know what I'm doing when I do it, that's the truth. And I guess the bitches who do it for a new hat, I guess they do it deliberately, too. The strange part is it only makes me puke about myself—not Gwen. It makes me love her even more. Christ, I set the trap for her and then

I watch her. She tries all her tricks, too, to win short of what I ask. Last time it was to go on keeping the Record when she'd threatened to quit.

But I don't fall for her tricks. I stay aloof. I'm not affectionate. And then, finally, I can make her want it so bad that she'll keep the Record and, Jesus, something busts in me. About the time she's getting ready to give in I'm so sorry for her, I'm just so goddamn sorry for her, I don't know whether to bust out bawling or love her to death and it ends up some of both. Now I think of it, they've always been mixed up. The guy that can't tell his pecker from pity, that's me.

How is it I can stand to do it, though, when I know what I'm doing and still not have it disgust me? Well, I can't bear for Gwen to make enemies of them all. I can't have them all down on her. I had to make her be reasonable about moving here. The hot springs are here, the tobacco is here, the soap plant is here. If they'd stayed there, they'd have blamed her for it. The same about the Records. We've all got to do it or else we haven't anything to keep us together. Anyhow, it's better for her to tangle with me than with Arthur. I'm not a guy like Arthur. Arthur doesn't bend before the wind, not every wind, not any wind. He stays himself. He stays his own.

But couldn't I find some other way to get her to do what I want? How come I end up with only one method all the time? How would I get another *man* to do something? Well, I'd just talk to him, I guess. I can't talk to Gwen and I never knew it before.

We haven't got any laws, that's the thing. Maybe you either got to have laws or play tricks. It's too deep for me. I could talk to Erma, all right. Or maybe I couldn't. She got me puzzled today. I never knew her to be coy before. Arthur and I've been working on the ink supply. I thought maybe the root might yield a more concentrated dye than the stems, and Erma called them conception flowers. When I asked her how come, she blushed. It's been puzzling me all day. I never saw Erma blush before; it just isn't like her. She didn't answer, either. She—holy Christ, she must be going to have a kid. I never thought of it till right now. Sure. Sure, that's it.

A kid. What a place to have a kid. You hungry, kid? Just reach up in the tree. You want to go to the zoo? Look around, kid, look around. You want to work? Go ahead. Pick yourself a spot.

Maybe *we* could have a kid. Jesus, I could take him with me all over the place. It would be great. What would it do to my girl, I wonder? Would it make her more contented to be here? Would she settle then, if she had a kid? I want us to start living here. I'm tired of this fight.

ERMA'S RECORD, SIXTEENTH DAY, FIFTH MONTH, FIRST YEAR:

My feathermane is here! He has followed me to the new place, alone, and what a reunion we had. I think I have never been so touched and pleased by anything in my life. I longed to bring him with us from the old place, but Joe could not remember if his striped grass grew here or not and it did seem cruel to separate him from the others. It was so much the kind of thing that people are always doing in the world and it seemed unseemly and unnatural here to insist on it. All the same I did miss him terribly and I was flattered and pleased when he came all on his own to find me. He came bounding up to me and leaned against me and snorted in that way he has and while I ran my hands through his soft, feathery mane I was suddenly lighthearted and happy as I had not been for a long time.

I went running off to tell Arthur and while we were laughing together quite miraculously we were ourselves and not constrained. Close again. And these terrible days and nights before looked like a madness. I think now with cold terror that if it had not been for my feathermane's coming to break the spell, Arthur and I might have been caught deeper and become more entangled in this morass of bitterness and separation.

Now I see these last days in perspective and I can neither countenance nor justify my own behavior. How could I, how *could* I have let this thing happen to us? For surely it was of my doing. The fertile time, the valuable days, slipped by, and Arthur, I thought, took no notice of them, nor notice of the great importance I had put upon them. I can see now how it had become an obsession with me to become pregnant to the exclusion of everything else. The years that we have spent together, our love for each other, Arthur himself, even the new wonders of this land and our new house, they were all as nothing, they were all blotted out in this determination to be pregnant. It was as though there were nothing of value in the world except fecundity. As the fertile days drew near, such a tension built up in me that all day I could do nothing but wait for the night. And at night I lay alone, unnoticed and unloved. The first night I lay there awake and Arthur was asleep beside me and unaware of my longing. And I thought that perhaps he was very tired from the heavy work that day, and pinned my hopes on the morrow. But the next night he did not touch me and I could not believe this, for we have always known about each other. It has never been a matter for conversation; it has never been a thing to *ask*. I could not believe that I could lie there with such longing and Arthur not be aware of it. Finally, in impatience, I turned to him, and he said, "Go to sleep." I was humiliated and infuriated and I got up and stood by the door for a long time, but he did not come after me or ask what was wrong. I went back to the bed and for the first night in all our life together I lay beside him with anger and resentment in my heart. And again I did not sleep.

The next night was worse. I even thought of pretending to be ill, so as to have an excuse to wake him. I had not slept for so long that I did have a headache, and I found myself tossing like a spoiled child, trying to attract his attention. And then I was ashamed and after that I was angry. I would not tell him what was the matter. I longed for him to suffer for his neglect in some way. I vowed I would not volunteer the information, that I would *make him ask*. Could this have been me? He would not ask and I did not speak at all yesterday and last night there was nothing left in me but hatred, hatred for my own husband.

But when the feathermane came I was so excited that I forgot our estrangement for a moment and I ran to Arthur and we were talking about the feathermane and suddenly I remembered and I stopped.

"Why, we are talking again," Arthur said.

I sat down on the ground and I was so tired and—and I began to cry. But even then I still thought that I would have to explain it to Arthur, that he was not aware of what had been going on in my mind. How could I have been so blind? There was nothing for me to explain to him. On the contrary. Arthur sat down beside me. The feathermane lay with his head in my lap. Arthur began to stroke his head and, not looking at me, but watching the feathermane all the time, he said, "Erma, you've built this thing up to an impossible, unreal height. Don't you see? It simply had to crash before we could start again. A man . . . a man does not like to be used just for stud. It puts him in an impossible position. It turns his love into a conscious, directed, mechanical thing. It makes him—well, it makes him not a person any more."

"I'm sorry," I said. "Oh, Arthur, I am sorry. I don't know what is the matter with me."

"Don't you remember all our years in Drury together?" he said. "Don't you think of them as a good time?"

"Of course," I said, "but—"

"Well, don't you see," he said, "that if you put a child—not even a child, but just to be pregnant—ahead of everything else, then it's the same as saying all those years were as nothing, that our life was as nothing, that we ourselves are nothing?"

"I just lost all perspective of everything," I said. "I couldn't even think of anything else. Oh, help me not to do it again. Already now I am afraid of the fertile time next month, for fear I will do it again."

"No," he said. "No, you must not do it again. Surely the tension has broken now and next time we will be able to talk about it together if it is necessary." Then he kissed me and said, "And maybe it will not be necessary."

The relief was so great that I went right to sleep there on the ground, and when I woke up, the feathermane was there beside me and the land was covered with enchantment again, the way that I first saw it. I thought of our new house, so badly neglected these last days, and I thought of all the work to be done and of how it would be a pleasure to get a meal again. Our life was good in the old days and we did not have a child then. And besides (dare I think this way again?), perhaps it is still not too late, for tonight, surely tonight, we will be close again.

JUSTIN'S RECORD, FIFTH DAY, SEVENTH MONTH, FIRST YEAR:

I don't remember what it was I was going to write because just as I started Erma and her feathermane came in with the present of a freshly baked loaf of bread and I am seduced into a homogeneous appreciation of its odor. Today I am especially favored with the most perfect loaf. It is a great triumph, this loaf of bread, and its creator an amazing person. To sit here looking at this bread, smelling it, occasionally reaching out to touch it, is like being in a room with a personage, so much do I know of its history. I think of the girl's first efforts when she found the grain, the laborious grinding and the resultant unleavened, lopsided doughy mess, and of how, swallowing it politely and hoping not to die, I was reminded of Tommy as a child. Then, little by little, how the loaves have changed in appearance, how they have borrowed from the beer vats for leavening, how they have come to have a definite, even predictable, shape, a soul-delighting color and odor and taste. And now—even decoration. Atop this loaf in golden relief is the perfect form of a little animal, the mold being the empty entire back of the shell of the centaur-snail. Like a tiny alligator, standing on its spiral tail, there it is in perfect detail atop the bread.

How different she is from Edith, this girl, in everything—in their essential construction, in their very beginnings, like the difference between a beaver and a hummingbird. I think of how Edith used to dress to go out in the evening. Her dressing room would appear to be in the wildest confusion—dresses, hats, scarves, slippers all somehow managing to look alive like members of a ballet. Over the whole house there was always that air of hurry, the threat of delay, complications with the children, with the servants, with the telephone. Then suddenly, in the midst of all this, one minute before the time of departure, Edith's hand would dart out, she would pluck a scarf from the welter of confusion, twirl it about her exquisite, delicate head, secure it and—there. She would be magnificently distinctive in a way that could never be imitated. Edith only did the *last* thing, without trial and apparently without plan.

It is fascinating to me now to see her exact opposite in Erma, who, if she desires the far-distant goal of a loaf of bread, *begins* with bread. It is as though you had asked the two women to meet you at a street corner. Edith, like a hummingbird, would have darted, swooped, glided, fluttered, and sailed over the whole town, and then, at the exact moment, alighted at the corner, but never from the direction you had anticipated, while straight down the avenue, having begun at the end of the same avenue, you could see Erma coming toward you in a straight line at a measured pace.

You can see her coming, always, and it is startling what a picture of force this premeditation gives. It is awe-inspiring to have a look at that big forehead and realize that it is directed somewhere without doubt and without possibility of deflection. And it would be very much like having a friendship with an elephant or a steamship if it were not for the incongruous surprise of that wonderful laughter she has, which is likely to burst upon you at any moment, and if it were not for something else. For to want a loaf of edible bread and, through many blunderings, achieve it is no doubt praiseworthy, but it is neither terribly rare or inspiring.

The bread is not the end of it—that's the thing. I am sure that in the girl's mind she always thinks that's going to be the end of it and that what happens afterward is a surprise to her as well as to everybody else. As the loaf begins to emerge from its shapeless beginnings, as through many trials it comes to assume the desired character of bread, some new chemistry happens between the girl and her creation so that the loaf is no longer the end of a series of trials but becomes the beginning of a cherished, loved thing.

I can remember when it was first a real loaf of bread. Then one day it had the crude print of a leaf on the top of it, then a design of shells. Now emerges the perfect form of the centaur-snail where the dough has risen into the skeleton. It is a dear quality in the girl that runs through her fabric. It is as though the fierce and conquering dragon of mythology, once having subjected a village, had said, "Now you are my village. I will keep you warm with the fiery flame from my nostrils. I will breathe a fountain of sparks that you may have fireworks in the park on feast days."

I think of Tommy's baby blankets that Edith embroidered on the spur of the moment, without any plan, simply because they bored her the way that they were. How curious it is that out of rebellion or sudden anger Edith could produce on the instant a thing of art that, finished, immediately possessed a life of its own, while Erma, with the most painful, tedious, directed efforts, produces only an endearing craft work which lives only in relation to her. In music, now, where the things that belong together can be put together and the laws grow logically out of themselves, it is this one, Erma, you would give four sons to. Only in life do the hummingbirds bear sons. In art it is incongruity.

Perhaps Erma will have children here. The land here seems to demand it, abounding in, insisting on, overflowing with fecundity.

I am come now almost to the last third of the second movement of the symphony, and perhaps when it is finished, as Erma suggests, I will then turn my thoughts to some sort of means of making it articulate. I have thought some on a kind of rude pipe organ since we have wood and plenty of leather. With Joe's help it is quite possible that something could be constructed, all right. If only Joe could be made to desire a pipe organ in the way that Erma can desire a loaf of bread, then we would have something astounding.

Or perhaps I should turn my thoughts to the musical instrument first and get away from the symphony for a while. This second movement has led me strange places, so that for me at least the forms are demanding a new departure from what I have ever written before. Almost against my will, the music has begun to build up such an unresolved potential that the answering of it, the capping of it, demands a violence of expression I cannot quite seem to accept. In the original conception of this movement, in this time of innocence, I had never envisioned such a potential of tension as I have unconsciously written into it. Well, perhaps in time it will work itself out right, or in time I shall come to accept as right the way it is demanding to be worked out. But innocence and violence, they seem strange bedfellows to me.

ARTHUR'S RECORD, TWENTY-FIRST DAY, EIGHTH MONTH, FIRST YEAR:

Joe and I have just returned from a trip up to the base camp and, though what we found there was alarming, still, on the way home I got a new perspective on what we have accomplished here and it is very reassuring. I wanted to see how the marks of the base camp have stood up so as to have some idea of how long we dared to leave the new place if we contemplate further exploration, without losing to the jungle's unmerciful encroachment. Our suspension bridge across the river on the climb upward needed little repair, but we had to hack our way out on the other side. The access to the bridge was almost completely overgrown and it was with the greatest difficulty that we found any trace at all of our old camp. It is terrifying, the speed with which the growth has simply choked, demolished, and annihilated our traces.

We have talked some of having a Year's End Day feast on the spot, but it will certainly necessitate several days of clearing first. My calendar on the tree remained, and after some time I located the place of our old fire pit and, from that, the place where Erma planted the seeds of the firstfruits, which are now growing in riotous profusion. Otherwise the trip was discouraging as to the prospect of our taking any long exploratory trip and hoping to find anything on our return. It means some will have to go and some stay if we do any exploring.

How different are the faces of man's enemy in different places. Here it is the growth that is aggressive. It advances, encroaches, penetrates, and smothers. Yet in a place like the Salt Desert, the force is equally destructive but just the opposite. Destruction recedes there and pulls the houses after it. The nails are pulled *out* of the boards, the walls fall out instead of in. But the enemy is always there, whether it smothers or pulls, and for once I thought of the enemy as something other than Time.

As we looked down on the new settlement on the way home I realized that I rarely think of the old press and Drury any more. Instead of measuring the quantity of our Records against the quantity that I hoped to achieve in Drury. I saw the new settlement against the base camp, and our accomplishment looks tremendous. Joe and I stopped to rest as soon as we caught sight of it and, stretching there below us, it was very impressive. We could see the three really sturdy houses and the new clearing for the corral where are our first domesticated mossbacks, the house for the Records with its fire trench around it against the mildew. We could see the big roller stone for pressing the finished paper that has performed for three times in a row now without accident. The settlement seemed drawn together, armed in bravery against the jungle's destruction. I have not felt so mighty since in childhood, as the King of Per-Fec-Ti-On, I led my imaginary armies in mutilating victory against our enemy and then allowed myself the luxury of weeping for their dead.

It is possible that our five Records may prove to be more valuable than five thousand in some other place, so much is each detail of man's struggle intensified here. This is the first time I have seen it so or believed it.

Joe and I came on down to the settlement just at evening, and the smell of the food cooking had us crazy with hunger. We told our news over cups of the new batch of beer and a fine home-coming feast of two fat ballsleepers roasted with sharples, those small tart fruits of the texture of apples. They found the ballsleepers in one of the pit traps, which is very unusual. Ordinarily we see them only in the clusternut trees, where they sit chewing on the nuts rather like fat squirrels. When they were fished up out of the pit they were rolled into balls with their tails over their faces just as when we surprise them asleep in the trees, so perhaps the posture is a protection reaction to fright as well.

It was a great feast and a great day, with only one detail to mar it. Erma's pet feathermane, in a playful moment, knocked over my beer and I accidentally pushed him aside too roughly. Erma disappeared abruptly and I found her crying. It was stupid of me; I guess I had had a little too much of the new beer. These days just before her menstrual period now take very careful handling, and in my triumph of the afternoon I had let this slip from my mind. I hope for her sake that she is pregnant now, to bring an end to these periodic tensions that she tries so hard and so unsuccessfully to control. And I guess the fact that I too can now desire it is proof that I am no longer in exile but, like Joe and Erma and Justin, live here too. Poor Gwen is still in exile, though outwardly she conforms better than I had hoped, and, with the exception of Justin's symphony, which we are unable to judge, Gwen curiously enough, with her loom weaving and her leatherwork, has perhaps made a greater contribution than any of us.

One more triumph for this day. After seeing the destruction at the base camp I began to fear for the early Records, that our trench fire had not forestalled the decay of the paper or that the ink had faded, but I have just looked into my own and, though there is some evidence of insect destruction at the edges, the ink so far holds.

GWENDOLYN'S RECORD, FIFTEENTH DAY, NINTH MONTH, FIRST YEAR:

Oh God oh God oh God oh God oh no. No. No. I will take a knife or a pointed stick. I will rip it out with my bare hands. Oh, where are they? Where is my mother? Where are my sisters? Even the people at the office—even the police. Why does no one come for me? I never did anything to hurt anyone. Why should *I* be deserted? Why should I be left in the hands of fools and children?

JOE'S RECORD, FIRST DAY, TENTH MONTH, FIRST YEAR:

What have I done? The fact is, Erma is *not* pregnant. I was absolutely sure she was, and for the life of me I can't remember now what made me so sure. Why the hell didn't I ask her? Oh no, not me; not Bungle Brain Roberts. He never asks first. He acts first and then, after all hell breaks loose, he gets around to checking the facts. And does he pay? No, Gwen pays. Christ, I thought it would be so neat. Erma would have her kid first and by the time Gwen was ready we'd know all the answers and Erma'd be able to help her. Now my rabbit is all alone with her back to the wall and I can't get within six feet of her. I've had everything in the house thrown at my head, including a knife, and I can't say as I blame her.

And as I pull my head up out of the sand where I must have had it all these years and stumble in my carefree manner out of paradise, I learn that things are even worse. We not only will have no experience to help Gwen; we have no knowledge. Even when Erma said she was not pregnant I still held onto some vague idea that women automatically had some special fund of knowledge because they were women. But it turns out I picked this idea out of a cracker-jack box. It just ain't so. Neither of the girls ever saw a child born. They know which hole it comes out of and how long it takes to have one and, by God, that's all they know. In a last attempt to make Erma give out with some knowledge I said to her, "But that water that's always boiling in the storybooks—what the hell is it boiling for?" "To sterilize things," she said. "What things?" I said. "Well, the instruments, I guess," she said. "What instruments?" I said. "I don't know, Joe," she said.

"Well, it's one sure thing they don't boil the baby in it," I said, and then Erma began to cry. I would have felt sorry for her if I'd had room in me for anything but fear. "It's all a lie about women, Joe," she said, "though after they make it, they're taken in by it, too. There isn't any special knowledge that a woman has because she's a woman."

When I think of how many years of civilization it took to produce two girls so absolutely ignorant in the essentials of living and dying . . . Oh, shit. This won't help.

I've even been peddling my wares to Justin. He's had four sons and he's completely vague on all the details. "My wife was very modest," he said. "I was never allowed in the room until the doctor was gone, and by that time the nurse had everything all cleaned up. I seem not to have learned anything while pacing the hall, Joe. I'm sorry. But Erma will help you," he said. "Erma will know."

Christ, as old as he is, he believes it, too. Well, one thing. The chips are down. If Gwen needs knowledge, if she needs help, she's going to have to get it from me. It's squarely up to me and no mistake. There is no hospital, no doctor, no coupon I can clip to send for the handbook on easy deliveries. There's no midwife, no mother here.

The hell there is no mother here. The place is lousy with them. The thing to do is to build me a bunch of pens in secret, and I know the place, too. Then I'll catch every pregnant animal I find and pen it up and watch it. Now I think of it, I never even saw a calf born myself. I've got almost nine months. In that time I could learn a hell of a lot about how the animals do it anyhow.

I've got to find something to knock Gwen out with. She can't stand pain. The beer's too weak. There's that weed I got hold of hunting for tobacco. That's too risky, though. I goddamn near died. I could try it on some animals. Maybe there's some way to dilute it or take the poison out of it. If it turned out that it took a six-pound animal twice as much of the weed as a three-pound animal to go to sleep and still be able to deliver, I could get an approximate dose for Gwen's weight and then I could begin to experiment on myself. In nine months I ought to know.

I could begin with the sleeks. They're closer to rats than anything here and they're easy to catch. And for the next size I could use ballsleepers. We've found several of them in the pit traps lately.

When Arthur and I went back up to the base camp I saw one of those wildcats with the pale fur ruff around its neck. Maybe they've started to come back there since we left the place. I'd like to get hold of some of those howling dogs, too, or whatever they are. I only saw them once and then it was a whole pack traveling together at night, but we hear them now and then. Well, that would give me a graduated scale to work on. Just guessing, I'd say that sleeks weigh about 2 pounds, ballsleepers 5, ruffs 13, howlers 20, feathermanes 60, mossbacks 100.

Of course just finding them is nothing. I've got to find them pregnant. But from the looks of things around the place, it won't be too hard. I'll start on the sleeks first until I get somewhere with the weed or some other plant. Then it'll be time to hunt.

Just call me Doc, that's the ticket. Christ, I got to get to work. I got to get that bunch of pens built. I got to wade in through those flying knives and take hold of Gwen. There's nobody else here able to help me. Nobody.

ERMA'S RECORD, TWENTY-FIFTH DAY, TENTH MONTH, FIRST YEAR:

I do not know myself any more. Not so long ago I thought I had a quite unusual amount of self-knowledge and, what is more, reason to take pride in it. Now everything I do surprises me and everything I think horrifies me and what I dream terrifies me. I seem to be filled with violence and what is not violent is evil and what is not evil is petty. I feel bruised all through, and like a leaf in a hurricane I am completely at the mercy of anyone else's smallest word. I am lost and I cannot find anything of my own.

I had just come through another cycle of hope and the ensuing bitter disappointment with what I congratulated myself was some measure of control, only to learn that Gwen is pregnant. The thing that I long for with such intensity—she has it in loathing and rebellion and disgust. And it was too much for me.

I had no concern for her obvious fear—only envy and hatred. Her face is swollen from crying and coarsened by hatred, and I so feared I would strike her that I turned from her and fled. What possessed me? I ran until I was exhausted and, when I stopped finally, I found myself in the field of conception flowers. Oh, bitter mockery. I named them myself. I began to tear at them like a crazy thing, to pull their roots out of the ground. I worked in a frenzy until I was covered with sweat and dirt and stained with their juices and then I lay down on the bare place to rest my barrenness against a barren place. But even in this I could not have my desire. By my wanton devastation I had dislodged a whole world of fat and fecund crawling things. A fat green spider stood not two inches from my face where I lay on the ground, rocking her body and flaunting on her back at least two hundred babies.

As in the time of drought in my childhood I hungered for the sight of a barley field or a green tree, so now I long for a desert, for any desolate place, where I might lie for a moment in burning dryness, in desiccation. I will go mad in this rank and steaming, dripping bath of fecundity, and I am afraid of madness. Last night I dreamed that I sat before a mirror putting on a necklace and the pearls turned to eggs and grew to my skin and I lay on the ground trying to drink from a spring, but the water turned to a fountain of semen and I could not escape it, however I turned my mouth, for over my body while I had lain there the first fruit vines had grown in a tangling prison.

I am afraid and I need help, but when I try to ask for help something in me alienates the source of it. I said to Arthur, "Oh, I am so envious of Gwen." And he said, "Yes, it's too bad. It would have been so much better all around if you had had the first child."

"You blame me," I said. It was out before I knew it. What possessed me? I never in my life put anyone on the spot like that before. I was groveling for reassurance, any reassurance, and he did not see it.

"You must have misunderstood me," he said. "I only meant that you are so much stronger than Gwen, so much more courageous. And then of course you came here willingly and, if she had believed we'd be shut in, she'd never have come. It's that I feel responsible for her because, in a way, it's as though we had persuaded her under false pretenses, and because of that we're the ones who ought to be experiencing the unknown first. It just seems backward. Joe and I've been together so long and it's always been the other way around. I can't get used to it. I was always the one that made the plans. I was the leader."

I was embarrassed because of what I'd said to Arthur and the conversation seemed to have got so far away from the help I needed. "Maybe I'll get to keep Gwen company part of the way, anyhow," I said. And for a minute I believed it *again*. From whence comes this bottomless pit of hope? How can I hope again and again?

I went for a walk with my feathermane and I came upon Justin.

We sat and talked and a fortunate thing happened for me so that I got a little patch on my shattered ego, and now, as a result, I am calm enough to write the Record, a thing I could not do last night. How childish we are! How we do live on vanity! Soon I will come to the place where I will be so craven for reassurance that if anyone says to me, "How nice it is you have two hands, two feet," I will follow him about like a dog, licking his boots. Is no one free from this terrible servitude to his own vanity? Is no one really adult? That is the trouble with feeling a fool. The world looks full of fools to you. I am ready to believe that no man is so great or confident but that, at the height of his work, he could be thrown into utter confusion by any nobody's saying, "Your tie is crooked; you have a smudge on your nose."

But to return to my fortunate conversation with Justin and being made to feel valuable for a few moments. I asked him how went the second movement of the symphony and he seemed discouraged and puzzled about it. He says that though "Discovery" seemed quite easy to write, "The Time of Innocence" seems to have taken on a willful direction of its own and that he is puzzled by it. How I wish I could hear it. I am timid about asking to see the manuscript and perhaps I'm not good enough to tell from the score, anyway. And yet I think I know what he is talking about but maybe it is only because I myself feel frenzied, unsatisfied, all the time now. He says that the beginning of the second movement seems right to him so that he does not want to deny it or to change it, but that it will only develop itself into unresolved tensions and if he tries to force or violate these he runs into a wall of falseness.

Unresolved tension. I fell on the phrase as though someone had said, "I know your aunt," and, feeling almost an authority, I lost my shyness with him and was able to talk. "Has this never happened to you before?" I said.

He thought a long time and then he said, "Yes, something similar to this has happened before, never so violently, I think."

"What was it?" I said. "And what did you do before?"

"Well, once," he said, "in an opera about Lazarus and once in a concerto. And I never finished either one of them."

My heart stopped to think that it might happen to *The Green Kingdom*. I could not bear for it to be unfinished.

"Well," I said, "what holds you back? You say that the unresolved tensions keep demanding to go a certain way. Why is it you don't let them go?"

"Well," he said, "once you do that they set a mold and you can never start over again with the same freshness. It's as though you use up the energy that is allotted for that one thing and you can never summon it up in newness again to do it over."

"Perhaps it would be right, though," I said. "Why do you feel so strongly you would have to do it over?"

"I can't accept it," he said. "Something in me rebels. It isn't in my original concept. The logical sequel to discovery is a time of innocence, and, to me, that is a quiet, slowly growing thing. It is the way that I first conceived it, the way that I first heard it. And this tension, this violence that keeps obtruding itself, it seems foreign to me."

Now it seems unbelievable to me that I could have said it, but I had no feeling of self-consciousness, no timidity with him. I was thinking only about the music and I said, "You must be thinking of innocence as a thing that grows naturally into something else or as something that dies."

"And isn't that right?" he said.

"No," I said. "Innocence never dies. It is always murdered."

He didn't say anything for a long time. He lighted his pipe and puffed on it awhile. "Hmmm," he said. "Hmmm. Out of the mouths of babes."

And then he put his hand under my chin and lifted my face so that I had to look into his eyes. "So that's it," he said. "So that's it."

He put his big hand on my head. "I thank you, Erma," he said. "I thank you very much."

I wanted to cry. I don't know why. I was overcome with timidity to think I had contradicted Justin Magnus, about music of all things. I touched the feathermane to wake him and jumped up and ran home. Oh, it would be wonderful to be like Justin Magnus, to have a place always waiting where you could put your fervor and your torment, to get a concerto instead of hysterics, a lament instead of nausea. To have with you always an expandable vessel that would hold any amount and, holding it, come alive on its own.

A little talent is the cruelest possession in the world. And in me it seems there is to be no creation of any kind, not even the creation I felt myself perfectly suited for. For me there is no balm for this bruise. There is no rest for this tiredness. There is no place to put this awful weight. To be pregnant forever of this need to bear that never gets born. To wait forever in a railroad station on a train that never comes. Can I do it? Can I possibly do it even if every day I could wheedle a compliment out of someone? Even if a hundred times a day I could get someone to say, "Thank you, Erma. Thank you very much."?

ARTHUR'S RECORD, THE FIRST DAY OF THE SECOND YEAR:

Yesterday we had our Year's End Day feast up at the old base camp with, as they used to say at home, free fireworks. Provided by nature this time. Just as we started to eat, the sound of explosions filled the air. Joe and I hit the ground instinctively. I had on the instant a clear picture of the air filled with anti-personnel bombs. Erma and Justin said later that they had both thought it had something to do with the volcanic eruption at the entrance. When Joe and I rolled over and opened our eyes, there was Gwen jumping up and down, yelling, "They've come! They've come!" Finally Justin pointed to what looked like a spray or shower in the distance, and so we all started toward it. The source turned out to be a tree several of us had seen before.

The tree bears huge nuts about the size of coconuts, pointed at one end. We had investigated these earlier in the hopes of finding an edible meat similar to the coconut, but the pulp turned out to be inedible and, in that unripe stage, hard as a rock. Erma did make bowls from some, burning out the center, but it was a laborious process. Now all this hard pulp seems to have liquified and to have produced such a pressure as to explode the shells, sending the much enlarged seeds out in spurts and showers. They do not, of course, all go off at the same time, and so after we had calmed down a bit we were able to watch another tree carefully. It's quite a sight and the seeds are the most amazing part. Each one bears a perfect miniature parachute so that the direction of the seed floating toward the ground is always vertical. The lower end of the seed is a corkscrew, ending in a sharp point, and it penetrates straight into the ground. The empty husks are still hanging on the trees today. Dried, they should make good cooking fuel—an endless problem since the wood is always damp.

If this is an annual occurence I suppose that we just missed it last year. I hope that it does happen on Year's End Day every year because, once you knew what it was, it would be a festive thing. God knows we need festivities and it is good to think we have a real tradition started now.

Joe and I spent two days clearing the ground and it was well worth it. We had a tremendous feast after the fireworks, and then in the evening we sat around a big fire eating firstfruits as we had on our first night. It seemed a very long time ago, that first night, and quite prophetic when you remember that it was Gwen that night, too, who lay exhausted and frightened with tear stains on her sleeping face. This time, of course, over her disappointment that the fireworks had not been *them* coming for her. One cannot help but feel sorry for her. I am not sure that in her place I would do better when I consider that at this moment over a slight headache I have thought longingly of a medicine chest, a corner drugstore, a doctor, and my imagination has leapt alarmingly to the possibility that one of us might have a serious illness.

Still, though, I am sure Erma would have been quite different from Gwen, and it is a shame for both their sakes that Erma could not have had the first child. After Joe and I had worked for two days clearing the growth from the base camp and building the feast table and making a fire pit to roast the young mossback, and after Erma had worked so hard preparing all the special feast foods, Gwen suddenly announced she would not go. She did not feel up to the climb. This was no calm announcement, either, and with variations it went on all day. The more Joe pleaded the worse she got. I can't hold my temper with her, I know from past experience, so I didn't try. Erma did though, she told me. She went to her alone and Gwen suddenly flared out at her, accusing Erma of keeping secret some knowledge of contraceptives, apparently with the willful plan of using Gwen's experience to her advantage. It was not only the unjustness of the accusation that threw Erma off; it was the quite obvious fact that Gwen has been harboring this idea for some time and letting it fester in her. At least it does throw some light on the curious little cruelties and retorts Gwen has made to Erma.

It was a rough go for Erma and, quite unlike her, she took it lying down. Prospects for the Year's End Day feast looked very dark when Justin suddenly saved the day with his not very subtle diplomacy. You cannot help but admire the man, and yet it's disgusting to see him go into action. When you first meet him the overwhelming impression you get is the man's honesty and it is hard to swallow the sight of his calculated flattery in action, the more so as it is very effective. I suppose that I fear in my turn I may also succumb sometime to having the spotlight of his diplomacy turned on me and become in his eyes a fool, a puppet. Well, diplomacy is a quality I am completely lacking in, and living all these years with Erma, who is without tricks, has not served to develop it in me. While I can imagine myself stealing a man's coat, I can also imagine letting him kill me before I could bring myself to flatter him to gain an advantage.

Justin saved our feast day, but I don't know but what I would rather have lost the feast day than to see the sight of its saving. He walked over to Gwendolyn, picked her up in his arms so that in surprise she shut up for a moment, and then, in a voice I cannot begin to describe, he said, "But, Little Mother, of course you are not to walk that distance. We will carry you."

This, I realized, was the first time we have mentioned Gwen's pregnancy in front of her and I can see now that it was a mistake to have kept silent. We all talk of it all the time to one another, but never to or before Gwen. By our manner of avoiding the subject when she is around we have all fallen into an artificiality and a conspiracy, as though the girl had some disease. It was a shock to Gwen, too, to have someone treat her hysterical tragedy as a natural, accepted, talked-of thing that belonged to all of us.

It was fascinating in a way to see her weigh this new idea. The whole thing was translated to her face and, over Justin's shoulder, she gave Joe a crafty smile. It was like watching a fox think. She licked her lips and I'd swear she was tasting her new-found power.

By little gestures and deferences, Justin managed to create a kind of princess role for Gwen, and, except for the disappointment that the fireworks were not a rescue party, she played the role all day. Joe caught on pretty fast, and his imitation of Justin's imitation concern is apparently acceptable to the princess.

She has the whip hand over us all now, even though she hasn't begun to swing it seriously yet. It is revolting, but I have to admit it is easier this way.

Joe opened his eyes, was instantly awake, slipped out of bed with a continuous, silent movement achieved by long practice, and began to pull on his clothes. The sleek number 39 was ready to deliver and the last decanting of the braidstem concentrate had yet to be made. He pulled half a loaf of bread and a piece of dried mossback meat off the shelf and let himself quietly out of the house. It was still dark. Shortly after wessun he should be able to get back, if sleek number 39 would co-operate and if nothing had happened to the braidstem concentrate in the night.

He began to walk rapidly in a path so familiar now as to be ignored. He took some of the bread and meat out of his pocket and ate as he walked. It was all going on in his mind now, the anticipation of the day's work. He could see the animals in the pens just as he had left them yesterday. It was always with him. He could start it any place and it would go right on by its own momentum. His accustomed feeling of well-being settled down on him, and, reviewing in his mind the exact figures of the dosage for this time, he smiled.

Never before in his life had Joe experienced this thing—a work that made its own laws, that created its own labors, its own momentum. With the laboratory, all he had to do was start toward it. The events there, never quite predictable, would be already in progress and they would determine his own labors. All his life he had worked at work which he had had to make, to persuade to happen, so that the quantity might not run out. As with the printing business, so had it always been. With the laboratory it was just the opposite. Maybe I should have been a doctor, he thought. I should have found this out a long time ago.

The first light of wessun was beginning when he turned off the path and entered the enclosure he had hidden so well. He went straight to the sleek's pen. Not too late. From her bin he took out a handful of crisproots and fed her. Then, reassured, he fed all the other animals. There was still a good supply of mossback meat, the howler and the ruff had a sufficient pile of centaursnails, but the clusternuts for the ballsleeper were running short. During eassun, maybe, he'd get time to gather some. If only he dared tell Erma about the place, he could get some help. He could use help. Well, if he had good luck from the braidstem concentrate on the sleek, maybe he would tell them. He had to have something to go on, though.

By the feathermane's pen he stopped and stooped down. While she put up her head to nibble at the striped grass he held in his hand, he stroked her bulging sides. If only she'd hold off a little, not rush him too fast, so that he could multiply the braidstem concentrate by her weight factor according to the sleek's reaction and try it on her. He had a lot of faith in this new braidstem concentrate. So far, it hadn't shown any of the violent toxicity of either the clawleaf or the shambacco.

He went over to the pile of weights and inspected the balance, wiping it carefully free from dew. Then he took up his notes from the day before to check his figures on the concentrate. Under his left thumb, while he studied the notes of yesterday, were the pages of his long struggle to find an anaesthetic for Gwendolyn. The defeat that lay in these notes, the carelessness of the ones toward the front, the struggle of them, were not his chief concern. They were of concern to him now only when they were of use. For he had great faith in the braidstem concentrate; he had great hopes for it. Otherwise the sheets under his left thumb would have meant a too-great weight of discouragement.

Such, for example, as the early work on the first drug that he called joedope, the one he had accidentally found long ago when he was hunting tobacco.

sleek #3—mother dead in convulsions—no birth
ballsleeper #3—mother dead in convulsions—stillborn litter
mossback #3—mother in convulsions—live litter—mother died
next day

Or the notes on shambacco, tried out on a series of ballsleepers and discarded:

5 drops infusion #1—no effect—normal birth
10 drops infusion #1—light sleep, normal birth. Sleep did not
last long enough

50 drops infusion #1—vomiting. No sleep. Normal birth
 5 drops infusion #2—light sleep, normal birth. Sleep did not
   last long enough
10 drops infusion #2—vomiting. No sleep. Normal birth
Dropper used: thorn from thorntree
              thorn equal in length to my index finger.

Or the pages of agony on clawleaf which had looked so promising for a while but ended in the notes added later:

sleek #17————————————mother, paralysis
howler #17————————————mother, paralysis
feathermane #17————————mother, paralysis
mossback #17———————————mother, paralysis.

And there were, of course, many days not represented here in the notes: the first days of hunting and trapping, of selecting only the pregnant animals, the days of building their pens and gathering the endless food supply, the days before Joe was concerned with the drugs or the system of weights, the days when he simply sat and waited and watched while the sweat gathered on his upper lip and the little green cat eyes of the ruff looked up at him in fear and turned into Gwendolyn's eyes and the beautiful feathermane lay on her side and strained and the straining muscles were Gwendolyn's.

Now he didn't sweat like that any more. No longer were the eyes of the heavily breathing mossback Gwendolyn's eyes. Watching had become observing, and Joe was busy keeping pace. For he had great hopes for the braidstem. He had great hopes for it.

He measured out the dosage from the newly decanted concentrate and set it aside to have ready. Then he picked the sleek up from her pen and stroked her in a practiced way to keep her quiet, and took her to the balance. There in groups were the weights, so long worked on, so many times checked, ranging in the order of their mass: the lightest clusternuts, then the turtleshells (equal to seven clusternuts apiece), next the green Yearsenday bombs that they had discovered on their feast day in the ripe stage (each one equal to approximately twenty turtleshells), and last, the huge, identical riverstones, each one equal to five Yearsenday bombs and four of them being the average weight of a mossback.

Joe put the sleek back into her pen, checked the weights, recorded them—eight turtleshells plus two clusternuts—with the date, and then replaced the weights. He took up the measured dose of the braidstem concentrate and sat down by the sleek's pen to wait. With a terrible intensity he hoped that the dose would produce a deep sleep in the mother, a live litter, no vomiting, no death, no blindness, no paralysis. For, as he felt the hair rising on the back of his neck, he realized again that the time was getting short.

Arthur could not decide if it was worse lying down or sitting up. He slowly pulled himself to a sitting position and swung his legs over the side of the bed. The room rocked through a forty-five-degree angle and jolted to a stop. His hands hung limply between his knees and felt disembodied. He slowly curled the fingers of his left hand and straightened them out again. It didn't seem to be his hand, and he doubted that it would hold anything. For all the power he had over it, anything he tried to hold in it would slip right through his fingers. He could not remember how long he had been having these headaches or if they were all parts of one continuous headache. If only he could get some line on them, some connection. At first he had thought it was the beer, so he had stopped drinking it, and then he had thought maybe it was the tobacco. Then there was a series of foods, each of which had preceded one of the headaches. But the headaches went on. The thing to do was to go back over his Records and see if he couldn't find some connection. Had he mentioned the first headache? But the thought of the script flowing before his eyes was so nauseating that he lay down again.

And instantly the throbbing in his right temple had again the upper hand. This throbbing was in constant battle with a bell, a high thin bell, which rang in defiance. The throbbing would beat the bell with its whip until it had almost silenced it, only to find that the bell had skipped just out of its reach once more, still able to ring faintly and then confidently and then tauntingly. Arthur closed his eyes and the right eyeball grated through a painful arc under the bruised eyelid. He was very cold, and yet such a lethargy held him pierced down that he could not pull a cover over himself.

As Erma came into the room the light from the doorway stabbed at the throbbing, sought out the tender roots of his teeth.

She walked across the floor toward the bed and sat down on it, jolting and rocking the room.

"Are you any better?" she asked, putting out her hand to touch his head.

Arthur gritted his teeth in an effort not to jerk away from her, for he knew that she meant to comfort him and had no idea of the sound, like someone walking over gravel, caused by her fingers on his skin. She touched his hair and it sounded to him as though two rough boards were being rubbed together inside his brain. The feathermane had followed Erma in, and now he leaned his head on her knee, snuffling a loud sigh. Arthur looked up in irritation but he could not get Erma's face into focus. It was a blur, an underwater face. The bell had gained ascendency over the throbbing again. Erma touched his head, rubbing her fingers over the skin, leaving a trail of grating sound.

Arthur jerked aside. "Take that thing out of here," he said. "It makes such a hell of a racket."

"What thing?" she said. "Oh."

Later she and the feathermane went in search of Justin.

"Would you keep him overnight for me, Justin?" she said. "Arthur has another one of those terrible headaches and he says the feathermane makes so much noise. The slightest noise seems to be excruciating for him, but the feathermane isn't used to being put out and he kicks the door and cries in that weird wail of his. I should never have got him to be such a house creature. Now I've done it, I can't undo it overnight."

"Sit down, Erma," Justin said. "Of course I'll keep him, if he'll stay."

The feathermane sat beside Erma and leaned against her leg. She rubbed her hand along his delicate pointed nose. "Well, of course," Erma said to Justin, "I don't want *you* to be kept awake all night, either. I don't know what to do."

"You look so tired," Justin said. "How long has Arthur had this headache?"

"It started this morning, I think," she said. "I feel so helpless, not to be able to do anything. He makes himself try to work, and it humiliates him that he can't. He can hardly see. And—and Joe keeps disappearing. Oh, Joe does his part, all right, but he works in such a hurry, and then, if there's an emergency with the stone roller or any of the animals in the corral, why, he's not there."

"I've wondered about Joe's disappearances, too," Justin said. "He has an air about him, though, of such certainty . . ."

"Oh, you can't ask him," Erma said quickly. "It's strange, but you just can't ask him."

"I think you're doing too much," Justin said. "You look so awfully tired. I see you so often taking care of Gwendolyn. Is she really as ill as all that?"

"Oh, I don't know," Erma said. "She often doesn't feel like doing her housework or like cooking and . . . and I'm so well. I ought to be able to help her. It's just that now Arthur is so often ill, too. And it seems to me the mossbacks are always hungry or waiting to be milked."

"Well, I could do that," Justin said. "Surely I could help with the animals. I wasn't aware, I guess, how often Arthur is unable to do it."

"Well, that's it," Erma said. "If you started to help, he'd know I'd told you. I don't know why, he seems ashamed of the headaches. He tries to hide them from Joe, even, I think. And yet anybody can tell from looking at him that something is terribly wrong."

"At least for tonight I can take care of the feathermane," Justin said, "and perhaps later I can do more. But I think you should bring over a dress or a jacket of yours for the feathermane to have near him, and then perhaps he won't kick up such a fuss."

"That's a good idea," she said. "I'll do that." She held the feathermane's head up between her hands. "You're to stay with Justin now, you understand?"

By the time she had fed the animals and taken one of her jackets over to Justin's house, it was already eassun, and Erma ran down to where the others were waiting at the Record vault. She looked first for Arthur to see how he was and immediately knew there was something wrong besides the headache. He and Gwen stood facing each other in hatred. They were all looking at Gwen, and Arthur's hand, which he held pressed against his right temple, was shaking. His face was quite gray. Erma noted that the trench fire to protect the Records from mildew had not been replenished, and no one as yet had taken his own Record from the vault.

"I said I refuse," Gwendolyn said, "that's all. I just refuse. I won't do it any longer."

She smiled at Arthur in a scornful, arrogant way, and Erma was suddenly afraid he would strike her.

"But, Gwen," he said, "you can't. We have to keep the Records. We don't dare to—"

"*I* dare," Gwen said. "I won't do it any more and there's nothing you can do about it."

Arthur started to speak and then suddenly he closed his eyes and swayed a little. He shook his head. "Listen," he said, "let's all sit down and talk it over. It's—"

"You can sit and talk till you rot," she said, "but not to me. Do you think I give a damn for your Records? Do you think it makes any difference to me—*to me*—what you think? Or any of you," she said, looking around.

She made a little movement with her right knee as though to kick at Arthur, who now had sunk down slowly to half sit, half lean on the outer bank of the fire trench. "Why," she said, "why, it's ridiculous, all this fuss over—over nothing. Absolutely nothing."

She stepped back a little and laughed. "I'm not stopping anything," she said. "I never started. How do you like that? Did you think I sat down every day like a good girl and wrote down my thoughts for the professor? Did you really believe that's all I had to do? Why, there's nothing in those books. Nothing at all. Every day I write, 'Now is the time for every good man to come to the aid of his party' fifteen times. But I'm damned if I'll do that any more. I'm through."

She turned and walked away from them slowly, confidently, knowing well, all through her swollen body, that no one dared strike her now. No one dared cross her. No one dared even follow her.

She returned to her loom, where she had been interrupted every day to go down and join the others and perpetrate the farce. She did not like to be interrupted at the loom. She sat down before it and, once she had the shuttle in her fingers, they were all forgotten. The whole scene was forgotten. The shuttle in her fingers moving over, moving under, moving in, moving out, brought her, as it always did, its lovely soothing. It brought her forgetfulness. It brought her the dream:

They had blasted the wall with dynamite and carried her out, oh, tenderly, on a stretcher, and put her in the ambulance. Then she was in the big hospital in a clean bed and the doctor was coming into the room. She had on a white negligee and he took her pulse.

"I'm afraid," he said, "you're going to be bothered a lot by reporters. Do you feel strong enough?"

She smiled up at him. "Not too many," she said.

"My dear, it must have been harrowing," the woman reporter said. "Everybody thinks you're wonderfully brave. Now tell me about the savages."

"There weren't any," Gwen said.

"You don't mind, do you, if the photographer gets a few shots while I'm talking? Here, let me fix the pillow for you. How's that, Mac?"

GWENDOLYN ROBERTS
TELLS GREEN KINGDOM LIFE
FROM HOSPITAL BED

"Well, now, little girl," the doctor said, "I think really you've had enough of this pain. Take this pill and pretty soon you'll be asleep. We'll take good care of you. Good care."

Through a haze she could hear the nurses moving about the room. She could hear their voices echoing down the corridor: so brave, so brave, so brave.

GREEN KINGDOM
BABY WEIGHS SIX
POUNDS

In the hospital room now there were more photographers to take pictures of Gwen holding the baby. The room was filled with flowers.

GWENDOLYN ROBERTS
TO WRITE OWN STORY
FOR SYNDICATE

GWENDOLYN ROBERTS
TELLS OF LIFE IN GREEN KINGDOM
FOR RADIO AUDIENCE

EXHIBIT OF
GWEN ROBERTS' WEAVING AT
NATIONAL MUSEUM

She was tired, very tired, lying in the hospital bed. The doctor was bending over her when she opened her eyes. When he saw she was awake he smiled at her. "I told the motion-picture people they'd simply have to wait," he said. "No more today. No more for some time. You've had a long ordeal. You'll need good care for a long time."

Good care, good care, good care, *the shuttle said.*

The doctor's eyes were deep blue, wonderful eyes. Wonderful, kind caressing eyes. Good care, good care, good care. How did she ever endure it? So brave, so brave. *Shuttle under, shuttle over, shuttle in, shuttle out.*

Erma could feel her lips trembling in the silence. It was terrible to see what Gwen had done to Arthur and it was terrible to see him trying to grope through that pain for the right thing to say to Joe. But it was worse to know that she did not know the right thing any more for Arthur. Once she could have gone to him; once she could have spoken. Now—now she could not even help the headache. They were estranged and she was inadequate, totally inadequate. She went into the vault and got her own Record and Justin's and the two of them went quietly away, leaving Joe and Arthur there alone, face to face, to fight it out.

Arthur could not think through the pain. He could not even get Joe's face into focus to talk to him. And it must be done now. Now. A stand must be taken before the whole structure of their lives collapsed around them and they had no work any more, nothing to unite them.

"I'm sorry as hell, Arthur, but in her condition there's nothing I can do now. You know that. I think maybe after the baby's born she'll be different."

"We should have seen this in the beginning," Arthur said. "A civilization that exalts property makes laws to protect the property. One that exalts people makes laws for the protection of the people. Ours should have had laws to protect the Records in the beginning. The punishment for failure should have been understood. Now any of us can crumble."

"I don't think punishment would have made any difference," Joe said.

"Certainly it would. At least it's not too late to try. We must all agree on the penalty now and it must be enforced. Otherwise—"

"Penalty?" Joe said. "Punishment? Come *off* it, Arthur. There's nothing we can do about it. Nobody's going to put up a whipping post *here*."

Under the water where the pain was, where the throbbing was, the word *whipping* became alive to Arthur. The pain whipped the bell, the bell that was clanging constantly now under the water where no one would wait, no one would wait until the pain was gone. No one would give him a minute to catch hold, to say the right thing. Under the water, under the throbbing, he had become the pain and the bell—the bell was Gwendolyn. Under the water he was the pain lashing, lashing away at that monstrous belly which ruled them all. They must consult the belly. They must obey the belly. They must bow down to the belly.

"Joe," he said, "Joe. The Records have got to be more important than any one of us. Otherwise, we have no unity. We are only five creatures trying to stay alive. It is ridiculous to joke about physical punishment. There are many other ways."

"Wait till Erma is pregnant," Joe said. "Talk to me then. See what you've got to say then."

No answer. Arthur had no answer to make to that. Defeat. But he could not see. He turned and tried to walk away and ran into a tree. And suddenly he began to vomit.

"Jesus Christ, Arthur, what's the matter? I should never have said . . . What's the matter, *can't you see?*"

Arthur sat down very suddenly on the ground. "No," he said. "No, I have not been able to see for quite a while."

"You mean you're *blind?*"

"It's only temporary," Arthur said. "It's the headaches. It's happened before. It goes away after a while. I've had them a long time now."

"Hell, I didn't know it," Joe said. "You never said anything about headaches and I've been so busy in the laboratory that I . . . Oh, you don't know about the laboratory."

"No," Arthur said. "What laboratory?"

"Well, I've been working on some drugs, trying to . . .

Say, maybe I've got something. Maybe it would work on your headache. Could you hold onto me and walk? Come on. Here, this way. Hold onto me now."

"I can walk," Arthur said. Or, he thought, I could crawl.

The dose of braidstem, which earlier that day had produced in sleek number 39 (weight, eight turtleshells plus two cluster-nuts) a deep sleep lasting almost to the end of the delivery of a live, healthy litter, gave Arthur first a nauseating, bitter taste in his mouth, followed by a welcome feeling of warmth.

"Do you feel anything yet?" Joe asked.

"Sort of warm, that's all," Arthur said. "Been cold all day. I can see now. But then it never does last very long, the blindness. It comes and goes."

"Well, you sit there awhile. I've got to take a look at the feathermane."

After a while the throbbing stopped and gradually the ringing of the bell began to recede. Finally there was only a residue of dull pain, easily bearable.

"God, Joe, how long have you had that stuff? I feel almost alive again. What a relief!"

"Pain all gone?"

"No, but it's bearable now. Maybe another dose would fix it altogether."

"I don't know if you ought to," Joe said. "I don't know much about the stuff. Some of the other ones I've been working with are pretty bad poison. On the animals, anyhow."

"I'll risk it," Arthur said. "Give me another shot."

Joe came back with a torch for light and handed Arthur the second dose. Also he had his book of notes. "We'd better write it down," he said, "how much you've taken. If you have these very often, you ought to stick to the smallest amount you can until I get to try it on a big animal." He turned back a few pages. "You see here, in the clawleaf notes, what happened. This stuff might not be safe."

Arthur took the book from Joe and began to study it. Then he was asking questions. So long had Joe kept his secret, and worked in solitude, that he experienced first a shyness and then a feeling of pride to see his work in another man's hands. Then he began to talk and to say out loud the things that worried him, the work that must be done in the short time left. He saw Arthur turning back to refer to an earlier experiment.

"It's a funny thing," Joe said. "I've been calling them notes. I never thought of it till you came, but . . ."

"Yes," Arthur said, "it's quite a record. I can't get relief from a headache from the kind I keep."

"I wish you'd keep this one," Joe said. "I need help bad. I've been wanting to ask you for a long time but I've been so damned scared Gwen would get wind of it. I've got to produce the magical dose at the right moment, that's all. By a trick if necessary. If she knew about some of these, she'd be sure I was going to poison her."

"But you can show her," Arthur said, holding the book in his hands. "You can—"

"You can*not* show Gwen," Joe said. "You ought to know that by now. I've got to have a live child that isn't hated by its mother, Arthur, whatever I have to do to get it."

The feathermane number 39 would not deliver for some time yet, so it was safe to leave her; the two men walked back together.

"How's your head?" Joe asked.

"O.K., Dr. Roberts. I'll have a good night's sleep and be all right by tomorrow. Jesus, what a relief it is."

"It's a funny thing about tonight," Joe said. "I've been thinking . . . It's all so much like Pete Dobenski in Drury. Remember?"

"I'll never forget," Arthur said, and then he began to imitate Mr. Dobenski, Pete's father, the little man of many creases: " 'It iss nothing, Mr. Herrick—nothing. Only a detecktiff story that my boy he copy out for you.' "

When they got back to the vault, the trench fire had been replenished. Joe took his Record and started off. "Good night," he said.

"Good night, Doc."

Arthur sat down alone. The warmth of the trench fire was good, and he had a tiredness in him that made him dread the climb to his house. Suddenly he had a picture of Erma replenishing the fire that he had neglected, wearing on her face that worried, patient, martyred look he hated so, doing once more a piece of work that he could not finish or had forgotten.

Wait till Erma is pregnant and then talk to me. Wait till the world ends. Joe's house would be full of kids and Erma would still be tending that goddamned feathermane and nothing more.

He reached for his own Record and began slowly to climb toward the house. God, he was tired. He stopped once and leaned against a tree, and suddenly he longed for the golden days over the print shop in Drury where *his* had been the important Records and Joe had been *his* helper, where he did not have headaches and his wife was alive and desirable, where Gwendolyn's words had been Mr. Dobenski's and he had known the answer to them.

So habitual had the gesture become with him now that, even without the headache, he opened and closed the fingers of his left hand. The hand no longer felt disembodied, but something had slipped through the fingers—away from him. Gone.

Lying in bed in the darkness, awake and apprehensive and hardly breathing, Erma saw him come into the house, close the door behind him, and lean against it. Then he walked over to the fire she had left and sat down before it on the floor. He sat looking into the fire and clasping and unclasping the fingers of his left hand. Once he smiled and shook his head, and, though the firelight was very clear on his face, Erma lay there not knowing, not having any idea of what had happened to him, except that she could tell the headache was better. When the fire snapped, he did not jerk. Once, to look at him, she would have been able to tell at least who had won the argument, but now she did not have the faintest idea. She longed to get out of bed and walk over to him quietly, easily, as she had done a hundred times before, to touch him, speak to him. In the old days she would have called out to him when he came in the door, or, if she had not called, then she would have been asleep.

I must not spy, she thought. If I have let it be thought I am asleep, then I must be asleep. At least I must close my eyes and try to sleep.

Perhaps she had slept a little, for she did not know when he came to bed except that he reached out and touched her and she turned to him in glad welcome to put an end to their estrangement, thinking: It is over, it is over, and afterward we will be able to speak each other again. But suddenly in fear she opened her mouth to cry out and the fear became terror and the scream was frozen in her. For she did not know this man. Even the skin of his back was alien to her finger tips, and her hands recoiled from the touch of it as, in denial of their long history together, without tenderness, without caress, with no love and nothing, nothing familiar, nothing belonging to their so infinitely varied

rituals, he thrust himself upon her in measured, inhuman brutal-
ity, thrust upon thrust. She tried to get away, but he pinned her
shoulders in pain and submission.

This was beyond her experience, as terror had been until now
unknown to her, as madness was unknown to her. Was he mad?
Surely he was mad. Even in terror she could think that surely he
was mad. It was as though she were dead. A dead woman. And a
stranger. And he violating the body of a strange dead woman. No
end, there was no end to it. No end to it until the terrible darkness of unconsciousness began to beat against her numbness like
the waves of the sea. A dead woman. The body of a strange, dead
woman lying on the shore, washed up by the sea. And then not
even the woman, not even the stranger's body, but only the shore
of the sea, and the man alone now become a giant phallus, in terrible hatred trying to violate the very earth. Mercifully, at last,
the waves of the sea washed over the man, washed over the shore,
blotting out the scars in the earth, taking it all into its own cold
darkness.

Hours later, Erma rose up out of the dark sea into a fog of
chaos, and she rolled out of the bed and began to crawl along the
floor, leaving the man there in the bed, mad, asleep, or dead, she
did not know. There was no choice among these states, only the
fact now of a presence, a weight, that must be abandoned, left,
escaped from. She crawled into the kitchen, toward the pool made
from the hot spring. Saliva dropped from her open mouth and
she stopped and wiped her lips with the back of her hand in an
aimless way. Then she crawled on to the edge of the pool and
painfully, stupidly, let herself down into it. To bathe, to lie in hot
water, to wash again and again, to be clean of it, to be clean again.

She was filled with a sickness that the eyes cannot be closed
against, that the head cannot be turned away from, that cannot be
vomited up. If it had been his fist smashing into her mouth,
against her breast, splintering the cheekbone—if it had been his
fist. But if a phallus be used as a fist, be directed as a fist, then
does it not become a fist? It does not.

For a long time she did not want anything but the hot water,
and then later she did not want anything but to die. And then, a
long time after that, she wanted to be comforted. I will go get my
feathermane, she thought, and feel his gentle head beneath my
hand and see his eyes trust me. Then . . . then I can think what
to do.

She took whatever clothes she could find in the kitchen so as not to return to the other room, and left by the back door. It is too early, she thought, to go for the feathermane. Justin would still be asleep. Well, then, she would sit by Justin's house and wait.

I will tell Justin, she thought. I will tell Justin that Arthur is mad. But Justin would ask her, anyone would ask her: "How do you know?"

If it had been his fist. That you can say to anyone. But how can I say this? she thought. I do not know how to say it. *How do you know? How do you know your husband is mad?* Because he made love to me brutally—was that what she would say? Made love? There was no love in it. What should she say? Because I am afraid of him? No one would believe her because she did not know how to say it. If you have the experience, she thought, and no words for it, how can you speak of it to someone who might have the words but not the experience? It is because I am afraid, regardless of what he has done, she thought. And no one but me can measure how afraid I am or how much it means that I am so afraid.

"Come in, Erma," Justin said, opening the door behind her. "Your feathermane is safe, all right. Do you trust me so little that you come so early?"

She walked into Justin's house and sat on a stool while he kindled the fire. The feathermane bounded to her and she put her arms around him and leaned her head on his.

"Justin . . ." she said. But it was like yesterday in here. Everything the same. The incredible night began to slip away from her.

From the fire Justin turned his head and looked at her. "Yes?" he said.

It didn't show then. People would look at her just as if it were yesterday. No one would believe it.

"Thank you for keeping the feathermane," she said.

"Oh, that's all right," he said. "He's good company. Maybe I should have a pet of my own. You bring him any time you need to."

Need to. But she needed much more now. She must tell Justin. She must tell someone before she went back into that house alone. How will I say it? she thought.

"Have you had your tea yet?" Justin asked.

"No," she said. It isn't tea, Justin, she wanted to say. It isn't tea I need.

"Well, wait and have some with me," he said. "Sometime I

hope to make you a cup of tea that will be as welcome as the coffee you made for me that first day in Drury. I often think of that time, you know, and those cold grapes in that awful heat. I can taste them yet. Oh," he said suddenly, and it seemed to Erma that Justin looked strange, embarrassed.

Her face flushed and she thought, It must show. There must be a bruise or a cut on my neck. By the greatest effort she kept her hands from feeling of her face and neck. Abruptly Justin started toward his kitchen, stopping on the way to jerk up the covers of his bed.

And then she saw why he had been embarrassed. Beneath the mossback-hide robe over the bed she saw the sleeve of her jacket protruding, the jacket she had brought for the feathermane. Her jacket lay on the pillow, in the warmth of Justin Magnus' bed. It must have lain all night beneath his head. She turned her back on it at once and pulled the stool closer to the fire. My jacket is cherished, she thought. *My* jacket. He has taken it into his bed. All night it has lain under his head. And suddenly she was able to forget her terror and to think of Arthur, for he who is so rich as to have even his coat cherished can afford compassion.

What had happened *to Arthur* that he should have done such a thing? She could not leave him alone. She had to find out what was wrong.

Justin poured her some tea; she drank it and refused a second bowl. "I have to get back," she said. "I have to get back to Arthur."

"Well," Justin said, "you go ahead. I'll bring your jacket over to you later."

"You'd better keep it here," she said. "Then you'll have it the next time I have to bring the feathermane."

"All right," he said.

The feathermane bounded at her side, lifting his delicate hoofs high off the ground, angling for her attention, but she was hardly aware of him. Her jacket had been cherished and out of its empty sleeve she had taken her pride again and put it on and it cleared her head. The proud can afford compassion. The proud can take time to think. What had made her go running off like a frightened child? What had made her leave the house when there was something wrong with her husband? What had made her contemplate discussing her husband with another man behind his back?

She left the feathermane outside and walked quietly into the house. Arthur sat at the table alone.

"I'll make the tea," she said.

When she had built up the fire and made the tea she brought it to the table and put it before him and a cup for herself. All this time he had said nothing, made no move. Now she began to drink her tea and at last he drank his, too. Suddenly her heart ached for him, for the terrible thing that must have befallen him to make him look the way he did. The proud can afford compassion. They can afford to cry out in their hearts, "Tell me, tell me, and I will help you." They can afford to believe that there is nothing they cannot understand, cannot share.

At last she said, "There must be something you have to say to me, Arthur. Surely something terrible must have happened to you that you could so deny our history together. There must be some reason."

"I have no excuse, Erma," he said, and he put his hand up to press against his right temple. "There is no excuse. However, I have been telling myself that there is something relevant."

"And what is that?" she said. But there is nothing relevant to humiliation, she thought, except humiliation.

"Well, Joe taunted me about your sterility and obscured the issue with it, and then he put me in his debt, and it set me wild. But remember," he said, "please remember that I didn't say it was an excuse."

Your sterility. How easily he had said it. And Joe must have said it. It was not fair. Not fair to condemn her in only a little over a year. To accept something about her calmly and speak of it, as accepted, behind her back. To call it by a name—that made it different. If he had not spoken the word; if it had not been so final. Before the word she was proud and full of compassion. Before the word she could have gone to him and touched him. Now she silenced the denials in her mind and bowed her head, staring at her white fingernails pressed against the table's edge. Those who have been accused, accused unjustly and in a calm manner, without being consulted, they cannot afford compassion.

Finally she looked up at him and he sat there, still with that terrible look on his face, still pressing his fingers against his temple.

"Have you a headache now?" she said. For what good would it do to plead her case if he had a headache?

"I have," he said, "again. And Joe has the medicine for it."

"The medicine?"

And so he told her about the laboratory and the record of the laboratory work, the animals, the new braidstem concentrate, and gradually they began to speak together of this new thing like two strangers discussing the landscape.

"And now," Arthur said, "I must go get some more of the medicine and I hope it works as well this time."

He got up from the table and walked away. At the door he stopped and looked back at her, forcing himself to meet her eyes. "I will build you another bed, Erma, as soon as I get back. Don't worry. You don't have to be afraid."

Now was the time, if she were going to speak in time to stop the estrangement between them. Now was the time to go to him, to speak to him, to say, You don't have to do that. To say, I understand.

She sat where she was. "Thank you," she said.

When Arthur opened the door the feathermane slipped past him into the house. He went to Erma, but she was strange and did not notice him, so he turned from her and lay down on the hearth, tucking his delicate front hoofs under him. After all, he was home and in his own place and later she would notice him.

What if it's true? she thought. True! And I cannot even have those few delicious days of hope each month. What if they are right and I have to know ahead of me forever and forever that there is no hope? It was not fair. It was not fair of them to have accepted the word so easily, to have decided this matter. Why, there were lots of women—she'd heard of them—who had children when they thought they were sterile. Two, three, five years did not make it so. There was Sarah in the Bible. Of course there was Sarah and it was thirteen years, or maybe seventeen—she could not remember. And then there was that woman she had met once in Drury waiting for the city train with her little boy and the woman was embarrassed—she couldn't get over it. She began to explain as soon as they'd met. "Of course everybody thinks he's my grandson," she had said. "Why, my hair has been gray for years. My husband and I had been married for twelve years before he was born, and we'd given up the idea completely. I tell you I couldn't believe it. And neither one of us can get used to it. We planned our life differently after we thought we weren't to have children, and now, why, we hardly know what to do with him. We're afraid he'll break something or hurt himself and he makes us so nervous. Why, you know, it's embarrassing at our age. It really is."

"Twelve years," the woman had said. And Sarah. There was Sarah and there must be some others. Didn't she know about some others? There *must* be others she knew about.

They were wrong about her. They were all wrong. She knew they were wrong. She got up from the table and went over by the fireplace and took stealthily from a place where she had hidden them a bowlful of clusternuts. She did not like them, but Gwendolyn did. Gwendolyn was always cracking them and eating them. And once before, in doubt, Erma had gathered a little hoard of them, thinking they might have some power of fertility because Gwendolyn ate them, but she did not like them and after she got them home she had left them untouched; thinking it was like witchcraft, like hiding roots and charms in one's bed.

But now she began to crack them and eat them, standing there staring into the fire. She ate them faster and faster until, in a kind of crazy frenzy, she was stuffing her mouth with them. Suddenly she realized what she was doing and she sank down to the floor and sat there by the feathermane. He stretched his neck and nuzzled her, asking to be petted. She put her hand on his head out of habit, mechanically, and then she bent over and began to sob.

For that sickness she had endured sitting in the bathing pool, that sickness the eyes cannot be closed against nor the head turned away from, there are no words, and therefore, being beyond words, it is beyond tears. But now, for her, they had a word, a name, a label. She sat on the floor, bent over, her arms crossed, sobbing and rocking herself, back and forth, without comfort, while outside in the corral the mossbacks grew restive and milled about, waiting to be fed, and the ewes, waiting heavily and painfully to be milked, began to bleat in plaintive puzzlement.

In the house the woman sat on, sobbing and rocking herself without comfort, the taste of the hated clusternuts musty and bitter in her mouth.

CHAPTER FIVE

WELL, the last note, then. The end of it. The second movement finished. As though he had just heard it performed, Justin sat now at his desk, experiencing the breathless, waiting interval, buffeted by the reverberations of the mighty crescendo. So "The Time of Innocence" was come at last to its strange, incredible end. No, not incredible because, on its premise, it was absolutely logical. An incredible premise, then? But no. Did they not live out their days now, all of them, in just such before-shattering tension? Was it not true, as true as the words Erma had spoken when she gave him the key, that innocence does not die; it is always murdered? In their time and in this place, he felt it to be true, prophetically and horribly true, but for him, Justin Magnus, it was . . . not false. Certainly not false. But a departure. Certainly a departure.

From a strange place and a frightening dimension his eyes returned slowly to focus on the room, on the table, on the cup of tea before him. Slowly he placed the quill pen on the manuscript sheet. How long had the tea been there? Had he made tea this morning? He must have. There was still a small fire in the fireplace. Was it deepsun, then, or eassun already? What matter? He stood up and stretched his great stiff body and shook from his head the maddening echo of what he had just written. Should one write a thing so terrible and call it "The Time of Innocence"? He had in him a feeling of guilt as anguished as the clarinets slashing at the French horns, as though he had spoken an oracle that should never have been spoken, and now they were all condemned. He kicked off his clothes and walked into the other room. He stepped into the hot-spring pool and submerged himself. Then he stood up and shook himself and walked over to the fireplace to dry. He squatted down and began to throw wood on the fire. A great hunger came on him, and he went and got a piece of dried mossback meat and some bread and came back to the fire. He sat looking into the fire and eating ravenously, the drops of water glistening on his chest and head.

And suddenly he longed for Max Staats to hear the second movement. He longed to know what the critics would have said—not Rouf and Slausen and that crowd, but Kirkendahl. Kirkendahl and Max Staats. Would it seem impossible to them that he had taken such a departure? Could they swallow it? He longed to know. He longed to hear it performed, too—full orchestra and Orananzo conducting, and then, in the morning paper, what Kirkendahl thought of "The Time of Innocence." And afterward, to sit and talk it all over with Max.

Outside a ragman bird let out its raucous four-note call— *Any old rags? Any old rags?*—and brought Justin back to where he was. What was he thinking? Kirkendahl and Max Staats were in the world and, for all he knew, they might be dead. Certainly if they ever heard "The Time of Innocence" or "Discovery," or any of *The Green Kingdom,* he wouldn't know about it. Why had he written it, then? If he had resisted this for sixty-two years, why *now* had he broken loose from restraint? Wasn't it that very restraint that had made him great, or was it only that it had made him great in a certain way? He looked at the last piece of bread he held in his hand, smiled, tossed it into the fire. Then he yawned, got up, and walked over to his bed. As soon as he stretched out he fell asleep.

When he awoke, after an hour's heavy sleep, it was with the dream figure of Lazarus haunting him, Lazarus from the old unfinished opera. He thought he heard Erma calling him, and he pulled on his leather trousers and a jacket and went to the door.

"I thought I heard your voice," he said. "Come in."

The feathermane following her, she walked into the room, carrying some pieces of leather under her arm. "I'm making sandals," she said. "Let me see how your old ones are while Joe is with Gwen."

For they never left Gwen alone these days. One of them stayed always with her or near her.

"How is Gwen?" Justin asked.

"I don't know," Erma said. "She hardly ever talks any more. I think she is terribly afraid."

"Poor child," Justin said. "Wait, Erma, I'll make us some tea. It will do you good to sit a moment and it will get the cobwebs out of my brain. I just woke up."

"You're not ill?" she said, looking around the room in a startled manner, so unusual it was for him to sleep in the daytime. Then she saw the manuscript.

"Oh," she said.

"Yes," he said. "Yes, the second movement is finished."

"Finished! Oh, Justin, that's wonderful. How I wish I might hear it. You shall certainly have new sandals, then, for a reward, whether you need them or not."

Justin lifted up one of his feet and looked at the sole of the sandal. "Oh, I need them, all right. But you have so much to do. Hadn't I better wait awhile?"

"Let me have the old ones," she said.

Justin took off the sandals and, barefoot, began to build up the fire and get the tea bowls ready. While he worked she knelt on the floor and, with a bone knife, marked the outline of the old sandals on the leather. The feathermane pulled at one end of the leather to tease her. She pushed him away gently, but he came back again to the game.

"Justin," she said, "hold the beast a moment till I get this heel right."

Justin sat on the floor by the fire and held the feathermane away from the leather. "If you're not good," he said to it, "you will end up with a collar around your neck, as they do in the world. You wouldn't like that."

When she had the markings finished she rolled up the leather and gave Justin back his sandals. Then she picked up the bowl of tea and drank deeply.

"So you've finished it," she said. "And are you pleased?"

"I don't know," he said. "You look thin, Erma. Are you not well?"

"Oh, I'm all right," she said.

She looked up at him suddenly and smiled. He was fastening the old sandals on his feet and he wore on his face a look such as she had never seen before. His tea was still untouched.

"What is it, Justin?" she asked.

He jerked his head quickly. "Oh, I had such a haunting dream of the figure of Lazarus just before you came. I can't seem to shake it out of my head."

"Lazarus? That opera that you never finished?"

"Yes," he said. "Why, how did you know? Have I spoken of it before?"

"Yes. When you were stopped on 'The Time of Innocence' that time before because you didn't want it to go the way it was going. I asked you if you'd ever been through that before and you said yes, once on Lazarus, and that you hadn't finished it."

"Perhaps I was wise not to," he said.

"I always wondered what happened to Lazarus after the resurrection," she said. "Not ultimately, but just Monday and Tuesday and Wednesday. How can you eat your porridge and wash your feet in a miraculous way?"

"That's what the opera was about," Justin said. "The miracle came first. It was easily written. And then the golden days of grace when people came from afar to see the man and he spoke his testimony to them and children followed him in the streets. And then—"

"And then they began to doubt that it had really happened, I suppose," she said.

"Exactly," he said, "and the more they doubted, the more he tried to convince them."

"And was it there you stopped?" she said.

"A little before, I think," Justin said. "I never understood it because I had the greatest sympathy with the man and a real sense of his tragedy."

"But not his frenzy?" she said.

Justin frowned and his big head leaned over on one side. "Frenzy?" he said.

"Yes," she said. "When you spoke of 'The Time of Innocence' to me before, you called it unresolved tensions, but to me it is frenzy. And if, in Lazarus, it was frenzy, too, then I can understand why you did not finish it. The sympathy you had for him, the awareness of his tragedy—oh, I can see that in you. But I do not see you partaking of frenzy, Justin."

True, he thought. That was true. He turned his face from her, for he did not know yet if this were an accusation. He did not partake of frenzy. He stared into the fire and thought of this thing. The haunting figure of Lazarus receded from him and instead he saw himself walking up the hill toward his house from Max's, at one of the many times he had been called home for Edith. Even then, even in the worst of it, with the unearthly sounds of her screams in his ears, her frenzy had aroused in him, as always, a stoicism. He saw now how it was he had resisted Lazarus so long ago and how he had resisted the death of his sons to the point where he could not remember their faces. But he *had* finished "The Time of Innocence." He had done that.

He could not reconcile the two—the music he had made of their frenzy and his aloofness from it. Patience, he had thought. Time will take care of it. They are young, he thought. They cannot believe that the child will be born, that things will be better after the child is born. And gradually he had withdrawn himself from them and their problems, waiting on time, believing in patience, thinking that the years alone would bring wisdom, thinking that they would be easier without his interference. He kept the feathermane for Erma often but did not always translate this into Arthur's increasing headaches. He saw Erma going back and forth between her house and Gwen's and he discounted the tyranny of Gwendolyn's fear. He sometimes went to visit and admire Joe's laboratory and did not weigh the risks that weighed on Joe.

He was quiet for so long, staring into the fire, that Erma feared she had hurt him, speaking so bluntly, and she put out her hand timidly and touched his arm. He took the hand and held it in his own, and there, at once, he felt between them a most beautiful communion. No longer was it unresolved tensions, or frenzy, or a delicate question of his place in their lives. It was all quite simply translated for him into a mountain of work that had fallen on this tired girl, that he must help her with.

She used his hand to steady herself, and stood up. He stood too and looked at her. No need to tell her. Tomorrow she would know his help if, indeed, she did not already. Quite simply he put out his arms and she came to him and leaned her tiredness against him and he held her very still and quiet.

"Will you keep the feathermane for me again?" she asked.

"Of course," he said.

She arched herself back from him and looked up into his face. "Oh, how I envy you, Justin. What must it be like to eat out your heart and be nourished from it at the same time, to have the answers come before the questions?"

She dipped down and picked up her roll of leather from the floor and ran out of the door. Justin went out after her but turned the other way and began to walk in his long strides away from the houses.

He had finished it, or he had allowed it to finish, and thereby committed himself. By the very writing of such music he had partaken of their frenzy. He could no longer be aloof, he must remember that. And something else, too, he must remember, a thing he rarely thought of, a thing he had thought to shut out of his memory forever. He stopped abruptly in his tracks and stared down at his old sandals and the feathergrass beneath them. Was he not the man who had gone out to sea in a frail and leaking boat with no thing between him and the furious sea except the dead body of his beloved? Oh, he had known frenzy. He had not always had his stoicism. "The Time of Innocence" was, after all, not the first departure. It had a precedent.

But that—*that* she did not know about.

In the laboratory, the fifth successive sleek to be given the new braidstem concentrate gave birth to a live litter while lying with her eyes closed in sleep or near sleep, so that she suffered Joe to touch her body without alarm.

Time in the Green Kingdom came to be measured in weeks instead of months, and Justin took on himself the task of the firewood supply. Without explanation or question he simply appeared with it regularly so that a huge communal stockpile grew up. The ballsleeper number 40 (weight, one Yearsenday bomb) responded, as had the sleek, to a dosage multiplied by its weight factor of 2.41. And Justin took over the stretching of the mossback hides and the butchering, having fashioned for himself a new set of bone knives.

The weeks became days and the sleep of the ruff number 40 (two Yearsendays, twelve turtleshells; dosage factor 6.28) lasted through a count of three thousand and the birth of a live litter. Justin strengthened the walls of the mossback corral. He smoked a large haul of lace-finned fish over a slow leatherwood fire. He went into the deep woods and sought out the tough roots of the soap plants, bringing back two full baskets of their shavings. Still he was not tired, and at late eassun, when he found Erma milking the mossback ewe, her eyes closed and her forehead leaning against the ewe's side, he said to her, "Move over. I'll do it." Often now, and in unexpected places, when she reached out her hand to the work ahead, his had been there before hers. The roofs of their houses were reinforced with new tough leaves from the dewplant. There was fresh moss, a mountain of it, for their beds, and, in the laboratory, the testimony for the potency of the braidstem concentrate continued to mount:

howler #42 (4 Yearsendays; dosage factor 9.66) Sleep to the count of 4200. Live litter.

feathermane #41 (2 riverstones plus 2 Yearsendays; dosage factor 28.97) Light sleep to the count of 3500. Live kid. Mother responded to loud noise during sleep.

The days became wessun, deepsun, eassun, and dark, and Justin whistled to himself part of "The Time of Innocence" while he pounded with a huge stone the grain for their future bread. In the laboratory the mossback ewe lifted her four rivstone weight onto her feet and shook the grogginess out of her head from the 48.28 dosage of braidstem concentrate. She licked at her calf in a puzzled way, and nibbled delicately at the greengrain held in Joe's rejoicing hand.

Wessun became early wessun and late wessun, and the night became early dark and true dark, and Justin took to himself the metronome of Gwendolyn's waiting time. His afternoon visits were the one thing that could stir Gwendolyn from her apathy. She sat now combing her hair and braiding it in preparation for his coming. It was tiring and laborious, yet she would not have it cut and she could not suffer Erma to comb it for her without an upsetting show of impatience. While she could still be weaving, she had lived through the days somehow. But then at last she had grown so large that she could not sit comfortably at the loom, and the effort of lifting her arms had become so difficult that weaving had lost its pleasure and the shuttle its soothing. And then . . . then there was nothing.

The kicking, struggling infant could no longer be denied, nor the thought of it escaped from. They were not coming for her. They would not make it in time. And she would die. She would die. Without the loom there was nothing but apprehension, and then, quite suddenly, the panic turned to blankness and she merely stared in apathy. Dull questions bounced at her from the walls, from the ceiling, and she suffered Erma to bathe her. Before, she had been quick to anger, full of impatience, accusations, complaints. With the coming of the blankness she ceased to quarrel, and finally she did not talk at all.

So Justin found her and so he began to pit himself against her apathy. He had a magic about him that he could always make people wish to be what he thought they were, or what he seemed to them to think they were. To Gwendolyn, her pregnancy was an end in itself, and beyond it she did not think. Around her, the others also found any other concept impossible to speak about. Justin assumed, naturally and articulately, that Gwen was going to have a child and that she looked forward to it. He created for her a mother role and made her wish, in his presence, to play it and to play it with him. Everything else that she did and thought, she did alone in a place that none could share with her. She did not have the magic. She did not know the invitation.

Joe, of course, thought long and often of his child as a reality, but the words of his plans and his joy died in him when he confronted Gwen. Her fear made a kind of paralysis and it was infectious. Even the cradle that Joe made he had worked on in secret. In the evenings he brought her the food that Erma had cooked. He carried her to bed and sat by her side until she fell asleep. He built up the fires, brought water for her to drink. When she cried he comforted her and when she raged he listened, but he rarely spoke of the child. He could not seem to break past the barrier of her fear. It was as though to mention the child in the future would be to belittle Gwen in the present. It was like levity at a funeral. He tried and he could not shake it. He put his faith in the braidstem concentrate and kept his own counsel. He did not know the magic of invitation, either.

Gwendolyn was braiding her hair, waiting for Justin to come as he came every afternoon at eassun. She wore a soft, pale-green woolen robe that fell in folds about her body. It was made from one long piece of cloth, with an opening in the center for the head. The sides of the front piece were caught together in the back. Then, by ties at each side, the back pieces were pulled forward over the sides and tied in front. The two side draperies were then caught into folds by a series of tucks, and, with the movement of the arms, the folds rearranged themselves into newness.

As she finished braiding her hair she heard Justin's step. "Come in," she called to him.

He came across the room to her and held out his hands to help her stand. "Come along," he said. "We mustn't be late. And, besides, I have a surprise for you today."

"A surprise?" she said.

"I do, unless your own is too imminent."

"Oh, no," she said. "I think it's all right to leave the house."

"Of course it's all right," he said. "I can always carry you home if necessary. Perhaps I am even plotting that it will be my house that has the honor of the first Green Kingdom child."

He tucked her arm in his and they walked out of the house together and along the path they took each afternoon to the place where they fed the birds. The steps of this pathway were now all ritual to them. There was the place where he walked ahead of her and held back the branch of a tree that hung over the path. There was the little decline where he stopped and lifted her very gently that she might not stumble. And at the end, there was the big seat with the leather back and the footstool for her feet.

Then Justin left her and brought bread and grain from the house. He would walk away from her, throwing the crumbs on the ground and whistling the notes that the birds now recognized, and then he would come back and sit down beside her and quietly they would wait for the first birds to come. Now Gwendolyn threw the crumbs to them, enticing them closer and closer.

At first only the big stiltlegs had ventured near, but one afternoon a timid wingtucker had shown up at the feast and after him had come the darklings and the fat, waddling clownbirds, until now, if Justin and Gwendolyn were patient, they might be entertained by an endless variety. Today they were to have real drama, for two of the big stiltlegs reached at once for the same piece of bread. Their dark-green beaks, almost black, were touching and the tug of war had first one and then the other walking backward. One of the birds lifted a long leg and raked at the other. Momentarily losing his hold, the second bird flew at his rival's head. The piece of bread fell to the ground and, from between the legs of the attacker, a small bow-legged clownbird darted for the prize and waddled off with it. This happened so suddenly and the clownbird was so ridiculous with his stump tail dragging the ground that Justin and Gwendolyn burst into laughter and there was a startled uprising as all the birds momentarily disappeared.

"Wasn't that ridiculous?" Gwen said. "Oh, he was wonderful."

"That's the best show we've had yet," Justin said. "You wait here and, while they're getting their courage up to come back, I'll get your surprise."

"What is it, Justin?" she said. "Tell me."

He stroked a loose strand of hair back from her forehead. "You'll see," he said.

When he came back he spread over her lap the most exquisite coverlet she had ever seen. Even she, who did all the weaving and was jealous of it, who made most of their clothes (and very subtly used her talent as a weapon against Erma), even she had never seen anything so beautiful. Justin had taken the forest-green feathers of the darkling, the pure, clean green of the easterbird, the yellow green of the riverheron's plume and the turquoise crest feathers of the chichimingo and woven them into a floating swirl of color, studded here and there with the jeweled breast feathers of the male gemboys.

Gwendolyn lifted the coverlet, floated it up and down over her hands. "Oh," she said, "I have never seen anything so exquisite, so light and warm and beautiful."

And then, fine craftswoman that she had become, she turned it over. "How did you do it?" she said. "Oh, I see. But how painstaking, Justin!"

The quills had been tied and woven into a mesh of fibers from the spiked leaves of the soap plant. These fibers, stripped from the leaves after the fleshy part had been scraped away, they used almost as much as they did the wool from the mossbacks, though not for clothing. There was great strength to them but little warmth. It was Erma who prepared them and braided them into string and rope and handles for baskets and belts and fastenings and hinges. Often she longed to experiment with weaving them, but she knew that the loom was Gwendolyn's and her pride in it a jealous one.

"I left it this way so you could see it," Justin said, "though I suppose you'll have to sew cloth over the back to make it safe for the child. There are still some places where the quills are sharp in spite of everything. Besides—" he laughed—"for this you only have to tie thousands of knots. For that you have to sew, and I still cannot even sew enough to mend my own sandals properly."

He said safe for the *child*, Gwen thought, and quickly she tried to adjust herself and respond as he wished, as the people he knew had always, in spite of themselves, tried to respond to Justin in a way that would please him—with the exception of his son George. Gwen had thought the coverlet was meant for her, and now she turned it feather side up and bent over it to cover her confusion.

"Yes," she said, "yes, it is beautiful. I will put a back on it."

"My wife made a set of coverlets, I remember, for Tommy when he was little. There was one for each day in the week and she called them the creation blankets. They were very beautiful. I found an old one in the attic, I remember, after her death. It . . ."

He spoke to her of Edith and of the birth of his sons. He spoke of the creation blankets and Gwendolyn turned her face to him attentively, there in the quiet circle of the feeding birds who had gained courage once more, who came close and darted and retreated, fluttered and fought and advanced again. And Gwen thought with surprise, as he spoke so naturally of birth, as though it were a knowledge they shared: They must not have told him how I act. Erma must not have told him. Joe must not have told him. He thinks that I am like his wife. Four sons. Four times. He *must* know what to do. He must know.

In the laboratory, Joe took leave of the animals and checked over their food supply. Gwendolyn's time was very near now and he would not again leave her until the child was born. Arthur would feed the animals from now on. Joe felt a great happiness of confidence and achievement and gratitude that he had been allowed time to carry all the big animals through and try the dosage on himself. The braidstem concentrate, measured in duplicate in case of accident, was ready for Gwendolyn, hidden securely under the kitchen roof. Joe turned suddenly, impatiently, to Arthur.

"No, I told you before, Arthur. You're hitting the stuff too often. You keep trying to increase the dose. I told you that ruff bit me yesterday, the one I've had on it steady."

"A ruff bit you—what does that prove?" Arthur said. "Any wildcat will bite. They're fierce, that's all. I've got to have the stuff, Joe. I don't care if the ruff spit in your eye. What's the matter? Are you afraid I'll bite you?"

"You might," Joe said. "How the hell do I know? I told you before, I'm leery of the stuff. For a while your headaches got better and then they got worse again. For all I know it might even cause headaches. Why can't you lay off the stuff till we've had time to run ten or twelve animals through a series? You think I want to take a fool risk on you?"

Out of the corner of his eye Arthur saw the bowl. He turned

his back on it carefully and, with a change to affability, said, "I guess you're right, Joe. I'll lay off the stuff for a while and see how it goes. It's pretty tough, though, when you know there is relief, not to take it."

He could feel the bowl behind his back. He could feel a round place in his spine, pulling toward the bowl. He felt the sweat coming out on the palms of his hands and with a great effort kept from wiping them on his trouser legs. The thing was not to be tricked into giving away the fact that it was not now headaches but insomnia he needed it for. He was holding his teeth together, locking them in an effort not to be tricked into talking, admitting, pleading. The frozen circle in his spine that was the knowledge of the bowl of braidstem turned hot and began to burn. He felt himself moving backward, trying to match the circle with the bowl, trying to cover up the treasure, the prize, the thing he had to have. And in the end it was so easy.

"So long," Joe said. "Take care of the joint. I'll see you when it's over."

He picked up his book of notes and walked off, not even looking back. It was so easy, so deceptively easy. That was the thing. There must be some catch in it if it could be that easy. Arthur felt his knees collapse under him. He sat down on the ground and began to shake all over. At last now he could wipe the sweat off his hands. He turned his head cautiously to look at the bowl. It was there. Nothing had happened to it. Maybe Joe was coming back. Maybe it was a trick. He felt watched, spied upon. He forced himself to sit and wait. He began to count to himself. If Joe hadn't come back in five thousand counts, then he'd take it.

But it would be missed. In two days, three days, sometime it would be missed. He could water it down. He could take half. He dropped his head to his hands and shuddered with disgust. At least, not that—not the man who had traded everything he had for the cause of an accurate Record, not that man to water down a solution. Better just take it. Better brazen it out. Yes, I took it. Yes, yes, yes, I took it. What could they do? A thief is a fact, he thought. There is nothing you can do about it. It is over. A watered-down solution, that is a criminal process, a long torture.

It made him laugh to think of Joe's face. Yes, I took it. It made him laugh. He jumped up and lifted the bowl and started down the path. He saw the label as he lifted the bowl: *first boiling only; not filtered.* But the words did not penetrate. He walked down the path carrying the precious bowl filled with the blessed deliverance for nights ahead. Many nights ahead. He would hide it and use it sparingly, only a little in the beer each night, and for many blessed nights ahead he would not have to ask. Oh, for a long time he would not have to ask.

He smiled. He walked along the path smiling, happier than he had been for a long, long time. A few drops in the beer at night and he would not have to ask and he could slip down easily, quietly, heavily, into the dream. But the bowl was too full to carry. The precious drops slipped dangerously to the edge and, that they not fall wasted to the ground, he carried the bowl before him in both hands and walked softly, and, that they not be wasted, he sipped a few from the edge and savored even their terrible bitterness for the sake of the dream.

He did not know the town. It was the same town but he did not recognize it, could not name it. It was evening and he walked down the empty streets, seeing how the lights in the building did not make a mark yet in the summer-evening light. In the hardware store the woman stood waiting by the nail bin. In the doorway Arthur leaned against the evening light from the street, tasting the pleasure of the woman's body, of her easy balance, seeing how the muscular, upright quality of her made the nail bin fragile, like a flower. He knew in advance that the woman would reach out her hand to the nail bin and set one of its flower-petal tiers revolving and reach below and set another revolving, so that the bright sectors would catch the light.

Even through the dream, though, he knew he had to get the precious bowl home, hidden, safe in the house. The blessed, bitter fluid he must hide for the future.

"What do you want nails for?" he said to her, to the woman twirling the tiers of the nail bin that was like a giant flower. "What do you want nails for?" he said to his woman, fecund, receptive, and waiting. "What do you want nails for," he said to her, "when I have your house built already and waiting for you?"

She turned away from the nail bin and began to walk down the path with him.

"Don't spill it," she said. "Don't let any spill. You have to be careful. You have to be secret. You have to hide it away."

She had never walked down the path with him before like this. She had never leaned against him, helping with her heavy, fecund, muscular body to steady the bowl. He knew that he had to hide the bowl, but he wanted her to come into the house with him and he was afraid to ask her, for she had never walked the path with him before, never seen the hated feathermane bounding out toward him, leaping, jumping, jeopardizing the bowl and the precious fluid.

"Down!" he yelled. "Down, damn you!"

The woman had disappeared and he was alone, holding what was left of the precious fluid out of the featherman's reach, turning to protect it from the feathermane's leaping. He kicked at the feathermane and felt the fluid coasting over his hand, spilling, and then he lost his balance and fell on the ground in a red fury of hate and the bowl was broken and he had his knife in his hand.

Now he slashed. Now he was on top. He cut the feathermane across the throat, and, when he saw the blood, he laughed and slashed again and the woman came back and laughed too and she said, "Cut him again. Cut him here. Cut him here. Slash him again. Stab him."

And then the woman ran toward the jungle, turning back to call to him, "Come on. Follow me."

*

Once he had finished "The Time of Innocence" Justin had thought to be rid of this crescendo of tension, but it only lessened temporarily and began to build again in him. He thought, when he threw himself into the domestic work, that the anxiety would abate, but he managed only to keep pace with it. He worked without stopping, but the wood pile mounting higher and higher seemed only to be the personification of his apprehension. Each day he worked more, harder, faster, and he thought, It is the child. It is the waiting for the child to be born because I spend so much time with Gwendolyn. All of us feel it. All of us are waiting.

But he knew that was not true, and today he thought that perhaps this feeling was only to make it untrue what Erma had said, that he did not partake of their frenzy. Had she said it in accusation? He would go look for her. He would speak to her and reassure himself. He would look at her and cast out this apprehension that tormented him.

He put down his ax and went to the mossback corral but she was not there, and it seemed to him that the land was unnaturally quiet. He went to the oven and she was not there, and, walking faster, he went to the grinding stone and to the cheese cellar, but she was not there. And *this* was it. Alarm for her. Not Gwendolyn, but Erma. For months he had had this fear in him, it seemed, and he had called it music, he had called it birth. He had called it everything but what it was.

He turned to the path to her house, and, when he came on it, the scene of violence, he stopped and heard his heart pounding while the breath went out of him and, yes, at last, it was like a relief to him. The thing had happened. The dread was no longer unknown.

She lay alone, her body thrown over the feathermane's, and all about them in the trampled, twisted grass the agony of struggle and violence and blood. Her clothes were cut and torn. Justin lifted her up and carried her limp body easily in his arms to his own house. She is alive, he thought. She is alive.

It seemed to him an act many times rehearsed, utterly familiar, as though he had dreamed all this again and again. In his house he put her down gently on the bed and went for a bowl of hot water. He knelt beside her and began to cut away her slashed, bloody clothing. Then he bathed her with the warm water. None of the wounds was deep, and most of the blood must have been the feathermane's.

She would open her eyes and shudder and say, "Why? Why? Where has he gone? Before my very eyes, Justin. Oh, why?"

And then she would lie back and close her eyes again while he went on carefully bathing her body, as though he had dreamed it all, as though he had known it all long ago. He saw how the skin was tight over the sharp hipbones, and he thought, How she has changed. How thin she has grown since I saw her dancing in the field of conception flowers. And it did not shock him to know that all this time he had held that memory accurate and secret in his mind for comparison.

Many were the visions he had had of her, seen, throttled, buried, sublimated, and called music. Long had the tortures of his insomnia been cast into the odor of her jacket in the night, cast into a mountain of work by day. Now the blood of the mutilated feathermane, flowing on the tortured grass, had set him free. The music and the wakefulness, the sweat—they ran free in a mighty river called Erma, called by his beloved's name, and the tension, the mounting, uncensored crescendo of tension,

burned in the flowing, freedom-making blood of violence and became desire.

Under her eyelids she felt the fire pulling her, felt his silence.
She opened her eyes and looked at him as he knelt beside her.
She lay of no weight at all in his two hands. He said her name. He
said her name aloud, the name of his beloved, and he saw the blue
veins stretch over her thigh as she reached to him, and then he
felt her body stiffen under the sound of the scream they had so
long awaited, so long been attuned for.

"It's Gwendolyn, Justin," she said. "It's the baby."

Justin took the high-pitched wail of the sound of Gwendolyn's fear into the bones of his hands and his hands held fiercely
the body of his beloved. "Yes," he said.

But he did not mean yes, it is Gwendolyn. He meant yes,
that was the sound! That was the sound he had written to resolve
the tensions. That was the sound of the end of "The Time of Innocence."

"Erma," he said, "tell me what to bring from your house."
(At least he could save her the sight of the mangled feathermane.)

"The clothing is hanging on the wall by my bed, Justin," she
said, "and by the fireplace you'll find a basket already packed
with things I will need."

When he returned she dressed quickly and silently and
picked up her basket to leave. At the door she hesitated. "And
Arthur?" she said.

"Go on," he said. "Go on to Gwendolyn. I will take care of
all the rest."

He closed the door after her and stood alone in the quiet
room. Slowly he reached for his pipe, filled it. He walked over to
the fire pit and got a light.

*That it should be given him. That it should be given him to
taste once again in his life.* He inhaled the smoke deeply and let it
curl out of his mouth.

"Edith," he said. "Edith, could you believe it? Could you
believe it of me, the way that I love that girl?"

*

On the twisted, tortured grass before the empty house of
Arthur Herrick lay the mangled body of the bleeding feathermane. A hanging tendril of the ferntree near him brushed across

his neck and lay, like a part of it, against his mane. High above, in the tree, the crested chichimingo cut the silence with its name call. In the body of the feathermane, a breath faltered, fluttered, trembled. A lime-and-turquoise butterfly spiraled down, alighting for a moment on the sharp edge of a broken piece of the braid-stem bowl. Slowly the eyes of the feathermane opened a little. He had never seen blackness before. The stench of the acrid braid-stem tortured his sensitive nostrils and, in the blackness, he longed to escape it, but in his delicate hoofs there was no answer to this desire.

Over his motionless head, through the blackness, came a high, strange sound, a sound never heard before in the Green Kingdom. A cry not like any other cry.

Later, in the blackness, the ground shook and the smell of the big man came close, bending near, making a clinking noise and freeing a new wave of the torturing, acrid odor.

Once again, in the darkness, the feathermane lay alone, longing for escape from the biting odor, longing for the nearness, the presence of another, a familiar and more comforting smell. Oh, where was she for whom, in the darkness, he hungered? Where was she for whom he had forsaken his own kind, his herd?

The memory of the herd is never quite lost, not even in the blackness where, once again, a faltering breath fluttered, trembled, and troubled the body of the feathermane. Against his mane the hanging ferntree tendril shivered with the weight of the lime-and-turquoise butterfly, newly cheated of its former perch on the piece of braidstem bowl, while, high above, the crested chichimingo crouched in silent fear at the repeated, wailing cry of the sound never heard before in the Green Kingdom. Blurred green-ness oozed into the blackness, bringing to the feathermane a quieter, deeper, more sustained breath.

Because he had not been able to answer Justin's letter for lack of an address, Max Staats left it stuck in his desk blotter for several weeks. Many times he read over the phrase, AND OF COURSE, IN THE MEANTIME, I'LL KEEP YOU POSTED. When two months had gone by without his having heard, he took the letter from the blotter and placed it in the middle desk drawer, hoping that in this way he might avoid the painful concern that he relived every time he saw it. But there was no similar drawer in his mind that he could close upon the thought of Justin Magnus. He made a feeble try at angrily damning Justin for his inconsiderateness, but it was no good. Justin was not an inconsiderate man; he was careless of details, yes, but not inconsiderate.

But he might be a sick man, Max thought. Well, even so, he had four companions. Surely they would not abandon a sick man. Perhaps they had had to return, though, to their work. Were they wealthy? How otherwise could they be away from their work for months at a time? They must have had to return home before Justin was ready to leave, and perhaps it was after they had left him that Justin had become too ill to write. But why had he not had someone send a telegram?

Max shoved his work aside impatiently. He could not concentrate on it, now that he had the idea that Justin might be ill somewhere, alone. For it would have to be illness, not death. It could not have been an auto wreck, or any public kind of death; that would have been in the newspapers. Even if, alive, the name of Justin Magnus could not command money or a popular fame, still, dead, he would certainly be newsworthy.

One night quite late Max found himself actually walking up and down his study. It was an action so out of character for him that the knowledge of it outweighed his dread of interfering, and before he could change his mind he checked the facts with Justin's letter and put in a long-distance call to Arthur Herrick in Drury.

"That phone has been disconnected," the operator said.

Max reached into the desk and pulled out the letter. After all, there had been two other people besides the Herricks. And then he remembered as he read: MR. AND MRS. HERRICK AND TWO FRIENDS OF THEIRS.

"Thank you, Operator," Max said. "That will be all."

He replaced the receiver, took off his glasses, and sat a while with his fingers pressed against his closed eyelids. And two friends of theirs, he thought. Two nameless friends. He could not help smiling. How like Justin that was. Something else occurred to Max, and that was that the name Arthur which he had remembered from Justin's old itinerary might not be right. After Edith's death he had destroyed the itinerary. But his memory for names was excellent; he had always been proud of it.

What could he do? He could not go to Drury until the end of the school year. It would take his entire summer if Drury offered no clue, and he had to comb the whole state from which Justin had sent his letter. It was a maddening situation and he of all people surely the least suited for the role of tracking someone down. Should he report Justin's disappearance to the police? He could not bring himself to do it. Perhaps Justin had decided to disappear; other men had. Who was he to question Justin's right to do just that?

He sat at his desk, quietly, having come to a full consideration of the weight of the problem. Outside, the sound of the sea won over any others. In the room there was only an occasional sound of Max's drumming his finger tips on the desk as his mind weighed and discarded yet another plan.

It was incredible. Five people. Exactly as though the earth had opened and swallowed them up. Exactly as though . . .

From this night there was a change in Max Staats. It was not that he ceased to be concerned over Justin, or that he didn't still watch the mail for a second letter, but he knew that the indefinite kind of anxiety which had led to that particular night had been chewed over to its limit of any possible resulting action from him, and he put an end to it. Gradually, the volumes on his desk began to gain companions. The slender Schroedinger was now pressed into a stance of attention against Von Neumann by its strange new companions—Joly's THE SURFACE HISTORY OF THE EARTH, Knott's THE PHYSICS OF EARTHQUAKE PHENOMENA, and, newly arrived in the mail, S. Arrhenius' ZUR PHYSIK DES VULCANISMUS.

3. Time of History

CHAPTER ONE

THERE are some people whose nightmares serve them as re-hearsals for behavior so that, when life becomes for them a nightmare, they have known for a long time how to act. So Arthur, waking to see the blood on his hands and on his knife which lay across the twisted, jungle root that had tripped him, looked behind him once with stealth, and then, grasping the knife, fled headlong, deeper into the jungle as, in many rehearsals, he had fled from the bear down the pathways of a crumbling park, fled from the Thing through the maze of a steepled, marshmallow building, fled from fleeing down many a narrow, twisting, night-city street.

Gasping and fighting, hacking with the bloodstained knife against the entangling, embracing jungle growth, torn by thorns, lassoed by vines, knocked about by the caprice of hidden roots, he fought on, wastefully, crazily. Yet he never erred in his direction. He stopped to urinate as though to drain off also, in this way, the terrible pain in his chest, but his body recoiled from touching himself with his blood-caked hand, and in anguish he bent forward, thinking: Whose blood is that? What have I done? Whom have I killed? *Which one of them?*

After this, he was more careful of his strength. He cut a path before him, he planned his steps, he no longer ran. But always the direction stayed the same. Now and then, with the knife upraised, he would pause and think: I must remember, I must remember. He stopped again, took leaves and scrubbed his hands and wrists, and after this he walked slowly, not thinking at all. He walked. Behind him was the settlement, and that he was going away from. Ahead of him was nothing that he knew. He walked into nothing. Later, he was not even walking; he was only moving. Finally, on the ground, he lay huddled and slowly burrowing for warmth, knowing neither the wetness nor the sharpness of the

razor grass. He awoke as a sick animal awakes. He was stiff from
the cold, painfully aware of the smarting cuts from the razor
grass, and suddenly ravenous. He crawled toward some berries,
hanging from a low branch, crammed them into his mouth, thinking that he must control himself, that he must eat only a small
quantity of any one thing lest he be poisoned as Joe had been.

Joe. Had it been Joe? He got up slowly from his knees and
stood upright, trying desperately to remember. He could remember Joe's standing in the laboratory, saying . . . What had he
said? He heard a sharp, crackling noise and turned in fear to
look behind him. The jungle seemed to have closed in on him in
the night. *But if he had killed Joe, then whom would they send
after him?* When they came for him what should he do? Should
he run or fight? What would they do with him? Even now, what
were they planning to do with him? He began to move stealthily
onward in the same direction as yesterday, and unconsciously he
accelerated his pace. He put up his hand to brush aside a hanging
rope vine and saw it turn into a snake, its terrible eyes on a level
with his. When he had escaped that, he stood in fascination to see
the spiked edges of a huge plant clamp shut upon the body of a
little animal, inexorably imprisoning it. Arthur shivered in his
own sweat and gave himself over to the panic of his own body. Of
the greatest, most primitive, importance it became to protect his
own body. Perhaps this is not real, he thought, this terrible plant;
is it created only by my own brain? Have I gone mad? And is this
why I can't remember? As though to taunt him, the evil spike
plants, like iron maidens of the Inquisition, sprang up everywhere. Cold and shaking, Arthur went toward one. If I touch it,
he thought, and there is nothing there, then . . . then I am mad.
He reached out his hand to touch the hard, gourdlike surface,
and the instant clamping of its jaws so threw him off balance that
the end of one finger was caught in the vise. He felt the thorn
pierce through his nail and, not knowing, he screamed. He pulled
himself free, pressing in agony upon the split nail with the fingers
of his other hand.

Under the pain he felt himself flooded with warmth. He
straightened his sagging mouth. It was real. He could go on,
then. He could keep on trying to remember. Without planning,
he kept the straight direction. In the beginning, to guide him, he
had at his back the settlement. But all the time, without knowing
it, he had under his feet a compass. He walked always downward

as, in many rehearsals, he had always fled downward. But now every hanging vine became a snake; every plant or tree trunk he brushed against was capable of piercing him, holding him prisoner. When one discovers himself horrible, all about him he sees the horrible; he walks in a horrible landscape. The blood from his finger drew many swarming insects, and he fought frenziedly a cloud of them until, swollen and maddened by their stings, he fell exhausted on the ground.

On the third day he became aware for the first time of the jungle noises. He could identify nothing in the clamoring, deafening racket, except once, when he heard the howlers. And this is where they live, he thought. This is why we so seldom find them in the settlement. He did not know if, before, he had been deaf or if, in his fear of madness, he had had no ear for anything but himself. Then he began to torture himself, trying to remember if he had not heard something in the days before. Even the number of the days before—he was uncertain if it were two or three or how long it had been. It occurred to him that he might have been wandering for a long time, that they could not find him or that, in truth, they had never sought him. Perhaps they would abandon him, as primitive tribes abandon the old and sick. Was it not, after all, more logical, preferable from their point of view, saving themselves the necessity of passing sentence? Who among them could hold him prisoner? Who among them *remained* to hold him prisoner?

His pace slowed and became automatic. His concern with safety left him; his fear of the landscape left him. He began instinctively to use the jungle for his progress. He ceased to hack at it blindly or to fight it. His hands sought narrow passages; his body turned and slid through openings. He began to move as jungle animals move. He tasted the absolute loneliness that only the abandoned know. It made him old, but also it made him unhurried.

How good a thing a prison is, he thought; how necessary the madhouse. Once inside, the crime, the act of lunacy, becomes of the past, accepted. One need never pit oneself against it again. Instead, there is a new thing. One pits oneself against the prison; one's war is with the keeper. The prison makes possible a future. One may, in some way, coerce or satisfy the prison. One may outwit the keeper. Freedom, then, is once again, the only way it can be endured, a promised thing. For if they had abandoned him, then he was free, absolutely free, a condition he had thought much of. And yet, in the end, absolute freedom must be synonymous with absolute flight. For if a man pause long enough to recognize a friend, to see a familiar place, if even once a bird should eat out of his hand, then he is not absolutely free. No man can endure freedom unless it be in jeopardy. No man can flee forever unless he believe in the existence of his pursuer. If it should be true that he had this absolute freedom, Arthur knew he could not endure the weight of it. Only in nightmare does one seem to flee forever.

That night he took more care. He tried to pile some branches into a semblance of a bed. On the fourth day he missed tobacco and hungered for it, and on the fifth day he longed for a fire to keep him warm, to keep at a greater distance the packs of howlers. But he could not stay still long enough to make the tedious search for powdery dry substances, nor had he the patience to ignite them by friction.

So in this manner Arthur Herrick moved onward, always in the same direction, gradually downward, eating what little came to his hand, spitting out the acrid and the bitter. And on the seventh day he came to the green river, swifter and wider than the river by which they had first camped. He thought of swimming it and sat on the bank to study the current. Gradually he heard the sound of the river, and, except for that of the howlers, it was the first familiar sound he had heard in all this time. He hungered for tobacco. He hungered not to be abandoned and he hungered for an end to uncertainty. He stood up and spoke aloud.

"I shall not cross that river," he said. "I'm going back."

Had not the jungle growth over Arthur's path served as a vision floor to the high-flying birds, they would perhaps have stopped their yacking, yawling crying long enough to take note of the movement below them. Yet it would not have seemed movement to them. In relation to the swiftness of a bird's flight, it would have seemed that the two men stood still, for the distance between them was constant. Behind Arthur moved Justin, tracing and studying the signs he saw. Always between him and Arthur there was the distance of one day. When Justin came to a widened, trampled place, he put down his blanket and stayed. The first day, it is true, he had advanced with hurry. In his mind he had as yet no plan and no design, only a quest. But when, under the canopy that served as a vision floor for the jungle birds,

he came upon the first place where Arthur had slept and began
to study the signs in the trampled grass, he lost some of his feeling of urgency. He was tracking down a live man and one who
was not so insane but that he had kept to a straight line in his
flight and had stopped to rest long enough to leave a strong imprint on the grass.

"You must let me be the judge of whether or not time is an
element of importance in this," Justin had said to Erma when he
left the settlement. "It is likely that a period of time away from
the settlement is more necessary to Arthur than your peace of
mind is to you. You will have to endure it as best you can. You
will have to trust me in this and promise me that, under no condition, will you or anyone else follow us. I think I am on familiar
ground. I think I have experience of value that the rest of you
don't have."

Justin hoped now that Erma could remember her promise
and wait a little longer, for, as he progressed along the path, eating where Arthur had eaten, sleeping where Arthur had slept, he
saw that the more time elapsed, the easier it would be. Almost as
though one could see the effects of the unfiltered braidstem concentrate falling off, the signs along the pathway changed character. The skins and hulls of fruits increased and then ceased to be
strewn in a line and became grouped in certain places. As the bed
places showed greater evidence of thought and preparation, the
path became more difficult to follow. Along here, Justin saw, Arthur had ceased to fight, had begun to use the jungle, be part of
it.

When he came to the bed that had been made of piled
branches, he studied it a good while. Beside it he found a piece
of broken sandal lace and a small, exact square of ground from
which all the vegetation had been carefully removed. He elabo-
rated somewhat on the structure of the bed, spread his blanket,
loosened his sandals, and carefully pulled at the vegetation to
enlarge the square.

I won't go any farther for a while, he thought. I will stay
here for a day, just in case. It is so much better to be met than
to be caught.

The next day Justin heard the expected footstep just as he
was shaking out his blanket and spreading it over the bough bed,
and the picture flashed into his mind of Max Staats making a
bed for him on the first day he had walked to the sea after his ill-

ness. He and Max had been embarrassed then, as he and Arthur, he knew, were soon to be. He dreaded the encounter and sat down hurriedly on the blanket to make his position as clear as possible. He sat with his back to the direction from which Arthur came. When he heard the abrupt step, the startled exclamation, he turned and looked up. He was surprised to see how composed and relatively rested Arthur looked. Though his face was white and thin, there was nothing frantic in it.

"Hello, Arthur," Justin said. "I've been waiting for you since yesterday."

"Did you come alone?" Arthur said. "There's no one with you?"

"I'm alone," Justin said. "Sit down, Arthur. I see that you sat here two days ago and pulled the growth out of this square while you were thinking. I enlarged it some. Strange the way a man insists on right angles."

"Here's my knife," Arthur said. "It's all I have."

"There's no need, Arthur. Keep it and sit down for a while."

But Arthur could not sit down. He took a couple of steps so as to stand directly in front of Justin. "And Joe," he said. "Where is Joe?"

"He's at the settlement," Justin said. "He's a new father, you know."

"The baby then," Arthur said. "Is the baby all right?"

"Very much so," Justin said. "A boy. They did me a great honor; they said I might name him for one of my sons."

"Erma?" Arthur asked. "Was it Erma?"

"I asked Erma not to come," Justin said. "She's needed there very badly."

"Not Gwen!" Arthur said.

"What do you mean?" Justin said. "I don't understand what you mean."

"Which one did I kill, then? You've named them all."

"Why, no one," Justin said. "You've killed no one. Did you think you had?"

"Don't lie to me," Arthur said. "There's no need. Look, I came to with a peculiar sense of horror and I saw blood on my hands. I know I saw it. Whose was it?"

"I suppose it was the feathermane's blood," Justin said. "Sit down now, Arthur. Don't you remember fighting with the feathermane?"

Arthur seemed merely to fold up and sink slowly to the ground. He looked at Justin with an utterly puzzled look. "No," he said. "No, I don't remember anything."

"That's curious," Justin said. "That's exactly what Gwen said after the baby was born: 'I can't remember anything about it.' "

Justin looked down into the pale, questioning, suffering face before him. "Come," he said, "lie down on the blanket awhile. I can see this is a shock to you. Why don't you rest while I go to hunt for some food? Then we'll talk it over."

Arthur had heard this tone before from Justin. His hands began to tremble and he tried hard to control them. Then he knew. So had Justin spoken to an obnoxious and difficult Gwen; so had he managed her like a puppet and made her tractable. Even then, Arthur realized, he had been afraid that he would some day be the recipient of this man's artifice. Even then he had doubted him. Arthur struggled to get up and managed to get onto his knees. Now his eyes were on a level with those of Justin, who still sat on the bough bed.

"Don't you understand?" he said to Justin. "I was coming back of my own accord, because I couldn't stand the uncertainty. If you hadn't been here, I would have returned. Even now, I offer you my knife. I'm harmless. I *want* to go back. There's no need to trick me. There is no need."

Justin stood up. "I don't know how to get you to believe me," he said, "nor do I know why it is easier for you to believe that you killed a man than that you killed a feathermane. I suppose there is nothing for it but to go back to the settlement so you can see for yourself that they are all alive. There is not one person less than when you left. There is one more."

Arthur looked at the ground. "I believe you," he said. "For a feathermane—my God!"

He put one hand up to his head and suddenly started to laugh. Justin walked away to search for food and left Arthur alone to strike a new balance between his capacity to carry and the shrunken size of his burden. When he came back, Arthur lay on the blanket asleep, completely abandoned to exhaustion. Justin bent down and flipped the other half of the blanket up over him. He ate alone without disturbing Arthur and finally went to sleep himself. When he awoke Arthur was still sleeping, but at the first movement of Justin's he sprang off the bed and stood in frightened animal awareness until, puzzled by the blanket entangling his feet, he realized where and with whom he was.

"For a moment I didn't remember," he said to Justin. "Wessun—that was the worst time."

"I found some kind of berries," Justin said, "and what I think is a relative of our sharples. You had no dinner last night."

"Thanks," Arthur said, reaching for the fruit, waiting to taste it until he had asked. "You did say that I had killed no one, harmed no one?"

"You *killed* no one," Justin said. But he saw that his subtlety was lost on Arthur and decided to postpone elaboration until they were on their way.

"Only the feathermane," Arthur said.

"I'm not positive of that," Justin said, "but I suppose he died. You see, when I came on the scene I found Erma in pretty bad shape. She had tried to protect the feathermane, apparently."

"Erma was there?" Arthur asked. "Who else?"

"No one," Justin said. "I took Erma to my place to rest and, just then, Gwen began having her labor pains, so Erma went to her. Later, I went back to bury the feathermane and I noticed that he was still breathing. I didn't see any point in moving him then. He seemed too far gone and not in conscious pain. And while I was looking at him I found the pieces of the bowl."

"Bowl?" Arthur said.

"Yes, I took the pieces to Joe and he smelled of them and said you had taken the wrong stuff from the laboratory, that you had got some unfiltered braidstem. He couldn't leave then, of course, with the baby coming."

"Wait a minute," Arthur said. "Something is coming back to me. I'm beginning to remember that I asked Joe for some braidstem. We had an argument, I think."

"Well, take your time over it," Justin said. "Maybe it will come to you. What do you say we get started? They're anxious, you know. Joe knows you had something toxic. Nobody knows what has happened to you or what state you're in."

"Of course," Arthur said. "I'm ready. It is so difficult to imagine how they do feel. You think of imagination as being such a remarkable thing, and yet it's really very limited. Here, I'll carry the blanket, Justin. You know," Arthur continued, as Justin stepped ahead of him in the direction of the settlement, "you know, back there, I even discovered that it's impossible to feel remorse if you cannot remember what you have done."

"You must have had a terrible time," Justin said, "and yet I was surprised at how composed you looked. I suppose mostly I was surprised at how clean you looked. You're not as dirty as I am."

"Oh, the river," Arthur said. "I forgot to tell you about the river. After I made up my mind to come back, I had a swim in the river and washed off a great deal of the dirt."

Justin stopped and turned around. "A river? Is it far?"

"It's a day from where we were last night. It's wider than our river at the Yearsenday Place. It seemed a kind of sign to me. I knew that I would never cross it and that I must come back."

"I would like to see it," Justin said, "but we must not take two more days when they are all so worried. You must remember, they don't know that I have found you."

"How is it that they are worried? In what way do they think of me? You say that only Erma saw it. What did she see? What did she say?"

"I don't know what she saw," Justin said. "She said only, 'Why? Why?' over and over again. Then almost immediately the baby was coming and no one had time to talk. By the next morning when I started out I knew already which direction you had taken and that your condition was doubtless due to the toxic braidstem and was, I hoped, temporary. And also, of course, by then the baby had arrived and I saw that Erma was going to be able to take over."

"You said it was a boy?"

"Yes."

"That's what he wanted," Arthur said. "It seems strange to have waited an event so long and then to have missed it."

On the day they came again to the evil, spiked, imprisoning plants, Arthur said, "I never thought I'd be glad to see those things again."

"What are they?" Justin asked. "I guess I was too occupied trying to keep on your trail. I missed them."

"Look out!" Arthur said. "I almost lost a hand on one of them. Wait until I get a stick; I'll show you how it works."

"I keep thinking of it," Justin said that night when they camped. "That damned plant!"

This night they had not even bothered to make a brush bed, but had thrown themselves down on Justin's blanket. Now Justin sat up and rubbed the calf of one leg. "I must really be getting old," he said. "My legs ache as though I had been running all day. It's good to think that by this time tomorrow night we'll be at home with a fire and tobacco and a hot bath."

"My legs ache, too," Arthur said. "I think we've been going steadily uphill all day. Do you suppose it could be that the river I came to, that second river, is a continuation of our river?"

"But," Justin said, "the settlement is below the river at the Yearsenday Place. If that river were continuous with the second one, then it should run near the settlement or through it, wouldn't you think?"

"I'd like to know where it does go," Arthur said.

"It's strange, really, how little we do know of the Kingdom," Justin said, "how slightly we have explored. We're not such adventurous creatures as we think we are."

"I suppose it's always so," Arthur said. "In a wilderness the first thing is to try to make oneself comfortable and safe. And then when the house is built, the animals domesticated and the crops planted, the comforts become responsibilities."

Arthur heard Justin's heavy breathing and knew he had fallen asleep. As Justin had said, by this time tomorrow night . . . And so at last Arthur came to face the fact of home. But home was not, as it was for Justin, a picture of fire, tobacco, and a hot bath. Wakeful and alone in the black silence, Arthur thought of home, and home was the face of Erma. Home was Joe. Home was Gwendolyn. The sweat on his hands was cold and it was no longer possible for him to lie still. As quietly as possible he stood up. He wiped his hands on his trousers and took one step. Then he realized that, in the darkness, there was no direction in which he could move. Two paces in any direction would immediately entangle him in thorns and vines. No light shone for him from any direction. In the distance he heard a howler give its unearthly wail, and he brought his back foot up even with the other one. There was really nothing for him to do, as long as the blackness held, as long as this clear wakefulness held, but to stand in that one spot and occasionally to wipe the cold sweat off his hands.

A faint green luminosity slowly supplanted the darkness. Justin's voice startled him, asking, "How long have you been up?"

"All night, I guess," Arthur said. He found that he was very stiff, and with difficulty he stretched himself and sat down. "I have been thinking," he said at last. "I'm not going back with you, Justin."

"No?" Justin said. "Where will you go?"

"I'm going back to the river, the second river, I think. But that's beside the point. The point is that . . . Well, I don't know how it has taken me so long to come to it. But you see, I thought I had killed a human being. One of you or all of you. When you think you have killed a human being and find you have killed only a feathermane, it seems like no crime at all. But last night, as we really got close to home, I thought for the first time of killing a feathermane in relation to no crime at all. In fact, for the first time I thought of it as it must seem to them."

"I see," Justin said. "Well, if it is more time you need, Arthur, why, there is really no need for us to hurry this last piece of the journey. But aren't you omitting an important factor?"

"You mean the toxic braidstem? That I made a mistake? Yes, I tried that. I tried getting out on that first, naturally, but it won't work. It's like explaining someone's outrageous behavior by saying he was drunk. Why was he drunk? Because he drinks too much. And why does he drink too much? There is an answer somewhere in the man. In me, too, there is an answer. I mean to wait until I have it or have given up hunting for it. I can't face them—that's what it amounts to."

"I think you underestimate their ability to make allowances," Justin said.

"Allowances?" Arthur said. "I can't be someone you make allowances for. Can't you understand that? I've never had allowances made for me. I've made them for other people, always."

"Oh, well," Justin said, "they have to be made for all of us at some time or another, surely."

"All right," Arthur said, "maybe that's what I'm supposed to learn on the river, but I don't know it now. I'm not ready."

"You plan to go back to the second river, then?" Justin said.

"That's only to give me something to do," Arthur said. "If I find my answer before I find out where the river goes, then I'll come back this way."

"And if you don't?" Justin said.

"Well, I suppose I'll come out somewhere, even if it's only on the river."

For a moment Justin toyed with the idea of trying to get Arthur to start out from the Yearsenday Place, properly outfitted.

with food and warm clothing and perhaps even a boat. But he knew, even without trying, that it was futile and transparent, for Arthur had admitted already that the river was not the important thing. Justin thought of what he might say. In the end, he said the only thing he could say with honesty.

"Well, you'll take the blanket, at least. I shan't need it any more." And then he stopped himself in time from the next thing he thought of, but not in time to hide his embarrassment.

"Yes," Arthur said, picking up the blanket. And then, saying it for him: "Of course, I have my knife."

"Well," Justin said, "I'll be getting on then, Arthur. I . . . I trust your search won't take too long."

"I don't know," Arthur said. "I don't know how long it will take."

There was, for Justin, a momentary flash, a sudden answer to a quest that *he* had made long ago. Standing there in the old and familiar frustration of wanting to say what cannot be said, of reaching for what cannot be touched, he was for an instant transplanted to the old railroad station, saying good-by in answer to George's jerky, half-wave. For the first time since the boy's death George had a face, and it was his own. For an instant Justin remembered it clearly. It eased him somehow, made his head clear.

"Erma," he said. "I'll tell her, of course, that you're all right. I'd like to be able to take her some message."

Arthur swung the blanket up over his shoulder and settled it into place. "Sure," he said. "You tell her I'm taking my forty days and forty nights. She'll understand."

Then suddenly he turned and started back the way they had come, back toward the second river. He put one hand up in the air and, turning his head over his shoulder, called back, "And thanks, Justin."

It was incredible, that gesture, that aborted wave, how here in the jungle it summoned up for Justin the sound of many people hurrying, the feel of bricks beneath his feet, the smell of trains, the sound of bells, the imperious voice of the loud-speaker.

Now that he had been made aware of it, Justin realized that his way was uphill, without doubt. But even uphill there was only one more day of it. This night should see him in his own house by a warm fire, drinking hot tea, smoking. And Arthur? Where would Arthur be? Justin wished that the anticipation could have been all pleasant, but he felt himself a failure to be returning alone. Last night he had fallen asleep with the greatest sense of accomplishment, and then, in an instant, this morning, the whole structure was destroyed. How could he have slept through it all while Arthur stood alone there in the night, unable to face the thought of going home? If he had talked with him in the night perhaps there would have been a chance. In the very beginning, he should have begun to discuss the home-coming with Arthur. Well, it was futile to go over it now. He had made a mistake. He had overestimated the time or underestimated the man. At any rate, he was returning to Erma empty-handed, bringing her a further period of anxiety.

Once before he had gone toward her, hoping to bring her something. He could remember sitting on the train reading her letter before he had ever seen her. Another time he had been moving toward her—and walking too, then, as he was walking now—only it had been raining. He saw her looking up from the table in Drury, aghast at his wetness. He saw her suddenly at the top of the stairs, reaching a hand down to him. Pictures of her began to flit through his mind, and he stopped to rest and catch his breath. It was as though, upon returning a borrowed book and being asked how he had liked it, he had replied without enthusiasm, "Oh, all right," only to have the lender exclaim in amazement, "But, man, did you not know it was in code?"

The old pictures from Drury and from the journey to the Kingdom had never been examined in the code of his love for her. They were *his*. They were his to ponder on, to turn this way and that, to delight in.

He began to walk again, deliberately bringing out now, from their hidden places, his treasures. But he could not keep them in chronological order; they kept coming up out of place, as though they had been released from prison. And the clearest of them all, the one that stayed longest, the one he didn't even know he had, was of Erma kneeling before him in the room at the old Westgate Hotel. He could see the white part in her hair as she bent over his swollen ankle. Under the water her fingers, as she turned her hand, had become toothpicks. He could remember how curious it had seemed that the fragile toothpicks could feel so firm and secure against his skin.

No matter with what disappointments Justin was returning, he was still going home. The joy that he could no longer restrain accelerated his pace. The wilderness thinned and, in defeat, went away.

*

Already the baby had begun to stir in his cradle, before Erma had finished washing Gwendolyn's breakfast dishes. As she dried her hands hurriedly her body was leaning in the direction of the fireplace. Without realizing it she moved always a little aslant, these days, in a kind of tired trot, never quite upright, never actually falling down, always behind in the race, always tired. She hung the baby's blanket on the warming stick before the fire, and with the muscles of her shoulders she tried to will the baby not to cry, because she hadn't yet brushed Gwendolyn's hair. How could she escape the early matinee today? Wasn't there an excuse her poor, tired brain could concoct? Maybe Joe would come in time to be the audience. She went in to Gwendolyn and leaned over, ready to help her out of bed.

"Come on," she said. "Better get into the chair. He's starting to fuss."

"Oh, dear," Gwendolyn said. "My hair isn't even brushed yet."

"I'll brush it for you," Erma said. "He isn't really crying yet. Wouldn't you like to sit up this afternoon? Not go back to bed after the feeding? We could move your chair in by the fireplace."

Gwen leaned her head back against Erma, closing her eyes to enjoy the more the delicious, gentle strokes of the hairbrush. "I don't think I'd better," she said. "I get so dreadfully tired and dizzy when I'm up, even to get as far as this chair. I'm so afraid something might happen to the milk."

With her eyes closed, Gwen put one hand on her full, swelling breast. She smiled smugly, almost comically. "I have a lot now and I wouldn't want to do anything that might change it."

Don't say it, Erma thought. Don't say anything. But her impatience showed in the brush strokes, no matter how hard she tried to control them.

Gwen was quick to feel the difference. She let her head slump against Erma's body. "Dear Erma," she said. "You're so good to me. I'd have died without you. I know I would."

Two tears squeezed out from below her eyelids and lay upon her cheeks. She opened her eyes and looked up at Erma. "Darling," she said, "do you forgive me for all the crazy things I said? I must have been out of my mind. I was so frightened, so terribly frightened. You don't know. You don't know what that fear is like."

Erma's hands were trembling so violently now that she could no longer wield the brush. She leaned over Gwen and kissed her lightly on the forehead. "Of course," she said. "It's all over now and the baby is wonderful and you're fine. Everything is fine."

I'm going to cry, she thought. And then the baby began to cry in earnest this time. Erma fastened her mind on him and started toward the cradle.

Joe came in from outside. "What's the matter with the baby?" he said. "I heard him cry."

Erma bent over the cradle to lift the child, and instantly he stopped crying. She wrapped him in the blanket from the warming stick. It was wonderful the way he stopped crying as soon as she lifted him, so wonderful that it made a smile in her tired, drawn face.

"Nothing," she said, looking up at Joe. "Nothing's wrong with him except that he's hungry."

"Oh," said Joe. "I thought there was something wrong. It's funny how he shuts up when you lift him. It couldn't be that he knows you already, could it?"

"No. Not really," Erma said. "Here. Do you want to take him in to Gwen?"

"No. I'm all dirty," Joe said, stepping back, flattening himself away from the child. "I've been in the corral."

As always these days there came a moment of silence between them.

"Any news, Joe?" Erma asked. "Anything?"

"No," he said. "No sign, Erma."

She started to turn away.

"Erma," Joe said. "Erma, I ought to go, don't you think? Wouldn't you feel better if I went to see what—"

"No," Erma said. "You promised. Justin said, no matter what happened, you were to stay here. You agreed, you know you did. Gwen would be terrified to have you go."

"I guess so," Joe said. "You couldn't take care of her and do everything else too, anyway. Justin must have thought of that."

The baby began to fuss at the delay and Erma moved close

to Joe, so that she wouldn't be heard. "Can't you get her to sit up awhile this afternoon, Joe? I feel sure she ought to be trying to get up now. She's all right."

"Oh, I don't know, Erma. Let's not hurry her. After all, it's only been two weeks."

"But I . . ." Erma began. "Well, all right," she said. She turned to carry the baby in to Gwendolyn.

"I'll be in as soon as I'm washed," Joe said.

She wouldn't have to be the audience, then. Joe would be there to admire. After she'd given the baby to Gwendolyn, she put fresh blankets on the warming stick and began to prepare the baby's bed, dreading so terribly the moment when she must go back into the other room, the *new* room, and wait, like a servant, witnessing that defenseless adoration in Joe's eyes. She laid out a clean diaper for the baby and began to put the freshly warmed blankets into the cradle. Suddenly she leaned over the cradle in despair, shutting her eyes tightly, thinking, I must not drop tears on the blanket. And then she turned and ran out of the house. Two minutes, five minutes, a quarter of an hour—oh, if she could be alone, if she could be away from their sight. Surely, she thought, as she ran into the smeared landscape, surely, between the two of them, they ought to be able to manage just once to get the baby back into the cradle and covered up without her.

She stopped running and wiped her eyes, forcing the smeared landscape into focus. Very slowly, as though she were being watched, she turned her head toward the house she had left. Then, bending over, she began to run as fast as she could. In her own house, she tried not to see the evidences of neglect, the work that cried out to be done, while she filled the bowl with warm milk and grain. This she carried cradled in her arms, hiding it, her whole body stiff with deception. Once she had her own cabin between herself and the other she began to run again, uphill, in the direction of the Yearsenday Place. She turned from the path and, crawling on the ground, pushing the bowl ahead of her, she worked her way to the small, well-hidden clearing. Here she stopped again, alert as an animal is alert, listening, peering behind her. Satisfied, she crawled the rest of the way.

The feathermane lay asleep on the blanket she had brought. Kneeling beside him, she listened to her own heartbeat, watching to see if he breathed. When she saw that he was still alive, her panic and her hurry left her. Slowly, with an excruciating tenderness, she bent over him and touched his head.

He was very thin now, and his many angry scars made ridiculous horror of his beauty. When he opened his eyes slowly, they were blurred and clouded. He did not try to get up, but he made a low sound of greeting. At this, she smiled and put her head down beside his. Then she sat up and, taking some of the warm mash on her fingers, held it to his mouth. Still lying on his side, he licked her fingers slowly. She fed him as long as he would take any, with a gentle, intense concentration. After a while he closed his eyes and refused to eat any more. She took grass and wiped up the drops he had spilled, making a fold of the blanket, so his head would not lie in the dampness. Then she pulled one edge of the blanket over him and pushed the bowl out of the way.

His wounds would not allow him to be held. She knew this. The intensity of her love must not be transmitted. It must be held prisoner in her own body. She bent over him, inhaling the odor of his mane and the odor of his wounds.

"Please," she said, "please, please, please don't leave me. Please don't die. I'll make you a safe place. I'll hide you away where no one will ever find you. I'll take care of you. Just please don't die."

GRADUALLY, the lives of the five people in the Green Kingdom came to achieve a structure, a kind of sculptor's armature
from which, in time, a form might grow that could not possibly
be the life of any one of them. Within this structure there came
to develop many other structures, both those that grew predicta-
bly and according to plan, and those that added to themselves,
accidentally, without design, like the language they spoke and
wrote. Even in the Records, west-sun, their name for morning,
gradually came to be written, as they spoke it, "wessun." There
was in progress without, often, their being conscious of it a blend-
ing process, softening riverstone to rivstone, east-sun to eassun,
Year's End Day to Yearsenday. From being names to identify
certain creatures, the names "chichimingo," "howler," "mossback" became the actual creatures, as though they had named
themselves.

There was the growing structure of the child called Tommy,
predictable and according to pattern. Justin knew, when he returned alone from the wilderness, that he would never wish the
boy to be called George. If it could be done by naming, he would
wish for Joe just such a child as his Tommy had been. For the
Green Kingdom, too, he would have wished that its first be such
a child as Tommy, with Tommy's capacity to embrace. At the
time of Justin's return the baby was a small bundle, infinitely
flexible, weighing one yearsenday bomb, eight turtleshells and six
clusternuts. His pale-blue eyes were unfocused and his tiny curled
fists moved aimlessly. Of the many other structures that were to
grow with him later, only the symphony was well under way. The
place of the feathermane, which was to become Erma's sanctuary,
was as yet only the crudest shelter, its future unforseen. The third
movement of the symphony, "The Time of History," not yet on
paper, would belong to the structures of plan, like the calcifica-

tion of the child's bones and, later, the boat that Joe and Arthur would build together. These were different from the structure of Erma's sanctuary and different from the structure of Gwendolyn's fear of and resistance to the boat. Within the aggregate structure of their lives together there grew these two separate kinds of structures: the structures of recognized plan and the structures of accident, the structures that grow in light and those that flower in darkness.

When the child was not quite two months old he weighed one yearsenday bomb and eighteen turtleshells. Real tears came when he cried, and he made delicious cooing sounds that sometimes coincided with questions asked him. What Joe liked best was to feel Tommy's feet push against him when he held him. The child had great possessions now: a powerful kick, tears, a smile, and, when Arthur Herrick arrived home at last with his tales of the great river on which he had spent thirty-nine days and nights, Tommy turned his head to him and followed him with his eyes across the room. To Tommy, he looked a thing-moving. Who can say even if, to Tommy, he looked a *bigger* thing-moving than the sprouting clusternut seed that Erma dangled on a thread above him and laughed to see his eyes follow back and forth? And to Tommy it was not seen at all, certainly, how quickly she hid the seed in her pocket if some other thing-moving came into the room.

The boat at this time had not been begun, since Arthur Herrick had just come home. Therefore, neither had the structure of Gwendolyn's fear of the boat begun. But Justin had chosen the leatherwood trees for the pipes of the organ and he had begun to write down, according to its pattern, "The Time of History."

These things would be from now on constantly developing and entwined together, like the separate strands of a coiled rope. And around them, weaving in and out of them and encircling them, would be the structures of the individual lives and the structure that their lives together made. It is a special sense, this awareness of structure. It was partly his quest for the knowledge of structure that gave Arthur Herrick his quiet air of puzzlement. He was preoccupied with the structure of the great river he had followed for so many days. Yet in his preoccupation he went about his work, caring for the cattle, doing the chores, taking much of the load from Erma, helping her. He was gentle, quiet, kind. There was never any embarrassment in his manner, no apology, no uncertainty. It seemed to Erma incredible that she could ever have been frightened of this man. Sometimes she had the feeling that she must have imagined the violence, the fear and frenzy of former days. There seemed to be no place of reality for her.

In the night she awoke suddenly, feeling herself suspended in space, belonging nowhere except in an infinite, unnamed loneliness. She tried to find some criterion of reality. This happened often and, as she did each time, she went back to the last night they had slept in the same bed. Surely the shock and fear of that night were real. And Arthur had called her sterile. Yes, that was real. Then came the mutilating of the feathermane. That had happened, or else why had she stolen away this very day to his place? Even now her muscles ached with the digging she had done in enlarging the cave, making it more secret, more secure, now that the feathermane could stand and walk a little. Had she not this very day carried there some of the sprouting clusternuts to hoard among her treasures?

She put out her hands to feel of the bedclothes, to anchor herself, to make this lost sensation of floating in suspended nothingness go away. Quietly, in the darkness, she sat up in bed. If those things were real, then it was real that Justin had held her with the strength of love in his hands, that from the depths of him he had, in love, called her name. Erma sank back on the bed. Slowly she exhaled and stretched her hands flat, feeling the tiredness of her muscles. They were real, all those things. Almost three months had somehow been gone through since those things. And for one month now she had lived with this stranger. If it had been that Arthur had been lost in the jungle and this strange person, called by some other name, had appeared, how much easier that would be. She felt such comfort in his presence, sometimes. She closed her eyes and thought: *Let this be real. Let this person be real.*

And now she sat up again, as though she were some mechanized figure, made to transcribe this arc at regular intervals. As on other nights, she gave herself the only touchstone she could believe. Tommy was born, she whispered. Tommy was really born. She made herself think only of the thing she had noticed that day, of how Tommy's hands had opened out like flowers. Surely it didn't happen all at once, this unclenching of the tiny fists. She must have missed the gradual steps. She was aware that her own fists were clenched, and, in the darkness, she let them uncurl slowly and lie palm up, relaxed. How like it was to the thing that had happened to Arthur. Somewhere, beside the mighty green river that haunted him, had he stood alone and let the fists that held his entrails and his brain and heart slowly uncurl and rest, resigned, accepting, waiting?

In the darkness, Arthur spoke. "Would you like to have a fire to watch while you are thinking, Erma?"

"Yes," she said. "Very much. I didn't think you were awake."

"I knew you were," he said. "You sigh so sadly. Are you sad, Erma?"

He knelt before the fireplace, kindling the fire from the last of the old embers. When it had a good start he pulled the covers from his bed and spread them before the fire. "Come on," he said. "It's warm now. We'll sit here awhile together. Would you like some tea?"

She came over to the fire and sat down on the bedcovers spread on the hearth. "I was just thinking about Tommy's hands and how they've changed," she said, taking the teapot Arthur handed her and putting it on the fire. "I noticed only today. His fists aren't clenched any more." She clenched one fist and held it toward the firelight and slowly let it uncurl. "They did that," she said. "It's quite wonderful to see. It's as though he had just let go of the womb and waited for life to fill up his palms."

Arthur put his own hand under hers, fitting it to hers, palm up. "This seems so real here," he said, "sitting by the fire waiting for the tea. I hope you stay awhile."

"You too, Arthur?" she said. "Everything is unreal for you, too?"

Arthur poured tea into a cup and handed it to her. She took it from him slowly, almost ceremoniously, as if the act had some charm to unlock the prison of her puzzlement. "Perhaps that's why," she said. "Perhaps that's why I feel comfortable around you now, more comfortable than with any of the others."

"In spite of the fact," he said, "that you think it should be the other way around."

"No, not exactly, Arthur. It's just that I would never have believed that people could go on, day after day, being comfortable with one another, when . . ."

Arthur drank his tea and put his cup down on the hearth. "I

know," he said. "I never would have believed that people could be reconciled without a reconciliation, or feel settled together when, between them, nothing has been settled."

"The frightening thing is," she said, "that no one seems to notice. The others all talk to me just as if it were possible for me to pay attention. *It doesn't seem to show.* Why, one could go through life in this terrible fog. The thinking part seems not to be essential. There are whole days, maybe weeks, that I can't remember at all. And yet, I surely washed Tommy's diapers and gave him a bath each of those days, or Gwendolyn would have complained. And I surely got the evening meal and fed them each day. But if you told me it had been six months you were gone, it would be just as easy for me to believe. And it is entirely possible that I put Tommy down on a rock somewhere and went off and forgot him."

"Oh, no," Arthur said. "No. The two things are not comparable. Not at all the same kind of thing. But then, of course, if you had, Joe would have been there only a couple of seconds later."

Erma laughed at this. It was funny how passionately Joe took to his new paternity. And then suddenly she stopped laughing. "You see?" she said. "Here I am, laughing at a joke, just like—just like anybody."

She put her hand up to her head, where the volume of confusion pressed hard against her skull. Arthur saw her lips tremble with the helpless spasm of tears to come. He sat down beside her and put his hands on her shoulders, turning her body so that she looked directly at him.

"But you remember Tommy's hands and how they opened today. You told me about that. You're paying attention to the really important things."

"But I told you it happened today," she said. "And I don't know, really. I'm not sure. Don't you see how frightening it is?"

Under his hands he felt her shoulders tightening. He felt the rising tension in her, saw her eyes completely filled with the question of her own existence.

"Yes," he said. "Certainly, I know how frightening it is. You came so late to know fear, Erma, later than anyone I know. Close your eyes now and lie back here by the fire. You're shivering. People always treat shivering as though it were caused by the cold. We will, too. We'll be conventional. Let your fists uncurl the way that Tommy's did. That's right. Take a deep breath. You never learned the weapons for fear, you know. You're used to the quick attack on what threatens you, the sudden victory. This is a subtler enemy."

He saw her chest swell as she breathed deeply. He saw her shoulders sink back against the covers. "That's right," he said. "Another one, now, deeper yet."

She opened her eyes and looked into the fire a long time. It was clear that she believed she was not going to cry. Then she turned her head and looked up at him. Her eyes held a great tiredness in place of the terrible question.

"It's just that I don't feel like an individual any more," she said. "I feel like an automaton that something is pushing around."

Arthur lay down beside her, not touching her. He put his arms under his head and, looking up at the ceiling, said, "Well, then, let's imagine that it isn't the individual that matters, if individuality seems unreal to you. Let's say it's only the distance from the center that matters. In the center is reality, or an awareness of reality, and around it are concentric circles of existence. Then if, for some reason, you get thrown to an outer orbit, that explains why reality seems far away to you. Or, on the other hand, if reality seems far away, it only means you're on a farther orbit. And with anyone on your orbit you can be comfortable, because reality is the same distance removed from both of you."

Erma sat up and reached for the teapot and filled her cup. In the old days she would never have let him get by with that, she knew, twisting and turning words inside out and around and around to cover up something that wasn't straight. "As you say," she said, "on the other hand, if you are comfortable with someone, it only proves you are on the same orbit. Not that you know each other. Do you want some tea?"

"Yes," he said, "please." He sat up and took the cup she handed him. He was well aware of the sharpness in her voice. He looked into the cup and then he looked up directly at her.

"It's not a very good trick, I know," he said. "But it's worth a night's sleep. It's a picture. They go around, after a while, those orbits. They all revolve slowly. It's soothing."

Erma drank her tea, watching him over the top of the cup. How old he looks! she thought. He looks like my father.

"But it is a trick," she said aloud. "Isn't there any other way than with tricks?"

Arthur leaned across her and set his cup down on the hearth. How carefully he puts the cup down, she thought, so that it makes no noise.

"Certainly there is a way without tricks," he said. "You say, then, that it is not the distance from center that matters. It *is* the individuals, that they should know one another, as you have always said. That they should know themselves, as I have always said."

"Yes, suppose you say that? Then what do you do?"

"You do just what you've always done, Erma. You reach in all the dark places and bring everything to light the way you've always done. I only wanted you to know that, from the orbit I'm on, it's a hell of a reach to the center."

"I do know, Arthur," she said, "but I feel closer to the center right now than I have for a long time." She lay back against the covers and stretched herself. Almost, she could feel her brain begin to awaken. It was good to have felt that little touch of anger with Arthur. She could not remember how long it had been since she had felt anger at anything. Perhaps tomorrow she would not have to write in the Record, as she had today, *Nothing. No thoughts.*

Arthur got up to put more wood on the fire. Standing there watching it steam and ready itself to catch, he said, "Of course, you understand, because Justin must have told you, that there are some things, like the feathermane, that I can never reach because they are gone from me forever."

"But, Arthur . . ." she said.

"I know I should have told you in words, 'I'm sorry I killed your feathermane,' but what would it mean? How can I be sorry for something I have no memory of?"

Erma put up her hand to stop him, and in her mind she heard the words she must say: *But, Arthur, he is not dead. You didn't kill him.*

He did not see her hand. He was talking into the fire, forcing himself the way she forced herself to get dinner for all of them every night, to get to the end of it, to get the door closed on them and be in the undemanding quiet with Arthur.

"I simply have no memory of it at all," Arthur said.

But if she told him . . . Then she must reveal the secret place. She must explain why she had kept it so long secret. Even

to the others. Wouldn't they think she had tortured Arthur cru-
elly?

"I have no memory even of wanting to do it," he said. He
squatted down before the fire and poured himself more tea. "Of
course," he went on, "that's not what you're thinking."

How could she bring the feathermane back and say simply,
"He wasn't dead after all; he's been alive all the time"?

"You're thinking that that's not the beginning, that's not
the start of it. You're asking me to reach much farther back in
time than that."

And if she did bring the feathermane back? The scars. He
wouldn't look to the others the way he looked to her. He'd look all
scarred . . . terrible. How could she make Arthur face those
scars day after day?

"I know," Arthur went on, "that eventually we'll have to get
back to the beginning of the headaches and even . . ."

But this moment with Arthur, so long awaited that it had
worn the waiting out, didn't it demand honesty to match honesty,
reaching to meet reaching, whatever the cost?

Such times Erma had had before, and rationalization was no
part of them. And lies were no part of them. She moved nearer
Arthur, sure of her impulse, motivated by the old openness. He
turned toward her his shockingly old and different face.

"Arthur . . ." she said.

And then she found herself, as in a dream, or as a helpless
figure in someone else's dream, putting her fingers on his lips.
"It is not necessary, Arthur," she said. "Surely if we are in the
same orbit together, all this is not really necessary."

He put his arms around her and held her close to him. What
have I done? she thought. What made me say that?

"Thank you, Erma," he said against her ear.

"I am so tired," she said, "so terribly tired."

"Come," he said. "We will lie down by the fire."

She lay with her head turned to the left, staring into the fire.
On her right she could feel Arthur's nearness, but she dared not
turn her head to look at him for fear of losing this delicious
drowsiness that had fallen like a heavy net over her. How long
had it been since she had known drowsiness? Each night she
floated into unreality and fought it, and then in the morning there
was a time she did not remember. That was her sleep, not like

this, not ushered in with languor, not announced and deliciously promised. The firelight blurred before her eyes. I don't feel evil, she thought. I don't feel sad for the deceit. I feel rested. I feel easier than I have felt for a long time. She let her heavy eyelids fall against the red flames, and smiled to think of the feather-mane, safe now, wrapped in the warmth of her deceit, walled about by the cave of her lie. Tomorrow, she thought, I will finish smoothing the wall behind his bed.

Her delight in the cave seemed in danger, with Arthur so close beside her. Under the mesh of drowsiness she stretched herself and opened her eyes to the fire.

"Tell me about the river," she said.

"All right," he said. "Well, there was magic and mystery in it, and a million changing qualities. But mostly power. Once I came on a flock of birds on the river. While I stood there they all took to the air at once. What a sound it was, the air in their wings. After they were gone, I could still hear it, deeper, stronger. That's what the river sounds like."

Erma turned on her side away from the fire and its distracting visions of the cave. She felt Arthur's surprise and knew his misinterpretation of it. She made of the misinterpretation an opiate and of the opiate a thing to cling to fiercely, and by the clinging she corrected the interpretation and felt her fierceness cradled in care and wonder, asking and demand, and a sudden joy.

It was, Arthur knew, an emotionally powerful thing to have witnessed all those birds lifting into the air at once, and, he supposed, even in the telling, some of the emotion came through. He still had the sound of it in his ears as he felt himself dropping headlong into sleep, and, to make a tempo for it, he felt the heavy pulse beats under the arm he had thrown carelessly across the quiet body at his side.

Erma stretched her arms above her head and folded them for a pillow. She flexed one knee and let the heel of her foot pull it back down slowly. She looked at the sleeping face of the man beside her and felt the weight of his arm across her body.

It was as he said. The orbits did begin to revolve after a while if you thought about it. And, as he had also said, it was soothing. She turned her head to the left and saw the last small battles of the flames. Oh, I don't know, she thought. I don't know why people have to be so bloody serious about everything.

Very gently she moved his imprisoning arm so that she could turn on her side, and, as she settled herself on the unaccustomed bed, she decided that tomorrow she would not work in rebellion like an ill-treated servant. Tomorrow there were many things that had long needed doing. She would make a sharples pie, a good deep one, crisp and tart, with a piece of spicebark in it.

*

When Justin had carved out the wooden bells for Erma to use to summon them all to the evening meal, he had not thought to answer their striking with such a feeling of unpleasantness and dread. He had found pleasure in their making, born of a jest; and the problems involved had interested him, as they related to his search for materials and techniques in building the organ. Each bell was made from a different wood, and, working on them, he had imagined the pleasure of hearing their curious tones across the distance, summoning him to the evening meal. But of late the meals had become more and more of an ordeal for him. It was to be expected that Arthur's home-coming would be accompanied with a certain amount of strangeness, just as Gwen's new motherhood was to have unpredictable accompaniments. These things he did not suffer from. He reckoned them to be problems of time, necessary to their living, and of the accepted pattern. What made him uncomfortable, even angry, what was not of the pattern, was Erma. No one ever before had given him the feeling that to feed him was a chore. That his simple wants should be a weight to anyone was an enraging thought. It was as though Erma had said to him of late, "Eat. Eat and be done with it. Get it over and get out."

It was true that Gwendolyn did not help her and that she had too much to do. Still, for himself, he was too old to mix emotion with his food. In the most trying circumstances, he had always been able to produce some quality of leisure—a little grace and ease—with the meals he ate. Angrily, he wished for the courage to withdraw from the group, to eat some fruit, some dried mossback, and a cup of tea in his own house. But of course that, he saw now, must be Erma's position. She too must wish for the courage to say to Gwen, "The lying-in is over. Tomorrow I cease to wash the diapers. Tomorrow at wessun I cease to wait on you."

Even so, yes, they must be in the same position. Still, that did not make the sound of the bells joyous to him the way he had anticipated when he carved them and tried their tones and hung them from the limb of the lacetree by her door. But as soon as he stepped inside tonight he felt the difference. As such, he did not notice that everything in the house had that day been scrubbed with soap and that the orderliness of small things had been re-established; but he felt the lightness of the room and of the girl's step. He saw it reflected in them all, a feeling of expansion, almost gaiety.

"What a sight," Justin said, pointing to the roast dowager hen as he took his place at the table.

Arthur picked up his knife and touched the crisp brown skin of the bird. "It's a shame to mar such beauty," he said.

The odor of the roast dowager curled up about their heads. "Is Tommy asleep?" Erma said to Gwen.

"Yes," Gwen said, turning her head toward the cradle in the corner and then back to the dowager hen. "Not Esmeralda?"

"Esmeralda or not," Joe said, "I'll eat her. I'm starved."

"No, it's not Esmeralda," Erma said. "It's a perfect stranger. It was a wild one. Arthur got it today."

Around the blade of his knife the juice circled and ran. Arthur began to serve the food. "I give you my word," he said, "one and all. It is no one we know."

"Aside from sentimental considerations," Erma said, "I wouldn't dare cook Esmeralda. She's the only one who lays eggs in a predictable spot. The others hide them anywhere."

It was good to see them all enjoying the food, Erma thought. When she brought in the pie it was still hot and giving off the odor of the spicebark.

"Ah," Justin said, contemplating it, "how the gods chasten one. On my way over here I was formulating a complaint to the management. Now my unworthy intentions stand ashamed before this masterpiece."

"He's just bucking for a bigger piece, Erma," Joe said. "Don't fall for it."

"Complaint?" Erma said.

"I miss the designs on the bread of late," Justin said, "but if this is the price, I withdraw my complaint."

"The bread?" Erma said. Now that was a curious thing; she couldn't remember when she had stopped ornamenting the loaves. There hadn't been any decision. But it was true. For a long time, it seemed to her, just to get the number of loaves in and out of the oven had been all she had had time for.

"I was thinking," Justin said, "if you had the services of an expert stoker for the oven on baking days, such a person as—" he looked about the table gravely—"as myself, then perhaps you would return to the ornamentation."

There. He had blundered again somehow. It happened often these days that, at some casual word of his, Erma's face would suddenly flush. His feeling of anger against her returned. He was not a man who went around embarrassing people. What could possibly have upset her? Each time it happened, he was more at a loss.

It is true, Erma thought. All this time I did not love the bread and now, because of a lie, an evasion, a falseness, I suddenly love the bread again. "Oh, well," she said, flipping her hair up from the back of her neck in an angry gesture, "I need a new design."

"A new design?" Justin said. "Well, I admired the old ones very much, particularly the centaur-snail."

"Is there more tea, Erma?" Gwen asked.

Justin watched Erma look into the pot and nod to Gwen. He could see the mysterious anger draining out of her and the deliberate, controlled way in which she handed Gwendolyn her filled cup, but what she felt called upon to steel herself against he had no idea. Then Erma leaned back in her chair and, frowning a little, spoke directly to him in a completely different manner.

"I guess it isn't just a new design I need," she said. "It's that I need a design of having made the old designs—or do I understand 'The Time of History' correctly?"

Justin took his clay pipe out of his mouth and leaned forward. "You understand it exactly," he said, "and that is the best I ever heard it stated."

"What's this?" Arthur said. "What's 'The Time of History'?"

"Why, that's the third movement of the symphony, Arthur," Erma said. "Didn't I tell you about it?"

"No," Arthur said. "I'm 'way behind. I didn't know you'd started the third movement, Justin. But I have wondered what would come after 'The Time of Innocence.'"

Joe smiled across at Erma and, leaving the table, walked over to the cradle and stood watching Tommy sleep.

Justin reached into the pocket of his leather jacket for tobacco and filled his pipe, carefully pressing down the crumbled leaves into the bowl. "Oh," he said to Arthur, "I amuse myself with these names. It's going to be the same music if I call them one, two, three and four or . . . or whatever I call them. I have no critics here to accuse me of being literary, and, having named the first movement, I enjoy seeing if the music makes of itself a structure which suggests to me an idea."

"Is he asleep, Joe?" Gwen said.

"Yes," Joe said, returning to the table. He pulled from his pocket a small piece of wood and his knife and began whittling.

"You mean," Arthur said to Justin, "you mean you have the music first and the . . . the idea of it afterward?"

"Certainly," Justin said, taking his pipe out of his mouth. Seeing the incredulous expression on Arthur's face, he frowned. "I suppose that seems backward to you."

A tingling of excitement ran through Erma. We are enjoying ourselves, she thought. Even Gwen has put her hair up neatly, and by herself for a change. Could such wonders of comradeship be accomplished with a sharples pie, with a house clean and in order? She was flooded with affection for all of them. She wanted to make them warm and comfortable, to give them fresh tea, to let their talk flood into her. Reaching for the teapot, she shifted her feet for balance and, like the pattern of a vine's growth, felt the memory of the night coil through her thigh and reach toward her belly.

"I seem not to have thought about it before," Justin said. "It's not primarily a thinking process, you know. One clamps onto whatever is accompanied by a conviction of authority without bothering to analyze how the selection works or what gives birth to the conviction."

"Well," Arthur said, "what were the things, then, that suggested the idea of history to you? You said the *structure* of the music—"

"I hated history worse than anything at school," Gwen said. "If the teacher had been a woman, I'd have failed every term."

Tommy set up his first tentative whimperings. "There he goes," Joe said. "Why don't you sit over by the fire, Gwen? I'll fix you a chair."

"But . . ." Gwen said.

They had never sat this long after dinner before, and, by Tommy's feeding time, had always been in their own place. Certainly she would not sit with her breast bare here. Her indignation was unnecessary; Joe had placed a chair near the fire so that her back would be toward the others. He carried the baby over to her and then rejoined the group around the table. So much did he want to stay in the room that he felt himself wanting to hover and placate. Almost angrily he sat down with the others and asked Erma for more tea.

"I'm making fresh, Joe," she said. "It'll just be a minute."

"You were speaking of structure," Arthur said, "and ever since I returned from the river I have been obsessed with the question of its structure. Lately I have come to be preoccupied with the conception of structure in general, the structure of anything."

"Well, there you give me some help," Justin said. "Because the fact that the third movement is primarily a matter of structure is part of where the idea of history came from. You see, the first movement—or, that is to say, the theme of the first movement—that is simply there. You have it. It comes. It is. One really has nothing to do with it. Now to accept this is to accept with it a kind of ghostly mold of forecast."

"Then you do have some kind of over-all plan?" Arthur said.

"To state it that way is too definite," Justin said. "It isn't that one knows what will fit the mold in advance; it's that whatever will not fit is so certainly cast out. After all, the mold is only a kind of hint. It's flexible."

Squatting before the fire, making the fresh tea, Erma knew again the awareness of strain in her thigh muscles and found it pleasant.

"I need a fresh diaper, Erma," Gwen said.

"I'll get you one," Erma said, starting up, so that she spilled a little of the hot tea on the hearth.

"Well, now," Justin said, "we'll see what can be fished out of the teapot." He smiled up his thanks to Erma. "Why don't you come and rescue me?" he said to her. "You and your design of having made designs."

"Maybe you could do better on beer," Erma said. "How's the new batch, Joe?"

"Sure," Joe said, "that's what we need." He put his knife and the wooden object back into his pocket. "Hand me a torch. The new batch is maybe a little green yet, but there's still some of the old. I'll go get it."

"Well, can you tell me," Arthur said, "what is the quality of history in this new music?"

"I doubt that I can," Justin said, "before the beer comes. But perhaps you can tell me the qualities of history in history, and I'll be able to find the parallels."

"Well, the most obvious," Arthur said, "would be repetition. Men find themselves doing what has been done before."

"But not exact repetition," Justin said. "Now there are many times when the themes of the first movement and of the second movement do appear again in the third. But sometimes they are inverted, or . . . well, twisted upon themselves, or are in a different tempo."

"Like the chair you sat in when you were little," Erma said. "And when you go home again later to see it, the least important thing about it is that it is the same chair."

"Yes," Justin said. "The least important thing is the technical part."

"And then there are the holidays, the festivals," Arthur said to Justin.

"But these are details," Justin said, "as far as the music goes. The main thing is—how shall I say it?—a deliberateness. It's not only that one becomes aware of the structure, but that the structure begins to insist, to thrust itself on your attention."

"It's something to do with the time," Erma said, "the tempo."

"What you are trying to say, I think," Justin said, "is that in the second movement one is aware of the melody, of the musical events, as though they were pushed forward by the tempo, or floated on top of it, while in 'The Time of History,' the melody moves against the stream of time. At war, so to speak, with the tempo. That's what I meant by the structure's forcing its attention on the listener."

Justin made a gesture with his hands of pushing against the air. "A deliberate structure of resistance shows," he said. "A struggle against acceleration, the antidote to frenzy."

Gwen carried the sleeping child over to its crib and returned to the fire, turning her chair so that she could see the others. There they were, still at it. Arthur was only getting started. How ridiculous they all were, arguing about history, as if any person in his right mind did not know perfectly well what history was. She wished that Joe would hurry and come back so that she could ask him to build up the fire and get her something to put her feet on. For all any of the rest of them noticed, she could sit there and freeze. It hadn't been like this when she was pregnant; it certainly hadn't. At least tonight the food had been fit to eat, for a change. Quite good, really, for Erma. And the room had been cleaned up and set to rights, too. But of course it still looked like Erma, careless and bare, not really comfortable. It was disgusting, somehow, the way they had never got another room built on, so that anyone, coming in, could see their two beds there. Of course, they didn't sleep together any more. Even before Arthur had gone off into the jungle there had been two beds there. And no wonder. It only confirmed what she had always felt about Erma. That she was sexless, cold. It was no wonder Arthur drank, or that he had tried to kill her. After all, one could hardly blame him. He still drank; she was quite sure of it. He had Joe fooled, and maybe the others; but he didn't fool her. It would serve Erma right if somebody else gave Arthur something to think about besides that river. And it wouldn't be hard to do, either.

A pleasant languor settled upon Gwendolyn, and sleepily she heard their voices recede in waves, still talking, talking. She set her teeth together and stretched her head back, pulling her breasts upward. She turned her head to the fire and smiled and wondered what a little mother's milk would do for Arthur Herrick. She looked over at Justin, tasting the incredible blue of his eyes. Had he? Had he asked his wife, as Joe had last night? It was probable all men did. She looked at Erma, sitting at the table, listening and alert, one hand held up like a white bird, ready to fly away. Something Erma Herrick wouldn't know about. Gwendolyn had a great urge to laugh aloud, remembering how Joe had begged her last night, "Let me taste; I want to know what it's like." That's what she'd tell him if they didn't get off the subject of history pretty soon. If this dull talk went on much longer, she'd tell Joe her breast was sore. Which one had it been? Oh, yes. Well, it did hurt a little. She'd tell him.

Joe came straight to her as soon as he had put the crock of beer on the table. He put his hand on her head. "Tired?" he asked. Then he went to work on the fire. He brought her a stool for her feet, without her asking. Pulling a cover off one of the beds, he tucked her in. Like a child with a naughty secret he leaned over her and said in a low voice, "Say, can you have any beer? I mean . . ."

"I don't think I'd better," Gwen said. "It might—"

"Make the kid drunk?" Joe said. "I was wondering about that."

She looked up at him and smiled. "I'd better not," she said. "Tired?"

Gwen lowered her eyelids and smoothed one hand over her breast. "A little," she said.

"Why don't you take a cat nap? Go ahead."

Joe pulled the wooden object and his carving knife out of his pocket and sat down at the table. "This my beer?" he said.

"What are you working on there so industriously?" Justin asked, reaching out his hand toward Joe.

"Rattle for the kid," Joe said, turning it over in his hands before he passed it to Justin. "The handle's still too thick."

"Let me see, Justin," Erma said.

"You know," Joe said, "I hunted all over the Kingdom for something that size. They must be unnatural qualifications. Everything that's light enough for him to lift is small enough for him to put into his mouth. And anything that's too big to go in his mouth is too heavy to play with."

Gwendolyn uncrossed her ankles and turned her head away from the fire. Well, at last they were off the subject of history. "Honestly," she said, "the time he's put in on that rattle, he could have built another room on the house."

Justin ran his big thumb along the polished surface of the handle. He shook the thing to hear the rattling of the seeds so cleverly trapped inside. And then he handed it over to Erma to examine.

"You know," he said, "that rattle makes me think. Why don't we have a big room where we can meet in the evenings and do work like this? We've most of us got something going all the time. We need a kind of social hall."

"That's a good idea," Joe said. "A place where we could all spread out and not be under Erma's feet. It wouldn't be anyone's house. It would be a place where you could go if you felt like being sociable. And you could get the hell out when you felt like it. We could move your loom over," he said to Gwen, "when you feel like weaving again. It would be good for the kid to have some —some place to go."

Justin smiled. "Yes, Tommy'll be needing a social life just any day now. But seriously, the dampness is defeating me on the building of the organ. I'll have to build a place for it. My own place isn't big enough."

"And the Records," Arthur said. "We have to keep a fire there all the time. Why don't we move them, or build the room around them? We could save a lot of time if we had all the things that needed to be kept dry under one roof."

"It's a wonderful idea," Erma said. "A kind of general drying-out room. To say nothing of the concerts we could have while we were working."

Joe reached over to take the rattle from Erma's hand. "Sure," he said. "A combination diaper and music hall."

Gwendolyn threw the coverlet back, disentangling herself, and went over to the table. Well, now, if they were going to have a room. Yes, she could see how it would be. The organ would be at one end, and in the evenings she would sit at the loom weaving while Justin played for them. A pang of the old homesickness for Drury came over her, of how she would sit with her sisters around the radio in the evenings while they manicured their nails and got their clothes ready for the next day.

"Erma, dear," she said, "would you fix me a little tea? The pot's cold and I daren't have beer, you know."

Would they still all eat together when they had the drying room? she wondered. And would she be expected to do half the cooking? But surely not. After all, Erma had no children. They surely couldn't expect her, Gwen, to look after Tommy and cook for five people and do all the weaving, too.

"Thank you, Erma," she said, taking the fresh cup of tea. "Everything tasted so good; it was such a wonderful dinner. You don't know how wonderful it is to be sitting up late and feeling human again."

What had he said? What was it Arthur said? Gwen leaned toward him, staring, trying to quiet the shaking in her arms.

"I could work on it in the evenings," Arthur said. "I guess I'd have about the same problems building a boat that you're having with the organ, Justin. We could plan the lighting better than we did in the houses. Now that we have plenty of oil, we could make it really light in the drying room, and we could work in the evenings."

That's what she had thought he said. Gwendolyn clasped her hands together under the table. Arthur was going to build a boat. He was going to go back to that damnable, mythical river, and he wanted to take Joe with him. Not possible. It was not possible. A wildness began to beat in her. Under the table she struck her fists on her thighs. It was not possible that the two of them could be sitting here calmly, *calmly*, planning to build a boat, planning to take a hazardous journey. Weeks, now, they were talking of. Exploring. They were going off and leaving her. Just like that. They were going off and leaving her. Oh, she could kill Joe. She could *kill* him. There he sat, running his hands over that goddamned rattle, looking at Arthur with that idiotic smile on his face, saying, What? Saying, Would it have to be built to weather rapids?

She'd have to be careful. She couldn't fight them this way. She'd have to get control. She got up from the table carefully and walked over to the crib. Standing with her back to the others, she let her eyes go wild, let them be fists beating on a wall, let them be footsteps scurrying crazily. She made her back broad and, leaning over the crib, pinched the sleeping baby until he woke and cried, putting an end to the talk at the table.

WHILE it was still dark Erma crept silently out of the house and stood waiting for the pre-wessun light, by which to see the path. She pulled the hood of her coat over her head against the dew and threaded her way silently in and out among the ghostly shapes of the trees to the field of greengrain. Here she filled her skirt with the cool, damp, striped grasses and, holding it against her body, she walked silently to the tool house, where she got out the wooden shovel. Gradually the contours of the land began to emerge and round themselves into shape, while the figure of the woman cut itself into the soft gray space. She carried the shovel over one shoulder. Her hood loosened itself and fell back as her body quickened with joy and her pace accelerated with anticipation. As the earliest light of wessun became a fact she left the path and, dodging through the thorntree thicket and among the dense vines, came to the entrance of the cave.

This fastness, this safe place, had she made for him in the hillside. Little by little she had dug farther into the hillside, dumping the loads of dirt into the hot springs nearby. Behind a dense façade of vines she felt her way to the place in the hillside where the block of sod must be moved away. Laughing with anticipation, she put her foot on the first step that led down into the cave. The feathermane came to meet her, sleepy and stiff, reaching with his delicate nose for her caress.

"Ah, my lovely," she said, "here's your breakfast." She sat on the ground and spread out her skirt, that he might bury his head in the fresh grain. Here for a while each day she began to live. Her eyes devoured him while he snuffled among the grain in her lap, choosing the freshest, the most succulent heads. When he had had his fill, he would make a small sound of satisfaction in his throat.

She put her arms around him. "Ah, you are warm," she said. "Lovely and warm."

She gathered up all the scattered remnants of grain and carried them over by the water bowl. This clay bowl she had sunk in the ground so that she need not fear his knocking it over and being thirsty in her absence. Surrounding it were circles of sprouting clusternuts, which she had first brought there because she had thought them beautiful, and later cultivated because she found he liked the taste of the delicate shoots. She lifted the bowl out of the ground.

"I'll get you some fresh water," she said. "I'll be right back."

When she returned the feathermane was lying on his bed of mosses. When she came to sit by him he made little movements with his hoofs and, putting his head on her lap, sighed heavily and closed his eyes. With her hand resting on his head Erma looked about the walls of the cave and began to talk. "They're going to have a room," she said. "A Drying-Out Room. The Records are to be moved there and there is to be a big fireplace, not a pit like those we have in our houses. Justin's going to finish building the organ there and Arthur's going to build a boat. Gwen will be weaving at her loom and Joe will be sharpening his tools and making new ones, I suppose."

She leaned down and grazed her cheek over the soft mane. "But what shall I do there?" she said. "How can I take my work there?"

How easily she spoke of them all when she was here in the cave. Yet, when she was with them, her mind ran constantly back to the cave, as though to rest itself. How often of late she had sat with them while her mind's eye had been roving over the walls of the cave, seeking out the rough places, planning the next place to dig. It was lovely here. She smiled down at the feathermane and, gently moving his head off her lap, stood up and reached to the wall where his halter was hung. Knowing the movements, he got stiffly to his feet.

"Come now," she said. "We'll go for your walk."

Slowly he climbed up the dirt steps to the entrance. It was something she waited for each day, to see the light strike and glance off his polished, spiral horns. How beautiful they were, almost translucent.

They walked around an outjutting of the hill, never very far

away from the entrance. Erma suited her pace to the feathermane's uncertain, faltering steps and planned where next she
would work on the cave. There were still rough places on the
back wall, and, in anticipation, she felt the shovel in her hands
and how it would be resisted and in which spots. When they re-
entered the cave, Erma had always to wait awhile to accustom her
eyes to the darkness. When she could see she began to study the
rear wall, looking for the place where she could best begin to
smoothe it.

Was it a trick of the uncertain light? A shadow? The halter
dropped from her hand and she moved quietly to the wall and
reached her hands up to feel if the bulge were really there.

The fathermane stood where he was, waiting for his halter
to be taken off. Erma's hands began to scratch at the dirt. She
picked up the shovel and cast it aside; then she ran out of the
cave and returned with a pointed stick. The feathermane was
puzzled by this change in their routine and, when Erma remained
oblivious to his efforts to gain her attention, he finally lay down
warily. Her hurry upset him, made him alert and restive.

She was not digging; with the pointed stick she was tracing
a sweeping arc and smoothing it out with the palm of her hand.
Presently she began to hum. Taking this for reassurance, the
feathermane let his head sink on his folded hoofs and slowly he
fell asleep, still wearing his halter.

Out of the wall, under the hands of the girl, began to emerge
the belly of a woman, rounded, full, and voluptuous.

FROM THE RECORD OF ARTHUR HERRICK, SIXTEENTH DAY,
NINTH MONTH, SECOND YEAR:

For a moment I thought I had it. Out of a conversation with
Justin I got a feeling that soon, in another moment, I would grasp
the structure of the river, that I would have it figured out. But now
it is gone. The slightest thing can throw me off. I have mislaid the
shovel and Joe will be sure to notice it. He guards the tools as though
they were his right arm. Is it possible that I have momentary lapses
of memory, as once I had a big one? How would I know if I did? I
suppose I have simply put the shovel down somewhere (I did use
it yesterday at the manure pile; but it is not there) and I will stumble over it shortly and call myself a fool for this anxiety. But once the
mind has failed for any reason, the slightest things are suspect.

Tomorrow we begin work on the Drying Room. It is to be built over a bed of ashes. Once it is done, Joe and I will start work on the boat. And when the boat is done, I shall know the river, all of it. I do not care how long it takes. Nor, in a way, do I care if I never return. But this I must do. I must know the form of the river before I die. When Justin was talking about "The Time of History" music I kept feeling that the symphony and the river are related, or even that the symphony holds the key to the locked secret of the river. Somewhere there must be a beginning, a *discovery* for the river, a spring, if only I could find it. Somewhere it, too, must have a time of innocence, where it follows the contours of the land, instead of making them; motivated by a course it did not make—as they say in the music that the melody is carried along, pushed along by, rides on the crest of, the tempo.

But Justin says that the third movement, the history music, is against the tempo, resists it. But a river does not turn and run upstream, back upon itself. A river is a fact, not a symphony. One should be able to predict a fact and have the prediction verified.

*

As at some point a mighty river gathers together its forces and takes on a character capable of making its own form—no longer nebulous, no longer easily diverted—so did the structures in the Green Kingdom begin to assume form and rigidity. As the behavior of the child and his explorations into life paralleled the secret, hidden processes of his blood and bone, so did the structures of light and darkness draw closer to each other, borrow from each other. From the separate houses and the separate lives, from the caves of memory and secret desire, like strands of a raveled rope, did these structures tend more and more to be pulled toward and focused on the Drying Room. Made of sod bricks and raised on a platform above a bed of moisture-absorbing ashes, it was larger than any of the houses and lacked only the fireplace wall to be complete. They planned this to be of the large rivstones, similar to the one Joe used for the largest weight in his laboratory, though that one he would not allow to be used.

Erma joined the three men in the laborious trips to the river, carrying back to the Drying Room more than the weight of the stone, carrying also the secret knowledge that the female torso on the wall of the cave emerged now complete, the great, fecund belly supported by massive thighs. It pleased her to stand in the water searching for the stones, to allow the water to rise on her thighs to the height where those of the cave figure emerged from the wall. Once the walls of the cave had been only dirt to her, an enemy in fact, to be pushed back, an impediment to safety. Now, beneath her hands, they had come alive, bringing her a joy she had never experienced.

In such a manner had the rattle emerged for Tommy, in focus, out of the blur he lived in. He held it in his two hands and learned to know the sound of the seeds trapped within it, as a little later he would know it as *his* thing to hold and to hear. As the rivstones were piled one on top of another to make the huge fireplace, which was to be such a great improvement over the fire pits of the houses, so did Tommy build, one upon another, the trials of the pattern that made him reach out for the rattle and successfully grasp it in his hands and, cautiously, gropingly, seek the satisfaction of putting it in his mouth. But ahead of him and around him his father had planned well and carefully. The fireplace drew and the rattle would not go into his mouth.

After the first time she had forgotten the shovel Erma never risked taking it again. Gradually she fashioned her own tools, a simple wooden scraper and three bone chisels with different-sized ends for the carving. Now, in the cave, she brought the scraper down on a flat surface rhythmically and, when it struck an obstacle, felt a thrill of exploration at what might emerge. Today the men were helping Justin to carry in the first pipes of the organ and they would not miss her. She began to explore the obstacle with her bare fingers. It was a root projecting through the wall of the cave. She cleared it of dirt and held the largest chisel poised to cut it away. But in that instant she had seen it as a hand, reaching in anguish toward the great torso, crying out in emptiness for the fruit of the swollen belly. She dropped the chisel and, with a handful of moss from the feathermane's bed, began to cleanse and polish the root hand.

One evening in the Drying Room, after they had eaten, Erma watched Gwen at the loom, weaving. Her fingers hungered for her own work and she wished that she might now be polishing the root hand in the cave. How different it was from Tommy's hand. Tommy could sit up now if she put her hand behind his back. He would rock from side to side and squeal and, when she held out the rattle to him, he would reach for it with one hand and gravely, with concentration, transfer it to the other hand.

"Don't get him excited," Gwen said. "It's time for him to go to sleep."

Erma took her hand from Tommy's back, easing him down into the crib. The baby rolled over onto his abdomen, and she straightened his coverlet and went over to sit by Justin. Arthur and Joe had begun to work on the boat at last, and the main skeletal ribs jutted against the firelight. Even Justin had work in his hands this night.

"What are you making?" Erma asked him.

"A flute," he said. Putting it on the floor beside his stool and taking out his pipe, he smiled at her. "This will come as a blow to you, I know," he said. "But—" he motioned toward the great pipes of the organ— "really, it is more my size."

"You mean," Erma said, "that you've given up the organ?"

"Well, temporarily, at least. At best, it was a poor substitute for an orchestra, and at worst, it is something I don't know how to finish. I seem to have been overly ambitious." He reached down for the crude flute and placed it across his lap. "Yes," he said, "this is more my size."

"And now I suppose I shall never hear any but the flute part of 'The Time of History,' " she said.

"What one needs," Justin said, pointing with the flute to the crib, "is to have been Tommy. Now, Tommy, if he makes music, will make it *of* the Green Kingdom, instead of about the Green Kingdom. And he will have a different feeling for what to make music out of. There is something here, you know, which is right for the sound of the chichimingo's call, just as surely as the chichimingo is here."

The Drying Room was a step forward in their development. It made a new cohesiveness in their lives that they had this well-lighted place to meet together in for the evening meal. It made their own places more private and it gave them all a sense of shared accomplishment. But to Joe, the most important thing was that it gave Tommy a little wider world, a bigger group, like visiting relatives, like having some place *to go*. Tommy could reach for his rattle with one hand, and he could transfer it from hand to hand. He discovered the joy of banging it on the sides of the crib, looking up in a puzzled way when Gwen said no. There was the time when suddenly he knew how to throw it away. A little later, he knew how to throw it away and look after it to see where he had thrown it.

The processes of growth are not always perfectly synchronized, and there was a small space of time when he could throw it on the floor and look at it, but he could not want it back yet. Perhaps it was here, just before he knew to want back what he had thrown away, before it had occurred to him to reach and cry for its recapture, that Gwendolyn took to leaning back from her loom and folding her hands in her lap while she stared at her enemy, the boat. Who can place these moments exactly—the moment before wanting is born, the moment when fear becomes enmity? Was it before or after Yearsenday? They did not go to the Yearsenday Place this year because the baby was so small (he had two teeth on Yearsenday, though; they all remembered that), and so they had missed the bursting of the bombs. But they had a feast in The Room—no one called it The Drying Room any longer—and, in honor of the occasion, they had firstfruit melons.

As deep and as dark as the cave that sheltered Erma's joy was the secret place of Gwendolyn's fear of the boat. The men were stretching mossback hides over the ribs now; and often, in fear and hatred of the boat, Gwendolyn would sit back from the loom watching them, feeling that it was her own skin they stretched and sewed to the gunwales with leather thongs. And soon, to heighten her displeasure and add nausea to her fear, she smelled everywhere the odor of boiling pitch. It seemed to Gwendolyn there was no escaping it. Even in her own bed she could smell it. It had a penetrating, cloying odor, this sap which the men scraped off the sweating gum trees and melted down for the boat. It personified her fear, this odor. Because it brought the boat near completion, it helped to crystallize her enmity. She would listen to no talk about the boat, though in these days little else was talked of. If anyone spoke to her directly of it, she laughed and made jokes about it. She had something to battle it with, to draw attention away from it, and to delay the work on it. For Tommy had developed a dramatic sense and he liked an audience. He could pull himself up by the sides of his crib, he could creep and, by reaching up for Joe's hands and pulling steadily, he could stand. He could say "mamma" and he could play peekaboo. He could say "dada" and play patticake. And he had discovered the third dimension; the rattle would go into his milk cup.

Now this was a wonderful knowledge to Tommy, that things had insides, that some things would go into other things. He

babbled to celebrate it. He squealed and crowed and yelled and
shivered with the delight of exploration. The special powers of
the index finger asserted themselves like the fingers of light that
Erma had set into niches around the walls of the cave.

Seeking through the shadows, the fingers of light darted and
explored, showing up new contours, promising the work ahead
faster than she could keep up. Teased out of the dirt walls by the
fingers of flame, a conception flower emerged, the udder of a
mossback cow, the plumed head of a riverheron, the shifting, enticing shadows of work ahead. There were many moments in the
cave now of unspeakable joy when she must leave the work and,
unable to contain her excitement, run to the feathermane and
hold him close to her in exultation while she laughed aloud. Even
the dirt that sifted down from the chisels and the scraper seemed
different to her from other dirt. She took to piling it up before the
huge torso that she had first worked on. In time, it came to assume the appearance of a low altar. No longer did Erma come to
the cave for solace and comfort; she came to be alive. Sometimes
her exultation was greater than the feathermane could hold and
she thought it must show to the others. Often, as Justin neared
the end of "The Time of History," she wished to share her
knowledge of creative processes with him, to say, "I know, I
know." But always something restrained her.

When the boat was ready for its first testing only Arthur,
Erma, and Joe went up to the river with it. The others stayed behind.

"It was good of you to stay and keep us company, Justin,"
Gwen said.

Justin and Gwen had eaten the noon meal in The Room.
Now they sat over their tea, watching Tommy crawl about the
floor, exploring and babbling to himself. Once in a while he
would pull himself up and try a few tentative steps.

"It's been my experience of boats," Justin said, "that several
immersions are always necessary. I'm sure we'll have plenty of
opportunity to see it tried out. You know, Tommy will be walking
all over before we know it."

"Yes," Gwen said, "he's into everything as it is. I would
have had to be after him every minute if I'd gone to the Yearsenday Place with them. It's really too hard a trip for a little baby,
and he would have been sure to fall into the river."

She went over to the child and picked him up. "Come now, Tommy," she said. "It's time for your nap."

Tommy did not like naps any more. He did not like to stop playing. He howled.

"It's not very restful for you," Gwen said to Justin, "and you must be very tired. I saw your lamp still burning when I got up this morning. Did you finish 'The Time of History' last night?"

"Almost," Justin said. He got up and walked over to the mantel and took down his flute. Then he pulled a stool over near the crib. "Perhaps he'd like a lullaby," he said.

Tommy's crying stopped at the first sound of the flute. His big eyes stared in fascination. Justin began to play *The Lullaby of Edie-Davie* and *The Strictly Family Music*. It was very pleasant and quiet in The Room, and Justin found great pleasure in the old songs. Unreal and dreamlike, old domestic scenes came back to him without pain or bitterness. Even after Tommy's eyelids became too heavy for him, Justin played on quietly. He was in a remoteness of fatigue from having worked all night on the symphony. It seemed to him that outside this room there was the sea, and next door lived his friend Max Staats. He was quite unaware of Gwendolyn, and, had he seen her move from her table to the loom and sit there quietly with the shuttle in her hand, he would have taken her for Edith.

The mood of the music was infectious, and Gwendolyn sat at the loom wrapped in a languor of peace and shelter. How good Justin had been to put Tommy to sleep, to stay with them when the others had gone off to try out the hated boat with never a thought for her. How was she supposed to manage by herself all day long? What did they expect her to do—leave the child alone while she milked the mossbacks? Oh, it was really disgraceful, their expecting her to come along on a foolish trek up the mountainside with a baby less than a year old. That boat, that damnable boat was all that anyone cared about or talked about. She was sick of the sight of it. She wished it would split into a thousand pieces. No wonder The Room seemed so pleasant to her today. The boat was gone, and for the first time in weeks her nostrils were not being insulted by the stench of the boiling pitch.

"That one is lovely," she said to Justin. "What is it? I never heard it before."

"Oh, that," Justin said, startled into identifying The Room

and Gwendolyn, "that is 'The Tree House.' I used to play it for my own children when they were little. They used to sing it. Well, that is, all of them but George. George never sang."

"Will you teach it to Tommy later on?" Gwen said. "I want him to have things like that, you know, songs and rhymes and . . . and the things we used to have."

"Perhaps he'll make songs of his own," Justin said.

"Where would he get them?" Gwen said angrily, and then abruptly wished she had not.

Justin turned his head away from her and, lifting his flute to his mouth, closed his eyes on the present. Like a wall, he thought; she was like a solid concrete wall. He began to play "The Ninescah."

> *Once more before I die, I want to see the Ninescah*
> *Once more before I die, I want to walk by the Ninescah.*

He heard Gwen's gasp of delight and kept his eyes closed, the better to remember the old song.

> *I'll wade in the shallows where the shining minnows are,*
> *Swim out to the bare backbones of the white sandbar.*

Justin thought of the world so seldom any more. It was only by the greatest effort of projection that he allowed the notes of the flute to pick out slowly from the past the song his mother had sung to him, which he had correctly guessed to be a part of Gwen's heritage.

> *Hunt for the rotten log where my father caught the cat,*
> *Though he was a grown man and didn't laugh out loud at that.*

> *Hush, Child, my father said,*
> *You'll scare the fish away.*

> *Oh, I'll have it back again some long and summer day.*
> *For surely on the banks of the Ninescah*
> *The wild sand plums are still purple in the sun.*

He opened his eyes to ask, "How does it go?" and saw Gwen completely defenseless, the silent tears sliding over her cheeks, making them shine in the dim eassun light. Justin put his flute away on the mantel and went over to her.

"Come, now," he said. "I didn't mean to make you sad." He

took her hands in his and said, "You're very often homesick, aren't you? I forget about it. I'm sorry."

Gwendolyn leaned over and put her wet face on his big hands. "Always," she said. "I am always homesick. I never forget. Never for a moment."

Justin felt awkward and guilty and, as always, sorry for the girl. He patted her shoulder clumsily and noted the sharpness of it.

"Stupid of me," he said. "I should have known those old songs would make you sad. We'll light the lamps and have it a little cheerier in here when the boy wakes up. Let's stir about, now. I promised to milk the cows, you know."

Gwendolyn released his hands and stood up. "You mustn't think I didn't love your playing. I did. I just got carried away."

When Justin came back from the milking Tommy was awake and sitting up in his bed, talking to his rattle, cooing, making little pleased sounds.

"I wonder how they made out with the boat," Justin said.

"I suppose they'll be coming back soon," Gwen said.

But, staring into the fire, so near the reassuring presence of Justin, she hoped not. This was the pleasantest day she had had in a long time, and she wished it might continue. How kind Justin was.

"We used to have such good times with the birds," she said to him. "The baby takes up all my time now. I've been meaning to ask you, do you still feed them?"

"Oh, yes, generally," Justin said. "I put food out for them still, though I don't go regularly any more."

How beautiful the birds had been, Gwendolyn thought. She could remember how Justin used to help her over the broken place in the path, how he had made the feather coverlet for her. Really, the only relative peace she had ever had was when she was pregnant. First they had had to leave the base camp to explore. Then they had had to move their tent to the settlement. Just when she had almost succeeded in getting a decent house around her, there had been all that stir about Arthur, everything so upset, Erma so absent-minded, nobody giving her a thought. And now . . .

She put her empty cup down on the hearth and got up to go to the door. Angrily she looked out to see if they were coming. *Now* there was this nonsense about the boat. What were they thinking of, going off to a weird, unknown river for weeks, months—who knew how long? Really, was there *no peace?* Did nothing stand still and stay settled long enough for you to catch your breath? It was disgusting. The only time at all when she had ever had a moment's peace was . . .

"Here they come," she said to Justin. "They've got the boat and it must have leaked in a hundred places, the way they're walking."

Erma would be tired, then, Justin thought. Suddenly he realized that the remains of their lunch were still littering the table and that no preparations had been made for the evening meal. The accumulated fatigue of the night came over him. He went over to the crib and lifted Tommy into his arms.

"Come on," he said, "we'll go meet your daddy and hear about the boat."

Carrying the baby, Justin walked with Gwendolyn to meet the three approaching. Erma saw him and waved but she did not increase her speed any. Joe and Arthur carried the boat over their heads.

"Here," Justin said to Joe, "I'll trade loads with you."

Joe flexed his arms to get the stiffness out of them before he took the baby. "Hi, kid," he said. "You didn't miss much."

Justin felt Arthur, behind him, adjust to his step. "How did it go?" he called back.

Joe, walking ahead with one arm around Gwendolyn, answered him. "She's got five leaks. We'll have to plaster her good with pitch."

"She rides high, though," Arthur said. "I think she'll take a good load of supplies."

Justin and Arthur carried the boat inside The Room and put it on its rack. Arthur rubbed his stiff arms and went over to the fire. "Is there any tea?" he said to Gwen. "We're all soaked through."

Justin saw Erma scan the table and pick up the teapot from the hearth. "Here," he said to her, "I'll make some fresh. You sit down and rest."

"Hey, what's the matter?" Joe said. "Look at him wiggle."

Tommy was fairly dancing in his arms. His fists were clenched with his great effort and all his being stretched out, away from Joe. He opened his mouth several times and impatiently he pointed out the return of something that had been missing all day from his accustomed world. Finally he said it: "Boat"!

Gwendolyn slipped quietly out the door and started for her own house. The others were delighted with this new word, this first real word; and under their encouragement Tommy began to chant his triumph.

Behind Gwen, growing fainter as she began to run for shelter, planning how she could say she had gone to get dry clothes for Joe, she could hear the hated word in her own child's newfound voice: *Boat! Boat! Boat!*

The boat was tested again and found to have one leak only. Again the pitch boiled and permeated the air. Again the boat was tested, and pronounced almost perfect. Every cubic inch of its contents was planned and replanned in the evenings. The odor of the pitch faded; the remnants of it, blended with that of the mossback hides, became the odor of the boat.

Even this was drowned now by the bunches of candleflowers set all about The Room. Fragrant peppervines hung from the rafters and mingled with the fresh, exciting odor of Tommy's first birthday cake. He had lived in the Green Kingdom thirteen months. He had six teeth and he needed a new bed. He could say "mamma" and "papa" and "boat." He could say "mine" and "milk" and "cup," besides many words exclusively his own. He weighed an even rivstone; and when he pulled himself up to his full height he could look a plumed riverheron straight in the eye.

These were great things to celebrate and Tommy was much aware of the excitement. He pointed to all the new things and was silent with wonder at the present Justin had brought him—a tame pet ballsleeper. Once Tommy had ventured to touch the animal he was wild with excitement over the softness of it, so that he frightened it back onto Justin's shoulder, where it stayed most of the evening. His excitement mounting, Tommy sat at the table with the others and spat out the taste of his birthday cake, it being unfamiliar. He knocked over his milk cup and cried and suddenly fell sound asleep against Joe's chest.

"I'd better take him home to his own bed," Gwen said, "where it's quiet."

"These great celebrations," Justin said, "are very exhausting. And I warn you, Gwen, it doesn't ease any with the years. My wife used to dread the children's birthdays worse than any of the holidays. We often considered not telling them when their birthdays were. But we always weakened."

"No, Gwen," Joe said, standing up with the child in his arms, "I'll take him. You stay and celebrate."

It was a statement made with a rare tone of finality for Joe. This night he wanted very much to put his son to bed. He found himself much affected by the fact that Tommy was a year old. Just for this one night he did not look forward to hearing Arthur's endless plans about the voyage. He threw a blanket over the baby and stepped out into the damp cold darkness, his feet seeking the familiar path. His arms tasted the weight of the child's sleeping body and relished the fact that this day it amounted to an even rivstone. How rare it was, such a moment. How seldom he was alone with his child. He wished to stand here in the quiet night and let the solemn time prolong itself. There was a sadness to this time, not at all unpleasant, and somehow familiar. He remembered the present that Justin had brought, the pet ballsleeper. There in the darkness, standing quietly on the path, holding his sleeping son in his arms, he remembered the scrawny kitten, above the print shop in Drury. He heard himself say, as he had said that day to Erma, "It isn't that you can't go to circuses any more; it's that you get so you don't want to."

Poor thing. Poor sterile thing. She had seemed to him then the wisest, the most maternal person he had ever known. Who would have dreamed he would come to resent her so, even to hate her at times? Who would have guessed it would be Erma Herrick's fault that his son should grow up with none but a ballsleeper for a playmate?

Inside the festive room Gwendolyn sat with the others, listening to Justin playing on the flute. While she listened, Gwen looked about The Room, enjoying the evidences of festivity. Now and then her eyes fell on the boat and she lifted one eyebrow and smiled a little. While she was of the group, listening to the music, she had only feelings of virtue. After all, was not this sacrifice to be made for her son, that he not be deprived of his father? But while she stood by the boat, putting on her coat, waiting for Justin to bring a torch from the fireplace, she could not resist her triumph. She turned her back on the others and, holding the sides of her coat apart for a minute, she allowed the boat to see its fill. Deliberately, slowly, she fastened the coat around her and

smoothed it down. She nodded her head at the boat emphatically
and spun on her heel.

"Thank you, Justin," she said, reaching up to take the torch.
"Good night."

Over the room hung the silence of a finished festivity and
the echo of Justin's flute. Over the boat hung the unspoken announcement of Gwendolyn's triumphant pregnancy.

CHAPTER FOUR

H o w often do we walk alone the pathways of desire and, by the very repetition of the act, believe some fraction of its history to have been shared. How easily do spatial landmarks serve to map the mind's geography, transforming coincidental longings into memory's events. *Here in this place, beloved,* the lover says, *I long for you.* The graduated sieves of Time receive this cry and let it sift successively to finer particles: *This place, beloved, brings forth thoughts of you.* Finally, the powdered dust that stays suspended and will not fall to any further sieve cries out: *This was our place.* In vain the fists of accuracy beat on memory's prison; in vain the voice of accuracy protests: *Not then! I could not have known that then.* The fists grow fur. The voice cries into a gray velvet ear that does not transmit.

Justin walked slowly along the path that led to the conception flowers. On this, their night of phosphorescence, he was thinking of Erma and of the other years. The time he had seen her unexpectedly among the conception flowers and the times he had expected her and not seen her were all blurred together, like the white night mists that curled about his body, erasing and drawing in his presence capriciously.

Here by the path was the giant leatherwood tree which held, like an old friend, so much of their past. Naked and hiding, he had sunk his fingernails into its bark to know again the anguish of physical desire, while he watched the girl dance and laugh to herself. So many times casually he passed the tree when the flowers were not blooming, and always it gave to him the music of "The Time of Innocence" until it seemed to Justin that he must have written it there. Long ago the scars that his fingernails had made had healed over. The tree kept all its knowledge secret. Justin leaned against the tree and turned his back toward the flowers. In case she came this time, he would rather see them first with her. Besides, he knew that he was too early for the first phosphorescence.

Why did he subject himself to this? he wondered. Why, after all, hadn't he simply asked Erma, "Are you going to see the conception flowers tonight?" Only a few hours ago he had spoken with her. Even now, possibly, she was in The Room, sitting with the others, and he could go and say to her . . .

But how could he ask that woman anything about Erma? When I stand here by this tree waiting each year, Justin thought, I wait for someone who does not exist and who will never come. Instead of the vague resentment and the questioning that he so often experienced in her presence and brushed aside, Justin forced himself to see her as she had been that very day and the day before and for how long he could not say. What could have happened to make this woman out of that girl? What had turned all her muscles to tendons? It was not that he was without sympathy for her or that he would not continue to try to know the nature of the rack on which her tension increased. It was not that he would forsake patience with her surprising evasions and secret motivations (she who had had, above all things, direction). It was only that he would know better now than to wait here again, or to seek further among the living for a girl already dead. His pipe had gone out. He put it into his pocket. "Ah, well," he said He put one hand against the tree, turned to find the path, and, just to make a fool of reason, there sat Erma with her back to him, watching the static flowers in terrible alertness.

"Erma," he said, fearful of startling her. "Erma, dear, you're here?"

She put up one hand and beckoned him, but she did not take her eyes off the flowers. He went over quietly and sat on the ground beside her where she had made a place for him. The flowers had not unfolded yet, and he saw that she intended not to miss a second of this thing. He watched her watching and he heard the beating of his heart; he felt his eardrums tremble from the silence. It seemed to him that he would laugh, that he would protest in some way the having associated always with this girl the glass-splinter quality of hysteria. It was so ludicrous to have received the news of Edith's death while he and Erma were eating scrambled eggs. It was an absurdity that the sight of Erma's shining hair under the lamp in Drury should be also the memory of water squeezing through the seams of his shoes. It must be the hands of a freak who remembered Erma's flesh as part of Tommy's birth. Now he must accept forever, like a giant standing among blown glass, the essence of their union. Had he not already accepted the ending of "The Time of Innocence," and said reluctantly that, yes, the structure of this music was inevitable and that, since he had made it, it must be his own? If he had admitted that, then he must admit also that the eating of scrambled eggs in the sunlight had killed his wife, the holding of Erma's body in acceptance of love had released Tommy from the womb. Forever now he would be like a customer in a grocery store who incongruously finds the grocer watching on a seismograph the progress of an earthquake. Surely, some day, it would go away from the man, this terrible desire to say, "I want a loaf of bread." Perhaps also the desire for the bread would leave him and he too would want to know about the earthquake.

Justin's eardrums grew accustomed to the silence. The noise of his heart's beating muffled itself. He knew the increasing darkness and he knew that it is possible to live in any world if only you know the laws and the rules that prevail there. He heard the girl exhale in a prolonged, whispered "Oh!" when the first huge phosphorescent petal unfolded. It said they could breathe now. It said their shoulder blades were no longer made of glass.

"Why did you not come last year, Erma? And the year before?"

"You?" she said. "You were here?"

"Yes," he said. "Of course. I come every year."

He put his hands on her shoulders and turned her body toward him. In the dim light the sharp outlines of her face were blurred and softened, but he could see the questioning, puzzled look in her eyes. How could he have been angry at her? His hands on her shoulders gentled their hold. "But of course," he said, "how could you know? I never told you, did I?"

"No," she said. Her body began to strain toward the flowers again, as though to get back her solitude. An impatience possessed her, a resentment that, even here, one night a year, she could not be free of interruption. Never could she be alone and free from anxiety at the same time. Always there were claims on her, if she were outside the cave—and inside it, she must be constantly alert for the sound of danger, the stumbling footstep. Now Justin was trying to tell her something. He was trying to force her back into another time and distract her from her mission. She had to have some of the pollen to take back to the cave. If it held its glow there were wonders she could do with it on the walls. But, even if it didn't, it belonged there. She had promised the figure above the altar. She had promised to bring Her some of the glowing dust.

"What is it, Justin?" she asked of him fiercely. "What do you want?"

It surprised him how easily he could feel anger, what a great reserve he had of it, ready. How dared she tempt his wrath this way—this tired, gaunt, harassed, petulant . . .

"I?" he asked.

He pulled her around by the shoulders easily, knowing with delight how his fingers must be bruising her. He held her in his arms, so that she was lying across his legs, so that he could look directly down into her face. And he waited for her struggle that his muscles might lock the more joyfully to imprison her.

"I want the phone not to ring in Drury," he said. "I want Gwen not to scream when I am holding you. I want to kill your husband. I want them all to die and leave us alone. I want to see you dance again among the conception flowers and not stay hidden behind a tree. Yes, I was here. Yes, I was behind a tree watching you dance, hearing you laugh. I want to follow you in the early mornings. You know what I want," he said.

She leaned against him without anger, without fear. He looked at the flowers and felt the muscles of his arms relax. He could feel her tears tracing a slow, hot pathway down the side of his hand. And presently he realized that he was rocking her, rocking, rocking, rocking.

"Here's one," he said. "Right close." He lifted her up slowly so that she could lean on him and watch the conception flower. The spiral movement of the stamens was just beginning. In rotation each bent in its arc and showered its glowing sparklets over the waiting pistil. It was close enough to touch. Still leaning against him, Erma watched.

"Which tree was it?" she said.

He turned his head. "That one," he said. "The leatherwood. The scars that my nails made in the bark were all grown over by the next year."

Under her hand Erma felt the skin of his arm bunch itself into goose flesh at the memory of that night.

"I named them," she said. "You knew that, didn't you? I

named the flowers. That's why I couldn't bear to come last year and the year before. It seemed such bitter mockery. I still hoped then."

She could say it like that, he thought, in the past tense.

It was less urgent now, but still she must gather the pollen as she had promised the huge figure in the cave. Like the blades of a machine that still rotate after the power is cut off, she began to search about her for the leather pouch she had brought. She could get dust from this near one, perhaps, and not even have to move. Also, that would make it unnecessary to get the dust on her clothing and so profane it. And now she knew why she had been so irritated to find Justin here. It was that the dust had to be gathered in a certain way; one must not profane it. It must not touch clothing before it entered the cave. Almost, she had an inkling then of what had happened to her hope, of how it had been translated to ritual: light becomes darkness; desire made superstition. Her fingers found the leather pouch and she put the hint of knowledge away from her into another place. Her place was a narrow equilibrium, essential to her life.

Justin felt her go away from him and saw her busy herself with the leather pouch, making the mouth of it wide. He felt her back no longer lean against him, felt her spine dismiss him. He felt his anger coming back to him, getting him ready.

"Don't, he said. "Don't go away from me, Erma."

"I *have* to," she said. "I have to gather some of the pollen in this pouch."

"I'll help you," he said. "Here, let me hold it while you . . ." He reached to take the pouch from her hands and she jerked aside.

"No!" she cried. "Not a man! A man can't touch."

He stood where he was, feeling himself recoil from her, resisting a desire to turn and run. *Witch.* She is a witch, he thought, and told himself to be sane. He told himself to look at her, kneeling on the ground, holding her hand over her mouth to keep back more of the dangerous betrayals.

She had lost the narrow equilibrium. She had put words to a wordless charm. Now she would be punished. Now, beneath her delicate equilibrium, the ground would become like the leaves of a polished table, sliding apart, revealing the abyss under her feet. *No, no, no, no, no.*

Justin walked over to her and squatted down, so as to be on

a level with her. But she turned her head away from him, her hand still clutching at her mouth to keep it quiet.

"Erma," he said, "put your hand down. Turn your head around. Listen to me, Erma. I'm going to my place. Get control of yourself. I will go to bed and you will tell the others that I am sick, that you are taking care of me. I will be with you all night, Erma. I will be with you. I will not let you go to pieces. Believe me, I will not let you. You be there," he said. "You be there by the time I get a fire going or I'll come after you. Do you hear me, Erma? I'll come after you. And if I have to come after you I'll have to tell them why."

She turned her head toward him slowly but her eyes were cast down. She took her hand away from her mouth and reached it toward him, so that he could lift her up. It was like ice in his, but it responded to his pressure. It grasped his for support to stand upright.

"Did you hear me, Erma?"

"Yes," she said. "Go away. I'll be there."

When he was out of sight she wiped her hand on her skirt. Then, being careful to touch all her clothing by the side toward her body, and holding each piece between thumb and forefinger, she took off all her clothes and dropped them, one on top of the other. She carried the pouch into the center of the flowers and set it on the ground. Then slowly she circled each giant flower of those nearest the pouch and, with her foot, tipped each stalk to shake its glowing burden into the pouch; she bent over and pulled the leather thongs tight and carried it back to the place where her clothes were piled. She dressed as quickly as possible, using no care now where she touched the clothes. She looked about for a place to hide the pouch and hesitated before the leatherwood tree where Justin had hidden to watch her dance. "No," she said aloud. "Not there."

She chose a smaller tree, marked its location carefully, and left the pouch in a low crotch. The strangeness and the desperation seemed to have left her. She walked in the direction of Justin's place without looking back. When she was in sight of the house she stopped near a dewplant, putting her hands, warm now, in the cold water of the leaf. She splashed her face, smoothed her hair, retied her sandals, and straightened her skirt.

She stood in the doorway of Justin's house, collected and a little defiant, so that he would know, when he lifted his giant head from the despairing hands that held it, that she had seen him so. She felt it gave her an advantage. For a moment she weighed the possibility of pretending that she had not seen him before, making him guess if she did not remember, making him guess if he had imagined it. But she knew that was not safe with Justin. Arthur, yes. She must not get them confused. Justin . . . with Justin she would do best to be cautious, to wait and make him speak of it first.

"Hello, Justin," she said.

His head jerked, and then he quickly covered his anxiety with his old manner as he got up and came toward her. "Come in, dear," he said. "Now I have planned it all out. You had best go and tell Arthur that . . ."

She closed the door behind her and, moving slowly, sat down before the fire. "It isn't necessary," she said. "He was asleep when I left. I'll tell him in the morning."

"You're sure?" he asked.

"I'd like some tea," she said.

It set him off, having her change like this so fast, made him fumble with the cups. He was prepared to offer asylum, comfort, undemanding peace, protection. Now, apparently, it was not to be permitted or even acknowledged that these were needed. Perhaps they were not; she *seemed* in control of herself now. He sat down and lifted his cup of tea from the hearth. He turned away from her and looked into the fire. Then he leaned back against his chair and felt the good, slow anger seep through him. How many times she had angered him, and, retreating in frustration from a battle he thought not his, how many times he had been defeated by her. But this time he would win. Even without looking at her he knew the small, betraying signs of her defeat: the tense cords of her neck, the too erect posture, the winging out of the nostrils to hide the sound of her breathing. Here, at last, was a battle on his own ground; here was an adversary of his own kind.

He drank his tea and relished the smoky, bitter tang of it. There was no hurry. If this night were not sufficient, then he would take tomorrow and the next night and the next. But in the end he would win. Whether she loved him or not hardly mattered. If she hated him, it would be a hate he could understand. If she resisted him, it would be a force he could match evenly. If she fought him, the weapons would be familiar. A wave of sorrow went over him for the battles he had fought on strange terrain with foreign weapons. Edith, George, even Arthur Herrick. He had been doomed to failure. And why had he never known it until now? In the world, it had always been so for him. Even here in the Green Kingdom he had continued in the same way. Always, he had followed and waited for his cue. He had slipped into the hollow someone else made for him. He could feel himself waiting by Edith's bed, holding himself suspended, waiting for her to give him the cue and tell him where they were in Time. Just so, he had slipped along Arthur Herrick's path, waiting for Arthur to let him know what the danger was. It was not that now Justin felt he should have done any differently. It was not the weapons that were wrong; it was the foe. Always, the adversary had called him from some unfamiliar place of darkness and always he had followed where the sound beckoned. He had *moved* that his answer could be heard.

Now, at last, and he might have died without knowing it, it was given to *him*, the summoning. It was *his* time to stand rooted where he was and compel another to be drawn toward him. As if he had in his hands silken cords that were attached to her, he could surely draw Erma Herrick back from the hidden place where she had wandered, *because she did not belong there.* It had been wrong since the moment they entered this place, how he had seen himself as the old one, the father who must not interfere. No wonder that his music had always had power. From *The Knife and the Grapes* to *Lazarus*, through all the symphonies, did not each one hold, besides its own peculiar mystery, his fury of the battle that could not be fought, his wrath against a weapon designed for other hands, his hatred for a path so fragile that it crumbled beneath his weight?

He put his cup down quietly on the hearth and turned toward Erma. He felt the force of her resistance, head on. He could have laughed to think that he had tried to be this woman's father. If there were such a man to be Erma Herrick's father, then he could be his, Justin's, father, too. They were the same kind, he and Erma Herrick, and, whether they were lovers or enemies, they did not make deals with death or trickery. Before they became reconciled to indirection, they would be marked by the sickness of it. They did not assimilate poison. Eventually, they would vomit it. Not for very long could they live with a wall between their left hands and their right. Before the mortar should set, the fingers would scratch and tear at the wall. And when the nails and the flesh were gone, the bleeding bones would still demolish it.

"Why must a man not touch the leather pouch, Erma?" he said in a low, unaccusing tone. "And why did you have to have the pollen with such urgency?"

He saw her eyes betray her, saw them gaze at the distance to escape. He felt the confident, anticipated spring within his joints and he knew that he could easily block her path.

"It does not matter," he said. "You will tell me in time." He made her eyes look at him and stay still. He willed her to feel that the hand over her mouth was foolish and he waited for it awkwardly to descend in a jerky path to her lap.

"You must know," he said, "that I love you for myself very greatly. But that is not of importance right now. If I hated you, it would be the same. Still, I would know you."

He saw her frown and move her head from side to side, beginning protest. He reached out and put his hand on her sandal. He closed his hand around her ankle and knew how easily he could splinter the bones.

"I know you," he said, "and I know what will kill you. I will no longer stand by and see you smothered or destroyed. I am prepared now to go to the others and make them admit your right to live with me, either here or cut off from them completely."

The small, foreign marks of her postural defenses were melted away and her head was bent forward a little in attention.

"You must know this," he said. "But also you must know that I am equally prepared to defend your right to live completely alone, if that is necessary to you temporarily, or as long as you will. You must assert yourself, Erma. Then I will see that your demand is met. I will defend your right to it. I will protect your hold on it. You do not have to live in stealth and hiding, Erma. There is no one here strong enough to make you do it."

Now she leaned forward a little more. "You?" she said. "You love me?"

"How could you not know it?" he said in anger.

Her head shook slowly back and forth in disbelief. "How could anyone love me?" she said. "What I have become?"

She slumped forward slowly and the palms of her hands turned upward, outstretched and vulnerable. The abjectness of her misery roused such a fury in Justin that he longed to strike her.

"Stop!" he said. "Stop whimpering." He grabbed her by

the shoulders and pulled her to her feet; but if he had let her go, she would have fallen. "Stand up," he said. "I tell you, if I let go of you, you will fall, and, if you fall, I will surely kick you."

He felt her knees stiffen to take her own weight.

"All right," he said. "There is some fight in you still. Not much, but some. Girl, do you not know there is enough strength in your hands to strangle a man? Why should you cringe from any creature?"

She was standing alone now and she looked directly at him. There was a sardonic smile on her face, a contempt for his incomprehension. "Why not?" she said. "I cringe before Gwen. I cringe before what I have made of Arthur. I cringe before the trees that bear fruit and every fertile creature on the landscape."

"You poor, blind fool," he said. "Do you think your womb matters to me? Do you think that I am a boy, eager to breed? Do you think a bed is the proof of strength? There is a womb of the spirit. Had you forgotten that? You knew it once. You carried it once. What have you done to yourself?"

She stood there, staring past him, lost to him.

"Go to bed," he said.

"Justin, I . . ."

"Go to bed, for God's sake. Lie down and cover yourself."

She did as she was told, quietly. He could feel her there as he paced back and forth before the fire, waiting for the angry blood to quiet. He too must bully her, torture her, taunt her, accuse. Slowly he became aware of her quiet breathing, and he went over to the side of her bed and knelt there. She had covered her face, but there was a part of her still exposed. One hand lay outside the coverlet, still testifying, still asserting. He thought of her hand under the water, bathing his ankle in the old Westgate Hotel on their journey to the Green Kingdom. Now the shapely fingers were gone. The tendons stood out in great ridges from the years of milking mossbacks. The years were here recorded— the years of kneading bread to feed them all, the years of stoking fires, the years of hacking comfort from the wilderness. Little beads of knots were strung along the cracked joints. Justin bowed his great, gray head over the eloquently scarred hand and stared at it. When had this hand had time for the spirit? When had it ever had sufficient help? He owed his life to it; and yet, it did not accuse him. It did not adulterate his compassion with guilt. It simply said, "I know you. Hello."

She slept in restless protest against some enemy or danger,

too intimate to watch. Unable to see her, in sleep, even more vulnerable than awake, Justin sat with his back toward her. When at last the irregularities of her breathing had settled down, he was himself so eased that he dozed in his chair. The deep quiet alarmed him into wakefulness and, when he went over to the bed, Erma seemed miraculously transformed, as though he had dreamed her. In her restlessness, her hair had come loose and it fell about her face, softening the features, denying the years. Justin could not remember how long it was since she had begun to wear her hair tied back in this gaunt, unlovely way. Nor would he have guessed that such a little thing could so transform a face. In the dim light, with her hair loose and tumbled, and with her eyes closed, it was possible for him to believe that this was the same person who had come here with him. In her sleep she smiled, but as soon as she opened her eyes and took in Justin and the room he could see recognition quench the look. She reached mechanically for the leather band with which she bound her hair.

"No," he said. "Leave it this way awhile longer."

He put his hand in the thick mass of her hair. She sat on the side of the bed, leaning against him, and he could literally feel her taking on the moments of the dreaded day ahead.

"You could go back to sleep," he said. "There's time still. You slept only a short while."

For answer she shook her head, went over to the fire, and poured herself some tea. "I was dreaming of us," she said, "all of us, when we first came here. Does it seem to you we had a lot of time then, Justin?"

Still half in her dream, she didn't listen for his answer. "In the dream," she said, "we were at the Yearsenday Place and we all had the most wonderful amount of time—hours and hours of it. And everybody moved slowly and smiled. No, that isn't right. Gwen had something in her hand, I think. I can't remember, but she wasn't smiling."

"Erma, dear," he said, "don't frown so. Are you hungry?"

"No," she said. "Oh, Justin, it was so beautiful. Remember? Do you remember that first morning? How gloriously fresh and leisurely it was?"

The radiance drained out of her face and she began to look about her on the floor as though she would find that day like the misplaced band for her hair. "What happened to it?" she asked querulously.

"To the past," Justin asked, "or the band for your hair? You're still half asleep."

"Oh, either one," she said, leaning back in the chair. "Is it wessun yet?"

"No, you've plenty of time. Go back to sleep, why don't you?"

But she would not sleep now, for had he not said last night that he loved her, and was not that enough to make her forever wakeful? Or was that, too, part of the dream? No, now she could remember his angry accusation: *Have you forgotten the womb of the spirit?* It had not been achieved without anger and humiliation, but it had been no dream and that was enough to make her waking different forever.

"If you're not going to sleep any more then," Justin said, "and it looks as though you're not, we must get right to plans. Here," he said, "have some fresh tea. Now, I have been sitting here thinking and it seems to me we must get you a vacation— get you quite away from everything."

"Why, that's not possible, Justin. How—"

"Of course it is possible," he said. "It has to be. We have to put a stop to your doing anything for a while and then you'll be able—"

"But Gwen's baby will be here in two months. Have you forgotten?"

"No," he said, "I hadn't forgotten."

The blunt finality of his tone was a wall before her, and frantically she wished to fling against it: *The bread! Who will bake the bread? Who will milk the mossbacks? The cheese. The washing. Tommy. Who will take care of Tommy? Who will watch over Arthur?* In the quiet which she could not shatter she felt the wall growing higher, forcing her into helplessness. How could she live without her work? She could see the chokevines grown into the houses. She could hear the mossbacks, unmilked and unattended, bleating. Nothing done right and all progress lost, to be so tediously recaptured later. She could see her way to the cave blocked and the feathermane waiting . . . waiting.

It was like a sickness in her, this awful need to get to the cave. The little lips inside her eyelids whispered in desperate entreaty to the Woman in the cave: "Save me, save me."

"Have you never thought of dying, Erma?" Justin asked.

"What?" she said.

"Death," he said. "Surely, here, where there are so many unknown things, you must have thought of dying."

She took a cautious breath and let her toes loose their hold for flight. This was safer as a subject than vacations. If he wanted to speak of death and dying for a while, until it was time to go to the cave, well . . .

"No," she said. "I never thought of dying."

"Well, think of it," he said. "Think if you died tomorrow."

"All right," she said.

"Do you really think we would all lie down and die, too, Erma? Do you think the new baby would remain unborn? Or that no one would ever be fed again? Or the fires not lit?"

Could even She soothe such hurt? Could the beloved feather-mane comfort her for this? Erma did not think so. There surely did not exist, anywhere, adequate comfort. It was not a wall Justin was building, then, to press upon her, to shut her off. The wall was demolished, and in its place there stretched an endless waste-land.

"I don't see how it can possibly give you any pleasure," she said to him, "to prove to me that, in addition to being inadequate, I am also unnecessary."

"Oh, that I did not say. You misunderstood. It is you who are necessary, not your work. You can fool the others by the sub-stitution, perhaps, and surely you must have fooled yourself. But it is yourself I need and not your work. And you don't allow me to choose both. They don't go together any more."

Now was the moment to run. She knew that. Run to the cave. But Justin's words were sweet to hear for a few seconds more. And surely he did intend a few safe sentences before she must make good her escape from the dangers of change and thinking. On the endless desert where she must henceforth live, if Her comfort could not avail, she would have these sentences. They would be her water and her meager shade.

Justin took the cold cup from her hands and put it on the hearth. He filled one of the clay pipes and laboriously lighted the tobacco. Then he hitched his chair forward a little.

"You see, my dear, it isn't that I underrate your work. With-out you we should all be less clean, I know. That would happen immediately. Our comforts would dwindle and our graces would fall away. We would soon be each man for himself, and that would mean meat and berries. The bread would not be baked, the ovens would go cold, and the good sharples pies and all the products of stored, planned things would become memories. The herds would suffer. The strong ones would break loose and leave us. And one day the cheese would be gone, the last of it stolen, probably, by one of us."

Erma leaned forward and reached out her hand for a pipe. He filled her a fresh one. It was safe to stay a little longer. These were good things. He knew that she cared for their comfort and their cleanliness. These were her things; this was her work. And they valued it. At least, Justin valued it.

"Oh, yes," he said. "We know who defends our domesticity, who guards our agriculture. And if you were gone, I feel sure, in time, these would go."

This was sweet to hear, yes. She closed her eyes and exhaled. It was quite a lot to have done, for a sterile woman—a woman who had humiliated her husband and left the children of his friend without playmates. It was pretty good for a coward who lived at the mercy of a shrew and a drunkard with only her pitiful prayers in a dark cave for solace.

"Yes, we should become nomads, I think, in time," Justin continued. "The settlement would crumble to the chokevines; the Records would return to vegetation. 'The Time of History' would be only in my head, I expect, instead of the stack of manuscript sheets you so carefully collect and keep in order in The Room."

Erma put the pipe down on the hearth. Well, then? Well, then, where was the complaint? If this was hers—and it *was* hers —and if he thought it good . . .

A small voice warned that questions opened the doors for dangers and questions decrease Her power to comfort. A smaller voice warned that questions are themselves the danger. Still she leaned forward and postponed fleeing.

"But don't make the mistake," Justin said, "of thinking that a nomad existence is the same as death. Nomads are different from settlers. No doubt they are less clean. Certainly, they are less comfortable. Their records are inadequate and their music does not seem to grow. But no one ever said that they were less *alive* than the settlers. That is what you must remember, Erma. With all your work, you have not made life; you've made comfort. And, if it destroys you, the price of comfort is too high. I would give all my comfort and I would deprive the others of theirs gladly to hear you laugh out loud, just once again, to see you lie down on the ground and look about you aimlessly, with pleasure."

"I don't know how," she said. "I have forgotten how."

"It will come back to you," he said. "Trust me. It will come back to you."

"You know, it would be Joe who would do it," she said.

"Do what?"

"If I died tomorrow. While you were talking I was thinking Joe would be the one to take over, to postpone the nomad existence. You know that dream I had? The way we looked then and the way we look now? All the rest of us seem a little smaller now, except Joe. When you think that he even wanted to bring dynamite and was never very keen on coming . . ."

"Yes, Joe has grown here, most of all."

"Well, he got what he wanted," she said, "although he didn't even know he wanted it."

"How was it you said that, Erma?"

"I said Joe was the only one who got what he wanted."

"Oh, no, my dear," Justin said. "The question is not: Did he get what he wanted? The question is: What did his wanting get?"

She tasted this on her tongue and in her ears. "I don't understand," she said.

"Desire," Justin said, "is always in the process of being fulfilled in some manner. As soon as you stop thinking of a man as being fulfilled, and think of him as incidental to his desires, then you will see what I mean. All that is necessary is life. If you live, your desires will be accomplished in some way; and, while you live, desire is always being accomplished. The hungers of the heart are always fed, if only upon themselves. To desire even a pair of red shoes will mark you in some way. You have only to begin the wish and already the process is set in motion, the desire is somehow being accomplished. Whether *you* acquire red shoes for your feet or not is an incident of doubtful outcome. That your desire moves you in some way toward redness, or toward shoeness, is a certainty. So you live. That is all that is necessary."

In all his life's uncertainty and fumbling, he had never had anything so clear as he had this. He was pleased and comforted by it. He must make Erma see, for surely it would console her about the child and she could, perhaps, accept the part of being an instrument not of the child but of the longing for a child. It was from this came the designs for the bread, the decorations on the oven. Out of her desire came her care for them, her gentleness, even her mysterious ritual among the conception flowers, perhaps.

"Oh, Erma," he said. "You must see how it is not the longed-*for* but the *longing* that is the powerful force, the real creation. It is not the thing desired but desiring that truly grows. Desire is never constant, never still, never static. Never can it be nothing; and always it is moving."

She leaned back and looked away from him. The eager questioning look was gone from her face. The fire had died down and the faint, cold light of early wessun crept up the folds of her dress and curled about her quiet head. Justin saw on her face such a look of resignation and finality as to make him believe she could not possibly have understood him correctly. He would make a concrete example. He would tell her about herself and her longing for a child. And it would comfort her. One corner of her mouth hinted an ironic smile and she nodded, as though to someone who stood beside him.

"The hungers of the heart," she quoted him, "are always fed."

But it was not said in triumph, as he had said it; it was said in a quietly bitter and sardonic way. She moved her head slowly and looked at him.

"I can see them," she said, "like mountain goats, constantly grazing, even by night. They never sleep. They never rest. They are never satisfied. They graze on and on. Their teeth never stop grinding the tender grass."

A chill came over Justin. How had it happened that his triumphant discovery had been turned into a relentless gnawing? He had had her wonderful attention of old, quickened to life again, for a little while. Right here in this room, only a few seconds ago, she had been young and alive and known to him. What had he done to make her withdrawn, old and sorrowful—and an enemy?

As though she followed his thoughts, she began mechanically to smoothe back her hair and to twist it up in the way he had come to hate.

"Oh, it is horrible to think of," she said. "Horrible."

The chill spread up his spine and seeped around his neck. He knew he must act. He must fight or he would lose her again. All the night's progress was being dissolved before his eyes, and yet he could focus nothing, except that he must prevent her finding the leather band for her hair. She stood quickly and her hands found the leather band at once in the bed covers, while Justin sat, frozen and unable to move. Her hands finished binding her hair, and then they began to tidy the bed, hunting out the wrinkled places, all by themselves, without direction. Once they stopped moving, while Erma, bent over, stared at the coverlet of the bed. *So that was all her cave was.*

Then her hands resumed their cleverness. Justin knew it was the wrong way and the wrong moment, done without planning or thought, but he made himself jump up from his chair and go to her. He pulled at her arm.

"Wait, Erma," he said. "I'll go with you and I'll tell them. We'll tell them together that you have to have a vacation, or . . . or whatever you want."

She turned and looked at his hand on her arm until it dropped away; and then she looked at his face. "No," she said quietly. "What I wanted was peace and you have destroyed it."

She began to move slowly toward the door, away from him.

"Peace!" he shouted after her. "I won't let you want peace. That's for the dead. That's for the sick."

At the door she turned toward him, a dark shadow against the cold early light. "I know," she said.

He walked as far as the door, and he knew it was futile to stand there in the early morning shouting in anger about peace after the lonely, moving figure. The mists rose about her and blurred her; and yet he could still count the evenness of her slow, rhythmic steps, as though she walked upon his chest. He could not go after her and he did not know why. He leaned against the door for a long time and no plan occurred to him. He stumbled over to the bed and fell upon it. He stared at the ceiling and it gave him no explanation. Outside the crested chichimingo called and set off the screaming of the shrillerjays. A mossback gave a muffled, blurred announcement of the day and Justin Magnus sank into a deep sleep. When he awoke, it was late eassun. The birds were quiet, his house was cold and he was hungry. He sat on the edge of his bed, staring at his feet; and it came to him that there was simply something that he did not know. It would not be required of him to live in a stupor, staring at a wall, but to watch and learn. The essence of this terrible mystery was not that he could not fight it; it was that he did not know what it was.

Something secret had become his enemy and to have an enemy made it easier.

Before wessun, next morning, in the darkness, he stood waiting. He knew that Erma often went out by herself in the mornings, before the rest of them were awake. He had known this for a long time and he had never thought it concerned him. Now he waited for the first promise of light to make the corner of her house known to him. He felt her presence, rather than saw it, and, very cautiously, at a safe distance, he followed.

Why would she, who was always tired, begin immediately to climb the old Yearsenday path? he wondered. For it was the most difficult of any she might have chosen. Justin had not been on it since the last Yearsenday feast. Perhaps he would learn something earlier than he had expected. If he had thought of them at all, he had always imagined her walks as being slow-paced and rambling. While he had not expected to discover much by following her, he intended to be thorough. He meant to be with her at the oven, in the stable, in the cheese shed, at the soap press, the washing spring, in The Room. He, who had never in his life opened a letter belonging to another, who had, in fact, been glad to be spared and had actively avoided knowledge of another's privacy, he now meant to know, without even an apology, the most intimate details of Erma's life. By day he would follow her and by night, if necessary, he would spy on her. For it came to him, there on the silent path, the certain knowledge, as though a rising wisp of mist had frozen in a picture of it, that if he did not kill the thing which menaced her he would some day kill her.

Swiftly he pressed himself into the landscape and stayed motionless, for Erma had stopped on the path and turned to look all around her. Then, somehow, before his eyes, she vanished. He was no more surprised by this than by the knowledge that he had been able to move so quickly and effectively into hiding. All his life he had stumbled and knocked into things. He had been cramped by the chairs he sat in, stifled by the rooms he lived in and so inefficient in his movements as to gain for himself much chaffing and several nicknames.

One has only to become a spy, to carry anticipated murder in his hands, for his feet to become as sure and silent as the tiger's. Crouch, spring, and frozen immobility are instantly his possessions. The teeth of evil are narrow and pointed; the predatory swoop is swift and efficient. So much do we all believe this that a buck-toothed man may achieve great mischief undetected, and a lithe, slit-eyed man must possess incredible virtue to be accorded ordinary courtesy. Even the elephant and the weasel have been endowed with personalities and motives with which they are entirely unconcerned. And yet, perhaps because the knowledgeable moments are not compatible with contemplation, there is thoroughly embedded in these conceptions a universal confusion. The fat, gentle quail becomes crafty and clever and full of deception at the approach of an enemy; and no one has ever shown that the incidence of survival in wars is higher for card sharps than for buffoons. The jolliest buffoon finds that his friendly belly will slide over the jungle growth as silently as a serpent's when he believes that a crackling twig can stop his laughter forever.

To fear death, or to seek to inflict it, look remarkably alike in silhouette. Who can tell, seeing the coyote against the moon, if he follows the rabbit or flees the hunter? Is the cat, seen alone, stalking the mouse or avoiding the dog? Does the hawk truly swoop upon the chicken or seek escape from the sky's starvation? Does not the cutthroat, following an unwary victim, himself look like a wary victim, fleeing? Do not the spy and the spied-upon move much in the same way? And, if it were not so, who could have thought of counterspies?

Justin himself, creeping upon the spot where Erma had disappeared, no longer knew if he sought Erma's enemy or Erma as his enemy. And not till long afterward did he know that Erma's destruction and his own would have been indistinguishable. Though he still thought of himself as he had been in the world, out of long habit, he had not really stumbled for a long time; and the leather jacket which he put on every morning had long been lined with alertness.

Here was the spot where she had disappeared, and here, at an angle, began a small, zigzag path, through a tangle of thorn trees. He crouched to get his bearings, for the walls of the path did not allow for penetration in the way of the Yearsenday path. The path delivered him into the midst of a small grove of sweating gum trees. Already his hands were covered with the sticky fluid as though these trees pressed upon him a token compensation for the many jagged pieces of his coat which had been claimed by the thorn trees.

And now he knew that what he sought was in some way

secret, for who would walk for pleasure among sweating gum trees? Even if one sought the pitch, there were other, more accessible groves. At the edge of the grove there was a small clearing. Suddenly the mist lifted and Justin saw Erma. She was not far ahead of him, standing by a hillock covered with greengrain. He flattened himself on the ground and saw her examine the landscape. The inspection was automatic. She has grown careless, he thought. That makes it easier. He stifled the sound of his surprise when she knelt down and lifted a square of the hillock's grain-bearing soil out of its place. He saw her disappear into the hillside.

So there was a cave. How long would she stay there? He must move out before she returned, or she would stumble on him. Yet he knew that, if he hurried, he would trip on the vines. And it would be better to meet her straight on than to be found fleeing. After all, he had found her out. Why did he not go into the cave after her?

Now it was too late. She was coming out. And behind her, on a leather halter, the feathermane stumbled, blinking against the light. Justin lay where he was and smiled. So she had got herself another pet. His witch was a soft child and needed a kitten, a warm thing to cosset. He would wait until they were out of sight and then he would go back. He would have a good head start. Just then the feathermane turned, and the light caught his flank, showing up the long, silvery worm of a scar.

At home, lying in his hot bath, soaking the pitch off himself, Justin sought escape from the feeling that his knowledge was, somehow, monstrous. Surely it was the same feathermane that Arthur had killed—or tried to kill. Why should he, Justin, be so angry that he had not been told? Why had it been held secret?

And why not?

The girl had something to love and she kept it to herself. He didn't presume to understand it, and no one asked him to. He picked a piece of pitch gum off his wrist, grimacing painfully as the hairs were pulled out with it. At any rate, he understood now why she wore her hair in that severe way. He had better forget the whole thing and leave well enough alone. He stood up from the hot spring and shook himself.

But why the pollen in the leather pouch? Why the panic? Why must a man not touch it? Some more secrets of her own, he supposed. He cursed himself for the care he had taken in the bath, because he was going right back to the same place, and he knew it. What he had seen explained nothing. Not the madness at the place of the conception flowers. Not the desire for peace, for death. Nor the fact that, for her, it was horrible to think of the hungers of the heart, gnawing by day and by night. There was more. What it was was surely in the cave. He knew that. Or some clue to it was there. However much he dreaded going, there was really nothing else for him to do.

This food he ate, this tea he drank would never taste quite the same again, he felt sure. Yet he did not linger over them. He took a long coat with him, the old one with deep pockets, in which he could protect his hands from the pitch and the thorns. Having established where all the others were, and that Erma had returned to the settlement, he set out.

Now that the light was better and he was prepared he made his way through the grove of sweating gum trees with greater ease. After some time, he found the loose square of sod and entered the cave. The entrance was small for him and he reached out to replace the sod block as an extra precaution. It was too dark for him to see anything and, not to alarm the feathermane, he felt down only a sufficient number of steps for comfortable sitting. There he waited in the darkness.

A strong, sharp animal odor came to him, mixed with the musty smell of the damp earth. His eyes began to sting and he felt cold. How did she stand this blackness? Yet when he lowered his head he could see his own feet. Then he felt in front of him and knew he had been facing a wall. He slid down the steps and pushed himself under the wall with some difficulty. Here there was a floor under him, seemingly level, extending for some distance. And the light was much better.

He saw movement in front of him and he sat still so as not to alarm the feathermane. Yes, it was the feathermane; and he sounded restless. Justin distinctly heard him snort. But in the dimness he could not judge distance yet. Where did the light come from? His eyes traveled upward and—he could not judge how far away—he saw three slits of light and the paths they cut into the cave. The three beams of light gradually grew clear to him, and, as his eyes became adapted, the beams converged startlingly on the nest of the feathermane, plucking his spiral horns and his mane out of the darkness. Now the boundaries of his moss manger showed against the darker earth and the cave fell into place around it. The walls were still blurred in shadow for Justin, but he could tell where they were and that the floor was level and continuous. In a feeling of pure applause for the dramatic effect of the beams of light converging on the feathermane, he forgot Erma. The sudden beauty of it made him forget also the strong, musty odor and the smarting of his eyes. When he remembered them, he thought of the cave in terms of Erma's having made it.

Or perhaps someone helped her? It seemed an impossible accomplishment for her to have made alone. He tried to estimate the size of the cave. He could stand straight in it, even here, and in the center the ceiling was vaulted. But first he must make peace with the feathermane, who was moving restlessly about on his moss bed. His head raised, the animal sniffed the air questioningly from side to side. Justin stood up and began to move slowly toward the animal. He meant to speak reassuringly, but the first sound he made was so distorted he could not bring himself to try again. Could Erma talk here? he wondered. Had she got over the eeriness of it?

The feathermane allowed his approach, turning his head away. Justin sat beside him and saw on the flank the scar he had seen this morning. He reached out to touch the animal and saw the flank tremble. He began to whisper and finally he saw the scar cease rippling and he put his hand on the animal. Gradually he eased himself toward the animal's head, and, yes, he was certain now that it was the same one. How in God's name could it have lived? And was this horribly scarred head beautiful to her? He patted the mane mechanically, not wishing to touch any of the scars for fear they might even still be tender.

She was a strange girl, a strange, mystifying girl, and who would ever know her? The feathermane sighed and lifted his great eyes toward Justin.

They were quite blind.

Justin exhaled a sound of surprise and the walls distorted it so that who can say—for Justin could not—whether it were a cry of terrible pity for the woman that she must crawl into a dark hole to pour her love on a scarred, blind thing, or terrible anger against those who had forced her here, or, who could say—for Justin could not—whether it were desire for the woman, more exquisitely acute and simplified than he had ever known before?

His hands partook of the light and he put his head in them and closed his eyes against the confusion of his thoughts. All of it hidden . . . hidden. How would he ever understand her now, a person who could leave this cave and go straight to the ovens or to carry Tommy in to be bathed? It was frightening to think how she would talk to them all in The Room this very night, how her face would give no clue, how she would sit calmly writing in her Record as usual. No, he could not understand it. It made him feel excluded and abandoned not to have been trusted with this knowledge. He felt very much alone. Well, he thought, it was what he got for prying into what had been meant to be secret. He had really learned nothing that he could understand, and, ignorant, he had been better off. Better to go now and leave it. Better to have stayed away in the first place with the belief that he could help her, that there was something he could do. He lifted his head slowly and saw that he had been transported into nightmare.

The walls had come alive and they seemed to be moving and twisting. The confusion was terrible. All he had seen before, which had so moved him, was nothing to this. He wished for the strength to close his eyes and crawl out blindly into a familiar place before he had ever seen, but he knew he could not do it. He knew he would stay and see, in hypnotic fascination, what he would never be able to make unseen. He let the feathermane distract him; he put off the moment. He saw before the feathermane a wooden bowl filled with water and sunk into the ground. All around it, the sprouting shoots of clusternuts asserted the fact of birth in process. Behind the bowl rose the altar. Here were carved in relief the spiraling conception flowers. Seduced by their motion, Justin allowed an impersonal admiration to possess him. He forgot that they were Erma's and, in that moment, his attention was caught and his vulnerability insured. He went over to touch them, and so he felt the top of the altar where the fire trough was.

Here, he saw, the dried dung was burned. It was clever of her to come in the early morning when any smoke escaping through the slits would be confused with the rising mists. He wished very much that he dared to light a fire here to see this as she must see it. He groped among the warm ashes which she had carefully used to smother any glow. What if he were discovered? What if he did give the place away? Why not? Wouldn't he welcome it, really? He blew on the tiny coals, half hoping, half fearing they might catch. In the gloom he began to feel his way

around the walls, making out the body of a mossback lying on
its side, a ballsleeper on a ferntree branch above a thick field
of greengrain. Excitement took possession of him.

That she had this! From the simple designs on the loaves of
bread no one would have guessed, no one would have known.
Here a root had been polished into a hand, strained but powerful.
Far to the right, was not that the crested chichimingo poised for
flight? Such life it had; one could predict the course of flight.
It was too much. There were too many things to take in. Everywhere, he saw, the walls were covered. Even near the floor, chokevines tangled together. He was exhausted. It was too much to
take in all at once. His eyes were burning from the effort to see.

This was discovery, all right, of the greatest importance.
Now he must go and speak to her and he must find when it would
be safe, in the greatest humility, for him to return with her and
see it all. Many times, many times it would take before he would
be able to take so much in. Now he wanted to see no more. Justin was pleased to see that the feathermane stayed quiet. He
located the tunnel that led to the steps. That was very clever, that
arrangement. This girl—who would ever have thought these
riches of complexity were hidden in her? Now he had only to
quiet his excitement so as not to be incautious and then to crawl
through the opening toward the steps. He would stand here a
moment with his back to the wall and rest.

And the huge torso above the altar leapt at him from the
wall. Her thighs moved and Justin was afraid that She would walk
over him. He was afraid that Her shivering, distended belly would
burst open and spew him with unknown liquid terror. Yet part of
his brain kept saying it was only the fire trough that had finally
burst to a small life. He wished to extinguish the fire, or else to
heap it into a great blaze. He wished to run, or to stay and see
everything. But he did nothing, for he could not keep the distractions from possessing him. Small spurting flames called life
up from the walls capriciously, life he had not seen before, and
all of it of a lushness not apparent in the gloom. Awareness of
the workmanship was not possible when the vegetation steamed
and coiled upon itself and the birds leapt up unpredictably in
answer to the flames. Now it could be seen that, in this living lushness, this surfeited abundance, the mossback was in labor and the
bellies of all the animals were distended in unbearable crescendo.
All of them, all of them. Wherever there was a root polished into a

hand or a foot or a hoof, it never rested, but strained under tension, reaching from the wall. All of them strained in the same way, he saw. Yes, there and there and there, all of them pointed toward the figure above the fire, begged of Her. Justin too strained toward Her, riveting his eyes on the undulating umbilicus. Suddenly he leaned over and vomited on the moist, dank floor. And the sweat dripped slowly off his forehead.

Outside he lay on the ground, not remembering the steps or the tunnel. He was an emptiness of no thought, with hardly the energy to dread re-entering the fetid, smoke-laden, writhing darkness below. Yet he must. He must smother the fire and bury his vomit. Not to protect Erma's secret from detection but to protect himself from Erma's knowing he had seen it. That he had defiled her temple and jeopardized her solace did not occur to him at the time.

In the dim light, where the three fading beams converged, the old feathermane nursed the chill in his bones and tried to recapture the comfort of a day not twice interrupted by strangeness. He stretched his neck, snuffled a long sigh, and shifted one hoof stiffly. He moved his blind eyes in a circle, innocent of the strain and tension before them.

Alone in his darkness, he rested his meager maleness in a room of lush, gravid female unrest.

Oн, то have back again his ignorance of yesterday, Justin thought. To be innocent of this knowledge—what would he not give? He walked about in his room. The late eassun light was fading and the evening mists were rising, yet he could not bring himself to light a torch or to make any other admission that it was time he should go to The Room. How could he face her? And yet, how could he not? If he did not appear, Erma would be sure to come by. If he said he were ill, then she would send for Joe. Joe had become their doctor, dressing their wounds and cuts. Joe was the one with the level head. Perhaps it was Joe he should tell. But could he do that to her? Even now, could he go behind her back? No. He must tell her first, before the others. He must tell her how dangerous, in a community of five, is a secret thing.

He must go now. Sometime he must face her in this new light. One night's respite would not help him. In a community of only five adults, there is no way to avoid one of them. Now it was growing darker. He could not stand here forever, like an adolescent boy, saying to the darkness, "So that's what women are like." He did not bother to shut his door and stepped out on the path to The Room at a fast pace. Suddenly he stopped and gave a sharp laugh and then went on again. *He* had told *her* that desire was always accomplished somewhere. He had told *her* of the heart's hungers. How she must have laughed at his innocence.

"No," he mumbled to himself. "No, that was not true. She had not laughed."

But this thing must be stopped. This secrecy must be exposed, brought out into the open. Something terrible would happen, he knew it. Simpler, really, if he demolished it himself, killed the feathermane and then said to her, "It is done. I have destroyed it before something terrible happened."

"Justin, Justin," Tommy called, running to him and reaching his arms around the big man's leg.

Glad of the diversion, Justin lifted Tommy into the air. "So I am late," he said. "Did you eat all the food?"

"Soup," Tommy said. "We had soup."

He must make himself move across The Room now as if nothing were different. Yet, from the doorway, everything was different. In the light they all seemed cut out by sharp scissors, like new paper dolls. Joe and Arthur sat at the table, still eating. But Gwen had already begun her game of solitaire; and she barely glanced at him. And Erma? She was at the fireplace, bent over the kettle. Food from her hands? He must take the bowl from her hands. He put Tommy down and the boy began to pull at his trousers.

"Eat," he said. "Eat soup." Then he began to run in circles around Justin, saying, "No, no, Tommy. Burn, burn."

"Tommy," Gwen said, "be quiet."

Somehow, Justin had taken the bowl of soup from Erma and found himself sitting at the table with Joe and Arthur. He lifted a spoonful of soup, but his hand was trembling and he put the spoon down.

"You're not feeling well, Justin?" Erma said.

He could feel her moving toward him and he thought, *If she touches me, if she touches me* . . . But the desire to flee or to cry out became, in translation, only the slightest averting of his head. And her hand on his forehead was exactly familiar—warm and rough and dry and (how could this be?) comforting. The same as it had always been.

"I'm all right, my dear," he said. "Just didn't sleep well last night. That's all."

"What you need," Arthur said, "is some of Dr. Joe's combination snakebite cure and restorative tonic."

"Fix you right up," Joe said.

"No, thanks," Justin said. "I know. It's only the magic salve in liquid form."

"Well, you have to admit the magic salve did all right by your leg the time you chopped it instead of the wood."

"I do," Justin said. "I do. But that was outside. Inside, I draw the line."

The spoon, now, and the bowl, they were absolutely devoid of ornament. How was it no carving showed on anything here?

Why this schism above and below ground? Justin reached for a piece of bread. The loaves had never taken back their designs. The night they had talked of this, had she had the cave, even then? She must have. Surely her margin of safety must have run out. If he knew, the others would in time. Bound to happen.

"Joe," Erma said, "can you help butcher tomorrow?"

Joe, now, Justin thought. What would Joe do if he found the cave?

"That's right," Arthur said. "The meat's low and Erma wants us to get the butchering all done and over with, so it won't come right at the time . . ."

And Arthur? Justin looked at Arthur, now nodding his head toward Gwen. What would Arthur, who could not even speak of birth or pregnancy—what would he do?

"Sure," Joe said, "that's right. We ought to get it out of the way before the baby comes. Which ones do you think, Erma?"

"I thought Molly's calf," Erma said. "And maybe even Molly. The herd's too big. There's more milk than we need and the cheese shed is full."

"Of course, now we'll be one more," Joe said.

"It could be twins or triplets," Erma said, "and we'd still have cheese for a lifetime."

"Oh, my God," Gwen said. "Don't even mention such a thing."

"No fear," Joe said. "I'm sure there's only one heartbeat."

Arthur turned toward Joe. It was on the tip of his tongue to ask, How do you know? When suddenly he knew. Would it never end, this pregnancy? He could not bear to look at her any more. And now the thought of an ear, perched atop that distended mound . . .

"Gwen!" he said, too loudly. "Do you want some beer?"

"Sure," she said. "Thanks, Arthur. Hand me over the cluster-nuts, will you? I'm hungry again."

That was the kind of thing that haunted Arthur now. He ought to do something to get rid of it. That ear, disembodied, lying perched on a belly—he would see it like the other things, until vines grew out of it and curled up toward him.

Was his own control much better than Arthur's? Justin wondered. It was a hard time for them all, truly. Gwen was very difficult and held them all under the whip of her ill-nature. Surely she had not been so fat the last time. He watched Arthur carry the beer over to her, saw her lean back and stretch herself.

"Tommy play cards," the boy said, reaching for the table top. "Tommy play." He picked up several of the cards and began to hit them on the table.

Gwen turned quickly and jerked them away from him. "No," she said. "Don't touch, Tommy."

Tommy relinquished the ones he had and reached out for others.

"No, I said." Gwen slapped the boy's hand.

As soon as he cried, Joe went over and picked him up. "Come on," he said. "You'd better sit with me awhile." He ruffled the boy's hair. "Get sleepy, kid," he said. "It's bedtime. Where's your ballsleeper?"

"Over there," Tommy said. "He won't play."

"Well, then," Arthur said, "it's Molly's calf tomorrow. That'll get us through, won't it, Erma, until . . . until after?"

"I suppose so," she said. "But be careful of the hide. We'll make the baby new shoes out of it."

Tommy's head leaned on Joe's shoulder and his eyelids were beginning to droop. "Tommy wants shoes," he said.

"Yes," Erma said. "And Tommy shall have new shoes, too. Regular moccasins, this time, with fringe around the top."

"Finge?" Tommy asked. "Don't want finge."

"It's coming out," Gwen said, slapping the cards down in hurried succession.

"Watch it, Gwen," Arthur said. "Remember how fast you wore the last deck out."

"I don't know why I get so excited," she said. "So it comes out. What have you got?" She let the cards fall out of her hands. She stretched herself and leaned back. "Oh, what I wouldn't give for a movie, for a magazine, any magazine, for a radio."

She closed her eyes. Too late, Erma, clearing up the dishes, noticed Tommy squirming down from Joe's lap and heading for Gwen's chair. Because she had put the dangerous cards down, Tommy took it to be a safety signal. He did not know yet that the worst times of all began with this desire for a movie, a magazine.

"The knives are in a mess," Erma said. "I don't know if they'll even get you through tomorrow's butchering. We need new ones."

"We need new ones, all right," Joe said. "I suppose we

really ought to call a halt and begin a search for something better than bone."

Knives, Justin thought. What had she used? He could remember no tools in the cave. But she must have had tools. And careful ones, too. It seemed even a greater accomplishment when you thought of that.

Tommy began to ease himself into the chair beside Gwendolyn. She did not open her eyes, but only moved aside a little. He decided that meant making room for him.

"And so," Arthur said, "in our time of history, we come to metals. Shall we have the iron age first and do them in sequence?"

"It does seem odd," Justin said, "that we've never found anything harder than bone."

"Oh, it's surely there," Joe said. "The trouble is that everything's buried under such a mess of leaf mold and vegetation. It would be a hell of an operation, and there always seems to be something more urgent."

"I've thought of it," Erma said. "Maybe we shouldn't. There were civilizations that never found metal, that stayed right where we are."

"And look what happened to them," Arthur said. "They all died out."

"Well," she said, "look what happened to the ones who found metal."

"Maybe you've got something," Joe said. "I'd hate to feel obligated, just because I dug a hole in the ground, to work myself right through arrows and knives to steel and rifles and tanks."

"Better not to have the choice," Justin said.

"No," Erma said. "One shouldn't know history ahead of time. It's too hard."

"It's corrupt, somehow," Justin said. "As if you knew already . . ."

He could feel the flush of color coming to his face. He would have to be careful or he would give himself away. It was so surely a description of the cave.

He knows, Erma thought. She did not know how it was she knew that he had been to the cave, that he had seen Her. But she did. *What will he do?*

To his left Justin could feel Tommy and Gwen. If he were to reach behind him for his harp, he could perhaps distract them and sidetrack an explosion. Across the table from him were the men. Yes, it was a serious decision and an interesting problem, this, of whether or not they should deliberately search for the things that would change their life. But he turned right, toward Erma, because he could not help it. How far would she commit herself here?

"Yes," Justin said. "You take a primitive, now, or a prehistoric man, and he wants something—"

"So he makes a picture of it," Erma said. She stopped her work and sat leaning a little forward. Perhaps she could find out how far he would go and how much, really, he knew.

"Yes," Justin said. "And then he brings presents to the picture. And at first, the presents are things that will help him get what he wants."

"Oh," Arthur said. "You're creating religion."

Both Justin and Erma jerked their heads in irritation. This was *theirs*. This was their intrigue, their secret war. Justin fumbled in his pocket for his pipe. And it was then he realized that he still had on the old coat he had worn to the cave. He looked up at Erma and saw her staring at the pitch stains on it. She knows that I know, he thought.

"Who has a pipe?" he asked. "I've left mine."

"Here you are," Joe said. Joe handed him a filled pipe from the mantel and lighted it for him. Something wrong with the old boy, he thought. Off his food, too. Joe looked over at Gwen, who was, he hoped, sleeping. Should he move Tommy or not? He turned his back to the others and looked into the fire. *Death.* One of them might die here. He had not thought of it before. Just by numbers, he supposed, if any five people spent ten years together, you could guess one of them would die. He looked at them all, one by one. Who would it be? It made his guts turn.

"I assume," Arthur said, "you're making the analogy with the metals. That is to say, only the innocent, the primitive man, can create a pure religion, for he must not know what is happening to him while it is happening. Any man who knows this sequence of events and instigates one of them does so with a knowledge of corruptness."

"Might make life a good deal easier," Joe said. "A few copper pans, a good knife blade . . ."

"And," Erma said, "even corrupt religions are justified by some, because they make life possible."

It was a deliberate, baiting taunt. Justin did not answer it.

He looked her straight in the eyes, and he smiled. All right, they would fight. This was better.

Arthur had not so enjoyed himself for months. It was good to forget Gwen's pregnancy for a little while. Usually, she made it impossible. Perhaps it did not obsess the others as it did him. But one more night that he had to watch her was gone, and his nervousness was forgotten. "Well," he said, "to mine or not to mine—is that the question? Have we decided? Tell me, Justin, do you think it is more or *less* corrupt to decide ahead of time what you are mining for?"

Justin threw back his head and laughed. Instantly Joe moved to shush him; but Gwendolyn had not been asleep. Now she sat up abruptly, jerking Tommy as she did so.

"At mines," Gwendolyn said, "I absolutely draw the line. What next? The houses have to be built. Then we have to have a drying room. Then a new corral. Now butchering again. Then we'll need knives again. When are we going to stop all this and get *on* with it?"

"With what?" Justin said, taking the pipe out of his mouth.

"With getting out," Gwen said. "What do you suppose? Out! Out!"

Everything in Joe yelled, *Wait. Wait till she has the baby.* But he knew they would not. What was he thinking of? Mooning over death by the fireplace. He should have had her out of here. He should have known.

"We've got boats," Gwen said. "We've got harps and looms and flutes and toys and, before I know it, we'll have a coal mine. Years, *years* go by and nobody gets started on a way out."

It stopped everybody. Justin could not even remember when anyone had last mentioned the possibility of getting out of the Green Kingdom.

She has not changed at all, Erma thought. And, really, I knew it all the time.

"Why," Gwen said, "with all the energy you've put into one damn thing after another, all of you, we could have tunneled through a mountain by now. Don't pull on me, Tommy. I told you, it hurts Mamma."

Justin felt Joe's urgency, begging them all to placate, to lie. Perhaps, in his place, he would have done the same.

"It was you, Justin," Gwen said, "who told me we could see light and so there must be some way out the top."

"But, Gwen . . ." Justin said.

She threw off the coverlet that had been over her legs, and she sat up straight, so that Tommy could sit behind her. Her voice was angry and her face, now fat and swollen, became flushed and mottled. "With all the building that's gone on here in four years," she said, "we could have had a tower to the sky by now."

"It might not be sky," Arthur said. "We see light, but we don't see the sun. We see moonlight, but we don't see the moon. The shadows are not sharp and all the light is diffused. I've thought a lot about it."

Erma turned toward Arthur. Did he, too, want out? Very possibly he wanted to escape her presence. If not by getting out, then on the river. Yet he did not accuse, like Gwen. He had never told her. She was suddenly so very sorry for him. Quietly, to himself, he had thought a lot about it.

"At first," Arthur continued, "I thought it was because of the mists that the light is always the way it is. But sometimes now I think there may be ice up there, solid ice over the top."

Joe looked up automatically, even though his eyes came only against the ceiling. That was Arthur for you, all right. Figuring things. It was something, thinking you might be sitting under pure ice that let the light through.

"Well, crack it," Gwendolyn said. "Suppose it is ice? What of it?"

"It might be miles thick, Gwen," Arthur said. And then he leaned back in his chair and smiled. "It might be some rare kind of crystal that only lets the green light through."

This was like it. This was like old times, Joe thought. Well, no. It was not. He must not let himself get carried away. Gwen was ready to blow her top. And inside Gwen there was his child, needing quiet, needing rest.

"I think Gwen is quite right," Justin said. He knew this would startle her, and he sat up straight and looked at her. "If all of us concentrated on this one thing to the exclusion of everything else, I'm sure we could get out."

"Of course," Gwendolyn said. "Why, even prisoners with only a little teaspoon dig their way out of concrete buildings."

"And so," Justin said, "since we haven't done this, but have let ourselves be distracted by all sorts of endeavors, one would assume that we do not really want to get out. Or, as perhaps you would put it, my dear, that we really prefer to serve our sentences."

"*Who* doesn't want out?" Gwen said, getting to her feet. "*Who* doesn't?"

Tommy slid down from the chair quietly and stood watching his mother. His thumb slid into his mouth.

"Who *does?*" Justin asked. He looked at each one of them in turn. "Who does?"

Gwen took a few steps toward him. Her face had gone white. She saw Joe starting toward her and she flashed him a look of warning. Behind her, Tommy stood perfectly still.

"*I* do," Gwen shouted. "*I* want out. And I'll *get* out in spite of you. You can all rot in this hell-hole, if you want. You can lie to me and smile and try to make me like it. But you won't help me. All right, don't help me."

Tommy began to walk backward, quietly, to where his ball-sleeper lay curled in a corner. "Hell-hole," he said to it. The ball-sleeper curled itself tighter to efface this disturbance. Tommy knelt down and began to hit it. "Hell-hole," he said. "Hell-hole, hell-hole, hell-hole."

"I'll make a hole in this place I can get out of," Gwen said. "I'll make a tunnel if I have to beat it out with my head."

The ballsleeper bit Tommy and he screamed. Now Joe could move. He went straight for Gwen and she leaned against him, sobbing. Erma went to Tommy.

"Somebody put Tommy to bed," Gwen said.

Justin reached behind him for his harp and, without bothering to tune it, struck as loud a sound as he could. That stopped Tommy's crying. Then Justin tuned the harp and began to play quietly the best sea chantey he knew. He couldn't remember when he had felt so good. And he knew he would never know why.

Joe and Gwen had gone now. Erma had rocked Tommy to sleep and taken him home. Arthur had gone to see to the trench fires. Usually Justin helped him, but tonight he waited. He thought Erma would come back to The Room. And she did. She sat beside him and he let her wait.

But now he must put aside sea chanteys, for this was serious. Now they must speak of the cave. She would not speak first, he realized that. How would he begin? There was so much, there were so many things to ask her.

"What is Her name?" he asked.

Her name? Erma thought. But Her name could not be a word. Could it be, even, a sound? Her name was a knowing. If the guts weep, if entrails cry, if tears hang forever caught upon unblinking eyelids somewhere in the hidden inner silences where there is no hand to brush them away, then Her name would be this knowing. But the tears would not be salt, not thin, not even liquid. Of some kind of molten heartscald, or granite; of iron, perhaps. And the shape not smooth, not meant for flowing. No. Jagged, many-faceted they would be. Yes, if the entrails weep such tears, and there is a substance of such a jagged, many-faceted hardness, then that is the knowing and those tears are Her name. But it is soundless, this name. If anyone speaks it, it speaks itself in the silent, absolute darkness of cavities within cavities.

"Her name?" Erma said. "I don't know. I don't know if there is a word for Her."

There was another long silence between them, and Justin put his harp away and replaced the pipe on the hearth.

"And you will not tell?" she said. "You will not give me away, Justin?"

"I cannot promise that," he said. "I don't know."

"But you will let me know first?" she asked. "Before you do?"

"Yes," he said. "That I promise you."

CHAPTER SIX

ALTHOUGH the inference could easily have been drawn from the structure of his own music, Justin was not given to philosophical interpretations of music. Yet this night, separately, he and Joe, unknown to each other, sat awake, staring into separate fires, giving a vivid demonstration of the great differences between a time of history and a time of innocence. One of the most characteristic attributes of the historical period is the rich variety of the alternatives to action. The innocent's contemplation is here expanded to include the contemplation of projected action. It does not occur to a child that he has also the choice of *not* running after the ball. Nor can you make youth believe that the urgency of his action will go away from him as the alternatives increase. The alternative to an urgent decision or an immediate action seems, to youth, to be nonexistent, or it may seem to be death. And death is of today for the innocent. But in the time of history there seem always to be many alternatives, and perhaps that is why death is of tomorrow. To contemplate death is to contemplate it either out of innocence or out of history, as a thing that could be of today or a thing that could not be until tomorrow.

So Justin sat alone, wondering how so much time could have gone by—weeks and months—and still he had not told the others, nor had he forced Erma to tell them, about the cave. And in his own house Joe also sat alone, knowing that he must bring an end to Arthur's hopes. He must tell him that he could not go with him on the river. Even though Gwen's pregnancy was safely over and the baby, Kathy, had somehow got to be five months old, still, in all this time, Joe had never found the right moment to tell Arthur that he could not go with him, that he would have to go alone.

No doubt their separate decisions were made even harder for Joe and Justin because they had fires to watch and live flames to follow with their eyes. Fire is, of all history's tools, perhaps the most convincing that death is of tomorrow and decisions can wait. It is only the innocent who have no time, whose actions seem to have only one alternative. Those who can value the past —they have time. Nations, too, being made of men, come to believe they have plenty of time and many alternatives. Death will wait until tomorrow. Decisions wait. Action waits. Everything will wait except their apprehension. The deeper men go into the time of history, the more does their apprehension become a component of their days. And, especially, of their nights. So do they love fires and court sleep and cherish the soft blanket, the thick wall, critically selected food and, above all, thoughts of themselves at work. For these are the great obscurers. These blur the connection between their apprehension and their reluctance to act. A virtue to explain indecision and a vagueness to clothe apprehension—this is the desired combination that makes of death tomorrow's thing. But some men stay a little innocent here and there, in spots. Enough to make rents in the obscuring veils, enough to find sleep and their questions incongruous.

Justin knew it was dangerous for the cave to remain secret, and yet, why could he not bring himself to tell? Had he really been right to suffer such apprehension about it? His feeling of imminent tragedy had faded of late. For one thing, there was the change in Gwen. Once her confinement was over she seemed to let them all off the hook. This baby she did not leave to Erma to care for, as she had Tommy, but much to everyone's surprise she would suffer no one to do for it but herself. She had become a doting mother and, of late, had been good company. Justin did not pretend to understand the transformation; he simply gave thanks for it.

Why, then, was he sitting up in the middle of the night with this feeling that it was necessary to force the issue before them all? Why did he not summon all his strength and deal with Erma alone? If she would destroy the cave, if the feathermane were killed, would that not be best? And what would that do to their— he had no name for it, for what went on between himself and Erma. He had pleasure in this forbidden secret shared; there was no sense denying it. To know that she knew that he knew of it had sharpened his whole existence. The deviltry in her when she handed him the leather button off his old coat—there was no other word for it.

"This is yours, isn't it, Justin?" she had said in front of all of them, smiling at him, enjoying his discomfort.

Almost every night in The Room there was some occasion for them to look at each other knowingly. If carving were mentioned, or caves, or leather buttons—well, it had certainly given spice to his evenings, there was no doubt of that. And how would it be for him if he were the one to persuade her to destroy the cave, if he were the one who must draw the knife on the feathermane's throat in cold blood? Where would their clandestine knowledge be then? What would take the place of mischief in her eyes upon him, the destroyer?

Justin cocked his head at an angle and raised his eyebrows. What was that? He turned abruptly, as though turning his back on something. No. He would not be seduced by music. It was no time to lose himself in the fourth movement, or whatever this was in his head. It had happened before to him, when he should have been most intimately concerned with reality, that he had allowed himself to be drugged into music.

Ah, that? So that was how it was to go? Well, it surprised him a little. Yet it was in the proper sphere. It . . .

He reached out his hand very slowly for his pipe and let the spill and the tobacco find their own aimless meeting while he listened. But he would not have it. He would not have this happen. He would deny it. Even if he lost it, lost the whole fourth movement, he was not to be seduced from some plan of action, some decision. He could drown himself in this. He could give in to it and become oblivious while someone blundered on the cave by accident, and then—then what would they do to her? This he could not forecast, but it was clear to him, had always been, that something terrible would come of it. Something irretrievable would be done. He did not know . . .

It was very irritating, this music. He did not seem to succeed in denying it. It would not go on but insistently began to repeat itself. And he supposed it would go on repeating until he wrote it down. But that he must not do. Then he would be lost and the girl in the cave and everything else would recede from him. There was this to think of: Was not her cave a creation of her own? Very strange he had not seen it as a work of art before. It was without restraint, of course, profligate, overblown. Yet it was native to a land that was without restraint. In the strongest way he had always believed that new creation should not be interfered with, not be dictated. Was her cave, then, to her, the same as his symphony to him? Who was he to say to another, "What you have created is not good, is evil, will bring tragedy"? If this were a valid basis for destruction of art, would not most of the world's art have been destroyed?

This did not change the feathermane. The feathermane was no work of art. The poor, blind, disproportionate thing had now grown to be a monster or a Christ Child—he did not know which —but it was not a work of art and he could not theorize away the fact of its existence and the danger.

No, not that way. That was not valid from the preceding phrase. He must have missed something. If he could note it down, it would be clear immediately what was wrong with that figure. From the beginning it . . .

He knew he could not resist it. Surely in the temptation of all the saints combined, there was not such a diabolical distraction from duty as this insistent, demanding music. It came out of the very walls of the room, numbing his brain, seducing his muscles with deadly languor, sharpening his ears with its error. It *was* in error there. Right there. And the error had been three times repeated.

He stood up and walked a few steps and then he stopped. Change the tempo, then. Would that do it? Now, from the beginning . . .

Urgency found itself betrayed by the music. Belittled and humiliated, it loosened its embrace of Justin, and, kneeling at his feet, it clung with impotent fingers to the front of his jacket, to the fold of the jacket pocket, to the hem, to the knees of his trousers. Then it lay dying on the floor where his heavy feet trod back and forth upon its fading body, unknowing. For the error was not truly an error. It did belong; but in an altered form.

And so Justin began to write "The Fulcrum." In later years, when it would come to his memory, this part would never stay in its context, would never be the beginning of the fourth part of *The Green Kingdom* but would remain always, for Justin, as a catalyst of remorse. Why had he stayed alone with his temptation if he knew—and he did know—that he would succumb to it? Why had he not, even before "The Fulcrum" had begun in his head, talked to Joe about the cave? Even if it had been a violation of his promise to Erma, it always seemed to Justin in later years that he could have trusted Joe with the knowledge of the cave.

Never would he be able to free himself from the belief that it had been obvious that Joe would have been the logical one to tell.

Probably Joe would have been glad for any interruption that night. He was even glad when Kathy whimpered, and, by moving very fast to comfort her, he prevented Gwen's awakening. You couldn't think about a person the way he was thinking about Gwen, or plot against them the way he was plotting, and have them looking right at you. The thing was not so much if he should give her the stones or what he should tell her about them. Those were questions he had thought about on other nights like this. All he cared about now was whether it would work. It seemed to Joe that it went back to that night in The Room, when Justin had been off his food, and Joe had found himself thinking about death. He'd thought a lot about death lately. Death and Kathy. He did not understand how these two had come to be so mixed together in his mind, and he knew it was too hard a thing for him. It was the kind of thing that Arthur liked to mull and chew over. But then he didn't suppose that he and Arthur would ever talk about it. It was a bad thing he was going to do to Arthur to-morrow and it was worse to have put it off so long. Yet he couldn't rightly say it was Kathy who had made him such a coward. If that were so, perhaps he wouldn't mind.

No. It was Gwen. It was Gwen who had made him return in secret to the site of the entrance, above the Yearsenday Place, and start the digging of a tunnel. Oh, it was too hard for a guy like him to figure out. He stood up and pushed one of the logs farther into the fire with his foot. Then he went over to the crib and watched Kathy sleeping.

How could you make a perfect thing like that out of spite? Never would he forget that scene. Never could he find it in his heart to forgive Gwen. He was aware of how, by constantly ministering to Kathy and worrying over her, Gwen was trying to win back his love. It gave him a mean feeling to withhold it. It was not a power that he cared to have.

"Why should I be glad?" she had said, turning her head away from the newborn child he had carried so carefully in to her. "It's no good to me *after* it's born."

Joe's mind always stuck there, on her having called the baby *it*. In some stubborn fashion he clung to the belief that all this meanness in him could have been washed away if only Gwen had said, "*She's* no good to me." He felt that, if he had been a good doctor, a wise man, or even a foolish but kind man, he would have erased her words from his mind, calling them drug talk, nonsense or untruth. But he was none of these, he thought. He had been an unwilling contestant, holding a consolation prize in his arms. He hadn't had enough wit to leave the room but had stood there, letting his love be killed and his fatherly joy poisoned, while Gwen spat at him the words he could never unhear. It was not his seed she had nourished, but a plot to keep him home. It was not his child she had carried, but a temporary triumph in a contest against Arthur Herrick and a boat.

And out of this kind of filth could be made eyelashes and a lip's perfect curvature. Out of such things could be forged this violent partisanship that he felt for Kathy. Here in this crib lay the center of whatever fierceness and strength had been left to him.

It was here, here in the Green Kingdom, that Kathy belonged. He would take her with him into the high places to gather the rare plants that would heal. She would ride bareback on a feathermane some day. She would be friends with all the wild creatures. And she should have a little playhouse of her own, hidden away in the ferns. He would never leave her. He must watch over her so that she would never know that she had been conceived in trickery.

Joe turned and went back to the fire and sat down again to chew on his old problem. Surely a man had a right to want his daughter to grow up seeing him with important work to do. He reached into his pocket and took out a wad of leather and began to peel the edges back. Then he shook the stones free in his hand and moved them back and forth to let the firelight play on them. Even if the bribe would work on Gwen, who knew how long it would work? Well, he could try, that's all. He didn't know if they were emeralds or glass and he didn't care. But would they look like emeralds to Gwen? And, if they did, could he prolong her greed so that, if he were lucky, he could let the green veins lead him in a continual and productive zigzag? The walls, which looked to Gwen like a prison, were equally forbidding to Joe because they now seemed to him to be full of doors. His great fear was that he would not be able to avoid finding a way out.

This was their land, his and Kathy's, and to stay in it was worth any price to Joe. He shook the stones together in his hands like dice, and suddenly he smiled. And if it were not for the baby sleeping, he would have laughed out loud. For someone who hated the world so much, it was funny to find himself wishing so greatly that he could be in it for a night. Though he had never known any of them when he was there, still he knew there were men in the world who knew what he wanted to know. The reason he knew there were was because he could remember so many cartoons about guys buying diamonds to get back into beds they had got kicked out of. Emeralds, especially, were in cartoons. In one way or another, guys were always buying a little more time in a place they didn't want to leave. Well, now, if he could be in the world for just one night without anybody's knowing, that's what he would do. He would find a rich man who had tried to buy something with an emerald. All he wanted to ask him was "Does it work?"

"What are you doing up like this?" said Gwen, coming into the room and going directly to the crib. "Did she cry? Is something the matter with her? Why didn't you call me?"

"She's all right," Joe said. "I was just sitting here thinking." He turned his hand so that the firelight played on the stones. Though Kathy was a quiet sleeper and rarely uncovered, he knew that Gwen got up three or four times every night to cover her and he knew his protest was futile.

"What's that in your hand?" Gwen said.

"Oh, it's just some stones," Joe said. "Pretty, aren't they?"

Gwen knelt down on the floor beside him. "Let me see," she said, taking them out of his hand. "Why, they're warm."

Without looking away from the fire, Joe could feel her settling down. He could tell exactly what she was thinking. And he knew exactly how she would look. The pity of it was that, even now, when she had become the enemy of everything he loved, her greed still had for him a kind of purity about it. The craftiness would make her eyes more alive and, as she bent over the stones, the way she would sweep back her black hair with the back of that long hand could even yet strike through his hatred.

"Do you think—do you think they could be real emeralds?" she said.

"I don't know," Joe said. "I never saw a real emerald in my life."

Gwen squirmed a little closer to the fire and, with the back of her hand, pushed her hair away from her face. "I have," she said.

Well, of course, he should have known this. But he had forgotten. In the days when he used to marvel at how she never drew a breath without knowing also what time it was, he used to think, too, that it was astounding, the concrete information she had about things she could never possibly possess. She knew the proper way to clean furs that she would never be allowed to touch. She knew how to distinguish real pearls from their imitations, and yet she had never known anybody who owned a real one. She knew the comparative durability and price of the hides of jungle animals whose diets and whose homes had never touched her curiosity.

He'd been a fool to try, Joe thought, because undoubtedly Gwen had the acid test for emeralds filed away in her mind along with all the other baffling, puzzling things that had always given her her strange authority over him.

"They look like emeralds, Joe. They do, really. Where did you find them?"

"Deep," he said, "quite deep. Under a layer of . . ."

She reached out and grabbed his wrist. "Does anyone else know?" she said. "Who was with you?"

"Why, no one," he said.

"You're sure, Joe? You're sure you haven't told Arthur? Or Erma or Justin?"

Joe reached down and took the stones from her hand. With exaggerated care, he wrapped them in the piece of leather and put them in his pocket. And then he turned and looked directly down at her. "Why don't you go back to bed?" he said. "Kathy's all right. You fuss over her too much. I told you before."

"All right," she said.

Joe helped her to her feet and stood watching her leave the room. For a moment his warm leather jacket turned into a tail-coat and his moccasins became shining, soft, thin-soled dress shoes. His taut, anxious guts relaxed into a moderate paunch. And on his upper lip a clipped gray mustache exuded a virile, expensive odor. Well, it was like he thought. By the time something got into the cartoons it was almost bound to be true. He patted the riches in his pocket and walked jauntily over to the crib. He was scared, as always, to see that the long, soft eyelashes and the curious cheekbones would create, once again, Gwen's same terrible beauty. He leaned over the sleeping child and whispered, "O.K., Kitten. She bit."

Then he gave the fire a quick glance of inspection and

walked quietly out the door into the morning mist to betray the
hopes of his friend and so prolong for yet a while the life that he
wanted for his daughter. She should have a playhouse among the
ferns, yes. And he would sit there and tell her how good girls can
be when they are really good and how great is their power.
Through the early-morning mists he walked to his rendezvous
with the only man who had ever depended on him. And he tried
to think who the great girls were that he would tell Kathy about,
the ones he had known or even heard other men tell of, the ones
he had read about in books or seen in the movies. He stopped and
stood still and swore. For the greatest of all the good girls, the
greatest of them all, was Erma Herrick when she was young.

"And if you had seen her," he would say to Kathy, "when
she lived above the print shop in Drury in that bare, scrubbed
place—the way she could light a spark in you, even if you were
dead."

And then he was no longer talking to Kathy, but was walking alone and knowing for the first time the full extent of what
had been done to Erma Herrick. What had they done to her?
What had they done to her, while he stood by and watched?

By the time he and Arthur had done the chores and assembled the pitch-gathering gear, it was full wessun. And yet Joe
had not found the right time to tell Arthur that he could not explore the river with him and that, as long as Kathy lived and
needed him, he could not enter into adventures that did not concern her. Well, he did not suppose it would make any difference
if he went to gather pitch again or, for that matter, helped caulk
the boat or test her or even launch her, so long as Arthur understood that he would have to make the journey alone.

"Now this is the place I told you about," Arthur said. "The
grove is smaller than the other. But we won't need very much this
time. And if one of these trees would flow right, we might have
the whole weight of the load downhill."

"Well, I don't know," Joe said. "At least the old grove
doesn't have these damned thorns in the way. And we've already
got the flow trees cut. Here you have to start testing all over
again."

"Well, let's just cut two or three, Joe, while we're here. If
they don't flow right off, we'll give it up and go back to the old
place."

Now, Joe thought. Right now. Before they got busy. Before

they began anything, he must tell him. "Arthur," he said, "have you got any tobacco with you?"

Arthur took his pouch from his pocket and turned to hand it to Joe.

"Christ, what happened to your neck?" Joe said. "You got blood all over it."

Arthur put his hand up to his neck and then examined the blood on his fingers. "I thought I felt something back there," he said.

"Sit down," Joe said. "Hold your head on till I have a look."

If that wasn't just like Arthur to go and hurt himself at a time like this. Just when he'd got himself all worked up to talk things over. Joe's hands busied themselves, trying to find the source of the blood, while his mind tried furiously not to remember all the other times he had brought water to this man's fever, dressings for his wounds and audience for his despair. He tore a leaf off a tree and slapped it roughly against Arthur's neck. "It's just a scratch," he said. "Hold that leaf on it till it stops bleeding. And hold still."

"Did I give you the tobacco?" Arthur asked.

"Yeah," Joe said. He sat down on the ground beside Arthur, fixed him a pipe and handed it to him. Then he began to blow on the small firebox which he carried hung from his waist. This was as good a time as any to tell Arthur. Perhaps if he had to hold that leaf slapped to his neck he wouldn't be able to think of such tough arguments. Joe couldn't remember a single argument he'd ever won against Arthur.

"I've got to tell you something, Arthur. I've got to get it off my chest."

"Sure, Joe. What is it?"

"Keep your hand on that leaf," Joe said, "or we'll be here all day."

"I forgot. Now what's eating you?"

"Well, I told you I'd help you build a boat. And I did. I told you we'd launch it. And we will. I'll help you fit her out and see that she's safe and tight. But . . . What the hell are you staring at?"

Arthur pointed and stood up. He forgot about the leaf, but it stuck by itself to the coagulated blood. "That's a path, Joe," he said. "Do you see it?"

Joe walked to the point Arthur indicated and knelt on the ground. "It is," he said quietly. The path was arched over with thorn trees. In the dim light Joe explored its edges with his hands to verify the vegetation. It was, as he thought, tanglevine. That could only mean that the path had either constant or very recent use. He crawled along one edge of the path, peering at it closely. Then he sat back on his heels and looked up at Arthur. The leaf was hanging at a crazy angle from Arthur's neck and this seemed a component of Joe's foreboding.

"It isn't an animal path," he said.

Suddenly it seemed to him that the trees were full of eyes and that the two of them, armed with nothing but pitch buckets and a couple of knives, could be seen and heard. He stood up and said, a little too loudly in the stillness, "Whatever it is, it wears sandals."

"What if?" Arthur said. "What if, all this time we thought we were alone, there have been other people here?" He leaned over to protect himself from the thorns and started down the path ahead of Joe.

"Wait," Joe said. "Wait, Arthur. We ought to go back to the settlement and tell them our location."

But Arthur was moving steadily ahead, wanting to find out something, wanting to know. That's the way it had always been, Joe thought, as he moved steadily behind him. You could never make Arthur listen when he had his mind on something, and you could never walk off and leave him alone, either. Yet Joe knew that whatever had made the path could not be something familiar or easy to understand, else he would have known about it by now.

Lulled into security by long habit Erma sometimes let days go by without discarding the dead greengrain that filled the chinks of the door block. It was this that Joe spotted. And it was Joe who lifted the big block out of the wall of the temple, while Arthur slipped down ahead of him into the strange, musty darkness.

Arthur could feel Joe standing behind him. "Can you see?" he started to say. But the words, drowned in their own echoes, became meaningless shouts. He lowered his voice almost to a whisper. "Can you see anything, Joe?"

"Don't look ahead," Joe whispered. "Look out to one side and don't move till you can see what your feet are on."

"My eyes burn," Arthur said.

"Something's burning in here," Joe said. "Wait. We'll see it after a while. Don't move till you can see."

This was Joe's greatest concern, for they had been in this

situation many times before and he knew it was almost impossible for Arthur Herrick to hold still.

"There's something or somebody alive in here," Joe said, "and it is probably watching us."

Since he could not move his feet lest he slide into a cavern Arthur began to move his hands restlessly in exploration of the wall against which they leaned. "This is a church, Joe," he said. "Some kind of temple. I'm sure of it."

"Hold still," Joe said, "and wait. We'll soon be able to see."

Arthur Herrick was afraid, yet nothing could have made him leave this place. Under his cold, restless hand there were strange carvings that he did not know. In his eyes there was still only burning blackness; in his ears, the sound of his own breathing; and in his nostrils, a heavy, exhilarating odor that he could not identify. He became aware of the three shafts of light and he followed them down to where they converged on a pale-green radiance. Somehow he bore the tension of waiting for the pale radiance to move.

There was a wrongness today for the feathermane. *She* had already gone, and her going and her coming again were not so close together as this. When she came, the earth did not cease to shake until her hand was on him. Now something waited there, beyond his blindness, and made sounds. On his neck the hairs of his mane warned him, even before the odors identified themselves and set off an old trembling. He was like a blind man who feels himself to be in a room with a silent robber and can only whirl about helplessly, saying, "What? Who is it?"

Feathermanes do not have any reflexes of guile. They do not freeze or mock death. All warnings are, to them, warnings to leap, to flee. But leap where? asked the brittle, folded bones. And flee where? asked the scarred, blind eyes. Not to leap and not to flee, this is to wait in trembling. Even so, he struggled to his feet and tried to sniff out the direction of the danger. Now the dread odor became sharper and the old memories crowded upon the feathermane. He remembered this man and remembered the knife that had made his eyes blind. Even *she* had been afraid then. Old postures of the past possessed his stiff bones in caricatures of battle stance. Although he trembled in fear and felt the certainty of no escape, his head bent down with some ferocity and one hoof grew restless. He took a tentative step forward and snorted to clear his nostrils for the scent. If memory is the name for it, the

warmth in his blood retold for him a mating season of his youth
and he, victorious, leaping over the green hills. The odor came
closer, and noise with it, and he was old and in fear and desperate
with no escape.

When it stood up, Arthur could see that the living thing was
a feathermane. Much as he wanted to explore the temple, study
the walls and learn who had made the carvings, he could not now
do otherwise than to keep advancing on the animal. He had the
feeling, against all reason, that it must be the same one.

But why would she have told him that it was dead?

The scarred eyes looked up at him—so it seemed—in re-
proach. And the years that Erma had lived with him, knowing
this, produced in Arthur such an utter bafflement that he turned
around to ask Joe if he had known.

The feathermane's horn nudged him, and Arthur whirled in
a fury upon the poor, blind thing that now seemed to symbolize
every unjust humiliation he had ever suffered. He had his hand
on his knife. "*This* time," he said. His fury made him deaf to
Joe's shouting.

"Come back, you fool." Joe's voice was too loud and the
walls only blurred it.

Consciously ignoring all the alarms set off by his instincts,
Joe moved forward. He knew what he was doing, as he had known
all the times he had done it before. He knew that it was senseless
and could have been avoided; but he knew that now, for him,
there was no choice.

The feathermane charged suddenly, felt his horn go into
something, be caught, felt the man off balance and on the ground,
twisting beneath him. They were out of the light shaft now. In the
dark confusion Joe held to the feathermane's throat and pushed
Arthur free. He could smell blood and he knew that the horn had
gone deep, knew there was no stopping now, no truce. He knew
that he, Joe, must kill Arthur's enemy without benefit of hatred,
fury or enmity of his own; but only because there was nothing
else to be done.

He strove to pull the animal away from the body, into the
light. It was not to be possible now. No. Nothing but to kill now,
and as quickly as possible. To strangle, to grapple, not to lose
hold of the sweaty hide, but with a clear head to plan the
strangling. Not to slip and lose footing, and not to hope that
Arthur would be able to help him.

There was no help for him, except that his muscles must grow stronger to meet the new power in the animal. Again the animal found strength to attack the air with its horns and to shake off the force that held it. And now Joe knew he must gain on the animal or his advantage would be lost. He must get his hands on the windpipe. Now he must expose himself to the horns for the great advantage of bringing his thumbs to press in the crucial moment of the kill.

Yet he could take no triumph in the gasping of the animal. He only waited for the moment when he dared believe the breathing was near the last, the moment when he could reach for his knife and slit the throat, speeding the time of release from this sweating, dark struggle.

Then he thought it was safe. He disengaged one hand to reach for his knife. He felt the impact of the whole animal's last great lunge, and he knew that he had been mistaken. He felt his knife cut flesh. But the full weight of the animal was on him and its tremendous dying thrust had found him. He knew.

There was surprisingly little pain. Gored, he thought. I'm gored and the thing to do is not to move. And at the same moment he knew he could not move. He could still see dimly where the shafts of light converged. They seemed a long way off. The struggle had taken them to the foot of the altar and now he looked up and saw Her whose name is a knowing, immobile, unconcerned.

Erma was a deep one, all right. He had never really known her. Maybe she would be coming soon. If it was soon, and if she had a light, there might be some hope for him.

He was aware of the feathermane across his body, growing heavier and heavier. But if Erma didn't come for a long time, then . . . well, perhaps this was it? He guessed so. He guessed it could be like this. Bleeding to death in the dark among strange pictures. No sense. No sense to it.

The conception flowers on the walls began to wave and recede. He knew what that meant, all right. He thought he heard Arthur groan. But he did not trust what he heard. The only thing he trusted was if Erma came in time. But then, if she couldn't, well, it was that way and there was nothing he could do about it. Nothing at all. And not to close his eyelids would make no difference either way. So he let them close. That way the crazy pictures were gone.

But Kathy! Kathy.

He would have cried for Kathy if there had been any tears. He would have said her name if there had been any breath. He would have shouted an obscenity if the blood in his mouth had not stopped it. But he thought it. As long as he could think, he thought of all the ways there are to call oneself a fool. As long as he could feel, he felt regret.

Ah, Kathy, Kathy. This is a fool's way to die.

At The Room, the others did not begin to feel uneasy until after they had eaten and made fresh tea, because it had happened before that one or another of them had not come in for the evening meal. Gwen was the first to voice their anxiety, though it was in the form of anger, for the delay must have had to do with the boat. Not until it was true-dark did Erma begin to be concerned. Joe was with Arthur this time; and that, of course, made it different from the times when Arthur was late and alone. She went to the door and looked out into the darkness, for it was their custom that if one were lost or in need of help he should light a signal fire after dark. She saw nothing and took refuge in the memory that in this place of mists and dew and dampness, a firebox could not always be made to work. She said that she would help put the children to bed, and, picking Tommy up in her arms, she followed Gwen, who carried the sleeping Kathy.

When they were gone, the apprehension became a certainty in Justin's mind. It seemed to him that he had always known, as with slow, heavy movements he put on his coat and pulled the hood up around his head. He walked across the room heavily; and at the door he met Erma.

"Where are you going?" she asked.

"To the cave."

"Wait. I'll go with you. Justin, wait. You don't know where the lamps are. You don't know how to make a light there." She began to run after him, but he could find nothing to say to her. So heavy was the dread that lay on him, there was no respite left for speech.

Since the moment he had allowed the first note of "The Fulcrum" to seduce him into keeping his knowledge secret, he had known that it was a tragic decision and that, after it, nothing but tragedy could follow.

ARTHUR HERRICK lay in The Room where they had brought him, his body bound in a kind of cocoon made of bark strips. The seas of fever, unconsciousness, and delirium parted once again and cast him up. Each time he stayed awake a little longer before his unspoken questions tired him into sleep. He did not know how long he had been here, or even the nature of his illness. But he knew that he could not move. He was able to remember from the times before and to know, when he opened his eyes, what he would see. Erma's face would be there before him, ransacked with grief and fatigue as he had never known it. Erma's hand would be on his forehead. On his dry, crusted lips would be the blessed wet coolness, dribbling precious moisture onto the tongue.

"Don't speak, Arthur. Don't try to move. I am here. I have to give you the water very slowly, because you are hurt. You are hurt in the chest and we don't know how badly yet. Be quiet, darling. Be quiet. You will live. Don't try to speak. You are much better; you are getting better each time. Close your eyes and sleep, sleep."

Justin came into the room quietly and stood behind Erma, so she could lean on him. "Did he wake again?" he said.

Erma nodded her head. And then, automatically, she stood and walked over to the table and sank onto the bench. Justin took her place by the bedside. Erma poured herself a cup of tea. It was cold. With the slow, drunken motions of exhaustion, she filled the kettle and put it on the fire.

"Is Gwen still in the cave?" she said.

"No, I finally persuaded her to go to her house. The children are asleep."

"And Joe?"

"I have to go back," Justin said, "as soon as you've had your tea. I came for the shovel."

She lifted the kettle slowly and poured the water into the pot. She poured two cups of tea and brought one to Justin. The boiling water sloshed over her hand, but she did not feel it.

"In the cave?" she said.

He took the tea from her and drank deeply while she returned for her own cup. "Yes," he said. "I've got to work fast, before Gwen gets there again. I had hell's own time getting her loose. My hope is that she'll sleep long enough for me to have done with it. When I get back you can take a rest while I watch. And then you can get us some food."

She got the shovel for him and came to the chair. "All right," she said. "I'll take over now."

Automatically, they changed places, as they had been doing constantly for the last two days. She checked to see if the sweetened water was at hand, if the improvised urinal was still empty, if the bandages were where she could reach them, while Justin stood by her, leaning on the shovel. Then they stared at each other in startled anguish, and stayed frozen, while the high, eerie wail of a howler cut the silence.

"Oh, God!" Justin said.

In their minds was the same picture. Rarely did the howlers sound this close and, whenever they did, there would be the mangled carcass of a mossback or some other animal who had died in the night. Justin, for all his fatigue, moved quickly toward the knives hanging above the fireplace.

"No," Erma said. "Fire. Take torches, Justin. They are afraid of fire."

"You're right," he said. He took from the stack of torches one which he lighted immediately, and two for spare.

"Don't leave Arthur," he said. "I'll be back as soon as I can."

Alone, she heard the howlers slit the night again and felt the coldness on her neck. She tried to settle herself and reached for Arthur's wrist. The pulse. Concentrate on the pulse. There. It seemed to her to be a little slower. And that was good. She sat in the threatened silence and her fingers were ears, listening to Arthur's pulse. Suddenly she bent forward, so that her bones might shield this terrible sphere of grief that lay somewhere inside her. It was Joe who had told her the howlers were afraid of fire. It was Joe who had known everything they needed to know.

She had dozed and started guiltily when Justin came in. He walked over and sank into her chair and put his head in his hands. She could hear how heavy his breathing was.

"You look so awfully tired, Justin," she said. "Is it done?"

"Yes, it is done. It was very difficult."

"The howlers," she said, "were they . . .?"

"No, no. They weren't inside. They were circling the entrance, though. Three of them. Mean-looking fellows. You were right. I threw one of the torches at them and they ran. I left one burning on the grave. We'll have to keep one going, I'm afraid, all the time for a while. It's a very ugly idea for Gwen to think of. Perhaps, if she didn't hear them, it might not occur to her what the torches are for."

He closed his eyes in weariness. Erma stood behind him so that he could lean against her if he needed to.

"Justin," she said, "I don't know how to ask you. I ought not to be able to think of him, even. But I have to know."

"The feathermane? I couldn't get him loose, Erma. The horn was stuck in so fast. I buried them together. No one need know, I think, but us. I couldn't take the time to file through the horns."

She put her hand on his shoulder. "It's all right," she said. "Joe wouldn't . . . he wouldn't . . ."

She began to cry silently. Justin stood up slowly and took the shaking body in his arms. "You are not alone, Erma," he said. "I bear the guilt with you equally."

"No," she protested. "No, Justin."

"We can neither of us afford to think of that now," he said. "There is too much to do. Will you get me something to eat, please?"

"Yes, of course. Can't you sleep a little now?"

"No, I must go out as soon as I eat. How is Arthur?"

"His wound has stopped bleeding, I think. And his pulse seems slower."

"Have you tried the broth yet?"

"No. Not yet. I'm so afraid of his choking. I thought, if the bleeding stopped, we could prop his head up next time he woke and try it. I'll fix you something to eat right away."

She moved away from him and wiped her eyes with her hands and shook her head to clear it. "Come on over to the table," she said. "Just watch if his eyes open, that's all. I think he'll sleep quite a while longer."

She had got her second wind and went about building up the fire and preparing the food with some efficiency. Grateful to find herself once again capable of this summoning, she ladled out soup for Justin, cut the bread and began to slice the cheese.

"Why do you have to go out again?" she asked. "Couldn't I do whatever it is? Couldn't you sleep now?"

Justin looked at his hands, grimed with the cave's dirt. But he was too tired to wash. He wiped them on his trousers roughly and picked up a piece of bread. "It's the boat," he said. "I have to get it out of here."

"The boat?" Erma took her hand off the knife handle.

"Yes. Gwen has told Tommy that Joe has gone away in the boat. And so . . . And so I've got to get it out of sight."

Erma opened her mouth to speak and then closed it, biting her lip. She resumed the slicing of the cheese. "Oh, dear," she said.

"I know. But it's done now, Erma. She has already told him."

"But I don't see how you can manage it."

"Well, we'll see. We'll see. You eat something now, Erma. Come. Sit down."

"Gwen is awake, then? Did you talk to her just now?"

"Yes."

"How is she?"

"She was in surprising control of herself. It's forced, but . . . well, it's a relief from the other. Eat, Erma."

She swallowed a mouthful of soup obediently, and then put down her spoon. "And Tommy thinks," she said, "that Joe just went off like that and . . . and left him?"

"No. Not like that. He's supposed to have gone into the World and to be waiting for them."

"And we . . . we all have to keep this lie up, too? But, Justin . . ."

"We have no choice, my dear." He nudged her and nodded toward Arthur, whose eyes were open.

The pain, the pain, the pain, the pain. Nothing would come clear, except the pain, for Arthur. The pain and the thirst, and then the belief that, if he stayed motionless, he would not die. *But there were things he knew. There were questions.* If he could hold his breath, the pain would not hurt so. But he could not. He had to breathe. At last, dreading the pain it would cause, he took a breath. Water. Erma. He couldn't understand. Erma and Justin. Justin and Erma. Erma and then Justin. But where was Joe? It was Joe he wanted. Joe was the doctor. These two, they couldn't be trusted to know enough to keep him from dying. Why didn't Joe give him something for the pain? Why wasn't Joe taking care of him?

"Oh."

"Don't hold your breath, darling," Erma said. "It only makes it worse later. I know it hurts, but you are really much better. Your wound has stopped bleeding. I'm going to raise your head a little bit. There. Can you stand that?"

There was something he knew about Joe. Something he did not want to know.

"Could you stand it a little higher? I'm going to give you some broth. You would get well faster if you could swallow this."

She put the spoon to his lips.

There was something he knew about Erma, too.

"Swallow, Arthur," she said sharply.

His great ringed eyes stared at her, as he swallowed one spoonful and then another and another. And she managed to hold her hand steady, while she saw the stare turn into recognition, and then question, and then hatred. So closely did it coincide with the broth that she felt as though the broth were going straight into his eyes, warming them, making them alive, making them hate. For one mad second she thought, I could control it. I could shut off this hate if I withheld the broth. But she went on methodically easing the dribbles of nourishment into his mouth, feeling his eyes blast into her cheekbones, into the hand that held the spoon, into the hollow of her throat.

"There now," she said. "That's enough. In a little while I'll give you some more." She made her eyes look into his. "Could you tell me if you want your head lowered again, Arthur?"

He made no sign. The unmistakable hatred in his eyes remained the same.

"Would you rather I left your head propped up this way? Can you tell me?"

He opened his mouth to speak. No sound came out. Erma bent over him closely. He could not speak. He tried and it hurt to try. And it hurt even to think of trying. He could not speak. That changed the look in his eyes.

"You can't speak?" Erma asked. "Is that it?"

He rolled his head from side to side and tears rolled out from under his closed eyelids.

"Try to sleep," she said. "A little later it will be all right."

She looked across to Justin, who sat motionless, watching. Soundlessly she formed a message with her lips: *He can't speak.*

Justin lifted one hand in the air and she took his signal to compose herself.

Quietly the tears rolled down Arthur's cheeks. She wiped them away and took his wrist in her fingers, for something to do. The wound must be deeper than they thought. Would he never speak, then? Never be able to accuse her, except with his eyes? How he must hate her. How terrible it must be for him to be at the mercy of someone he hated and could not accuse.

Except for a while, after Arthur Herrick had returned from the wilderness with the spell of the river still upon him, he had always been quick to act, sudden of decision, impulsive. The time he had spent in the wilderness alone had given him a temporary change of pace. Though the desire to contemplate on his thoughts had supplanted his characteristic urge to communicate them as fast as they came, even this experience had not made him greatly observant. Now he found himself in a unique position. As he began to believe he would live, and as his inability to speak partook less of panic and frustration, it seemed to Arthur that he had never noticed anything before in his life. He had always brushed away or stepped on any insect without even thinking of it. Now that the pain in his chest and side had made any such sudden movement impossible, he found himself, one day, observing the progress of a small, green, visored beetle on the floor near his bed. With such bell-toned clarity must painters see the world, Arthur thought. But surely it must be only at certain times for them, else the impact of each day would be too great to bear. Awake and motionless at dawn, he heard a solitary chichimingo call, as though to him personally. Perhaps it is the fever, he thought, and I shall lose all this.

He had discovered that a half-sitting position was much less painful than reclining, even for sleeping, and one day as Erma was leaning over him to raise his head even higher her face as he had known it fell apart and became a composite of planes. There were short periods each day when the pain would be less insistent, and Arthur began to look forward to these as a time of rediscovery of his world. He saw the stones of the hearth, the tools hung on the wall, the texture of the blanket that lay over him, all with a discreteness he had never experienced. As his communication with inanimate things became more intimate, it ceased to bother him that Erma and Justin and Gwen spoke increasingly less to him. Somehow he found this a source of relief.

It would have been a great effort to listen to them; he was glad to be left motionless to watch, in between the times they ministered to him. Sometimes it seemed to him that he was gradually receding from them, until he should become a part of the wall. And then one day he really saw their faces, and the deep, unmistakable grief that was written there. Whether it was that he had never before possessed such power of observation, or whether real grief is so rare a thing, he knew that such a depth of it he had never seen. And so the knowledge which had been competing with his pain and his speechlessness and his preoccupation with himself at last commanded his whole attention. There was no need to ask about Joe. Their faces shouted not the statement of Joe's death but, for each one, each one's loss.

Arthur felt a deep and vicarious regret for Joe, that he would never see this evidence of how greatly he had been loved. He would never have believed it, Arthur thought. And then the very real sense of his own personal loss swept over him and he closed his eyes against the tomorrow which would be so greatly laden with this positive absence. And the day after, and the day after, for all the many days.

"What is it, Arthur?" Erma said, coming to him and kneeling by the bed. "Is it the pain again? Shall I give you another dose of braidstem?"

He was glad that he could not speak and need not explain the nature of his pain. He opened his eyes and looked at Erma. So his face, too, must look like the others now. What would they do? How would they live without Joe?

"Oh, it's your side again. I'm so sorry. I'll mix some medicine for you," Erma said.

He had not known until then that he had moved his left hand

across to the right side of his chest in answer to her question. But he was glad to have the pain misinterpreted. There were so many ways of speaking. Perhaps men were wise to confine their feet in shoes lest, while they were not watching, their toes should suddenly begin to spell out truth in the dust. He kept his hand imprisoned between his arm and chest while he swallowed the medicine slowly. Then he smiled at her, closed his eyes, and let his head drop back, so that she would leave him. He could feel her hesitation and her desire to bring him some unknown, further comfort. He suffered her hand to lie on his forehead and to stroke his hair in a message of her defeat and sadness for his pain. And then he felt her move silently away from him.

He lay and waited for the braidstem to dull his new knowledge and to postpone the taste of tomorrow. *Would their faces have borne such grief for him?* If it had been Joe who lay here, and he—he who lay wherever they had buried Joe—would their faces have worn such sorrow? Would their heads be bent forward so with the weight of *his* death? Would their hands dangle so uselessly from their wrists as they walked or stood about in a room empty of *him?*

His head moved restlessly from side to side on the pillow. As Arthur had discovered, there are so many forms of speech. It would be well for anyone who wished to speak neither with his voice nor with his eyes to see also that his feet were confined in shoes, his hands gloved and chained to his sides, his shoulders put under a yoke, his neck held in a clamp, his eyebrows paralyzed and his mouth frozen. Perhaps even the hairs of the head should be covered with a neat cap. If any part is left free, it will speak. If any part is left free, then all parts may as well be left free and open and all confining guards be relinquished.

Somehow, they lived through those first days. The mossbacks got milked, the children were fed, listened to, even played with. The torch was kept lighted on Joe's grave and Arthur was constantly nursed. Of the three adults able to move about Gwendolyn's motions seemed, to Arthur, the busiest and the most effective. At intervals one of the three would drop onto the temporary bed and fall into a deep, short sleep. The routine of their days was shattered, except as the livestock and the children demanded, and their meals were of the most cursory type. No one went in search of fresh fruits for the table. No one cared for variety. When the

children were around the adults talked, but otherwise they worked
in silence. Except in the barest questioning about his food, his
position, his comfort, no one spoke to Arthur except Tommy.

"Why you no talk?" Tommy asked.

"Tommy," Gwen called, "come away from Arthur. Arthur
doesn't feel good."

Tommy moved a step farther away from Gwen. "Why not *he*
go the World?" he said.

Gwen came over to the bedside and took Tommy's hand.
"Where's your ballsleeper? He hasn't had any supper."

"Don't care," Tommy said, jerking angrily from Gwen's
grasp. "Don't care."

He ran over to the now gaping, empty corner where the boat
had been and sat down on the floor. Soon he was in an imaginary
boat, going faster and faster. The boat began to circle around and
around and make him dizzy. "Tommy," Gwen called, "what are
you doing? You'll wake the baby."

Justin came over and swooped the boy up in his arms. "Let's
go," he said. "Let's go bank the fires and check the corral and
do our chores."

Outside, Justin sang a note into the night and looked at
Tommy. Tommy yelled an imitation. Justin sang another note
and this one he let roll about among the hills. Tommy put his
head back and yelled louder. From the great chest and the small
throat came the nonsense sounds, alternately, until laughter was
achieved, and breathlessness. And then Justin set the boy down
on the ground. "Run," he said. "Run and I'll catch you."

The fires were banked to the child's mounting excitement.
The corral was secured on the peak of it. Its pace diminished on
the way back to The Room. And suddenly exhaustion set in. Justin carried the boy in his arms, ashamed that such a small weight
should so soon make his muscles ache.

In The Room he found Gwendolyn sobbing and clinging to
Erma. "I can't," she said. "I can't go back there alone. I can't
stand it. I can't stand to be there alone."

"Why don't you stay here?" Justin said, looking at Erma.
"Why don't we all stay here together for a few days?"

"Yes," Erma said. "Yes. Why not? I'll go up and get the
baby's things, Gwen. You stay here by the fire."

Gwendolyn dried her eyes and reached up for Tommy. He
stirred only a little at being transferred and put his thumb into

his mouth. "Well," Gwendolyn said, "would it be too much trouble? Will it disturb Arthur, do you think?"

They had forgotten about him again.

"Oh, I don't think so, Gwen," Erma said. "The nights are very long for him. Probably he would be glad for someone to— for some company."

She went over to Arthur's bed. He was asleep and she sighed with relief. She must remember, she *must* remember not to talk about him as if he were—as if he could not understand or could not hear.

"I'll help you, Erma," Justin said. "Let me finish this pipe." He turned to Gwen. "We might as well bring down the beds. You ought to have your rest."

"Keep an eye on Arthur, will you, Gwen?" Erma asked. "He should have more broth, if he wakes up. It's there on the hearth." She went over to the wall and got her coat. "Ready, Justin?"

It was the first time they had been alone and they walked in silence toward Gwendolyn's house. Neither of them could begin speech between them, and yet the night was full of things to be spoken. At last Justin took her hand and locked her arm with his. At the house, which would hold so much of Joe for both of them, they paused, dreading to enter without having first spoken to each other.

"Well," Justin said. "Well, my dear."

"I never thought," Erma said, "that a thing like this—that Gwen and I would have been drawn closer by a thing like this. I would have thought—"

"You must remember," Justin said, "that, ever since the beginning, her chief reason for any action has been not to be alone."

He held the door open for Erma and she went over to the fireplace to make a light.

"Oh," she said. "I thought, perhaps, that grief had—"

"Because she has not blamed you for Joe's death, you are ready to lose your judgment completely and assume that she is the same as yourself. Don't mistake her panic for grief, Erma. Nor her ignorance for forgiveness. There is a great deal more to come after the shock is over, whenever that may be. And you should be on your guard."

"Ignorance?" Erma said.

"Yes, ignorance," Justin said, lifting up Tommy's bed impatiently, in order to stir Erma into some activity. "How would she know the cave was yours? How would she know the feather-mane was the same one? How would she know? From *me?*"

"Oh," Erma said. "But Arthur will tell her."

"Perhaps not," Justin said. "Will you get the baby's things together now, Erma? And some blankets?"

"Of course, Justin. Of course. I'm sorry."

She put down all her questions and forced herself to concentrate on the task ahead, lest Gwendolyn say she had forgotten some essential.

"You go ahead," Justin said. "I'll come behind with this. Then we'll come back for Gwendolyn's bed."

She trudged on obediently, not daring to cause delay, until Justin himself stopped to rearrange his load.

"But, Justin," she said, "even if Arthur could never tell her, I must. There must not be any secrecy ever again among us. We are so few now."

And She is dead, Erma thought. *She whose name was a knowing. But I must not say that.*

"There's Tommy's ballsleeper," Justin said. "Better bring him along."

She squatted down to make a lap for her bundles, and picked up the ballsleeper, putting him on top of the pile. "I've got him," she said.

She walked on quietly, thoughtfully. Had she need now to be careful of what she said, even to Justin? She had expected that all of them would accuse her and she dreaded their accusations. But when they did not, she thought she must surely accuse herself before Justin. And now she had the feeling that he would not allow it. But if she were not to be accused, not even allowed to accuse herself, then how could she be absolved?

She took a deep breath and adjusted her burden. Then she lengthened her stride so that she might, for a moment, where the path turned, be alone.

There was no absolution. No amount of accusation, or absence of it, would alter this. There was no absolution and it had been cowardly of her to wish Justin to assume this burden. No one living wanted it.

I have to live with it, she thought. No one can take it away from me. No one can make it right. Because it wasn't right. It will always be there. *It is a part of me.*

Şince Erma had not been aware of the change in her posture

in the last two years she was not now aware of how her back was straightening, how her head was lifting. She had not known of the tentative qualities that her footsteps had assumed; she was not now aware of the firmness of her tread on the path or the lengthening of her stride.

The most valuable one among us is dead, and dead because of me, she thought. This is not knowledge that can be absolved or transferred or disguised or forgiven. It is not to be pitied; it is to be *carried*. From now on. Forever. Carried by me. Alone.

And so Erma Herrick was precipitated by the death of her friend—out of the realm of darkness and secrecy into the structures of open light. Thus did she embrace the time of her history and join herself with those who own themselves to be responsible for what they do and able to live with what they are. It is a small and quiet-spoken group in any world, made up of people like Justin Magnus, people like Joe Roberts. Usually they can recognize one another because of a certain distinguishing gravity which they possess in common. In these people, this quality is not the accompaniment of sadness, nor is it at war with gaiety. Rather, it is like the air they breathe.

CHAPTER EIGHT

E R M A had gone to the ovens and Justin to the woods, for the settlement was nearly out of bread and fuel. They would not be back for hours. The children were down for their naps and Arthur was asleep. The Room became terribly quiet and Gwendolyn was afraid. I must work, she thought. I will clean the place. But she dreaded to make the first noise in the quiet. Maybe Arthur would wake up soon and she could talk to him. Even Arthur would be better than no one. She would not be able to stand it if she didn't talk to someone. She put the kettle on to boil and sat down by the fire to wait. When it began to hiss the quiet grew less terrible. She could wake up Tommy, but he would want something. The fingers of one hand creased a fold in her skirt over and over. She pulled her chair closer to the fire. What should she do? What should she do? She looked over to Arthur to see if he might not be awake. What would she say to him? She could make tea for him and something to eat. That would please him.

Between Gwendolyn and the things she needed or wanted, there had, all her life, been a person: the person who got them for her. She had never asked herself, How will I do this? But always, Who will do it for me? Even the job she had held in the city near Drury had meant to her an employer who gave her money and not the work she did. The conception of one's facing the world directly, without this intervening figure, had actually never occurred to her. Also, she assumed that all other people in the world, including the intervening figures, functioned in this manner, since she knew of no other. Whatever she failed to achieve she accredited to her improper choice of the person to achieve it for her, or to her incorrect means of persuading the person. She was absolutely consistent in this. Just as if she had been born with an inability to see color, she had never seen herself directly in contact with her needs. She naturally assumed that her children would acquire their fulfillments through her. What they reached for, she handed to them. When they reached for her, she picked them up. They were easier to care for and control and less frightening than she had imagined they would be. She was not afraid of them, but they were sometimes afraid of her. This had been one of the great surprises of Gwendolyn's life.

And now that the person, the necessary intermediary, was gone, to whom should she turn? Kathy and Tommy and herself—she did not think, How will I take care of them? She thought, Who will take care of us now? Arthur? An invalid who was, perhaps, dying. Justin? Too old. He too might die, and she would be left helpless once again. Besides, he was not . . . he could not be counted on to be . . . manageable. She had really been afraid of him, ever since the night he had said they did not want to get out of the Green Kingdom. He might flatly refuse to help her. Then what would she do? Erma? Erma was more pliable than Justin, but then . . . Oh, why had not Arthur died instead of Joe?

She must get back to the World, that was it, where there was a wider choice. Someone safer than an invalid or an old man. She must take her children to safety, away from this place of murderous beasts and terrible loneliness. But how would they live in the World, until she found another Joe? Tommy stirred in his sleep and she went over to look at him. He was too small to dig a tunnel. Who would dig the tunnel for her?

Joe had promised her that he was digging a tunnel. Why did he die before he finished it? But why there, in that place? It did not seem to her the cave was a logical place for a tunnel. The emeralds! She felt under her clothing, where she had them tied around her waist. Since she had taken them from Joe's pocket, she had scarcely thought of them.

With emeralds, she could get anything she needed in the World. Even if she had to bide her time until the wall opened again. They would be rich in the World. *Rich.* And there must be more, many more emeralds here. She would take all she could carry, all the children could carry, and she would never tell. She would use only one at a time and sell each in a different place. Then, when Tommy was grown, she would tell him where they were and he could come back, if they needed more. She leaned back in the chair and closed her eyes and sighed with relief. They were rich. She had never put her faith in a *thing* to get things

before and, since things had never disappointed her, as had people, she was inclined to feel overoptimistic. If you have emeralds,
she thought, you don't need people.

But if Arthur was with Joe, then Arthur must know about
the emeralds. Joe said he hadn't told anyone that night. But he
was probably lying. Or maybe he only told Arthur later. He had
always told Arthur everything in Drury; it used to make her
furious. Arthur knew about the emeralds; she felt sure he knew.
Perhaps the others did, too. Perhaps she would have need of them
all before she could find the emeralds.

She got up and walked over to Arthur's bed chair. He was
sleeping. He knew. Of course, he knew. *And* he couldn't talk. She
walked quietly to the other end of The Room, deep in thought.
The loom was dusty and had been pushed back against the wall
since Kathy's birth. She had need of a loom now. Her hands
longed for the monotony of it to help her plan how she would go
about things. She got a cloth and began to dust the loom slowly,
carefully. All of them needed new clothes and they would be
pleased with her if she began to weave again. They would be
pleased.

She began to ready the loom, and, while part of her mind
was occupied with the cloth she would make and the construction
of the pattern, a plan ran around her brain. It was always easier
for her to have her hands busy when she was planning anything.
Quietly she began to hum. After a while she left the loom and
walked over by Arthur and sat down.

"Arthur," she said quietly.

He opened his eyes instantly and his lips began a movement.
He winced and then smiled and nodded to her.

"Oh, I hope you weren't asleep," she said. "I thought I saw
you move. Would you like a drink of water?"

He nodded.

"Are you hungry?"

He shook his head no.

"I thought we might have some tea together," she said. "I've
put the kettle on. It's awfully quiet with everybody gone, isn't it?
I suppose they won't be back until late. I've just been dusting the
loom. We all need clothes so badly and it would be good for my
nerves to have something to do."

Arthur looked over at the loom.

"I could make you something first, if you like. What would you like? Trousers? A jacket?"

Arthur pointed to his chest and shrugged his shoulders. After all, what did he need clothes for? He, least of all. But he did not want to seem uninterested. He knew that it was good for Gwendolyn to be occupied at the loom. And he, himself, enjoyed watching it and listening to it. It would be companionable, cheerful to have it going.

"The water's boiling," she said. "I'll be right back."

The bread was not fresh, it being the end of the supply. So she toasted it over the coals and spread it with butter. To the buttered toast she added a few sharples and some nuts.

"This is cozy," she said. "Are you warm enough?"

He nodded yes. And then he began to eat and to drink very slowly in small bites and sips. He did not eat any nuts, because he was afraid of coughing. He was really afraid of the toast, but he did not want Gwen to know it. He smiled at her. It was very nice of her to do this. It seemed to him that they forgot about him all the time.

"Arthur," Gwen said, "before they get back, I wanted to tell you something. They feel I oughtn't to talk about Joe. I get to crying and . . . well, I understand. I can't seem to realize it. It just doesn't seem real."

Arthur put out his hand and she put hers in it. She lowered her head and, obviously, controlled herself.

"But I wanted you to know, Arthur. I wanted to say it."

Arthur held her hand tight to encourage her. His throat began to ache with the words of sympathy he could not speak.

"I wanted you to know that I know you did all you could to save him, Arthur. We all know it. You were hurt so terribly yourself. Why, you might have been killed, too. Oh, dear, I've upset you. I didn't mean to, Arthur."

No. It was Joe who saved me, Arthur tried to say. *I was the one. I rushed in, like a fool. It was my fault. My fault.* Paper he must have. Ink. Make her understand.

"Oh, you want to write something? I'll get the paper. But, really, it's all right. I only wanted to thank you."

She began to get frightened. What if he got to coughing? What if he had a hemorrhage while they were gone? What would she do? She went for the pen and ink and paper, but her fingers were all thumbs. What if they came in and found him all excited like this? What would they think she had done?

"Here it is, Arthur. But, really, I don't think you should. Why don't you wait till later?"

He took the paper from her feverishly and dipped the pen. Of course he thought they would all have taken it for granted . . . The paper slipped and Gwen held it for him. To keep the wound from being pulled open, his right arm had been bound to his side so long that he could hardly move his fingers. Impatiently he transferred the pen to his left hand. Oh, but it was so much to tell, all with his left hand. He couldn't begin to do it. The effort to write brought sweat out all over his face. He began to breathe rapidly and finally, coughing and frightened, he lay back in his chair and let the paper fall from his hand.

Gwendolyn began to wipe his face, to cover him up, to fret over him. "Oh, never mind, Arthur. Try not to cough. It was too much for you. You rest. I'll sit here beside you and maybe you'll sleep. Try to sleep. Forget all about it. It's too terrible to remember. I know you did everything, everything you could."

There, on the floor, she made out the awkward scrawl: *Everything so confused. Can't remember how*

How could he tell them? How could he ever tell them, he thought, if he couldn't talk?

Gwen drank a cup of tea while Arthur lay quietly, dreading another spell of coughing. "There," she said. "You're all right again. I'm glad. You had me worried. We won't speak about anything sad again, I promise."

He smiled at her gratefully. Poor Gwen. It was good of her to sit here by him.

"I suppose Joe told you all about the emeralds," she said.

Arthur raised his eyebrows.

"The emeralds. You know, the ones Joe found. I suppose that's what you were doing in that cave."

Arthur shook his head no.

"But Joe told me you knew all about them, Arthur. It's all right. You can tell me."

Now he was angry. How could she keep pressing him? He didn't know anything about emeralds. Why didn't Erma come back and take her away?

"Listen, Arthur. There isn't much time before they get back. I have to know where those emeralds are. I'll make any kind of deal you say. But don't just keep shaking your head no, no, no. I won't stand for it any more."

She had lost all control of herself and Arthur was afraid of her. She grabbed hold of his shoulders and he winced with pain. She began to shake him. "You always took everything away from Joe in Drury but you're not going to get away with it here," she said. "You're not going to die on me too before I find out. I won't let you. You tell me. You can talk. I know you can talk. I've heard you groan in your sleep. You can't fool me. *Where are those emeralds?*"

Arthur began to struggle and cough. The pain became so severe, as the old wound tore open, that, mercifully, he fainted.

"Gwendolyn, what are you doing?" Erma said, dropping her armful of bread and running to her. "What's the matter with him?"

"What is it? What's wrong, Erma?" Justin said, coming in after her.

"Oh," Gwen said. "Oh, I had the most terrible time. He . . ." She threw herself in Justin's arms. "Thank God you're here," she said. "He was like a madman. Oh, he must be clear out of his mind."

"Get *back*, Gwen," Erma said, working over Arthur, chafing his hands. "Get out of the way."

"You should never have left me alone with him," Gwen said. "Oh, Justin, it was terrible. He was going to get up and go out. I tried . . . I tried to hold him."

Now he was coming around and Erma knelt down to take his pulse, anxiously watching his face.

"He kept saying something about emeralds," Gwen said to Justin. "Do *you* know anything about any emeralds?"

"No," Justin said. "I don't understand it. Come on. You'd better go sit down and calm yourself."

"Do *you* know anything about any emeralds, Erma?"

"No, Gwen. Be quiet. Can't you see he's broken his wound open again? Go get me some bandages. We'll have to bind him up again, Justin."

"I'll get the things ready," he said. "Gwen, bandages."

Bandages. She must get bandages now. She had to mind Erma, be nice to Erma, help Erma. They didn't know. They didn't know. She must move fast and do everything quick and fast.

"Arthur," Erma said, "do you know me? Oh, my poor dear."

"Why is the bread on the floor?" Tommy said, waking from his nap. "Can Tommy have some?"

"Erma dropped it," Gwen said, "because Arthur is sick. Mommie will pick the bread up and Tommy can put on his shoes and then we'll go and play so we won't make any noise and wake Arthur."

"Is Arthur sick again? Can he talk yet, Mommie?"

"Put your arm in your coat now, Tommy, and be quiet. Mommie'll talk to you out of doors."

"Can Tommy have some? Can Tommy have some bread?"

"Yes, yes. Be quiet."

"Well," Erma said, when Gwen had left The Room, "what do you make of it, Justin?"

"She's lying," Justin said. "But it won't do to press her. Only put her on her guard. We'd best just let it lie and hope when Arthur is better again he can tell us what happened."

"But she said he talked. Do you suppose he did, Justin?"

"Don't know. When I pressed her, she said she *thought* he said something like 'emeralds.' She couldn't be sure. You know, he does make sounds in his sleep."

"I can't understand it," Erma said. "I just can't understand it."

"Don't try. He's alive; that's the main thing. He'll tell us in time if he remembers. If he doesn't, it'll just have to be a mystery, that's all."

"But he's been so quiet, so patient. He's so weak. I can't believe she had a struggle with him."

"Feverish patients are sometimes very strong, Erma. We've no idea what we're dealing with there. Something must have moved from the wound to his vocal cords. It could be a piece of bone, perhaps. It could be almost anything: a rock, dirt, a leather button pushed into the wound. All we can do is wait."

"And watch Gwen," Erma said. "He's afraid of her. He heard her voice and shook all over. If we can't ever leave them alone together, Justin, how can we possibly manage?"

"We can't do a thing tonight," Justin said. "I don't think that he really lost much blood. We'll have to be on our guard for a while. Here, I'll finish cleaning up. You need to rest. Lie down. If Arthur wakes up, I'll call you. I promise."

"Oh, I am tired, Justin. I'm just now beginning to shake

from the shock of it. Did somebody pick the bread up off the floor?"

"Yes, and it's very good, too. Why don't you have a piece of it with some tea?"

Erma washed her hands and sank down at the table, suffering herself to be waited on. "I don't know why you should have to clean up all that mess, Justin, after cutting wood all day. Did you get a lot?"

"Enough for a while. It helps to have us all in one place."

"I wish I had enough bandages so we could just throw those away," Erma said. "But we're so short."

"I see Gwen has been at the loom," Justin said. "That would ease things a good deal, if she had something to busy herself with. Now, can't you lie down, Erma?"

"Oh, no, Justin. The tea helped a lot. That was what I needed. I ought to get dinner now."

"Our widow can get dinner when she returns," Justin said.

"Oh, she'll be too much upset, Justin. Didn't you hear her say we should never have left her alone with Arthur?"

"She will get dinner this night," Justin said, "or she will go hungry."

"Oh, Justin, you mustn't be too hard on her. Maybe it's true, what she said. Maybe he did—"

"That's so," Justin said. "It is possible that he had a sudden fever, a delirium. However, she will get dinner, or we will all eat bread."

"But I couldn't sleep now, Justin. I feel as though I could never sleep again."

"Go sit by Arthur, then, and stay off your feet. I'll tell you what. I'll go up to my place and get my flute. Would you like that tonight, after dinner? Maybe it will keep the children quieter."

"That would be good, Justin. I wish you could play 'The Fulcrum' so I could pay close attention to something and get my mind off Gwen."

"Ah, not 'The Fulcrum,' my dear. You really can't play 'The Fulcrum' on a flute."

"Just think, Justin, I've never even seen the score. It is finished. *The Green Kingdom* is finished and I've never even seen the end of it."

He transferred the tub of bandages to the fire to boil. Then he went over to Erma and put his hand on her head.

"It will keep," he said. "It will wait."

Tommy and Gwen tiptoed into the room elaborately, and Tommy came over and stood between Erma's knees. "We got firstfruits for dinner," he said.

"How is Arthur?" Gwen asked.

"Asleep," Erma said. "Better."

"I'm so glad. Now I'll get dinner so you can rest, Erma. I know you've had a shock. I hope Kathy doesn't wake up and start crying."

"I see you started to work at the loom," Erma said.

"Yes. It would be good for my nerves. And besides, everybody needs new things. I'll make you something beautiful, Erma. I'll make you a warm robe, first thing."

*

Gradually the sense of living always in a state of emergency lessened, and the thought of catastrophe constantly impending gave way to the next chore. Arthur's wound slowly mended and his needs came to be part of the daily schedule, fitting into the changes dictated by the growing children. Gwendolyn, Justin, and Erma managed to do what was necessary and, when necessary, to stay out of one another's way. The community life in The Room settled into a pattern. A few moments of pleasant comradeship graced it now and then; what gaiety or surprises there were came from the children. There were no great moments, no great joys, but this was accepted by all as the necessary price that there were no great emergencies and no tragedies, either. Essentially The Room, the community life, was a means of staying alive. It promised tomorrow and nothing else. In the days the people worked until they were tired. At night, generally, they slept. Except for Arthur, of course, who often lay awake in the night, half sitting.

Today he had walked out of doors for the first time. He was very tired; yet he could not sleep. Erma lay so close to him that he could reach out and touch her. How strong she is, he thought. How _young_ she is. She has taken Joe's place here. Soon, she had promised him, they would go back to their own place, and there would be just the two of them again. He would be glad to go. The Room had become so much like Gwendolyn's house gradually, it seemed to Arthur, that it was no longer the old place. And now that Kathy had begun to walk, it seemed to him that there was confusion everywhere. He did love Kathy, loved to watch her delicate, questioning steps. But then an invalid really shouldn't be around children. He thought of himself as an invalid now, easily and without question.

Yes, he would be glad to go back to their own house as soon as Erma could manage it. He was never comfortable around Gwen. He supposed she was still embarrassed over that time she had gone to pieces soon after Joe died. He never had figured that one out, and probably he never would. He supposed *they* had taken care of it—whatever it was. *They* had saved his life, coming in time. Erma had said she would tell him all about the cave and any other things he wanted to know when they were home. It seemed so long ago. Once he had been full of questions, but now, now he could hardly remember what it was he wanted to know.

The ballsleeper ran across the room and hopped up onto Arthur's bed. He let it settle and then he petted it gently. It was welcome company in the long nights, and usually it came to him when he was awake. He felt it curl itself into a ball under his hand, felt the warmth of it gradually sink through the blankets. He could not remember that he had ever had a pet of his own. That seemed very odd to him. Almost all boys did have pets. Erma had always had pets, she said, even before he knew her. Probably when he was a boy they could not afford the extra food for a pet and that was why. Here there was plenty of food.

Suddenly he remembered what it was like to be an invalid in the world he had left. Not able to work all this time, he would surely be in a charity hospital—in a ward—and Erma would come on Sundays to see him. But on the other hand, they might have been able to save his voice. And they would have treated his wounds properly so that he would not be bent over to one side and always, after any movement, in pain.

He put his hand on his throat. How was it possible that the horn going into his lung had injured his voice? There had never been a wound on his throat. He had asked himself this a thousand times. When the pain left, they had thought he would be able to speak again, but he had not. He had puzzled himself to exhaustion over all the possible explanations he could think of. From the site of the wound to his vocal cords must surely be a distance of four or five inches. If the horn had gone in that far, they would never have been able to get it loose from him. The twisted thing would have torn him apart.

The fire leapt up in a pointed wave of flame and the ballsleeper stirred. Arthur put his hand on it to soothe it. Then he pulled himself more upright. Something seemed to excite him, make him lean forward.

How slight a shift is the crucial one that sometimes brings into focus the pondering of many nights' thoughts. In the shadows against which men pit their listening minds there wait, so tantalizingly, the hulking shapes of the almost-known, the sensed, the not-quite understood. They wait their time of ripening and laugh to see how men give magic credit to some coincidence and say it summoned them to their giant's order. *And then one day I was watching a scrap of paper in the wind,* men say. *It came to me,* they say. *So simple a thing. An apple fell. My mother's kettle,* they say. *It seemed so easy, so clear. I was petting a ballsleeper.* The hulking shapes move ponderously and confidently out of the shadows toward order when they are ready, and have their quiet joke.

At the base of the ballsleeper's neck Arthur's questioning fingers idly traced the cowlick's path in the fur and his fingers remembered the tendrils of the chokevines. His fingers remembered the pointed, corkscrew seeds of the yearsenday bombs and the pattern of the centaur-snail's tail that used to ornament the loaves of bread. His fingers remembered whirlpools. In the air above the animal his fingers traced, as he had so many times imagined, the tortured, winding path that his wound must have described at the bidding of the feathermane's horn.

He reached down excitedly and touched Erma.

"Yes?" she said, sitting up. "What is it, Arthur?"

He leaned toward her and put his hand under her chin. He smiled at her and winked. Then he reached for the pad of paper and pen he kept fastened to his bed chair. She could feel the excitement in him and, though he smiled and seemed happy, she was alarmed. He was usually in pain when he woke her in the night, or thirsty. Tired and sometimes petulant, but not like this. She got up on her knees so that she could turn the writing pad to the firelight. He would be so impatient if she could not make it out. Sometimes when he was in pain the message was so scrawled that she had to take the pad loose and carry it over to the fire or else bring a light. And this always awakened Justin.

But Arthur had meant there to be no doubt about this message. There was only one way, he believed, that he could have walked for thirty-nine days on the river, upstream, without crossing near the settlement. On the pad he had printed in big letters: THE RIVER IS SPIRAL.

He watched her face as she looked up at him. "Why, I suppose it is," she said. "Isn't it strange that we didn't know that before?"

Arthur was nodding his head in excitement. He began to hit his fist on the arm of the chair, so difficult did he find it not to be able to release his excitement in speech. The river was spiral. That was its structure. His mind had wanted to tell him, that's why he had been kept awake. He had been close to it before, one night when they were talking about the structure of the third movement of Justin's symphony. How was it his feet hadn't known right on the river bank itself?

He was very happy. Erma reached up and kissed him. Tears of happiness shown in his eyes. Now he could sleep. He closed his eyes and leaned back, keeping hold of Erma's hand. Now, even, he could die. Because he knew the structure of the river; he knew the shape of the thing he loved.

Erma felt the happiness in the thin hand and waited for its relaxation. The theme of "The Time of History" came to her and she let it sing in her mind. Tomorrow she would tell Justin that the river was spiral. I don't believe Arthur ever had a delirium the way Gwen said, she thought. I don't believe he spoke. If he could possibly speak, this is what he would have said, that the river is spiral.

But now was not the time to bring up that old scene with Gwen to satisfy her curiosity, she knew. Gwen was absolutely under Justin's control, and it had best be left alone. Erma had, that day, been to her old house and seen the dirt and disorder there. But, more seriously, she had noted the chokevines, penetrating the line where floor joined wall. What a job it would be! And it would mean more work for Justin, to have an extra wood supply. But she had promised Arthur. Arthur wanted to go home. And here she could never tell him all the things she owed him.

"It is not a prehistoric cave," she would say. "Not something I found. Not the way you think, Arthur. I made it."

She would tell him how she made it and, as well as she knew, why. Whatever he asked, she must answer. Yes, they would go back to their own place and she would save their house from the chokevines. Maybe Tommy could come there to play without Gwendolyn's constant nagging. She loosened her hand from

Arthur's and lay down again to sleep. Arthur would live now, there was no doubt about it. Six of them were alive. And she and Justin had done it together. The worst of it was over.

She heard the little footsteps and made a place beside her for Tommy. He crawled into her bed, as he so often did, and lay in the warm circle of her arms. "I want Joe," he said.

He would wake Arthur, Erma knew, because when it started this way it wasn't made to disappear by warmth and silence. She got to her feet, picked up the child in her arms, and took him over by the hearth. There she set him on her knee and looked into his face.

"We'll sit here and talk," she said.

"Why did he go, Erma? Why did he go the World?"

"It was because of the way he was made, Tommy. He couldn't choose not to."

The boy leaned against her and put his thumb in his mouth and stared at the fire. "Is it lonely in the World, Erma?" he said.

Even I, Erma thought, even I know better than to tell a child of the loneliness that is to be found in the World.

"We miss Joe, don't we?" she said.

In the way that Erma was alerted for Tommy's footsteps, Justin was alerted for hers. He crossed his arms under his head, so that he could see better, and he lay there in the quiet room, watching Erma and Tommy against the firelight. Since Erma had ceased going to the cave she let her hair fall loose again about her shoulders and the firelight made it deeply alive. She wore a long, full gown, and yet the soft folds of it could not erase the angular concentration of her body as she bent her full attention on Tommy.

Justin had never cared for Madonnas in painting or in sculpture. The submissive faces, the somnolent postures had seemed to him a portrayal of self-hypnosis, complacency or, perhaps, infectious boredom, caught from the infants they contemplated. This is more the way he would have painted a madonna: with animation, with the most vital attention, sharing a conspiracy with a child in the middle of the night.

She is all right, he thought. She is herself again. Better than herself. Long had he waited for her. Longer yet would he wait. The tableau in the firelight was blurring and becoming hazy before his eyes as sleep began to lay its hundred hands upon him. How pleasant it was to be able to fall asleep gradually while watching a tableau. The fact that Erma whispered to the child so that he could not hear what they said as he watched them, sillhouetted against the waving heat haze of the fire, lent to the quality of enchantment. So long had they all fallen asleep in the terrible state of vigilance for the emergency, or in the stupor of utter exhaustion, that the simple pleasures of peace and order had partaken of the exotic for them.

And now, for a while, they might have a little respite from emergency. Arthur was going to get well; he felt sure of it. And all the rest of them were well. They had made it through five years, all of them but Joe, and now they could begin to live again. Five years. What had happened to Max Staats in five years? he wondered. There was no reason to believe that anything had happened to Max. After all, Justin thought, it is really not so long, in the World's time, five years. The change in Max's life would probably be imperceptible. No doubt he was still teaching at the university, still living in the same house, working at the same huge desk, sleeping in the same bed. Justin smiled in the darkness to think how his own bed would look to Max Staats. He thought of the long discussions he had not only heard in the World but had partaken of, about the fabrication and construction of mattresses. Not to mention my clothes, he thought, or my beard. He thought of the pleasure it would be to appear, right now, just as he was, at Max Staats's door and to walk across the room slowly and see Max peering behind his thick lenses, his mouth open, half rising from his desk.

Justin remembered carpets and rugs, the feel of them, their colors, their designs. He remembered the carpet in his grandmother's house that bore the geometrical record of the sun. He thought of the sun and of how, in the World, you could feel it, if you moved in and out of shadows. He thought with wonder of the sharpness of shadows.

And at last he slept, this giant of a man, in The Room which he had helped to build. Here in this place, on one of the last nights of their communal living, which they had chosen because of their emergencies, slept also the woman he waited for, the invalid, the widow, the two children. Here they lay resting, unvigilant after their last emergency and vulnerable to the next. If there should be one among them to see that food for the future is not really progress, that tomorrow's warmth is not the same as the mind's assessment, he should awake now.

Now, before the crested chichimingo calls.

They had discovered and explored. They had named the birds and the fruits and the fish and the trees and the animals. The structure of the river was known to them, and from it, perhaps, the limits of their land could be forecast. They knew what could be used for their future; they knew how to store grain and wood, how to preserve meat and how to insure milk and cheese supplies. They knew the seasons of flowering and of fruitfulness and how to alleviate pain and keep themselves clean and how to succor conviviality. They knew some of their enemies: the howlers, the chokevine, the dampness. They knew the value of festivities. They marked the children's birthdays; they took account of their own milestones. The finding of tobacco they commemorated, the day of discovery and the day that Joe died. And all these things they recorded.

These things are, perhaps, a little more than being cast off the treadmill; but only a very little. And, after all, they are the plans that insects can make. They are very nearly the same as the clusternuts hoarded by the ballsleeper; they are not really what the minds of men are for. The future was, for men at least, surely meant to be something other than a stored bin.

You who lie resting, as well you deserve to rest, without pain and without fresh grief, here, among the things you made for your use and comfort and pleasure, if there is one of you who could awake now, this is surely the moment.

Quickly, before the crested chichimingo calls.

Before the day lulls you with living as it does the insects and the furred mammals, the birds, the trees. There should be a difference, an essential difference, between them and you. *Quickly, quickly.*

Very slowly the fire in the room died down to that critical point beyond which its light would no longer distinguish the walls that separated the people inside from the darkness outside. In that darkness, high in the lacetree, a crested chichimingo stretched itself and felt in its throat how it would feel to call when the right moment should come.

Even with his new and expanding interest in geology, Max Staats still devoted one evening a week, as he had for many years, to the study of his journals of mathematics. As he scanned their tables of contents, trying to get a comprehensive current picture, he sighed and shook his head. The same names. The same OLD names. Where were all the young men? Where were the young men who should be speaking here from the short, golden original time that is now and then given to them? He didn't need to ask; he knew. They were buried in secret projects, out of communication even with one another and often, he felt sure, duplicating one another's work. In all his years of teaching he had been privileged to have two really original students, and their names, too, were buried. One of them, sending to Max for a character reference, had at least cleared up the mystery of why Max could no longer reach Drury on the telephone. What had once been Drury was now a gigantic secret project behind a high, locked wall. The town itself had been moved to a distance and renamed.

But aside from the two truly original ones, there were the excellent and the very good, the competent and the adequate ones. And not one, to his knowledge, had gone into teaching. It saddened Max very greatly, and he felt it a personal failure that he had not been able to imbue them with a sense of potentiality, had not been able to help them penetrate beyond a very limited sense of the future into assuming some responsibility for the future's future.

In his neat, small hand he made notes of the references applicable to the specialized bibliographies he kept current. Mrs. Johns, unchanged in the five years since Justin had disappeared, came into the room.

"There's a man at the door," she said. "Says he's a reporter. It's something about Mr. Magnus."

Now and then, through the years, Max had been through this. Usually, it was someone from one of the Sunday music sections, trying to glean reader interest with a new tidbit about Justin's disappearance. Justin's sons had been killed over and over, Edith's insanity had been scraped threadbare, and Max always did his polite best to see that the flurries were as short-lived as possible.

But this time it was different. This time the reporter brought news. In the great uranium boom, many unknown regions were now full of prospectors, geologists, and amateurs of all sorts. Two of these had stumbled onto Justin Magnus' abandoned automobile, and tomorrow's headlines would be shouting imaginary bandits and massacres.

Max took a short leave from the university and flew out to the scene. The car itself had been roped off from the curious who now milled about in large numbers (it had been a great time for old Fish-face; he had sold thousands of sandwiches and given rise to a score of false rumors), but the car had been picked absolutely clean of luggage or any other clue before the state police had arrived. The paint was gone from the license plates, but the registration slip, enclosed in plastic and fastened to the steering wheel, still gave out enough information for definite identification. It was Justin's car, all right; Max was satisfied of it, but nothing indicated whether Justin had been in it when it was abandoned at this spot. The state police seemed confident that if there were a hastily dug, shallow grave anywhere near, it was sure to be found soon, for the mountains were crawling with amateur prospectors.

These Max listened to, wherever he found them in little

groups. He was listening for tales of the old prospectors, tales
of earthquakes, volcanoes, of any kind of upheaval or legend. But
he listened in vain. He did hear, at last, of the Indians and the
mountain fever, and he decided that if they had had the
knowledge he wanted, it had been burned with them. He
answered the questions the police asked, he identified the car,
and he kept his own counsel. On the last day he did a little
climbing on his own, and in a pocket of solitude he cast his silent
questions at the mountain and knew his reluctance to leave the
place. He had only to have the slightest accident, to trip on a
stone, to lose or break his glasses. Then he would be helpless.
He had a sudden comic picture of himself prepared for exploration
in the wilderness, a solitary figure with twenty-five pairs of
glasses fastened to his clothing and his body in all strategic
places.

He returned to the abandoned car, took his leave of the state
police, went to the airport and returned to the university. To all
who spoke to him of Justin Magnus he agreed, yes, it was a
very sad thing. But he did not believe it; he did not have the
conviction. He saw Justin's house sold for taxes and he held his
own counsel. For in all the lies and babbling that old Fish-face
had done about Justin, once he had learned he was famous, he
was firm on one point and that was that there had been five
of them. And if there were five of them . . .

This was all Max had to go on, and yet it gave him pleasure.
Now again, in the huge room in the evenings, he could get out
the recordings of Justin's music and let the sound swell about him
without that terrible sense of loss. Why not, if it gave him
pleasure, IF THERE WERE FIVE OF THEM, why not hope his friend
still lived? Wasn't history full of little bands of people going
into the wilderness? And how had they fared?

It was a subject he knew almost nothing of, but once he had
started on it it seemed that history was full of nothing else.
An entire shelf of the old journals of mathematics had to be
carted to the attic to make room for the new studies, for the

material seemed endless, and though Max ended each volume in
a state of rage, he could not stop, once he had started. Accustomed
to abstractions, he regrouped and refocused the unique powers
of his mind to study, in a way they had never been studied
before, the endless number of little bands of human beings: the
Shakers in New York, the followers of Dr. Keil in Oregon, the
Icarians in Illinois, the Rappites and, later, Robert Owen's
New Harmony in Indiana, the Promised Land of Saba, the Welsh
in Patagonia, and more, and more.

Always the dream. Always. And always, too (and this is
what made his rage), the terrible limitations put upon it by
the dreamers themselves. It was as though there were some
universal law that any man who had a vision must be compelled
to incorporate in it the seed of its own death. It was not the
obvious ones—those who had implanted the rule of celibacy
right from the beginning, thus insuring their own end—but
the ones who could not see the celibacy of the mind, that so
enraged him. And yet, in a way, it brought him a little comfort
for himself. For, if this were universal, or almost universal,
then he need not feel that he alone carried the blame for what
had happened to his students. It was not his alone, then, the
fault that whenever variation promised, new limits to variation
threatened.

But of all the groups, the settlers, the colonists, the
eternal sporadic risings and movings of the dreamers who would
not prepare, who would not learn from the history of others,
who would not (it seemed even deliberately) serve potentiality,
but always some smaller goal—of all of them, none had been
so small as five.

Had they, then, any chance?

4. The Fulcrum

SOUNDLESSLY Erma Herrick stepped onto the veranda and looked out on the early wessun quiet to see if Tommy were coming for breakfast. The soft mists were devouring themselves and the bath-dampness left on Erma's skin caused her to shiver pleasantly. By her hand, where it leaned on the log railing, the soft, furred leaves of a firstfruit vine asserted themselves against the night's invisibility. Their gray-blue color coincided in her awareness with the odor of smoke from the breakfast fire.

Smoky color, she thought. I must remember to tell Tommy about the smoky colors and the big department stores in autumn and how the windows had yards of fabrics tossed in folds to show the new season's colors and of how the women would be full of a wanting of this newness and of getting ready for something. Tommy was so eager to know about the World now, so full of questions all the time. "For what?" he would ask. "What were they getting ready for?" And how would she answer, for she could only remember the feeling of it? "Oh, for winter," she would say. "They were getting ready for winter." She had already told him about winter, about snow. Getting ready for the death of the vegetation. Was it for this that the World's women needed new clothes and had inside their bodies an excitement to feel vanity reborn after the long summer, to anticipate being desirable, being loved and warm in a snug place?

It would be too difficult to explain that it was somehow mysteriously exciting to have death in the vegetation all around you. But then, of course, if she told him this, she must also tell him that those fine fabrics had not been available to her in the World, because of the money. Perhaps, when he was six, she would try again about the money, but it was altogether too difficult for a five-year-old boy who had been born in the Green Kingdom. She would remember forever her utter defeat at his questions:

"Wasn't there any food at all, Erma?" "Well, why didn't you just go there and take it?" "How could they keep you from getting it?"

She saw a piece of the landscape detach itself, taking on a familiar jogging movement of Tommy astride the feathermane, and she went in to stir the porridge. Circling the wooden spoon through the thick coils of porridge, she thought of how it was Tommy, really, and not just her memory, who had given her the smoky-blue color; for, like the wooden spoon in the porridge, he had broken the even surface of her seeing and made it full of change and variety. Justin thought that, being born here, Tommy did not see the Green Kingdom the way the rest of them did. Erma tried to remember how it had looked in the beginning, all green, of a sameness. Then, little by little, they had seen the blue-greens, the yellow-greens, the gray-greens and the forest-greens. But Tommy, when he was first talking and learning his colors, would go into a very fury when they called two different shades the same name, and finally Justin had said he believed the shades were distinct colors to Tommy.

Knowledge destroys uniformity. Intimate living experience begets variety, creates change. To know anything, alive or dead, intimately, is to trade its wholeness for a constantly changing variety. Who welcomes this exchange creates adventure; who retreats from it fears life; who denies it asserts death. The threads of the same cloth are not alike to the microscope, and even the nothingness inside a bubble is different at the center from what it is on its walls.

Erma ladled the porridge into two wooden bowls and set them on the hearth, and then she went into the shed for a skin of cream. Nothing you know will stay still, she thought, and so, if you don't want things to change, you have to keep from knowing them. She took the bowls out onto the veranda as soon as she heard the feathermane's hoofs, and, when she had put the things down, she waved to the boy who was riding toward her with one of his hands caught in the animal's mane for hold.

"Perhaps," Justin had said about Tommy's color naming, "the spectrum is within us and we make it of whatever we have."

"How bewildering, then, would the World's spectrum be to Tommy," she had said, "if he can make all this out of green."

"But still," Justin had said, laughing at her difficulties, "still not so bewildering as money and poverty."

"You, Justin," she had said then, "you're going to get the task of telling him about war. That I won't even attempt."

She could remember it so clearly, how Justin had stopped laughing, looked very thoughtful, and then said, "No, my dear. War he would find quite easy to understand. Not nearly so difficult as money and poverty." She supposed he was right. He had been right about the boy's having a feathermane to ride. She had not thought Gwen would accept the sight of the boy riding one of the same animals by which his father had been killed. Yet it was Gwen who had made it into a pony. Justin was much more often right about Gwen than she was. It would be Justin she would tell about remembering the fall colors and about getting ready for the winter, instead of Tommy. She had to keep remembering that Tommy did not want her remembered emotions; he wanted to know about the *things* in the World.

They were exactly right for each other now, the boy and the animal. In another year or two the boy would be too large. "And what will he ride then?" Erma had asked. But Justin had answered, "He'll make himself an airplane, no doubt. I wouldn't worry about it if I were you." Now she watched Tommy slide effortlessly off the animal's back and come to sit by her.

"How is your pony today?" she asked, pouring the thick cream over his porridge and handing him the bowl.

The feathermane nudged at Tommy's elbow and the boy moved aside to protect his porridge. "Go away, Pony," he said. "Go graze yourself."

His wrestling with the World's idiom was a constant delight to Erma. Now that she saw he was beginning to eat, she left him to go into the house.

"I'm going to get my tea," she said. "Watch my porridge for me, will you?"

She could tell from the sound of the house that Arthur was still asleep, and she took her tea out and sat down again by the boy, glad to share this time with him alone.

"Erma," he said, "what is vaccination? You get it when you go to school, I think."

When she had done the best she could with it, he asked, "Do ponies have it?"

"I think so," she said. "But for different things. Not the same diseases."

So much did she cling to the child's love that she had never found the courage to tell him that ponies had not been a part of her life in the World.

"Yes," Tommy said. "That's what she said, too."

Erma blushed and looked into her teacup. She had never learned how to avoid these traps he set for her or how to handle the discovery of them. He often had good reason to verify the things Gwen told him and he had yet to learn any reason why he should not.

"Was Kathy awake when you left?" Erma asked.

"She crawled into bed with Mamma," he said.

And Mamma? she longed to ask, but could not. How glad she would be when Kathy, too, was big enough to come to her for breakfast on the mornings when Gwen could not get up.

"The baby can get Mamma awake," he said. "She pulls her hair and cries. She keeps at it till she wakes her. Erma, I lost my ballsleeper."

"Oh, Tommy, that's too bad. I haven't seen him this morning. Did you have him last night?"

"No, not last night, either. I can't find him any place."

The ballsleeper represented a series of three pets that had blended into one in the boy's mind. It seemed to him that he had always had the same one. But now, Erma realized, now that he was five, it was different. Almost certainly the animal was dead as the others had been.

"I'll help you hunt for him," she said, "a little later."

It was not starting out well, this day—the ballsleeper probably dead, Gwen with a hang-over, and Arthur not up yet.

Tommy had finished his breakfast and was restless. "Shall I go see did Justin make his breakfast yet?"

"Yes, do that," Erma said. "Why don't you ride your pony over very quietly and, if Justin's awake, tell him we have porridge ready if he'd like some. You'll remember now!" she called as the boy jumped astride the feathermane. "Remember to be very quiet."

He leaned back and waved to her. "Justin doesn't care," he said. "Not even if you jump right on his stomach."

"Oh, Tommy," she said.

But the boy was gone. The ground mists had risen and she knew that soon they must find the ballsleeper. Perhaps, if Justin would help, they might be able to get it buried without the boy's knowing. But Justin would say that wasn't right, she knew. Justin would say that Joe wouldn't have shielded the child from death. Erma could hear the mossbacks bawling and she hoped fervently that Arthur would feel up to doing the milking when he woke up, so that she could start right away to hunt for the ballsleeper before the beetles found it.

Justin knew that when Tommy was sent to ask him to breakfast it meant, in the private language he and Erma had, that Erma thought he should look in on Gwen in The Room to see if Kathy needed care. When Erma went herself it always made things worse. Justin did not think he was much better at it. The one who could get Gwen on her feet the quickest was Arthur. Justin sat up in bed and ran his hands through his thick, gray hair. "All right," he said to Tommy, "tell her I'm on my way."

But Tommy did not leave the bedside nor, Justin realized, had he jumped on the bed or pretended to pull him out of it or played any of their other games. He shook his head and looked at Tommy. Reaching out for him, he pulled him between his knees and held him there. "Now," he said, "what's the matter with you?"

"I lost my ballsleeper."

"Oh," Justin said. "Well, we'll have to see where he's got himself to."

He walked past the boy and into the next room, where he stepped down into the hot spring bath. He splashed the water all over himself, drenched his head with much snorting, and jumped out, shaking the water from himself. Tommy handed him his towel gravely. He had not laughed at the snorting as he usually did.

"I couldn't find it last night, either," he said. "Do you think a howler got him? Do you think anything happened to him?"

Justin pulled on his trousers, rubbed his head with his towel, and reached for his pipe and tobacco. "Don't know, Tom," he said. "We can't know till we find him, can we? Fetch my jacket, will you, while I get my pipe lit? Now we're off. Did you look by the ovens?"

"No."

"Well, we had a fire yesterday. Maybe he got cold and decided to sleep by the ovens. You go up and see while I have breakfast with Erma, and then you come back and tell me."

Tommy was near tears, and Justin lifted him up and carried

him out the door. "I see you brought Pony," he said. "Well, it will be no time until you're over at the ovens and back again, then. If the ballsleeper isn't there, then we'll go . . . oh, I don't know. We'll go all over," he said. "We'll find him."

He waited until the boy had turned off toward the ovens, and then he put his pipe in his mouth and set off for The Room. It was still called The Room, though Gwendolyn and her children had taken it over completely and there had never been the faintest hope, really, that she would return to her old house. So far as Justin knew, she had never gone back, for the place was overgrown with chokevines. Some day the woodborers would have turned it all to powder.

Damn the woman, he thought. If everything was quiet when he got to The Room, he'd go have his breakfast first.

Erma, sitting alone on the veranda, lifted the cup of hot tea to her mouth and felt the trembling in her hand. For this torment she lived. To preserve this ache in her loins she would have fought above all other things. It seemed to her now that here in the Green Kingdom in their first years she had moved about without it, unaware of it, except in rare flashes. Now it was with her always, as though all senses had been sacrificed to it and all nourishment converted to the hairs of her skin that they might become antennae of fiery awareness for the nearness of Justin Magnus. One area only of her body, and the matching part of her brain, were excluded. These were her shoulder blades and a small knot in her spine where lived the awareness of Arthur's needs. Now these were devoted to pressing back upon the house. These were concentrated in delaying Arthur's awakening with its early-morning cough and gasping and need. All else pressed forward for the first glimpse of Justin. She was aware of the dichotomy as though a wedge had been driven vertically through her. She was aware of how the wedge intensified the torment. Yet her whole life was devoted to the torment, to the savoring of it, the prolonging of it, the control of it, and sometimes, for the sake of self-preservation, the escape from it.

Oh, why had they built their houses so that one could not be seen from the other? She cursed this fact again now, having to wait until Justin should come to the turn in the path, as on sleepless nights she cursed it. It seemed to her that if only she could walk out and look over toward his door, see his light at night, it would ease her.

"I did it deliberately," Justin had said. "How else do you think I could have endured it?"

For of course, in those days, not knowing, she had flaunted her domesticity before him. In those days she had been Arthur Herrick's wife and—and had she really not known? She could not remember what it had been like to live without this torment, before this torment. Nor was she able to believe in any life without it. Though Justin was. Justin believed in easing it, ending it. Soon again, now, he would press her to action, to speaking. "Not yet," she had said last time. "Not yet."

Then he was there, in sight, at the turn of the path, carrying the baby in his arms. Erma waved to him and, on the tempo of the torment, went swiftly, soundlessly, into the house to get the breakfast ready. With the small, unelectrified portion of her back she continued to press against the fact of Arthur's awakening, although it told her that there had been a stir of the bedding, the first formless cry of demand.

Reaching to take the baby from Justin, she felt the streak of fire from his touch on her left arm. The outside of her right little finger came alive when it grazed the hairs of his wrist. These, and a small area on the inside of her left knee where she had leaned against him for support, seemed all that was alive of her. And yet those places were sufficient to hold the squirming baby; they were sufficient for her movement across the few steps to the veranda.

"Naked, mad, and hungry," Justin said. "She's all yours."

"There's your tea," Erma said, nodding toward the cup while she wrapped the baby in a clean blanket. "Here, Kathy. Here's your milk." She kissed the child and patted her and held the cup for her and then looked into Justin's eyes.

"Gwen?" she said.

"Out cold," he said. "A real stupor. The baby's been up quite some time, I'd say, from the litter about. It's going to be a rough awakening. Arthur will be able to go over?"

Now she was holding the porridge bowl and suffering the child's awkwardness with the spoon. "I don't know yet," she said. "He's still asleep."

"You've seen the boy?" Justin said.

"Yes. It's too bad. I'm afraid the ballsleeper's dead."

"I sent him to look by the ovens," Justin said. "When he comes back, I'll go with him to hunt."

"Oh, good. I promised to, but—" she looked at Kathy—"it doesn't seem likely."

The first coughing came from the house, and Erma looked at Justin, listening with a diagnostic ear for the sound of it.

"Yes," Justin said, handing her his empty cup to be refilled, "it looks to be one hell of a day."

He looked at her and smiled, and involuntarily his lips moved in caress. He saw her listening for Arthur and struggling with the child, and, as always now, the rage filled him that she could not cast off her enslavement. But if he pressed her, she would say, "Not yet, Justin. Not yet." Part of his rage was the fear that, through his clamped teeth, he too would be tempted to ask for her pity. Christ, did she never think of how little time *he* had left? Surely he could not live forever. Then he relaxed his jaw. No, she did not think of it. He did not seem to her a dying man that one must be in a hurry to love or miss loving altogether. And he was glad of it.

"I'll do the milking," he said, "before I go off with Tommy. Don't worry about it."

"Thanks," she said. "Ouch, Kathy! What are you doing, you rascal?"

Kathy was pulling at Erma's jacket. She had pulled at the waist of it, tried unsuccessfully to unbutton it, and then had started to explore under the skirt. "Emeralds," she said. "Want emeralds. Kathy wants emeralds."

Erma had just bent over to set the child down, so that she could go in to Arthur. Now she lifted her head and stared across the child at Justin. The shock of it, after all this time, brought such a confusion of memories and questions that neither Justin nor Erma could speak. They did not notice that Tommy had ridden up, slipped quietly off the feathermane and was suddenly slapping Kathy's hands.

"No, Kathy. No. Mamma will spank you. Mamma will whip you for that."

For what? Justin longed to ask. But no one could have heard him. Kathy, surprised, turned an angry face to Tommy and began to scream. Her sturdy, naked little body was all aggression and her beautiful dark eyes were full of rage. Erma picked her up and carried her into the house. There was no need to be quiet for Arthur now. "I'm coming, dear," she called to him. "I'm coming."

"Well, did you find your ballsleeper?" Justin asked.

Tommy turned away in embarrassment. Now they thought he was bad to hit Kathy. But . . . but it was so. He knew it was a very bad thing to mention the emeralds. He could not remember why. There in the misty recesses he knew something, but he could not say it.

Justin saw the boy squirming and saw the sweat come out on his upper lip. So there had been something to that scene between Gwendolyn and Arthur, then. No one had ever mentioned it. He shook himself. This was no time for speculation. "Well, Tommy," he said, "we'd better do the milking before we go off anywhere. Come on."

Tommy ran ahead toward the corral. He was glad to escape the mists of something . . . something. Even the loss of his ball-sleeper was better to think of.

"Do mossbacks get vaccination, too?" he asked. "Do they, Justin?"

*

Gwendolyn lay on her side, her head buried in her arms, her back to the room. The curve of her back was contained in a huge, gray shell that extended in an arc from the floor to the ceiling. The gray shell, thick and murky, and made of clouds, waited hovering for Gwendolyn's body to touch it. It was made of her dread of the morning. Through her thin dreams Gwendolyn felt it there and knew that she had only to touch it by an aimless movement to make it collapse about her, its grayness engulfing her. By the slowest contraction of her muscles she made herself smaller, further from the shell. She was dreaming of Kathy. But instantly Kathy turned into her baby sister, who was lost. She ran crying to her mother. "Mamma, the baby is lost." But her mother said to her, "That is not for little girls to worry about. Papa and I will worry about it. Now you must change out of your school clothes and put on your play clothes."

It was too silent on the other side of the gray shell. Too silent. And a fury seized Gwendolyn against Tommy. Where was he? Why did he not take care of Kathy? He was big enough to take care of her for five minutes in the morning. No one helped her. She was so tired. Just one morning you would think . . . Oh, damn them, damn them all.

She jerked one arm angrily and touched the gray shell. It

fell like fog about her, clinging to her, and she began to cry. Through her tears she saw Arthur, quietly straightening up the havoc that Kathy had made. He brought her a cup of hot tea. Well, that was a break, anyway. Not to have Erma looking at her with her supercilious air, or Justin seeing the mess in the place. At least Arthur couldn't *say* anything to her.

"So I drank too much last night," she would have said to Erma or Justin if they had been here. "Who has a better right? What do you know about loneliness?" But now she didn't need to say anything because it was Arthur, and Arthur was sorry for her. He was the only one.

Arthur took out a pen and his pad of paper and wrote: *Cheer up, Gwen. It's only three and a half more years.*

"Only?" she said.

These yours? he wrote. He pulled the emeralds from his pocket.

She felt for the bag tied around her waist and knew its emptiness. She snatched the emeralds from him. This had never happened before.

"Where did you find them?"

Arthur pointed to the floor by the table.

Kathy! What a stupor she must have been in if Kathy could get that bag open without waking her. Oh, the brat. The little brat. And now Arthur knew! Her face colored at the memory of how she had tried to force him to tell her about the emeralds. Had he forgotten? She stole a look at him but no anger showed on his face. He was a sly one. She could never tell what he was thinking. She would have to be careful.

The shock of finding the leather bag empty had momentarily dispelled the gray fog, and she drank her tea hurriedly and handed Arthur the empty cup to be refilled. "Thanks," she said. "Arthur, why do you do this? Why do you help me like this?"

Why not? he wrote.

Well, that was Arthur for you. He could have written *sorry for you* or . . . or . . . oh, almost anything. But not Arthur. He wouldn't give her the satisfaction. Now he turned and left her, and, while he was gone, she restored the emeralds to the bag around her waist. He came back with her hairbrush and handed it to her. She threw it on the floor and buried herself in the bedcovers. "Oh, what's the use? What's the use?" she cried.

She could hear Arthur pouring the beer and she stopped crying and sat up. He handed her a note.

No use, it said. *Let's have a beer.*

There was this about Arthur. He would drink with you if you had to have a little in the morning. Not sit there and stare you in the face. Now she would be all right. Just one cup of beer to settle things. She reached out to retrieve the brush and began to brush her hair. They would never know, the others. She'd have a bath and get into a clean skirt, get her hair done up. Then she'd thank Erma for taking care of Kathy. They'd have a hard time accusing her of anything. "I couldn't sleep last night," she'd say.

A hurry began to insist inside Gwendolyn, a hurry to get the place in order before anyone came. It didn't matter about Arthur. But when the others came in for dinner she'd have to be able to convince them they were wrong. She'd clean the place up, have it sparkling. "I've got a surprise for dinner"—that's what she'd say to Erma. Not anything about Kathy at all. Just act surprised Kathy was there. And then be busy. Keep talking. A surprise for dinner. A party. "Let's have a party," she'd say. "Because I'm feeling so good." That was it.

When she was bathed and freshly dressed she found that Arthur had gone. She had counted on his being there, and finding the place empty put a damper on her plans for a moment. She poured herself another cup of beer and felt her hands getting steadier. She began to make up the bed and set the place to rights in a frenzy of activity. She stopped in sudden hunger and crammed down a piece of bread and cheese. But it was something sweet she wanted and there was no time to hunt for it. Sundaes— that's what they'd have for a surprise. She'd fix the place up like a Helmquist Drugstore with a counter. She could write the menus up on the wall. And pictures of the week's special. Caramel, with crushed clusternuts. She'd be a waitress and take orders. While she worked feverishly to get The Room all in order, cleaned and aired, the plans scurried in her mind, bigger and bigger: the cash register she could make out of paper, the table setups, the cloth to wipe the counter, the order pad tucked at her waist.

She smoothed back her hair and straightened her skirt and started on a run for Erma's to get Kathy. Clinging desperately to her enthusiasm and clutching in her hands the clean clothes for Kathy, she tried to think what she could use for substitutes, how she would make a pudding shaped like ice cream. And then, close to Erma's house, she slowed down to get her breathing under control, and to rehearse the announcement that would make them all forget the morning, carry them away and make them doubt their own morning judgments. Because it would be all right. She would wear a cap like the Helmquist waitresses wore. The cap would make them gay. The cap would protect her.

Justin wished Erma had not had the foresight to pack them a lunch. Then he could have used hunger as an excuse to end the search for the ballsleeper. He had got himself into more than he had bargained for with Tommy and he did not know how to get out. Who would have guessed the boy would turn so strange and deep on him once they were away from the settlement? Having had four of his own, he knew he should not have been so surprised to meet once again the ubiquitousness of a small boy. But that was so long ago, he thought. I had forgotten.

Tommy was not really hunting the ballsleeper any longer; they both knew that. For the first hour or so he had actively sought him, had spoken of little else. When he had reached his limit of a sustained search he fell silent about the ballsleeper. It was then that it had come to him, an awareness of this golden opportunity.

"Maybe he went in the church," Tommy said.

"The church?" Justin asked.

"Yes, down in the cave. My mamma's church, where she goes."

Justin caught the crafty look on Tommy's face. He knew he was being used to accompany the boy to a place he was afraid to go alone. But how did he even know about it? When had Gwen told him it was a church? And what was it he wanted there? Certainly the ballsleeper was a pretense. Justin supposed he had better find out, though the thought of seeing the place again was not pleasant.

"Well, all right, Tommy. We'll have a look."

For answer he got a look that there was no mistaking, no matter how long ago it had been—a triumphant look that said, "Mamma cannot punish me if you are there."

"I tell you, Erma," Justin reported later, "I tell you he's been there before. And more than once. Something is eating the boy, tearing him apart. It was like . . . like meeting death for the first time." Justin rubbed his face with one hand.

"That's what you look like," Erma said. "Justin, can't it wait? Tommy's asleep now. He's exhausted and you are, too. After you finish your tea, why don't you lie down and rest a while before you tell me?"

"Rest?" he said. "No, I couldn't rest."

He looked about the Herricks' cabin as though it were absolutely strange to him. "I could wash, I suppose," he said.

"Sit still, Justin. I'll bring you a hot towel. Tommy was so dirty I could hardly bear to put him to bed that way, but I didn't have the heart to wake him. How far did you carry him?"

"From the old house. Joe's old house."

"You went *there?*"

"Yes, he wanted to go. I thought he would begin to talk, but he can't."

Erma went over to him and put her hand on his shoulder. "Wait," she said. "I'll be right back."

While she wrung the hot towel almost dry in her quick hands, apprehension filled her. She hurried in to Justin and held the steaming towel before him. He buried his face in it and was silent. From the kettle Erma refilled her cup and quietly sipped the hot tea while she waited for him to be able to tell her. At the back of her mind was the awareness that she should be milking the mossbacks, but now they must wait.

At last Justin lifted his face from the towel. "Good," he said. "That was good." His face was red from the heat as he handed the towel to her. She gave him a pipe and held a light for him.

"Thank you, my dear," he said. "Well, now, I'll try to be less confusing. Where is Arthur?"

"He's helping Gwen. She's planning some kind of surprise."

"Surprise?"

"Yes, for dinner. You know, all gay and full of enthusiasm."

Justin groaned. "Oh, God! Again?"

"Well, anyhow," Erma said, "she's all right."

"Personally, I prefer the stupor," Justin said.

"Justin, you went to the cave? You say Tommy goes to the cave?"

"Yes, and it was uncanny, Erma. He went straight to Joe's grave and stood there."

"What did he say?"

"Nothing. I kept waiting. But first, Erma, fill my cup, will you? There's such a lot to tell; I realize now there isn't time. And there's the milking, too. I'll help you."

"You'll not," she said. "You'll rest."

"Never mind that," he said. "But before the child wakes or someone comes, how is the wood?"

"Low enough," she said. "Tomorrow? It ought to be a good time. Gwen never pulls these two days in a row and I can leave the children."

"All right," he said. "Tomorrow, then."

To replenish the wood supply was the one occupation at which they could ever count on being alone, for the work was too hard for either Arthur or Gwen, and in the years they had lived here the near places of supply had been exhausted. If he had to-morrow to tell her, Justin thought, then he need not try to tell it all now. He could take one thing at a time.

"You've not been back?" he said. "You've not seen it?"

"No," Erma said. "Not in two years. I would have thought that it would be destroyed, overgrown."

"And you didn't know Gwen was in the habit of going there?"

"No, Justin, no. She's so afraid of death. I don't understand it."

"Well, there you are," Justin said. "That's how little we know her. I don't want to know her. I never did. I've tried not to. And now, now somebody has to. She has done something to Tommy. The boy's . . . Erma, it sounds fantastic, but I swear, if he were older, I'd be sure he is thinking of suicide."

"Tommy? Why, Justin, what did he do? What did he say?"

With difficulty she kept herself from jumping up and waking the boy to hold him in her arms for reassurance.

"Say? Do? I don't know, Erma. Hardly anything. Perhaps it's my imagination. It's a feeling I have. He suggested we look for the ballsleeper—in the church, he called it. His mamma's church. He showed me the way there and he was excited. I'm sure he's been forbidden to go there. It was obvious he wanted me to go there with him. Perhaps he wanted me to catch Gwen there. Anyhow, he showed me where the lights were and then he went over to where Joe's buried and walked all around the grave. I can't remember to keep up that foolishness Gwen insisted on about Joe's going to the World in a boat and I thought it likely I'd made a slip in his presence. I decided if Tommy asked me about it I'd tell him the truth and have it out with Gwen. Surely he knows, really, that Joe is dead, don't you think?"

"I don't know, Justin," Erma said.

She was much shaken by old memories. When Justin had said *he showed me where the lights were,* it had come to her suddenly how it used to be to light them, how she would go to the feathermane and then look up . . .

"And She," Erma said. Is She still there, Justin, above the altar?"

"No," he said. "Down at the base, near the floor, there are some traces left of the carvings. Tommy pointed them out to me. He said, 'There used to be pictures here.' "

Erma had thought to have wiped it all from her. She had thought of the cave as her place of madness, her time of being lost, before she loved Justin. She had thought it a pit from which Joe's death had rescued her. But now she felt tenderness and was surprised to feel it. Even in madness, if one has carved well, there must be a tenderness for the carving, she thought. And a loss, a feeling of great loss if it be gone.

"Crumbled, then, Justin? Already? So soon?"

Even in his great tiredness, Justin knew the loss to her, knew that she was not thinking of Tommy. The feeling for one's own work, under whatever conditions, this he could always recognize.

The cabin was taking on the eassun gloom. The fire should be lighted. The mossbacks should be milked. The others, the others, as always, were pressing upon their time together. Justin reached out and took her hand. "No, my dear, not crumbled," he said.

"What then?"

"Dug," he said. "They have been dug out. I thought they had crumbled, too, at first. And then I saw marks, purposeful marks, and I thought, Desecration, anger, hatred, destruction."

"Yes?" she said. She stood up to shake the gloom from her, to make herself know the time and the tasks ahead.

"The boy told me," Justin said. "Gwen is digging the walls, Erma."

"Gwen? What for?"

"I don't know." Justin stood up, too. "Well, tomorrow I'll

tell you the rest. I'll do the milking now so Tommy doesn't wake up alone here. You'd better get him cleaned up so he won't get into trouble over it."

Erma followed him to the door. "But, Justin, Joe's house. What about the house?"

"It's full of beer crocks. Gwen drinks there, apparently. Or did. There are spider webs on everything. I don't believe she bothers to keep it secret any more."

"And Tommy? Did he see them?"

"Oh, yes, but he didn't seem surprised. He just walked around and touched things. There again I thought he would ask me about Joe, but he didn't. All he said was 'I used to live here, didn't I?' "

"We must get him to talk, Justin."

Justin held Erma close to him for a moment. Then he started toward the corral. "Tomorrow," he said. "Tomorrow we'll talk it all over."

*

His mother had made them all laugh and play with her, so they would not notice if he left the table and went off by himself to play the World. And it was safer if he pretended to be drawing pictures, he knew from experience. He did not know why his mother was cross with him when he played the game because she had really given it to him. As soon as he had his colors and paper at the little table he looked about for the ballsleeper and then the memory of the day suddenly smote him. For a moment, so much was the rhythmic petting of the ballsleeper a part of the World game, he had forgotten. Dead, then. Was it dead? And would beetles eat on it now, lying alone in the darkness? Tommy got up from his chair and went over to the shelf where were kept his treasures, and from here he took a small, polished object, cupped it hidden in his hand, and returned to his drawing paper. He could not remember why the fulcrum was enchanted or why holding it in his left hand and stroking the smooth surface of it with his thumb was, like petting the ballsleeper, a secret ritual that made the World open to him smoothly, easily. Justin had given the fulcrum to him, he knew that, but it had long ago become his own. He had heard the strange word again and again while Justin was writing the fourth movement of *The Green Kingdom*, and finally he had asked "What is it? What is fulcrum?"

"Well," Justin had said, "there are lots of them, but I could show you a simple one," and he had whittled a wooden prism for him and set a splinter atop the ridge. With his big finger he had tipped down one end of the splinter. "And this is life," he said. And then he had tipped down the other end. "And this is death," he said. "But see here what can be done." And then he had spanned his hand to keep the splinter horizontal, and with the other hand he had slid the prism back and forth, back and forth. This, now, was gone from the boy's memory, as were all conversations that had to do with death. Also, the splinter was gone from his memory. All that remained was the little prism which he called his fulcrum and which, long ago, he had worn smooth by the rhythmic rubbing of his thumb.

Entrance to the World was also to be gained, but not so easily, in other ways besides rubbing the fulcrum and petting the ballsleeper. There was looking at the fire through his eyelashes and watching a stick move under water and, he had been very surprised to learn, walking in a circle around that forbidden place in his mother's church.

Now the door was opening for him. Now the people in The Room were going away, away, away, and it was time for him to think the magic words: *The night will be brighter than the day.* Yes, the night would be brighter than the day, this they had all told him. This he knew. And also, from his mother, he had that word *easy.* Everything would be easy. They would not gather the firewood; if they were cold they would touch a button on the wall and warmth would wrap them. They would not milk the mossbacks or drive them to pasture or clean the manure from the stalls. In the morning there would be bottles of a strange stuff, glass, waiting for them. They had only to open the door. And the door would have a lock on it. And the lock would have a key. And the house would have a staircase, a waxed staircase. They could slide down it. They could slide down a pole at its side, too. This was called a banister. It was one of his favorite words. *Banister, danister, your sister is a fanister; silly baby ganister.*

Even their play they would not have to make themselves, but they could go into a dark room and sit there motionless, *easy,* and watch other people play. The theater was on the corner of his street, always, and next to it was the school where also they could sit, *easy,* and have lessons and vaccinations put into them. And here, the most exciting part, there would be many, many other children like himself, all the same age. A whole roomful of children, just his size. Next door to the school was the church, and it was not very clear to him what you did here, except that there was music. Here also one just sat and waited and received. Next to the church was the circus and this perhaps was the best of all. Everything went on at once and it had a smell and sawdust which he knew about. The animals talked and people flew through the air and went whirling around and were shot out of cannons. Oh, it was glorious and, like the other brightly lighted wonders, all *easy*, all his to be had simply by sitting and receiving, because his mother had the emeralds. He supposed that his mother would rub the emeralds to make it happen. Perhaps he would have to touch them, too. But it was the emeralds that would make it *easy*. This he did know. Yet it was not a thing his mother would talk about unless she had beer and they were alone. And then it was their secret.

The street itself was smooth, like a table, and easy to walk on. You didn't have to walk, though. There were so many things you could ride: ponies, trains, streetcars, buses, escalators. Sometimes he rode on these for the fun of it. You could even fly if you wanted.

But not after the circus. He might ride in between the theater and the school or between the school and the circus, but after the circus he always walked because this was the best part and this he liked to be slow. At the end of the street, all by himself, in a quiet place, was his father, waiting for him. His father would be eating peanuts, not out of a leather bag, but out of a paper sack with stripes on it, and he would be feeding pigeons. Pigeons were larger than gemboys and much more wonderful. And his father would see him coming down the street and his father would wave to him.

And the night would be brighter than the day and there would be no work. But this Helmquist Drugstore. Where did it fit in? He had never heard of it before and it jarred everything. Should it be next to the church? Or after the circus? The street must be a straight line. He knew this. And he cared passionately for accuracy. Should he ask?

He left his corner and went over to the table. "Where was this Helmquist Drugstore?" he asked Erma. "By the theater? By the school?"

"Where?" she said. "Oh, they were everywhere, darling.

There were hundreds of them, all alike. Every time you turned around in the city, there was another one."

"What have you there?" Justin said. "Let me see."

Tommy had not realized that he had carried his paper over with him and, looking at it, was even more surprised to see that it was covered with angry, jagged lines. He did not remember drawing them, but when Justin looked at it so very seriously and asked what it was a picture of, Tommy found he knew, all right.

"It's my ballsleeper," he said. "He goed the World."

"Give me that," his mother said, "and you, Tommy, you go to bed. Why are you up so late? Running off all day and then staying up half the night. Go to bed."

*

Erma could hear Justin moving quietly about in the darkness hitching the mossback to the woodcart and she rose, relieved, from the bed where she had lain awake all night waiting. She was never able to sleep the night before they went for wood. Quietly, without making a fire, she dressed and assembled the supplies for the trip.

Briefly she touched Justin and swung the bag of provisions onto the cart. They walked ahead of the mossback, and Justin spoke to the animal to follow. Then they slipped into step with each other and began in quiet haste to walk away from the settlement. They would not speak until they were out of hearing. They walked until the pre-wessun light had touched the night mists, and then Justin stopped.

"Well," he said, "about here?"

Erma pushed back the hood of her jacket. "Yes," she said, "this is fine."

Here Justin made a small fire and here they would have the first cup of tea together. But still they would not speak of anything dear to their hearts or any subject that would entrap them, nor would they touch each other. For they were not really young, these two. They did not believe that a day together was to be had at a god's caprice or that, because of their love, they were to be granted favors. They did not believe that the work would be easier if they postponed it, or that it might somehow miraculously need never be done at all if only their happiness were great enough. No, they were not really young. Yet they were not really old, either. They knew that the price of their being together was simply that the work of gathering wood was too hard for the others; yet they did not count the price too high. And, though neither had slept the night before, they did not complain of weariness. No, they were not really old, either.

They sat sipping their hot tea, glad not to have had to share food with anyone else this day.

"That cart," Justin said, "is really a disgrace."

"Yes," Erma said. "Like everything else that Joe made, it is slowly disintegrating."

"We seem all to be maintainers," Justin said. "Joe was the only inventive one. We just patch what he made and continue what he began. Perhaps one of the children will save us from complete disintegration."

"Oh, Justin," Erma said, "did you hear what Tommy said last night? That his ballsleeper had 'goed the World'? He knows, Justin. He knows about Joe. You were right to be so concerned about him."

"Well, we must talk about it," Justin said.

"Of course," Erma said. She began to clear up the tea things. They must not start talking about Tommy now. First, the wood. Then their time would be their own.

In the place where they had prepared it before, by sawing and burning at the base, the big tree had been attacked by wood-eating insects so that now it was ready for felling. They prepared a tree for the next time before they began work on this one. Then with their poor tools they began to cut the wood into lengths that would fit into the cart. Their labor was exhausting. It was stupidly wasteful and they knew it, and yet they knew that, when the wood was gone the next time, they would not have found a faster, better, easier way, nor discovered another fuel to substitute for it. The most they would manage would be to try to sharpen the edges and keep in some state of repair the tools that Joe had made and the ones they had copied from his. There was not extra breath for talking. They labored in sweat and silence with brief rests. But, as much as they could, they hurried. They hurried to be done with it, to pay the price of their only quiet, free time together.

At last the cart was full and the mossback tethered nearby to graze. They spread a mossback hide on the ground and, in exhaustion, they lay resting. Erma fell into a deep sleep. When she awoke Justin had a small fire going and tea made.

"Have a cup," he said. "It will wake you up."

"You look awfully clean," Erma said.

"I've had a bath," he said. "There's a hot spring near. Finish your tea and I'll show you."

When Erma returned, with her hair wet and shining and all the grime and sweat washed off her, Justin was smoking his pipe. He motioned her to sit beside him. "Well, now," he said.

"Yes," she said, "now we can talk. We've earned it."

"You sound so righteous," he said, smiling.

"I feel righteous."

"Tell me," he said, "do you feel more righteous because the axes are dull?"

She stopped the cup halfway to her mouth. "Do you suppose I do?" she said. "Is that why I'm so stupid about never doing anything about the tools?"

"No," he said, "I think your mind doesn't run that way, that's all."

"I'm just not Joe, you mean."

"None of us is," Justin said, "unfortunately. I suppose the remnants of every single group that ever tried to make a settlement could have told us the same thing. It's the Joes that are essential. For every man with an idea, for every man with a map, you need about ten Joes."

"Why is it," Erma asked, "that no one seems to realize this beforehand, when the plans are being made, when all the excitement and the promise are new?"

"I think it's because the value of people like Joe is that they improve the places where they are," Justin said. "They don't lead either in seeking adventure or seeking escape; they get there out of loyalty to someone who does. They don't lead. They don't exhort and kindle. They hunger less to escape from where they are and hope less for the wonders ahead. They follow, and they fight."

"And," Erma said, "they die."

The quiet of the woods fell about Erma and Justin. The tiny life of the cooking fire was magnified.

"Justin, what about Tommy? What can we do about Tommy?"

"Well, Erma, it isn't Tommy that needs the doing to or for, I don't think. It's Gwendolyn. And Gwendolyn I have never known what to do about. There was a moment, that last night we were all together in The Room, that I had a distinct feeling that I should—I don't know how to say it. I was awakened, I remember, just before wessun. It seemed so urgent to me that *that* was the moment to seize hold, to act, and that if the moment were lost, I should regret it deeply."

Justin was not looking at her. He was looking into the fire, but Erma turned and looked into his face.

"What, Justin? What did you feel you should do?"

"I am ashamed to tell you," he said. "The only thing that came to me was that I should kill Gwendolyn."

"Kill? Oh, Justin!"

"I know," he said. "It seemed such poverty to have no other plan, no better plan at my age, with my experience, than to kill something because it was different. The most primitive answer of all."

"But you didn't seriously—"

"Of course not," he said. "I couldn't accept it, that there was no other way. Besides, it is not in me to do it. If they want to hand out answers like that, they should at least hand them to someone capable of carrying them out."

Erma reached up her hand and touched his face. It was sadder than she had ever seen it. "Of course you couldn't kill," she said. "Of course not."

"No, I could not even if all our lives depended on it, which they very possibly do."

Erma threw a few more twigs on the fire, for his mood had chilled her. Then she sighed deeply. "Oh, Justin," she said, "where did we fail so miserably with Gwen? We were not evil people. We were all of us capable of making many adjustments to her, if she could make none to us. How is it we all suffer now, and the children, the same as though we had been full of hate?"

Justin turned away from the fire and stretched his legs, trying to break the depression of his mood. "Well, this I have thought a lot on," he said, "and it does not seem puzzling to me. It seems logical and consistent."

"How?" Erma asked.

Justin relighted his pipe and sat puffing it for a few moments. Then he looked directly at Erma. "In the first place," he said, "we did not really believe in the Green Kingdom. If we had—"

"But I did, Justin, in Drury."

"Did you?" he asked. "Really? If we had all acted as though we really believed in it, Gwendolyn would never have come."

"I don't know, Justin. She might have, if Joe came. She might just have told herself we were wrong rather than be left behind."

"Yes, if Joe came," Justin said. "But if we had been sure, it is doubtful that Joe would have come."

"Yes, it was he who wanted to bring the dynamite, you remember."

"And it was Gwen who talked him out of it."

"But I don't see, Justin, how that helps now."

"I want you to see, Erma. I want you to see."

He turned toward her and put his hands on her shoulders and waited for her to turn her face up to his. "I want you to see," he said, "that we can't help Gwen now, that we can't placate her. Our vacillation got her here. More of it will not save her, nor us. I want you to give it up. To admit it's a failure. Let go."

"But how, Justin? How?"

He crushed her to him so that he could not see her questioning eyes. "Oh, Erma," he said, "I want us to live for ourselves instead of dying for the others while they die, too."

He could feel her trembling and he knew that he was holding her too harshly. "We cannot ever win with death," he said, "because we cannot kill. We have to give it up. We have to let them die their own way and see that we live ours. Can't you do it? Can't you come away with me, right now, straight away?"

She was so long silent that he released her at last and, watching her bowed head, he felt the hope go out of him.

Erma felt the slow, tired tears of despair start down her cheeks, making the fire smear and glide before her. She looked across it at the cart, symbol of her life. Here in this wonderful promised land everything, like the cart, had fallen into disintegration. It was true that they fought the disintegration with bandages, like the poor rope about the cart. One must stop bandaging disintegration, she knew that. One must fight disintegration with a whole thing, a live and positive thing, with love.

"Surely," Justin said quietly, watching her, "surely it cannot be that you do not love me."

She shook her head, clearing her eyes for a moment, bringing the fire and the cart into sharp focus. "Surely not," she said without looking at him. "You know that."

"Well, then?"

A kind of desperation shook her, scattering the despair. To

be given to see the answer so clearly as now she saw it—to see this, and to be so fettered. She turned to Justin. "But not yet," she said.

And how long, how long did she think he had? Justin wondered. But he said nothing and watched her. Finally she looked up at him and spoke timidly, as though he would scold her.

"But Arthur?" she said. "I cannot leave Arthur, Justin. Not yet."

"Why not?" he said, and he said it coldly, in anger, lest he soften and plead with her in the urgency of his little time.

"For the same reason that you could not have left Edith," she said. "You know you could not, Justin."

"But I loved Edith," he said.

"Well?"

"You?" he said. "You are not telling me you love Arthur?"

"Love?" she said. "Oh, what has love to do with it? I am Arthur. I was Arthur. Perhaps it would be the same with a stranger if he were in such need."

And then she too grew silent. For, after all, the anger would not really sustain her. "Of course," she said quietly, "of course I have wanted to go away with you. I have dreamed it and planned it, but . . . I suppose this will shock you. I thought Arthur was dying. I still think he is. I thought it would never be necessary to leave him."

Justin desired to laugh. "Surely," he said, "this is not the quality of passion. Do you really see me sitting around waiting for everyone to die off? Must we outlive Kathy, too? Tell me, Erma," he said—and yet, while he heard himself saying it, he wondered that he could be so cruel—"tell me, can you imagine Isolde saying to Tristan, 'Well, after King Marke is dead, perhaps we can get together'? Is that how you see us?"

"Oh, Justin! Isolde didn't have to betray Tommy's trust. She only had to choose death. I would be glad to die for you, or with you. I can't desert Arthur or leave Tommy in the name of love."

Justin reached out and put his arm around her, holding her head on his shoulder, all desire to wound her gone. "I am chastened," he said.

"Besides," Erma said, "Isolde had a potion. They always had potions, all those lucky people. They weren't responsible. They . . . Damn you, Justin, you're laughing." She pushed away from him and looked up into his face. "I can feel you laughing inside."

"I can't help it, Erma. I just heard—"

"The music, I know," she said. And suddenly she stood up and tore at the silence of the woods with raucous mimicry of an Isolde, whining in complaint, "How can I leave them? What shall I do?" And as suddenly she stopped and knelt on the ground and hid her face in her hands. "I don't really like being a caricature," she said.

And so here they were again, past quiet despair and anger, and so arrived at the familiar truce. Even this laughter, even these tears—they had lived through them all before. And now they would comfort each other and steal from the dying and disintegration what little of their love was left to them before eassun should demand their return.

"My dearest one," he said, comforting her, holding her, "you cannot help the way you are. It is you who are heroic and Isolde becomes the caricature."

Erma lay quietly on the ground in his arms, her head on his shoulder, being comforted. Then she became quiet and turned on her back. "It's all a lie," she said. "Don't give me credit for anything. There have been many times at night when I longed to leave the house and come to you. There have been many times when, for love of you, I would have walked off with Arthur strangling in a cough, or Tommy with no one to hear him, or Kathy hungry and wet."

"Then why have you never done it?" Justin said.

This was not familiar. Here they had never been before, and Justin became alert for the answer. Erma rolled over and leaned on her elbows. "The truth is, Justin, I am afraid of Gwendolyn. I'm afraid to be happy in a world she lives in. I'm afraid to show love before her."

She had never understood it before. For she knew that she loved Justin enough to leave Arthur, and she was brave enough, if that were the word, to desert and betray both Joe's children. But she was afraid to show love before Gwendolyn and her fear was unreasoning and very powerful.

"You make it easier for me, then," Justin said.

"What do you mean?"

"I hardly know," he said, holding her very gently, turning her body slowly so she faced him, drawing her surely and powerfully into the circle of his arms while yesterday and tomorrow died within them and life for them became this moment. Now. For them the fire burned without consuming twigs, birds communicated without sound. Without firmness the ground supported them, lifted them up, cast them onto a gradually expanding spiral of answer to their questioning history. To the complications of their natures, an answer was promised them of extreme simplicity. For the frenzy of their frustrated waiting, an answer lay ahead, infinitely soothing. When the bones should become fluid, an answer would be given them. Cast off the wide, ascending spiral into timelessness, they floated through the answer. They became the answer.

Against the dampness in the air Justin pulled a cover over the body of his beloved. For the first time in seven years he saw her not as a separate being. He experienced her as part of himself. He knew the serenity of her quiet face. He knew also that she was not asleep. Yet not for anything would he have wished to disturb her or to force response from her. In seven years he had never looked on her without knowing in himself some demand. To protect her, to call her, to possess her, to fight with her, to comfort her. Now there was no need to do anything about her or to her or for her, now that he was part of her.

He moved away from her quietly, arose, dressed, and walked off into the forest. He did not need to tell her that he was going in search of fruit for them to eat. He did not need to tell her that he would return. He did not have to hear her say "Good-by" or "All right." In seven years he had never been without this need and now he knew a quiet freedom. In his mind he heard himself singing. Yet not for anything would he have broken the quiet with a real sound.

It had been about here that he had seen the firstfruits, he remembered. He knelt down to explore under the furred foliage for ripeness, and he smiled to himself to think that there were still mysteries. At his age, to have a mystery—it was a fine joy. For of his limited knowledge he knew no reason why it should have been today. They had gathered the wood a hundred times together. Why had it not been at any other time? Why had it not been at any one of the times when they had lashed out in anger at each other? Justin found a ripe melon and it said to him that he was fortunate to possess a mystery.

Erma was exactly as he had left her and he was glad that she had not bustled about or made the fire alive. What need had they for comforting things? Separate people need comfort. Her eyes were open and he broke the fruit in half and handed it to her. Again his heart rejoiced in the freedom of not having to say what was obvious.

Erma turned on her side and leaned on one elbow to eat the fruit. He sat beside her and, bending to kiss the curve of her shoulder, he thought in how many ways he had been saying all his life, "I have returned" when he had returned, and of hearing someone else say, upon seeing that he had returned, "I see you have returned."

Erma sat up and leaned against him. She moved her head slowly to see as much of the land as possible. "It is all beautiful again," she said, almost in a whisper.

Justin lifted her up and they went about the necessary preparations without having to say, "It is time to go" or "We must get back." Her movements were slow and deliberate, and now and then she would stop and lean against him or, reaching up, lay the palm of her hand flat against his cheek. Together they pushed against the old cart to ease the burden on the mossback. Once it was started, Erma turned back to see once more the place. *These leaves. This grass,* she thought.

Justin waited for her to turn back to him. "I'm sorry I can't make a new cart until tomorrow," he said.

"But you feel you can?" she said. "Oh, Justin, is it false, this optimism? I feel as though everything is really very simple of solution, that we had only to confront all our problems and they would slink away. Is it foolish to feel so?"

For a moment, seeing her hand at her throat, the question in her eyes, Justin saw her as a separate person, outside himself, and he felt the terrible old need to shield her, to cover her vulnerability.

"No, no," he said. "We must believe that every time we are proved foolish we will be able to recapture our faith that we are not."

Holding his beloved close lest she show him her vulnerable eyes and so become again a person separate and entire, Justin thought, That is the mystery—the capacity to recapture, a thousand times over, one's belief in one's competence. It is not even necessary to recapture the competence.

He felt her relax against him and then lean back and look into his face. "Is that all we needed," she said, "all this long time, just to feel competent again?"

"It is no small thing," he said.

They fell into step and began the homeward walk in silence. "What is that, Justin?" she said later. "What are you whistling?"

"Oh?" he said. "Oh, that is *The Legend*, I think."

"I've never heard it before."

"No," he said. "No, it's quite new."

THE seed of *The Legend,* or at least the cupped earth that nestled the seed, was the World-play of the children. Justin had come upon Tommy instructing Kathy in the practice of looking both ways before crossing a city street. The incongruity of their anxious watching beside the narrow footpath which had for traffic one cart, one feathermane, four adults and an occasional darting woods creature had startled Justin and set him to remembering his own childhood games of being in the Green Kingdom. By the time the music was with him, and the feeling of a legend which endlessly turns itself inside out, he had forgotten its connection with the children. Had not the music come to short-circuit his impression he might have added it to the growing list of alarming signs about Tommy. The truth was that Tommy and Gwendolyn and even, at times, *The Legend* were blotted out of Justin's mind by the great reality of his love. The thought of Erma, now that she was his, would constantly engulf him like her presence itself. This long-awaited acknowledgment of their love was very different for Justin from what it was for Erma.

"I long for an ocean," Erma had said to him, "or for a desert. For something big or violent enough to receive my feeling. This gentle landscape, this softness, I feel I might break it."

Yes, Justin thought, it was very different for her. One had only to look at her to see the difference. She seemed free, exultant, unafraid. Perhaps, he thought, between two people who have long waited for each other there is a constant level of anxiety, and now that she is free of it I must take it on. So it had always been with him—that what was his to love he feared for. He could not help it. Before that day they had gone for the wood it had seemed to him that it would be the simplest thing if only Erma could be his. They would say to the others, "We will live together now." And if she could not, then they would leave the others and go away by themselves. Before that day Gwendolyn had seemed to him a pathetic, irritating creature that he did well to avoid as much as possible. He had thought Erma's fear of her exaggerated.

Now he pushed the sheets of *The Legend* aside, for his growing alarm made further work on it impossible, and he tried to reason with the dread he felt. What was this fear of Erma's which he seemed to have taken on from her? Surely she was not physically afraid of Gwendolyn. This he would find hard to believe. What was it she had said? Not that she was afraid of Gwendolyn but that she was afraid to show happiness before her. And what did this mean? Erma herself had been unable to explain it, had called it unreasonable. What was it then she feared Gwendolyn could do? Could Gwendolyn command one not to love? He did not know himself why he now felt a fear of this woman. What *could* she do? Probably no more than get drunk again and make things difficult all around, as she had before. But her drunkenness was only a nuisance and not the cause for such a feeling of anxiety as he now felt. Justin got up from his chair and walked about the room. His pipe had gone out and he relighted it and found himself wishing for the millionth time that Joe had not died. To have brought only one Joe to such a place as this—that was the fundamental error. In the World, now, losing Joe, Gwendolyn would have had a chance of finding his substitute. At least her difference would not have been so magnified.

Justin knocked out his pipe on the hearth and extinguished his oil lamp. He lay on his bed, hoping for sleep. Well, perhaps at Yearsenday some solution would present itself. He had said to Erma that if they were all together at Yearsenday, having a celebration, perhaps the memory of former years would make them closer. But he did not feel hopeful of it now. He lay in the darkness longing for the presence of his beloved, that she might come to him and lie beside him and still the agony of his longing and the irony of his depression. It seemed to him against all reason and rightness that in the seven years of waiting for her he had been more confident of their union than he was now. Now that she was his, now that she was unafraid and able to lean upon his love, he was afraid for her, and the problems they faced seemed hopeless. He could not remember ever having been so depressed.

FROM THE RECORD OF ERMA HERRICK, THE LAST DAY OF THE THIRTEENTH MONTH OF THE SEVENTH YEAR:

Tomorrow we are all going (even Arthur) up to the Yearsenday Place to celebrate the new year. Justin has hopes that a celebration may bring us all closer together so that the children, especially Tommy, will feel more of a family around them. The truth is we have not one real family here. We are all keepers of children: Gwen of Tommy and Kathy; I of Arthur; and Justin of all of us. I wonder if there ever was a society built like that, where everyone was a keeper of children. You'd think if there were, all the laws would be *about* children. We don't have any laws at all.

I remember when we first came here we were supposed to be keepers of Records and Arthur and Joe had that terrible fight about laws for the Records. We couldn't make Gwen keep the Records then and now we can't make her take care of the children, either. How do they make laws work in the world? Is it easier with more people? I don't see how we can make Gwen do anything. And if we could, by force, wouldn't it be even harder for the children?

Gwen gets worse and worse and of course it's all reflected in Tommy. Several times Gwen has suddenly appeared in my house, glared at me, and said, "I know what you're doing and don't think you can get away with it." I have no idea what she means. Kathy doesn't seem to notice much yet, but Tommy keeps going off by himself. He misses meals and sometimes he won't talk at all.

There are times when I feel we should just take the children away from Gwen altogether and hope that she doesn't drink herself to death in the next three years so that she can leave. But I'm afraid to try this. So is Justin. He doesn't know why, either. I don't know if it's that I'm afraid Gwen might harm the children or what.

And then, what about Arthur? The children make him very nervous. I tried to talk to Arthur about Tommy because, with Gwen the way she is, it's so hard to keep track of the children all the time and I thought perhaps we all ought to go back to The Room together the way we were after Joe died. I just couldn't get to Arthur. I told him about the strange things Tommy's done lately and Arthur wrote on his pad: *It's cold in here.* So I fixed the fire and got him a jacket and tried again, but after listening awhile he wrote: *Let's have some tea.*

He is so wretchedly ill, I suppose it is asking too much for him to be concerned about a small, healthy boy who can ride a pony all day without getting tired. And perhaps I make too much of it. Lots of people in the world have grown up out of homes where the mother was drunk and the father was dead. And at least Tommy doesn't have starvation here. It is terrible to know that however much I love Tommy, my power to help him is limited because, to him, I'm not his own. I'm always an outsider.

Even as I write this, I am anticipating tomorrow with pleasure because I will be with Justin all day. Surely, with the power of so great a love, Justin and I together will be able somehow to make things better. It seems to me now that in the name of such a love it is more impossible than ever simply to walk off and leave the situation. It should flow over Tommy and Kathy, over everything, making them happier, fuller, richer. Surely, if Justin and I live together, it will have to be with the courage to do it here among the others. Yet I do not feel despair. Perhaps because Justin shares my feeling now and I do not have to defend it.

Some day, I know, this love will refuse denial and I think I will know the right time when it comes.

———————

At first Tommy thought it had been fun while they were fixing the food, and Erma had even brought a bundle of greengrain so his pony could have Yearsenday right there with them. Justin had told him again about how they came there before he was even born. Arthur drew him a funny picture of how scared they had all been when the Yearsenday bombs went off. The picture had his father in it with his arms over his head. He wished some Yearsenday bombs would go off now and make them stop fighting.

His mamma was mad at them all because they were spying on her, she said. He didn't know if he wanted them all to come and live in his house or not. He guessed not. Because then it would be harder to keep away from them. Sometimes it didn't seem right what his mamma said—that they were going to take him away from her and hide him and never let her see him any more. Why would they do that? They'd better not try that. He'd get on Pony and ride away fast and they could hunt for him and call for him but Pony would run faster and faster and they would never catch him. And then he would hide, maybe in a cave like his mamma's church.

Arthur saw the boy slipping stealthily away and envied him. Justin was a fool to try this. Why hadn't he let well enough alone? Gwen knew what they were up to. She was the wrong one to try to fool.

"Just leave me alone, that's all I ask," Gwen said. "Yes, I'm lonely. Of course I'm lonely. I'm lonely for Joe. But I don't want three of you spying on me and telling my children what to do. They're mine. Remember that. Mine!"

"There's no call for a tirade, Gwen," Justin said. "After all, this is a holiday. I rather thought you'd like the idea, but if you don't . . ."

Tommy had made it successfully without being noticed. At least no one called him back. He made his way quietly down to the river. Was it here that his father would come for him in the big boat and take him back to the World? Yes, it was here. His father knew he would be here on Yearsenday and so he would come today. In a big boat. And he would see him a long way off and wave to him and call him: "Hi, Tommy!" And then he would go running down the shore to meet his father and his father would say, "Jump on, Tommy," and Tommy would leap from the shore to the boat and his father would catch him and then they would turn the boat right around and go to the World.

But it was hard to run on the shore because the jungle grass tangled around his feet and tripped him and, besides, he could not see very far. Which way would his father come from? Upstream or downstream? If he were out in the middle of the river he could see a long way. He could see his father coming and he could wave at him. If he had a little boat he could go to meet him. If he had only a raft he could go out in the middle of the river and see his father coming.

Kathy, trailing far behind, finally caught up with Tommy and found him intently trying to lash four small logs together with ropevine. There were drops of sweat beading his upper lip, and his short leather jacket bore the stains where he had wiped his hands free of the ropevine juice.

"What doing, Tommy?" she said, flopping on the ground beside him.

"Oh, Kathy, why you always have to trail me? Why didn't you stay with Mamma? Go back."

"No," Kathy said stubbornly. "Mamma's mad. What's that? What's that, Tommy?"

"It's a boat, that's what it is. And you leave it alone."

"Boat?"

Did the word echo through the Kingdom? Did it find its earlier, no less significant mate? And did the two spoken word-boats clasp hands and dance in evil mischief and laugh in evil glee at the havoc their sound had wrought? This small word, heard in such hatred by Gwendolyn so many years ago, the first word Tommy had ever spoken, a word which filled his mother's nostrils with the stench of boiling pitch gum and the jealousy of a hated rival, was now not heard. Neither Gwendolyn nor Justin nor Erma nor Arthur heard it, caught up as they were in Gwendolyn's accusations.

"Boat?" Kathy repeated. "Boat. Boat."

"Yes, it's a boat," Tommy said. "I'm going to meet Joe. My father is coming in a big boat and I'll be on this one, see, and I'll jump off this one on the big one and then we'll turn around and go to the World. No, Kathy, you can't go. No."

Kathy cried to be so rudely pushed off the boat, and she cried louder to be left alone on the shore while Tommy slid the fragile raft into the shallow water and, kneeling on it, held himself small and anxious, the tip of his tongue touching his upper lip.

Slowly he saw the shore moving back, saw his baby sister, still crying, getting smaller and smaller. Then his head jerked back with the surprise of the current and he leaned forward to hold onto the raft with his hands. For the first time he began to doubt if he should have tried to meet his father.

The water seemed to be moving faster and faster, bent over as he was to hold onto the logs, and it made him dizzy and he closed his eyes. The current caught the raft and twisted it a quarter turn and Tommy, tightening his hold by reflex, felt himself falling. Trying to right himself, he overturned the raft and felt the cold water wrap itself about him. He fought now, reached for the raft, bumped his head on one of the logs, got his head out of water long enough to scream, bobbed under again and fought for a handhold on the log.

The current speeded him faster and, in one place, turned him around and around and pitched him against the raft. Then the current slowed, the river became peaceful, and Tommy, sinking through the dappled-green reaches of the filtered light, saw his father standing on the big square boat. Floating through the deepening reaches of the slowly moving river, Tommy smiled because he had not known his father had hair that shone like highsun on the greengold tree or that light would drip from his outstretched hand. He reached for the hand. He reached for his father's hand.

The secret, winding, mysterious river took his body into its arms and held it secretly with its other secrets. The river washed him and cradled him and tumbled him over the shallows, causing the boy's square hand to rake a scar on the serrated shallows, causing minnows to kiss the strands of his hair. The river sang into the boy's ears its song that was like many birds taking to the air at once. The river transported him over the polished horns of feathermanes, over glistening rocks. Once, if the body of the boy had wanted them, it could have taken coins and a key thrown there many years before by Justin Magnus. It could have pocketed the fired clay handle of a pot made by old Grandfather Magnus and thrown into the river in anger when the pot broke.

The river tossed this boy, this son of Joe and Gwendolyn, for now he was the river's son. The river carried him, pushed him and pulled him to the other side of the Green Kingdom, where, in life, he had never been. Then it circled the Kingdom again. At last it put him down gently on the shore not far from the place where Arthur Herrick waited five days later.

But a piece of his jacket it kept a little longer, and this Arthur Herrick saw and recovered, because he was watching for it. Of all the days there had been in the three years since Arthur Herrick had imagined the river to be a spiral, when he might have verified its structure with a marked stick or any other floating, inanimate thing, he had never thought to do it. But (how many days ago?) standing there at the Yearsenday Place watching Justin and Erma diving into the river near where the small raft had been found, he had known this was what had to be done. He had walked off and left them, leaving a note for Erma when he passed his own house. For they would never stop diving, never stop trying, it seemed to him, until they were drowned themselves. He could not stop them then. Surely they had stopped by now. Arthur could remember Justin's swollen, purple face, could hear again the hard, tortured breathing, see the thick gray hair on his chest matted flat.

Once again, before he sighted the jacket, he doubted the rightness, the wisdom, of what he had done. What if, after all, the two rivers were separate and not a continuous spiral? Wouldn't his leaving be only a running out? Shouldn't he have stayed with the others and somehow lived with them through the time when uncertainty became certainty? Or was there a chance still that there was no tragedy at all? Had Kathy been lying, as Gwen insisted? How much can a four-year-old child know? And of what it knows, how much tell? The more they questioned her, the more different directions Kathy had pointed. But surely Gwen was wrong to say it was all made up, because how could Kathy, who could not even remember Joe, how could she have made up the story about Tommy's going to meet Joe?

Arthur Herrick sat on the ground and shuddered with pain, remembering in every detail the senseless, needless death of Joe in the cave. Months at a time he succeeded in blocking this knowledge from his mind, but now it sat there with him beside the green and secret river. He shook himself and tried to say that Gwen was right because she was the boy's mother, that Tommy had run away to be naughty, was hiding somewhere watching them make fools of themselves. How glad Arthur would be to be on a fool's errand, to know Kathy a liar as her mother said. But he could not believe it. He knew somehow that there was nothing needed now but verification of the terrible truth. This man, who had so long lived with guilt and sickness about which he could not even make an audible groan of complaint, sat by the same river near the same place where he had stopped more than five years before in his coward's fleeing. I was here when Tommy was born, he thought. In so little time a boy can live out his whole life, while a man's slow disintegration is hardly perceptible.

Toward the spot where Arthur sat waiting the river, with maddening slowness, tossed on its surface the piece of jacket. As soon as he saw it he had much work to do and no time for thinking, but, just before he saw it, even through the crushingly tragic memories he suffered, he was aware of a feeling of surprise that he had made it here, this long journey. In anxiety and shock he had done a thing he thought himself physically incapable of. Even when he plunged into the cold water to retrieve the piece of the boy's jacket, Arthur had been thinking with amazement that he was farther from death than he had thought.

*

Even though Erma had warned him and he had sat with an old, exhausted Justin for an hour listening to his description, Arthur was still unprepared for the Gwendolyn who waited for him. She sat in a chair near the fire, erect, carefully dressed, her hair done smoothly, her face a mask. She received Arthur with formality and, with a studied graciousness, inquired if he would like tea. She ignored completely the piece of Tommy's jacket which Arthur held out to her. She was absolutely sober, and this he found a greater shock than the contrast of her face with Erma's.

Kathy leaned against her, still curiously impressed with this new personality. And as Gwendolyn talked she reached out and stroked the child's dark, shining hair possessively. Finally Arthur folded the piece of jacket and put it into his pocket. They had told him, warned him, but he hadn't believed it. He'd thought surely that Gwen would break when she saw the jacket.

"I've missed you, Arthur," Gwen said. "Are you sure you won't have any tea?"

Arthur shook his head no. Then he wrote on his pad, *I buried Tommy. The grave is marked.*

Gwen handed the pad back to him with an apologetic smile. "Something seems to have happened to my eyes recently, Arthur. I can't read this. I need glasses, I suppose, though I hate to admit it."

Although he had dreaded an emotional scene of grief, Arthur felt now he would have preferred it to this blank wall of unacceptance. Justin and Erma had told him that, cruel as it sounded, they were persisting in the truth, thinking that this shock reaction of Gwen's was temporary and surely, soon, must break. Well, let them try, Arthur thought. It was too much of an effort with pen and paper. Perhaps it was a merciful thing, this refusal to admit the child's death. Who could wish her to admit it? Not he.

He wrote, *Is there any beer?* And this Gwendolyn was able to read instantly, without noticing any discrepancy in the fact.

"Oh, no, Arthur, I'm sorry. The beer has had to go, you know. I'm being punished; I suppose you've heard. I'm being treated like a naughty girl. Teacher won't let me have my boy back until I prove I'm a good, obedient child. Oh, never mind, Arthur. Don't feel sorry for me. After all, they're in power here. I have to face it. What can I do against them?" She looked up at Arthur with a disarming smile. "The thing to do," she said, "when you're beaten is submit gracefully."

She turned to Kathy, who stood silently watching her, and put her arm around the child. She kissed her on the top of her head. "Do you want some milk, darling?" she cooed. "Are you hungry?"

Kathy shook her head, and for a moment Arthur felt that she too might pull out pad and pen in order to communicate.

"You know, Arthur," Gwen said, "I can't tell you how relieved I am that you're not entering into this moronic nonsense with teacher and his loving girl. I could certainly use an ally, not to mention a friend."

Arthur tried to smile at her. He tried to make some contact with the woman's eyes, but they were out of focus. Now she laughed bitterly.

"Oh, I know their game. They're trying to punish me. I know. But I don't deserve this. They know where to hurt, all right. The cruelest way. I drink. I admit it. Why shouldn't I? Who had a better reason to, I'd like to know? And now they've hidden my son away and told me those dreadful stories to punish me. Well, I'll play their nasty little game. They're so smug. So self-righteous. As if I didn't know what was going on between them."

Suddenly her body became tense and the left corner of her mouth drew down in an ugly snarl. "Really now," she said. "Really, which do you think is worse for a little, innocent boy to see—someone drinking a few cups of beer, or an old man fucking someone else's wife?"

Arthur stood up. If he could not say to the bitch, "Shut up! Shut up!" at least he could go away.

And instantly Gwen was transformed into a demure, maternal creature. She pulled Kathy, against the child's will, onto her lap.

"Oh, darling, you must excuse Mamma. Mamma should never have said such a naughty thing. Mamma has to be a very good girl now and toe the mark for teacher and his sanctimonious friend."

Kathy began to struggle against her mother's locked arms, but Gwen continued to smile on her benevolently and hold her. Over the child's head she looked up at Arthur's angry face.

"Oh, for Christ's sake, Arthur, sit down. You can't run out on me. I have no one left. No one. But don't be mistaken. I'll get my boy back if it takes me a year. I'll be sober. I'll be a model housewife."

She pointed to the loom which had been moved out from its corner, dusted and repaired. "I'll even weave their goddamned cloth and make their clothes for them. Until I get him back. And then, when I get him, all I say is, let those two watch out."

Gwen, Arthur wrote, *I have to go now. Do you want anything?*

Arthur held the paper out toward Gwendolyn, but she pretended not to notice it. She was holding Kathy's face very close to her own.

"Who do you love, sweetheart? Tell Mamma, whose girl are you?"

But Kathy seemed to have been struck as dumb as himself, Arthur thought. Her eyes were closed in embarrassment, her whole sturdy body given over to wriggling to escape from this demanding voice saying, "Tell me, tell me, tell me who you love, Kathy. Tell Mamma."

Arthur pushed his note before the child's face, fearing for the child suddenly, knowing that she would not say it now, could not.

Gwendolyn let the little girl slip away. She read Arthur's note and became again the parody of the polite hostess.

"Oh, do you have to go, Arthur? I'm sorry. It was so kind of you to come."

Then she turned away from him in dismissal and stared into the fire. Arthur stood uncertainly a moment. He put his hand on Gwen's shoulder and took it away again. Then he began to cross the room, away from her silence. As he put his hand on the latch, Gwen called out, "Arthur!"

He turned and saw her running toward him across the room, took the impact of her body, let it cling to him, felt his head nodding yes, yes, while she spoke rapidly in a low, intimate voice into his ear.

"Arthur, please come back. Please. I'm so lonely. It's the nights. The nights are so terrible. Arthur, don't make me humiliate myself like this. Please say you'll come back and sit with me, just for a while, a little while."

Who could say no? Arthur thought. Not he, certainly.

"No, Kathy dear," Gwen said. "You stay with Mamma. Mamma's very lonely. Arthur's going to go away awhile and then he's coming back and keep us company. Won't that be nice?"

Once the door was closed on Arthur, Gwen lifted the child into her arms and carried her over to the fire. There she sat with Kathy on her lap. In a calm, low voice, patting the child's hair, she began to talk to her.

"Kathy, when Mamma asks you who you love, what do you say?"

Kathy turned her head away and tentatively tried, with her chest, the barrier of Gwen's arms.

"Don't look away from Mamma, Kathy, do you hear? Say, 'I love you, Mamma.' Now. Say it."

Kathy did not feel stubborn any longer, only frightened. And if she could have said it, she would have. She felt herself shaken warningly.

"Say it, Kathy."

The child looked up at Gwen, her eyes wide with fear. But she could say nothing.

And now Gwendolyn's voice became menacing. "You'll say it. Do you hear me? No one can stand this. No one can live without someone to love them, do you understand? No one. Joe gone. Tommy gone. The others all against me. You're all I've got. You've got to love me."

She carried the child over to a corner of the room and placed a bench across the corner, so that the child could not get out. Then she stood back.

"There," she said. "You stay there. Like me. Alone. With your back to the wall. See how *you* like it." She began to back away from the child. Kathy found her voice immediately—not to speak the magic words, for she had forgotten all words, but to cry in protest as Gwen gradually walked backward. Kathy cried louder.

Gwen stopped walking and stood watching the screaming child.

"Say it," she said. "Say it, and I'll let you go."

The sound of her own voice crying had brought back to Kathy something familiar. However unpleasant, it was no longer so strange to her that she couldn't find an answer to it. The answer, which had followed tears before, was rage.

Gwen stood watching the child's face become red with her screaming, saw her beat her little fists on the heavy bench, kick at it.

"Say it, Kathy," she said in a gentle, persuasive voice. "Say it."

Suddenly the child stopped beating on the heavy bench, stopped screaming in rage, and silently stood there urinating.

"That's all right, darling. You just stand in it then. Mamma won't move until you say it. Mamma won't get you dry clothes until you've said it."

Kathy stared at the pool of urine on the floor. It had been a surprise to her, and now she was too tired to go back to her rage.

She was very tired. She slid one damp thigh over the other and began to whimper, tiredly, hopelessly.

"Say it, darling," Gwen said, feeling close to victory now.

The whimpering began to grow. It grew into an experimental cry, the experiment became a confirmed behavior, and finally the tears became tired, loud words. "I love you, Mamma. I love you. I love you." And then she could not stop saying it. Like an old, mad parrot the child cried, "I love you, I love you."

Instantly the bench was taken away and her mamma lay on the floor, kissing her wet feet, holding her wet legs, clutching her, holding her tighter and tighter. And her mamma was crying like a little baby.

There are few adults who can match the compassion of a four-year-old child once that child has successfully survived a burden greater than it thought it could bear, has seen the thing it feared turned suppliant at its feet and has known its own terror turned to power. Such compassion was Kathy's. With great grace, through her tiredness, and in spite of her uncomfortable wet clothes, she put her small fat hand on her mother's shoulder and almost in a whisper said, "Mamma hungry? Mamma want some milk?"

So craven for love had Gwendolyn become that she counted this a triumph, and so long had it been since she had had any triumph that it made her glad. It seemed to her that while she had stood there in anger before the trapped child she had felt alive for the first time in years. During the days and weeks which followed it seemed to Gwendolyn that life and energy were flowing into her, that she had made a great discovery and that henceforth her life would be different. In her excitement she forgot to eat, felt no need to drink, and entirely overlooked the fact that what she thought of as her victory had been over a four-year-old, frightened child. For now it seemed to her that all her life she had been put upon, had taken what other people doled out to her and had been the butt of their displeasure—all because she had never had the sense to seize what she wanted, to demand what she needed, all because she had kept her hatred secret and hidden and tried to work around it. Now she saw anger as a blazing deliverance for herself. She felt herself filled with the energy of hatred. She would fight. She would never be tired and listless again. She would never escape in drunkenness again, leaving others to seize an advantage over her. Now she would always be alert, awake, on the defensive, and ready at any moment to summon the fire, the wonderful, blazing hatred that filled her with new life.

She began to imprison the child even more carefully in the net of her attention. The few things that Kathy had learned to do for herself, Gwendolyn now did for her. The new energy she felt within herself, like the alertness of a trapped animal, made her quick of movement so that she seemed, to Kathy, to be everywhere at once. Not a move did the child make but Gwendolyn saw it. The sudden change, the abundance of attention, being novel and something to be manipulated, was not unpleasant to Kathy. She submitted to being dressed, to being bathed, even to being fed, with a questioning kind of tolerance, for it was all new. She demanded to be told stories of the World and to be rocked to sleep. All her demands were instantly met. But then she demanded that Gwendolyn listen to the tale of Tommy and how he had gone away in a boat. She found herself back in the corner again, trapped behind the bench. Gwen stood before her, holding the bone bread knife.

"I'll cut off all your pretty hair if you lie again."

Deliverance was much quicker this time, and Kathy's long, black hair was safe, for the child was learning very fast. They were, in fact, learning of each other from constantly practicing on each other, but Gwendolyn did not know it as a mutual process and drew further confidence as she put the knife away and fondled the child and fastened flowers in her hair.

Also she took confidence from her own body as she constantly lost weight. As she moved more rapidly about the house, the increasing lightness of her body reminded her of her youth. The years of heavy stupor fell away from her and her old vanity returned. She would sit at the edge of her bathing pool looking at herself, holding her breath so as not to ruffle the water, and become lost in the slowly waving image of her own face, for in her mind a plan was forming, a conquest more difficult than victory over Kathy, one that would need greater subtlety. The stakes were higher now and the desperation was growing.

The truth was that Gwendolyn had grown afraid that harm would come to herself, that she would die, that some terrible thing would happen to her. She had never thought much about death before, certainly not her own, and now she thought of it constantly. In the night she would awaken suddenly and it seemed to her that her heart had stopped beating, but if she moved for help she would die, and she would lie in the darkness holding her breath in terrible fear. She began to read dreadful significance into her loss of weight and thought herself wasting from some obscure disease. During the day she worked frenziedly in the housekeeping of The Room, at the loom, keeping constant track of Kathy, so that it was mostly at night that the fear came; but even so there were times during the day when she would suddenly be stopped in her tracks, a nameless dread hovering over her, and she would wring her hands. Kathy would come to her then and stare up at her, and Gwen would pick up the child and babble to her and caress her, trying, usually successfully, to distract herself.

But for some time now Gwendolyn had felt incompetent to assume responsibility for herself; moreover she felt it an injustice that she should have to. It took more than the powers she had to keep a constant watchfulness against the dangers that might, at any moment, pounce upon her. She wanted someone else to feel responsible for her, to be *made* to feel responsible for her. And she chose not the most responsible person but the one over whom she felt the greatest confidence of victory. In her disordered, bewildered mind she began to lean toward Arthur, and her fear taught her to take encouragement from any small sign and to read pathetic confirmation into the frailest gestures.

*

It would often come over Justin during the day, perhaps in the middle of some chore, this overpowering desire to see Erma, to touch her. He put down his pen in the midst of a page of *The Legend* and, taking his pipe, went out to look for her. At the cabin Arthur wrote out for him the information that Erma had gone after sponge moss and spicebark, and so Justin had a good idea of where he would find her. Even so, seeing her gave him a shock, and for a moment he felt himself back six or seven years in time. Just so, then, had he caught his breath at sight of her, for the strength of his desire. She stood reaching up for the bark of the tree to put into the small basket that hung from her shoulders by a leather strap. At her feet was the larger basket, now half full of the soft green moss. The thing that had startled Justin was the feathermane standing by her side. Now the animal, which had been Tommy's pony, sensed his presence, and Erma, turning to see what the animal saw, saw Justin and came toward him smiling. Wordlessly they met and kissed and held each other for a moment, and then they moved apart and Justin fumbled for his pipe.

"It gave me such a start, seeing you with a feathermane again," he said.

Erma sat down on the ground and shifted the big basket to make a place for the feathermane. Cautiously he knelt down beside her with his head on her lap. She put her hand lightly on his mane.

"Poor Pony," she said. "He missed Tommy so. He wouldn't eat and I thought he would starve to death. He kept hunting and hunting for Tommy."

"Much the same state we were all in," Justin said. "I shall be eternally grateful to Arthur for establishing a certainty. Bad as it is, the death is not so terrible as thinking the child might be lost somewhere, or trapped, that if one dived again or hunted the banks, or kept trying . . ."

Erma reached toward him and put her hand on his knee.

"Forgive me, my dear," he said.

"Sometimes I envy Gwen," Erma said, "that refusal, that ability just not to have it be so."

"Can she really not know?" Justin said. "It doesn't seem possible. And yet, of all people who should find it possible, I should."

"Because of Edith, you mean?" Erma said.

"Yes, but they're nothing alike, you know. It doesn't help at all. Edith was . . . well, Edith was insane."

"And you don't think Gwen is?" Erma said.

"No, I don't," Justin said. "Oh, I don't know anything about it. All I know is she's nothing like Edith. Edith was convincing. You'd find yourself seeing things her way."

"Yes, that's it, Justin. Gwen isn't convincing. I know that in some part of her mind Gwen understands everything we say."

"Yes, the way we feel toward Gwen is probably a more accurate measurement of her condition than anything we're able to observe in Gwen herself."

"It's the same with Arthur," Erma said. "Like the feathermane. I don't know how I know that it's all right for me to have this feathermane in the house in front of Arthur. I just know that it is. He's not going to kill this one and I don't have to hide it in a cave. That's all over."

"When I stopped at your place," Justin said, "Arthur was up and dressed and I could hardly believe how well he looked."

"I know," Erma said. "Every day he does a little more. Who could have believed that he could make that journey to find Tommy's body? He didn't believe it himself, he told me. He actually thinks of getting well now. He has hope."

Justin saw her smile of gladness and turned away. He plunged his hands into the basket of damp moss and lifted some on his hands. This moss, dried, they used for scrubbing in all the cleaning jobs about the cabins, since the weaving of cloth was too laborious for such purposes and the sponge moss so plentiful. It had, when damp, an odor like that of burned almonds, and, in the silence, Justin became aware of this odor blended with that of the freshly gathered spicebark. It was like a cloud all about them. He tried to lose himself in it to distract himself from the dread that had been growing in him for weeks now. He was ashamed of what he was thinking; he was ashamed that he would not be able to keep from speaking of it.

"Erma," he said at last, "you are right about Arthur. Those things, those terrible things he did under the influence of the braidstem, even the use of the braidstem, are quite impossible for him now. As you say, one just feels it. For so long he has been wrapped up completely in himself and his illness and his needs, like part of the sickbed itself. But it isn't true now. He changes every day. It's as though—as though he were returning at an accelerated pace to what he used to be."

This, Erma thought, could this be Justin? She would never have expected to hear Justin Magnus stumble over what he had to say, unable to look at her. She watched him compressing the sponge moss in his giant fists, rendering it quite useless.

"Erma, I found myself dreading Arthur's recovery, balking at knowing that he has to be treated like . . . like a person now. Suppose he got well, that he looked and acted just as he used to, Erma, would you . . . ?"

And now it was Erma's turn to look away, to feel the quick tears in her eyes, for the knowledge that Justin Magnus needed reassurance. All the rest of them had needed reassurance, often, at different times. She herself, most crucially and cravenly, had needed to be told her barrenness was not of the spirit. But that Justin Magnus should be in doubt—it was enough to make the very rocks weep. For Justin there had been no time of having lived secretly in a cave, no time of having been in very different health, no time of having been with or without braidstem, with or without a mate, or children. No one remembered Justin as thinner or heavier or in any way different from what, to their knowledge, he had always been.

Erma turned toward him. "I don't think that to belittle the love I once had for Arthur would reassure you, just as it would not make me glad to hear that you loved Edith with anything less than—"

"But Edith is safely dead," Justin said. "She isn't here before my eyes, turning day by day into the very person that I once loved."

Erma reached up her hand to touch Justin's cheek and felt the feathermane shift his head on her thigh. "You forget," she said, "that even if Arthur is, I am not returning day by day to the person who loved him."

"How can you be sure?" he said. "How can you know?"

"Oh, Justin, how foolish this is. Already, for several minutes now, I have known that I will come live with you."

"You will come live with me now?" he said.

"Yes," she said, "as soon as I have spoken to Arthur. Today or tomorrow, whenever the time seems right. It doesn't matter exactly when, does it? The thing is, I know it in myself now. Not to go away from the others, you understand. I could not leave Kathy. But I will come to live in your house with you."

Suddenly she put out her hand and they shook hands very solemnly. And then she bent her head over his hand and kissed it and tears fell on his hand. "What made me do that?" she asked. "Like . . . like some kind of bargain?"

But Justin did not answer her, for it had not really been a question. He held her head against his shoulder, and when she was quieter he lighted his pipe and passed it to her to smoke.

"Shall we go now and tell him?" Justin said. "Together? Or would you rather I went alone?"

"Oh, no, Justin. No. I must tell him myself when . . . when I think it is right. You must be content to trust me to know . . ."

But she did not finish her sentence and fell into silence, letting the clay pipe grow cold in her hands. "You see," she said, "he has not really returned to the old days after all, Justin, for in the old days he would have known all this. I would never have needed to tell him anything. He would have told me."

"I should be with you," Justin said. "I think it would be better."

Then he too fell silent, for these things were, after all, details, arrangements, trifles, compared to the fact which he was only now fully accepting, the long-awaited fact that his love, in a cloud of spicebark and burned almond mist, a feathermane asleep against one thigh, had said that she would come and live with him now and be his. Yes, she had said it. She had shaken his hand on it.

CHAPTER THREE

I T W A S a small room, dark. Through the only window the night lights of the city could be seen dimly, as through fog. The room was filled with sadness, with a feeling of his hopelessness which he shared with the woman. Arthur Herrick sat awkwardly on the edge of the bed, his arms clasped around the thighs of the woman standing beside him, his head against her hip. He could feel the rough cloth of her skirt against his cheek. Although he knew that she shared his feeling, there was an unyieldingness about her body. Under the skirt he could feel her muscles hard and tensed, pulling stubbornly away from him. Yet her hand rested willingly, even tenderly, on his head.

"Explain," she said. "You must explain to them."

It was then he saw that one of the walls which he had assumed gave onto the street was not a wall at all, but a curtain, falling into folds. The woman pulled herself gently from him and went over to the curtain. "They will listen to you," she said. "They must."

She pulled the curtain back slowly and he saw then that what he would have expected to be the open space on a street was, in reality, an assembly room, and that this room he had taken for a bedroom was the rear of a small stage. He got up slowly and moved forward onto the stage. Lights came up and he found himself beginning falteringly to tell them. As the seated listeners settled down and more of them turned their faces attentively to him he found himself grasping a hold on his thoughts and he began to speak surely and forcibly. Suddenly they were with him and he found himself speaking with fluidity, with such a beauty of language that the words seemed sensuously to caress his lips as they left his mouth. He stood straighter, his arms moving easily to help the words communicate his ideas to the listeners unmistakably, so that they could not fail to understand.

So Arthur Herrick awoke, as he had many times recently, to find his eyes filled with tears for the beauty of the words he had spoken in his dream. As starving men live over in memory the subtlest detail of flavoring and texture in the foods of past feasts, so Arthur, in these later days, had come to relive conversations he had had. Almost he could fondle sentences with his fingers, so clearly did they come to him at times, and the feeling of clothing an idea so that another might know it was almost literally sensuous. He did not particularly distinguish between his sexual impotence and that of his speech, except to count the former as part of the latter, and to feel, perhaps correctly, that the disappearance of one impotence would mean the end of the other. He was keenly appreciative of the fact that for anyone who, like himself, had lived always for and by and with ideas, it was the cruelest torture to have his communication with others reduced to a statement of physical wants. He desired communication, with a hunger so overpowering that at times he must use all his control not to smash with fury the pad and pen he wore strapped to his belt like some kind of chain. So long he had been content to be taken care of, to be fed, bathed, kept alive and not questioned; then gradually he had grown stronger so that, without realizing it, he had been ripe for hope when Tommy had drowned.

Even such tragic corroboration as finding the boy's body was still corroboration, and it was corroboration of an idea of the river's structure, an idea which he had himself conceived. In that arduous return journey from the child's grave to the settlement, Arthur Herrick had been amazed at his physical capacity; he became a man who has been given back his life. It was then that he began to hope to speak again. At first he felt confident of controlling this hope, of keeping it within bounds, of nurturing it and helping it to grow. Then the dreams had begun and, with them, the secret savoring and reliving of remembered conversations: of sitting across a table from Joe, talking, of pitting himself against the wall that was Mr. Dobenski, of talking with Justin about structure. By this time the hope was out of control; it engulfed him. No longer did he feel that he might some day speak again if he were patient and careful. The hope of speech beat on him its demands so that now, *now*, he must try and, trying, fail and, failing, be reduced to impotent fury.

In recent weeks the hope had taken on new character and Arthur came to believe that what he could not accomplish alone he might perhaps achieve with help. He knew that the river was a continuous spiral. This he had thought out, believed in, and this Tommy had proved. And every continuous spiral must of a certainty find itself a vortex. If he were to give himself to the vortex it would certainly spew him somewhere, and perhaps if he lived there would be doctors there. With their help he would speak again.

The alternative was to wait almost two years for the split to open again and lead them back the way they had come. Every day this waiting became more impossible for Arthur, and every day his belief that the river would lead to a quicker deliverance was firmer. There was one thing that convinced him more than anything else. That was the fact that Gwendolyn, who wanted escape from the Green Kingdom more than anyone, who had never, from the first day, wanted anything but to escape from it, feared the river above all things. It seemed to Arthur that its being so exactly consistent with Gwendolyn's life and character —for she had always feared and turned from the very thing that would mean her salvation—was a kind of confirmation that deliverance lay, and had always lain, by way of the river. The river, the river, the river. In his mind Arthur heard himself saying the words over and over and felt with a sensuous and agonizing pleasure the touch of his lower lip against his teeth in memory of the time of his speech.

He was alone in the cabin. On the hearth were the tea things which Erma had left ready for him. Shaking off his dream, Arthur washed his face and prepared breakfast for himself. The essence of each thing he touched, ate, felt spoke with an exquisite insistence to him. All the things which he had so long ignored, or simply endured, he knew, now that he planned to leave them, with an individual awareness: the texture of the coarse bread, the surface of the tea mug, the call of a stiltlegs outside the cabin. All the facts of their existence he experienced now, and often their whole history would come flooding over him. This cup would call up the first cup, the first tea, the first camp. It seemed to Arthur that the years were full of their history and he felt a traitor for having so long denied it. Since Joe's death he had himself been only a protest against death, living from one demand to the next, denying past, denying memory, denying future. But the gates were open now and the smallest things crowded upon him at every moment, so that he could look at nothing about him, perform no act, but that he felt the years in the Green Kingdom to be full of the richness of their living history. He became surfeited with remembering. At times he would stop whatever he was doing and hear in his head the words *Why, we had everything. Everything necessary.*

At such times he found it hard to believe that it had been he, above everyone, *he* who had turned against this paradise and made it into a trap for himself. He found it hard to remember why. Why was it he had fought against this life, this history? He could not fathom it. He could remember his hatred, but he could not remember why he had had it. It seemed foreign, as though it had happened to some other man. He was overwhelmed with sadness that it was only now—when he must leave it all—that this sense of participation was coming to him, that he could think of as *ours* the great accomplishments: the clearings, the houses, the corrals, The Room, the food stores, the cloth, the paper, ink, sandals and, yes, the deaths, the sorrows, the troubles.

Why, yes, they had had everything necessary here. They had experienced everything. A rich history was theirs that they had made and lived for. But he knew, even if now it reluctantly was coming to belong to him, he had missed his chance to belong to it. He knew that. He had missed his time here. The question was not how to live out the time in holding under control this knot of regret; the question was: Was he to be given another chance?

He thought he was. Not here, of course, but in some other place. At least he must make a try for it. That he must go to the end of the river was inevitable. Whether, at the end of it, he would be swallowed up in the vortex or spewed out upon some place where there were doctors who could restore his speech— either way, this knot would be at last dissolved. In the silent cabin so pregnant with the documentation of their years, Arthur walked over to the hearth, poured himself a fresh cup of tea, and returned to the table.

Yes, the river was his inevitable destiny. Perhaps it had always been. For even, very early, almost at the beginning of their time here, he had wanted to explore the river. He smiled now at the boat he and Joe had so long worked on, the boat that must long ago have been crumbled under the weight of choke-vines and eaten by insects. How complicated that boat had been, how foolishly constructed. The memory of the long months he and Joe had worked on the boat flooded over him. For Tommy had shown him, even in dying, that it was a raft that was needed, the simpler the better, and this could best be made at the bank of the river.

But these plans were not today's work. Today's work he had already planned, and for the beginning of it there could not be a better time than this, while he was alone in the cabin before he had spoken to any of the others. He reached now for his Record book, tried the point of the pen against his finger, and with deliberation removed the top from the ink pot and began to write.

This is my final Record. This is the last time. It has long been clear to me but some inner demand makes me say it here as a kind of test of finality. My work, the work to which I gave the struggling years of my youth, the best that was in me, the work to which I was willing to sacrifice my wife and my friends, was based on a fundamental error. I am not the first man who has had to face such knowledge. I would like to believe that I will learn to face it with better courage than some others have and that I will not devote all the time after the fact, as so many others have, in trying to destroy and discredit the work of other men. Perhaps the kind of Record which I believed in is not possible for any man. I do not know. But I know now that it is not possible for large numbers of people chosen at random. And the reason is that it violates some essential law of man's nature because it is an enemy of action. Whatever is an enemy of action cannot be undertaken casually, but must be weighed carefully in full knowledge of the cost involved by the person who takes the risk. The tools for seeking self-knowledge are so puny and few as compared to the formidable barriers of infinite variety which are thrown up tirelessly against such knowledge that my work is hopeless.

It was a hard thing to come to; harder to accept. But the People's Library can only be in existence, as it always has been—or mainly so—by the writings of men about other men, and not about themselves. In short, I no longer believe that a man can know himself in his own present time and I feel sure now that he was never meant to. In my own Record, the times of great crisis, the moments of real significance, are missing. There is no Record of my having killed Erma's feathermane, because I conveniently have no memory of it. But even more significantly there is no Record of my planning to steal, if necessary, the braidstem, nor any notation of the increasing quantities that I was then in the habit of taking. Neither is the fiction destroyed in the Record that I took the braidstem for headaches or any admission that the braidstem ceased to help the headaches after a time. Joe's death and the fact that I caused it are not recorded at the time they occurred because (again, conveniently) I was injured and I could not move my right arm for a long time after the acute phase of the injury. But these things, of course, could be (and were) chewed over in retrospect. They have not caused the deep sadness. What is gone, because I never had it, is the knowledge of how whatever wisdom or acceptances or reconciliations with life I have came to me in my long journey alone on the river. Perhaps, with everyone, this kind of understanding or whatever it is must come in the back door while one is not looking. You know something about what you can do and can't do, about what you can take and can't take, and something about how you must seem to other people, and you don't know how you know.

In short, a man can't be his own psychiatrist. At least, most men can't, not to the extent that it could become a way of life, because it is fundamentally against the protective measures that function outside of recognition, on a biological level. So, it was no fluke that I failed in Drury. Pete Dobenski was perfectly logical because he *dared* not be otherwise, not because he desired to make me fail. A larger group would not be any different. And what has happened to the Records here in the Green Kingdom is not exceptional, not because the group is small. It is because we are living organisms championing in different degrees what is on the side of life. My own Record's defeats I have mentioned. Joe very early came to use his to record his *own* work, his laboratory findings. And Justin long ago told me that he writes music almost entirely in his, *in order that he can anticipate keeping it with pleasure.* He told me, I remember, that all he could claim for it was that *any other musician* would be able to follow the state of his emotions (not his thoughts) with fair accuracy. Gwen of course never tried from the very beginning and only lately have I come to understand that she had no alternative.

The one thing I cannot understand is why, or how, Erma continues to keep hers, apparently in the same spirit in which she began. I have, of course, never seen it. It is impossible for me to tell myself that she never understood the work from the beginning and simply was satisfied always to keep a daily diary of the world about her. It is ridiculous to think that a woman who created that cave with her own hands, out of herself, would be happily satisfied to skim the surface and speak with me as though she knew of the depths. I do not understand it. I never will. I do not know how it is that she did carve upon the walls of a cave in the ground what other people sweep under the rugs of their brains. But if Erma's Records were the absolute living embodiment of the plans I had for my lifework, still it would not signify. There are not enough like her to make the work have any broad meaning. And their numbers cannot be increased by coercion. Nor, if it were possible, should they be.

For here is what I know now. The real Record, the only one that can be nearly universal, is here, all about us, and always has been. It is the cup on the hearth, the cheese stored in the shed, the sandals on my feet; it is the shape of the oil lamp on the wall. It is Kathy and Tommy. The keeping of a true Record cannot be a man's lifework. Records are kept in truth as a *result* of men's lifework. And I do not say that this is the best way necessarily; I say it is the only way possible for most living men when they are primarily concerned with living.

And so I have done it. I have written my last Record. I have said in the baldest way possible that I am a man whose work was based on a fundamental error, and therefore I am a man who has no work. I have no children and, in reality, no wife. And I have no friend because, in my carelessness, I killed my friend. And the blame for all this, if it is a matter for blame at all? It is mine and cannot be made out to be any other's. And so there is only one thing left, then, the slimmest chance of another chance to be concerned primarily with living. It is time now, very soon, to find out if this also is based on a fundamental error. This writing is the last essential thing before the ultimate decision to go.

———————

Arthur closed the book, put down the pen, and replaced the top of the ink pot. For some time he sat motionless. At last he shook his head impatiently and sighed. Well, then, if the time had really come, and the few tools and supplies he needed were ready, as they had been for some days, why, then, did he delay? What held him?

For one thing, the new clothing which Gwendolyn had promised to make for him, though she knew only his present need and not that he planned to travel in the clothes. But this he recognized at once as an excuse. When a man goes to seek something which has always been there and will be there tomorrow, it is hard for him to choose of himself the moment of leaving, unless something outside himself conspires to urge him. What am I waiting for? he thought. Surely I, who brought them nothing but sorrow and death and the tedium of my care—surely I do not hope for one of them to wish me farewell and bon voyage?

As he cleaned up his breakfast dishes he thought: Is this the last time? Will tomorrow be the last time? The sound of the crockery had a sound of finality about it. For a moment he had a picture of himself breakfasting alone, on the raft on the river, and for the first time in several days the picture filled him with excitement. He moved over to his cobbler's bench and began the work that would finish the new sandals he was making for Gwendolyn. He had made new sandals for all of them now. When these are worn out, he thought, will they remember? How will they think of me then?

He worked quietly, patiently, now and then straightening himself out of old habit to ease the discomfort in his chest where the misshapen scar tissue pulled.

Erma came in with a basket of firewood, which she put down on the hearth. "Have you had breakfast?" she asked him.

Arthur nodded and smiled at her.

"Good," she said. "You started a new kettle. I'd love some tea. Are those Gwen's?"

She picked up the one finished sandal in her hands. "They're beautiful, Arthur. Kathy's were the prettiest of all. All the same, I'm glad you didn't make mine out of this hide."

Arthur looked at her and smiled and then returned to his work. He would have liked to touch her, but knew it was too dangerous a thing for him. He was so often filled with pity for Erma, and he was frightened that to express it would loosen a flood of emotion that he could not control. This hide had come from a stillborn calf. It was there, always, between them, the memory of his failure to help her, to share with her her sterility. Would it all have been different if Erma had had children, the way he used to think? He doubted it. He shook his head and pushed himself back from the bench angrily.

It came to him to take his pad and write on it: *I'm going, Erma. I'm leaving.* But he did not. He was afraid. He knew that if she were to reach out and touch him he would beg her to come with him. He knew he would not be able to help himself. If she refused, how would he face the rejection of it? But if, as she might—as he knew, even now, in spite of everything, she might —if she accepted, then how could he face the guilt of it? No, better the way he had planned. Much better. The need to fall on his knees before her, to beg her forgiveness for all the times he had hated her, made him grab up the finished sandals. Waving them toward Erma in a gesture of explanation, he went out of the cabin. He had found it much easier, of late, to be with Gwendolyn. With Gwen he was not in constant danger of breaking down. She seemed to have lost much of her old animosity toward him, though he had done nothing to lessen it. Perhaps Gwen, too, was undergoing a softening process with the years, similar to his own. To whom would she tell her fears when he was gone? he wondered. Well, that was not his worry. He would be glad to hear the last of her headaches, her heart complaints, her fears of a brain tumor. At any rate, with Gwen, he did not have to keep reaching for his hated writing pad. All one had to do was listen. Gwen talked. Well, he could take a day or two more of it. Nobody got new clothes without paying some price for them, and this was his. He found Gwen sitting on the floor by the hearth trying with a wooden pestle to masserate a bowl of the heavily scented swamp-star flowers. The Room was filled with the heady, sultry odor. Gwendolyn's long, damp hair, freshly washed, hung down her back, drying.

"Oh, Arthur," she said, "I was wishing you'd come. Here, you pound awhile. It's harder work than I thought. I'm making perfume. I decided today I had to have perfume, that I'd die without perfume."

Arthur wondered how she had managed to get the swamp-stars, for he knew she loathed the dark, mucky places where they grew. He held the sandals out to her.

"Put them on," she said, thrusting out her bare feet. "They're lovely, Arthur. Thank you. You really shouldn't let me have them until I finish your suit."

Arthur knelt a little awkwardly and put the sandals on her. She was vain of her feet, he knew.

She suddenly moved close to him and placed her hands under his face. "Smell," she said.

Arthur raised his head from her hands and leaned back to escape the heavy smothering odor, and as he did so he looked into her eyes in the hope of communicating his distaste of the too strong perfume. But what he saw there stopped him. Absolute surrender showed. Something unforseen had happened and Arthur felt himself trapped and unable to move. He longed for Kathy to enter The Room and deliver him.

"Arthur," Gwen whispered, "don't leave me."

How did she know? Or was it only that she asked him now not to leave her, not to leave this room? He had never seen such obvious entreaty in his life as he read in her eyes. The awkwardness of having to take out his writing pad would be a slap in her face. He could not bring himself to do it.

What does she want of me? he thought. But it was unmistakable, the entreaty in her eyes, the waiting silence. Even he, impotent and sexless as he felt himself to be, even he recognized this naked surrender. But surely she knew about him, he thought. He had long taken it for granted that they all knew. The fear that he might be put in a position of explaining it to Gwendolyn so shocked him that he was able to break the silent spell, move jerkily aside and lift onto his lap the bowl of flowers. There was enough fury and embarrassment in him to grind them to a powder easily, he thought as he reached for the wooden pestle. But Gwendolyn put her hands over the bowl and waited for him to look at her.

"Never mind, Arthur. It won't work, anyway. I've tried before. The perfume always rots or ferments or gets a scum over it. It always fails." She buried her face in her hands and began to weep. "Everything fails," she said.

Arthur was less frightened now. Her weeping he had seen before. He put his hand on her head and was suddenly filled with sympathy for her such as he had never felt before. At the same time he raged at his speechlessness, for he longed to comfort her despair. He longed to tell her what he himself had so recently discovered: all the moods and insight and wisdom that to him were summed up in the words *Why, we had everything. Everything necessary.*

For a moment he believed that if only he could tell Gwendolyn about this, if only he could explain to her all that the phrase meant to him, he could somehow help her in a way she could accept. He could not remember now why he had always resisted this woman, often hated her, feared her, held her in contempt, for the quality of her despair was formidable and demanded attention, even respect.

Slowly, as though under the weight of her great hopelessness, she lay back on the floor and stared up at the ceiling, not weeping now. Her eyes were so filled with sadness that Arthur Herrick felt himself drowning in them and knew the abyss was more than he could alleviate, more than any man could touch. A whole man, perhaps, might tackle it. For himself, it would be hopeless.

"I want to die," she whispered.

If he had had speech then it would not have helped him any, he realized. He reached out to stroke her hair, finding with surprise how alive it felt to his hand, for Gwendolyn lay so flat against the floor as to seem already dead. Suddenly she reached up and clung to him.

"I'm afraid," she said. "I'm afraid of my thoughts. Arthur," she said, pressing herself close against him, "don't leave me."

He lifted her so that he might be sitting up and held her in his arms. What could he do? For a moment, so well had he shared her despair, he found himself tempted to relinquish the river, relinquish hope of speech, and take on this woman's sorrow for his own, simply because it fitted her so poorly. It came to him that this was what Joe had been trying to tell him. It had never occurred to him to wonder in all these years what it was, on that fateful day, that Joe had been trying to tell him.

"Listen, Arthur, I've got to tell you something," Joe had said, but he, Arthur, had had all his attention on the path to the cave. He had not heard until now the hesitation, the apology, the entreaty in Joe's voice. And not hearing, he had led him foolishly, carelessly to his death.

"Don't leave me, Joe." That was what she must have said. And Joe had agreed as a moment before he had been tempted to agree. Arthur felt himself filled with hatred for the woman who had managed to give him a suppliant, weakling picture of Joe. Here, clinging to him, wrapping him in despair, drinking in his pity, was the enemy of all exploration, adventure, the enemy of man's trying and questing, the woman who ate hope and breathed out despair. And now Arthur knew that he was saved, that somehow he would escape her, that his hatred would cut through her sorrow and free him.

Gwendolyn felt his arms stiffen and, in desperation, she tore open the front of her dress, freeing one shoulder and one bare breast. "Love me," she said. "Love me."

It was as though his brain had become a rabbit pen and the sight of Gwen's breast opened the door, so that his thoughts, like rabbits, went hopping about in all directions and he must gather them all in individually before he could act. His attention flew from one irrelevant distraction to the next, and he was aware of their irrelevancy, he was aware of the inopportuneness of his thinking at all at such a moment. Yet he was powerless to help himself. He must act. In some way. He must touch her, grab her shoulder, touch her face, make her understand that she had asked the one thing impossible for him. Odd to feel nothing, not even disgust, nothing except the panic at being distracted until no action was possible. How long could she wait with her eyes closed like that? If only he could speak! Say, "Gwendolyn"; say, "No, Gwen." Say . . . anything. And maddeningly he fell to thinking of his new clothes, and hated his inability to stop thinking of them. For if he had to go in the old ones, as he surely would now, he might have saved himself all this. He might have left this morning. Why hadn't he? The situation seemed almost hysterically funny to him, as though he were keeping a firing squad ready and in prolonged suspense, his white handkerchief held aloft, while he explained that he must list the names of all his cousins first.

He saw Gwen open her eyes and he knew that already it was too late. Never would he be able to make her understand, for even if he could bring himself to take out his writing pad at such a time, what would he write? *My brain is full of rabbits; never mind the new pants.*

Gwen jerked upright, away from him, and got to her feet. "So I amuse you?" she said. "I'm funny?"

Now it was possible for Arthur to move at last. He stood facing her, shaking his head, reaching out to touch her. She whirled away from him. "Don't touch me," she said. "You . . . you . . . How dare you laugh! Don't deny it. I saw you. You've always laughed at me, haven't you? I've always hated you, always. You hear? Always!"

Her voice grew louder until at last she was shouting at him. Her face was contorted with fury. She made no gesture to cover herself but left the dress hanging from one shoulder. Arthur knew it was impossible—he could never explain. There was nothing to do but leave. He put out his hands, palms up, shrugged his shoulders, and moved toward the door. Behind him he heard her still shouting, threatening something, but he did not look back. Once outside he breathed with relief and then started toward his own cabin. There was so much to do now, now that the time had come.

On the way he met Kathy, the skirt of her dress filled with swampstars, her legs and arms caked with the swamp mud. So that was how Gwen had got them. She had sent the little girl for them where she herself was afraid to go. It occurred to Arthur that he ought to take the exhausted child home to Erma, feed her, clean her up. But, after all, by tomorrow he would be beyond helping any of them or harming them either and so why not today? He waved to Kathy and went on.

By the time the tired child had trudged home and managed by herself to lift the heavy latch on the door with one hand while she held the swampstars safely bundled in her skirt with the other, Gwendolyn's rage had risen to its violent frenzy and at last spent itself so that, entering The Room, Kathy's "More flowers, Mummy" said itself, unanswered, to a silent room. Something was wrong, she knew. She put down her skirt and heedlessly let the flowers fall on the floor at her feet. She could see her mother across the room sitting naked on a bench by the fire, staring. Cautiously the little girl began to move toward the familiar figure which somehow looked unfamiliar. Her mother's hair was cut short, all choppy, and there at her feet was the big pile of it. Had Mummy told a lie, then? That was the way you got your hair cut off, she knew. But what had her mother said? It was very bad to tell a lie. It was so bad it made you wet yourself. She moved a little nearer, but still her mother did not seem to notice her. She was looking right at her but she didn't see her. Why was Mummy holding the big knife across her naked legs? Didn't other people cut your hair off if you lied?

Now the child noticed that the floor was covered with broken dishes and crocks. And there was a stool overturned. She went over quietly and set it upright, and then she sat down on it. When her mother saw the mud on her she would scold, she knew, but that would be better. She moved the chair up a little. "I got mud on me," she said.

Her mother did not answer, did not move. Kathy remembered that she was very hungry. Among the broken dishes on the table she found a piece of bread. This she carried back to the stool and, sitting down, began silently to chew on it. Now she remembered the flowers she had dropped at the door and, passing a little nearer her mother, she went and gathered them up and put them with the ones that Arthur had earlier been pounding. Kathy then began to pick up the broken dishes and to carry them over to the corner of the room. Each time she crossed the room she skirted a little closer to the staring figure on the bench. At last she went up to her mother and took the big knife out of her loose hands and put it away. Then she picked up her mother's dress from the floor and took it to her. Gwendolyn made no sign of recognition and the child spread the dress over her lap. Then she bent down and picked up the heavy pile of hair from the floor and held it out to Gwendolyn.

"Put your hair back on, Mummy," she said.

But the staring figure made no move. At last the child let the long hair fall from her hands and, knowing nothing else to do, crawled quietly onto her bed and covered herself. She put her thumb in her mouth, knowing she wouldn't be scolded now, knowing she wouldn't even be seen. Just as she was falling asleep she remembered what it was that she had to tell her mother, that would surely make her notice, make her talk. In the swamp she had seen an emerald stuck down in the center of a big plant, but she had been afraid to get it. When she woke up she would tell her mother about the emerald, because now she was too sleepy and too cold. She sucked her thumb and pulled herself into a small knot and fell asleep.

Slowly Gwendolyn's body bent forward. The arms leaned upon the thighs, the head fitted into the upturned, lifeless palms of her hands. Was there, then, no alternative? Gradually her eyes came to focus on the pile of hair on the floor. Tears fell out of her eyes and dropped onto it, glistening there a moment. What of the knife, then, the knife? She looked at her empty hands in wonder. The awareness of the changed weight of her head came to her. She put up one of the lifeless hands to confirm it. She reached for the dress which had slipped to the floor and put it on. In a daze she walked about the room until she saw the knife safely put away on the mantel. A great fear came upon her that she could not remember having put it there. She heard her own heart beating in her panic. Someone. Anyone. She must not be alone. She would run to find them, talk to them. An excuse. She must have an excuse. She ran across the room to find the new clothes for Arthur. She would take them to him, then say they had to be fitted, say . . . Memory returned. The memory of her humiliation, the memory of Arthur's laughter. The memory of rage.

Her hair. They would notice her hair. Well, let them. Let them know, then, how she had been treated. Let them know.

She was breathing hard now, fastening her dress, moving about The Room, picking things up aimlessly, putting them down, and in her erratic movements moving gradually closer to the door. That would be the test, then. Yes, she would put them to the test. She would say, "Yes, I cut it off with the butcher knife," and then watch them. She would test them. If only one of them said a word of Christian pity, only one of them, one word, then she would be saved.

And if not? She was out the door now, running, running toward Erma's house. If not, then it would be on their heads. Then it was their fault, their fault, and they would suffer for it. Let them pass the test or suffer. She could make them, all of them, suffer for it.

*

Erma came into her house, the grain bag still over her shoulder, to put on the kettle before finishing her chores so that as soon as she had finished them she could have a cup of tea. The fire was almost out; Arthur was not in the cabin. She took a spill from the mantel, blew upon the coals to light it, and touched it to the wick in the lamp. As soon as it flared up she saw the letter.

"My dear Erma," she read, and, forgetting the fire and the tea, she sank down onto a bench, letting the strap of the grain bag fall off her shoulder while she read.

I am going away now, Erma, and, as much as any man can plan, I plan not to return. Certainly I can guarantee at least that any claim I have upon you is at an end and I hope that you will feel free to live your life in all good conscience according to your desires. I know that you love Justin and I know that Justin has long loved you. That you should live freely in this love is my wish for you and yet I know you so well, Erma, that I know there would be no better way to poison this for you than to make you believe that I am clearing out for your sakes.

It is not so. I go for the river itself, to know it, but also in the hope that at the end of it there is a way out. And that, once out, I can find the way to doctors who can restore my speech. When I was without hope and only waiting to die, it did not matter. Now that I have begun to recover, the idea of speechlessness is intolerable. I would rather be dead than without hope of speech.

So you see it is not a mistaken martyrdom which motivates me. Long ago, when I first realized that, not having children, we would be second in importance to Joe and Gwen, I acted stupidly, criminally. I accused. I contributed to and primarily caused your beginning feeling of inadequacy which was to have such disastrous results for all of us. Between us there have been anger and bitterness, guilt and love, hatred and contempt. But there would always return devotion in some degree and sympathy for each other. In all the ways you have appeared to me you have never seemed ridiculous and so, I hope, I never have to you.

Even now I think that if I wanted you to come with me you would come. You must remember that I did not want it so.

I thank you for the long months of care and nursing. The bitterness, dear Erma, has oozed out of the wound slowly, with the pus and blood and pain. Of the long list of things that I should have asked it for, I ask forgiveness for only one thing: that I consistently and seriously, and in all respects, underestimated you.

As I should have loved life, as I should have loved you, Erma, now do I love the river, whether in its vortex lies a hope of speech or not. After much sorrow and waste and the contemplation born of long illness, I love something without question. I cast myself upon the river in a frail craft with only the most receptive curiosity to learn whatever it has to teach.

This I hope for you, you who were my girl, that you too may live again with joy and curiosity.

ARTHUR

In the dim light of the room Erma bent forward to read the postscript:

For one who has taken so little responsibility before, I suppose now this concern will seem trivial; but today I saw Kathy returning from the swamp with swampstar flowers. I don't think she should go there alone. There are spike plants there.

A.

So Justin found Erma when he came in, still sitting holding the letter in her hands, the hearth cold, the lamp smoking, and the grain bag on the floor beside her.

"What is it, Erma?" he said. He went rapidly over to the lamp and adjusted the wick.

"Arthur is gone," she said.

"Gone? Where? Where could he go?"

"To the river. Alone. Oh, Justin, I feel such a failure."

Justin came over to her and put one hand on her shoulder. "You need your tea," he said, "before you tell me. I'll build up the fire. It's cold in here. Arthur's all right?" he asked. "There's no emergency?"

"Oh, no," she said. *"He's* all right."

Justin heard the emphasis on the word, but he busied himself with the fire. Erma wanted time. It was a surprise, though, all the same. He brought Erma the tea and sat down opposite her.

"You remember, Justin? You remember I said that if Arthur had been like himself there would be no need for me to tell him about us? Well, he knew. It was not he who was unseeing; it was I."

"But how could you have known his plan?"

"Oh, there are many little things, now that I think back. I should have known. I should have, Justin. How is it possible to live so many years with one person and not know the most important . . . ?"

In her mind she kept hearing over the phrase from the letter: *the surest way to poison it for you, the surest way to poison it for you.*

"But did he say why, Erma? Will he be back?"

She shoved the letter toward him. "Here," she said, "you'd better see for yourself. I'm reading things into it. I feel . . . I feel angry and I'm sure there's nothing angry in there. Oh, I don't know," she said. "I don't know how I feel. Why couldn't he have told me?"

It was while Justin was finishing reading the letter that Gwendolyn burst into the cabin. The familiar scene of two people drinking tea before a fireplace instantly calmed her, as though she had reached safety. Immediately she craved a cup of tea, too.

"Where's Arthur?" she said. "I brought his new clothes. They have to be fitted."

"Sit down, Gwen," Justin said. "Here. Have some tea. Arthur is gone."

"Gone?" she said, the cup arrested halfway to her mouth. "What do you mean?"

"He has gone to the river," Justin said. "Apparently he's not coming back."

Gwen looked from one to the other quickly. Her hand shook and she spilled the tea. Would they blame her, then? Did they know? Did they know it was because of her that Arthur had gone off to drown himself? That was rich. That was a funny one. That Arthur should be the one to kill himself instead of her. Somehow this had saved her, she knew. And she need not die. She began to laugh and the more the others stared at her in silence, the more she laughed.

"Shut up, Gwen," Justin said. "Stop it!"

They did know, then. They blamed her. Immediately she stopped laughing and began to cry.

"It's all my fault," she said. "I didn't mean to drive him away. It's because of me he's killed himself."

"Gwen, what are you talking about?" Erma said. "Arthur hasn't killed himself. He thinks there's a way out. Oh," she said in exasperation to Justin, "oh, take her away. I don't know what she's talking about. I want to be alone for a while."

Justin lifted the hysterical woman to her feet. "Come on, Gwen," he said. "Come on. I'll go over to The Room with you. Can't you see Erma's upset? Can't you see she needs to be alone?"

"*Erma's* upset!" Gwen shouted. "It's always Erma, Erma, Erma! Nobody ever notices if I'm upset."

"Come on," Justin said.

Weeping more quietly now, Gwendolyn followed Justin out of the cabin.

"I see you've cut your hair," Justin said.

Gwen put one hand up to her hair. "Yes," she said. "It was too heavy to brush. It was too much bother. I thought maybe it had something to do with my headaches."

"Well, it's quite becoming to you," Justin said.

What was it now about her hair she had been planning to say? Some test. Well, never mind now.

"Erma is really suffering, isn't she?" she said.

Justin looked at the girl sharply, though it was too dark now to see the smile that he knew must surely be on her face.

"She just wants to be alone," he said.

Alone, in the cabin, Erma brushed the unsettling scene with Gwen out of her mind. She couldn't be concerned with it now.

She picked up Arthur's letter and folded it and sat there knocking one edge of the letter against the table.

"Well," she said aloud, "well . . ."

She reached for the strap of the grain bag and put it slowly over her shoulder. Then she stood up and slowly walked out of the cabin to feed the flock of dowager hens. They cackled about her in great confusion, but she had no greeting for them. She spread the grain down mechanically and, in her numbness, didn't hear their noise.

*

In the days that followed, Justin had occasion to be reminded often of Erma's words to him: *I'm afraid to show happiness before Gwendolyn. I don't know why.* The enormity of this obstacle to their happiness, which evaded definition, infuriated him. He had brought himself to grappling with it, after the long time of avoiding it, placating it, giving it temporary expedients. In Erma's absence, partly to distract himself from his concern for her, he was trying to pay his full attention to Gwen in a last desperate effort to understand her. The fact that Arthur's disappearance had not simplified but had complicated their lives had been a great shock to him. There was a time when he had thought if only Arthur Herrick could be removed from the scene there would be no obstacle to his union with Erma. But he saw now that Erma's leaving Arthur for him would have been much simpler than their leaving Gwen alone. This was clearly unthinkable. For a long time he had planned the house he would build for himself and Erma away from the settlement and its record of tragedy and failure, its constant demands of work to be done. Clearly now this could not be. What happiness could they expect with each other based on the abandonment of this frightened, desperate woman who really could not be trusted to care for her own child?

Arthur's leaving had not simplified Erma's immediate problem, either. The numbness had hung onto her. She had been lost in it. And then, finally, she had come to Justin and said, "I have to go after him, Justin. I have to put an end to this somehow."

"Well, then," he said, "if you have to, let me go with you."

"No, Justin," she had said. "No, I have to be alone. I have to be alone when I see him. Besides, you know that if we both left, Gwen would go out of her mind with fear."

"Erma," Justin said, "you're not thinking of going with him?"

"No," she said. "Of course not. I can't explain. It's just that I can't seem to start anything new. I can't begin. And I'm angry all the time. Why should I be angry now? Years ago I had things to be angry about. But now . . . There's nothing vindictive in that letter. I've read it over and over. It's a very generous letter; it's one he might have been capable of writing years ago. Except that then he would have talked it over with me, not left a letter. I'm full of this anger all the time. It's destroying me. Old things keep going around in my head. I seem unable to control them."

"Maybe it's right, Erma. Maybe you should have been angry long ago, seen Arthur as an enemy and fought him, and, because you didn't, perhaps it's all coming to a head now."

"Oh, I don't know, Justin. Maybe it's just that I don't believe it, that I want to satisfy myself he's really gone. I keep thinking I hear him, you know."

"Well, I suppose you must go and satisfy yourself," Justin said. "But I shall worry about you. Will you promise to come back as soon as you possibly can?"

"I can't promise anything, Justin. I'm so baffled. I didn't know I'd feel like this. I don't want to come back until I'm different. Until I have this finished, somehow, over and done with."

Justin had taken her in his arms then, very gently, because in so many ways she still seemed very young to him. "My dear," he said, "I'm afraid that's not possible. Human things don't seem to get finished like that. You would not have me deny Edith's existence, would you?"

"No," she said. "No, of course not. But you don't feel all the time that you failed Edith, do you?"

It was a serious question. He had not asked it of himself for a long time. "No," he said finally. "No, I don't feel that way about Edith. I do about the boy, though," he added. "I didn't ever get over it about George."

"I don't even know what it is I want to say to Arthur," Erma said. "Or perhaps it's something I want him to say to me."

*

"What are you thinking about, Justin?" Gwen asked.

They had just finished dinner, and Gwen, coming from putting Kathy to bed, had joined Justin before the fire. They took all their meals together now, and in fact were together almost constantly, for, even when Justin must work outdoors, Gwen would follow him out. Always she walked on a precipice, fearing to be alone for any length of time.

"I was wondering about Erma," Justin said. "Wondering if it isn't about time for her to be back."

"Back?" Gwendolyn said. "Why, of course she won't be back. You ought to know that. She never meant to come back."

Sometimes the woman was so transparent, Justin thought. It was very deceptive; it gave you the idea that you knew what you were dealing with. He remembered the ease with which, once they were alone together, she had accepted the fact of Tommy's drowning. Not to accept it had made Arthur an ally with her against Justin and Erma. As soon as her ally was gone, then she must drop the accusation against Justin and Erma—that they held the child captive. For she must have a new ally. Yet Justin knew this oversimplified the situation. He knew that such a statement of it connoted a conscious planning which surely had not been there.

It was deceptively easy, too, how quickly one got the illusion of having been helpful to the woman, of having changed her. For it was quite easy to produce outward signs of improvement in her: tidiness of the house, cleanliness of her person, care of the child (even oversolicitousness), responsibility for meals and even an obvious desire to please. All these changes had been very quickly wrought since the night he had brought her home, half hysterical, to find Kathy asleep in bed, covered with mud. All that one needed to do to achieve this apparent miracle was to devote all of oneself, all the time, to her. This Justin found very difficult and knew he could never do for any length of time. In the last years he had become much attached to solitude and he found constant company exhausting. After he had tucked Gwen and Kathy both in at night, as though they were of the same age, and banked the fire, he would walk to his cabin and fall on his own bed wearily, only to wake in a few hours from a dream of concern about Erma.

"Tell me, Gwen," Justin said, "I've long meant to ask you. Why did you destroy the walls of Erma's cave?"

He watched her head jerk up, the short hair framing it softly, making her face more childlike even than of old. He saw her body stiffen and ready itself. He had been trying this now for some days, in the moments when they were alone together, to throw some sudden surprise at the girl, hoping to find, in her offguard answers, some better understanding of her.

"Erma's cave?" she said. "Why Erma's cave? It's my husband who's buried there."

"Yes, of course," he said. "I called it Erma's cave only because she made it, you know."

"Erma made it? Why, Justin, how could you believe such lies? How could she have made it? You know perfectly well it was an old cave that had been here for God knows how long. Joe found it himself."

"No, Gwen, I'm sure Erma told you about the cave. You must have misunderstood. But that's beside the question. What I wanted to know was why you destroyed the work."

"Why, the emeralds, of course."

"Emeralds?" Justin said. "Oh, they're real, then. I remember your having spoken of them long ago."

Gwen jumped up and went away a moment. When she came back she handed Justin a small leather bag. "See for yourself," she said.

Justin fumbled with the knotted string and finally poured the stones into his hand. It was all so baffling, everything about this woman.

"Come over by the fire," Gwen said, "so you can see them in the light."

Justin moved over to the hearth and sat down. He held the stones in the palm of his hand. They meant nothing to him, except a memory of some unpleasantness early in Arthur's illness, and again a scene with Tommy and Kathy at breakfast; but he saw that Gwen was kindled with excitement. She knelt on the floor before him, staring at the stones.

"I meant to keep them all to myself," she said. "They were my secret. But now that you know, you'll help me, won't you? There must be more. There *must* be. But I wore myself out hunting them. And then I . . . You'll help me, won't you?"

"Where did you find them?" Justin said, turning the stones in his hand to catch the firelight.

"I didn't find them," she said. "Joe did."

"But how could he have told you he found them in the cave, Gwen? He was never in the cave before that day and he was killed before we got there."

It had always angered her that Joe had kept this to himself. It was humiliating. Now she stood up and turned away from Justin. She walked back and forth in front of the fireplace.

"It must have been there," she said. "It must have. What else would he have been doing there?"

"Then he didn't tell you where he found them?" Justin asked. At least now he had the answer to his question. It was not wanton destruction, not grief turned to hatred that had made her destroy the wall carvings; it had been to her a simple mining operation.

"No," she said, "of course he didn't. He wanted it to be a secret. He wanted to have power over me. Oh, how he must have laughed to see me digging away at those walls when there was nothing there. Nothing!"

What had he been hoping for? Justin thought. Had he really thought that in a few days he could make a human being out of a woman who was ready to accuse her husband of dying for spite? Again he heard Erma's words: *I'm afraid to show happiness before Gwen.*

Justin got up impatiently and reached to the mantel for a pipe, leaving the stones lying on the hearth. He lighted the pipe and stood watching Gwen touching the stones. An overwhelming depression settled down on him. How was it possible that this frightened, irrational child had the power to tyrannize two people as strong as Erma and himself? How had they ever allowed it? Why had they not, long ago, ruthlessly trampled her to death? Her power was very real. This pitiful, irresponsible creature had, because of the smallness of their numbers, the power to regulate his meetings with Erma, the power to make their love furtive, to make their joy guilt. As he had sighed a thousand times before, he sighed with the deepest regret: if only Joe had not died.

"Well, tell me," he said. "What did you plan to do with them, then?"

Gwen looked up at him in surprise. Then she stood up. "Do with them? Why, we would be rich. Do you realize what they would be worth?"

She put one hand up to her temple to help her remember. For once, surely, it had been very clear to her what she would do with the emeralds. Once she had explained it all to that little boy, to Tommy.

"Why," she said, "we could have anything we wanted."

I can't just walk out of here and leave it, Justin thought. I can't erase her, I can't escape it. I can never be rid of her so long as she lives.

"Come and sit down with me, Gwen," he said.

When they were seated he reached out and took her hands. "And what is it you want?" he said. "You tell me, now. What is it you want?"

Why is it, Justin thought, why is it I never asked her this before? For one moment, out of his tiredness and discouragement, he had a wild hope that the woman would say, "I want your eye; I want your arm," and he could pull out the eye, tear off the arm, and say to her, "Here, take it, take it, and leave me in peace." But he knew it could never be so easy.

Gwen had been sitting opposite Justin on a low stool. Now, her hands still in his, she slipped to the floor and knelt before Justin, looking up into his face. The room had become very silent. The moment prolonged itself. Justin, waiting for her answer, looked down into her upturned face. Gwendolyn's large, dark eyes spoke unmistakable, trusting appeal. Yet she said nothing.

If Kathy would only awake now, Justin prayed. If Erma would return at this moment and deliver him. But nothing interrupted the woman's intensity and for Justin the scene took on a feeling of unreality, as though Gwen were not a woman at all but some beautiful, inarticulate animal trying desperately to communicate with him. We are carved out of stone, Justin thought, this silken, appealing, inarticulate animal and I, and we have been here ten thousand years.

At last Gwen spoke, her voice a harsh whisper in the silent room. "Justin, do you remember how we used to feed the birds together before Tommy was born?"

"Yes," he said, "of course I remember it. It seems a long time ago, doesn't it?"

The spell was broken. He could move now. He straightened himself in the chair and patted her head affectionately. He saw with gratitude that the fire was low and knew that in a few moments he could move across to the hearth on the excuse of replenishing it, and, from there, he would be very cautious. Certainly he would never again ask her what she wanted.

"And do you remember the little coverlet you made for me out of the feathers? I've always kept it, Justin."

"Oh?" Justin said, his mind on the fire and escape from those great, appealing eyes that would not leave him. "I would have thought it fallen apart by now," he said, "or molded. I'm afraid the workmanship was pretty clumsy."

"You asked what I wanted, Justin, a while ago."

"Yes," he said.

"Well?"

"Well, what, child? You're very strange tonight, very sad and quiet. What is it?"

"That's what I want, Justin," she said. "I miss Tommy so terribly. I'm so very lonely. I want another child."

He had thought himself beyond shock, as old as he was, as much as he had lived through. An unreasoning anger rose in him so that he pushed the girl aside and went to the hearth. He busied himself with the fire in an effort to gain some sense of control. His fury was turned upon himself, for now he saw the idiot role he had played, hoping to understand this woman, believing he could direct her toward some kind of acceptance of his love for Erma. He could see how this must have been planned, how, as Erma's return had grown imminent, Gwen in growing desperation had seen herself in competition where she had, she believed, only one advantage.

Behind him he heard her low laughter and he turned abruptly. Gwen sat on the floor, her arms around her knees. She was fighting against tears, summoning anger and contempt to save herself from humiliation.

"Well," she said, "don't tell me you too are going off to the river to drown yourself."

"You're mistaken," Justin said. "Arthur's going had nothing to do with you. It was planned months ago."

Now Gwen sprang to her feet, anger blazing in her eyes. She stood directly before Justin. "Oh, it didn't?" she said. "What do you know about it? What do you know about anything? Tell me," she said, "am I that ugly? Am I so repulsive that this has to happen to me twice? Well?" she shouted. "Well, do I have leprosy?"

Justin put his hands on her shoulders and began to shake her. "For the love of God, Gwen," he said, "be quiet!"

At last the anger went out of her eyes and he felt her resistance crumple. She began to whimper and finally she sank down onto the hearth and buried her face in her hands.

The anger had gone out of Justin, too. She had always been able to arouse pity in him, even when her craftiness and plotting were most obvious. No matter how much, through the years, she had aroused his anger and his contempt, there was always at the end of it this appeal she had for him. As he told Erma later it was, he thought, the awful inadequacy of her weapons compared to the size of her battle that moved him.

"I'm going to make us some tea," he said. "You see if you can't get hold of yourself, and then we'll sit down together and talk."

"Talk," she said. "Talk." And she began to laugh. But the laughter, Justin was grateful to see, did not reach hysterical proportions and soon died out, leaving the room quiet except for the magnified clatter the tea things made.

Justin drew up a chair, lighted his pipe and sat down. "Gwen," he said, "I want to talk to you seriously about the future."

She looked at him in a dazed way. "Future?" she said. "What future?"

"Yours," he said. He began to speak with a seriousness and an authority that he did not by any means feel. "I want you to put your mind on the future," he said. "I want you to begin planning for it now. Why, do you realize that there are only about two years left before you can go back to the World?"

"Two years," she said. "It might as well be two hundred. I will never live to leave here."

"Why, of course you will," Justin said. "You are a young woman, Gwen. You will have more children. You will marry again. You will be happy again."

"Two years," she said. "You don't understand."

"But, my dear, look what you have lived through already. Look what you have endured. Surely the worst that will ever be asked of you has already been asked."

"No," she said. "Not two months. I can't endure it. You don't understand."

She seemed to be very sleepy. Her shoulders, so erect when she had been angry, now drooped. She spoke slowly in extreme lassitude and she stared at the floor.

"I wish you would drink your tea," he said.

Slowly she lifted her head and looked at him out of dull, dead eyes. "Why?" she said.

"Well, because I think it would make you feel better."

"You want me to feel better so that I can suffer more?"

"Not at all, Gwen. Why should I wish you to suffer?"

She continued to sit bent over, staring at the hearth. Once she sighed as though to express the despair of all those abandoned everywhere, and once she gave a bitter little laugh and stretched out her hands to the stones on the hearth.

"Why did I think they were emeralds?" she said. "Any fool can see they're nothing but glass. There's no light in them. No life."

It was like the Kingdom itself, she thought. Why had they called it the Green Kingdom when there was nothing, wherever you looked, but this gray sameness, like an eternal fog, closing in, closing in?

*

Erma had correctly calculated that Arthur, wishing to experience as much of the river as possible, would set his raft afloat near the Yearsenday Place and would, sometime later, pass by Tommy's grave. She had herself been camped uphill some distance from Tommy's grave and waited now for sight of Arthur's raft. When she saw it she found herself running back uphill, out of sight, instead of standing on shore to welcome him. Did she not, then, after coming this long way, mean to speak to him? She still did not know. She counted on Arthur's tying up near this place. If he did not, but went on by, then perhaps she should call out. She did not know yet.

She had traveled this long distance, on foot, alone, heavily laden, sleeping uncomfortably at night, eating only cold food— for what she did not know. She seemed to have no future, no past, and to be caught for a present in that moment of reading Arthur's letter. Some sign, she felt, would surely free her, but what she wanted of Arthur, or what she intended to say to him, she still did not know. Even as she ran hurriedly uphill to be hidden, she was aware of relief, of a gladness that Arthur was still alive, for the knowledge that the river did not necessarily claim every body for its own.

From her vantage point she watched and forgot to breathe until the pulsation in her ears made her remember. Arthur leapt ashore, lightly, easily, as she had not seen him move in years. He pulled the raft ashore and then he went over and stood awhile by Tommy's grave.

Now, Erma thought, now I must go to him, not stand here like a spy, watching. But she did not move.

Arthur inspected the raft and appeared to be making some kind of repairs. Then he took a bundle from it, went some little distance away, and from the bundle took food.

I could go sit with him now, Erma thought. We could eat together. But after moving a few quiet steps downhill she reached another, better view of the raft and stopped again. And then she drew in her breath sharply. For Arthur, finished with his meal, had taken a mossback hide from the raft, spread it on the ground, lain down on it, and *crossed both arms behind his head.*

He had not been able to lift his arms above shoulder height since the day of his injury, the day of Joe's death.

Quietly Erma climbed uphill to her own camping place. He can lift his arms, she thought. He leapt from the raft to the shore. He built the raft as well as Joe himself might have built it. She could not get over the shock of it. And why did I come back up here? she thought. Does it mean I do not want to see him at all? That I want him to go away now, out of the Green Kingdom if that is possible, or to his death, or wherever he goes, with no word of me? He can lift his arms, she thought. He does not seem like a sick man any more.

Hardly realizing what she did, she chose from the store of things a loaf of bread (the last one) and a warm wool shirt of Arthur's which she had brought with her, and then she turned back toward the shore.

Still undecided, she moved very quietly downhill, stopping to watch at each place where the raft was in sight. But the sleeping figure drew her on. Finally she left the sheltered area and came out onto the sandy shore so that there was no escape for her. She moved across the sand silently until she was very close to Arthur. He lay sleeping as she had not seen him sleep in all these years, his head cradled on his arms, a look of absolute peace on his face.

He is happy, she thought. He is truly happy. She put out her hand tentatively to touch him, but stayed the motion. Who was this man? It seemed not possible that it could be Arthur, Arthur who suffered nightmares, who, even in sleep, protected his injured side and always lay with his left arm thrown protectively over the scar of his old chest wound. This surely was not even the same man who strode angrily up and down the print shop in Drury, frowning and defeated over the keeping of Human Rec-

ords. Who was this man who built a solid raft and stowed away
his gear in such rigorous order and leapt lightly ashore? Who was
this man who surrendered his body to sleep on the ground with
no roof over him and slept without fear?

Erma let her hand drop to her side, for it was no one she
knew. Then quietly, stealthily, she moved over to the raft and,
not to disturb the order, wedged the bread, wrapped in the warm
shirt, between two other neatly rolled bundles. And then she
skirted the sleeping figure quietly, carefully, and made her way
across the strip of sand to the shelter of trees and vines and high
junglegrass.

Now she could run, now she dared to move fast, now she
dared to breathe. She climbed until she was safe from detection
and then she rested. Here she could look back on the sleeping
figure. For a moment she wished that she had brought paper and
pen. But after all, what would she have written? What had she
to say to her husband that could not better be said by a loaf of
bread and a warm shirt?

She climbed to her camping place, quickly rolled up her
bedding, and fastened it over her shoulders. From here she could
no longer see the shore, no longer know if Arthur still slept or
walked about or had set out again on the river. Without hurry
she began the steady walking pace toward home. She did not
know how it had happened, or why, but she was freed from her
anger. Some question deep inside her was satisfied at last and
finally answered. And now I can go home, she thought. Now I can
go home.

Not until the next day did Arthur Herrick come upon the
bundle wedged between two others. The river had widened here
and the current was very slow. He swung his arms for the pleasure
of knowing the absence of the old pain, and looked about him.
The beauty and variety of the shores he passed were satisfying
beyond dreaming. He knew now that he had been right about
the structure of the river. It was his to explore as he had always
wanted to explore it with Joe. He had *thought* of how it would
be and it was the way he had thought it would be.

Moreover, he was gaining health each day. And this, too,
he experienced to the fullest. And he knew ever-increasing hope.
For if he had been right so far, why should he not be right, too,
in thinking the river must lead out of the Kingdom and into a

place of doctors and returning speech? Even at the Yearsenday Place he had torn his writing pad roughly from his belt and thrown it away.

And something more he experienced that, since the days of the war when he had first known Joe, he had never really possessed. That was the feeling of knowing himself able to manage the physical requirements of his world. Even if his world at that time consisted only of one small raft, he was equal to what it asked of him and he felt he would be equal to what it might ask of him in the future. The vortex, of course, lay ahead, how many days, weeks, he did not know. And the vortex was unknown. It might ask of him his life. He was, he thought, prepared for that. At least, if death came then, it would come quickly. And in his new state of well-being he found the idea that death might be waiting for him far preferable to the old way of his living, when he had been content to wait for it.

To be right and to be free, to be gaining in health and to be hopeful, to know oneself equal to the demands of one's environment and no longer to wait on death—what more could a man ask? Or, as Arthur in the quiet, satisfying days put it to himself: to feel oneself integrated, at last.

Was there something more needful? And if there was something more, was it to be found in the small bundle wedged in between the others? Moving silently on the smooth, green water, the raft rode lightly, well made and sturdy, carrying on its surface this confident man who, puzzled now, began to unwrap the once familiar shirt to find there the loaf of coarse bread, kneaded by his wife's hands, taken by his wife from the oven, and surely carried by his wife to the end of a long journey where he, this free and confident man, had lain sleeping. Arthur Herrick sat in the middle of his raft, floating quietly down the green river, holding in his arms the loaf of bread. The muscles of his throat contracted and the tears fell silently down his face and dropped onto the warm shirt.

She wished me well, he thought. He looked up and about him at the blurred trees and the silent, plumed riverherons on the shore. He had the bread in his hands and lifted it. It was as though he said, "You witness this, you trees, you birds, you great silence upon green water. Bear witness. She wished me well. My wife wished me well."

CHAPTER FOUR

ALONE in his cabin, Justin paced back and forth in a torment
of anxiety. He poured tea for himself and forgot to drink it. For
the hundredth time he opened his door and peered out into the
blackness, thinking he heard some sound that might mean Erma's
arrival. Yet she would not come at night, he told himself. It would
be foolish to think so. All the days of her absence he had clung
to the belief that she would arrive today.Why had he ever allowed
her to go? What idiocy had made it seem reasonable that, if she
must go, he should stay behind? For Gwen's sake? He had done
Gwen nothing but harm by staying. In any case, he did not care
for Gwen's good now. He cared for nothing but this fear that,
after all these years of waiting, he had somehow allowed himself
to lose Erma. He knew that if he tried to find her now he might
miss her in the darkness, but at the first wessun light he would go,
promise or no promise.

He spread a blanket on the floor and threw tobacco and a
shirt, dried shavings, and food on it, and while he did so he saw
Erma lost, saw her suffer an accident to her food supply, saw her
attacked by howlers. But he knew she would not get lost. If anything happened to her food supply, there was food all about her.
Howlers? They were so wild no one could get close to them. Unless, of course, Erma had fallen, had hurt herself . . . Justin
stopped his preparations and admitted that the picture of himself
bending over Erma lying injured on the ground was false and
that he had thrown it melodramatically upon the screen of his
mind hoping to obscure the very simple picture of Arthur's sig-
nifying to Erma that he was afraid to go alone and of Erma's saying, "All right, Arthur. I'll go with you."

Justin was filled with anger at Erma. Could she really deny
their love so easily? He believed she could. At this moment he

believed that any stranger could say to her, "I'm afraid to die alone," and she would say to the stranger, "Oh, never mind. I'll die with you."

And then so quietly that, in his fury, he believed it to be an hallucination the door opened and Erma, very wet and dirty, her pack fallen lopsided across her shoulders, entered the room.

Justin held her in his arms as though to promise himself that she should never again escape him, not even for an hour. Such was his hunger for her, so long held leashed, that he kissed her eyelids, her throat, her mouth, and would have crushed her had he not at last noticed her protest.

"Oh, Justin," she said, "I'm so dirty."

He began to laugh. He helped her off with the lopsided pack. "Oh, so you are dirty?" he said. "Well, do you know nobody cares?" He held her close to him again and then held her off, looking at her. "Yes, you are very dirty indeed," he said, "and scratched and bleeding, too. And no doubt in need of hot tea and good care, but at the moment I'm so glad to see you I can't think of anything else."

"What's this?" she said, pointing to the blanket on the floor where Justin had begun his preparations.

"I was coming for you," he said. "I couldn't stand the waiting."

There were so many things to do at once: to build up the fire for her, to make tea, to pick up his blanket and supplies from the floor. "Be patient," he said. "I'll get the tea in a moment."

"Don't hurry," she said. "It's just so good to be home. Just to sit here."

"If you knew," Justin said, "what I have imagined, the horrors. I've seen you dead a thousand times. You must never never do such a thing again. Whatever possessed you to come at night? It was foolish of you."

"I know. That's how I got the scratches. But last night—no, I mean this night, don't I?—I couldn't bear to make camp when I knew I must surely be close. And then, once I could see your light, I couldn't possibly have stopped."

"You're not eating," Justin said. "How long since you ate?"

"I'm too excited," she said. "And I'm not tired any more. Do you realize this is the first time I've been away from the settlement in all these years? Do you remember in the World how it was to come home from a journey, how your tiredness would leave you, and people would say you must be tired, but you'd go on talking and not be able to stop? Oh, it is good to come home!"

"Yes," Justin said, "I remember coming home that time I went after Arthur."

"Justin, you wouldn't believe it. Arthur can lift his arms above his head."

"You saw him, then? You talked to him?"

"I saw him. But I didn't talk to him. I am free of the anger, Justin. My bitterness is all gone. If you could have seen him, asleep on the ground, so . . . so trusting. He's never been able to rest out of doors before. And his arms. That was really the most important thing for me, to see his arms under his head, like this."

"You mean, all this time, it hasn't been—"

"No, I don't mean that at all. I mean something has happened to him on the river. He's doing what he wants to do. And the raft, Justin, the way it's packed. It looks as though Joe had done it."

"And you didn't speak to him at all?"

"No. I meant to. I watched him a long time while he was asleep. And then, well, then I found I was glad for him, and I didn't have anything to say."

She looked into the fire. Now the hot tea was beginning to have its effect and some of the excitement was dying. "I suppose," she said, "that's very hard to believe—that someone could travel so far to say something and then be content to say nothing."

"You are content?" Justin said. "This is all that matters."

"Yes, I am freed from that anger."

"Now, how about your bath?" Justin said. "And then you'll sleep."

"Justin, how's Kathy? And Gwen? They're all right, aren't they?"

"Well, I don't know."

"Nothing happened?" Erma said, her relaxation banished instantly.

"Oh, no. They were both alive and physically unharmed when I left them a few hours ago."

"Well, then?"

"I've bungled things with Gwen," Justin said. "But we'll talk it over tomorrow."

"Kathy?" Erma said. "She's not hurt Kathy!"

"No, the child is all right. We'll talk about it tomorrow. I want you to sleep now."

"First a bath," she said.

"All right. First a bath."

"I'm crazy to see Kathy," Erma said. "I brought her a present. I found the most beautiful stone by the river."

"You'd better have two presents," Justin said. "One for Boodoo."

"Who's Boodoo?"

"Boodoo is the new imaginary playmate. Boodoo has to be fed when Kathy is fed, has to be put to bed at night. I've been very busy taking care of Boodoo lately."

"Thanks for the warning," Erma said. "I'll be sure to have a present for Boodoo. Where did the name come from?"

"I've no idea. I don't even know if Boodoo is a he or a she. All I know is Boodoo's feelings are very sensitive."

He could not bear to tell Erma now that Kathy had been convinced by Gwen that Erma would never return. Tomorrow, tomorrow would be plenty of time. Let her rest now.

In the hot bath she remembered a strange bird that she must tell about and she must know about the cow and the bread supply.

"You've been gone only thirteen days," Justin said. "Things really haven't changed much, you know."

"It seems years," Erma said.

"It seemed forever to me only an hour ago," Justin said. "But now it is as though you had never been gone."

Now that her face had been scrubbed, the signs of her fatigue leapt out at him. There were dark-blue splotches under her eyes. Erma did not remember falling suddenly asleep before the fire while she was drying her hair. Justin carried her to his bed, covered her carefully, and then discovered that he himself was in that state of extreme wakefulness beyond fatigue, as though if he stayed awake he could hold off tomorrow. If only she might awaken tomorrow to taste the pleasures of the day in leisure and they might begin to live their love, the ghost of Arthur Herrick lost forever, settled by the river. In only a few hours this reunion would no longer be secret. Gwen would have to know that Erma had returned and—what then? He had told himself that if only Erma should be returned to the settlement alive, nothing else could matter seriously again; yet already he dreaded the dawn.

He found himself wishing that, while she slept, he might carry Erma to some safe place and hold her prisoner there as once she had hidden the feathermane away, deep in the fastness of a cave.

*

Boodoo was sitting on Kathy's bed when she awoke. "Hurry up and get dressed," Boodoo said. "You aren't dressed even and I'm already dressed."

"I don't want to," Kathy said. "I want to have breakfast in my nightgown."

"All right," Boodoo said, "but hurry up. I'm hungry."

"I'm hungry, too," Kathy said. "Quit pulling on my nightgown. Quit it, Boodoo!"

"Why don't you put your sandals on backward? I've got mine on backward."

"You shouldn't wear your sandals backward, Boodoo. You'll fall down."

"I don't care," Boodoo said.

Boodoo led the way and Kathy followed, dragging her clothes behind her, slapping awkwardly in her backward sandals.

"Why isn't there a fire in the fireplace?" Boodoo said. "I'm cold."

"I don't know, Boodoo."

"Why doesn't your mother get us some breakfast? I'm hungry."

"I'm hungry, too, Boodoo."

"Why is your mother sitting there like that? Why doesn't she say something?"

"I don't know, Boodoo. She does that sometimes. Leave her alone."

"I'm going to pinch her," Boodoo said. "I'm going to see if she'll wake up."

"Don't, Boodoo. Leave her alone. I'll take you over to Erma's for breakfast."

Kathy began to put on her clothes hurriedly so she and Boodoo could go over to Erma's house before Boodoo did something naughty.

"Just a minute, Boodoo. Wait till I get dressed."

"You forgot," Boodoo said. "Erma's gone. Erma won't get breakfast."

Kathy stopped dressing. "Oh, I forgot."

"And she won't come back," Boodoo said.

"She will too," Kathy said. "That's a lie, Boodoo."

"She will not. Your mother said so."

"I'll get you some bread, Boodoo. Here, eat this."

"Thank you," Boodoo said. "Let's have some cheese with it."

"All right."

"What would your mother do if you stuffed some bread in her face?"

"I don't know, Boodoo. Leave her alone. Turn around this way. Don't look at her."

"Look on the hearth, Kathy. Look at your mother's emeralds. Why don't you pick them up and put them back in the bag?"

"No, Boodoo. She doesn't like anyone to touch her emeralds."

"I'll bet she wouldn't even move. I'll bet you could get them and she wouldn't even notice."

"Yes, she would, Boodoo. She'd scold me."

"Well, then? If she scolded you, then she'd see you. Then she wouldn't be like that any more."

"You do it, Boodoo."

"All right. You come with me. . . . I touched them," Boodoo said. "Did you see me?"

"No."

"I'll pick them up and put them in the bag. Is she going to scold? Is she watching?"

"No, Boodoo. She didn't see us. Put the bag down."

"Why don't you go lean on her knees and see will she notice you?"

"No, Boodoo. Her eyes scare me. Let's go away, Boodoo. It's cold in here."

"I know," Boodoo said. "They're prolly old, the emeralds. Prolly when emeralds get old they're no good any more. Why don't you get her a new emerald?"

"Where, Boodoo?"

"You know where. Down inside that big plant in the swamp."

"I'm scared to go there, Boodoo. It's sinky."

"I'll go with you," Boodoo said. "I can hold onto you and then you wouldn't sink and I could pull you out if you did and you could reach down inside that plant and get that new emerald."

"I don't know, Boodoo . . ."

"I bet if you brought a new emerald and held it up in front of your mother's eyes, she'd look at you."

"You think so, Boodoo?"

"Sure. I bet she'd say, 'Kathy, where did you get such a beautiful emerald?' "

"You think she would, Boodoo?"

"And she'd say, 'Sit on my lap, Kathy, and I'll give you a big kiss for your emerald.' "

"Really, Boodoo, you think she would?"

"Come on, let's go. Let's hurry."

"All right, Boodoo. Wait till I turn my sandals around."

"I'll turn mine around, too," Boodoo said, "and we'll go get the emerald."

"Do you think we should tell Justin we're going to get the emerald, Boodoo?"

"No. He'll make us wait for porridge and wash our faces and all that. We have to hurry. The emerald might be gone."

"All right, Boodoo. I'm ready. You help me open the door now."

They raced each other to the swamp.

"I won," Kathy said.

"Not very much," Boodoo said.

"I know," Kathy said.

"You really are a better runner than me," Boodoo said.

"It's awful sinky here, Boodoo. It's sinkier than I thought."

"I'll hold your hand," Boodoo said. "Where was the emerald?"

"It's down inside that big plant," Kathy said. "It's all shiny."

"Can you see it?"

"Yes, I can see it. It's 'way down inside."

"Nobody got it," Boodoo said. "Good. Nobody got it."

"Do you really think my mamma would kiss me?"

"Sure. Your mamma will say, 'Kathy, what a beautiful emerald. Come sit on my lap and let me kiss you.' That's what she'll say."

"Hold onto me, Boodoo. I'm going to reach for it now."

"I'll hold onto you," Boodoo said. "You'll hold the emerald in front of your mamma and she'll say . . ."

Kathy's tiny hand, reaching for the glistening pistil, touched the vital trigger and the awful arms of the spike plant clamped on her arm. She screamed and struggled and fought with the pain, but the plant held her firmly, impersonally, the same as if she were an insect, the same as if she were a careless bird. And then, mercifully, it began to inject into the wound its paralyzing fluid, so that the pain lessened and the slow dissolution of the flesh began. With the numbness and the lessening of pain, the child's screams stopped and she looked about for Boodoo to help her, to pull her free. But Boodoo was gone.

*

With great reluctance Justin put his hand on Erma's forehead and began to smooth back her hair. "Erma," he said, "Erma, you'd better wake up."

So long had she dreamed of such an awakening that she kept her eyes closed to postpone the pleasure of seeing his face, and stretched luxuriously. Then she opened her eyes and reached toward Justin, but one look at his face arrested her movements.

"Justin, what is it? What's wrong?"

"Oh, my darling, I would have given anything—anything for it not to be like this."

Erma, now fully awake, sat upright in bed. "What is it, Justin? Tell me."

"It's Kathy," he said. "Now, wait; it's nothing yet. It's just that I can't find her and I'm alarmed."

"But your face, Justin. Are you telling me—"

"No, no. My face looks this way because I didn't sleep, that's all. I've been over to your place for some clothes. Will these do? And while you're dressing I'll get some breakfast ready. We may have a rough day ahead. I want you to eat. I need your clear head."

While they talked Erma dressed, brushed her hair, and tied a leather thong around it. She washed her face and ate her breakfast, all the time trying to slow the beating of her heart, to make her movements deliberate and efficient. "I suppose you've been all around the house, of course," she said. "There's no chance she's just playing somewhere?"

"I don't think so," Justin said. "I would have heard her. She can't have got very far. It's early yet."

"But Gwen?" Erma said. "Doesn't Gwen know how long she's been gone? When did she miss her?"

"Gwen's having one of her spells. She may have been sitting

there all night. I'm perhaps to blame, Erma. Last night, Gwen and I . . . Well, I don't want to go into it all now."

"Never mind, Justin. You mean she won't answer you about Kathy now? She might have frightened Kathy."

"I'm counting on you to shock her out of it," Justin said. "The sight of you might do it and then we could get some sense out of her."

"Why? Why me?"

"Because she's got it in her head that you'd gone for good, that you wouldn't be back."

"Why didn't you tell me?" Erma said, jumping up. "Did she tell Kathy that?"

"I'm afraid so. I thought I would start on the idea that the child had gone to find you. You see, it must be something special. She's never done it before. She's always there in the morning, waiting for me."

"You really think she might have gone after me?"

"Yes, I do. Now that I think back, she stopped talking about you rather abruptly. God knows what has been going on in her head."

For some minutes now, just out of range, an impression had been nagging at the edge of Erma's consciousness but she was unable to identify it. She began to walk about the room.

"I need to smoke," she said. "Have you got a pipe?"

Justin fixed the pipe for her, lighted it and handed it to her. "I would have given anything," he said.

"Oh, not now, Justin. We're wasting time. Justin, I don't think you're right. It . . . it doesn't feel right to me. Kathy wouldn't leave Gwen to hunt me, no matter what Gwen did. Children don't . . ."

And then it came to her, the source of that unsatisfying impression. "The swamp!" she said. "I'm going to the swamp."

"The swamp?" Justin said. "But why?"

"Because of Arthur's letter. Don't you remember? At the end of the letter. I read it a thousand times; I ought to know. He saw Kathy coming back from the swamp alone."

"Yes," Justin said, "I remember. But why would she go there so early?"

"I'm going," Erma said. "You go the other way if you think that's right."

"You ought to see Gwen first," Justin said. "If you can get

her to talk, maybe she knows something that would save us hours."

"All right, I will."

At the door she turned suddenly and ran to his arms for one brief moment. "We've got to find her," she said. "We've got to!"

But Erma did not find Gwen in The Room, for Justin had done better than he thought with Gwen. The word that Erma had come back had slowly penetrated the gray veil of Gwendolyn's numbness, leaving in its wake the cleansing fire of hatred, the awareness of the missing child, and the desperate need to find Kathy before Erma did. The knowledge that Erma had returned after Gwen had condemned her to the river was maddening enough, but that she might return and, the very first thing, find reason to criticize—that knowledge brought forth such a fury with Erma, with Kathy for having put her in this vulnerable position, with everything, that the bonds of her lethargy were dissolved. Full of an energy she had not known for many weeks, Gwen summoned her wits to find the child, to have her returned safely to The Room before Erma should find them. Let her say one word, she thought. One word.

Erma could hear Kathy's screams before she saw her, and she ran blindly toward the swamp, calling, "I'm coming, Kathy. I'm coming!"

But Gwendolyn had arrived before her. She stood as close to the child as she could get without leaving the safety of a firm piece of ground, and pulled on the child's free arm. Each new wrench opened the wound of the imprisoned arm, allowing the viselike blades of the plant to bite deeper and deeper into the child's flesh, and with each bite the child screamed.

"Gwen, stop it!" Erma called. "Don't you see you're making it worse?"

Gwen dropped Kathy's free arm. Maddened at having failed in her plan, she turned on Erma in a rage, her face distorted with hatred, but the words of her hatred refused to come and, instead, the knowledge of being once more in the wrong before this woman made her the victim of impotent weeping.

Erma had no eyes, no time for Gwen. She pulled at a dead log and shoved it into the swamp. Then she stepped into the sucking mud and jostled the log into a position under the child's feet, which were slowly being sucked down. Very gently she held the little body and spoke quietly to the child: "There, darling. There, now. We'll get you out. See, there's something under your feet. You must be very quiet and hold still so we can work. Now, quiet, darling, quiet. We have to figure out the best way, so it won't hurt so much.

"Gwen," she said, "go get Justin and the ax. Hurry! Justin's started toward the old river path. Go ring the bell."

"Go yourself," Gwen said.

Erma felt Kathy's free arm tighten around her neck, saw the look of panic in the child's eyes.

"Don't be afraid, darling," she said. "I won't leave you. We'll get you out. Go on, Gwen," Erma said in a quiet, controlled voice. "Go get Justin. Ring the bell. And if you can't find him, don't wait. Get the ax. We'll have to cut the plant down, you can see that."

Erma had now sunk in the mud up to her knees so that it was necessary for her to look up at Gwen, who stood on the last margin of firm earth, still unable to make herself set foot in the frightening, sucking mud.

"I won't leave her," Gwen said. "I won't. You can't make me."

Suddenly Gwen lurched forward and caught Kathy's free hand from around Erma's neck and began to pull on the child. "Pull, Kathy!" she cried. "Pull. You aren't trying. You can get loose."

Erma did not remember later how she had extricated herself from the mud, how she had pulled herself up on the bank and found herself standing with her hands around Gwen's throat.

"Let loose," she said. "Let loose of her."

In her mind Erma was measuring how much harder she must press on Gwen's throat to make her loosen her grasp. When she felt Gwen let loose, saw the child's hand fall free, she shook Gwen from her, the way a dog might a rat, and threw her on the ground. Then she turned immediately to the child.

Gwen lay on the ground, staring, her mouth open. "You tried to kill me," she said.

"I will if you don't go get the ax. Never mind about Justin now. It's too late."

Gwen crawled along the path, her hand at her throat. Gradually she got to her feet and began to walk slowly away, quietly weeping. In a way it was wonderfully thrilling, because it made her right at last. She had always said they were trying to kill her, they wanted her dead. She had always said so. And now it was true.

Erma turned her whole mind on Kathy and the terrible problem, for she had no faith that the ax would be brought or that Justin would come. Mercifully, exhaustion had come to the child, and momentary unconsciousness, so that she no longer struggled. Yet this meant also that the whole weight of the little body hung from the one arm and the log under her feet was useless as a support, for the small knees had buckled and already touched the greedy, sucking mud. Erma found another log and tried to wedge it into the plant's opening. If only she could pry the plant open. Yes. That was what she must do. Sweating and fighting the mud, she maneuvered the small end of the log into the space under the child's arm, and could have cried when it slipped free of the edge. She tried to harness her panic and make herself strong to try again.

And all this time she should have been supporting the child's body, she knew, so as to keep the wound from tearing even larger. At last the end of the log was wedged into the opening of the plant, and Erma climbed onto the slippery bank where she could get better leverage. She kept murmuring reassurances to the child, though she felt sure she could not be heard. From the bank she lifted the large end of the log and began to feel her way with it, trying for a slow, steady pressure that would wedge the arms of the spike plant slowly apart. She was prepared for the moment when the child might be let suddenly free and fall face downward into the swamp. She was geared to move fast, then. But she was not prepared for the fragile, rotten spot in the log, near the small end, not prepared for it to crack suddenly, throwing her off her feet, and all the work gone for nothing. She jumped to her feet in an agonized prayer to something, to someone, for help of any kind, and, tasting the salt in her mouth, she knew she was crying.

The taste of her tears steadied her. She took off her jacket, as she should have done at first, and wrapped it around the child's cold body. In the tiny, limp, free wrist she found an unmistakable pulsation. And then she could see that everything had not been lost, for the broken-off piece of log was still wedged in the plant and, while it was not enough to spring the vise, it had spread it enough to give her a foothold.

With her own body she supported the weight of the child.

Her arms around the child, she grasped the edge of one giant half of the plant. Pulling her legs free of the mud, she was able to get her feet wedged against the opposing half of the plant. She took a deep breath, bent her knees, and then began the slow, steady pressure of straightening her legs so as to push the two sides of the plant apart. Slowly the leg muscles bunched themselves and slowly the legs began to press toward straightening. Sweat gathered on Erma's forehead, on her lips. The color of her face darkened and the cords of her neck stood out. In the final analysis, she had more faith in her own body than in any system of levers made from logs. At last the straining muscles, the screaming tendons, translated a message of slight change. The vise began to give.

The farther Justin moved away from the settlement the less confident he became that the child had come this way. Finally he did not believe it at all and turned back. Surely if Erma's feeling had been correct, they would have found the child by now. But if they had, wouldn't they have rung the bells to let him know?

He went first to The Room, hoping by some miracle that they would all be there, the child safely returned. Gwen sat in her accustomed chair before the cold fireplace.

"Gwen," he said, "did you find her? Where's Erma? Where's the child?"

"Justin," Gwen said, "it's so horrible . . ."

"Oh, my dear, what is it? What has happened?"

"Erma tried to kill me," she said.

"Gwen, what has happened to Kathy?"

"Really, Justin. She did. Look here. Look at my throat. She tried to strangle me."

"Where? Where did it happen?"

"She's so strong, Justin, so cruel. You wouldn't believe—"

Justin grabbed the woman's shoulders and began to shake her. "Tell me where they are!" he said.

"You, too?" she said. And she began to weep hopelessly.

Why am I wasting time? Justin thought. He loosened his hold on her and left, running as fast as he could toward the swamp.

Erma came toward him slowly, stumbling drunkenly, holding in her arms the limp body of the child. Justin took the child from her and they turned toward The Room.

"Is she alive?" Erma asked. "Is she alive?"

"Yes, dear," Justin said. "Yes, I think so." He noticed that Erma was stumbling more and more. "Hold on to me, can't you?" he said.

Erma's arms were still outstretched just as they had been when Justin lifted the child off them. Now she stared at them stupidly. "I can't feel them," she said.

Justin halted then and saw the cuts across the palms.

"Spike plant," Erma said. "She was trapped in it. My feet, too. It must have cut through my sandals. There's something . . . you have to know for Kathy's sake . . ."

"You mean it isn't just the injury, that Kathy's been poisoned by the plant?"

"Yes," Erma said. "It's . . . it's . . ."

Justin shifted the limp body of the child over one shoulder so as to have an arm free with which to support Erma. "Lean on me," he said. "We'll soon be there."

"Sorry," Erma said. "Sorry . . ."

"Don't try to talk. Think about The Room, Erma, about getting there. Gwen!" Justin called, pushing the door to The Room open and half lifting Erma over the threshold. "Gwen!"

Nothing but silence met them. Damn the woman, always missing when she was needed. Well, if she had gone off to sulk somewhere he certainly couldn't leave here now to hunt her. He guided Erma to a chair and then he put Kathy down on her bed. She gave no sign of life at all, and Justin covered her with a blanket because he did not know what else to do. It was coming now, a clearing of his brain. He must concentrate on Erma. She must not slip away into unconsciousness. Everything, everything depended on Erma. If he saved Erma, Erma would take over with the child.

"Erma," he said, shaking her, "Erma, you have to stay awake." He built a fire and made tea. While he waited for the kettle to boil he rubbed Erma's legs and arms. Constantly he talked to her, without knowing it. Every time that Erma seemed to be falling asleep he would yell for Gwen, yet he knew somehow this was hopeless. Only one idea filled him, and that was that everything depended on keeping Erma awake. Once he had pulled Erma back to awareness, then . . . then she would know what to do. He began to force hot tea down her throat. He bathed her face in cold water. Once he had a moment to feel, as they all felt in times of crises, a terrible longing for Joe.

Slowly it came to Erma that it was not Justin she fought, but something else, and that she and Justin fought it together. It was not Justin but sleep that was the enemy. She must not sleep. She was beginning to believe this now. She must not sleep. She must drink the tea. It was because of her hands, her feet. It was something to do with this deadness slowly creeping over her. She fought because Justin said she must and because some instinctive reservoir of fighting came alive in her in answer to Justin's desperate ministrations. And slowly the dulling clouds began to recede and the numbness gave way to sharp pain. And with the pain came immediate clarity of mind and memory.

"Kathy!" she said. "Where is she?"

"You're back," Justin said. "Thank God! Will you be all right, Erma?"

"Where is Kathy?"

"She's on her bed."

"Bring her here to me. Now. Now!"

Justin carried the little body to Erma.

"Bring her bed," Erma said. "My hands are stiff."

Erma knelt on the floor beside the little bed and watched the child. Slowly she pulled the clothing away from the mangled shoulder.

"Why is there so little blood?" she said. "I don't understand it."

Justin brought water and soap and cloths and, at Erma's direction, bathed the wound. Then they bound the arm to the body so that it could not be moved.

"There," Erma said. "She has been spared that pain at least. Now we must try. Didn't you give me tea, Justin? Do you suppose it helped?"

"I don't know, darling, but I'll make more."

"Make it strong," Erma said, never taking her eyes off the child.

It was not really the tea she was counting on, nor the patient rubbing of the child's skin, nor the warmth of the blankets. It was her own will that she counted on. She would *will* the child to live because . . . because the death and the dying and the waste must stop. She had fought once before and won and what had it been for? For a feathermane in a cave. For an animal. While around her the human lives were carelessly allowed to be wasted.

"She has to live," she whispered. "She has to live."

"My darling," Justin said, "do not feel it is in your hands."

"It *is* in my hands," Erma said angrily. "It was in my hands to prevent it. It was in my hands to save Tommy, and why did I let it all happen? Why, Justin?"

"Don't blame yourself, Erma, please. What could you have done differently?"

"Don't stop rubbing her, Justin. Go on. I'll tell you what I could have done. I could have had this anger years ago. I could have put up a fight. I tell you, the dying has got to stop."

An overwhelming anger filled Erma at last, a devastating hatred for her own history of gentleness. Had it come too late, this anger? Now that she knew what was necessary, was it too late?

"I think her eyelids moved," Justin said. "Did you see it?"

"Yes, I saw it," Erma said. "Kathy, Kathy, wake up. Open your eyes."

Erma held her breath while she searched for the tiny pulse, but the sound of her own heart blotted everything else.

"Now the tea, Justin. And can you prop her up, do you think?"

"Just tell me what to do."

"Hold her like that. There. Now I can put some on her lips. Kathy," she said. "Kathy, swallow this. Kathy, open your eyes."

But there was no response, and when Erma saw the child slowly slipping from her she realized that Justin, in his exhaustion, was relaxing his arm.

"Justin," she said. "Justin! Don't give up."

"Let the poor babe rest, Erma," Justin said. "Can't we rest a little?"

"No," Erma said. "No. Go rest if you want. I'll hold her."

"No, no," Justin said. "It was only for a moment."

"I'm sorry, Justin. I didn't mean to speak to you like that."

"It's all right. My arm is asleep. Let me change positions."

"Where *is* Gwen?" Erma said. "She could be doing this and you could rest. You've been up all night."

"I don't know where she is," Justin said, "but I think we're better off without her."

"No, we're *not* better off without her. It's her voice I need. It could reach something in Kathy that I can't. Go find her, Justin, and bring her back, by force if necessary. I've got to have her."

"Now?" Justin said.

"Yes, now! Go on, Justin. Find her."

"All right," he said. "All right."

At the door he paused to steady himself. What is the matter with me? he thought. I can't fall down now. I would never get up.

Alone with the child, Erma renewed her efforts and found new resources of will within herself. The mighty anger against death, so late in coming, grew within her and seemed boundless. "Kathy," she said, "Kathy, Kathy, you must live. You have to live."

She supported the little head and patiently, again and again, dampened her fingers in the tea and put them on the child's tongue. At last she was rewarded with a choking sound, a moan and a fluttering of the eyelids. The tiny free hand doubled itself into a fist and made hint of belligerence. The hand of the injured arm attempted to do the same and sent a sharp, clear message of pain to the child's brain. Startled eyes looked into Erma's for a moment.

And now it was as though Erma had done nothing before. Her whole effort became concentrated in getting the precious drops of fluid down the throat. The accumulation of a spoonful was a major triumph. So intense was this struggle that Erma did not notice how long Justin had been gone. Her voice was worn out with endearments to the child, yet she did not notice, for at last a regular breathing had set in, and with the drawing of each breath Erma felt herself replenished.

At last she was aware that she could hardly see the child and she knew that she must build up the fire again and light the lamps. It was then she realized that Justin stood beside her.

"She's alive, Justin," she whispered. "She breathes."

Suddenly Erma was leaning on Justin, crying hoarsely in her exhaustion.

"You did it," Justin said. "I didn't think you could. Surely you could rest a little now, eat something, if I am here to watch her."

"I'm not tired," Erma said. "You rest. You . . . you were so tired before, Justin."

"I got over it," he said. "Come, lie down now. I must fix the fire."

"I'll sit here a moment," she said, "by the hearth. I feel cold now."

The firelight flamed up and, as Justin lighted a lamp, Erma

saw his face. "What is it, Justin? What happened? Did you find Gwen?"

"I found her," he said.

"Well, is she coming?"

"No," Justin said, turning from the lamp and sitting down on the hearth.

In the quiet of The Room there was no sound except the child's breathing. Erma became aware again of the sharp pains in her hands and feet. A quietness came upon her and she looked at Justin. She stood up slowly and got his pipe for him, filled it and handed it to him.

"You'd better tell me," she said. "Where did you find her?"

"In my place," he said, "hanging from the ceiling. Naked. She took the tether rope from the milk house. A clumsy thing. Ten times as strong as she needed."

"Was she dead when you found her?"

"Oh, yes," Justin said. "She was dead all right."

The fire snapped in new life and Justin and Erma looked away from each other in embarrassment. Erma stood up. She turned aimlessly and walked over to the table. There was a bowl on the table and she shifted this a little to the left and then placed it back where it had been. Once she looked over at Justin, who sat staring at the floor. Then she looked at her hands and flexed the fingers, trying the stiffness caused by her wounds.

Slowly she turned toward the little bed and let herself be pulled there. She knelt by the side of the bed and watched the child's quiet breathing and saw with terrible happiness the change in her color. But she kept her back to Justin lest her sense of possession for the child appear indecent and unseemly. With an exquisite control she lowered her head and placed her cheek against the child's good arm.

CHAPTER FIVE

I T O F T E N happened in these days that Justin felt himself to be an instrument, played upon. A cello, perhaps. Yes, a cello, at the mercy of music of such tremulous sweetness that the instrument must surely be shattered by the experiencing of it. That, so close to seventy, one should have an experience absolutely new was a wonder to him. In the constant presence of Kathy's approaching death he found himself experiencing a new life of an enchanted quality. And yet it was difficult to remember any other.

Here these three remnants of other people's families—Erma, the child, and himself—lived in a kind of golden, idealized family state, playing tricks with time and their own history. Often his past seemed to Justin a strip of heavy silk, thrown into folds which, sinking one upon another, coalesced. It sometimes seemed to him that Joe had been killed in the war with his sons and that it must have been in the old house by the sea, next door to Max Staats, where he had cut down Gwendolyn's body. The present, like oil on water, seemed to spread out in all directions. It promised, against all reason, to extend into an indefinite future and it seemed slowly to spread over all their days in the Green Kingdom.

Yet no man, wishing for himself a time surrounded and enfolded by tenderness and love, would deliberately seek to make it of such ingredients: a child slowly dying, a woman defeated in her basic beliefs. But of course he had not made it, he who felt now so often like a cello played upon. What had made it, this golden interval in his life? Whence came this sense of boundless time, of the moment's enjoyment spread in all directions? Where had it begun?

He was engaged in the task of arranging and preserving his manuscripts in preparation for moving them from his old place to The Room, and he had dragged them outdoors to have a better

light. There were no materials for making a fire in his place, and
so long had it been abandoned that he found it unpleasant to
spend any time there. All life, all warmth were now centered in
The Room about the bed of the dying child. They had decided to
salvage everything of value from the cabins, center their lives in
The Room, and allow the other houses to succumb to the chokevines and return again to the Kingdom. But the chore of the
manuscripts Justin had postponed until now. He sat on a low stool,
in the late wessun light, the pages all about him, a stack of leather
skins spread over his knees.

He had brought Arthur's shoemaking tools with him and
was engaged in making some crudely sewn leather bags for the
manuscripts. Around him in a circle were the sheets of "The Time
of Innocence," "The Time of History," "The Fulcrum," "The
Legend," a series of experimental notes, and the beginning of
"Death of a Hero," a memorial to Joe, unfinished. This one Justin
picked up and studied for a while, tasting the pleasure of having
the leisure to do so. As he scanned the page he rested his chin in
his hand and remembered that, yes, certainly, he had had a
beard when he began "Death of a Hero."

He looked up from the manuscript into the green distance
and thought over this clue. Yes, shaving had something to do with
the beginnings of this new and golden time. When was it he had
shaved off his beard?

It was the day, that terrible day, of Erma's defeat, when all
at once he had seen her give up hope for Kathy, seen the fight
crumple in her and be supplanted by a quiet so profound that,
simply for something to do, he had gone out and sharpened all the
bone knives and, trying one on a hair of his beard, had decided to
shave. It was to keep himself from talking, more than anything
else, from profaning with small words of comfort this awful
capitulation in the quiet woman. The quiet of it—that was the impressive thing. If she had been rebellious, angry, self-accusing, as
she had been before over the delirium, over the wound's not healing, he would have had words for her.

The child's delirium had been a very early effect of the poison, and in it she had relived her fear of Gwendolyn, of standing
in the corner crying for Tommy, of being punished for touching
the emeralds. Erma had not been quiet then. She had worked un-
ceasingly, bathing the child's dry, feverish skin, moistening the
parched lips, crooning, comforting, never resting, never taking

off her clothes. And, when it was over, bursting out in self-accusation.

"Why didn't I know?" she had said. "Why did I allow such a thing, Justin? There is no excuse for me. That baby lived in terror right before my eyes and I made no effort to save her."

"What should you have done differently, dear?" he had asked her.

"I should have taken her away from Gwen. Tommy, too. Why did I let her lie to him about Joe? Why did I sit by and let it happen?"

"You weren't alone," Justin had said. "I did the same. We all placated her. You're looking at it in retrospect. At the time we tried not to interfere with her. I suppose we all had hope that she would change."

"But why did we allow ourselves that stupid hope? It should have been a simple matter of choice—of choosing for the children and sacrificing Gwen. Why couldn't I have had the courage to see long ago it was a matter of choosing? Why didn't I kill Gwen? She died anyway."

To Justin now it was like remembering another life to remember Erma's anger and how he had answered her: "Why, my dear, we didn't see it all that clearly then because we couldn't have. And you didn't kill Gwen because it is not in you to kill."

"It is now, Justin," she answered him. "If I had made it my business to know then what she was doing to Kathy, it would have been in me then."

"No, dear. It is not in your nature. If it had been possible for you to kill, you would have done it when you had your hands around her throat."

"I should have," Erma said. "I should have believed I knew better than Gwen what was right for them. As soon as Joe was dead I should have known. But if not then, at least when Tommy was drowned—I should have seen that it was the loss of fifty per cent of the next generation and not a study in parlor manners."

"You are holding yourself alone responsible," Justin said, "when really you are only a small part of it."

"I do hold myself responsible," she said. "Tommy is dead and Kathy is—who knows?—crippled for life, perhaps, and they are all the children there are! And I . . . I had some idea of being polite to Gwen, of not interfering. What place did such expensive delicacy have *here?*"

It had been impossible for him to get her to rest, but he had taken her a little food. "Try to eat a little something," he had said, "and then we'll talk."

"All right. But I don't see how talk can ever make me reconciled to not having acted. And now it's too late."

"It's this expensive delicacy you mentioned," Justin said, "that's the whole crux of the matter. It is expensive. Perhaps it is too expensive. It's civilization. Do you imagine you are the first to believe, after the event, you should have taken authoritative action? Do you not know every thinking person has been in this place where you find yourself, asking the same question? Do you not know that when my sons were killed in the war, one after another, that I knew I should have taken them all when they were little and hidden them away in a cave somewhere, without friends, without learning, without thinking for themselves, just to have kept them physically alive?"

"Well?" Erma said. "Perhaps you should have."

"Yes, it's a valid point. There is an argument for exalting a very limited idea of life above everything else. It is, in effect, embracing the primitive and denying civilization."

"I *am* primitive," Erma said. "I believe in life."

"In emergency," Justin said, "we all believe; we are all primitive. But to be primitive is to live in a constant stage of emergency."

"Haven't we?" she said.

"It seems so in retrospect, I know," Justin said. "But even if we had not had any of it in actuality, we have an *idea* of ordered, planned, fruitful existence, with continuity, and this the primitive hasn't."

"It was a false idea," Erma said. "I wish I had given it up long ago and recognized the way things are."

"Perhaps it is false," Justin said. "The point I want to make, Erma, is not how true it is, but how *old* it is. You didn't choose this expensive delicacy, as you put it, all by yourself. The thing I want you to see is that your choice was hundreds of years in the making. When you berate yourself for not having seized authority over Gwen, over the children, you're denying your history. You're denying the centuries behind you. If you are wrong, history has to share your wrong, civilization has to share it. I have to share it."

"I know what you are trying to do," Erma said. "You're trying to spread the guilt so thin that I can get out from under it. Thank you, but no. It won't work. The fact is there to confront me: Tommy is dead. Foolishly dead. Dead because I didn't force Gwen to tell him the truth and because I didn't take him away from her and tell him myself."

"Tommy is dead," Justin said, "that's true. But the idea of how Tommy should have been told the truth is still alive, you see."

"What good is it," Erma said, "if there are no more children to try it on?"

"Well," Justin said, "I did not expect to convince you or even comfort you in a time of emergency. It's just that I wanted to talk to you about it. But, here now, we haven't tried it the other way around yet."

"What do you mean, the other way around?"

"Well, suppose you had been sure you had the right to seize authority because you had the power to do it."

"You mean, what if I had taken the children away from Gwen?"

"Yes, suppose you had."

"Well, they would be alive now."

"Barring accidents, yes. How would you have managed Gwen, then? You don't suppose she would have admitted you were better suited?"

"Well, I would have fought her. If necessary, killed her."

"And what would the children have thought of that?"

"Oh," Erma said. "Yes, I see. Well, suppose they had feared me? Lots of children in the world fear their parents and they are alive."

"That is questionable," Justin said. "It all depends on what you call alive. But we'll say that physical life is enough for the moment. And that gradually the children came to trust you or at least in fear *had* to trust you. Don't you think it would have become a habit, this taking on of responsibility, all alone? Don't you think the next time you would have known better than they? Better than anyone? Do you think you could have given it back, some of the responsibility, let them have some?"

"I don't know, Justin," she said. "Maybe they would have

had to fight me for it. But they would have been alive to do it, that's all I'm saying. It may be all right to pussyfoot around in the World assuming people are responsible for what they do. In the World they've got children to waste in experiments. Here we haven't. This isn't the World and I acted as though it were."

"Yes," Justin said, "we brought it with us because we were of it. You may be right that what we brought was wrong and dangerous for this place. I only want you to see that the error is not yours alone, that you have to share it with the World, with history, with me."

"All right," she said tiredly, "all right. But you won't change me now. You won't make me give up on Kathy, you understand. Even now, so late, you may as well know that death is my personal enemy. I'm going to fight. I want Kathy to live the same as I want life for myself, on any terms, under any conditions, just as I wanted it for the feathermane, and fought for it, and won. And I mean to win this time and the next and the next. I mean to be forever angry."

"I would not change you, my dear," he said. "You don't have to fight me, too. I'm on your side."

She had meant to be forever angry and it was not he who had changed her. Even had he known in advance how their life would be now, and the advantages it would have for him, still he would not have changed her.

Justin pulled down the leather flap enclosing "The Fulcrum" in its case and stacked this one on top of the other finished ones. They were not very neat jobs, he had to admit, and what they would have been without the help of Arthur's shoemaking tools and Gwendolyn's needles he could not think. Strange that the two of them left alive here, he and Erma, would be the unhandy ones, without dexterity. What Erma had produced in the cave, out of a spiritual turmoil, had never been translated into any household utensil, and the organization and deft construction that he put into his music never showed up in a fishnet. How would it be with them, he wondered, when all the things the others had made were worn out and broken beyond repair? He did not believe that the two of them would develop new talents when this time came, because there had already been time enough and occasion for this to have happened. He thought it more likely that they would learn to do without the things. How pleased they both had been to find, near The Room, two depressed contours in a mossy bank into which their bodies fitted. Erma's even had a projection to serve as an elbow rest. Here they went when the child was sleeping, to sit and enjoy the late eassun light. They would fit themselves into the contours of the bank and congratulate themselves about their comfort. Neither of them had made a chair. This very stool he sat on now had been made by Joe.

Justin heard the chatter of a ballsleeper near him and, looking up into a nearby tree, spotted the animal. He reached into his jacket pocket where nowadays he always kept a few clusternuts. He threw one onto the ground near his feet and made a chattering noise in imitation. The ballsleeper studied him carefully, its absurd furry head held to one side, and moved cautiously to a lower branch of the tree.

The work in Justin's lap lay untouched, for, of a sudden, he remembered the day of his shaving, the day of Erma's quiet, the day before the golden time had come upon them.

"The wound is not healing," Erma had said. "It's not healing properly. I have to admit it."

She had the wounds in her own hands and feet to go by, and they had healed some time ago, leaving white, tough scars that were insensitive.

"Of course, the child's wound was much deeper," Justin had said to her, "and then, too, the poison might have been less intense by the time you got there."

"I wish I knew what else to try," Erma said. "I was so encouraged when we whipped the fever and the delirium and for a while I thought she was improving, but now I have to admit it isn't right."

Justin had seen for some days that the child was not improving, had in fact shown less appetite and greater lassitude, but he knew that Erma would not give up and he was surprised that she would admit, even, that the wound was not healing properly. Erma worked with the child every moment Kathy was awake, encouraging her, trying in the face of all the facts to find some sign of life in the injured arm.

"Think about this finger, darling," she would say, pointing to one of the lifeless fingers. "Can you think about it for Erma? Could you try to do this?"

Kathy would try. It was heartbreaking to Justin to see how she would look into Erma's face and try to please her while, involuntarily, the finger on the good hand would make small, jerking movements.

"That's the way, Kathy. You are trying so wonderfully, I can tell. Rest awhile now. We'll try again later. Would you like a little milk to drink?"

Kathy would shake her head, tiredly, no, and Erma would sponge the drops of sweat from her forehead. Justin could feel Erma fighting down despair, could see her straighten herself and breathe in strength, replenishing the fuel that fed her will. He dreaded the fury she would heap on him if he suggested that she should not force the child to try any more; yet he felt for the child, for her terrible fatigue. Perhaps, he thought, there was something he could do to ease things a little, to make the child happier to be awake, something besides a criticism of Erma which, he knew, would only reinforce her determination.

And so he had found a tiny ballsleeper and made a pet of it, as once he had for Tommy's birthday. He had brought it to Kathy and tucked a store of clusternuts under her good arm, so that the ballsleeper would snuggle close to the child at once. And he had been rewarded with a light in the little girl's eyes they had not seen for many weeks. The ballsleeper slept on the child's bed, it washed its face with its soft paws for her delight, it interrupted the careful grooming of its long, soft tail at the child's slightest movement. The pet was a great success, and, though Kathy did not laugh out loud at its antics, she would hold it cupped in her good arm and put her face against it and hum and murmur to it.

"You love your ballsleeper very much, don't you?" Erma said, sitting beside the child's bed.

It was one of those innocent questions people ask of children, knowing the answer, not even expecting an answer. And Erma, making conversation with her beloved invalid, had no inkling of the answer coming, nor the change it would make.

"Yes," Kathy said, her eyes on the beloved ballsleeper. "I love him. He doesn't push me. He doesn't make me move my fingers."

This was the moment of Erma's awful quiet. She had opened her mouth to speak and then she had closed it. She had put her hand on the child's head, lightly, and smoothed her hair and then she had taken her hand away. She sat quietly with her hands in her lap and Justin ached with pity for her. He longed to take her into his arms and try to soothe the hurt in her. For it is hard knowledge to learn that the child you want life for does not want what you would give it, wants love instead. It is hard knowledge to find that a fragile, sick child, with its good hand on the silken fur of a ballsleeper, can so innocently wound you deeper than any adult has ever been able to do, and permanently render useless what you had believed to be your greatest strength.

Justin had seen Erma's eyes, naked and vulnerable, searching his, and then he had seen the quiet of this knowledge descend on her, snapping one by one the threads that held her angry, fighting spirit together. It was then he had gone out of The Room and started to sharpen the knives for something to do, and, testing one on a hair of his beard, had decided to shave.

That night, after Kathy was asleep, Erma had come to his bed, had lain close to him, holding to his collarbone with one tight, articulate hand. She had kissed all the places where he had scratched and cut his face. In inarticulate silence they had waited through those moments of profound sadness until the time for words had passed them by.

The wild ballsleeper in the tree had descended to a lower branch, still eying Justin. Without any sudden movement Justin slid his hand into his pocket, extracted another clusternut and tossed it near the base of the tree. Then he returned to the measuring of the leather in which to wrap "The Time of History."

Yes, it had been after that night that their golden time had come upon them. Very slowly, bit by bit, all their lives changed. It was as though some last sharp splinter of Erma's fighting will, in defeat, had punctured a wound in a swollen reservoir of love within her so that at first it had begun to seep out of her toward the child, the child's pet, and then to himself and finally to engulf everything in The Room. No more did she demand of Kathy that she try to move her fingers; no longer did she demand of him that he testify to the child's recovery, nor of the fire that it burn, nor of dirt in the house that it be gone. Everything she approached with the greatest tenderness. Everything and everybody became slowly suffused in this golden fountain of love that poured from the woman like honey from a broken comb. Sometimes Justin saw her reach for and seem to caress a loaf of their bread with the same tenderness that he received, and he was content to have it so.

The Room had changed, too. Sometimes Justin forgot about it when he was away, and, coming back to it, was startled to enter this child's paradise.

Now, with the task of the manuscripts completed, and the strange ballsleeper advanced to within a few feet of him, Justin gathered up the tools, the leather scraps, the manuscripts, and started home. Earlier he had noticed conception flowers in bud near the path and he planned to take some of these home with him. When either of them was out of The Room they always thought what they could bring back, as though it were a shrine they returned to with some tribute. And so, in a way, it was. The child's bed had become the center of their lives. To make it warmer for Kathy it had been moved near the fireplace, and to make the nursing easier Justin had elevated it so that the bed had actually taken on the appearance of an altar. Around it were all the child's pets. The ballsleeper had had added to its company a stiltlegs, a chichimingo, and a ragman bird. By the bed they had made, for her pleasure, a miniature garden, so that there might be constantly new things happening for her to watch. Seeing the scene afresh, Justin was often reminded of paintings of holy infants surrounded by wild creatures. Of every kind of bird he had taken the very young because of the greater ease in taming them; and, short-lived as some of them were, he felt sure they would all outlive the child. It seemed to Justin that each time he returned to The Room her skin had become more transluscent, as though inside her there was a slowly increasing amount of light and that, at the moment of her death, this inner light would blaze and glow. Everything in The Room was centered about the child's bed, every beautiful thing moved near for her pleasure. It was hard to remember that The Room had once had different functions. Justin stood in the doorway, breathing in the beauty of the scene.

Erma came to him swiftly, silently, the way that she always moved now. She kissed him and took from his arms the leather-wrapped manuscripts, and then she leaned against him while they looked at the child. It was curious how she seemed to have given up words as a means of communication and used instead a touch, a kiss, a smile, a sudden leaning of her weight against him. She put the heavy manuscripts down on a table and held out her hands for the flowers. Then together they moved toward the high bed. He felt her holding the flowers with that same caressing tenderness with which she reached for the loaf of bread, and felt himself sinking once again into that hypnotic, enchanted spell.

"Look, Kathy, what Justin has brought you," Erma said. "Conception flowers."

Justin bent over the bed and kissed the child's forehead. She smiled up at him.

"I didn't realize it was time for them again," Justin said.

"I didn't either," Erma said. "They're always nineteen days after Yearsenday, and we didn't celebrate this year. I suppose that's why we forgot."

"I don't know if they'll open after they're picked or not," Justin said, "but I knew that we wouldn't be going to see them, so I thought we might as well try them indoors."

While Erma went to put the flowers in water, Justin went through an elaborate ceremony of greeting each of the pets in turn, and then he sat down where he could see both the child and the miniature garden. For the base of this they had used Arthur's old shoemaking bench and on it placed a layer of soil covered with moss. Seedling trees, when they grew too large, were supplanted by others. A bowl of water sunk in the moss became a lake and by its shores stood a miniature Kathy carved from wood. Little by little, in the evenings, had been added a carved feathermane, a plumed riverheron, and a ballsleeper. The live ballsleeper, Kathy's pet, left Kathy and jumped onto Justin's shoulder from where he began to explore. Finally he succeeded in extracting a clusternut from Justin's pocket.

"The tray will be ready soon," Erma called.

Justin stood up, lifted the ballsleeper back onto Kathy's bed, and then, very gently, he lifted the child and put pillows behind her so that she might sit up for this, the high spot of their day. The little body weighed almost nothing now. Each day Justin's big hands felt the tragedy of it. As Erma approached the bed carrying the big tray the birds all began to twitter in anticipation. Justin moved the table near and got a stool for Erma. The tray had on it a pot of tea, cups, a fresh loaf of bread, some cheese for Erma and Justin. Around the edges there were many small dishes. There were piles of grain, berries and fruits for the birds and a stack of clusternuts for the ballsleeper. Dotted here and there about the tray were small servings of the child's food. It was, by now, a long ritual, conceived at first in desperation when

Kathy had refused food. While Erma poured tea and sliced the bread, Justin began the feeding, a tidbit for the stiltlegs and a tiny bite of egg for Kathy, a little grain for the chichimingo and a small sip of broth for Kathy. And so it went, while Erma drank her tea. Then she would take her turn at feeding, while Justin drank his tea. It was a slow process, getting any nourishment down the child, yet there was never any impatience or anxiety allowed to show. They had the time now. They had all the time they needed. When Kathy refused to eat they would stop for a while and play with the garden or carve a new animal for the landscape. And they did not speak of their own concerns. They lived in the garden. They spoke with the birds and the ballsleeper and the child, and, when the great, dark eyes in the waxen face showed pleasure, they were gladdened. They developed in themselves an infinite patience. It was here, most often, that the feeling returned to Justin of being an instrument, played upon. It was here that he felt it the strongest, this boundless flood of love washing over the babe, the birds, the ballsleeper, the portions of green-grain, the berries, even the very cup in his hand.

When Kathy became too tired to eat, and slipped down on her pillows, Justin would call to the birds and carry the tray out of doors and they would fly out after him. Then he would lift Kathy in his arms and hold her while Erma straightened and cleaned the bed. While she made the child ready for sleep Justin would take his old harp or sometimes the flute and play upon it until Kathy slept. When the child was asleep Erma would put her hand on Justin's shoulder and then he would stand up quietly and get their pipes while she put on a warm jacket, and they would go to their hollowed-out resting places in the mossy bank beside the house. Sometimes they would not speak at all, but sit together quietly smoking and resting. Then Justin would go to do the evening milking and get in the firewood for the night, and Erma would return to the child. Later at night, when the chances were best for Kathy's sleeping, they would have their evening meal. But there was always with Justin now—and he supposed Erma shared it—this sense of time, this lack of urgency, that he had wanted all his life.

"I was thinking," Erma said, "isn't it odd that Kathy has never mentioned Gwen? Has she ever said anything about her to you?"

"No," Justin said. "She seems to know, somehow. Or perhaps she doesn't want to know. She hasn't talked of Tommy, either, has she, except in the delirium, right at the beginning?"

"No, she talks so little. And that only about the ballsleeper and the birds and her garden."

But we don't speak of the past, either, Justin thought. We are impaled on the present moment for as long as the child still breathes.

"Do you remember," Erma said, "during the war, I think it was, when they used to have those demonstrations of iron lungs on the streets in the cities? Did they have them where you were?"

"Yes," Justin said. "It was to raise money, I think. They'd let people walk through them. Oh, and the sound, like some monster breathing."

"I used to be fascinated by the crowds around them," Erma said. "They would keep circling. People couldn't seem to bear to get outside the sound of the breathing. They would wander off and then keep coming back."

"Sometimes you frighten me," Justin said.

"Why?"

"You seem of late to be able to read my mind, as though it weren't necessary for me to speak. I was just thinking before you spoke of how we seem to be impaled on the present moment. I want to plan ahead for us when . . . when all this is over, as it surely must be soon. And I don't seem able to."

Erma put her hand on his arm. "I cannot think beyond it. I cannot imagine it," she said. "Please, don't make me try."

That evening, while the child slept, Erma and Justin sat watching the huge buds of the conception flowers.

"I wonder if they will open," Erma said.

Just then the ballsleeper let out a plaintive little squeak and, jumping down from Kathy's bed, began to run restlessly back and forth.

"What's the matter with him?" Justin said.

Erma started toward the bed, but already the birds had set up a restless twittering. She bent over and touched the child. "Justin," she said. "Oh, Justin."

It was true. The child was dead. So long had she been approaching death, and by such gradual steps, that it had seemed to Justin there could never be a final step. And so it must have been that death, at last, approached the child. Very quietly, very easily, shortly before her fifth birthday, Kathy died in her sleep in the time that it takes a conception flower to open, unnoticed, unfurl its huge petals and begin the spiral ballet of its stamens, delicately touching, one by one, the central pistil. In the silence of The Room the shining green pollen showered down unseen. In the time that it takes a conception flower to open, the last of a good man's progeny can disappear from the living, the last of a new generation be gone from the land.

FROM THE RECORD OF JUSTIN MAGNUS, THE TWENTIETH DAY OF THE FIRST MONTH OF THE NINTH YEAR:

Kathy died last night. We buried her this morning beneath the spicebark tree where she used to play a lot before her accident. Howlers had already started to circle the settlement by dawn and we have set out all the oil lamps we can spare on the grave. Erma did not want the child put in the old cave where Joe and Gwen are buried, for which I don't blame her; and, anyhow, the entrance must be all overgrown and lost by now. Erma has no tears yet. She seems frozen somewhere beyond them. I must get her away from here soon. I must take her away.

Who would have thought that death had any new trickery for Justin Magnus? And yet the variety of death is endless and the surprises of grief are as great as those of life. Because the child's death was not violent, not unexpected—as Tommy's had been, or Joe's—Justin had mistakenly thought there could be no abruptness to it. The increment of the child's sinking was so constant from day to day and so gradual that Justin had thought it would seem the same the day after her dying. He had thought somehow that it would be another day, like the others, with only a little less of the child alive, the way that it is with flowers fading. He thought that he knew and so he had not prepared himself, had not even thought of himself in this quiet day, whose moments seemed so long.

He was even aware that Erma was moving quietly about, making tea for them, while he was recording the child's death, and he saw that she made the tray the same as she had every day and was even aware that she was carrying it out of doors so that the birds would follow her. She's taking it to the grave, he thought, so that the birds will be with Kathy still. And this seemed right to him, a gesture filled with a gentle, bearable sadness. He closed his Record and went over to the mantel to get himself a pipe. While he was lighting it he thought of following Erma and of being with her when the birds settled on the little grave, but without realizing what he did he picked up his harp and carried it over to the accustomed place.

The tea was making at the accustomed time, the bread was ready. The fire in the hearth, the stool he sat on, the little garden —everything was in its accustomed place. Who, moving through this quiet house, touching familiar things, feeling a familiar hunger for tea at the accustomed time, would be guarded and watching for trickery? Without thinking, Justin ran his hand across the strings of the harp as he always did, and looked up at the bed to see the child's ethereal face, as he always did.

So Erma found him, a bent, broken figure, leaning over his harp, sobbing. She ran to him and cradled him in her arms and waited, and at last he lifted his head from his arms and, staring down at the harp strings, said, "I forgot she was dead."

Erma rose slowly and stood behind him, letting him lean his huge, heavy head against her. "Go on and play," she said. "I wish you would. Play while I move the bed. I have to do it some-time and tomorrow will be harder."

Justin rubbed his big knuckles across his eyes and lifted the harp. "Wouldn't you rather I helped you?" he said. "It's heavy."

She felt his head move from her body and knew that he did not need her for support now. She moved over to the bed with her back to Justin. "No," she said. "I'd rather you played. I'd rather it wouldn't be silent."

Erma stretched her hands forward and made them touch the little pillow, and then she concentrated on the music, one note at a time, while she began to take the bed apart. There has to be a time when you touch the emptiness, she thought. There has to be some certain moment.

That night they lay together in the big bed, staring into the darkness, not sleeping, not talking, and at last they became aware of the mossback bawling in the corral.

"My God, I forgot to milk her," Justin said. He got up and began to dress. "I'll have to go, I guess."

"I'll come with you," Erma said.

"No, darling. No. Please. There's no need of that."

"I'll get you a torch," Erma said.

Justin walked first to the grave to see that all was well. In the heavy dew the small lamps sputtered, but it was enough. The grave had not been molested. He turned to the corral. The mossback, hearing him, changed her bawling to a scolding puffing.

"Hold still, damn you," Justin said. "I'm here now."

The mossback at last stopped lifting her feet and pushing about and, as the milking progressed, subsided into quiet sighs. Justin leaned his head against her warm side. "All right," he said. "All right, now."

As he left the corral he set the pail down carefully and started to close the gate. Why am I closing the gate? What does it matter now? he thought. Even now, will we not be able to leave here because an animal is waiting to be milked?

"Come on," he said to the mossback, "come on. You're free. No gate. No fence."

The mossback, puzzled, backed away from him.

"Freedom is hard to face, eh?" Justin said. "What would become of you if Erma and I both died? Consider us dead. Consider we never came, and act accordingly."

The mossback looked at him in the light of the torch with her great, stupid eyes.

But we aren't dead, Justin thought. We do know. And we did take her calf away. We'll have to drive everything we've domesticated into freedom or kill it before we go. The thought of witnessing more death, even that of a mossback or a hen, made him angry, and in his tiredness the weight of the milk bucket added to his anger. He stopped and poured the milk on the ground. "We don't need it," he said aloud. "We don't need milk any more. The child is dead."

Let the grain rot in the storehouse. Let the moss grow smooth over the grinding stone. Let the gates of the corral yawn open and abandoned and the hens run foraging for themselves, toughening their muscles now that there would be no one to eat them. Let the hearth grow cold. And leave it. Leave it, gladly. For these are the comforts that come at high price and these are the comforts lovers do not need. What we need, Justin thought, Erma and I, what we need is to look on a landscape without history, without demands or memories.

His torch was burning short and he roused himself from his solitary thinking and returned to The Room. With his hand on the door he thought that if she were awake now he would tell her this. And they would begin to plan this very night where they would go. With a kind of awe he realized that they had outlived all the demands on them. They had outlived them all. And, knowing this, he knew that, when it was necessary to kill the mossback, he could do it.

CHAPTER SIX

"'A N D my love lay sleeping on a bed of fragrant fern.' What
is that?" Justin asked. "Is it a song? It keeps running through my
head."

"It sounds familiar," Erma said, "but I can't remember any
music to go with it. 'And my love lay sleeping . . .' "

She stretched herself and folded her arms behind her head
for a pillow. "It's a lovely bed," she said. "Aren't you tired,
Justin?"

"No, dear. I feel very much awake. And you?"

"I'm glad to lie down."

They were camped, this their first night away from the
settlement, at the Yearsenday Place, because Justin had seen
Erma's fatigue and had known they must not try to go farther.
Before they left the settlement he had been impatient to be
away from familiar things, but as the day wore on and he became
sure that nothing now could call them back, his impatience left
him. What did one more night mean, after all? It would be a slow
process, bringing Erma back to life.

Outside the settlement, on the uphill climb, where she was
away from the routine tasks, the toll of Kathy's long illness and
death showed on Erma in startling ways. Her movements were
slow and she was very quick to tire. She seemed not to notice
anything about her, yet she did not protest at going on. Even
though he knew in his own body how it was with her ("It feels
like a rock here," she had said, "in my chest, day and night, a
jagged rock that won't dissolve"), still Justin did not doubt they
had been right to leave the settlement. It had become an obsession
with him, the fear that he might break his leg or that the drying
wall for the Records would crumble and have to be repaired or
that some wounded animal would stumble into The Room and
have to be nursed.

The smokehouse had been secured as well as possible with a wide trench around it, the corral and the pens had been emptied, the child's grave, unlighted, had remained unmolested for three consecutive nights, the best possible protective measures for the settlement had been taken, and the decisions made as to what they would take with them. But not until the leaving had actually been accomplished did Justin's dread lessen. The leaving had not been easy on Erma.

Justin put another piece of wood on the fire and then turned toward her. *And my love lay sleeping on a bed of fragrant fern.* She reached out and put her hand in his.

"I'm glad I didn't build any of those houses I planned for us," Justin said.

"Yes," Erma said. "Each one would have been another place to leave."

"Exactly," Justin said. "And this way, if we build it on the raft, we'll have our house with us."

"Tell me about the others, though," she said.

"Well, there was one. Maybe you've noticed. Downhill from the settlement. It's a place we've been for soaproot a couple of times. There are five trees together that enclose a space about the size of a small room."

"Spicebark trees?" Erma said.

"Yes. I had the space all cleared once, I remember. I was going to train vines around it. It was a natural room."

"When was that?" Erma said.

"Oh, I don't remember exactly. A long time ago. There have been so many of them, places I would earmark when I was out hunting wood, or walking alone. I've always wanted to take you away, to myself, to a place that I had made for you."

But he did remember, and very well, the time he had cleared the space enclosed by the five trees, and he did not want to speak of it with her, for he remembered it in terms of the cave, in terms of Arthur Herrick. He felt her hand relax slowly and he slid his own away gently so that she might fall asleep. He filled his pipe and lighted it and gave himself up to his thoughts with anticipation of pleasure. He had lived through this before, many times, and yet he had never been able to capture the experience in the process of happening. This night, beside the fire, with this enjoyable wakefulness and the great relief of having escaped the settlement without mishap—this night he might devote to exploring this puzzling phenomenon: of how the same amount of time could be relived an infinite number of times in different terms.

It would be happening to them in the days and months to come that their histories would be subtly rewritten *in terms of each other*. This night he had caught it happening, that a time in the life of Arthur Herrick had become the space enclosed by five trees he had cleared for Erma. And he knew now that it would occur again and again to them, that they would be rewriting their past in terms of each other. And, having had this night to think of it, he knew that, when it came again, it would give him conscious pleasure. For no one, not even someone as old as himself, can anticipate which of the events will emerge, or what things from out one's past will elect to jump their moorings and join a new procession of events rewritten by lovers in a context of their own.

And my love lay sleeping on a bed of fragrant fern. No, it was not a song. It was a poem, a poem remembered from a time before Erma was born. And there was more of it with him now in the quiet night.

> *And my love lay sleeping on a bed of fragrant fern*
> *While I watched the night away beside the fire.*

It was a poem that had been read to him many years before by a young woman lying on an elegant man-made couch, a woman who had never been any closer to a fragrant fern than to finger one delicately in a florist's shop. But these were memories which did not elect to jump their moorings and become a part of Justin Magnus at the moment, neither the woman nor her name. Not the couch, nor the color of it. Only the sound of the words came to Justin to describe for him, with pleasure, this woman that he loved, who this night lay sleeping beside this fire, in this land.

Justin caught two fish for breakfast and took the ease with which he had got them into the net as a good omen. He left them cooking over the fire and went in search of a firstfruit melon. When he came back he saw that the fish were done. He called Erma softly. Immediately she sat upright.

"Kathy?" she said. "Did she call?"

"No, dear," Justin said. "No."

Erma looked about her, seeing the trees where she had expected the walls of The Room. "Oh," she said. "Oh, yes."

"We'll have breakfast soon," Justin said. "I had rare good luck. Look."

"Fish," she said. "You must have been up for a long time."

"Long enough to make tea," he said. "Here, have some."

She drank deeply of the tea, hoping the pungent steam of it would curl about her brain, erasing the dream and the disorientation and the great reluctance she felt to face the day ahead. "Justin," she said, "did you know where you were when you woke up? I thought I was in The Room and—"

"I know, dear. You asked for the child. It may be so for a long time, but one of these days you will wake up and know instantly where you are."

"Did you?" she asked. "Are you out of The Room already?"

"Well, no, not exactly. I didn't sleep. There is so much here in the Yearsenday Place."

"Yes," Erma said, "all the times . . ." She stood up, then, and stretched. Not far away she could see the giant leaf of a dewplant, brimful, and she decided to wash her face and comb her hair before breakfast.

After they had eaten, Justin said, "How do you feel? Do you want to stay on here today and rest?"

"You'd like to go, wouldn't you?"

"It doesn't matter," he said.

"Yes, let's go on. I keep remembering all the Yearsenday feasts and Tommy. Let's go on to a place where you can sleep."

"Oh, it wasn't unpleasant," Justin said. "I wasn't pacing up and down or anything. I just lay here quietly watching the fire. But I would like to go on if you feel up to it. I would like to leave everything familiar behind us as soon as possible."

"All right," she said.

Suddenly, unaccountably, she was filled with anger at him, because of the way he had said *everything familiar*, as though it were of no account, as though he belittled it. She thought with longing of the child's grave and of how, if she were at the settlement now, she could be close to it. She thought with longing of the familiar house and of the great peace of resting in it, of being able to locate what was needed, of having whatever she touched be familiar to the hand. Why had she been dragged away

from what was, after all, *everything she had?* Why was she made
to walk on and on and on in this endless fight against the wilderness, when behind her there were all the good things of home?

"Darling," Justin said, seeing the tears in her eyes, "what
is it?"

"I don't know what's the matter with me," she said. "I
shouldn't have come. It's too soon. I don't see how you can be
in a hurry to leave the familiar things. They're everything.
They're all we have."

"Surely you don't mean that," Justin said, looking at her,
for he could not bring himself to ask her if she valued his love,
which was here, less than the clay pots or the bread oven at home.

Surprised at her own outburst, Erma closed her eyes and
put her head in her hands. Of a sudden she had remembered
Justin, bent over his harp, caught in grief for Kathy. How was
it that in her heart, a moment ago, she had seen Justin and herself
in some ridiculous competition over who grieved the more?

"No," she said, "of course I don't mean it."

Justin came over and sat beside her and took her in his arms.
"We can go back, dear," he said, "if that's what you want."

"How is it," Erma said, "that grief got the reputation for
being an ennobling thing? It has only made me childish and unpredictable and—"

"It's one of the classic myths," Justin said.

"The dead have all the dignity," Erma said.

"In the times of crises, anyhow," Justin said, "it often looks
that way, as though the survivors were engaged in a grotesque
ballet to wrest some dignity away from the dead and have a little
for themselves."

"It would be merciful," Erma said, "if you had some way
to obscure from yourself the knowledge that a selfish, childish
demon had taken possession of your mind and your heart."

"It's only a temporary possession, my dear. Believe me."

"Justin, there's something I have to know."

He reached out and took her hand. He saw her swallow painfully and awkwardly and felt the answering convulsive movement in her hand.

"I have to know," she said. "Was there really never any
progress with Kathy? Did she just go steadily downhill, and was
it that I imagined all the hopeful signs?"

Justin looked down at the woman's hand in his. With his free hand he began to trace the pattern of the veins. What did she want of him? For the child's death to Justin was an accomplished fact and he did not care for the accuracy or inaccuracy of his observations. He cared only for Erma, that she should be returned to living. Did she want him to say that he, too, had anticipated Kathy's recovery, or was it that she wished him to say, in effect, that his vision had not been obscured and therefore he loved Kathy less? Perhaps it was this that she wanted, that she might have cause for anger toward him, for accusation, so that she might have something against which to pit her fury at death and so rid herself of some of it.

But this was not Edith, this was not Gwendolyn who sat here beside him asking this formidable question. This was Erma. And, no matter her need, he must not seek the answer that would reassure but the answer that was true.

"Darling," he said, "we didn't have a dispassionate observer here with us. We had only ourselves. There isn't any absolute scale when hope of life is involved. You're asking something impossible of me."

She locked her fingers with his, then, and raised his hand to her head. Against the hardness of his knuckles she rubbed her forehead roughly back and forth. Then she sat up and breathed deeply.

"Of course," she said, "of course. Oh, Justin, do you remember how beautiful she was, how she would look up at you and . . ."

Now, at last, the jagged stone in her chest began slowly to dissolve and be eroded in the long-delayed weeping. And Justin got up quietly and began to fold his fishnet and put the knives back in the leather case and make their possessions ready for transporting. For he knew that the time had come for them to be going on into strange places and that the hold of the settlement had been weakened.

It was their plan to continue uphill by easy stages, staying in any one place as long as they liked, and crossing successive coils of the river until they reached one too small to carry a raft. Here they would follow the river downstream until they found suitable materials for the raft, and at this place they would make a camp until the raft should be finished to their satisfaction. From that time they would live on the river.

The days of the uphill climb added one to another. And slowly Justin and Erma became aware that the landscape was changing. The chokevines and tangleroots disappeared from underfoot. No more did they see swampstars or the evil spike plants, and the climbing became gradually easier. At last they put away the heavy knives and, when they had no longer to hack out the path before them, they began to have time to look about and to glean old conversations that had been left unfinished long ago. Their vision became cleared for newness in the landscape and their spirits prepared for surprise. What was happening to them and what was happening to the landscape was like the falling away of the leaves of the heartglow.

This curious plant, which grew only sparsely near the settlement, had at first been a disappointment to them. A strong central growth forced the outer leaves into a furled sphere, similar to the growth of the World's cabbage. But the taste of the leaves, in what they had mistakenly believed to be the ripe state of a vegetable, was unpleasant and bitter and the texture coarse and unpalatable. They had lost interest in the plant as a food and, when later they saw its outer leaves being pushed out and back and falling flat against the ground, they saw them rot there without question. But the heartglow produces, much later, in its center a solid, concentrated fruit of such a pale yellow-green in color that it is almost golden. The fruit has an exotic, delicious taste, and a silken but firm texture. So different was the core fruit from the outer leaves that several years passed before the connection between the two was made. The plant did not grow in profusion and, until they had cultivated it, required seeking.

So it was with Justin and Erma as they climbed steadily uphill away from the settlement and three times crossed coils of the river: there was a gradual falling away of the old leaves. The old demands, the responsibilities, the old frustrations and sorrows and memories of failure began to be forced back and down to make room for the golden fruit of the heart. The central core of their lives began slowly to grow and be filled with flavor and life and form and reaching. And what was not of the slowly expanding fruit of the heart gradually fell away, just as the jungle roots, the ropevines, all cloying, entangling and entrapping impediments to their freedom of movement, began to disappear from their path.

For the inner core, the heart's fruit, the prime moving force

of these two, was love. Not the need of it, but the capacity for it.
They were, simply, lovers, and all their lives they had been
lovers. They had loved music and weather and food and drink.
They had loved people and animals and birds and all live things.
Yet neither had so labeled himself a lover; they had only, separately, been aware that when they were not so motivated they
were not functioning well, or to their fullest.

The world has a poor regard for lovers. Whether it is because there are so few of them that they seem not worth protecting or that, being unprotected, there are so many casualties
among them is rarely debated, simply because they do not themselves recognize their uniqueness. Ask any man what are his
memories of deepest satisfaction, and it is likely he will speak of
moments of personal acclaim, of an individual goal recognized
and won. Rarely will the answer be a memory of love. The world
has poor regard for lovers and pits against them its subtlest
weapons. And what are the enemies of love? The marking of
time in small parcels is an enemy of love. Claims that seem duties,
demands, obligations are enemies of love. Acts of clutching,
grasping and holding are enemies of love. Cleverness is an enemy
of love. In a long life there are often remembered times of love's
brief and momentary triumphs over the enemies. And, in memory,
what is the essence of these moments? It is timelessness and the
translation of obligation into pleasure.

So it is in the world, where the central core of most people is
not love but something else, where often the core is split into two
or three separate cores which twist and writhe about one another,
where sometimes the central core is so splintered that it disinte-
grates altogether. And so it was for many years in the Green
Kingdom with the remnants of the World and the World's ways
they had brought with them. But now, for Erma and Justin, it was
no longer so. The marking of time in small, insistent parcels was
at an end. The golden fruit of the heart, kept alive by rare moments of struggle and reaching, was free at last to flower and
function, not for brief, sporadic, stolen moments, but fluidly.

It was as though their very breathing continuously polished
a bright jewel of great value.

Justin awoke just before dawn to an instant awareness of
where he was, an immediate feeling of well-being and caution not
to disturb the beloved burden. Erma lay with one leg thrown over

him and her head on his shoulder. This body he knew now, intimately, completely. He closed his eyes and treasured the silken warmth of it. Also he knew now that if he spoke to her in her sleep, she would not be startled, not make any sudden movements, for their voices belonged to each other in the deepest recesses of their beings. He knew that if he put his hand on the knee which lay over him and caressingly moved up the thigh and over the sweet mound of the buttocks, letting his warm, huge hand come to rest over the flat sacrum, that she would move closer to him in her sleep and smile. In the deepest recesses of their beings they knew each other's voices.

How very much her body had changed lately, Justin thought. He could remember only with difficulty the drooping of fatigue it had shown in the days of her life in the cave, the sudden awkwardnesses she had shown then. Even in the old days, when Tommy had been a baby, she had not been as she was now. She had had that manner of leaning forward, of trying to catch up. But slowly, as week after week they had climbed upward, as the lacetrees and the leatherwoods had given way to these stunted, twisted, strange new trees and the entangling, lush jungle growth underfoot gave way to the thick moss, studded with minute flowers, Erma's body had seemed to him to be growing younger.

They had not expected such surprise in the landscape as this. They had not known that it would be so cold, but both of them found it exhilarating. Would they make another loop of the river today, Justin wondered, and would this be the one where they would decide to build the raft? He found himself impatient to know the day. Not since he had been a very young man could he remember having felt such exaltation merely at the prospect of living a day. A memory of a room came to him, a bare, cold room where he had first lived alone, first written music that was his own. It had been cold there, too, bitterly cold in that room, and he could remember pacing about the cold room, watching the white plumes of his own breath, waiting for the fire in the stove to begin roaring, feeling himself and the stove to have kindred fires roaring and leaping within them, sharing valuable advance knowledge of the day to which the rest of the city had not yet awakened.

Slowly the pre-wessun light made the mounds of their bodies visible under the blankets. A circle of visibility spread out from them, like warmth from their bodies. And Justin held his breath to keep from laughing at what he saw. With his right hand he pressed gently on the hollow of Erma's back. He bent his left arm to cradle her shoulders closer. "Erma," he whispered, "be very quiet, but wake up. There's something you've got to see."

She moved against him and smiled in her sleep, and then, down the whole length of him, he felt her stretch. "Erma," he whispered, "don't say anything. Open your eyes, and look over there."

Lined up near their bed, projecting fuzzily out of the shadows, was what appeared to be a whole family of ruffs, their fox faces peering questioningly, their big neck ruffs of pale-green fur trembling with excitement. Very slowly, so as not to disturb them, Erma turned so that her back was cradled in the curve of Justin's body, and the two of them lay side by side, staring at the staring ruffs. At last Justin could stand it no longer and he began to laugh. With one startled bound the ruffs turned and disappeared into the shadows.

To awaken to a breath-taking moment of silent enchantment, to hear the first sound of the day one's own laughter and the laughter of one's beloved echoing through the crystalline, cold air, to taste in deep love the warmth of the beloved before the time of dressing in the cold air, to anticipate fire and hot breakfast—all this was given to them many mornings, until any memory of having awakened with dread or dullness, with fatigue or illness, faded into some other life.

"Well," Justin said as they were finishing breakfast, "do you want to go on, or shall I build up the fire?"

"I have to mend my sandal," Erma said, "but that won't take long. And then I'd like to explore a little farther. Are your sandals all right?"

"Seem to be," Justin said. "If we go much farther, though, we'll need warmer clothing."

"I had no idea it would be so different, did you?"

"No," Justin said, "I didn't. But from the looks of these scrubby trees we'll soon be above timber line and that will mean carrying firewood."

"Even if we got to another coil of the river," Erma said, "there wouldn't be anything to build the raft out of, would there?"

"No, I think we'd have to go back down to the last one for that, but while we're up so far I'd like to see what's here."

"So would I," Erma said. "Let's go as far as we can. Do you suppose we'll ever know what's over the top?"

"I doubt it," Justin said. "I've been watching those clouds up there. They don't seem to change any. Maybe they're always there."

"Isn't it strange to see clouds? We never saw clouds in the settlement."

She was rummaging among their gear, hunting for the leather thongs she needed to mend her sandal. A small, flat piece of wood fell out of the roll. She picked it up and studied the knife scratches on it. "Why, Justin, are you still keeping a calendar?"

Justin knelt on the ground, rolling up their blankets. He stopped and turned toward her. "Why, yes, dear. I thought I would keep track."

"But why, Justin? What does it matter to us?"

She found the leather thongs but did not begin work on her sandal. It seemed odd to her that Justin had all this time, in secret, been keeping track of the time, and now she saw an embarrassment in his manner that she didn't understand. She walked over and sat down beside him on the blanket. For the first time she felt really cold.

"Well," Justin said, "it's because of the opening. I thought we might better not lose track of it."

On the face of it, it was nothing. If he wanted to go on keeping a calendar, as they always had, what of it? And yet she could not shake off the sense of her surprise. Why had he kept it in secret?

"Just in case, you know," Justin said.

"In case of what, dear? You don't mean that you want to go back to the World?"

"Oh, no," Justin said. "I don't want to go back."

Erma moved closer to him, put her hands on his arms, and studied his face. "But you don't think I would go? You can't think I would ever leave you?"

"You're cold, dear. Go back to the fire and put on your jacket. Here, I'll help you."

"All right," she said. "Yes, I am cold."

Erma put on her jacket and pulled the hood over her head.

"We've never needed gloves or socks before," she said. She held her hands out to the fire to warm them and began to work on her sandal. But still the sense of something unsaid between them hung over her.

"It will be warmer when we're moving," Justin said. He picked up the small wooden board, made a mark on it with his knife, and slipped it into his pocket.

"Justin, what is it? There should be no secrets between us. There's something you're not telling me. I can feel it."

"Why, it's very simple, really. Don't distress yourself. It's just that we have to allow for the fact that you might be left alone here. You might want to get back to the World, and I wouldn't like it to have been my carelessness that caused you uncertainty or trouble."

Erma fastened her mind on the work of her sandal and tried to collect herself lest she blurt out the wrong thing. Had he, then, secretly and alone, been thinking of death while she, in the fullest time of life she had ever known, had been unaware? She mended the sandal as quickly as she could, put it on, and stood up so that Justin could make ready the firebox for the journey. But the weight in her heart could not be put away. She ran to Justin and put her arms about him and looked up into his face. "Have you been thinking about death all alone, without my knowing?" she said.

"No, no," he said. He held her close and pressed her head against his chest. "There's nothing to upset yourself about, Erma. I haven't been brooding. It's just that, once in a while, I remember that I am almost seventy years old. It's in the nature of things."

"But, Justin, why would you think I would want to leave our land, our things, ever?"

"Do you think you know now how you might feel then? You might be very lonely, you know. Don't be so sad. It's only that, in case you ever needed to get out, there ought not to be unnecessary obstacles in your way."

"But suppose, Justin, suppose *you* were left alone. You wouldn't want to go back, would you?"

"Let's stop this," Justin said. "We'll freeze to death and settle the question that way if we don't get moving."

"All right," she said. "What's left to do?"

But even after they had their packs on and had kept up a

brisk pace to keep themselves warm, Erma could not get it out of her mind.

"Is it your music you were thinking about?" she said suddenly. "Is that it, Justin? Do you want your music taken back to the World, the way Arthur hoped the Records would be some day?"

"Oh, I hadn't thought about it much. Sometime when we're on the raft we'll take a whole day and talk about it. Right now, in case you hadn't noticed it, there's ice on the ground and you'd better pay attention to your footing. In fact, I think we'd better turn back."

Erma had been so much concerned with her thoughts that she had not noticed the landscape. Now she stopped and looked about her. The low twisted trees had almost disappeared and patches of ice were dotted frequently underfoot.

"How bleak it is," she said. "Do you remember when Joe and Arthur were talking about how the top must be covered by ice?"

"May have been right," Justin said. "What about it? Don't you think we'd better turn back? There's no wood here for tonight. And it's really very cold. If we mean to make a real exploration of this region, we'd better plan it with some care."

"All right," Erma said. "But don't you think if we went just a little farther that we might touch a cloud? I would so love to touch one of those clouds."

"All right," he said. "We'll go on a little, but let me go ahead. Stay close behind."

The path grew suddenly steeper and they felt the exertion of climbing. Yet something pressed them on. They became aware of a sound they had not heard for years, the sound of wind blowing. At last they were walking on solid ice and Justin knew they must turn back. He stopped. Erma came up behind him and the two stood looking about them at the bleak, icy loneliness. Even if they had had breath for speech, the place was too awesome for it. Justin reached out to take hold of Erma so that he could get ahead of her for the descent, but he could see nothing, for the wind had suddenly swirled upon them a huge mass of clouds. In the white blindness the two of them moved instinctively to touch each other and, gropingly, found themselves in embrace. Sight gone, sound gone, all other senses obliterated, they stood wrapped in thick clouds, knowing only the solid forms of each other's bodies and, gradually, the warmth. It was a moment of discovery that would return to Erma many times, as though they had been given knowledge of the ultimate reality.

As suddenly as the clouds had obliterated them from each other and everything about them they now swirled away and left them locked in embrace, able to see. Without any words they turned and began the slippery descent. They did not speak again until they had reached the flower-studded green moss.

For four days now they retraced their path, until they came again to the third coil of the river, and then they began walking downstream. Here the river was narrow and the current very swift. They made three camps before they came at last to the place where they would settle and build the raft. Here the river had widened and made a gentle cove. There promised to be a good supply of logs suitable for the raft, and a gently sloping bank, pleasant and easy to explore. But especially had they chosen this place because the shore and a long roadway to it were beaten smooth by the hoofs of many animals.

Nearby grew the soaproot plant so that Erma, knowing a new supply was available, felt free at last to use all she had brought. There was a great washing of everything they had brought with them. She made new sandals for them both from the roll of mossback hide they carried. It was a pleasant, leisurely time for Erma, a time of mending and repairing, of taking stock, of curing shambacco and drying moss for the firebox's future appetite. They had made their camp a little distance from the worn watering place, behind a thin shield of tall grass, so that, night and morning, they could watch the procession of animals come down to the river. They grew to have individual favorites and to care passionately about the rivalries among the animals.

Without hurry, but carefully and slowly, the raft began to take form, the matched logs to be laced together securely.

"I've been thinking of putting soil on top of it, on part of it, anyway," Justin said.

"Like Kathy's garden," Erma said.

Justin reached out and touched her hand to share the memory of sadness. "Yes. Perhaps that's where it came from, that miniature garden on Arthur's cobbler's bench."

"Could we have a moss floor," Erma asked, "to sleep on?"

"That's an idea," Justin said. "But what I was thinking of more was that we might see if those reeds wouldn't grow up around the sides and back of the raft to make a kind of sheltered cabin."

"Living walls," Erma said. "How wonderful that would be!"

"Well, we can try it," Justin said. "It would be nice if a few riverherons would come ride with us, too."

And so they did make it, little by little, a river home in which everything except the logs and their lacings was actually living. The fast-growing reeds in time became tall enough and were flexible enough to be bent into a roof; a riverheron, after much enticing, came to explore and at last was joined by a mate, and these were to ride with them for a long part of their journey.

At last they had stored everything on the raft and reorganized the space several times. They had trimmed off the branches of the reeds which projected into the cabin, and over the floor moss they had loaded the soft ferns for their bed, the freshly washed blankets and hides. The last of the dried mossback meat, the last of the cheese, the last of the supplies from the settlement were gone. From now on they would live on the land and take what variety the river brought them.

It was a very great and exciting moment when they cast themselves upon the river. They stood together on the forepart of the raft, feeling the smooth motion beneath them, accustoming themselves to a new way of standing and of moving, letting their feet learn the knowledge of the rounded logs beneath them, and in all their muscles and tendons and joints experiencing a new system of balance and motion. There would be always with them that undersense of alertness for what might be ahead of change, of danger, of surprise, of new scenes.

At last their campsite faded out of view and they stood leaning together, and together turned to look ahead.

"Did you notice, when we cast off," Justin asked, "how the roots of the plants had grown around the sides of the logs?"

"Yes," Erma said, "so white and tight and twisted. Like a cocoon."

"Just so," Justin said, "all wrapped tight. I only hope they don't split the logs apart."

"Oh, no," Erma said. "It's a real Joebuilt job."

"Do you know where you put our pipes?" Justin asked.

"Certainly I know where I put them," Erma said. "That cabin is organized."

"I know, but you've organized it so many times."

"I'll get your pipe," Erma said. "I'll prove it to you." She turned gaily and kissed him and they had a sudden moment of seeking balance.

"We'll get our river legs soon," Justin said. He saw her safely into the cabin, and then he secured the long pole and squatted down on the floor of the raft. He had a great and pleasant feeling of pride in the raft and anticipation for the journey.

Erma came out carrying their pipes and tobacco. "I found the pipes, all right," she said, "but I had a little trouble with the tobacco."

Justin took the pipe from her. It was the first smoke he had had that day. "Where was it?" he said, smiling.

"I won't tell," she said.

"With the tea?"

"No."

"Come on, tell me."

"I won't."

"Look," Justin said. "Look up. Here comes your riverheron to ride with us."

"I hope *her* nest is in order," Erma said.

Justin smiled secretly to himself, for now he could identify it: the tobacco smelled faintly of soaproot.

The rudder, which they had had great trouble with because of the dullness of their tools, still gave Justin concern. He did not really relax until they had successfully negotiated two turns in the river. By this time he had the feel of it and had mastered the steady, even, muscular control to make it work smoothly.

Their eyes were washed with wonders: with flocks of stiltlegs and gemboys and strange birds they had never seen before, with hanging curtains of flowers they had not known. They moved through a series of perfumes and spice odors. They heard the sounds and songs and raucous calls of birds. And, under everything, always, there was the voice of the river that came to be like the blood in their veins.

"I wonder if Arthur made it," Justin said one day.

"Out of the Kingdom?"

"Yes. Do you think he did?"

"I don't know, Justin. For his sake, I hope so."

"There's a sandbar ahead," Justin said. "Would you like a swim? Looks like a good place."

"Fine," she said. "What's all that?"

"I can't see yet," Justin said. "It's odd there's nothing growing."

"It looks like . . . like driftwood," Erma said.

"Well, we'll soon see."

Here, for a reason of its own, the river had cast sand into a long island and, on it, for how many countless years, it had been tossing its burden of driftwood.

Justin and Erma stepped off the raft onto the island and began to walk among the strange, bleached, dead shapes, and Justin saw that, in Erma, some kind of significant excitement was taking place. She moved among the strange shapes worn smooth by years of the river's washing, stopping to run her hand along a surface, to kneel and pick up a particular piece, to return to one already seen. She seemed oblivious of everything else.

Justin turned and left her alone to wander among the treasures, for in his heart a fragile hope had begun to live, so fragile a hope that he dared not even state it to himself. He made a quick decision to arrange for them to stay awhile on this island, and that would necessitate a good deal of work. For the first time they had come to a place where there was no food, nothing growing to be gathered, and that meant he must fish. He gathered enough of the driftwood near where the raft was anchored for a fire, and then he went aboard the raft for the net. He would be willing to live on fish exclusively for several days, or if necessary to go without food, if the fragile hope should be realized.

Much later, while he was cooking the fish, Erma came to him carrying in her arms one large, smooth, beautiful piece of driftwood. "Look," she said. "Just look, Justin. I saw the fire, finally. And food. Oh, I'm hungry. I forgot all about food. Did you have a swim, too?"

"Yes," he said. "Here, your fish is done."

"Justin, I want to stay here awhile."

"I know," he said. "Why not?"

"Oh," she said with sudden impatience, "I wish I had my carving tools."

Justin turned back to the fire with quiet thanksgiving for the growth of his fragile hope. This was the first time Erma had ever mentioned anything that had to do with her life in the cave. And she had spoken easily and naturally of the tools left there and long ago buried and lost, he supposed. At last something from the deep recesses had emerged into the light. And to Justin this was very important.

"Tell me what you need," he said. "Maybe I can make some."

"I used to have a little chisel that just fitted in my hand. Of course it was only dirt in the cave, not wood."

"I'll see what I can do," Justin said.

By day they lived on the island and at night they went aboard the raft. And Erma continued to work on the carving, very happily and quietly. To Justin they were equally fascinating to watch, the carver and the carving, for when Erma would sit back from the carving to study it her own body would unconsciously borrow line from it, and she had a way of walking about the island, while she hunted for fine sand with which to polish it, that had a charmed, soundless grace. Lest this spell of creation be jeopardized by a monotonous diet Justin pushed off from the island in the raft one morning, leaving Erma alone, and went in search of food. Toward evening of that day he returned, the raft laden with berries and melons and nuts and the body of a fat, uncautious dowager hen. He found Erma sitting by the fire, the carving at some little distance on a mound of sand. Justin walked up quietly and sat down beside her. She leaned against him and he kissed her.

"Well, and is it finished?" he asked.

"Yes."

Justin sat for a long time looking at the carving. It had great power and surprising motion, and these were of line. Solidity of form, of material, the power and weight of the driftwood itself had all been sacrificed, carved away, deleted, so that in detailed examination one lost the power and motion momentarily in appreciation of extreme delicacy. The original piece of driftwood had stood some two feet high and had been as thick around in some places as his fist, yet Justin knew that the whole thing now must have the physical weight of a bird's skeleton. As soon as he turned away from the contemplation of its detail and let himself submit to the whole of it, that extraordinary sensation of powerful motion came back.

"It is really wonderful," he said.

Tempted beyond resistance, he reached out to trace one of the descending curves that glistened in the light.

"I remember learning that line," Erma said, "on the big torso, on Her thigh. I remember exactly how it felt."

And so, for Justin Magnus, there was a new experience: that of having the force of his love involved in (he would not have said *cause*) the rebirth of creation in his beloved. How wonderful to see how the too lush literateness of the dark cave had become, above ground, this restrained, powerful beauty, how the hidden, wound-licking process of secret consolation had metamorphosed into a joyous process of work. *And his love had been a part of it.* Hunger, all bodily needs, even the need to tell the news of the day's plunder now stored on the raft, went away from Justin.

"What shall we call it?" Erma said. "What does it look like to you?"

"It looks, to me, exactly like you. I'll call her Erma."

Erma turned toward him with a quizzical look on her face. "It does?" She turned again to the carving and contemplated it, her head on one side, a strange smile on her face.

"Why?" Justin said. "What does it mean to you?"

"Oh, a while ago, before you came, I thought what I would call it if I called it anything, and the only word that came was . . . was *pride.*"

"Well," Justin said, "you see, I wasn't far off."

"What did you bring back?" she asked, but did not wait for his answer. Jumping up from the sand, she ran ahead of him to the raft to explore for herself.

That night they had a feast by the fire and afterward swam naked in the shallow water and ran in the cold night air back to the roaring fire. Wrapped in blankets, they sat drying themselves and getting warm. A kind of greed came on them to have a great fire, a wasteful fire, such a fire as would even show at a distance the raft and its living house.

"I don't want to go back to the raft tonight, do you?" Erma said.

"No," Justin said. "I feel contemptuous of shelter and safety tonight. I wish there were stars, though."

She had called the raft a cocoon, Erma remembered, had loved the cradling of the tight, white, secret roots binding the logs. "Cocoons are for bursting," she said, "after all."

"Let us hope not this one," Justin said. "Not literally."

That night on the clean washed sand island the silent driftwood, so long bleached and powdered in death, became vicariously alive for a while by the play of light and darkness, by the extension of embrace, of rapture, of wildness and tenderness radiating out from the two lovers who lay by the fire. Here a wooden thigh would suddenly glow, the tip of a wooden breast twinkle in the firelight. There the long wavy roots, like coils of hair, would glisten. Alternately touched by fire and washed by the dark shadows of the bodies moving in locked embrace, the old, dead remnants of the river's loot moved and danced in the reflections of love.

And then at last the animated shapes were no longer washed by the moving shadows. The random lighting and showers of warmth trickled down from them. They wrapped themselves in shadow, became spiritless, dead, the river's driftwood once again, motionless under the murmur of the quiet voices.

"It is wonderful," Erma said, "how it isn't sleep love gives sometimes, but this clarity instead."

"I've always suspected that the great discoveries are made in this special time of clarity," Justin said, "but I've never been able to verify it."

"Do you suppose that now we'll never want to sleep under a roof again?"

"Not being butterflies," Justin said, "we have the happy privilege of returning to the cocoon any number of times, and of bursting out over and over again."

"I don't feel that way about the cave, though, and the carving. I feel that's final, that emergence. I'm above ground to stay."

"Yes," he said. "There was a great difference between that cave and a cocoon."

In his arms she shuddered suddenly and Justin reached out and covered her with a blanket and drew her nearness to him. "I cannot tell you what a gift this is to me—this day, your beautiful carving, this night."

With a movement of her fingers on his shoulder she said, wordlessly, "I'm listening."

"I never forget the bitterness, the stultifying sense of defeat I had with Edith, of having to admit that my love was powerless to dredge up the fearful recesses, to bring them into the light. I could go down into the dark places with her, but no matter how hard I tried I could not bring the dark things back up into the light with me."

"Is that how it seems to you," Erma said, "like dredging—that love should be a kind of lever to force the dark, hidden places up into the light?"

Justin held his two fists together and suddenly let his fingers spring apart. "Or like turning the soul inside out," he said. "It used to seem to me that love should have the power to do that, just turn the inside outside."

Erma turned and lay on her back beside him. "It doesn't seem like that to me at all," she said.

"No?"

"No dredging, no lever, no force. Just a light that gradually grows brighter and brighter and pushes the shadows back until finally all the hidden places become illuminated."

Justin turned to her and gathered her sweet fragility to the giant strength of himself. "All right," he whispered, "a light, then. But to be a part of it, to be part of it happening in someone else, that's what I've wanted all my life."

"A part of it?" Erma said. "You *are* the light, Justin."

In the darkness, in the shadows, the quiet forms of driftwood marked the stilling of the voices, marked the dying of the fire, marked the silken hypnotic voice of the river licking at the island's shore. But Justin's tears fell on the sand unheard, unnoticed, lost beneath the river's voice. And the sand drank them in and hid them, as though they had never been.

Eight months, altogether, they had spent on the river, or preparing for it, before they came out at last on the shore where Erma had bade farewell to Arthur and where Tommy's grave was. Here they made camp and, after all the time of strangeness in a landscape where the only history was their own, they found themselves caught up in a wave of memory for the old times, the old life. And such is the magic of lovers that this history was rewritten as though all their former times had been their own, together.

It was morning now and they were preparing to break camp and reload the raft. Erma found herself reluctant to begin the packing. "Justin," she said suddenly, "could we leave it, the rest of the river, the vortex, for some other time?"

"Not go on?" Justin said. He stopped his work, lighted his pipe and walked over to her. "Are you tired of the river, Erma?"

"No, it isn't that. I hardly know how to say it. I'd like to go back to the settlement. I want to spread out."

"The raft is pretty confining," Justin said, "especially if you start that big carving you've been planning."

"I know, there just isn't room. I'd like to be back in The Room again, wouldn't you?"

"I hadn't thought about it," Justin said. "I'd like to be wherever you are most alive. It doesn't matter to me where."

"But, Justin, won't you want to work again soon? I know you brought no writing materials on purpose and even kept your calendar on that board so we wouldn't feel compelled to keep Records, or to do anything, in this free time, but wouldn't you like to sit at the long table again with the fire in the fireplace and . . ."

"Well, yes, I suppose so, though I've been glad to have this time away from work."

"But you've been making those motions with your hands."

"What motions?"

"Oh, like this," she said, cupping her hand and rotating it, "as though you were feeling the surface of a ball."

"I have?" he said. "And tell me, Constant Observer, what does that mean?"

"You often do it before you write something. It goes before the whistling."

"Well, possibly so," Justin said. "I hope some day to go over 'The Fulcrum.' I'm in no hurry, though."

"I am," Erma said. "Just this morning, for the first time, I didn't want to get back on the raft. I wasn't excited about what we'd find ahead. Oh, Justin, think of the space in that big house. And we could have real bread again. I dream of baking sometimes—and of new clothes."

"And your cooking pot, I know," Justin said.

"Yes, my pot. I dream of that one fine pot, too. It was the only one I ever got shaped just right. I dream about my fine cooking pot and how the handle felt in my hand."

"The honeymoon is over," Justin said. "The woman is dreaming of cooking pots."

"I didn't think that the place where Kathy died could ever seem like a good place to me again, but it is, Justin. It's home, and I'm homesick, I guess."

Something in her voice so touched him that he took her in his arms and held her quietly. After a while he said, "All right, then, we'll go."

"Even the Records, Justin. I miss the Records. And all our things. I can't explain it."

"Why should you?" Justin said. "It isn't as though we couldn't come back here at any time we wanted."

"Yes, next year we'll have a vacation, and we'll see the rest of the river."

"There is something, though, Erma, now that we've seen the river and all it has to offer, and the ease of traveling with the raft. We could build a house on the river."

"No," she said. "There isn't time."

"Time?" Justin said. "What do you mean?"

"Why, I don't know," she said. "That just came out. I don't know what I meant. I guess I was just thinking of how long it took all of us to build The Room."

"It really is partly the settlement you want, isn't it? That feeling of going home?"

"I don't know, Justin. It's just that lately I've had such a longing for us to be in a place with space, to see you sitting at a big table, comfortably, to bake bread, to have room for my carvings. And I want to make some beautiful clothes to wear."

"Now I understand," Justin said, laughing.

"Don't you want to go back, Justin? Did you want to stay on the river? Do you dread the memory of the settlement?" She looked into his face questioningly.

"No place where you are could seem dreadful to me, Erma. It will be good to have bread baked by your hands. It is good to have your hands empty of bread. It will be good to milk a moss-back again; it is good to catch a fish. It will be good to see you in a robe that you make on the loom. It is good to have you naked. It will be good to work on 'The Fulcrum' again until it satisfies me, or to write 'Death of a Hero,' but it has been very good to be away from them, to let them stop, too."

Erma leaned against him and relaxed. "All right," she said. "I'm glad, then. None of the things I said about the bread or the clothes—"

"And the pot," Justin said, for it was this cooking pot that amused him most of all.

"And the pot," she said. "They aren't really it. I don't know why it is I want this so much, but as long as it is all right with you, I don't have to explain it."

"No," Justin said. "Even if it were that you wanted to return to the World, even to Drury in particular—that, too, would be all right."

"Oh, no," Erma said. "They don't seem like home. The settlement seems like home to me."

Justin put his hand on her head for a moment, and then he walked down to the raft. In a way it made him sad to think of beaching the raft, knowing the living walls would die and the white cocoon roots fall apart and rot. He would miss the raft. He was reluctant to begin unloading and, once aboard, he stood looking out on the river. How positively Erma had said the settlement was home to her. It occurred to him to question, for the first time in his life, what was home to him. A parade of houses slid through his memory: his grandmother's house, the little house that he and Edith had had where David was born, the house in Greece on the hillside where they had lived for a while when the children were little, the big house by the sea next to Max Staats, his cabin at the settlement, The Room. Which of them was home? Or was it this raft he stood on, the only one of all of them that he had made himself? Not one of them spoke to him clearly above the others. About none of them could he state, as Erma had been able to, "*That* one. That one is home."

This struck him as very curious, because certainly he was not a homeless person. Was it then that this thing that was so strong in Erma was missing in him and he had never known it? But if it were missing, then how was it he understood so well how she felt about returning?

He did not seem able to begin unloading the raft, and he decided to postpone it until they had talked over what they would need. He knocked out his pipe and leapt ashore and began to walk back to the camp. It was then that the answer came to him as Erma caught sight of him and waved. Home was not a place to him. It never had been. Home, to him, was a woman. And sometimes it was music.

"Have you started unloading?" Erma said.

"No," Justin said. "It seems so different when you think of it on your back, going uphill for six or seven days."

"Oh, let's go soon, Justin. I'm so curious to see what's left, what stayed through this time undamaged."

"Just our packs, then, just the minimum, and we'll beach the raft in case we want it soon again."

Together they walked up the long, hard path, the same that each of them had taken separately at different times in search of Arthur Herrick. Separately and alone each had pressed on against fatigue and discomfort, toward getting home where the other would be waiting. Now they climbed together, not toward a waiting person but toward an idea—an idea of home, a place of history, a place of roots and order and working space, a place where birth and death had happened, where animals and children had played and had small hungers satisfied, a place where the handle of a favorite cooking pot fitted the palm of the hand, and the harp leaned against the hearth, waiting to be restrung.

FROM time to time while they had been on the raft Justin had thought about "The Fulcrum" and found to his surprise that there was a part of it he could not remember. He had been glad enough to get back to it, once they had salvaged their house from the chokevines, because he suspected that the part he could not remember must be faulty in some way and needing revision. When he had taken the manuscript out of its leather case and located the unremembered section he had had the surprise of finding it absolutely new, as though someone else had written it. This had occasionally happened to him before, that the conscious mind had forgotten what the subconscious had cast up directly and without effort, so the experience was not alarming to him but provided a pleasant sensation of discovery.

And he found that he liked this part very much, and went back to the beginning of "The Fulcrum" with anticipation of going over it all carefully. There was little that he wanted to change or polish, but this little gave him an extraordinary quiet pleasure. It was better than he had thought. He decided to go back to the first movement and go over the whole symphony. "Discovery," "The Time of Innocence," "The Time of History," "The Fulcrum," they seemed to him to be the best work he had written, and if his whole reputation could rest on only one work it was this one, *The Green Kingdom*, that he would have chosen as always before he had said his *Second Symphony*.

He looked up from the manuscript on the big table, this quiet elation in him suddenly seeming a miraculous thing, for a picture had come to him of himself in a time before he had written *The Green Kingdom*, when he had been certain not only that his best work had already been done, but that all his work had been done. His future work and his future life he had been ready to abandon on the day that he had carried Edith's body out to the sea. Since then, he thought, I have had a whole new lifetime. It had never come to him so forcibly before, that he had actually lived twice.

Lost in his meditation, having still the music of "The Fulcrum" in his head, he did not realize Erma was in the house until she stood beside him, her hand on the back of his neck.

"You look so extraordinarily happy," she said. "I have to know, too."

He put his arm around her and leaned his head against her. "Oh, I like the symphony, for one thing, but I was just thinking how few men ever get a second chance."

"Or take it," Erma said, "if they get it."

"I remember sitting by the sea when I was at Max's house, holding your letter in my hand—how weak I felt, how sick and ashamed. I was finished. You could never have made me believe then that I had a whole symphony yet to go, a new world to see, a new love to love."

"For this moment," Erma said, "I have the perfect thing. Close your eyes and I'll be back."

When she came back she stood silently a moment watching Justin's face. He had turned toward the sound of her coming but obediently had closed his eyes. So openly did the lines of his face, the smoothness of the huge brow, the posture at which the head was held, all portray trust and the anticipation of pleasure that an intense wave of love washed over Erma and she found her fingers grasping too tightly the burden she carried.

"Come," Justin said. "What is it?"

She ran and knelt by him. "Hold out your hands," she said, "but don't be startled and drop it; it's warm."

"I know already," Justin said. "I can smell it. It's bread."

"Yes. The first real bread since we've got home. Look, didn't it come out fine?"

"I'm starved," Justin said. "Let's eat it. Is there tea?"

"In a minute," she said.

"The oven works all right, then, after all?" Justin asked.

"Seems to. There were some cracks where the vines had been at work, but after I got it clear of them I put on a thin coat of clay soup and it's as good as new."

After they had eaten at the table before the fireplace Justin reached out his hand in the way that was so characteristic of him, as though the hand had some kind of receiving apparatus of its

own for intelligence. When the hand fell falteringly on a pipe
and, accompanied by the pipe, journeyed a small way to the tobacco bowl and found it to be filled with tobacco, the hand assim-
ilated all this information and sent it by tendons and muscles and
nerves, letting the information seep into Justin's deepest senses
of awareness; and at last he realized they were truly home. They
were settled in.

"What are you smiling about?" Erma asked.

"Oh, at everything," Justin said. "How pleasant it is here.
It looks as though we had lived here forever."

"Look what I found when I moved the loom." She reached
into her pocket and pulled out of it Tommy's first rattle.

Justin took it in his hands and shook it to see if the seeds
so cunningly trapped inside still rattled. They did.

"I remember Joe's working on it," Justin said.

"So do I," Erma said. "We didn't have this table then. We
were all sitting around your work table and . . . and I had made
a sharples pie."

"Will you put the rattle with the other things?" Justin asked.
"Yes."

On one wall they had built new shelves where Erma kept
the children's things. Cleaned of their dust, repaired, oiled and
polished, here stood the childish monuments to the children's history: Tommy's "fulcrum," one of his boats, Kathy's doll, her colored stones, her little cup. Such a short time ago they would have
been like knives in the cruelty of their power to wound; now they
had become beloved, cherished objects.

Justin handed the old rattle over to Erma, knowing how it
would be cleaned and brushed and polished, thinking of the
pleasure with which she had found, since their return home, the
surprising number of their old things still serviceable.

"You are a born salvager," he said. "If ever we go back to
the World I'm going to buy you a whole junk yard all your own.
I can see you pawing your way through old beer cans and litter
and humming to yourself."

"Do I hum?" Erma said.

"You hum," Justin said, "when you find things that will
do for. I think that's what you always say—they'll *do for* something or other."

"It is strange about things, isn't it?"

"What do you mean?"

"Oh, that only people have them or make them."

"Thank God!" Justin said. "Can you imagine the litter? For every bird a broom to sweep the nest."

"And a broom closet for the broom and a hook on the wall of the broom closet," Erma said. "But it wasn't only that I meant. It's the way things don't die. I remember my mother had a silver dish that had belonged to her mother, and I used to touch it with a scary feeling to think it was still there after they both were dead. It might still be there after I was dead. I used to hold it in my hand sometimes and think, This dish will outlive me."

"It is sobering about things," Justin said, "but it's exhilarating about one's work, the thought of one's work outlasting oneself."

"Well, everybody's things were once somebody's work, I guess," Erma said.

"But surely there is a difference to you between your favorite cooking pot and, say, 'Pride,' which you carved from the driftwood, isn't there?"

"Not the difference there is to you, Justin."

They had had this discussion before many times, Justin holding that a useful thing, by its very usefulness, limited the future potentialities. A pot, if it lasted a thousand years, would still be a pot, but no one could foretell the interpretations that time would bring to a work of pure creation, nor the sparks of life to which it might give birth. To Erma, the line was not so sharply drawn.

The discussion was interrupted, for it was that hour of eas-sun when their pet animals were accustomed to come into the house for favorite tidbits and play and affection. The love with which the two people surrounded their living days was of such a boundless quality that it had spilled over to all the living creatures of the Kingdom, just as the house, the dishes from which they ate, and even, after overcoming her timidity of the loom, Erma's weaving had all become things of beauty. Without knowing exactly how it had happened they had accomplished a way of living never possible for them before, so that instead of working every waking hour to maintain themselves they now spent about a fifth of the day at this kind of work and had the other four-fifths for the creation or enjoyment of beauty. Not that they themselves had it so rigidly measured or even separated into two categories. To them, it was an awareness of the present moment, an appreciation that living or any part of love's pleasures need not be postponed. Somewhere on their long journey on the raft they had come into possession of the magic power that all men long for—the power to erase the distinction between preparation for living and living itself. Leisure and pleasure, living and love, were not now the hard-bought rewards of work that must be done first, for the work itself had become part of all these. Since they worked together, or for each other, their living days became a continuous process of experience in the present moment, so that the phrases *as soon as* and *after this is done, later on, first we must* disappeared from their speech.

Now Justin, sitting with a ballsleeper on one shoulder and a gemboy perched on one wrist, looked at Erma, who sat, as so many times he had seen her, with the head of a feathermane in her lap, and remembered her other postures. Her long hair fell loosely, softly, against the animal's glistening spiral horns as she bent her head over him. Could this really be the same woman who had once worn her hair severely pulled back, whose face was drawn and hard, whose body had seemed to be all tendons—a woman he had once wanted to strike, in fury at what she had done to herself?

Erma felt his gaze on her and looked up at him. "Darling," she said, "now that you like the symphony so much, do you feel bad about it's not being played? Should we try to get it out?"

"I hardly know how I feel about it," Justin said.

The ballsleeper, ignored, began to lick Justin's ear. "Stop it," he said. "That tickles."

"Oh, make him behave, Justin, and stop laughing. I want to know, really, how you feel about it."

"Down with you," Justin said. "Scoot."

The ballsleeper came back to bite at Justin's sandal and finally curled up against his foot and was quiet. Justin filled his pipe and lighted it, and the gemboy, knowing the smoke that was to come, flew up to the mantel and began grooming its feathers.

"While there is life there is ego," Justin said. "If I knew absolutely that the river led straight to a music publisher's or to Kirkendahl or to one of several conductors who would give it their best, I would certainly put the symphony on the raft and send it out."

"But you're sure you don't want to take it out yourself?"

"You're thinking of the opening's being so near now, is that it?"

"Yes," Erma said. "I could understand if you want to go out because of the symphony, if you want to be able to hear it performed. I could understand that."

"And you would go with me?"

"Of course," she said.

"And you? Do you have some reason of your own to go?"

"No," she said, "except to hear the symphony and have people heap praise on you. I'd like that."

"Well, then, it's settled," Justin said. "We stay here. The symphony stays here. But I'd like to go up for the opening, anyway, to see it, wouldn't you?"

"Yes," Erma said. "Who knows? Maybe other people will be coming in."

"After we have a chance to study the problem at the opening, don't you think we should begin work on a tunnel?" Justin said. "If we really wanted to stick at it, we could make a permanent opening so that you need never feel trapped here. You know, if we concentrated on it, we could in time make a permanent opening."

Erma pushed the feathermane gently off her lap and went over to sit on the floor by Justin, leaning against him, for she knew now that he was thinking of a time when he might not be with her and of the burden of a loneliness that might come upon her.

"I don't feel trapped," she said. "I never did. I feel especially favored. And I don't want us to devote all our strength and our living to digging a hole to crawl through. Why, it might take us a year, Justin."

"Yes, it might. I feel sure that that must have been what Joe was doing when he found the emeralds, or whatever they were."

"All alone," Erma said. "He would be missing such long times, all alone. No, I don't want us to live like that. I love the way we live now, with this sense of time, these pleasures, never having that awful tiredness. Besides, don't you think, if we did accomplish it, that we might destroy the whole Kingdom?"

"How?"

"Well, the climate, for one thing. The climate that seems to be responsible for everything—wouldn't it perhaps change? Wouldn't some of our animals go out and others come in?"

"I suppose so," Justin said. "If you tamper with nature, you never know what forces you're letting loose."

"That's it," Erma said. "I really don't want to tamper. I

even dread having the knowledge of the clusternut pile, in a way."

"Oh, to me that just seems a difference in degree, more effective than pulling and hacking."

The hulls of clusternuts had proved to be a good, hot, compact fuel for the outdoor bread ovens, and so it had long been their custom to pile them in a spot near the oven. While they had all been living in the settlement these hulls had been constantly used and supplemented and, the paths near the pile being well traveled, the peculiar properties of the nut had not shown up. But when Erma and Justin returned to the settlement after their long journey, the chokevines, the ropevines, the thick, jungle growth of all kinds had almost obliterated the buildings. The oven itself had had to be literally unearthed from a mound of tightly twisted vines. In all this overgrowth there appeared one startling bare spot. In a circle about the clusternuts, as far as the moisture leeching through them had spread out, there was an area where nothing grew.

"To think," Erma had said, "that I used to believe they had some magic of fertility because Gwendolyn loved them, and here the hulls have given us our first really destructive agent."

Now, by soaking the split hulls, they possessed a chemical that could preserve the house, that could resurrect the ruins of the buildings of their history. For the first time they possessed something which, separated from their own hands, removed from them, could kill, could destroy.

"Or," Justin had pointed out, "if you think of it so, can preserve." But whether one considers it as an agent of destruction or of preservation, it is a significant time in the history of a settlement when man has it within his power to dominate the landscape. And it was characteristic of their life, having as they did the leisure and the accord to be thoughtful, that this milestone gave them thought.

"I know what let's do," Erma said. "Let's make a copy of the old map and write up a short history of all of us, so it can be verified, and put it in a bowl or a hollow log and seal it and toss it out the opening."

"All right," Justin said. "How many landmarks can you remember in coming up the mountain?"

"There was the Indian Village," she said.

"And the mound of red rocks."

"And the ledge."

"And the bridge of shells," Justin said. "I think a hollow log is better than a bowl because it won't break, and we can smooth it off, maybe paint something on the outside so it will be conspicuous."

"We could send one down the river, too," Erma said.

"I like that notion," Justin said. "So, in the end, what the future holds for the Green Kingdom will be largely determined by the contours of the earth itself, how far the log we toss out rolls downhill, whether the log on the river floats or is snagged."

"It will take some doing to get all our history condensed into something that will fit the hollow center of a small log."

"Remember Name Rock?" Justin asked. "What a lot there was there, and they had to carve it out of stone."

"Oh, and what was his name, the one who was feeling well?"

"Joreth something, I think," Justin said. "Joreth Ames."

"That's right," Erma said. "Joreth Ames, well. If you could only have one word for yourself, what would you have, Justin?"

"Why, composer, I guess," Justin said. He reached down and lifted her onto his lap. "How about you?" he asked. "Who are you or how are you or what are you, in one word?"

Erma put her arms around him and held him close to her, and the time for words was gone from them for a while, there in the house they had salvaged and made beautiful, by the hearth where the pet animals grouped themselves in eternal tableaux. But in her mind's ear Erma heard herself answer: Loved, I would say. Erma Magnus, *loved*.

*

There was a pattern of pre-wessun sounds that Justin remembered with pleasure from his old cabin, in the days when he had lived alone there. And now he had a longing to hear them again, for in his memory they were associated with his work on "Death of a Hero," which was still unfinished. Although there were many birds around the house, so many of them had become pets that they had lost their wild habits and called now for attention from the two people. Also, the trees had been cleared in such a wide circle that the natural groupings of awakening animal life had been forced back to a distance which muted the sound.

So long had Justin's old cabin been abandoned that the

surrounding vegetation was again much the same as it had been before. Some days before they had used their new destructive weapon to clear the door, had forced it open and seen that the firepit could still be used. Earlier this day Justin had swept out the cabin and brought in new ferns for a fresh bed. Now they had only to carry over blankets from the house, their pipes and tobacco.

"Are you comfortable?" Justin asked.

"Yes, dear. But promise to wake me. Don't let me sleep through it."

"All right, I'll wake you if I'm awake myself. Maybe we won't get what I remember at all."

"Then we'll stay another night," she said. "Or more. We can stay until we do."

"But who knows? Perhaps it isn't the same," Justin said, "or perhaps I'm only remembering something that didn't exist."

"Did you often wake early in the old days?"

"Yes," he said. "I used to lie awake all night often, wanting you."

She turned to him in the bed, her movements releasing the fresh, spicy odor of the bruised ferns. "I remember the day I came here," she said, "so broken and frightened, and found my jacket under your pillow."

"I was afraid that you saw it," Justin said.

"It gave me courage; it made my life possible. I'm glad I saw it. Tell me, which bird would call first, that you remember?"

"The chichimingo, I think, and then . . . then there were three birds together. One of them had a tone much like that horn I made with the river reed. Well, we'll see what we get in the morning. The whole pattern seemed to me to be filled with solemnity, some profound awakening of the day; but without loneliness it may sound joyful now. We'll see."

"You think to start work on 'Death of a Hero' soon, don't you?"

"I'd like to. Now I'm so pleased with the symphony I'd like to tackle 'Hero' again. There is something so—I do not have words for it."

He did not know how much, even yet, Erma could bear to hear, though long ago he had told her the facts. But to Justin the tragic memory of Joe as a person, Joe Roberts, had become quite separated from Joe as hero, grappling in a dark cave with an adversary in such a final struggle that the man and his enemy could not be separated even in death and must share one grave. Forever intertwined their bones must lie while strange gods, not of their creating, crumbled down upon them. That the accidents which contrive the meeting of heroes with their adversaries are often made of neurotic fears and heightened by the thoughtless acts of lesser men does not detract from but only intensifies the reality of the hero's final struggle. For he is made to taste finality: to recognize the moment when there is only one action, without alternatives.

It made important music to Justin, this struggle without malice between the man and the scarred, blind animal, and, associated in his memory with the time when he had had the best grasp on it was the pattern of pre-wessun sound coming to the cabin where he had lain awake and alone.

He felt Erma's head become heavy on his shoulder and in the darkness he smiled. The nights he had lain here alone in sleepless longing and frustration, the memory of the children coming to awaken him, even the memory of cutting down Gwendolyn's naked body were all laid to rest. One thing there is that, in the potency of its memory, outlasts all others and that is the memory of work well done. Here in this cabin Justin had written "The Time of Innocence," "The Time of History" and most of "The Fulcrum."

In the darkness Justin smiled at the great goodness of the present moment and with anticipation of the morning when he might again hear that curious pattern of pre-wessun sound, and for the days ahead when it might be given him—the finishing of "Death of a Hero."

He was still smiling when the pain hit him, the very severe pain at the back of the skull.

"Erma," he cried impulsively.

"Love," she said in her sleep. "Yes, love."

Immediately Justin regretted having called her, and held his breath now, hoping she would slip back into the dark reaches; for, as the pain increased, he came very rapidly to know that this was of a great seriousness, and he needed time to think.

For could this be death, really? Death, for which he had so poorly prepared his beloved? A giant feeling of rebellion filled him against death, for he did not want to die, would never want to die, would rage against dying so long as Erma breathed. And this feeling of rebellion fought stupidly with the knowledge that there was enough wood cut for a week. A week—what was a week to the loneliness that lay before her? A momentary panic came upon him that he must prepare Erma, that he must tell her something, give her some weapon against the time ahead. But he knew this was not possible. If there has been an essential neglect in ten years of loving, it cannot be made up in ten minutes of talking, in any last message.

And if there has not?

This brought calm to his panic, or perhaps it was a little easing of the pain, but it came to him that if there has been only the best in ten years of loving, then the power of it must sustain the bereaved one. Or if that will not, then nothing will.

The calm, brought of acceptance of this knowledge, did not last long, for soon it was with Justin as it had been with the old feathermane in the cave. Scarred and blind, alone in the darkness, the feathermane had been aroused by the blundering of Arthur Herrick and, recognizing the odor of his old enemy, had wished to meet him on his feet. So Justin wished now to be standing, to be facing the enemy. With that same powerful instinct that motivates animals some depths within him urged him to stand, to be on his feet. And he found that movement was already impossible to him. So much did this infuriate him that he would have killed himself with rage, and saved death its subtler weapons, were it not that then he heard, and knew he heard, the continuation of "Death of a Hero."

He knew he would never write it and, more, he knew no one would ever know that he had heard it. But it was near worth dying for, this music, of such a quality that it brought the tears streaming down his face. The volume of it increased until it filled the whole room, demanding all his attention. He knew that Erma moved beside him. He could feel her hand upon his wet face. He could hear her voice, but the music blotted out her words. The music would permit no distractions.

With all the life he had now he was holding on to hear the end of the music, to last until the last note.

So died Justin Magnus, a little before wessun, the fourth day of the tenth month of the tenth year, the sound of his unwritten music in his ears, his fingers clasped tightly around the hand of his beloved, in the room where he had done the best of his work, in a land without shadows.

He was not ready to die; he never would have been.

"Justin!" Erma called to him. "Justin! Justin!" as she had been calling since the moment his tears had fallen on her hand, awakening her. For Erma there was no music of an unearthly quality, there was no answer to her call, there was nothing but the awful quiet until at last, in the pre-wessun hint of light, a lonely chichimingo called.

THERE is a state of shock in which the mind hangs in a desolate landscape like an abandoned gate swinging aimlessly in the wind, so that alternately and capriciously nothing can be admitted or everything can be. Was it for hours or for days that Erma clung to the body of Justin Magnus in full and terrible knowledge of her loss, only to turn suddenly to the belief that by the doing of some familiar thing she made this fact a lie? Building up the fire with her back to the bed, she believed that she had only to turn to the bed and find that Justin was sleeping. In the lonely wind of a desolate landscape the gate blew shut, and it was not so that her beloved was dead; it could not be. If she made tea for him, as always, then he could not be dead. But the broken cup lying on the floor said that he was dead. The gate swung open and Justin was dead.

For a while the question of whether he was or was not dead became lost in Erma's sudden, overwhelming feeling of fear. For once, in a moment of sanity, she had realized that Justin was truly dead and that the dead must be buried, and she had started out the door of the cabin to get help. But help of whom? Was it Justin himself she had thought to go for? He, who had buried all the others except Tommy, must he now be asked to bury himself? It was this that brought Erma to a realization of her absolute aloneness, and so to fear. At last in a floundering and stupid way she stumbled out of the cabin, aimlessly hoping for direction, for help of some kind. In an awful weariness she leaned against a lacewood tree.

"Justin is dead," she said to the tree.

And it seemed to her that that was what she must do. She must tell the trees that Justin was dead. The trees must know. Perhaps she might have gone on then with senseless compulsion, to tell each tree individually, if it had not been for the inter-

ruption. In the distance she heard the first howler's eerie cry
and a streak of ice shot through her, restoring a kind of animal
alertness to her mind and to all her muscles. She turned and ran
into the cabin, closing the door behind her and leaning against
it.

"Justin," she said. "Oh, Justin, what shall I do?"

She had loved his great size. She had loved to lean against
a giant, to be carried by a giant. She had gloried in his strength;
and now it was this which defeated her. For she could not lift him.
Even in the state she was in, had she been able to dig a grave so
deep she could not have dragged his body to it from the bed. She
pulled a stool over and sat by him. She could think of nothing
to do but wait, while the sound of the howlers gradually grew
closer to the cabin. The violence of her grief was succeeded by
alternate states of stupor and extreme fear. Perhaps she slept at
times. Now and then, mechanically, she replenished the fire. Gradually the giant figure on the bed lost all reality for her, as did,
at times, the room itself. Reality became centered in the howlers
outside who, by the second day, paced in a circle about the cabin.
She had no plan but to wait; she had no feeling but hate. Slowly,
within her, as the signs of the howlers' growing audacity increased, a hate smouldered, a rage that promised to grow indefi-
nitely until it would consume everything in the land.

At last the necessary ingredient was added for the releasing
of rage, for the translation of its growth into action. One of the
howlers scratched at the door of the cabin, and it was to Erma as
though its claws had ripped across the surface of her brain.

She sprang to the fireplace, picked up a log for a club and,
opening the door, sprang out among the ravenous beasts, yelling
her fury, and glad, glad to kill what had now become her beloved's enemy. She brought down the club on the head of the
first one that came at the door and the sickening sound of its skull
crushing seemed to echo endlessly through the Kingdom.

FROM THE RECORD OF ERMA HERRICK MAGNUS IN THE LAST
MONTH OF THE TENTH YEAR:

I think it was that sound that brought me to my senses. I was
glad. I was proud, as though I had done something for Justin. I
wanted to kill and kill and go on killing. There is so much I don't
remember about those days. I am still lost in the days and do not
know exactly how much time has gone by, but I think it was the

sound of that skull splitting that made me know what it was I must do, so that I went into the cabin and kissed my beloved and then set fire to the place. It is still burning. Every day I pile more wood upon the pyre, for I do not know how long it must take to be sure that the howlers do not return to claw over his dear bones.

Oh, my darling, it is so terribly lonely without you.

I have turned to the Record at last for discipline in the hope of finding some help in this terrible confusion that stupefies me. I must come to some decision about the opening. I know that it must be soon and since I am so mixed up in time I should go soon if I am to be sure to make it; but I do not seem able to force myself to get ready. There are Justin's manuscripts, which I must take if I go out, and the Records.

I have come to have such sympathy of late for Arthur and his desire to get to a doctor. I do not know if this is the menopause—could it be?—or does grief have this power? I had not thought the menopause would have such a sudden onset, and it seems to me forty is rather young, too. How I would love to speak to someone about it who knows. I really know nothing about it. It would be good to speak to another woman about it, even to Gwen. It is for such times as this, I suppose, and such questions, that people herd together in the World's cities: to indulge themselves in the belief that, however ignorant one is oneself, a real authority is always nearby. To know someone *who knows:* this was what Arthur hungered for so terribly. And now, at times, so do I.

Yet I do not do anything about getting ready for the opening, and when I try to make myself prepare for the journey an awful lethargy comes over me. If only I wanted clearly to go or clearly to stay. I want nothing, really. Only Justin.

I dream of him constantly, as I still dream of Kathy, so that awakening is a nightmare. Sometimes I think in a dream that Justin will tell me what to do. I have gone over and over our conversations about getting his music back to the world, trying to read into his words some indication of what he really wanted. And yet I know it is just part of my helplessness to try to shove the decision off onto Justin, even in death, just as at first I was so confused I started to the house to get him to bury himself.

There is no one, no one, to tell me what to do, and my own inner voices, upon which I used to rely so heavily, seem silenced, struck dumb. The animals would help me if they could. It was heart-breaking to see them seeking Justin, to see their awareness that something was seriously wrong. The feathermane still follows me about everywhere with that kind of questioning stance, and always comes and paws at me in a restless, disturbed way when I have uncontrollable spells of weeping. Perhaps I should ask of the feathermane, "What shall I do?" In my dreams Justin will not tell me and, waking, I ask of myself and get no answer.

The decision that Erma made, at last, was to postpone the decision. She packed the old cart with the Records and Justin's manuscripts. She took some clothing for herself, food, blankets, and for a long time she hesitated over taking Justin's harp, a toy of Kathy's, and "Pride," but in the end she left them all in place.

Since they no longer had domesticated mossbacks she pulled the cart herself by easy stages, resting often, and camped at last near the opening place to wait. Still she had not decided whether to go out. No clear desire had come to her, no direction. She had meant to leave her decision until after the opening, to stand in the opening between the two lands and see which called to her. Behind her, as she climbed, trailed the feathermane and Justin's pet ballsleeper. Often the gemboy that used to perch on Justin's wrist would visit the caravan.

At night Erma lay down in the cart to sleep, wondering if the opening would occur on the morrow, trying again to calculate the days from her hazy memory. Often she thought of the bitter argument that Gwen and Arthur had had over the discrepancy of one day between their two calendars. Her own calculations had an error of weeks, possibly. It was so typical of both Gwen and Arthur that they would have fought bitterly over an increment of time out of proportion to the action involved, and that neither one would be present for the proof. She wondered again if Arthur had actually made it through the vortex to the outside and, should she go herself, if she would meet him again.

Eight nights she lay down to sleep, no closer to a decision, no clear desire in her mind. On the morning of the ninth day she was thrown clear of the cart when it was overturned by the earth's convulsions, and, frightened, she lay on the ground trembling. The noise of the falling rocks deafened her and the choking dust blinded her. At last there was silence in the land. All animal life had disappeared. Even her pets had deserted her. Through the sifting dust she could barely make out the opening. Slowly, in the terrible silence, she crept forward, hardly breathing. At last she pulled herself up to her full height and made herself walk through the rock wall until she could look outside. She saw that the opening would be wide enough for the cart. After she had looked once, she could go back for it.

But she had forgotten how it would be. She stood in the opening, gazing out upon the World, and she had forgotten how brown it was, how, in comparison with the Green Kingdom, it seemed to be burned, hard, alien, and dry. All sense of hurry left her. In the eerie quiet she stood perfectly still and looked her fill, for at last the clear inner voices spoke to her.

There was no need to go back for the cart; there was no need to beg like a child for someone or something to tell her what to do. At last she felt one single, clear desire. She turned away from the World and, without turning back to see if anyone else should have entered, without waiting to see the opening sealed with lava, she entered her own land and began to descend to the settlement. For the first time in many months she felt something close to joy stirring within her. She did not stop at the cart, for in the freedom of having made the decision she could not bear to be hampered. She could return for the cart in the days that followed. Now, at this moment, she wanted not to be a beast of burden. She wanted to move freely, easily, confidently, even to run, in a full embrace of this beautiful land.

For this *was* her home. Where you have lived for ten years in the richest and fullest experience of your life; where crumbles the cave of your dark despair, defeated; where stands the house that you have made yourself out of a wilderness; where lie the ashes of your beloved: there is your home.

In the green silence Erma paused and looked about at the rich and beautiful land. In her grief she had been blind to it, and now, by her choosing and her embrace, it sparkled once again in all its richness. In the silence she spoke aloud, defiantly: "I live here. This is my home. I live here, whether anyone knows it or not."

About halfway down the slope the animals waited, their necks stretched toward her in questioning, and she ran to them and knelt on the ground and gathered them in her arms while the tears fell silently down her cheeks. That she could ever have thought to leave them, her own!

She had new eyes for the landscape again and cherished its magnificence as she had on her first day in the Kingdom. For so many weeks she had been at war with it. It had seemed the greatest cruelty to her that flowers could bloom after Justin died. Even at times it seemed to her that they flaunted their life before her. Now they were part of the land again. Erma stood and looked about her. For the first time since Justin's death she was possessed of serenity of the spirit. The decision was made and now it seemed to her that she should have seen all the time how very simple it would be, for there had not really been two alternatives. Even loneliness, she thought, in the land of one's history, even grief, is preferable to any other condition in exile.

"Justin," she said aloud, easily, without self-consciousness, "Justin, I really had no choice as soon as I saw that, for me, any other place is exile." She closed her eyes and felt about her the great arms of her beloved. Once more she possessed that incredible moment when they had climbed above the clouds and, blinded and faltering, had reached for each other in a basic recognition of the body's raw reality. It was the first time, waking, that she had had any memory of Justin alive. Only in dreams, before, had she been able to see him any other way than dead, with the howlers circling greedily about the room where he lay. This new thing, testimony to the power of love's memory, seemed to Erma to confirm the rightness of her decision. A warmth suffused her whole body, washing away the coldness of death, blotting out the discreteness of the wall that had imprisoned her in isolated survivorhood.

About her feet she felt the scurrying and panic of animal movements. She opened her eyes and, turning, began to climb back again, for it must have been the threatenings of the lava flow that the animals had heard with ears more sensitive than hers. Standing in the clouds of memory, locked in Justin's embrace, she had forgotten about the actual sealing. For her the Kingdom was already closed, and the physical fact of it was an anticlimax. She would not turn her back on it, though. At a safe distance and in quiet content she would witness this finality, as though it were a kind of confirmation of her own decision, like the seal put upon a bargain.

Now even her ears could hear the hissing sound, constantly increasing in volume. When the hissing increased to a great roar, and the lava spewed forth in a high jet, the dramatic qualities of the spectacle absorbed her, destroying her new-found serenity; and even though she was collected enough to know that, for her safety, she must retreat farther toward the settlement, she heard herself shouting in defiance, as earlier she had pronounced with calmness: "I live here. I live here. I live here whether anyone knows it or not."

Down the slope again, at a safe distance, she stopped to get her breath and heard her own breathing as the only sound in the land. Once more the wall's eruptions had quieted themselves. Once more all animal life lay hidden in fear. Silently the rain of dust dissipated itself. Everything in the land lay quiet, waiting.

It was then, at this moment of suspension, when no other creature moved upon the land, that Erma felt within herself, unmistakably, the quickening.

"No," she said aloud. "Surely it could not be."

But in the next instant her whole being opened in receptivity to the truth, and the many small verifying physical details of recent weeks fell into corroborating logical order, making an absurdity of her preoccupation with the menopause, so that it seemed to her she should certainly have known for some time.

Surely they forgave her, the great, fertile forces of this wonderful land, that she thought of herself first in the suddenness of finding that the very basis on which she had built many formative years of her life was in error. The soft life-giving mists, the fruit-laden plants, the smoothly flowing great river placing its richnesses carefully along its banks—these had never been questioned. These had never been accused. The massive mossback lying sheltered in tall grasses placidly licking her newborn calf— what could she know of irony? And the arrogant plumed river-heron who had never built a nest to mock her with its emptiness —what could she understand of the need to dig out a cave underground to hide one's suffering and, in the hiding, make strange, demanding gods? But surely, even without understanding, they forgave the woman that her first impulses, her first thoughts, were not instinctive acceptances, not placid identifications with natural impersonal forces, but highly individual scurryings, disorganized and pathetically oriented only to her own singular history.

They had been wrong, then, the others, Arthur and Gwendolyn and even Joe. They had been wrong all the time. This was one of the scurryings.

And surely she was forgiven when, scurrying away from the petty, singular preoccupations with herself, she thought of the child and in a moment of sudden panic turned back to the opening and knew with a highly personalized human fear the reality of the seal upon it. Surely they did not censure her that she behaved for a short time as less than an elemental force, lacking in dignity, without heroic stature. For if it is of their nature that they do not know irony, mocking, false accusation, then it is also of their nature that they do not censure, do not hold rancor, do not condemn.

But can they pity? Can a river know compassion? Can the fertility of the earth know sympathy?

Erma became conscious of the trembling of the feathermane's body pressed against her thigh, and she turned her back on the seal and reached down to pat the animal's head to reassure it.

"Well," she said. "Well, it is done now."

She began to walk, the feathermane close beside her and the other animals following behind. She did not hurry but moved rhythmically, steadily downhill toward the settlement. Once she had accepted the fact of the closing a great longing had come upon her to be at home, in the house, a fire roaring in the fireplace, and a pot of strong tea made. It was sobering knowledge, this, and already she had cast aside as useless the question of whether or not, had she known of the child before the opening, she would have made a different decision. She had made it; it was done now. She knew immediately that she would never risk the precious burden she carried to the unknown fate of the river's vortex as Arthur had risked his own life. Nor, no more than when she had thought she and Justin were alone, would she spend the days ahead burrowing a tunnel.

This was her land. She had chosen it for herself. And now she had chosen it for the child within her. She expected the hot tea and the fire at home to bring her calmness and patience for the time when her own reserves of strength and courage would come to aid her. She stopped suddenly and put her hands in dear embrace over the child, and for a moment closed her eyes, the better to savor the knowledge that had just come to her.

"Oh, Justin, Justin, I am not alone, and you will live again before my eyes. Could you have known? Did you know?"

How strange it was to smile again. As she once more resumed her steps toward home she put her hand up to her cheek. She knew that times of panic, moments of fear, questioning of her decision would return; but for now, for a few seconds, she knew a strange new joy.

Can a river know compassion? Can the earth know sympathy? Can the mists give comfort? And if they cannot, if these are qualities only humans possess, then what comfort is there, what help can there be for this lone woman in the time ahead of her?

There is her own strength and health, by which she had managed to survive all the others. There is her spirit, which had withstood the life underground in the dark cave of her own wounds and, being reborn in love, had emerged richer and wiser. There was the moment, culmination of long growing, when she had known that no one could absolve her of responsibility for the death of her friend, and she had taken it on herself.

There was the land about her, with all its riches of life, which she had loved and chosen, and learned to live with.

There were the years of history written into everything she touched and wore and used.

There was the great yearning for a child of her own body, which had evolved from desire and hunger through twisted craving into a spiritual acceptance, so that now the actual fact of its physical existence fitted into its spiritual counterpart as a miraculous abundance in excess of need.

But greater than any of these things, greater even than her own hard-won courage, was the memory of love. She had been given, in the days of his greatness, the love of a great man, and greatly had she loved him in return.

And perhaps, if the river cannot know compassion, the earth cannot know sympathy and the mists cannot give comfort—perhaps these things are enough. Let the hot tea comfort, let the years of having learned courage become courage's friend. Let the memory of love sustain, for, as Justin had known the night he died, if this will not, then nothing will. Not a river, nor the earth itself, has the power of the memory of love.

At last she was home, only a few minutes away from the fire and the hot, comforting tea. At the door she stopped and turned around and looked out at the rich greenness of the land she had chosen; for how would it be now? She had never stood just here before at this hour of eassun looking out just here, knowing that she was to have a child. Behind her waited the house, no longer a place of her loneliness and grief but the place of the years she had lived with Justin Magnus.

She was very tired. She took off her sandals which were muddy and stained from the long journey and, followed by the feathermane, went into the house. She started the fire at the hearth, put on the kettle to heat, lighted a spill at the fire, and walked about lighting the lamps. Then she sat down in Justin's chair and waited quietly for the water to boil. For the tea would comfort her and the memory of love would sustain her and the life that she bore within her would have the chances, the gamble, the promise and the potentialities that cherished, valued life asks everywhere.

So Erma sat, quietly waiting for the hot tea for which her tiredness hungered. And if the river cannot pity and the earth cannot know compassion, she could perhaps do without these things. For had she not, after all, been singularly blessed to have known that the land of her heart's desire does exist, that it had accepted her as she had chosen it, that it had given her love so that she might give it new life? Was she not, like the Green Kingdom itself, privileged to be a component of death's most formidable enemy: a condition of potentiality?

On the hearth the kettle boiled and Erma rose and reached out her hand to lift it. It was a simple, deliberate movement, the one most characteristic of her: a movement of answering, a movement of response.

Max Staats had gone upstairs to say good night to the young man, but he was already asleep and that was not surprising, Max thought, considering. Just as well he had not had Mrs. Johns move the things out of his sister's room, as they had for Justin, but had given Mr. Herrick the smaller guest room. For he certainly didn't need a view, Max thought. What he needed was sleep.

Coming downstairs, now, he stopped at the door of the kitchen. "That was a very good dinner, Mrs. Johns," he said.

"Well, thank you," she said. "Not that it mattered, good or not, to HIM."

"Well, I suppose," Max said, "our food is strange to him. He's been away for a long time in a . . . a different sort of place."

"And talk," Mrs. Johns said. "I never heard anybody talk so much. He didn't have time to eat for talking, that's what. I could hear his voice in the kitchen, on and on and on."

"Yes," Max said, "he's only lately got his voice back. He'd lost it, you know."

"Oh, no wonder, then," she said.

"Besides," Max said, "he had a lot to say."

He certainly did, Max thought, walking now into the big living room and closing the door after him in the hope of having some privacy to digest what he had been hearing for the last several hours. And I am no doubt the only person in the world who would believe it.

Anyhow, Arthur Herrick had thought he was the only one, and after what he had been through it was understandable.

When Arthur had found himself carried out of the Green
Kingdom and thrown with violence upon a strange shore he
had still been able to think that he was alive, and when he
heard his thought and realized he had actually spoken that
thought, he had believed for a short, foolish interval that his
troubles were over. He could not wait to talk and he had talked
himself into nothing but trouble.

Max sat in the big chair by the fire. He took off his glasses
and shook his head at the ridiculous odyssey he had heard. A
publicity stunt, of course, that's what they had thought. Advance
publicity for a movie to be called, no doubt, THE GREEN
KINGDOM. And the more Arthur talked, the more they were all
wise to publicity methods. So he had had to get rid of the clothes
first, he had thought, and he had been caught trying to steal
others. There had been quite a delay in the jail, for he had no
identification of any kind, and when he had tried to prove who
he was he had had the misfortune to mention Drury. And that
had led to another kind of delay altogether, the theft of the
clothes now made unimportant.

"I didn't understand then," Arthur had told Max "that
Drury—or what had been Drury—was right in the middle of a
secret military project. All I knew was I was saying something
wrong, and so I decided to quit talking. And that led to a
psychiatric examination, which was all right with me because I
knew it meant going from one building to another. That's how
I made it out, and I just kept moving. I knew I'd have to find
one person who would believe me, so I could stay out of jail
long enough to get some clothes and some money and some
identification. And then I remembered Justin's talking about you.
He talked about you quite a lot. 'My good friend Max Staats,'
he'd say. So I thought it was worth a try to see if you were
still alive."

Of course I am still alive, Max thought. Why wouldn't I be?
Nothing remarkable in that, even if Arthur Herrick had seemed
to find it so. What Max found remarkable was his own lack of

surprise. *It was as though he had been waiting all these years for nothing else. He had brushed Arthur's voluble explanations aside impatiently, saying, "Yes, yes, I know who you are. I believe you. Tell me—my old friend Justin Magnus. Do you have news of him?"*

And what news it had been! Another symphony. Complete. A whole new symphony was there, not to mention all the other wonders Arthur Herrick had told of.

Max put on his glasses and looked at his desk. *Absurd to think he could get any work done this night.* He stood up and started for the door, but it was just as absurd to think he would sleep. He checked the door to see if it were closed tightly, although he did not imagine that anything could possibly wake Arthur Herrick now. And then he put Justin's SECOND SYMPHONY on the turntable. Not for years had he been able to listen to it like this, with real joy in his heart.

He walked across the room and threw open the door to the sea and stood with the sound welling all about him. *And there is more,* he thought. *More. In that place. There is a new one, waiting. And it is mine to seek.*